As it turned out Kate got to Saint Laurent in plenty of time. The Chanel show was still running so she was able to slip in through the back and watch the finale. Strange to be a spectator. All those shows she'd done over the years and yet she could count on one hand the ones she'd actually watched. She gazed admiringly at the models pausing for the cameras and felt at the same time a greedy desire to be up there with them bathing under the hot lights, part of the magic. Funny how just a few years ago the idea of appearing on a Parisian catwalk would have filled her with terror.

It had never occurred to Kate to try modelling until her friend Joanna, who was trying to break into fashion photography, needed a volunteer. Kate, a shy and rather overweight nineteen-year-old, had reluctantly agreed to pose for her. After two days of experimenting with endless positions, lighting, clothes, make-up and hair styles at Joanna's house, Joanna announced that she was satisfied and began clicking furiously.

Emma Davison went to The London College of Fashion when she was nineteen and has been modelling ever since. She has had contracts with Christian Dior and Lanvin, and has worked with top couturiers including Yves Saint Laurent, Givenchy, Belville Sasson and Caroline Charles. She has also made many TV commercial appearances. She now lives in London. CATWALK is her first novel.

Catwalk

Emma Davison

CORONET BOOKS
Hodder and Stoughton

First published in 1994
by Hodder and Stoughton
A division of Hodder Headline PLC
Simultaneous Hodder and Stoughton hardcover edition 1994
A Coronet paperback

10 9 8 7 6 5 4 3 2 1

British Library Cataloguing in Publication Data

Davison, Emma
Catwalk
I. Title
823.914 [F]

ISBN 0 340 61352 1

Typeset by
Letterpart Limited, Reigate, Surrey
Printed and bound in Great Britain by
Cox & Wyman Ltd, Reading

Hodder and Stoughton Ltd
A division of Hodder Headline PLC
338 Euston Road
London NW1 3HB

For David
. . . my Catalyst

When from our better selves we have too long
Been parted by the hurrying world, and droop,
Sick of its business, of its pleasures tired,
How gracious, how benign, is Solitude.

Wordsworth

I have taken the liberty of mentioning real people in this novel in order to make the background as realistic as possible. My plot and main characters, however, are all completely imaginary, and have no relation to any real person, living or dead, or actual happening.

1

Kate Temple walked out in a wicked saffron satin suit to an explosion of clicks and flashes. The white runway, which seemed to stretch for miles, was flanked by photographers from the world's most prestigious fashion magazines. With her eyes fixed on the video crew at the far end of the ramp, Kate strode down arrogantly to a spontaneous burst of applause and gave a neat full turn.

Today was the launch of the French *haute couture* spring/summer collections. For four days the fashion world's *paparazzi* had descended on Paris to preview the new 'look'. Top designers, who had sweated for weeks over the length of a skirt, were about to present their creations. They were nervous and with good reason. The power of the magazine editors was phenomenal. There was a time when Donna Karan couldn't have sold a bagel, until *Women's Wear Daily* stepped in and hyped her collection in a major review. Twenty-four hours later, much to her own astonishment, Donna Karan had sold the entire collection. Now, dauntingly, more than seven hundred international journalists sat with pens or laptops poised ready to immortalise the supermodels (ironically more than the clothes) who earned as much as $20 thousand a day. With more than a thousand pages of editorial reserved, designers hardly turned a hair at the staggering fees the model agencies charged.

Back at the top of the runway Kate posed, hands on hips, head tilted slightly to the left, and waited for the lights and hearty round of applause to dim. Perfect! She felt powerful and acknowledged. There was nothing more intoxicating than the high of feeling thin and exquisite on a Paris runway. And today everything was working. At this moment she felt she could accomplish anything. The lights blackened, the music changed, and as new models walked on Kate disappeared behind a black and silver screen bearing the legend 'Christian Dior'.

Backstage was chaos. Models charged around in scanty underwear, throwing on clothes and accessories. Make-up artists waded through rails touching up lips and blotting noses with thick powder-puffs. Distracted, a security guard ogled the semi-naked girls with unabashed delight. Middle-aged dressers battled with seriously expensive clothes carelessly discarded by models struggling into their next outfits.

'*Attends!*' one dresser cried, waving a satin pillar-box hat in the air as a stunning Ethiopian wrestled to get a look in the mirror.

'Who's got my shoes?' hissed an infuriated voice, searching through her things strewn across the floor.

Models were notorious for pinching each other's shoes during a show. No matter how organised the assistants were, someone invariably messed up on the sizes.

'Diana!' the voice accused, spotting a suspiciously familiar pair by Diana's rail. 'You do this to me every show!'

An immaculate blonde mop appeared through the top of a dress and gave her a bored look. 'Just because we're the same size, honey, doesn't mean we share the same taste!'

'Use mine,' offered Cassy Peck, an anorexic-looking east-ender with a mass of chaotic ginger locks, who deposited a pair of gold sandals in her frustrated colleague's hand. 'Chuck 'em back for the finale.'

Readjusting the pads stuffed into her bustier, Cassy swanned off to find a mirror. A man with dyed-black hair and sixties sideburns was strutting territorially around the room in a Profecto leather jacket, obscenely tight black lycra shorts and a T-shirt emblazoned with the logo, 'Beat me, whip me, kick me, I'm yours'. He grabbed a model as she came off stage and started fiddling with her hair.

'Dar-ling! Stand still, for Pete's sake! Your bun's coming off.'

'I'm not surprised,' complained the model, pulling at a skin-tight body. 'You try getting this damn thing on and off without taking your head at the same time.'

'Don't tempt me!'

The hairdresser, who had been up at four to get to his first show and had a raging hangover, gritted his teeth. Another girl glided by with a black, spiky tuft sticking out at the back of her head.

'Hang on, Roberta!' he shrieked. 'You're not bloody well going on with hair looking like that!'

Snatching at pins from his sweating assistant, the hairdresser tore after the vanishing model.

At the top of the stairs stood Bernard Plassier, Dior's current *haute couture* designer, commanding the room as the models lined up to go on stage. Behind him an enormous board with sketches of each outfit outlined the running order of the show. Each sketch had a small piece of fabric and a polaroid attached to it along with the model's name and all the accessories she would be wearing. As each group came up Plassier shouted their names, his voice rising threateningly if they didn't immediately appear. Next to him two assistants acted like a couple of well-trained parrots.

'*Allez! Vite*, Kate!' one urged.

Calmly removing a long, glittery earring from her dresser's ear, Kate attached it to her own. A make-up artist with a peanut-size head and poured into drainpipe Levis patted her brow and nose with a damp puff. Kate tried not to think about how much it had already been used as she walked on to a change of music.

'Come on!' urged Roberta, now trapped beneath the Profecto jacket's monstrous can of hair spray. 'I'll miss my cue. Just back-comb the front a bit more for me. It's wilting.'

'That makes two of us, dear.'

Seconds later the restored Roberta disappeared through the backdrop while the two parrots, who were late getting her on and had been screamed at by Plassier, looked at one another in despair.

Cassy Peck, closely followed by Kate, came flying off the backstage clutching her embroidered satin jacket and legged it, naked from the waist up, back to her rail.

'Have you been roped into doing Vaubelle this afternoon?'

'Yes, and I'm bound to be late. You know what Yves Saint Laurent shows are like.'

Kate, already out of her suit, said to her dresser, 'No. Tights first, please.'

'And it's going to snow, which means the traffic'll be diabolical. Hardly worth making the effort for that cheapskate!' Cassy held the sides of her bustier together while she was zipped up. 'I dunno, bonking his son's not all it's made out to be. Sebastian Vaubelle's about as generous as his father is talented!'

Kate smiled. 'He's got some stiff competition today. They're going mad for Plassier's collection.'

'Where's Diana?' asked a parrot, pushing a group of models dressed in pink cocktail dresses into their running order. Then in a louder voice, 'I'm missing Diana!'

'Fuck!' came a voice from the background.

'She's coming,' soothed a top model from Brazil, casually rolling up the waistband of her skirt to make it shorter. A single mother of two, she was working her last season before retiring at the ripe old age of thirty-two.

'Why are you in your last outfit?' the parrots shrieked as Diana appeared in a full-length blue silk evening dress. 'You should be in pink!'

Plassier, checking the running order, looked as if he were about to have a heart attack.

'Change, quickly,' he ordered in a strained voice.

'She'll never make it,' one parrot squeaked. 'There isn't time.'

'Do it!' repeated Plassier, kneading together the palms of his sweaty hands, as Diana raced back to her rail, the priceless dress already half off.

Three dressers rushed to help her. The music changed and models started to dance as they waited to go on. They cast occasional critical glances into the mirror, double-checking themselves for flaws.

'Who sings this?' one of them asked.

'Black Box, I think.'

'Fab voice.'

'Kate!' Plassier barked. 'You're on.'

Kate winked at Bea Parker who was coming off stage in a black and white figure-hugging dress, the short skirt a froth

4

of matching feathers. Bea's skin was paper-thin and her features too irregular to be strictly beautiful (she was hard to photograph) but her eyes were a brilliant china-blue and she had a floor-stopping smile.

'Breakfast the minute we're finished,' she mouthed. 'I'm starving!'

Kate leapt up the steps, followed by a hairdresser with a comb and Plassier, pushing her none too gently towards the opening. Out of the corner of her eye she saw Diana already returning in a pink blur. It was her cue. Kate took a deep breath and walked out to loud murmurs of approval.

The forty-minute show, inspired by a Venetian summer, was a huge success. The journalists, clutching their scribbled notes, had already decided that this was the show of the week and were trying to escape before the stampede. After the finale Plassier reluctantly appeared to thunderous applause. Clinging on to Kate's arm he made the traditional walk down the runway with his 'bride', pausing at the end with smiles of relief for the cameras. The wedding dress, made especially for Kate and clinging to her like glue, was of clotted-cream satin, rippling with twists of silk cord. Behind her came the other models, smiling in earnest now that their job was done. Diana made it down first, still wearing the stolen shoes, and kissed Plassier to show her admiration. She made sure the photographers got a good shot of her at the same time.

Backstage Kate stood in her underwear and searched for her clothes. Her mane of dark-red hair, now released from its chignon, spilled down her back in thick, heavy curls, setting off the pale, almost poreless complexion. Bea emerged from her rail wearing a blood-red satin suit.

'Do we still have a hairdresser?' she yelled, to no one in particular.

Kate raised a tidy eyebrow. 'Why are you in your first outfit?'

'Plassier's roped me in for a press call and like a fool I said yes.' Bea supported herself on a rail with one hand as she struggled with a lethal satin stiletto. 'Don't worry. I'll be done in a couple of minutes.'

Pulling on a crisp white shirt and pale blue 501s Kate caught a security guard watching her across the room. She scowled and turned away. Her hands felt icy. I must buy some gloves, she thought, fumbling with a pair of thick socks. As she put on a neat ankle boot, she stopped to inspect her other long, narrow foot. It was marred by bunions and her painted big toenail was chipped. She made a mental note to touch it up before the next show. Horrid feet! Reminders of her ugly duckling days.

Two androgynous-looking models, already dressed, waved to her on their way to the portable latrines parked outside. 'Did you spot Elton John second row on the left? Next to that woman in the screaming-pink polka-dots and the Alan Rickman look-alike?' one asked. 'I'm sure he was wearing a wig.'

'Transplant. You *have* been in New Zealand a long time!'

Kate had forgotten that snow was forecast so when she stepped outside with Bea into the bitter cold she could hardly believe her eyes. It was like a fairy-tale, everything so clean and beautiful, grey Paris transformed into a startling white world. Worth a poem, Kate thought, stuffing hands deep in her pockets. People passed with bowed heads, bracing themselves against the swirling flakes. Only their muffled voices and boots crunching deep on the snowy pavements broke the stillness. Linking arms, the girls made the perilous walk to Bea's battered Volkswagen Beetle parked across the road. It's only distinguishing mark was the wire coathanger used as an aerial.

The Beetle skidded somewhat inelegantly to a halt in front of the Café Etoile and Kate's stomach gave a terrific growl as coffee and yeasty smells greeted them from the kitchen. Jumping a growing queue, they managed to find a table at the back of the room.

Kate sank gratefully into a chair. 'I'm not sure I can face the pool tonight.'

'Then don't go. I always think fashion week is like having a four-day workout with Arnold Schwarzenegger. Murderous!'

A waitress hovered. Bea inspected the menu although she knew what she would order.

'And while we're on the subject of stars, I saw Lucy Ferry at the show.'

'Doesn't count. I did a charity show with her last year.'

Bea yawned. 'What about Angelica Huston getting on a bus in the avenue Foch?'

Kate looked suspicious. 'Were your contacts in or out at the time?' She consulted the menu while Bea ferreted around in her model bag. 'Tea or coffee?'

'Anything, as long as it's hot and sweet. Hell! I've gone and left my Wonderbra at the show. I knew I'd forgotten something.'

'Do you want to go back?'

'Can't be bothered. I'll get the agency to chase it up later.'

A small, bird-like waitress wearing bright-blue mascara and reeking of cigarettes deposited a basket of croissants and two steaming omelettes on to their table. Bea, who had given up smoking a week ago, drank in the familiar stale smell. She still had a half-empty pack in the bag parked temptingly on her lap. Would one tiny puff count?

'Think of that new car your dad promised you and say to yourself, is it worth it?' warned Kate, reading her thoughts.

Bea's bag slid to the floor. At the adjoining table an enormously fat woman faced three *pains au chocolat*, an almond croissant, and a *café au lait*. Asking for low-calorie sweeteners, the woman caught Kate watching her and coloured. Kate shuddered inside. She'd never let herself end up that way.

'How was the photo-call?' she asked, spreading a thin layer of apricot jam on a warm croissant that snapped and peeled apart like cotton wool. Bea, less restrained, put three large dollops on to her plate along with a wad of butter.

'Tedious. I had to put on six outfits, none of them mine. Oh, but you did miss out on the most fabulous-looking man. Caused quite a stir with the girls! I saw him talking to Plassier, then he asked me and Cassy loads of questions. You know, what we thought of the collection, competition from other designers, were we doing the Vaubelle show. That sort of thing.'

'Journalist?'

7

'Don't know any journalists who wear black Valentino suits or Cartier watches, but definitely the cagey type. I was dying for him to ask me out for a drink, but then Plassier called us back to change and Mr Gorgeous just disappeared.'

'Without your phone number? Bea, you must be losing your touch.'

They exchanged affectionate smiles. Behind them the windows had fogged up. New arrivals left wet coats and umbrellas steaming by the front door and collapsed eagerly into vacant seats. Coming down from the show fever, Kate felt the beginnings of a headache and popped two Nurofen into her mouth. She longed for spring, for an adventure. These dreary, endless winter months when nothing ever happened!

'Are you doing the Dé d'Or Friday?' she asked, cupping the warm plump belly of the teapot in her hands.

'Can't. I've got that Cartier show in London and Mandrick wants us there a day early to rehearse. Lousy money but he's got a trip coming up in May and I've never been to Indonesia. Then there's the rent to worry about. I still owe you for last month's phone bill.'

'Forget it. They've been re-running my Ambassador chocolate commercial and the repeats have been great. So I can afford it.'

'Still, with all your handouts I'm beginning to feel like an Oxfam branch!' Bea scooped up croissant crumbs with her index finger. 'Incidentally, I bumped into a friend of yours the other day.'

'Oh, who?'

Kate broke into a half-smile, which was immediately wiped off her face when Bea said, 'Jean-François. He asked very affectionately after you. Now don't look like that. From what I've heard the man's loaded and supposed to be incredible in the sack. Don't you find him remotely attractive?'

'He's a useful spare man to go out with but he overdoes the cologne and his accent gets on my nerves. It's frightful.'

Bea giggled. 'I think he's fun but then I'm not as fussy as you.'

'True.' Bea's idea of fidelity was having only one man at a time.

Bea gave her a martyred look. 'One of these days I'm going to set you up with Mr Right.'

'Darling, there's no such thing.'

Bea fumbled for something in her bag and for a moment Kate was able to study her friend unobserved. Bea had a striking physical presence but seemed unaware of it, which was unusual in a model. It was one of the things she liked about her. Looking at her watch, Kate signalled to the waitress.

'We should go. I've got ten minutes to get to YSL at Palais Royal. Have you finished?'

'Yes. I'll drop you off. I'm not due at Lacroix until twelve.'

They both dived for the bill.

'Uh, uh. Definitely my turn,' Bea insisted, stuffing the last of her omelette into her mouth. 'You've been feeding me for weeks. Oh, and don't worry if you're late for Vaubelle. I'll cover for you. Now, what did I do with the car keys?'

The Volkswagen gave a great lurch as Bea started it without checking the gears. The windscreen wipers screeched like chalk on a blackboard, clearing the deluge of frosty-white powder. Peering through the dancing snow the girls zoomed down the Champs Elysées, narrowly missing an oncoming motorbike.

As it turned out Kate got to Saint Laurent in plenty of time. The Chanel show was still running so she was able to slip in through the back and watch the finale. Strange to be a spectator. All those shows she'd done over the years and yet she could count on one hand the ones she'd actually watched. She gazed admiringly at the models pausing for the cameras and felt at the same time a greedy desire to be up there with them bathing under the hot lights, part of the magic. Funny how just a few years ago the idea of appearing on a Parisian catwalk would have filled her with terror.

It had never occurred to Kate to try modelling until her friend Joanna, who was trying to break into fashion photography, needed a volunteer. Kate, a shy and rather overweight

9

nineteen-year-old, had reluctantly agreed to pose for her. After two days of experimenting with endless positions, lighting, clothes, make-up and hair styles at Joanna's house, Joanna announced that she was satisfied and began clicking furiously. They were all thrilled with the results.

'Isn't it amazing what lighting and a bit of make-up can do?' said Kate's mother, Sophie, who was leaving for a two-week jaunt to Venice and felt guilty about leaving Kate behind. 'Why not take them to an agency, darling? You've got nothing to lose.'

Not at all sure what she was letting herself in for but with absolutely no other job prospects, Kate stuck the shots in a plastic-sleeved book, spent hours tarting herself up and set off to one of London's top modelling agencies. Five brutal minutes later she was back out on the street clutching the rejected portfolio in her arms.

Nothing like a positive start to the day. Don't be discouraged, she told herself as she consulted her list. The second one was in Notting Hill Gate, which meant trekking to the other side of London. Having made her wait twenty agonising minutes, they too rejected Kate, but told her to try elsewhere.

It went from bad to worse. One by one they all turned her down. She wasn't tall enough, she had no experience, her nose was too small, eyes too big, she was too young, too old, too pale, not athletic enough, and the classic: 'Sorry, but redheads are difficult to market except in the autumn.'

Through the avalanche of criticism they all agreed she was overweight. Feeling about as popular as a traffic warden, Kate turned up at the last agency on her list. Prime was holding a major casting in the basement so there was no one available to see her. A booker, coming off the phone, suggested she left her pictures behind.

'I'll get someone to look at them later,' she said kindly, stubbing out her cigarette.

Kate carefully wrote down her telephone number, slipped it inside the book, and left.

Back at Onslow Gardens Sophie was preparing a late supper. Wearing a white apron over an expensive coat-dress, she hummed into the béchamel sauce. She tried to be sympathetic but she had holidays on her mind, day-dreaming of Venice and the beautiful silk lingerie she was dying to show off to her new lover.

'Never mind, darling,' she said later, gaily scooping out Loseley ice-cream, 'we can't all be Jerry Hall, and you shouldn't take any of it so seriously.'

However, the next day Kate got a call from Prime agency. They wanted to have another look at her. Unable to curb the surge of hope, once again she put on her best suit and her warmest coat and caught the bus to Pond Place. She was shown into a private office and introduced to Nigel, the owner, whose shoulder-length hair framed his round face. Kate was determined to charm him into taking her on. After all, he had asked her back. After a perfunctory nod in her direction, Nigel retreated behind his blue-rimmed glasses and inspected Kate's photos. This gave her an opportunity to view the brightly-lit room. God. It felt like an oven! She longed to take off her size fourteen jacket, but her waistband was straining as it was and she didn't want to draw attention to her bottom. Behind Nigel's head were two dozen exquisite faces, superimposed on a laminated headsheet and covered in Prime stickers. Kate swallowed nervously.

'Can you walk for me?' he said brusquely, taking his third call in as many minutes. 'No, start over there by the door towards the desk.'

Here goes. Sucking in her stomach, Kate teetered over to the door, cursing the ludicrously high heels Sophie had insisted she wore.

'They give you height, darling, and don't make your legs look so chunky.'

Sometimes Sophie's tact left a lot to be desired.

'Tony! How'd it go today?' Nigel was flicking through Kate's book at an alarming rate. 'See anyone you liked? What about Toya, the Latin American?' Kate, having made it elegantly back to the door, wobbled a bit as she turned. Had he noticed?

'Ah . . . Well, in that case, I've got just the girl for you,' Nigel swivelled in his chair and selected a model card from a row of plastic trays. Kate posed, a fixed smile glued to her face. Now what? Should she wait for him to turn back round or just carry on walking? As Nigel flicked over another page, his eyes on the model card, Kate wondered if she should point out that he'd just missed one of her best shots. He waved at her to continue. 'Only joined two weeks ago,' he said reading from the card. 'Just turned sixteen. You really should see her. Fine. Ten thirty tomorrow.'

Nigel hung up. He stubbed out his cigarette and immediately lit another. Next to the brimming ashtray were five packets of Saint Moritz and a half-eaten Marathon. How many did he smoke a day? After a few minutes he tossed her book on to the desk and Kate slipped gratefully back into her chair. Nigel studied her meditatively, resting his chin on his hands and gave her a brief smile.

Kate decided that she hated him.

'Right. To be honest we're mainly looking for girls with strong editorial books, you know, *Vogue* covers, tear sheets from *Cosmo*, that sort of thing,' he glanced down briefly at her photos. 'There's really nothing here that we could use. We'd have to start afresh.' The small ember of hope turned to ashes. 'On the other hand you've got unusual features and great hair, I'd be interested to see what a real photographer could do with you. But before any of that . . .' he paused dramatically to light a cigarette, 'you'd need to shift some weight.'

Surprise, surprise.

I can do that, she told herself, summing up her best smile for Nigel. Losing a couple of stone's a piece of cake. No, that was taboo. Cake thoughts and anything else that had calories in triple figures had to go!

More bookers called for Nigel's attention, phones rang, clients wanted to know which girls were available, faxes came through from every capital city, stunning models dashed in to collect booking details and cheques. One booker poked her head round the door and said she was thinking of taking on a peroxide blonde.

Nigel glanced at the model through his window next door and shook his head. 'Too short,' he mouthed.

12

The booker left with the bad news.

'Okay, okay!' Nigel yelled, making Kate jump, as yet another face appeared demanding his attention. 'Bloody hell! It's like Victoria Station in here.'

Kate smiled sympathetically and wiped a clammy hand against her skirt.

'Now, if you can loose a stone in, say . . . a month, we might be able to do something for you. You'll have to whack some hair off and get a new wardrobe. That suit . . . well, it's all right but a bit officey. Clients like you to make an effort. Tell you what, have a look at some mags for ideas. I can't promise anything. This is a tough business because every little girl wants to be a model. I get dozens of calls every day.'

He paused to drag deeply from his cigarette, blowing the smoke from the side of his mouth as Kate digested the sobering reality.

'One piece of advice I can give you is to avoid advertisements offering instant portfolios for a fee. They won't be any good. If an agency isn't recognised by the Association of Modelling Agencies don't touch it. It's the agency that introduces you to photographers and editorial magazines, sets up tests and organises a composite, which you pay for once you start work. That's one of these.' He held up a card about the size of a paperback, depicting black and white shots of a beautiful model. 'It's a sort of model's ID.'

Kate, baffled by so much information, wondered fleetingly if Sophie would lend her some money. She was going to need an awful lot of things.

Nigel, deciding he'd spent far too much time on this girl, stubbed out his cigarette. 'You get on and shift that weight. Then come back and see me.'

Three lines were flashing. He picked up the phone and waved her out.

Seizing this small chance to make something of herself, Kate tackled her weight reduction head-on. At first Sophie was amused to see signs of salad, rice cakes, soya milk, brown rice and cottage cheese replacing the cakes and double cream. She seemed genuinely pleased to see her only daughter finally making an effort with her appearance, but as the pounds flew off and Kate came down with a nasty bout of flu, Sophie's sympathetic tone changed.

'Really, darling, you're going to ruin your health if you're not careful. I do think you should eat more. Try a little bit of this nice cheesecake I made, mmm?'

'Mum! It's riddled with calories. Who's side are you on, anyway? This is jolly hard work.'

Sophie looked offended. 'Well, I just think trying to starve yourself is silly. There's no guarantee that this agency's really going to take you on. It might all be for nothing.'

But Kate persisted, weighing herself morning and night and haunting the bathroom mirror for signs of change. The first few pounds shifted effortlessly, but within a week Kate's metabolism ground to an abrupt, stubborn halt. Having made her decision she had expected her body to shrink as effortlessly as a deflated lilo. It didn't. All too often she would weaken, sneak out to McDonald's like a convict and order everything in sight. Then she began taking hunger-suppressant pills, and quantities of laxatives. She visited the local beauty salon three times a week for expensive G5 treatments, while small pads throbbed electrical currents into her thighs. She became depressed. She skipped meals and weighed herself three times a day, sinking into a further depression when the scale needle refused to budge. She developed spectacular stomach cramps, blinding headaches, fatigue and irritability. Spots appeared on her normally unblemished skin, so she went to a dermatologist who put her on a three-month course of oxytetracycline. She became irrational and cried a lot. Sophie was quite unsympathetic.

'What do you expect?' she said in an exasperated voice. 'You're a healthy, strapping girl, Kate, you can't turn yourself into something you're not. Now, come and have a proper meal. You're being anti-social.'

'And you're making this impossible for me!' Kate had howled, her nerves in shreds. 'Just because you're a perfect size eight! It's not bloody fair!'

'Oh, Kate. Don't be silly!'

Sophie's voice followed Kate as she rushed upstairs, slammed the door and threw herself on the bed. She doesn't understand, she wailed. I'm never going to be rid of this beastly body, ever!

One afternoon, three days before her month was up, Kate returned from her daily, hateful jog to find Aunt Rose having tea in the garden with her mother. Ruskin, the King Charles spaniel, having successfully chewed up one of Kate's shoes, lay panting in the grass. But on seeing Kate he gave a great woof of delight, causing Sophie to jump and spill her tea. For a moment Kate stood in the doorway, shielding her eyes from the bright sun, then she called out to Rose. Her aunt glanced at her politely. About to take a bite of Sophie's newly-baked Victoria sponge, her expression changed as she recognised her niece.

'Katie, darling, is that you?' Aunt Rose looked shocked. 'My dear girl, what have you done to yourself?'

Kate's face fell. She'd had no time to change or wash her hair. I must look awful, she thought in despair. She tugged diffidently at her baggy sweat pants.

'I'm sorry,' she said, scuffing her feet in embarrassment, 'I've just got back from my jog. I didn't know you were coming.'

She looked reproachfully at her mother.

Sophie saw her daughter as if for the first time and found her transformed. All of a sudden her clumsy, podgy girl had become a beautiful woman! Sophie felt a sudden stab of jealousy. But wasn't this what she had always wanted, a daughter she could be proud of? She poured Kate a cup of tea to cover her confused emotions.

Kate had lost slightly more than sixteen pounds and now weighed a very acceptable nine stone. Now on a dairy-free, fruit and vegetable-dominated diet and still on the prescribed antibiotic pills, Kate's spots had cleared up, the red hair which she usually wore in a stream around her face had been pinned back revealing high cheek-bones, cat-like green eyes and a long, slender neck.

Rose, ten years older than Sophie, and looking it, turned to her sister in amazement.

'Why, Sofe, she's the spitting image of you! I've never noticed it before, Katie darling,' she said with wonder in her voice, 'you're a really beautiful girl,' and she put an affectionate hand out to Kate's cheek. 'Tell me now, what on earth are you doing jogging, for heaven's sake? Nobody keeps fit in this family. We're all absolutely bone idle.'

Two weeks later Kate was back in Prime agency filling out model forms. They wanted complicated body measurements so she had to get one of the bookers to help her on inside leg, hat and glove size. As she hadn't made any commercials Kate left that bit blank. Underneath was a list of specialist talents. Please tick any of the following, the form read: ride a motorbike, tap-dance, sing, horse-riding, para-sail, scuba-dive, snow ski. The list, reading like an application for the Olympics, was endless. Finally she put down: write short stories and poetry, grade five in piano, good French and can drive anything with wheels. That, she thought, would have to do.

Modelling, she soon discovered, was far from glamorous. The reality was a daily slog around London, often in appalling weather, lugging her heavy model-bag which housed everything from shoulder pads, portfolio, make-up and costume jewellery to a selection of tights, shoes, the essential A–Z, and her first composite card: a natural-looking headshot with her name, measurements and agency details on the front, a body shot on the back. The Prime bookers, although helpful, often gave her the wrong address (usually miles the other side of London with no nearby tube). Kate was forced to splash out precious money on taxis, then found herself at castings she was quite unsuited for. She was often kept hanging about to show clients her portfolio. She joined the cattle-calls where models not only walked for clients but had to endure embarrassing scrutiny from a sea of other girls waiting to do the same thing. She tried coming off the antibiotics but within a week her skin had erupted and in a panic she went running to the dermatologist. He told her not to worry, that acne was a common occurrence in girls of her age and promptly wrote out a prescription for a further three months.

Some work started to trickle in, enough to feed her ambitions, but mostly Kate tested with photographers to build up her portfolio, undeniably the most important 'prop' as it showed clients the model's photographic versatility and experience. Photographers wielded enormous power, because without them models didn't get the attention.

Then, at last, came an opportunity to work in Paris. Prime felt she needed more editorial shots for her book and most of the good photographers were in Paris. Editorial sessions paid as little as £20 an hour but they gave aspiring models prestigious exposure which would lead to advertising bookings and could earn them anything from £500 a day. So Kate's card was sent off to a top agency in the rue François Premier, just off the Champs Elysées. They liked the look of her and suggested she flew over for the collections. Kate seized the chance, seeing it as a dream come true and a way finally to escape from home. In Paris her agency helped her find accommodation by putting her in touch with Bea. The girls soon became inseparable.

The first months were tough. Both were constantly broke, their modest earnings going straight back to the agency to pay for new model books, composite cards, headsheets, bikers ferrying their books to clients, and tax: the costs seemed endless. Bea's modest top-floor flat was in an eighteenth-century building in the avenue de la Grande Armée, with ornate wrought-iron balconies and facing a truffle shop that sold glacé fruits, *fougasse* (tiny biscuits) and pâté de foie gras – which Kate found irresistible – and a run-down but nevertheless bustling café where the girls often went for breakfast. The smell of baguettes and freshly-ground coffee wafted up through their windows, along with noisy arguments over double-parked cars. When one of the main pipes burst the girls went without hot water in their kitchen for five months. After each meal they would scrape leftovers into the loo and wash the plates in the bath. To save on food bills they accepted masses of dinner invitations.

Standing a willowy six foot in her bare feet, the Hon. Belinda Parker was enviably thin. She lived on an appalling diet of junk food, alcohol, Twix bars (she had been known to eat five a day) and Pepsi. It therefore came as a surprise to Kate to learn that she was also a fanatic keep-fit addict.

17

Those around her took for granted Bea's easy, outgoing nature, which she maintained with frequent trips to the gym to work off her stress. Although she was keen on mysticism and often carried a gold pendulum and a pack of tarot cards in her bag, Bea's main passion in life was men. She had been out with them all; men obsessed with expensive toys, obscure opera buffs, men with manipulative mothers, body-builders, Hooray Henrys, religious fanatics, married men, even male models. As a rule they simply had to be under thirty with good bodies and pretty faces.

'Not actually sleeping with a man is a bit like having an appetiser and then forgoing the rest of the meal,' she explained to Kate, returning one evening from a date with a six-foot-eight Harlem Globe Trotter. 'It's not that I'm promiscuous exactly, it just seems such a waste to turn a beautiful man down!'

'Don't you worry about AIDS?' Kate asked soberly, munching some honey-coated peanuts, her feet propped up against the wall. They were having a late night snack in front of the television.

'You can't let it take over your life. I mean, a life of celibacy doesn't bear thinking about.' Bea played meditatively with a cigarette. 'I simply tell all my new men that I like my gifts wrapped,' and she pulled a box of gold condoms from her shoulder bag, waving them gaily in front of Kate.

'But none of them ever lasts more than a week.'

'They're only a hobby, Kate, rather like the gym. Why do you think I do yoga? Position isn't just a way to show your athletic prowess, it's brilliant for clitoral stimulation. You should try it sometime. It wouldn't hurt to let yourself go.'

'You're absolutely shameless!'

'I know,' said Bea, squinting at the television because she'd forgotten to put in her contact lenses and was too vain to wear her glasses. 'Oh, goody, a film! Have we got any more of those chilli crisps?'

2

Roe Lewis had been in Paris less than twenty-four hours but had already packed in three meetings and eight fashion shows. It was only when he got back to the royal suite at the Hôtel Crillon that he realised how tired he was. All the same, it felt good to be out of Los Angeles. For weeks leading up to his departure he had been putting in a fifteen-hour day at the Wilshire Boulevard construction site. The thirty-floor tower block, to be made into a business centre, was an ambitious project costing millions of dollars and they were already running several months behind schedule. Thank God it was no longer his problem.

The central heating was blazing. Removing his tie and undoing his top shirt button, Roe ran an elegant hand through his dark hair, overwhelmed by a sudden wave of jet-lag. He rested his head against the back of a chair and closed his eyes, which felt sore and tired. Pierre Bauget, his newly appointed personal assistant, was perched on the edge of the sofa reading from a typed schedule. His impersonal voice diminished as Roe's attention wandered.

For twelve years Roe had been working for Carl Elliot, chairman and founder of Cortes Enterprises, a vast privately-owned conglomerate based in Los Angeles. One of Cortes's subsidiary companies, a pharmaceutical manufacturer, had recently developed a line of cosmetics. Stuck without a well-known name to promote the line, Carl had bought into Vaubelle, an ailing *couturier* house in Paris, snapping up $30 million worth of its shares. Now, with fifty-one per cent making him Vaubelle's chief shareholder, Carl had the licensing rights to sell the sunglasses, hosiery and perfume which would follow the launch of his cosmetics. Roe's clever business acumen, fluent French and natural flair both for clothes and for women made him Carl's obvious choice as Vaubelle's new chief executive officer.

'Monsieur?' Pierre's pale, bushy eyebrows were moving up and down inquisitively.

'Go ahead. I'm with you.'

'I've arranged a meeting with the immediate staff and members of the Vaubelle family, as you requested, tomorrow at two. You have an interview with *Le Monde* Thursday afternoon and I've managed to delay the conference as you asked, but the press won't be put off for long. Then you have the Dé d'Or on Friday with Monsieur Claude and his wife. It's most important that you're seen together . . .'

'Are the notes I gave you on the Dior show typed up yet?' Roe interrupted. 'I'll need them for the meeting.'

'You'll have them first thing in the morning along with the amended report you make on Vaubelle.'

'What time does it start?' Roe asked, referring to the show.

'Four o'clock. It follows Lacroix, Léger, and Yves Saint Laurent.'

'Skip the first two. Just have the car pick me up in time for Saint Laurent. And as to my identity, keep it low-key. No point in starting a premature panic.'

Roe's voice dragged. The huge double bed, just visible through a side door, looked very tempting. The phone buzzed. Pierre picked it up and spoke in rapid French. Christ, the room was hot! In order to wake himself up Roe walked over to one of the great windows and opened it. He surveyed the white scene. Snowflakes had softened the edges of the balcony and covered an outside gargoyle. The faint slushy drone of traffic filtered into the room. It faced directly on to the place de la Concorde, where the rue de Rivoli meets the Champs Elysées. A bright-yellow Beetle suddenly shot out in front of a cyclist, spewing black soot from its exhaust pipe. That was French drivers for you. To his left the Jardin des Tuileries, practically buried in snow, flanked the right side of the rue de Rivoli. Close by sat the modest Jeu de Paume, once home of the Impressionist painters. In just over six weeks huge white fashion tents would be erected for the *prêt à porter*, less élite but much more affordable than the *couture*. He took several deep breaths, exhaling mist into the air, then closed the window. The room was immediately silent. Having forgotten Pierre, Roe was surprised to see him hovering in the doorway waiting for instructions.

'Monsieur, that was reception. They have a fax for you from America. I've asked them to send it up. Will there be anything else?'

'Yeah. Start looking round for an apartment. I'm not big on room service. And stick to French. I'm a little rusty and want to acclimatise my ear.'

After Pierre had gone Roe made some calls, then ordered coffee. Despite the fatigue he felt too keyed-up to sleep. He envied people who could take catnaps at the drop of a hat. Revived by three cups of piping hot caffeine he then spent half an hour on his Tai Chi. A fitness fanatic, Roe never let more than a day go by without exercise, keeping his lean, athletic build in shape by ruthless self-control and exercise.

It was at the Opéra, the highlight of Baron Haussmann's revamped Paris, that Claude Vaubelle was launching his spring/summer *haute couture* collection. The entire area was ringed by barriers. Security men were trying to control the select but frenetic crowd waving precious gold-embossed invitations. This was not a time to be bashful. People were fighting for a seat and one freelance journalist who got knocked over suffered a nasty graze on her knee.

'Look, will you stop pushing!' snapped an angry voice somewhere near the front.

Once through, the audience moved quickly into the marble main hall, leaving behind a stream of melted footprints and limp umbrellas. The massive ceiling was painted by Chagall and the walls glowed with huge gilt mirrors and Venetian mosaics. Expensive chatter echoed round the great hall as the audience awaited the start of the show. In front of them the runway, covered in thick polythene and draped on either side with gold silk, stretched eighty feet long. Loudspeakers crackled, lights flared briefly then dimmed, while a macho-looking film crew noisily set up their telephoto lenses.

Nothing looked ready, but then Paris fashion shows always started late.

On the far side of the screen Claude Vaubelle was making frantic last-minute changes to his collection. He was not in a good mood. Someone had messed up the running order, an error which had cost him fifteen valuable minutes. A model had gained three pounds over the weekend and couldn't get into one of her outfits. This meant a complicated swap with another girl. And now Louis, his Chihuahua, had just been sick under the accessory table – a nervous young man was trying to get the smell out of the carpet. Claude was getting hotter and hotter. He wiped away the thin beads of sweat lining his brow. He longed for a shower and to remove the blue wool pin-stripe suit he should never have worn. The white shirt printed with a yellow diamond pattern did not, after all, entirely disguise his thickening waistline, a reminder of rather too many prolonged and self-indulgent lunches.

Removing his jacket, Claude paused in front of a mirror. Not bad for a man of fifty-seven, he thought, smiling at his smooth, almost handsome reflection. Thank God he still had all his hair, which had been rather expensively cut at lunchtime and secretly dyed to disguise the grey.

Vaubelle, founded in 1879 by Jeanne Vaubelle, was the last existing Parisian family-owned fashion house. The eldest grandson of Jeanne Vaubelle, Claude, was born in Montreal unacknowledged as a part of the family. His mother had fallen in love with a glamorous but impoverished Canadian and eloped to Montreal. Less than a week later her father had died. The old matriarch, Jeanne Vaubelle, was overcome with grief and wrote to Canada begging her daughter to return. One year later, however, with no word, Jeanne's grief gave way to bitterness. She immediately disinherited her, refusing to acknowledge the birth of her grandson, Claude.

At the age of seven Claude took to sketching sophisticated women in beautiful dresses. For him they represented an impossibly glamorous world, one which he knew was his birthright and which he was determined to be part of again. Claude devoured the fashion magazines his mother left around the house, unconcerned that he did not share the interests of other boys of his age. With high school finished he won a scholarship to a school of fashion and design and changed his name back to Vaubelle. Keenly ambitious for money and public recognition Claude excelled in his work, quickly becoming the school's star pupil. Making clothes on the side for private clients, he saved enough money to move to Paris and at twenty-four presented himself at the Vaubelle house in the rue du Faubourg Saint Honoré.

Jeanne Vaubelle, who had not spoken to her daughter since the elopement, was secretly thrilled to see her grandson, particularly when he announced his wish to work for the house – there was no doubt he had the family arrogance. But did he have the talent? Jeanne, too old to work, had been forced to hand over the running of Vaubelle to a distant cousin. But the house had been losing business and desperately needed help. Claude was tried out as assistant designer for the next collection. The clothes were a success and with the birth of his son two years later the Vaubelle dynasty seemed set to continue. Over the next twenty-five years, with Claude running the *haute couture*, and later the *prêt*, Vaubelle re-established itself as a leading fashion house alongside the likes of Chanel, Dior and Ungaro.

These days, however, fresh ideas were harder to come by than in the days of his youthful inspiration, and with the present collection Claude had repeated old patterns that had been popular with his clients in past years. Thinking about it now he shrugged his shoulders and straightened his tie. Everyone knew *couture* never made any money. The only good thing about all the blood, sweat and tears was the publicity that followed. At least he could rely on that.

Satisfied with his appearance, Claude looked at his gold Rolex. He licked his finger, polished the crystal, then peered through the partition separating the makeshift backstage area from the runway. The room was packed. He inspected his audience. Most of them had obviously gone to great lengths with what they wore, each trying to outdo the other and dark glasses were definitely *de rigueur*. Photographers, who had spent hours waiting, jealously guarded their floor space around the catwalk.

'Look, goddam it! I don't want you sticking your head in my camera!' whined an American voice, as a very tall photographer pushed in front. 'Find your own goddam spot!'

Joni d'Akouri, Vaubelle's glamorous PR woman, as skilled at charming the stars as she was at cutting dead gate-crashers, guided expensively-dressed people to their seats. Status, in the fashion hierarchy, was determined by how close to the front you got. It had taken some up to twenty years to get promoted to the front row, though ironically it was disastrous as a viewing point because of the presence of the photographers. A few front seats reserved for important press and fashion magazines were still empty.

'Edouard! Where is he?' Edouard, one of Claude's minions, appeared, his brow damp with nervous sweat. 'I want to know what time was Saint Laurent's *défilé*?'

'Two thirty, Monsieur Vaubelle, but they started late. Three of our models have only just arrived. We might have to delay by fifteen minutes until the rest of the press arrive.'

'Mais non! Absolument pas! Just make sure we 'ave Anna Wintour. I don't care about the others.'

As editor of American *Vogue*, Miss Wintour was one of the most powerful women in fashion.

The accessory man joined them, his neck partially buried under bright chiffon scarves. *'Women's Wear Daily* has arrived. And Patti Klensk is here from NBC. She wants to interview you. Can she come backstage?'

Claude sighed heavily and nodded. *'D'accord,* Jean-Marc. Get Joni. They like each other. Just don't inflict Madame Baudis on me or we won't get started.'

Designers lived in dread of being cornered by the journalist Madame Baudis, who never drew breath.

At the back end of the partition three scantily-clad models peeked through tiny holes at the rapidly filling seats. Their hair had been pulled back into fierce buns, secured by dozens of tiny pins and heavy-duty hair spray. By the end of the day they would all have headaches.

'Isn't that Catherine Deneuve in the front row, two seats

along from Hamish Bowles?' one of them asked.

'I'm trying to find Donald Sutherland. Cathy said he's somewhere near the front.'

'I see him. Oh, look!' squeaked a third model excitedly. 'There's Sebastian Vaubelle sitting with his glam mother. Isn't he quite the most gorgeous thing!'

'Gay,' the second model sneered, checking for runs in her tights.

'He's not! He's seeing Cassy Peck. Went out with Caroline until he dumped her.'

'Caroline'd go out with Quasimodo if he asked her,' was the dismissive reply.

All the same, three pairs of eyes focused curiously on the pale, finely-figured young man in the first row, immaculate in a charcoal suit and lemon shirt. His elegant long legs were crossed and he held a programme to one side with both his hands. The slender, exquisitely dressed brunette at his side had shattered several hearts when she married Sebastian's father Claude thirty-two years before.

Joni d'Akouri approached the NBC journalist and her sweaty cameraman with a smile. Technicians were rolling back the plastic sheet covering the catwalk.

'Patti, can you interview Monsieur Vaubelle now? I warn you he's not in a very good mood.'

A video crew was busy filming the thirty fresh-faced models having their hair and make-up done. A couple of them waited for their make-up, one wrapped in her coat and wearing Carmen rollers, the other was plugged into her Walkman, feet propped up against the wall. While most of them sat resignedly having their hair tonged, back-combed or rolled into order, one model was proving difficult, insisting that the hairdresser used her own hairpiece. Jean-Marc stood looking on in exasperation. The girl was a top model from the States, costing them a cool $8 thousand for the show. Jean-Marc, over-worked and over-stressed, was sorely tempted to put his hands round her beautiful neck and break it.

'You can't be different!' he wailed, throwing carefully manicured hands in the air. 'Monsieur Claude will have a fit!'

'But I always wear it like this!' the model said petulantly. She placed the hairpiece on top of her head to demonstrate. 'Monsieur Lacroix loved it for his show.'

'But you're not doing his show now, *chérie*, you're doing mine,' snapped Claude Vaubelle, walking past with a veil. 'Remove the bird's nest!' Then to Jean-Marc, 'Where's Louis?'

'Edouard's taken him back to the house, Monsieur Claude.'

'And I don't want that girl doing my show again, I don't care 'ow many times she's been on the cover of *Vogue*. She has an attitude problem.'

Jean-Marc put an enthusiastic red cross against the model's name on his list.

The dressers checked their model rails from a list each of them had been given. It outlined which accessories went with which outfit, and the running order they appeared in. Despite the crush of people the noise level was relatively low, just the hum of hair driers and a buzz of models talking.

Kate appeared, windswept, having been held up at Yves Saint Laurent. An up-and-coming editorial model from Sweden had been booked for the show. Inexperienced and very nervous about working for such a celebrated name, the model had tripped and stumbled in her last outfit. The poor girl had been in such a state after the show, fearing she'd never work again, that Kate had stayed behind to comfort and reassure her. Now she had to worry about Claude Vaubelle whose intolerance for lateness was well known. Finding the rail with her name on it, she waved to a couple of models, kissed her dresser and dropped her heavy bag on the floor.

'*Vous êtes en retard!*' snapped Jean-Marc, rushing up to inspect her face. 'I was just about to call the agency.'

The chiffon scarves he'd been wearing earlier had all been allocated, and he was now handing out masking tape for the models' shoes to stop them slipping on the runway.

'Change the lips but keep the hair in the chignon. You'll have to hurry and for heaven's sake don't let Monsieur Vaubelle see you. He's not in the best of moods.'

He raised his handsome black eyebrows despairingly and sauntered off in search of more problems.

26

As a last-minute replacement, Bea Parker was the only model in the show who hadn't had her outfits specifically made for her. She was going through each one to make sure there were no problems. Her hair had been set in tight curls and swept up on one side. Her blue eyes now looked almost navy against the charcoal eye make-up and her alabaster skin was accentuated by bright red lipstick.

'Why do I always get the ones that need boobs?' she moaned, wrestling with a sequin bustier that was much too big. 'Kate should be wearing this.'

'I was. They swapped us.'

'Here,' said a thin, patrician model from India smoking near by, 'try these.'

She fished out a pair of falsies from her bag and gave them to Bea, who was eyeing a waiter handing out champagne for the models.

Kate collapsed in front of a cheval mirror.

'Can we have one of those,' pleaded Bea, 'I'm desperately in need of a pick-me-up.'

Roberta came back from the loo. 'I've got bloody thrush again. I'm going to have to tell Tim we can't have sex for a week.'

'Just a week? The only thing my vagina's seen for the last three months is a Tampax,' sighed an androgynous-looking blonde Amazon with 'Mike' tattooed on her left buttock. Wearing a man's white singlet and a bright wrap-over sari which gaped open to reveal one non-existent hip, she pinched a cigarette from Kadja.

'Take an extra one for later. I've got another pack in my bag.'

'What happens when Mike becomes Peter or James or Bill or someone?' Bea asked, also wondering curiously if the blonde Amazon's tattoo affected her work.

'Nothing. Mike's my five-year-old son. God, this make-up's foul. I should have done my own.' She inspected in the mirror the false eyelashes glued to her eyelids. 'How was Lacroix?'

'Lethal. He should have handed out L plates to go with his shoes. One girl actually fell off the catwalk.'

27

Bea inspected her profile in the mirror. If she breathed out she'd just make it down the runway and back without calling out, 'I'd kill for a cigarette!'

Kadja, feeling guilty, stubbed hers out and joined Kate in front of the mirror for a final check on her make-up. A photographer appeared brandishing a large Nikon. His jacket, with a 'press' tag pinned to it, was too small for him and the armholes revealed rings of sweat. All three girls turned to the camera and flashed toothpaste smiles.

'I never see Karen these days. How is she?' Kate, in a flesh-coloured bra and a G-string, was sitting cross-legged on the floor, her mouth stretched to a wide O as she carefully applied a second coat of lipstick.

Kadja lowered her voice. 'Still working for Bright Things though why a recovering anorexic would want to be a booker surrounded by models defeats me.'

'She's supposedly gaining weight but I've got more meat on my little finger than she has on both thighs! It makes me shudder even to look at her.'

'Poor thing. She must be so unhappy,' murmured Kate sympathetically, remembering the exquisite brunette who had been destined for stardom. 'Is there anything we can do to help?'

'Not really. In the end it's down to them. I took in a box of chocolates for the bookers last week. Karen joined in with the "how lovelys" and helped herself to one, then spent an agonising twenty minutes nibbling one side.'

'God.'

The audience were getting restless. They began a slow clap and the odd cry of '*Allez*. Show us something!' could be heard.

'We're starting!' announced Jean-Marc, swanning past with a pair of gilt sandals. 'First outfits, please.'

'I'm really not in the mood for this,' said the Amazon stubbing out her cigarette and hauling herself to her size eight feet. 'But I s'pose we'd better rock and roll.'

For over sixty years the Vaubelle building had dominated the corner of the rue du Faubourg Saint Honoré. Sales occupied the first two floors. The remaining six floors held the Attaché de Presse, the offices of the family, and four studios known as ateliers. One of the most expensive governing rules set down in *haute couture* was that garment workshops had to be in the same location as the *maison couture* – inevitably in Paris's golden triangle and the most expensive property in France. The first atelier was the fabric department, responsible for chasing up orders the designer had placed. The three others were where the clothes were made: in Rodriguez's studio a mostly male staff of eight cutters and seamstresses were in charge of tailored suits and coats; one floor down Monique and Colette made skirts, dresses and shirts, and here, unlike tailored clothes, which were cut on the table, evening dresses were draped on dummies. It was easier to work this way and the results were much softer. There were no men working in these rooms.

Claude Vaubelle's own studio took up the whole of the top floor. Along the ceiling ran track lights to spotlight designs. Huge sheets of cardboard, framed and pinned to the walls, were covered in fabric samples and sketches from old collections. Rolls of material were piled like timber in one corner. And on the wall facing the door were shelves stacked with sample boxes of buttons, zips and lace.

Staff, including the house models, had to wear white overalls, like doctors. Underneath the models' uniform consisted of flesh-coloured bodies, tights, and flat black pumps. Their *cabine* (the room they used to do their hair and make-up, make calls and relax when they weren't working) was on the first floor supervised by Madame Geneviève, and as the lift only went as far as the second floor they had to climb the four flights of stairs to the design studio.

At two o'clock the afternoon following the show the *maison* bristled with tension. Word had spread that an American hatchet-man had flown in to take over the running of the company. Claude Vaubelle, as head of the house, had been due twenty minutes ago but no one could find him. The meeting was being held in the main showroom on the first floor, a large, grey-carpeted room with four french windows. One of these was open. Against the back wall metal racks sagged under the weight of the samples worn in yesterday's show.

Everyone sat round the table quivering with nerves and indignation because they had had to cancel their lunch plans. Some scribbled nervously on pads, others talked in low whispers. Rodriguez and Monique hovered in the background, unsure if they were meant to sit down. Monique was particularly nervous because Colette still hadn't returned from her dental appointment and Pierre had made a lot of fuss about being punctual.

'I bet he turns up with a loud suit and a fat cigar just to prove he's a heavyweight,' predicted Marie-Claire, Joni d'Akouri's pretty assistant.

Joni, shattered from the build-up to the show, had hoped to slip off early for some much-needed sleep. She wore a severe black suit with the hemline around the knee, showing just enough leg to remind the men which side of the fence she rested. Her thick hair was swept back in a tight knot, still a rich, dark brown despite being in her late forties. She was chain-smoking, drawing tightly on each cigarette like a teething baby and expelling the smoke towards the ceiling in a whoosh. On her left was Richard Vernon, first assistant to Claude Vaubelle, an ambitious thirty-year-old who was going bald and had a complex about it. Joni held a hand to her nose to ward off the garlic fumes Richard exuded as he banged on about the poor press reviews. He had taken copious amounts, encouraged by his boyfriend, to combat a flu bug going round the house. It had to be said that Richard was a bit of a hypochondriac.

'It is not right making us miss our lunch break,' whined Richard Vernon's assistant, Brigette Buchman, as she popped another humbug into her mouth. 'I was supposed to haf lunch with Art and it will now have to wait until Sunday.'

German-born Brigette was overweight, had close-cropped, almost punky blonde hair and a face that might have been described as pretty if it were not for a liberal crop of acne made ten times worse by thick foundation and a weakness for chocolate.

'Where have you been for the last six collections?' said

Jean-Marc cuttingly. 'Time isn't your own in this business.'

He was a thin, twitching man in his mid-twenties with straight oriental blue-black hair, and smooth pale skin. Studying his fine, beautiful face, Brigette thought there was no justice in the world.

Richard glanced at his Tag Heuer watch for the sixth time. 'How long are they going to be? I've an appointment at three with the milliner which I've already put back twice. Brigette, go and check on what's happening, if anything,' he said in an exasperated voice, 'or we'll be here all night.'

'*Moi. Je le fais.*' Jean-Marc jumped to his feet and slipped through the door. He hated sitting still.

Sebastian Vaubelle, furious at being dragged back from the show celebrations, now sat in a sulky slump at the other end of the table. He had bitterly opposed the American deal and shared his father's contempt for Carl Elliot. Losing company control meant, in effect, a leasing-out of their name for a slew of items Vaubelle didn't even design. If Carl suddenly announced that he wanted to sell Vaubelle Barbie dolls there wouldn't be a thing they could do to stop him. The recession had crippled Vaubelle and the banks were putting on the pressure.

Jean-Marc reappeared announcing that they'd arrived and made a neat dive for his seat.

Whatever they were expecting, it certainly wasn't Roe Lewis. He strode into the room like a power-line – dangerous and crackling energy. He towered over an excited-looking Nicole, Claude's secretary, gorgeous in a pale-pink Chanel copy and exuding clouds of Anaïs Anaïs. Every female's heart missed a beat – Brigette was so overwhelmed that she choked on her humbug and swallowed it whole. The men checked him out with more suspicion, taking in the immaculate black suit, the alert, sinewy form, and the set expression on his face. Pierre followed him in, then two Hungarians with slick, double-breasted suits and square shoulders. To Richard, now sitting very squarely in his chair, they looked quite capable of pulling out revolvers from their breast pockets at the first sniff of trouble. Roe appraised the assembled company and launched straight in.

'I'd first like to thank you all for turning up at such short notice,' he began in a soft, beguiling voice. 'I know that after yesterday's show you're probably exhausted, so I won't take up too much of your time.'

Brigette, flattened with lust and struggling with the trapped humbug, was thinking how much better-looking Roe was than her boyfriend Art.

'My name is Roe Lewis and these two gentlemen with me are my attorneys.'

The heavies, who looked as if they had been dipped in cement, nodded curtly.

'You've no doubt heard rumours circulating about recent company problems. You will also have been told that they're nothing to worry about. But that's not the case at all. In fact,' he said bluntly, 'Vaubelle's been running at a financially disastrous loss for some time!'

Sebastian breathed in sharply. *Dieu*, that was quick. The American *did* mean business.

'Cortes now owns fifty-one per cent of Vaubelle and has asked me to knock it into shape. That's actually harder than it sounds because unless significant changes are made Vaubelle will be forced to shut down in two, three years at the most.' He scoured the sea of shocked faces. 'Yes, it's that serious. Somehow we've got to get this company back in the head-lines. I'm not a fashion designer, I'm a money man, but I've done my homework on each and every one of you here today.'

He paused momentarily for effect, letting each person round the table feel the full benefit of his disconcerting yellow eyes. He could have heard a pin drop.

'This company desperately needs new blood! For years there's been no sense of improvisation, no one prepared to take risks. And I'm not talking about gimmicks or special effects, because they're not working either. Take a look outside. The market is in a crisis. Designers who have dominated fashion for more than a decade are running out of ideas, and it shows.'

Richard shuffled uncomfortably in his chair. Marie-Claire, who had been running errands all morning and hadn't had time

32

for a shower, was conscious of her BO. She wondered whether to risk getting the bottle of Rive Gauche from the bottom of her bag.

'I watched yesterday's show. To be frank it was an unmitigated disaster! Fashion's constantly moving forward and you have to move with it or get left behind. If we're to survive, we've got to build the *couture* and *prêt* back again into something exciting, revolutionise the image of this house, not just with new ideas but with stuff that sells!'

It was quite a speech but Roe was not finished. There followed a ruthless attack on shoddy management, lack of initiative and the disgraceful amount of time taken off work, which left everyone's head spinning. Marie-Claire, bristling, felt he had no right to bully them in this way. Joni, who'd always prided herself on her professionalism, looked mutinous, while Sebastian was silently spitting with rage and attacked the side of his right thumb with the nail of his index finger. Everyone else was trying to come up with a clever retort in their defence.

'If you work here you leave your egos at home,' Roe went on, 'or you're out! We've got to pull together. Oh, and start wearing watches. Punctuality doesn't seem to count for much around here. Two members of staff haven't even bothered to turn up for this meeting!'

Brigette seemed suddenly very interested in her chipped nail-polish. A telephone rang and Pierre got up to answer it.

'*Monsieur, c'est pour vous,*' he said in a low voice to Sebastian.

Sebastian muttered a few words then hung up. At that moment there was a knock at the door and Colette made her untimely appearance. The right side of her face looked horribly swollen.

'*Je suis vraiment desolée, monsieur,*' she apologised in a tiny voice, catching a disapproving look from Pierre. Aware of the sea of glum faces watching her, she turned a dull red and sank into the seat nearest to Monique.

'If you work with me on this, we might just turn this house around,' Roe said more gently. 'I don't expect miracles but we will have to work hard and I must feel I can count on your support. You're all good at what you do, so in case anyone is worried, I don't plan on kicking anyone out.'

You could hear the sigh of relief half-way up the Champs Elysées.

Pierre then formally introduced everyone. Roe systematically made his way round the table firmly shaking hands. Joni held his hand slightly longer than necessary, then coloured when Roe spotted the used ashtray and announced that there would be a ban on smoking.

'OK, where exactly is Claude Vaubelle?' he then asked.

There was an awkward pause. Joni did not meet his eye.

'Wasn't he told about today?' Roe's penetrating look was directed at Pierre.

Pierre fiddled with his glasses and explained that Claude had had to attend a very important business meeting elsewhere.

'I don't care. Find him and get him here now! No excuses. Everyone else managed to turn up.'

Roe's voice was calm but his eyes were like granite. Richard, who had been bragging fifty minutes earlier about how he'd show the American upstart who ran what and that *nobody* pushed him around, started doodling very intently on the pad before him. Pierre picked up the phone. He knew exactly where Claude was.

Claude Vaubelle was in fact tucking into a very tender *filet mignon* and a third bottle of a 1968 Château d'Angludet at Le Grand Louvre. Louis, who had made a speedy recovery, was under the table chewing greasy bits of fat. Claude had invited two members of the English press, his beautiful wife Isabella, and his twenty-one-year-old daughter Leonora, just back from London, to join him in celebrating the completion of his show. When the *maître d'hôtel* quietly informed him that a car was waiting outside to take him back to Vaubelle, Claude thought it was a practical joke.

'Monsieur, they did say it was urgent. I believe you were expected half an hour ago.'

'*Chérie*,' Isabella urged gently, sensing his agitation, 'this man has just arrived all the way from America. It would be nice if you were there to greet him.'

34

Seeing the English journalists desperately trying to translate, Claude curbed his irritation and left the restaurant for the company Mercedes waiting outside. He was less restrained when he arrived at Vaubelle.

Not bothering to knock, Claude's short, stout frame barged into the boardroom.

'Just who do you think you are,' he said bullyingly, 'interrupting an important press lunch? I must protest at . . .'

He stopped in his tracks and glanced around at his staff listening avidly to an uncomfortably tall stranger. On the table were photographs and designs, which they were studying. Roe spoke without looking up. Trouble ahead, Joni thought to herself.

'Claude Vaubelle, I take it. Good of you to join us.'

All eyes were now on Claude.

'Could this not have waited?' Claude demanded pompously. 'I've two members of the press waiting for me. It really is a most inconvenient time for me.'

'Well, that would depend on where your priorities lie, I guess,' said Roe enunciating each word as if he were talking to the hard of hearing. 'All the same I hope you'll be more punctual in future. As for your press meeting,' Roe's lips tightened, 'don't you think a celebratory lunch is a little premature? I mean, a couple of paltry paragraphs covered yesterday's show and they weren't very impressive.'

Roe signalled to Pierre who handed him the press cuttings.

'Listen to this. "In the pursuit of individuality, Claude Vaubelle decided to eliminate trousers from his collection," says *Women's Wear Daily*. "They were not missed. He did add some evening styles from his ready-to-wear, including plaid capes and below-knee-length dresses, but on the whole there was nothing about this collection that we haven't already seen." '

Claude gave an audible snort.

'I've been running through some of the changes we aim to make for this season,' continued Roe, 'and judging by yesterday's cock-up on the runway you're going to need all the help you can get.'

Claude, who had never in his life been spoken to in this

manner, was speechless. Nicole, sick to death of Claude's rudeness, decided the American was very good news.

Later on, in his freshly-painted office which overlooked a clump of white roofs and the tip of the Tuileries gardens, Roe made a call to Carl Elliot in Los Angeles.

'He's fucking arrogant! No way can I work with the guy. I mean, he's repeated the same designs for the last four years. He's lazy! Christ, Carl, his own staff can't stand the sight of him. I want him out.'

'Can't help you, kiddo. They still own forty-nine per cent. You're going to have to figure out a way round it.' Carl Elliot's gruff voice echoed down the line, 'You'll find a way. You always do. Keep me up to date. If you need anything I'll be back from New York at the end of the week.'

Hanging up, Roe's thin lips pressed together determinedly. Carl was right. There were always ways out. All he had to do was find one. He gazed out at the heavy falling snow, down at the facing grey buildings and into brightly-lit offices. He could just see people packing up, finishing off their work for the day. Five floors below he watched Richard Vernon race across the road to a tiny, but packed corner café. What was he in such a hurry about? Boyfriend? How small everything looked compared to the vast sprawl of Los Angeles, none of which he would miss. It felt good to be back. Paris had always been his lucky city. Why, he'd clinched his first really big deal here.

Overcome suddenly by another wave of jet-lag, Roe glanced at his watch, noting that his next meeting was in less than an hour. No point in going back to the hotel to grab some sleep but, boy, could he do with some. Rubbing a weary hand over his face, Roe did the next best thing. He put his feet up on the desk, rested his head against the back of the chair and closed his eyes.

3

The much coveted Dé d'Or, otherwise known as the Golden Thimble, was awarded by a jury of top fashion journalists twice yearly to the best French *couturier*. This spectacular event, which followed fashion week, was to Paris what the Oscars were to Hollywood. Last year Claude Montana had made history after winning the award twice running, and his latest collection to storm the runway had received rave reviews from *Women's Wear Daily*. Much to everyone's surprise today, however, Jean Béger won the thimble, proving that as a designer he was light years ahead of the competition. Madame Chirac, the Mayor of Paris, presented the award.

Kate, representing Dior, was escorted by Bernard Plassier and flashed a professional smile at the sea of photographers flanking the front door. She wore a full-length velvet dress cut shockingly low at the back with a tulip-shaped skirt. When she walked it revealed glimpses of her long legs. From a distance it looked violet but on closer inspection the dress was deep blue with flashes of turquoise where it caught the light.

Bernard, never comfortable in crowds, acknowledged everyone with quick, irritable nods. Fiddling self-consciously with his bow-tie, he left Kate chatting to the towering ex-Chanel model Inès de la Fressange. Ines had become something of a legend in France after signing an exclusive ten-year contract with Chanel. She had a curiously masculine beauty, huge chocolate-brown eyes and an anorexic body which made clothes look sensational. Some years ago her amazing partnership with Karl Lagerfeld had come to an end after she broke her exclusive contract with Chanel. She became the latest in a long line of stars to personify La Liberté, national symbol of the Revolution. Her fame and beauty continued to grow, and now happily married, she had opened a smart new boutique selling shoes and handbags in the avenue Montaigne.

The champagne flowed, and waiters in blond curly wigs and gold-buttoned eighteenth-century uniforms handed round plates of smoked salmon and caviar. The huge gilt doors leading to the frosted garden were open but giant heaters blasted hot air into the room. Kate watched some of the world's most glamorous figures drift in: Ivana Trump sharing a joke with Joan Collins; and William Baldwin talking to Jacqueline Bisset, who looked stunning in an Anouska Hempel dress. Cindy Crawford arrived shortly after with a sheepish-looking Richard Gere, causing a considerable stir among the press. Rumours had been circulating that Cindy was pregnant. She certainly looked radiant. Beyond her, through the doors, Kate could see a large, frozen fountain and the ghostly outline of trees and clipped shrubs. The sky, like a great black mouth, yawned and issued a spray of tiny, bright stars.

Kate drifted away in search of a drink, stopping to acknowledge compliments from passers-by. Jean-François, a gaunt Lebanese with a ready grin and a sharp eye for pretty girls, disengaged himself from the petulant blonde who was boring the socks off him, and followed her.

'I was hoping to run into you. Why won't you ever return my calls? I loathe talking to answer machines.'

'I've been busy.'

'Even for me? You're a difficult woman, *chérie*.'

Kate laughed. 'Only because you can't bear rejection, Jean-François.'

Unperturbed, he moved closer, circling an arm round her waist. 'I think you are afraid of me, *tu sais*, which is a shame because we'd be really good together.'

'Save the clichés, Jean-François. I'm immune.'

'You're no different from any other woman, *chérie*, you just don't like admitting it.'

He was nothing if not persistent. 'Well, if you're so eager

to please me, why don't you grab one of those alcoholic trays. I could do with a nice strong drink.'

'Anything for a beautiful woman.'

As Jean-François pushed his way to the bar Kate scanned the room, wondering how she could get rid of him. A useful spare man, as she had told Bea, but Jean-François had a habit of pushing his luck.

Then, quite suddenly, she saw him. Kate caught her breath. Dressed entirely in black, he was, without question, the most devastatingly attractive man she'd ever seen. Less than a foot away from Jean-François, he grabbed a drink from the bar and quickly drained it. His handsome face lit up as he waved to someone. A few minutes later a diminutive woman in her early fifties approached him. They exchanged a few words, then he took the brunette's arm and they disappeared from view. Lucky thing, Kate thought wistfully, then was distracted by a deadly blonde professionally swinging her tiny hips across the room. She wore an acid-green sequin dress with more holes in it than a sieve.

'Can you believe it! Christopher Lambert's sitting outside the cloakroom!' she squealed. 'He asked me if I wanted a drink and I was so nervous I couldn't think of a thing to say!'

'Must be awful having that effect on women, Arielle,' said a man whose head was covered with snow. He slipped a territorial arm around her. '*Salut, chérie!*'

'Kate, have you met my wonderful fiancé, Michel?'

Kate, dragging her eyes from the spot she'd seen the man in black, found herself engulfed in a cloud of Aramis as Michel bent to kiss her. An obscene amount of gold jewellery flashed at her.

'I apologise for being so late. My car was frozen and I had to jump-start it. I hate snow!'

'You could have fooled me. Look at you, *chérie*, you're covered in it!' Arielle fussed tenderly with his hair.

'*Pas pour moi,*' declined Kate, avoiding a plate of cocktail sausages thrust under her nose.

'Oh, come on, Kate,' said Michel, his mouth full, 'don't tell me you're on a diet too. You girls will fade away.' He looked despairingly at Arielle, who laughed.

'Paul has an Italian mother, Kate. She can't understand why I don't want to be a size sixteen!'

They found themselves a table. Kate, who'd been on her feet since nine that morning, sank gratefully into a chair.

'Rough day?' Arielle asked sympathetically. 'I heard you got the Shiseido commercial. Congratulations.'

'Thanks. We had to shoot during most of last night. Only time the clients could fit everyone in. Lovely crew but it was exhausting. I didn't get to bed until five this morning.'

'I've been wanting to get into your bed for weeks.' Jean-François had arrived back with their drinks. 'Just got to find out what makes you tick.'

'The same as everyone else, Jean-François. Tick, tock, tick, tock.'

The orchestra was playing the slow movement of Mozart's *Clarinet Concerto*. The champagne started to take effect. Kate's gaze wandered back to the handsome stranger, now deep in conversation with the brunette. They were joined by a pretty blonde wearing a cheeky Versace number, whom Kate recognised as Claude's daughter Leonora. Though striking, she had inherited her father's rather bullish looks, which was unfortunate as her mother's beauty was renowned. Beside Leonora sat Claude Vaubelle in a navy suit and smoking a cigar. His right arm rested casually on the back of the brunette's chair and Kate watched his hand stroking the back of her neck. Obviously his wife Isabella. Goody. Kate's eyes returned to the handsome one who seemed to direct most of his conversation to Isabella. Kate tugged on Arielle's sleeve.

'Without being too obvious about it, any idea who the man in black is over there?'

Following Kate's gaze, Arielle then checked to see that Michel was out of earshot. 'No. But I wouldn't mind finding out. He's wonderful-looking.'

'Probably married with four children,' Kate sighed wistfully.

'Doesn't look the type to me. If you're interested I could always send Michel over to investigate.'

'Taking my name in vain?' Michel grabbed Arielle's arm. 'I

40

need to steal her away for a second.'

'Go ahead,' said Kate, 'I suppose I should do one final round or I'll have Plassier breathing down my neck.'

Letting her hair fall seductively over one eye, Kate breezed across the room, stopping deliberately to kiss an admirer just beyond the group. Claude smiled as she passed his table.

'*Charmante, chérie*, but you looked better in my dresses.'

Kate peeked sideways at the stranger. He cast a slow, lingering glance over her body and for a second their eyes clicked. Then he resumed his conversation with Leonora who was hanging on to his every word. Probably gay, Kate thought furiously and fled to the loo. No Christopher Lambert welcoming party for her. Someone else must have snapped him up. Pity!

The small bathroom was a nice surprise with its mosaic floor and salmon-pink walls. The overwhelming clash of perfume and hair spray, however, was less inviting. Neat rows of folded towels had been placed by the sink and an attendant sat on a stool reading a book about mass murderers. A saucer placed on the counter beside her for tips held one solitary franc. The rest lay hidden in the attendant's drawer, safely out of sight.

Kate joined the loo queue. As the hair sprays were exchanged for lipstick and powder, she watched the women preen before the mirror appraising their sex-appeal. Two Englishwomen at the head of the queue were grumbling about an amateur dramatics class they'd recently joined. The one talking had on an emerald-green silk dress which was too tight around her bottom and revealed the line of schoolgirl knickers. The other was buried in pink taffeta bows. She wore a wide-brimmed hat and was touching up her lipstick in a compact mirror. Their loud conversation was being broadcast to the whole room.

'Melanie says to be more aggressive with my part. "Dominate me," she said last week. I ask you! How are you supposed to dominate someone standing six inches taller than you! Especially when they're dressed as a centurion.'

'Sandra should never have got the lead. Keith obviously

fancies her,' said the woman in the pink bows, picking spinach from her teeth. Two loos flushed and the queue shuffled along.

'And have you seen what she's wearing tonight? Not that you can call it a dress, she's practically falling out of it. The tart! Oh, this is a lovely colour,' she gushed, distracted by her friend's lipstick. 'Where'd you get it?'

Kate dived into a free loo, noting with dismay that the flush had broken. Hitching up her dress and trying not to look into the stinking loo bowl, she unravelled several strips of pink toilet paper to cover the toilet seat. Squatting, yoga-style three inches above the seat and feeling the muscles in her legs clench, Kate peed loudly. She gave a wide yawn but tired as she was, she didn't want to go home. She wanted some excitement.

Back at the table Jean-François took her arm. 'I thought you'd gone.'

'Not at all.' She felt suddenly reckless. 'I want to go dancing tonight. Why don't you take me dancing, Jean-François?' Kate tilted her head to one side and gave him the full benefit of her green eyes.

'Great idea. We'll go to Castelle's. It'll give me an excuse to hold you in my arms until the sun rises.'

'I know what else he'd like to rise,' Arielle muttered to Michel. Michel stubbed his cigarette out and picked up a large bunch of keys.

'*Tiens, chérie. On y va.*'

Castelle's was packed. Michel, owner of a four-star restaurant and health club, used his considerable influence to get them a table in the back. Arielle's green sequins winked in the dark. The group followed him through a labyrinth of kitsch, gold frills, narrow staircase and magenta corridors. They passed the gaming-room and plush drawing-rooms hidden behind baize doors. Seated in the underground cavern reserved for drinkers and dancers more champagne arrived and Kate began to feel quite light-headed. She was dying to dance, but not with creepy Jean-François.

Arielle pointed out Jack Nicholson hidden behind his *lunettes*. He was lounging at his favourite table at the base of the stairs, which provided a stimulating visual angle of leggy young models ascending in micro-minis. Then there followed the usual, 'Oh look, there's so and so. Wasn't he going out with . . . *Chérie!* You're back from New York . . . It's been ages! . . . What have you done to your hair? I always said going blonde wouldn't suit you.'

Sounds of Otis Redding's *I'm a love man* drifted up from the dance floor one level down and Jean-François pulled Kate from her seat.

'Come on. I like this track.'

Kate consented. No one else had asked her. Dancing proved somewhat tricky with so many people on the floor. It was rapidly becoming a sweat box. Jean-François went into an orgasmic trance as he gyrated and bounced in front of her, unperturbed by the crowd. Kate was knocked by a couple of out-of-control enthusiasts behind her and kept flying into Jean-François. Then her dress started coming apart, much to Jean-François's approval. So much for dance erotica, she thought crossly. The music slowed and couples meshed together, girls resting their heads on partners' damp shoulders. Kate tried to escape but Jean-François was too quick, clasping her against his Bijan-soaked body.

'Relax,' he slurred into her ear as he felt her tense against him. 'I'm very attracted to you, *chérie.*'

'That's nice but must we play Sardines? I can't breathe!'

Frustrated hands explored her back and down over her bottom. Kate moved them back up to her waist but each time he'd drop his hands down again, squeezing her cheeks. I'm not enjoying this, she thought, gritting her teeth. Arielle, on the other hand, was having a fine old time bopping away with Michel. She danced well too. One song blended into another and Jean-François's arm tightened as if sensing her desire to leave. His eau-de-Cologne was overpowering and she could feel his erection pressing against her. That was taking liberties!

'*Kate, ma petite Kate,*' he murmured into her hair.

'Jean-François, will you take your flaming hands off me!'

In a breathy voice, 'Never. Not now I have you.'

'I'm warning you . . .'

'You smell good enough to eat!' And he buried his head in her cleavage.

It was the final straw! As her arms were trapped Kate raised her right foot and kicked him sharply in the shins.

'*Merde!*'

'Serves you bloody well right for . . .'

'You're pretty handy with those heels.' A smooth American voice behind her interrupted.

Mortified, Kate turned and found herself looking into the eyes of the stranger she'd spotted with Claude Vaubelle. Leaving Jean-François gaping like a Japanese carp, the man took her arm and swept her deep into the crowd of dancers.

'Out of the frying pan, into the fire,' said Kate in a daze, finding herself pressed against his denim shirt. Her nose recognised faint traces of Fahrenheit.

'That guy was practically mauling you.'

'Jean-François's not known for his subtle approach with women.' She raised her coppery-green eyes and gave him her most seductive smile. 'I'm Kate. Thanks for rescuing me.'

'Forget it. You gave me a good excuse to escape from my own table.' His hand, firm with long, bony fingers, pressed against the hollow of her back.

'Oh, that's right. You were sitting with Claude Vaubelle at the awards.' Subtle, Kate, very subtle!

'For a while. I left them talking about hemlines an hour ago.' He flashed her a lethal smile, then glanced at his watch. 'I'm supposed to be meeting someone here but he disappeared with a blonde an hour ago. Can't understand how he missed you.'

'Oh, I pop up from time to time.' She glanced away self-consciously.

'I'll bet you do.'

Out of the corner of her eye Kate could see Jean-François watching them moodily from his table. Arielle and Michel were still dancing together. She moved her hand up the American's sinewy arm, enjoying the reassuring dip and curve of his biceps.

'The truth is I'm not a great one for nightclubs.' Distracted by his nose which bore a slight suggestion of a hook, Kate couldn't think of anything else to say.

'Oh, I don't know,' the American said as they were crushed together by surrounding dancers, 'they have some advantages.'

As they moved around the dance floor his hair trailed over his haughty and expensive face. The overtones were English public school rather than American. Another devastating smile. It would take time to build up her resistance. She could feel her breasts squashed against his hard chest and the familiar tingling between her legs. Careful, Kate, slow down. You don't know anything about him. But already she felt out of control. There was something dangerous about this man. Dangerous because she sensed he could stroll into her life and take it over completely. A fast track came on, and bodies started thrashing wildly around them.

'Roe!' a squeaky voice yelled. 'Honey! Over here!'

A very pretty, slightly overweight girl with masses of black hair waded through the crowd towards them. She was dressed in raspberry velvet shorts trimmed with fur, black stockings and a velveteen bra that was too small for her. As she got close Kate realised the girl couldn't have been more than eighteen.

'Roe, you promised you'd only be gone a couple of minutes. You were supposed to get me a drink,' she said petulantly, her voice revealing traces of an Australian accent. Or was it New Zealand? Kate never could tell the difference.

'I think you've already had quite enough. Besides, it's way past little girls' bedtime. Beat it, baby, I'm busy.'

'So I see.' The girl glared at Kate. 'All sweetness and charm until something better comes along!' She pushed her way angrily back into the crowd.

Now that's two people we've upset, thought Kate, wildly excited, as she glanced at Jean-François. People pushed in front of them, laughing. A very drunk girl at a nearby table howled with laughter as a man poured a glass of wine down her front and started to lick it off.

'Don't you think it's hot!' Kate panted over the din of the music. 'There's no ventilation.'

'I agree. Let's go somewhere we can talk,' said Roe, steering Kate off the dance floor. 'I've got my car outside.'

'I didn't mean . . .' Kate stammered, side-stepping a burning cigarette. 'My friends. I can't just leave them.'

It sounded awfully lame. If only she had some of Bea's wicked repartee.

'You mean that guy you were dancing with? He looks overage to me even if he doesn't act like it.'

Kate gazed at the thin, sardonic mouth and wondered what it would feel like to be kissed by it. Taking her hand he lead her off the dance floor. At her table Roe's hand deliberately reached for her bag and coat.

'Hate breaking up a good party,' he said, helping her into the coat, 'so we're off to find one.'

Leaving Jean-François speechless with rage but not prepared to take Roe on, who though slim was twice his size, Roe ushered Kate through the back door. It was snowing outside. They walked towards a black Porsche parked across the road and she clutched Roe's hand. Well, it was tricky trying to negotiate three inches of snow in high heels. He held her door open and she slid into the seat. Climbing in the other side, Roe revved the car into action. The CD player screamed at them but he quickly turned it down and the dashboard glowed in the dark, looking like a Boeing 747 control panel.

'Where are we going?'

Paris flew past her window in a ghostly blur. The windscreen wipers whittled back and forth, keeping time with her nervous heart. Kate slipped her hands between her knees as if seeking warmth. She could still feel the shape of his hand encasing hers.

'That depends. Hungry?'

'Not really.'

'My place, then. For a drink,' Roe added, noticing her panic-stricken face.

Kate pulled her coat around her protectively, chewing the inside of her cheek. Away from the safety of the nightclub and other people she felt less sure of herself.

'It'll soon warm up, Kat,' he said, fiddling with the heater.

The car phone purred. Roe picked it up and spoke briskly into it, which gave Kate a moment to sneak a side-on look at him. He had surprisingly small ears for a man and there was a mole on his left cheek. Roe hung up.

'Actually my name's Katherine.'

'I know but I'm an uncouth Yank who likes to abbreviate names. Besides, Kat suits you. You're sleek and feline.'

'With all nine lives intact.'

'Oh, really?' He raised a neat eyebrow. 'Guess you've led quite a sheltered life, then.'

Kate giggled nervously and studied the window. For a moment they sat side by side like bookends feeling the space between them. Then, still worried about going to his flat alone, she said, 'I know a wonderful little café close by. We could go there for coffee.'

'Relax. You're quite safe,' he said, reading her mind. 'I'm not going to try anything. I've been around a lot of demanding people all day and I'd just like to go somewhere less noisy. Anyhow, from what I've seen tonight you're pretty capable of taking care of yourself.'

He glanced briefly at her shoes and smiled. One could win Academy awards with a smile like that, Kate thought, deciding not to be so weedy. Her ears were still humming from the club's loud music. Stretching her long legs, she removed from the floor some unopened post bearing American stamps, some literature from an estate agent, and an empty box of tissues. She flicked idly through the CDs in the arm-rest, none of which she recognised, and caught Roe studying her through the gloom of the car.

The car skidded into a corner, unnerving her. Changing sharply down to second gear, Roe accelerated on to the straight. Kate was impressed by the casual way he handled the powerful machine. She studied the fine dark hairs emerging from his cuff, the slim, masculine watch. She drew a hand up to her mouth and breathed against it. Honestly! Why must the French drench everything with garlic. And no mints left. Bea had scoffed the lot earlier on.

They came to a halt outside a smart-looking block of flats trimmed with wrought-iron balconies. A couple emerged from the hôtel Meurice next door and made a dash for a passing taxi. The woman slipped and, hanging on her partner's arm for dear life, gave a whoop of laughter as they skidded to the car. Snow danced around them like confetti.

Roe helped her out of the car and Kate waited for him to tap in the door code. The latch snapped free and she followed him into a small courtyard.

'Mind that step,' he instructed, guiding her up a musty-smelling side staircase that wound in a spiral to the top floor. Roe's flat was a surprise. The studio room was huge, but apart from two nondescript oil paintings, a leather sofa with matching armchairs, an enormous remote-control television and a music system, the room was empty. A newspaper open at the financial section lay on the stripped-wood floor alongside an open leather sports bag revealing a squash racquet and a pair of grubby trainers. Large french windows introduced a breathtaking view of the city below.

Kate walked round the room curiously, looking for something she could safely comment on. It was so big! You could land a plane in here. A typical man's room, she decided. Stark and anonymous. Where were all his things?

'I like it,' she ventured tactfully, wondering if he was moving in or out.

'It needs work but that'll come. I've got most of what I need.'

Roe approached her from behind and removed her coat.

'You're lucky. I share a tiny flat and there isn't much room for privacy.'

'Boyfriend?'

'Girlfriend. We're very close.'

'Sounds cosy.' Roe tossed her coat on a chair. Even his most casual movement was deliberate. 'What can I get you to drink?'

'Oh, anything,' Kate said following him over to the sofa. 'Wine if there's some going.'

She sat down, then, anxious in case he tried to kiss her and smelt the garlic fumes, asked where the loo was.

In the hall his answer machine was flashing furiously. Obviously popular, she thought, wondering how many of the

48

calls were from women. Sitting on the loo, Kate kicked off her shoes and massaged her frozen feet. Roe's bathroom was full of wall-to-wall mirrors. The floor, covered in black and white tiles, looked like a chessboard. There was a portable phone next to the loo and a large chrome shower with a five-speed massage spray. She contemplated calling a friend long distance but instantly changed her mind. The conversation would have had to be conducted in whispers. Used to Bea's clothes and towels strewn over the floor, splashed mirrors and a noisy extractor fan, this clinical room made her feel uneasy. After all, she knew nothing about this man. He might be a serial rapist or into knocking off old biddies.

After flushing the loo Kate searched for the toothpaste, but everything seemed to be hidden. Noiselessly she investigated the cupboards, looking for clues which would tell her more about Roe. It was wrong to pry, but she was doing it now so she might as well go on. She found a lipstick. Girlfriend? Horrid colour, she thought, putting it back. She could hear him talking next door. Must be using the phone. Underneath the sink she found four toothbrushes in a mug and opted for a red one. Studying her face in the mirror, Kate ran a hand through her hair. Her mother's sleepy greengage eyes gazed back critically. Oh dear. I look a wreck, she thought inspecting the full mouth and her long, aquiline nose which was covered in freckles – they drove Kate mad. Her right cheek bore the imprint of someone's lipstick. How much of the evening had she been walking round like that? Irritated, she rubbed the mark off and used Roe's brush to clean her teeth, then immediately worried about AIDS.

Music drifted through the speakers as Kate moved out to the sheltered balcony to look at the view. The sky was dotted with stars, the moon gazed dreamily through a curtain of wispy black clouds and in the distance the Eiffel Tower winked at her. Although it had stopped snowing it was bitterly cold and a gust of wind lifted her hair, blowing it across her face. She heard a champagne cork pop inside and turned as Roe emerged with a brimming glass and a tumbler holding neat vodka. No. Serial killers didn't look like that.

'I found some cheese in the fridge but it doesn't look too

good. I rarely eat in.' He handed her the champagne. 'Can you do without?'

'Don't worry. I'm really not hungry.'

'No, I guess you aren't.'

Kate smiled, he thought, uncertainly. She gazed up at him for a moment feeling the full force of his eyes wordlessly saying, your move. He was standing under the balcony light with his face partly in the dark. The severity of his black suit only served to set off the tall, slim build. She felt he could accomplish anything. He seemed so powerful, so confident with just a hint of danger. Who is this man, she wondered. They moved back into the warm drawing-room.

'You're very tanned.'

'Skiing last month. I'm going back soon. Do you ski?'

'No,' said Kate, wondering if that was an invitation. 'I never fancied those hats. They make you look like an overgrown Santa's helper.'

Roe laughed. 'Yeah. And they itch like hell!'

'Have you been in Paris long?'

'About a week. My company's based in LA but they needed someone to give the French a good kick up the rear. So here I am, a believer in change.'

'Me too,' said Kate, wondering again why there was so little of a personal nature here – no books, ornaments, photos, the sort of things her own flat was stuffed with. She resisted the temptation to ask what he did for a living. Sophie had always said it was the height of bad manners to ask a person their occupation, as you inevitably pigeon-holed them. He must be a merchant banker or something equally high-powered. 'What else do you believe in?'

'Freedom, beauty, power. Taking risks.' Then with an amused smile he asked, 'Are you always this uptight?'

Kate, attempting to hide the fact that he'd offended her, ignored the question. 'Men only ever seem interested in money and power.'

'And sex,' Roe said bluntly. 'It all amounts to the same thing in the end. Money makes men feel more powerful, therefore more sexually desirable.'

Kate raised an eyebrow. 'Well, they may feel it but most

50

rich men I know wear bifocals and platform shoes.'

Roe laughed. 'I've got no argument there. How about you? What turns you on?'

She answered slowly, 'Work, I suppose. I'm at my most confident when I'm on the catwalk. Not that the feeling lasts but while I'm out there, I'm in complete control.'

Roe smiled suddenly, amused at her earnestness. The strap on Kate's right shoulder had fallen, revealing smooth bare skin which he felt a strong desire to nibble.

'I didn't think serious girls like you existed. Don't you ever break the rules?'

Kate struggled to stay sober. 'Constantly.'

She gulped down the rest of her Laurent Perrier wondering if it would be her salvation of her undoing. She glanced around the room. 'What about your family?'

Roe's face was suddenly blank.

'It's just that I don't see any photos lying around,' she added quickly.

He poured more champagne and Kate didn't try and stop him. She felt awkward, inadequate suddenly in Roe's presence. The champagne helped to blur the edges.

'My mother left home when I was a boy and my father's dead. That's about it,' he said unemotionally.

'I'm sorry. Any brothers or sisters?'

'No, just me. How about yourself?'

'My mother's been divorced twice and now lives with her boyfriend in London. We're not very close.' She added, 'And I'm an only child too, so we have that in common.'

Roe studied her meditatively. 'That guy you were with tonight, the one doing an impersonation of an octopus. Is he your boyfriend?'

Kate flushed. 'Jean-François? God, no! He buys and sells very expensive antiques. Not my type at all.'

'What, the antiques or the guy?' His eyes challenged her. 'And just what is your type, Kat?'

'You!' Really, the champagne was making her unusually bold. Kate took another hasty gulp.

'But I make you nervous.'

'You do?'

'I just get this feeling you don't trust men very much.'

How the hell did he know that? Kate was suddenly on her guard.

'What happened to your father?'

'Found someone younger than Mum. Didn't last long, of course, but then men are never very smart when it comes to sex.' Roe didn't comment. 'I honestly don't know where he is or what he's doing. He and Mum lost contact years ago. She never really got over it, though she pretends she has. I can't say that my stepfather or any of the subsequent boyfriends have been much of an improvement, but then I'm not the one that has to live with them, am I?'

They gazed at one another and it was Kate who dropped her eyes first. Well, it was hardly surprising. She tried to ignore the hand he used to pull back her hair which tumbled between them like a heavy silk curtain. Out of sheer nervousness she knocked over a glass. As she went to pick it up, her head started to spin.

'Hey, take it easy.' Roe put out a steadying arm, taking the broken glass from her.

'Sorry about the glass. I think I've had too much to drink.'

'Forget it. No carpet to clean. Come here. Let me give you a shoulder rub.' He threw the offending glass into a bin.

'Oh, there's no need,' protested Kate in a panic.

Roe liked that. She wasn't as cool as she looked. 'Don't be so damned English. Come and sit down.'

Resting his hands on her shoulders, Roe began kneading her soft skin with firm but gentle hands. Kate's body stiffened as she tried to check sudden waves of lust. He was standing so close, Kate could feel the outline of his strong body against hers, his warm breath on her neck. I really should stop him, she thought as her stomach flip-flopped. He glanced outside; the sky was already turning the unadorned french windows a flat blue.

'Ouch. That hurt!' snapped Kate, pulling away.

'You're too tense. You've got knots the size of golf balls. Drop your shoulders and let your arms hang by your side. No, not like that. Relax.'

Relax! Did he realise the effect he was having on her. It

was just as well she was sitting down. Her legs had become liquid. When was the last time she'd felt like this with a man? Unable to help herself, Kate leant back against him and felt the champagne rush through her veins.

'Feel good?' Roe's voice sounded far away. She nodded and kept her eyes shut, waiting for the inevitable kiss. Roe, however, surprised them both when he said, 'I think I should take you home now.'

He wasn't sure why he'd said it. Perhaps it was because he felt tired after all the meetings, the jet-lag. He certainly hadn't had any sleep with Lucinda, the blonde air hostess he'd met on the flight from LA. Last night she had proved insatiable. But that wasn't it. Something about Kat made him back off. Her defensiveness perhaps? Her desire to control men yet at the same time revealing a vulnerable, childlike side? Which one was an act? Roe glanced down at the freckled, milky skin of her hands. She smelt of vanilla, innocence and toothpaste, which he found encouraging. A nice change from the kind of girl he usually took out. He'd enjoyed watching her at the nightclub. Christ, that had been funny the way she'd gone for that French dick. Practically put a hole in his leg. He had a hunch that she got too much of her own way. His instincts with women were usually accurate and he liked to keep the upper hand. Kate intrigued him enough to defer taking her to bed. After all, the promise of seduction so often outweighed the event.

Kate opened her eyes as Roe walked across the room and collected her coat. In a daze she allowed him to help her into it and followed him silently down to the car. What had she done wrong? Roe asked where she lived and slipped the Porsche into gear. It roared into life against the quiet backdrop of morning.

The trees lining the boulevard were scarcely visible in the early morning haze. The street cleaners were out sweeping up the weekend's snow from the roads, hunched miserably over their brooms against the biting wind. Café awnings flapped, pavements looked bereft without the tables and chairs provided for lovers and tourists during the warm seasons. As the Porsche zoomed across the river to the right bank Kate could just make out a few people setting up the animal and bird market along the quai Mégisserie. How could they bear to get up so early when it was so cold? An ambulance screamed as it flew past in the opposite direction. Kate shivered in her thin dress and patted a yawn. She wanted Roe to drive slower, she wasn't ready yet to give him up. He didn't speak as he drove, his aristocratic profile fixed on the icy roads.

Two skinheads were necking on the steps as Roe pulled up outside Kate's block. They glared into the car's headlights, then turned their bodies towards the dark. No sign of the Beetle though. Bea had obviously changed her mind about having an early night. Kate was suddenly oppressed by fatigue and disappointment. The evening had promised so much and failed in everything. He'd obviously lost interest.

'Hey.' Roe touched her cheek and explored her face with his eyes. 'I'm glad I ran into you tonight. You make a nice change from financial bureaucrats.'

'Yes, it was nice.'

How lame, but what else could she say? In the cold light of dawn he had suddenly become a stranger to her, something the night and alcohol had concealed.

He leaned across her to open her door. 'I'll call you.'

That's what you all say, Kate thought glumly, as the car shot off into the gloom. He hadn't even asked for her number.

4

Claude Vaubelle was in a particularly foul mood. Last night he'd attended an annual benefit for the Cancer Foundation. The President's wife had chosen one of his new *haute couture* dresses and Claude had been looking forward to the ensuing publicity. The fact that his clients were rich and famous gave Vaubelle a huge amount of free advertising. Unfortunately the beautiful, intricately-draped pink gown chosen by Madame Mitterand had also turned up on Maggie Hennes, a well-known television personality. Claude was livid. Only last week, having been notified of the President's wife's plans, he had called Maggie to warn her off.

'Don't worry,' she had reassured him. She had sounded frantic and he could hear a dog barking in the background. 'I'm flying to Yugoslavia this weekend, so I've had to cancel everything. You don't know anyone who wants to babysit a Great Dane, do you?'

But the trip was delayed and Maggie had forgotten her conversation with Claude. Madame Mitterand was frosty and avoided Maggie all evening. Cornered by the press as he was leaving, Claude was quoted as saying, 'It is unfortunate but I cannot control who wears that dress to which function. I can only warn my clients if I know someone else is planning to wear the same one. The decision, *enfin*, is theirs.'

On his desk was a copy of *W* with photographs of the President's wife and Maggie. At least they weren't in the same picture. Claude checked his diary. Sophia Loren was arriving at eleven thirty for a fitting. A long-standing admirer of the actress, Claude planned to take her to the Régence-Plaza for lunch. Nicole had pencilled in an appointment with a fabric firm at ten. Although the collections had only just finished it was already time to start work on the *prêt à porter*. The prospect depressed Claude. He lowered his hand to pat Louis, noisily gnawing a rubber ball under his desk.

He was also hoping to avoid the odious American who had been pestering him from the day he'd arrived. It was common knowledge that the two men cordially disliked one another. At their last meeting they had discussed the possibility of signing up a model exclusively with the house not only for the collections but to advertise the cosmetic range. No mean feat. Although Paris was stuffed with top models, few were equally good at print and shows. What Roe wanted was an equivalent to Chanel's once unique Inès de la Fressange. Claude had hated all Roe's suggestions of women with hour-glass figures, preferring his own androgynous types. After all, clothes looked so much better on flat-chested girls. He glanced at the thick pile of model composites lying on his desks. They could wait till later.

Nicole buzzed through to remind him that Edouard was waiting downstairs in the car.

'Call Sebastian and remind him he's having dinner with us at the house,' he ordered.

Somehow, they had to come up with a plan to oust the appalling Roe Lewis. Grabbing his coat, he instructed Nicole to put urgent calls through to the fabric factory. The phone was Claude's lifeline and he was visibly uncomfortable if he was out of reach.

At five past ten Claude swept into the fabric firm with Louis tucked under one arm, like a small Napoleon, his cashmere coat draped over his shoulders like a cape. Edouard, his thin assistant, trailed behind, shivering because he hadn't put on enough clothes.

'Can I take your coat?' asked the young woman behind the reception desk, who was waiting to show him the fabric line. A newcomer, she'd been warned that Claude Vaubelle could be difficult.

Ignoring her, Claude turned down the hall to the bright and airy showroom which he'd been visiting for the last twenty-four years. In the centre was a large, oval-shaped conference table covered in fabrics. Edouard and the salesgirl followed, watching him fling his coat dismissively on a sofa as only a person used to expensive clothes would do. He immediately asked for a phone.

'Bring us some coffee, Mademoiselle,' he demanded, planting himself squarely on the sofa, 'and water for the dog.'

The phone duly arrived and as Claude riffled through samples Edouard plugged it in over by the window and dialled 0 for an outside line. Claude, glancing at him out of the corner of one eye, frowned. Why did he hunch his shoulders in that repulsive fashion? The boy had absolutely no style.

'*Est-elle arrivée?*' he asked Richard on the phone, meaning Sophia Loren. 'Well, how does it look? . . . Have you tried her in the gold lamé? . . . Why not? It seems obvious . . . I want you to try it all the same. She must look incredible . . . I don't know. I've only just arrived . . . *D'accord*, call me back when she's decided.' His voice was expressionless, without the usual French upward inflection.

The salesgirl returned with his coffee and waited patiently for instructions while Claude helped himself to four spoonfuls of sugar.

Sophia Loren was being fitted for a dress for the Cannes film festival in two weeks. It was a major event for Loren, there to endorse her latest film, and would provide excellent exposure for Vaubelle as she would be photographed by dozens of magazines. Claude wanted her to wear a particular dress he was keen to promote. Vaubelle frequently loaned sample dresses to important women who were small enough to fit the model size ten, but Sophia was buying hers and even with a generous discount he couldn't control the one she would pick.

He snatched up a piece of bright floral fabric and asked the salesgirl, 'What is the price range on this?'

'A hundred and sixty francs a metre, monsieur.' Sensing his interest the woman peeled off several more samples laying them before him on the table.

Claude hardly paused, saying, 'Yes. No. Yes. Yes. Perhaps,' while his assistant frantically scribbled the style numbers of each approved fabric.

'You're the first to see this range,' the salesgirl said encouragingly.

'So anything we choose you'll give us exclusive rights?' He yawned without bothering to cover his mouth.

The woman began methodically taking more samples from a cupboard. Claude, who was in a hurry not to miss Sophia, snapped at her to speed things up. The phone rang shrilly. It was Richard to say that Loren had chosen a full-length embroidered dress with a plunging neckline. The dress was so heavy that it took three dressers to help her into it. She loved it.

'How does it fit? . . . Is she with you now? . . . Oh, so you can't really talk . . . *Tant pis*, get a polaroid at least . . . *Oui*, it's essential.'

As he talked Claude stood in front of the mirror holding heavy silk against him, cocking his head to one side as he inspected his reflection. Edouard kept his pen poised.

After another hour Claude asked the salesgirl petulantly if they were nearly done.

'Just one more group, monsieur.'

Again the phone rang. This time it was Annie who was in charge of sales for the ready-to-wear at Vaubelle. Two minutes later Joni rang, concerned about the story on the President's wife. Claude talked to her for a few minutes, holding up samples he liked as he listened, signalling to Edouard to write them down.

It was only after they had gone that the salesgirl discovered a wet patch on the carpet. At first she thought it was a leak in the roof, but after closer inspection she cursed Claude Vaubelle's wretched dog who had peed on it.

Back at Vaubelle at a quarter past two, Claude was furious to learn that Sophia had already left for lunch with Roe.

'Surely you've got the message wrong?' he snapped.

'She only had an hour and Monsieur Lewis insisted she lunched with him. He said you wouldn't have wanted her to wait. Would it be all right to take my lunch break now, monsieur?'

'No, it would not! I need you to write a memo.'

Nicole had to cancel lunch with a friend and make do with a sandwich at her desk.

Just after seven Roe climbed the stairs to the fifth floor. He had just spent four hours with Sebastian and two lawyers, going over figures in a long meeting with the Vaubelle bankers. The loan had been agreed only after complex negotiations and Roe now wanted to update Carl. Glancing at his watch, he calculated the time in Los Angeles.

As he turned into the long, grey and white hall that stretched to the executive offices his attention was drawn by two people talking intimately at the other end. A sixth sense warned him to keep out of sight. Pausing behind a large potted plant he identified Claude Vaubelle talking to Jean-Marc. Funny. Wasn't Claude supposed to be going to a cocktail party at six? And Jean-Marc should have been at home recovering from flu.

Roe slipped unseen into his office and buzzed Nicole. Claude had given her so much extra work that she had decided to stay late to clear her desk. Roe asked her to come into his office. Noticing the dark circles under her eyes and the weary posture he offered her a drink. Nicole accepted cautiously, unused to an employer being nice to her, and placed a selection of the latest English fashion magazines on his desk to browse through. She observed, curiously, that unlike Claude Vaubelle, who had obsessively filled the office with personal memorabilia and framed photographs of himself shaking hands with famous people, Monsieur Lewis had done little to change the room since it had been repainted. Apart from his name on the door there was nothing to indicate that it was his.

Half an hour later she was looking much more cheerful. Sitting with her legs folded on Roe's large sofa and nursing a second Kir Royale, she admitted the difficulties of being a single working mother. Over the years Roe had discovered that being an excellent listener paid dividends; lulling clients into a false sense of security and with little more than the occasional understanding nod, useful information was disclosed while giving little away about himself. Nicole, who was lonely and hardly ever had a chance to talk about herself, proved the point and opened like a spring flower under Roe's easy charm.

'How long has Jean-Marc been working here?'

'About a year. I remember he arrived when Madame Vaubelle went into hospital.'

'Employed by Claude?' Roe asked.

Nicole took a sip of her Kir Royale and nodded. 'Monsieur Vaubelle employs everyone here.'

'What about his wife? Are they close?'

Nicole hesitated, afraid of seeming disloyal. 'They go to many different venues but never together. Madame Vaubelle has all the money – the houses and cars belong to her.'

'And the children?'

'Monsieur Vaubelle is very close to Sebastian. Years ago Sebastian almost died in a boating accident. They didn't think he would survive. Monsieur Vaubelle went crazy, couldn't even work. It was in all the papers.'

After she had gone Roe picked up the *Harpers and Queen* Nicole had left, thinking hard. He had a hunch. His attention lighted on an article about the new working generation of the 1990s, and in particular on a young Argentine who had recently graduated in *haute couture* from the Royal College of Art. Already working part-time for New Girl, a trendy chain store in the UK, it seemed she was being head-hunted by an important designer who had wanted her to join his team. *Harpers* predicted that she would be the new Alistair Blair. Roe tore out the article and put it to one side.

Bea Parker during her best year had earned three times as much as the President of France.

Her parents, Lord and Lady Parker, were in their thirties when Bea was born. Feeling too old to handle their lively daughter after raising two sons, they had packed her off to boarding school. She hated it. Her school reports had detailed her failure to settle down, her bad influence on the other girls, her ardent plotting and domestic terrorism. After countless gatings, some fruitless spells with the school psychiatrist, being caught smoking pot in the loo and later embracing the gardener's son in the chapel, Draughton Hall had handed Belinda Parker back to her parents.

In order to please her father she had spent a year at Frances King's Secretarial School. But, hopeless at short-hand and bored with keyboards, she was more often seen at the local pub playing pool or darts with the boys. Next she switched to Cordon Bleu cookery classes, this time for her mother who loved to cook. Bea wasn't very good at that either and left with a pass certificate which concealed the fact that she was still unable to boil an egg. But it got her a job as a chalet girl in the Swiss Alps for a season where she discovered a penchant for skiing and for blue-eyed instructors with thick Swiss accents.

After that, the prospect of returning to London had seemed very dull, so when Bea was approached by a scout for a modelling agency outside Waitrose in Chelsea, she was quickly seduced by promises of exotic trips and huge modelling fees. Never one to do things by halves, she discarded her twin-set and pearls, cut off her Sloane-ish shoulder-length hair, and bought a wardrobe in black. It was her most successful career move. Two years later, having cornered a small London market, Bea packed her bags. She had always wanted to climb the Eiffel Tower (not to mention Gérard Depardieu). With the money her grandmother had given her for her twenty-first birthday she bought a second-hand Volkswagen and found a flat in the Palais Royal.

Her career took a sudden leap forward when she started going out with top photographer Sven Leisel. Leisel had a contract with American *Vogue* rumoured to be worth £4 million, and had an uncanny eye for new talent. Through him Bea was introduced to top designers who put her on the catwalk – the ultimate platform to stardom. However, the relationship with Leisel had ended on rather a sour note, and although Bea continued to get steady work she never quite achieved the dizzy heights of success so many had predicted. Perhaps, as she once admitted to Kate, she just wasn't hungry enough for it.

Now, she leapt out of a cab and thrust twenty francs at the driver. She was late. Not that it was her fault. They had made her wait over an hour to see the director at the Grand Marnier commercial casting. She'd almost walked out. But she was glad she hadn't. The client had obviously liked her, and the money would make an effective dent in her overdraft. She made a few mental calculations, promising herself the Karl Lagerfeld coat she'd spotted in his sale if she got booked.

Wrapping her printed Hermès cashmere shawl over her skinny black body-suit and blonde mop, Bea strode along the pavement as if she were modelling on a catwalk, head pointing firmly upwards, then spoiled the effect by colliding with someone carrying a suitcase.

'I'm so sorry,' she said politely, not really seeing the woman whose thighs strained through her cheap, flimsy skirt.

She strode past Eric, waving a cheery hallo. The Vaubelle doorman experienced the same flicker of desire each time a bony Amazon strode through the doors as if they owned the place. Most of them were too stuck up to give him the time of day, but this stunner even remembered his name. Eric's eyes glued themselves to Bea's tiny bottom as she glided towards the lifts. Christ, what a job!

Geneviève was just hanging up the phone when Bea burst into the *cabine*. She pecked Geneviève's heavily powdered cheek.

'What's the weather forecast like upstairs?'

'Monsieur Vaubelle has called down two times already. You were supposed to be here twenty minutes ago,' tutted Geneviève, trying to look cross. 'Get ready quickly, please.'

'I'm on my way,' soothed Bea, slipping into the clean body and white overall folded on her chair. She pulled out a book from her bag for later, then deciding she might get cold standing around in so little, grabbed her brightly-coloured shawl. In her haste she didn't hear Geneviève's murmur of protest.

'I wouldn't take th . . .' Geneviève said to the closing door. She looked glumly at the pile of Bea's clothes on the floor. When she'd come to Paris she'd imagined models to be fine, elegant women who wore *haute couture* every day, had their hands and feet painted by Chanel and their hair set by a personal hairdresser. They didn't drink from bottles, live off Danish pastries and read airport novels. And her a lady too.

In the studio upstairs people were scurrying around trying to look busy. Their closed faces indicated that Claude Vaubelle was around. Nicole, on the phone scribbling down sample numbers, waved Bea through. Entering, Bea felt as if she'd stepped into a pocket of Siberia. There was a howling draught and both windows were open. Hell, I'm going to freeze. She hugged the cashmere shawl around her for warmth. Judging from the white faces of Jean-Marc, Brigette and Richard, all standing defensively behind the desk, Claude wasn't at his most charming. Monique held up a half-made jacket by the window. Claude pulled rolls of fabric from their stack and threw them in a heap on the floor, while Rodriguez from tailoring stood by.

'This is not what I ordered! How can I create beautiful clothes surrounded by such inefficiency!' Claude said contemptuously, and threw down another roll with a bang.

He had been asked to remake a dress for Princess Yasmin Aga Khan. Unfortunately someone had stuffed up on the order and there wasn't enough fabric left to make it. Claude was now trying to come up with an alternative. He rummaged through several sheets of paper and pulled out a sketch.

'What about the mauve chiffon we used for this?' he suggested, brandishing a sketch to no one in particular. 'Do we have some left over?'

Brigette nodded. 'There's half a roll downstairs, monsieur. I saw it yesterday.'

'But will it do?' Claude demanded.

'I think so.'

'Then get it up here.'

Richard spotted Bea standing in the doorway. *'Monsieur, le mannequin est arrivé.'*

'At last!' said Claude turning. The flicker of a smile on his face fell away at the sight of Bea. 'What is that?' he asked in horror. 'Are you quite mad? Take it off immediately!'

Bea gawked uncomprehendingly as Claude reduced the

space between them in a second and snatched the shawl from her shoulders.

'No one wears anything but my designs here.' He looked like an aggressive Rottweiler. 'Can't anyone follow simple rules?' He marched over to the open window and threw out the offending shawl.

Bea, open-mouthed, glanced at Richard in disbelief, but he shook his head warning her to remain silent. He knew how notoriously insecure Claude was about independent designs encroaching on his own artistic space. Bea found herself propelled into the centre of the room, her white coat removed and Claude angrily throwing on a half-made dress Monique had handed him.

'This needs a three-quarter sleeve and I don't want any seams in these yokes here. *Tu comprends?*' he said to a trembling Monique. 'You just have to work the material towards the back, like this,' he explained, pulling taffeta roughly around Bea's non-existent bottom.

Claude's hand came out for a pin. Monique, glancing briefly at Richard sketching the dress, didn't see it.

'A pin, Monique! I'm doing this for your benefit, not mine.'

Brigette returned with the mauve chiffon. Claude removed the dress, which he gave to Monique, and held the chiffon against Bea.

'I don't know,' he said moodily. 'It doesn't work as well as I thought. Don't you think it's rather old?'

'It depends on the style of the dress,' offered Brigette.

'No, it doesn't,' snapped Claude. 'It doesn't depend on anything. It's just old.'

Why bother to ask Brigette's opinion in the first place then, thought Bea irritably. What an intolerably rude man!

Later on, unwinding over a much-needed bottle of wine and with the rescued shawl restored to her shoulders, Bea repeated the story to her friends.

'I came so close to telling the man what he could do with his precious job. He should be bloody grateful he could get a model to fit so late! I've a good mind to invoice him for the cost of dry-cleaning my shawl.'

'You're lucky it was only your shawl,' said her model

friend, 'I've heard stories where he's actually hit people in a rage. Honestly, what we have to put up with in this business. They think that because they're paying you they can treat you however they like.'

Meanwhile Joni d'Akouri was discussing Claude's latest advertising campaign with Roe and Steve, the campaign's art director. Joining them in her office were Marie-Claire and Nicole, who was taking notes. Claude Vaubelle should have been there too but after a series of further dramas in the studio he had gone home saying he was quite unable to work on designs a moment longer under so much strain.

'Maybe now we'll get some peace and quiet,' Brigette had muttered as he left.

Roe hated everything they showed him. The model used for the shots had lost almost a stone since the casting and it showed. Not only that, the mood in the photos was too stiff for Roe's taste. He was determined to erase Vaubelle's archaic image. They spread the photos on the desk, trying to work out a format which would detract from the harsh photographhy and sell the products.

'I hate to say it,' said Roe finally, 'but whichever way you look at it, it's a disaster. I thought the emphasis was supposed to be on accessories? All we've got are two handbags and some tacky-looking jewellery.'

'The original idea was not to use models at all but just have silhouettes,' explained Joni. She was furious with Claude for interfering with what was *her* job – it was her bloody neck on the line, not his. 'But then we changed it and most of the accessories were taken out because they detracted from the clothes.'

Roe looked at Steve.

'I could take it home over the weekend and play around with some ideas,' Steve suggested. He was desperate for a cigarette but had been warned of Roe's ban on smoking.

'There's not enough time,' said Joni, massaging her head irritably. 'The deadline's Friday.'

'Maybe we should re-shoot?' suggested Marie-Claire.

'Having spent 150 thousand francs on photography? That's

one hell of an expensive mistake!' snapped Roe. 'I'm just kind of surprised you didn't replace the model, Joni. This looks like a fund-raising campaign for Somalia.'

He suddenly thought of the redhead he'd met the other night. It might be an idea to track down her agency. Claude Vaubelle's taste in models, as in most things, it appeared, left a lot to be desired.

'Claude insisted on using her and the photographer,' said Joni, bristling. 'Just for the record they weren't my choice.'

'That figures,' said Roe angrily. 'Well, he's going to have to do better than this.'

He picked up a shot of the model standing in a garden and passed it to Steve. She was wearing a short green dress and her thin legs stuck out like bamboo sticks. A telephone rang. Marie-Claire picked it up.

'This is the nicest of the dresses,' said Steve, studying the shot, 'I'd hate to waste it. Let's crop just below the hemline so that we lose the legs but still see that it's a short dress.'

'This one's not bad either,' said Joni holding up a shot of the model swinging a wide-cut jacket, 'she's much better when she's moving. Maybe we could use this for the cover?'

'*Vanity Fair*'s on line one,' said Marie-Claire, flicking a switch.

'Tell them I'll call them back,' said Joni without looking up.

'Where was this shot?' Roe asked.

'Vienna.'

'It might just as well be Sunset Boulevard for the amount of background we can see. For Chrissakes, what's the point of going on location? Someone want a vacation in the sun?'

Joni looked upset. 'Well, you try working with a brick wall. I don't write the cheques around here. All my ideas were stamped on, and as for the weather, it pissed down for six days!'

For a moment Roe smiled. Then he said, 'When are the deadlines?'

'We've got to have the mechanicals in tomorrow,' said Steve.

'And where are these running?' asked Roe.

Marie-Claire consulted her notepad. '*Vogue*, *Elle*, and *W*.'

'Then nobody goes home until we make some sense of this mess. Sorry, guys, but that's how it's got to be. Make any necessary calls home if you've made plans tonight. Nicole, honey, could you fix up some coffee and something to eat?'

Steve was barely listening. Used to last-minute deadlines, he had his head bent over the trannies with Joni, already deep in conversation. Nicole left the room in search of food. Roe drained his glass of water, then picked up the phone. It was going to be a very long night.

Shortly before midnight Bea Parker let herself into the flat and was surprised to find all the lights still burning. Kate was normally in bed by eleven. Bea found her in front of the TV in floods of tears.

'Darling!' cried Bea, the picture of concern. 'What on earth's the matter? It's not that lech, Jean-François, is it?'

God, had he come on a bit too strong after the Dé d'Or? Kate had been very cagey about what had happened the next day over breakfast.

'No. I'm just feeling a bit down.' She grabbed a box of tissues and blew her nose.

'Your mother called, didn't she?' said Bea perceptively.

Another sniff. 'We had a blazing row and said things we're both going to regret! I don't know why, but we always seem to be at cross-purposes. Nothing I do seems to please her.'

'Mothers are like that. Just like men; you can't live with them, but you can't live without them either.' Bea removed a brown apple core from the sofa and put a consoling arm round Kate's shoulders. 'You silly goose, I thought something dreadful had happened to you.'

'Sorry.' Kate dragged a hand across her red, swollen eyes. 'Ignore me. I've got the curse and a case of the guilts because I ate two of your Twixs. How was Vitek?'

'Lovely. We went to a new place in Montmartre. Horribly over-priced, of course, but glorious food. Vitek, the beast, smoked the whole time, then rolled a joint during pudding. The *maître d'* had an absolute fit and we only got away with it because Vitek's so disgustingly good-looking. One man even asked him for his autograph, saying, "You are Rupert

Everett, aren't you?" Vitek coolly nodded and took the man's number,' Bea giggled. 'Afterwards we went back to his flat for coffee and looked at some snaps of his new man.'

'What's the flat like?'

'Wildly over the top. Wall-to-wall pink brocade. Pure Barbara Cartland.'

'Sounds awful,' said Kate, cheering up.

'Rumours were circulating that Bruce Willis was in the restaurant, so I spent a great deal of time fruitlessly trotting back and forth to the loo, hoping to spot him. Did, however, catch Emma Thompson and Ken Branagh holding hands on a nearby table. Do you think she might be pregnant?'

'How? Those two are workaholics. They never have time.'

'Good addition to my celebrity list though. Any messages?'

'Four. Three of them from Fabier. Sounds very keen. They're all written down.' Kate gestured towards the phone, 'Oh, and your agency cheque finally arrived.'

'It did? Hell! If only I'd got it this morning I could have paid it in and stopped a couple of cheques from bouncing. My bank's not exactly user-friendly.'

'I realised that,' said Kate pulling her feet up under her, 'the banker's slip's there with all the rest.'

'Oh, Kate, you're an angel! What would I do without you?'

'Replace me with three members of the opposite sex, I suspect!'

Later on, tucked up in bed with a hot water bottle, Bea wondered for the third time that night if it would be worth trying to convert Vitek. She'd fancied him for years. Kate would like him too. Must invite him round to the flat soon. All the same, when Kate had asked her what they'd had for dinner she had thought it wise not to mention the two portions of roast pork or the excellent duck paté she'd had. Sometimes, reflected Bea, it was tough living with such a beautiful purist.

5

The rain drummed relentlessly on the morning commuters pouring out of Hammersmith tube. Umbrellas opened in unison and Toby, struggling miserably with his coat and hangover, narrowly escaped a poke in the eye. He glanced at his watch and realised he was going to be late. What excuse could he give Yarnton this time? Not the truth, which was that he'd been up all night getting pissed at Annabel Gough's – her parties had a reputation for getting out of hand. Nor had he planned on spending the night on her sofa but he'd stupidly lent Guy his car to take a girlfriend home. Guy had not returned. Faced with camping at Annabel's or walking home in the rain, Toby had opted for the former. Besides, he hadn't brought any money with him and Annabel, quite inhospitably, had sloped off to bed with her latest toy boy. That was why he was now queuing in the dreary bus station behind the tube. When a vacant black taxi whizzed by Toby wondered if cabbies accepted Gold American Express. He couldn't remember the last time he'd been on a bus.

A group of schoolgirls wearing tartan mini-skirts and black opaque tights crossed the road. Laughing, they clutched at their pleated skirts to keep them from blowing up in the wind. Toby looked at his watch again. Nine forty-five. Where was the damn bus? He'd been waiting half an hour. A cold, wet trickle ran from the collar of his coat on to his neck and down his back. Toby shuddered. A woman standing behind him reading was shielding her book from the rain with a crooked black umbrella. She held it at an angle over her face, which redirected the rain on to Toby. Irritably, he edged forward out of its stream.

''Ere, Madge,' said a middle-aged woman in a plastic scarf.

She clutched a shivering Jack Russell, also wearing a hat, in a canvas shopping bag. 'Sharon lost 'er specs in Woolworths yesterday and gave Tim a tin of chicken-flavoured Kit-i-Kins for his supper. He only went and bolted the lot!'

'Oo-er!' said her shocked companion. 'My 'Arry says that stuff's made from 'orse meat and ain't fit to feed pigs!'

The Jack Russell (who lived quite happily on Kit-i-Kins) looked up gravely at Toby.

Another vicious gust of wind tugged at the umbrella, whacking Toby on the head. It narrowly missed his left eye. For the third time, he cursed the faceless girl and Annabel's party punch.

The bus drove through a wide puddle, drenching the frustrated queue. Toby politely let a group of old biddies get on before him then realised that the girl with the book had queue-jumped.

'Full up, sir!' The bus conductor blocked the entrance with his considerable weight as Toby reached the front of the line.

'But you can't be serious! I've been waiting here for almost forty minutes! I've got to get to Knightsbridge.'

'Sorry, sir, looks like you're going to have to swim for it.'

The conductor turned his back and rang the bell. The bus began to move away and in desperation Toby hit the side with his elbow as hard as he could. The bang vibrated and the bus came to an abrupt halt. Toby grabbed his foot in one hand and hopped up and down, simulating great pain.

'You all right there, guv?' the conductor called out.

'My foot!' Toby cried. 'You ran over my damned foot! I don't think I can walk.'

The conductor looked sceptical. But the lady with the Jack Russell came to his rescue.

'Poor little love, let 'im on. You can't expect 'im to walk all that way in that condition. We've got room. Come on, girls, budge up.'

The OAPs shuffled along and made a space. Aware that all eyes were focused on him, the conductor stepped aside. Toby hobbled on to the bus and sat down, smiling gratefully at the pensioner.

'There you are, ducks. You're a bit more comfy now,' she

said encouragingly and patted his knee. He looked a bit like her grandson. Funny about his hair though. Ever so odd. And he was only a young lad.

The girl with the umbrella was sitting opposite him, still buried in her book, which he now saw was *Madame Bovary*. He was able to study her more closely. Her heavy dark hair was tied back in a severe knot. She had warm, olive skin, a strong round face, rosebud lips that looked as if they'd been outlined in crayon and a big, slightly crooked nose. She wore small John Lennon spectacles that kept slipping down her nose, and her forehead creased as she read. It was hard to tell what her figure was like because she was so covered up. As the bus came to a stop she suddenly took off her glasses, slipped the book into her bag and looked up. Toby felt as though someone had hit him with a sledge-hammer. He found himself gazing into a huge pair of owl-like eyes, Latin and very warm. Her smile was instantaneous.

'South Kensington!' announced the conductor.

Grappling with her bags, the girl stood up. People were already climbing on and she had to push her way through the bodies to get off. Unthinkingly Toby got up and followed her.

'Your leg seems to 'ave recovered something miraculous, sir,' jeered the conductor as the bus pulled away.

He followed her along the Old Brompton Road, which the rain had cleared except for a few splashing cars, to a little health food restaurant. A tall, fair-haired man was lounging inside the doorway smoking a cigarette. As she approached he dropped the cigarette into a nearby puddle and took her bags. They entered the building deep in conversation. The sign on the door read CLOSED in large capitals. Toby stood for several minutes soaking up the rain, his eyes glued to the window, then he turned and retraced his footsteps, pressing his body against the wind.

It was noon by the time he got home and he was wet through. The phone was ringing. Quickly switching off the alarm, Toby threw his keys on the sofa and picked up the receiver.

'Hang on,' he said breathlessly.

He walked into the bathroom, tripping over a golf club he'd

left lying around. Bloody hell! He was always doing that. Turning the bath taps on, he removed several blonde hairs clogging up the plughole and returned to the living-room.

'Toby! What happened?' said a deep, authoritative voice. 'We were expecting you at ten.'

'Sorry, Yarnton. I know I said I'd be there but I got my foot run over by a bus.'

Toby balanced the phone between his ear and shoulder and began to strip off his sodden clothing. The house was a tip. Why couldn't Tanya occasionally tidy up after herself?

'That's terrible!' said Yarnton Miller. 'What were you doing on a bus?'

'Trying to get to you. Ran out of money at Annabel's last night.'

'So it was one of those.' There was disapproval in Yarnton's voice. 'You sound terrible. Did you get any sleep at all?'

'Not a lot.' Toby admitted.

'Drink much?'

'Does a bottle of rum count as much?' Toby's yawn came out as a burp.

'I'm coming over. Things can't go on this way any more, Toby, you're going to end up killing yourself.'

'I thought I was talking to my solicitor not my GP.'

'I'm also your friend and I hate to see what you're turning into. Ever since Camilla walked out you've been hell bent on self-destruction. You've got no job, no direction, nothing seems to motivate you. Why are you frittering your life away?'

'I resent that,' Toby said indignantly. 'I provide enormous support for my friends and Tanya takes up a great deal of my time.'

Rather too much time, Yarnton thought irritably. He didn't like Toby's latest girlfriend; an archetypal blonde, with her snub-kittenish face that was both helpless and seductive. It was obvious that she was using Toby as a stepping-stone. She treated the house in Campden Hill like a hotel. Why, Toby had paid for her entire Alaia wardrobe! It pained him to see the boy spend his whole time running round that girl when what he really needed was someone to run around him.

Yarnton felt a responsibility towards Toby whom he saw as the son he had never had. Philip Wilmot-Smith, Toby's adoptive father, had been a long-standing friend and when a heavy goods vehicle went into the side of his Bentley on the M4, instantly killing Wilmot-Smith and his wife, it was Yarnton who broke the news to their only son. In London at the time, the nineteen-year-old Toby was devastated and went on a two-week drinking binge. The results landed him in hospital. He was released a week later with little more than a bruised ego – but the drinking and partying continued.

Three years later when he graduated from Oxford it seemed as though Toby had calmed down and he was offered a job as a trainee at his father's investment bank. Popular with his contemporaries, Toby had a brilliant financial brain and showed every sign of making a phenomenal career for himself. However, he simply wasn't ready to take on the Wilmot-Smith empire. Emotionally immature and easily influenced, he got caught up in the wrong crowd who were quick to take advantage of his kindness and his money. Because of the drinking his work began to suffer, and when he bungled an important deal which cost the bank millions, Toby was sacked. But for Yarnton's professional skill and guiding hand he would have ended up squandering his entire fortune.

'Philip didn't leave you his money to spend it on a bunch of idle parasites!' continued Yarnton. 'Don't you think it's time you thought about getting a job? You could resume work for your father's bank again any time. You'd be bloody good.'

'No thanks. The stress would give me ulcers.'

He couldn't go back. He'd just make another mess of things.

'Well, I don't care what you do, just find yourself an interest.'

Toby, now naked, was shivering. The heating had gone off because he'd forgotten to reset the dial when he came in. He hated being cold. Lately he'd been thinking very seriously about moving abroad. He fixed his eyes blankly on a Ford Madox Brown painting showing two emigrants, part of an excellent collection he'd been building up for three years.

Tiredly he said, 'I appreciate the advice but you're over-reacting. I'm perfectly happy, just need some sleep.' He could almost see the resigned expression on Yarnton's face. 'Look, I promise to think about it. Why don't you come over for dinner tomorrow night? We'll talk then.'

As soon as he'd hung up Toby remembered that he'd already promised to take Tanya to the opening of some new film. There'd be hell to pay if he didn't go. She'd been harping on about it for days. He'd have to put Yarnton off until next week.

After a couple of calls to find out what had happened to his car, Toby poured himself a large rum and coke, collected the morning's post, which was mostly bills, and dumped the lot, unopened, with the rest gathering dust under the dining-room table.

His bath had overflowed. He pulled out the plug as he got in, burning himself because he hadn't run enough cold. Sipping his rum, Toby closed his eyes and let *Madame Butterfly* sooth away the day's tensions. Bliss. He hardly ever got to play it these days. Tanya hated classical music, preferring the, to him, incomprehensible Capital Radio. Why couldn't Yarnton just leave him alone. He had enough money to buy half London.

By the time Toby got out the water was cold. Wrapping himself in a £600 Ralph Lauren paisley silk dressing-gown, he walked into the bedroom and pulled close the curtains. He lay down, shattered, and tried to sleep. He should call Tanya at the theatre about tonight but frankly couldn't be bothered. Let her call him for a change. He was tired of doing all the running.

He closed his eyes. Images of the girl with the chocolate-brown eyes flickered through his mind.

'James, over 'ere and have a butcher's at this,' coaxed Pippa. She pointed to the pale blue Mercedes Sports parked across the road. 'Isn't that the same car that's been parked outside all weekend?'

'So it is. Wonder why? Nothing like a bit of mystery to get a girl's attention,' said James, a six-foot-two, lanky blond with mischievous blue eyes.

'It's mysterious, all right.'

Pippa Sparrow, raven-haired and pretty, was wearing black leggings under a tunic dress and Doc Martin's. She was up to her arms in orange peel, as the juicer churned out fresh supplies of orange juice.

'Might be one of them mass murderers!' she said ominously.

'I doubt it,' said James dismissively. 'If he was planning on knocking anyone off he'd have been a bit more subtle about it, wouldn't he, Rachy?'

Rachel Winger, returning to the kitchen, was carrying a tray of clean cutlery. She shrugged, pausing for a brief look out of the window. Her mind was on other things, notably the call she'd had this morning from a Mr Lewis. He had seen the *Harpers and Queen* article, he told her, and had a business proposition he wanted to discuss. As he was only in town for forty-eight hours she'd agreed to have lunch with him the following day.

James got up and started wrapping the clean cutlery in paper napkins. 'Maybe he's got a few screws loose?'

'Makes me go all funny, thinkin' about it,' said Pippa. Resting her head in her hands she was gazing thoughtfully out at the car. 'It's hard to make him out though. Them windows are ever so dark.'

'Well, don't make it so obvious that we're looking at him,' warned Rachel, pulling Pippa away from the window. 'Have you taken care of table nine yet?'

'Yer. He wants a nut rissole with mixed salad and a cup of Echo.'

'I'll do it now.' Hoping to distract Pippa, Rachel said, 'Wasn't last night's storm awful?'

'You're telling me!' James sighed dramatically. 'Tiles from our roof blew off in the night. Our bedroom got flooded so we had to sleep in the lounge. Didn't get a wink of sleep of course and poor darling Brad had his exams today.'

Pippa rolled her eyes disparagingly, ignoring the sound of the restaurant door opening. Let them wait. She'd been on her feet since eight. Instead she watched Rachel remove a tray of golden scones from the oven. The sweet aroma wafted around the room. Pippa poured dressing on to the salad.

'You want to hear about me drawing class. Mark, the luv, gave me a lift into college. Our male model was sick so Jude got one of the blokes in class to volunteer. Well, I couldn't look at him.' Her eyes grew wide at this point. 'I mean, him sat there in the altogether with his cock up in the air as hard as this job. Poor Jude didn't know where to look either. She spent two hours sketching his feet.'

Rachel laughed.

'Cor, Rachy, you don't 'arf make a good scone,' mumbled Pippa, stuffing a warm one into her mouth. 'Can I take some of them home?'

'Not unless you stop eating them now,' said James, putting them out of arm's reach. 'What about you, Rachy? Any more news from New Girl?'

'Head office rang yesterday and offered me a full-time job designing sports wear. I'm wavering. It's not quite what I was after, but it would be a great start and it'll look good on my c.v. Victor Halstein hasn't replied yet, which probably means he's not interested after all.'

'No it don't,' argued Pippa, 'and he'd be bloody daft not to snap you up.'

James carried a home-made carrot and ginger soup and wild rice salad out into the restaurant. Looking across the road Rachel focused on the blue Mercedes. The occupant appeared to be reading a paper. As a middle-aged woman wearing a quilted coat and thong sandals, which had received a few raised eyebrows, got up from her table to leave, Rachel noticed a large clamping van stop behind the car. Two men got out, one carrying the familiar orange clamp, and fastened it to the back wheel.

'Oh lord,' she exclaimed, 'they're clamping his car!'

'You're joking!' said James, walking past carrying empty plates. 'How very funny.'

They watched as a tall, skinny, grey-haired man got out of the Mercedes. His proportions were wrong somehow, gangly, and his arms, Rachel noticed, were too long for his body. He began arguing with the clampers, but it was soon clear that they weren't going to remove the clamp. The conversation became more heated and the man waved his wallet at them angrily. Rachel hoped there wasn't going to be a fight. She loathed violence. Nervously she began to giggle. The clampers eventually walked back to their van. The grey-haired man could only watch indignantly as the van drove off. After a few moments he turned and walked towards the restaurant. Rachel stopped giggling and made a hasty retreat into the kitchen.

James looked delighted. 'Perhaps now we'll get to solve the mystery.'

'You'll have to go and deal with him,' Rachel pleaded in a panic.

'Don't be silly. He'll just want to use the phone. Anyway I'm busy with the washing up.'

Pippa, the minx, had done a skilful vanishing act.

The door clanged as it opened and shut. The man walked to one of the tables, sat down and picked up the menu. Rachel reluctantly approached him. Despite the colour of his hair, he was no more than thirty. Rachel found herself staring into pale, denim-blue eyes. On closer inspection she could see he needed feeding up and a bit of sun, but he had neat Irish features, an intriguing air and she liked his smile. For some reason she had a feeling she'd seen him somewhere before.

'Hello, lovely.' The man put down the menu. 'I won't eat anything, just a cappuccino if it's not too much trouble. My wretched car's just been clamped outside your restaurant.'

'Yes, we saw. How awful for you. Do you want to use the phone?'

Golly. No one had ever called her lovely.

'Could I?'

'The phone's in the back. Use it when you like.'

'Thanks,' he said gratefully, searching his pockets for change. 'Is this your place?'

'Gosh, no. I just work part-time to make some extra money. I did design at college. That's what I'm interested in.' As soon as spoken Rachel regretted it. Acutely aware of her own scruffy appearance she noticed that his dark-grey coat was pure cashmere, the scarf an expensive silk. The shoes looked hand-made. She thought of the sodden M&S macs and Oxfam rejects hanging on the coatstand. No doubt he thought she was trying to impress him. But the smile on his face merely broadened.

'That's wonderful. Perhaps you'll make me something. I'm Toby Wilmot-Smith, by the way.' He proffered his cold hand. 'And you look like a Gabriella or a Francesca?'

'Rachel.'

She took his hand gingerly before removing the menu and cutlery. He was staring, making her wonder if there was something wrong with her. Not used to men paying her so much attention, Rachel felt embarrassed. Noticing a customer signalling for the bill she seized the opportunity to escape.

'I'll be right back with your coffee.'

'No rush,' he said, watching her go. He liked the way she walked, her hips swinging gently, her hands pulling her sweater over her generous bottom in a self-conscious manner. Rachel. He tried her name out in his mouth like a boiled sweet. It felt new, uncertain, risky almost. He definitely liked it.

The restaurant was filling up now. Businessmen on short lunch breaks parked themselves in groups of twos and threes and signalled impatiently for service. A group of tired matrons collapsed in a bunch, littering the floor with shopping bags. It looked as though they'd cleaned out half of Peter Jones. The afternoon rush was on. Toby sat watching the kitchen door. One of the women stopped Rachel as she came out.

'Where's the loo, dear?'

'Down the stairs, first on your left.'

'I'm having a small bash this weekend. Will you come?' said Toby, surprising himself as much as Rachel who had returned with his coffee. Her fringe was sticking up at the sides where she'd pushed it out of her eyes and she had flour on her chin. She looked tired.

'I couldn't possibly. No, really, it's very kind of you to ask but . . .' She stood lamely by the table twisting a silver crucifix chain around her neck. There was nothing for her to do but she felt it was rude just to walk away. He still had his coat on and she wondered if she should put the central heating up.

'Why not?' Toby persisted. 'Look, I know it's not the done thing to ask out a complete stranger, but I'm quite respectable, you know. You can look me up in *Who's Who*.' His mouth twitched. 'How else am I to get to know you? I could pick you up from work and promise to bring you home safely.'

The woman returned from her trip to the loo, adjusting her straining skirt as she walked. Out of the corner of her eye Rachel caught Pippa winking at her through the glass panel on the kitchen door. James had slipped out for a quick puff. Toby saw her hesitate and played his trump card.

'I must get some credit for approaching you. I've been plucking up the courage for three days. Besides, how many men get their car clamped on your behalf? Come on, Rachel, live dangerously for one night and if you hate it, you need never see me again.'

Rachel hovered, noticing that one of his blue eyes was in fact a muddy green. Why not? There was something about this odd man she instinctively trusted. She accepted but refused his offer of a lift. Toby scribbled down his address on the back of a napkin. He then made a quick call to the de-clamping squad and paid his bill.

'Now don't even think about not coming,' he threatened at the door, 'or I'll have to come back for more parking tickets next week.'

As he hailed a passing taxi five minutes later, Toby panicked. Where the hell could he hold a party? Certainly not at his house. Tanya would have a fit! She flirted like mad with all his friends but he was never allowed to do the same with a pretty girl. Would Annabel help him organise a party after he'd thrown up all over her Persian carpet the night of her party? He'd have to do some serious sucking up to get round her. So much for being impulsive.

At twenty-four Rachel had never had a proper boyfriend.

Growing up in Argentina she had been painfully shy and kept very much to herself. She used to invent private games, imagining herself as a fairy princess swept off her feet by a hero. Dressing up in her mother's clothes, she would dance and sing to the polo ponies grazing in neighbouring fields. She spent hours day-dreaming about England, her father's country, which evoked so much mystery and romance.

Rachel was a curious mixture of both her parents. Her mother, a sultry, Isabella Rossellini type of beauty, had bequeathed Rachel her chocolate-brown eyes with well-defined eyebrows and olive skin as well as a talent for cooking, drawing and making clothes. But Rachel had her father's build, which was stout, and his Scottish nose propped up her small glasses. The bridge of her nose was narrow but thickened in length from her cheek bones, tipping downwards above her lip and had a small bump in the middle. Rachel hated her nose. It was everything the fashion magazines said it shouldn't be.

She had won a scholarship to the Royal College of Art. There she developed the skills she'd inherited from her talented mother as well as her passion for clothes. Since she was never going to be beautiful she would design clothes that would make women feel beautiful. Separated from her father as a baby, she was fiercely independent on the one hand, deeply insecure on the other, and to those who didn't know her she could seem unapproachable. Rachel worked ferociously, sketching, always sketching. Having few friends she avoided parties, feeling shy and unattractive. Instead she retreated into her designs, striving to perfect her talent. Night after night, locked in her Hammersmith studio flat, Rachel worked, trying to ignore the violent arguments from the floor above and the mind-crunching music coming from next door. Rachel was desperate to move but her restaurant wages barely covered the rent and New Girl had offered nothing long-term. For the moment she was stuck. Toby's party would be her first evening out in months. She felt a flicker of excitement and planned to make herself a new dress for the occasion.

★ ★ ★

Roe arrived at Trescalini's a little before one. He was shown to a discreet table in the green room which had a sun roof shaped like a dome. Exotic birds flitted in a gentle whirl of vibrant green, peacock-blue and scarlet so that customers instantly forgot the wintry day outside. Bird sounds mingled with baroque music and the clanking of plates and cutlery. Despite the recession the exclusive restaurant in Holland Park was full. Roe ordered a bottle of Chablis and made a couple of calls on his mobile phone. So far his search for a new designer had been fruitless. He'd investigated some of the big designer names, but they were all over-exposed. No, the time was right for a complete unknown.

He spotted Rachel long before she saw him. Of course he had the advantage of having seen her photograph in *Harpers and Queen*. Still, he thought, as she fumbled with her coat and umbrella, she was less pretty in the flesh and heavier. She shouldn't wear those glasses. Her eyes were her best feature. Sensing her discomfort, Roe stood up, caught her attention and waved her over.

'Am I late?' she gasped, slightly out of breath. She placed her portfolio on the floor next to her chair. 'I had problems getting away, then it started to rain and I couldn't find a taxi.'

Roe pulled out a chair. 'Relax, I was early. Have some wine.'

'This is a treat,' Rachel said, as she settled into her seat and Roe poured her a glass. She thought, what an incredibly attractive man. 'I'm normally the one taking the orders.'

'You must find that frustrating. Wouldn't you rather be designing full-time?'

'Well, that's the plan. I've been offered a permanent job with New Girl. But I was hoping to get taken on by Victor Halstein. I find his work inspiring but I haven't heard from him and, to be honest, getting any kind of work is a relief. So many of my friends are having problems.'

Roe liked her honesty. After the recent conniving and bitchiness at Vaubelle, Rachel made a refreshing change.

'Well, *Harpers*, for one, sees you with a glowing future. Tell me, you're from Buenos Aires?'

'Not exactly.' Rachel was having trouble coping with his

extraordinary amber eyes. 'My parents met in Buenos Aires. My father was out there on holiday and they had an affair. He brought her back to Scotland and I was born rather impulsively eight months later.' She smiled ruefully at him.

'I don't get it.' Roe, puzzled, watched her play with her fork. 'I thought you were brought up in Argentina?'

'Oh I was. My dad had taken up golf professionally but was having trouble getting his career off the ground. I suppose the pressure of money and being saddled with a baby was too much for them both. Mum was seventeen and Dad only twenty at the time. Anyway the marriage ended after two years and my mother returned to Argentina taking me with her. I think the cold weather got to her in the end!'

'As a southerner myself, I can relate to that.'

'I'm probably making all this sound horribly unromantic, but they were very much in love at the time. And I know Dad has regrets about it all.'

Rachel lifted her glasses from the bridge of her nose and rubbed her eyes. She was allergic to cigars and someone was puffing an obscenely large one near by.

'Your parents must be very proud of you,' said Roe, signalling for the waitress.

'I owe a lot to Dad,' she gushed. 'His career finally took off and when I was fourteen he brought me over to live with him and his second wife in Edinburgh, and put me through school. I think he felt guilty for not having been around when I was a child. Anyway I got a scholarship to the Royal College and a flat, and I've been living in London ever since. It's a struggle, but Dad helps with the rent when he can. He has two more children and a house in Argyll. That's where they live now. So, there you have it,' she said, embarrassed because she'd monopolised so much of the conversation, 'my entire life history in five minutes. Not very exciting, is it?'

'I suspect there are a few gaps to fill, but I get the general idea. Does your father still play golf?'

'Oh lord, yes! Perhaps you've heard of Jack Winger?'

'*The* Jack Winger! He's a legend!'

For a second Rachel looked smug. Then she shrugged. She was used to the reaction her father's name provoked.

'I didn't make the connection. You don't use your mother's maiden name?'

'Most people can't remember Sanchez-Terrero.' The name rolled off her tongue very quickly. 'Winger's easier.'

A harassed-looking waitress finally appeared to take their order. Rachel, who was horrified by the prices on the menu and sympathetic to the girl because the restaurant was clearly under-staffed, asked Roe to order for her. At a neighbouring table were a young man and his mother. As she lectured him about his impending divorce, her dyed hair floating in blonde clouds around her temples, she applied pink frosted lipstick to her pinched mouth. The man, looking depressed, was slowly ploughing his way through a second bottle of wine. Poor thing, thought Rachel.

Roe asked to see her portfolio. He skimmed through it so quickly the first time that Rachel's heart sank, but then he went through it a second and a third time much more methodically.

'These are very good.' It was all he said but privately Roe was staggered by how fantastic her designs were. 'I notice, though, you've kept them low-key.'

'Deliberately,' said Rachel with confidence. 'Designs should be interesting, but in the end women want to buy clothes they can wear.'

'You must work very hard.'

'It never feels like work because I love what I do above everything else.'

'Everything?' Roe asked, raising an eyebrow. 'No romantic ties?'

Rachel shook her head and coloured. Good, thought Roe. That should make life easier. He drained his glass.

The waitress had brought over two piping-hot pies topped with thick puff pastry, new potatoes and a dish of baby vegetables. Roe zipped up her portfolio and placed it back on the floor, explaining his motives for inviting her to lunch. He launched into a brief history of Vaubelle and of his own involvement with the company. Rachel, whose nerves were in shreds, found she'd suddenly lost her

83

appetite and picked at her pastry. Then came the bomb-shell.

'What!' She dropped her fork on to her plate with a clang. Several startled people turned to look in their direction.

'How would you like to be the new Vaubelle designer?' Roe repeated evenly. Just for a second Rachel, with her O-shaped mouth, John Lennon spectacles and huge, incredulous eyes, reminded him of an owl.

'I'm speechless. I don't know what to say!'

'Yes will do for a start. I'm offering you a six-months contract on a trial basis, with work to start on the *haute couture* immediately. You won't have time to make the *prêt* in March, but that's OK. We'll just skip a season.'

Rachel was having trouble taking all this in.

'But what about Claude Vaubelle? Do you mean that I'll be working as his assistant?'

'Claude Vaubelle's taking an early retirement. Family commitments,' Roe said with an impudent smile. 'Don't give him a thought.'

He stabbed two potatoes with his fork and popped them into his mouth. The waitress returned to their table and, noting Rachel's untouched plate, asked if everything was all right. The heavily made-up woman with the frosted lipstick got up unsteadily from the next table to leave, followed by her equally wobbly son.

'So. What do you say?' said Roe. The amber eyes were pinned to Rachel's. 'It would mean flying out to Paris by the end of the week, which doesn't give you much time but I'd like to get things going. Think you could handle that?'

'Oh yes! I want this job more than anything! God, I'd be mad to say no. But what about my commitments to New Girl? I can't just walk out.'

'Have you signed a contract yet?' Roe asked cautiously.

'I do that next Monday.'

'Then you're not committed. Let me handle the details. You just concentrate on being ready. I know you'll be real anxious to tell everyone, but until I've announced your replacement to the press, keep this to yourself.'

84

'Oh thank you! Oh yes, I will!' The penny still hadn't quite dropped.

'Oh, just one more thing,' said Roe in such an ominous voice that Rachel's heart stopped. 'Next time I buy you lunch, young lady, I'd like you to eat it!'

For the first time since arriving at the restaurant, Rachel really laughed.

6

It was hardly surprising that the month which followed the *prêt à porter* was a slow one. For three weeks models, ranging in age from fifteen to their late thirties, had flown to Germany, Milan, London, Paris and New York for up to sixty shows. They had lived in hotel rooms and airport lounges, swallowed fast food and undrinkable coffee, ordered 5 a.m. wake-up calls, then spent the rest of the day cat-napping behind dress rails or on fitting-room floors. These beauties had lived in an exclusive, vacuum-sealed world where nothing seemed real and the only people they could rely on and understand were each other. They moaned about the fees and the latest diets, showed off new cards and editorial spreads in magazines they called tear sheets, and announced what they were going to do when they gave it all up. They commiserated about children and exes and advised on how to handle partners who found the modelling profession a threat. They put up with the boredom, the persistent demands of make-up artists, hairdressers, designers, photographers and choreographers, all trying to turn them into fantasy creatures, the envy of the rest of the world. And out of their fees came the agent's twenty per cent, the air fares, taxis, food expenses, wardrobe upkeep and accommodation. The collections over, they could pay off the overdraft and give in to fatigue and the repetitive feeling of appalling anticlimax. Then the long wait for next season. This pattern of life never changed.

For Kate that month was unbearable, not helped by the weather which remained cold and wet. Although it was now April signs of spring still seemed a long way off. With little to occupy her gloomy mind she caught up on long-overdue letters and ate too much chocolate. She couldn't explain her moodiness but whenever the phone rang (mostly for Bea) the caller got his head snapped off. It didn't help that Bea seemed to have a different man each night of the week.

Like many models Kate felt that the less she worked, the less she existed. By Friday, however, the weather had improved and to combat her restlessness she went to the Pontoise swimming pool and worked on her laps. After an hour she hauled herself out of the deep end and dangled a leg on the poolside. Watching fellow-swimmers from the corner of her eye she ran a critical hand along her upper thighs and buttocks, which had tiny silver snail-trails of stretchmarks. They were there to rebuke her for years of dieting.

Sports, particularly swimming, held no happy memories for Kate. By the time she was ten she could no longer be described as merely plump, her weight had suddenly ballooned and showed no sign of budging. Sophie's way of dealing with it was, like Bea's parents, to send her daughter to a boarding school, and, like Bea, Kate had hated it. She became the victim of schoolgirl sniggers and whispers in the changing-room. Their stares crawled over her like leeches and what had once been a niggling mistrust of her body now developed into a full-scale loathing of it, with all its bumps and hair sprouting in dangerous places. She lost count of the number of times she had used the curse as an excuse not to swim, only to have to watch the girls splashing and shrieking from the gallery. How she had longed to join in.

Unable to cope with their relentless teasing, Kate withdrew from the other girls, and because she was so homesick her academic work deteriorated. Her mother received frequent calls from the school complaining of Kate's inability to keep up, but Sophie, now divorced from her second husband, was caught up in the fever of a new love affair and turned a blind eye. Kate took refuge in food.

She was allowed to keep a pet white rabbit at school in a shed behind the tennis courts. The rabbit was the one thing Kate had of her own and she lavished affection on it, talking to it for hours and calling it Camelot after her favourite book. An incurable romantic, she read anything she could get her hands on, devouring historical novels under the bed-covers with a torch she'd sneaked from home. The stories featured long-haired heroes in black capes and ludicrously frilly sleeves which got wildly flicked about – their faces were always anonymously dark. Powdered heroines wore plunging necklines but kept their ankles primly hidden. Everyone swooned, dropping white handkerchiefs with personal emblems all over the place. There was always a happy ending. Snatched by wicked barons, Kate dreamt of rescue, sticking her own face resolutely over the heroine's. She spent endless nights under the duvet, tent-like, writing short stories; one of them she bravely submitted to her English teacher to read and was thrilled to bits when she won first prize in a local competition – she had sent a copy to Sophie who put it aside to read but it got inadvertently thrown out with the Sunday papers. Kate craved popularity but most of all she dreamt that one day she would meet someone who would truly love her.

Someone yelled out nearby. A handsome youth climbed out of the pool and gave chase to a shrieking nymphet in a bright-pink bikini. Kate's thoughts again returned to Roe. What a fool she was to have let him go without her number!

Bea found the whole thing rather amusing. She had never seen her normally cool friend go to pieces over a man. But she soon found herself the recipient of Kate's wrath, after spending an hour and a half on the phone.

'For God's sake, Bea! Can't you find anything better to do than spend the entire morning on the phone,' she snapped. 'Our bill's going to be horrendous!'

'Stop pouncing. It's like living with a kangaroo on heat.' Bea collapsed on to the sofa. 'He's either tied up with work or playing it cool to get you really interested. Smart man. Of course you'll now have to make him wait at least two days when he calls.' She unwrapped a fruit and nut bar and devoured it swiftly.

'If he calls,' said Kate mournfully.

'Oh, he'll call. And stop chewing your nails. You're supposed to be a vegetarian.'

But as the days slipped by Kate's hopes faded. On Saturday night she went to an agency party with Bea. They were picked up by a couple of German lawyers and got drunk on Stolis vodka. Bea disappeared with a Rod Stewart lookalike, winking at Kate as she swept out in a borrowed metallic Muglar tube dress. It was daringly short, but despite six inches of snow outside, Bea had been determined to wear it.

Early on Kate had learned that physical beauty opened many doors. She had revelled in smart dinner parties and social events, discovering the power of her physical charm but allowing nobody to take her out more than once or twice. Much better to stay aloof and keep the upper hand. But recently the novelty had worn off. Throughout the evening Kate found herself repeatedly thinking of Roe Lewis, who from a safe distance had become the object of her fantasies. Again and again, knocking back the vodka like orange juice, she re-enacted the scene in his apartment, giving it a different ending.

Bored by the German lawyer banging on about corporate law, Kate drank too much and lost her date on her way back from the loo.

On Sunday Kate woke up feeling as if she'd been dipped in a pot of glue. Her mouth tasted foul and her eyes were stuck at the corners. Staggering into the bathroom she found a white-faced Bea in the bath clutching a chipped mug of tea and a fat Jilly Cooper novel. Her feet were propped up against the taps.

'Don't say a word!' croaked Bea, raising a feeble hand, 'I'm feeling too ghastly for words. Can't even rouse myself for the divine Rupert Campbell Black.'

Kate stood on the scales and checked her weight, grimacing in the mirror. Violet circles ringed her eyes and a large sneaky spot had erupted overnight on her chin.

'What's the time?' she yawned loudly.

'Ten. I think we should splash out and keep the heating on today. Otherwise I'm going to spend the whole day in bed.' Bea ran more hot water professionally with her toes. 'Did you see you've got a three-hour booking with Cacharel tomorrow? Wish they'd throw a bit of work my way. I promised the bank I'd pay off my overdraft by the end of the month.'

'Did they leave any details?' said Kate, noticing that her friend had lost weight. Where did all that food go to, for God's sake.

'It's all on the machine.'

'Damn! I'll have to change my doctor's appointment again.' Kate sat down on the plastic loo seat and stared at the floor. She felt sick.

'Still planning on having your coil taken out then?'

'It's funny. I've recently gone right off the idea of having anything artificial inside me. Never used to bother me but you read so many horror stories.'

Bea shuddered. 'Give me a straightforward condom any day. Oh, if you want some tea, there's a fresh pot of PG tips in the kitchen. I couldn't face Lapsang with a hangover. And we need to descale the kettle. It looks like a bad case of dandruff.'

Half an hour later Kate was sitting on the living-room floor in a bright-blue face pack, waxing her legs. The spot on her chin was looking quite angry now that she'd given it a good squeeze. Bea, in leggings and one of Kate's Calvin Klein vests, was munching burnt toast and peanut butter, which she dunked into her coffee. She was reading cartoons while on the television flickered an old Pinewood movie dubbed into French. Neither of them was really watching it. Kate, whose breakfast had been a glass of Alka Seltzer, was carefully applying another strip of hot wax to her leg when the door-bell rang. Bea ignored it.

'Bea!' said Kate when it rang a second time. 'I can hardly answer it like this!'

'Okay, grumpy. Keep your mask on or you'll crack. It'll be Martin from downstairs wanting to borrow my eyeliner. That makes it the third time this week. Wish he'd buy his own.'

Two minutes later Bea's head re-emerged round the door making an agonising face.

'Sorry,' she mouthed.

Kate's expression turned to horror as Roe Lewis, looking

even more god-like than she remembered, walked into the room with Bea trailing close behind. In her panic, Kate knocked over the waxing machine as she got up, spilling the hot liquid all over the floor, and smudging it into the carpet.

'I'll do that,' said Bea, intervening. 'Go and get changed.'

'Won't be long,' stammered Kate as she fled to the bedroom.

'No hurry,' said Roe, slipping one hand in an exquisitely-tailored trouser pocket and sinking on to the sofa.

'I've a feeling we've already met. Would you like some coffee?' she heard Bea ask, as the door closed. Bea never made coffee for anyone! She hoped he took it black. They'd run out of milk.

Damn, damn, damn! Kate rushed to the bathroom mirror and started to cry. Oh, and I wanted to look so good for him. How dare Bea show him in without warning her! Ripping off the last of the wax she dived into the shower, yelping with pain as the water scalded the tender skin of her calves. Water went everywhere as Kate scrubbed her hair and washed away the remains of the ghoulish blue face pack. She wrapped herself in a fluffy bath towel and with shaking hands tried to apply some make-up to her now flushed face, cursing when she smudged mascara under her eye.

Kate dripped into the bedroom and opened her cupboard. She threw several outfits on to the bed. First she put on her jeans with an Hermès shirt and a wool fitted jacket, but then decided that was too casual and changed into a navy coat-dress. No, she looked as if she was going to a funeral. Then came the emerald-green catsuit that was too dressy and the silk trouser suit that wasn't warm enough, until in the space of fifteen minutes she'd tried on and rejected her entire wardrobe. Bea popped her head round the door and Kate signalled frantically for her to come in.

'God, Kate. No wonder you've been so worked up. Thought I recognised him. He's the dreamy man in the Valentino suit I spoke to after the Dior show. The one we thought was a journalist. He's only been here for half an hour and I'm already running round like a housewife. Why are you standing there in your underwear?'

'Come and help me!' Kate pleaded, urgently pulling her further into the room. 'I haven't a thing to wear!'

Bea lifted an eyebrow at the sea of clothes surrounding Kate's feet. 'You could have fooled me!'

Perhaps she'd invite Ray over for the afternoon. All this excitement was making her horny. She could wear Kate's new Joseph sweater – having sneaked it on yesterday she thought the colour really suited her.

'I personally like the green catsuit,' she said finally.

'No.'

'What's wrong with jeans?'

'You've seen what he's wearing!'

'Better to be understated and cool. Oh, all right,' she said, at Kate's darkening face, 'why don't you wear the camel suede dress? You can borrow my jacket, which looks great with it, but only if I can wear your new sweater.'

'Anything. Just go back out there and talk to him, for heaven's sake, or he'll think we're terribly rude.'

Five minutes later Kate found Roe engrossed in a heated political debate between Mitterand and a United Nations representative on the television.

'Sorry I was so long.' She picked up her bag. 'Where's Bea?'

'Still here.' Bea, with her mouth full, emerged from the kitchen. 'I was just making more toast.'

Roe took Kate's arm and smiled, appraising the transformation.

'You look great. Sorry to rush you but I made reservations for one thirty. Thanks for the coffee,' and he rewarded Bea with one of his smiles.

She winked, none too subtly, at Kate.

'Have fun. I'd like her back by midnight please.'

'Nice girl,' said Roe as they took the lift down to the ground floor. 'Body's in great shape. Must work out a lot.'

'Skinny genes. Bea was born perfect.' Please don't let him fancy her.

'Where are we going?' she asked, trying to keep up with Roe's long strides.

93

'Somewhere we can talk. I've a few unanswered questions.'

'Sounds as if I'm going to be interrogated.'

'You bet,' and he put his arm round her waist, his hand resting on her hip as if it were the most natural thing in the world.

He took her to a tiny restaurant on the left bank overlooking the Seine and Notre Dame. Most of the snow had melted revealing purple and orange crocus buds and shrubs which were shooting up in the gardens. They had the best view in the place from a window-seat covered in Viennese striped cushions, fringed with burgundy tassels. While waiters efficiently flambéed veal and arranged exotic desserts, Roe ordered for them both. Lobster soufflé, perfectly risen, was followed by thin slithers of bream with orange, aubergine and tomato ragout, and sugar-browned potatoes. Kate noticed that he hardly touched his food, pushing it to one side after only a few mouthfuls. Embarrassed by the sight of her own licked-clean plate, she refused the dessert menu the waiter brought over.

'You've got to try Hubert's speciality. People only come here for the dessert,' insisted Roe, brushing away her protests.

'But what about you?'

'I'm not a sweet man.'

'I think you're very sweet.' Kate dug her spoon into the burnt topping of her *crème brûlée* and tasted it. 'This is ambrosial!'

They talked for hours, oblivious of the admiring glances from other lunchers, and Kate hardly noticed the gun-metal grey sky outside or the waiter pouring the remnants of the second bottle of wine into their glasses. Sometimes she let her mind wander, not really taking in a word he was saying, just enjoying how much the yellow eyes and beautiful mouth made her think of bed, and how she envied the glass his long, capable hands were holding. Roe signalled the waiter and ordered more wine.

'I really shouldn't,' Kate said weakly. 'I'm not much of a drinker. Alcohol sends me out of control.'

'Now that I'd like to see!' said Roe, filling her glass to the brim.

'Where did you learn to speak such good French?'

'My mother. I was brought up in Houma, New Orleans. You seem pretty fluent yourself.'

'About the only advantage of having had a French step-father.' Kate checked herself as she always did when she felt she was saying too much. She pleated her hands together and rested them defensively against her mouth.

'Vous désirez, monsieur?' asked the waiter, looking for a cigarette to light, a plate to clear away, anything to get another look at Roe.

'You want more coffee?' Roe asked.

'Mmm. Please.'

'Encore deux cafés, Jean. Merci.'

Jean beamed and dissolved into the background.

'I think you've got a fan,' said Kate, shifting the attention back to Roe. 'Tell me about your parents.'

'Not much to tell. My mother left home when I was six. She'd had enough, I guess. For most of their short marriage my parents weren't speaking. My mother hated my father because of his drinking and womanising. Guess I can't blame her for that. When he died they couldn't track her down and the only relative I had left was my paternal uncle. He didn't have a clue. I mean, what do you do with a messed-up kid of seven? So I went to the orphanage. It could have been worse, I just wish there'd been a few girls around.'

'Did you ever manage to find your mother?'

'She could be dead for all I know. Who cares? It was all a long time ago.'

Roe drained a glass and smiled but his voice was suddenly bitter.

'I expect you ran riot?' said Kate lightly, fighting a sudden urge to touch him.

'I wasn't exactly angelic – picked up some bad habits from my father – but I was pretty shy as a boy. Didn't talk much. My big break came through Cortes – that's Carl Elliot's company. As soon as I was old enough I escaped to Los Angeles. Started out collecting rent-rolls for one of Carl's

95

restaurants, then moved on to scouting for real estate. I've been working for him for twelve years.'

'I've never worked for the same person longer than a month.'

'Carl's tough but he's got real staying power. I learnt everything I know from the guy. He's in pharmaceuticals, restaurants, real estate, you know the sort of thing. Big time. Always looking for something new.'

'Married?'

'Yeah. On his fourth divorce.'

'With number five lined up, no doubt.'

Roe's eyes shifted. 'We all have our weaknesses.' Why did that sound like a telling off? 'We're pretty close but on the whole I prefer your sex. Word of advice. Don't ever trust a man.'

'Sounds as if you're warning me off already.'

'No. You can make an exception of me.' He smiled suddenly, the determination in his face softening.

Jean came back with the coffee and a plate of sticky Florentines.

'As to my staying with Cortes, when I decide to go for something I push hard, and I push to win. My problem, Kat, is I don't always like the result as I also hate responsibility.' He fixed her with his eyes, challenging her.

Kate sipped her Pouilly-Fuissé slowly, not really listening, but she liked the sound of her nickname. It had an intimate, long-term feel which made her look at Roe with real interest. Did he feel the same about her? Funny, she wasn't normally attracted to handsome men, and Roe really was indecently good-looking. She watched him pour the wine, talk to the waiter, occasionally tilting his head in her direction to make her feel included. Each gesture fluid, confident, controlled. Roe seemed to dazzle everyone. Including me, she thought giddily, trying to imagine what he looked like without his clothes.

Crossing her legs under the table, the suede dress hitched up around her thighs, Kate caught her tights on a piece of splintered wood. She looked down. The hole, which exposed her pale skin, was small but might get bigger and she kept

96

running a hand over its surface. Even as a schoolgirl Kate had hated flaws. For years she had harboured a terrific crush on a school prefect who had all the attributes Kate so thoroughly lacked. She had seemed so sophisticated with her ability to talk to boys, always being exquisitely dressed, teachers giving her special privileges because she was so beautiful and prizes for being the brainiest, the most athletic, the most popular. Everyone wanted to be her friend. Once Kate had eavesdropped on a conversation during which the prefect had mentioned two pet hates: chipped nail-varnish and laddered tights. Kate thought this was some vital clue to her secret powers and had never forgotten it.

Roe, called to the phone, broke her train of thought and Kate took advantage of his absence by waving over the waiter. They'd been in the restaurant for three hours.

'Mademoiselle?' Jean was instantly at her side.

'Is there a chemist open close by?' she asked hopefully.

'Ah,' Jean had spotted her ladder. But Roe was already back.

'What's up?'

'Oh, nothing. I think they're about to close the kitchen, that's all.'

Roe sat down, thinking that without her professional make-up she looked about twelve. 'What were you like as a child?'

Kate smiled. 'Hideous! And very badly behaved. At least that's what my mother always said.'

'Then I don't think she and I would get on.'

'You say that now but then you haven't met Sophie. All my friends fall in love with her.'

'Roe, honey,' cooed an expensive voice, 'I was wondering when I might run into you.'

A beautiful woman, wrapped in a huge mink coat and matching hat to set off charcoal-black eyes stood by their table.

'Jody!' Roe stood up and kissed the intruder. 'What a nice surprise! How was Tokyo?'

'In a word, cold. Hope you're still planning to make our drinks party.'

'Sure thing. Jody, this is Kate Temple.'

'Hi.' She gave Kate a careful once-over before turning back to Roe. 'About seven suit you?'

'Yeah,' said Roe easily. 'I'll call you at the hotel.'

Jody gave Kate a perfunctory smile, and in a wave of Joy, drifted off.

'Old friend?' Kate enquired, trying not to sound overly curious.

'Something like that.' He watched Jody leave. 'She looks well.'

'She looks like an Eskimo.' Kate disapproved of the real fur. 'She'd be shot by animal rights campaigners in London.'

'Hey,' he said, reaching for her hand, 'what's going on in there? You disappeared again.'

'Did I? Sorry.' She was still thinking about Sophie and why it was her mother lavished attention on everyone except her.

'That's okay. Just fuels my curiosity about you.'

Kate giggled, happy to have his attention on her again.

'You don't like talking about yourself much, do you?'

'I'm not used to so much interest. Oh, I'm noticed by men,' she waved a dismissive hand, 'but it's always about getting me into bed or having me on their arm like a prize because of what I do – a sort of status symbol.'

'Don't knock sex. Going to bed with someone is usually the best way of getting to know them.'

'Not always,' Kate replied, wondering if in this instance he was right.

Jean appeared and wordlessly slipped something in Kate's lap. She lifted the edge of the tablecloth and was astonished to find a packet of Christian Dior sheer black tights.

Outside, after a quick dive to the loo to change, they walked along the busy river holding hands and watched boats pass under the Pont Neuf.

'Christo apparently used seven miles of rope to wrap that bridge.'

'He wouldn't have been much fun to play Pass the Parcel with,' said Kate, gazing up at the grey duvet of clouds.

Some hardy Japanese tourists weighed down by Sony cameras asked Roe if he'd mind taking their photograph with

Kate. There was much excited giggling and a lot of shuffling around as Kate was a good six inches taller than the orientals. Roe took the picture and returned the camera.

'You have virry pretty wife!' said the man with the camera. The group nodded a vigorous agreement. 'You have virry many children, no?'

'No,' said Roe putting his arm round Kate, 'but it's a nice idea.'

In an extremely anti-social manner the sun skulked off behind a patch of clouds and refused to come out for the rest of the afternoon. It didn't matter. Still gloriously drunk and ignoring the rude, bullying wind that whipped them from the river Seine, Kate couldn't imagine when she'd last been so happy. She wanted this day to stretch out for ever.

Roe took her to the zoo and was astonished when Kate admitted it was the first one she'd visited. She hated the idea of animals in captivity. With only a few visitors they had the place practically to themselves as it had been the coldest March in almost twenty years. In a moment of madness they bought heart-shaped ice-creams and popcorn in red boxes, which they fed to each other. The chimps huddled together in small groups with their backs to the spectators. At the far end of the cage two of them lazed together in the grass nibbling at each other's ears, picking fleas affectionately from their fur. They seemed oblivious of the cold. In the distance they could hear the fierce growl of a lion.

'I can't believe I'm still eating. I'm ravenous!' said Kate through a mouthful of popcorn.

'You're ravishing. I wish you were eating me,' said Roe, steering her towards an elephant.

The magnificent animal, with skin like a gnarled old tree, swayed relentlessly from side to side. Dignified, prehistoric and once mighty, he looked like a defeated king. It was worse than Battersea Dogs Home.

'That really upsets me. He should be back in Africa, not hemmed in like that.'

'If it wasn't for zoos,' Roe said, 'many species would now be extinct. Most of these animals were born into captivity and don't know any different. At least this way they're protected by people who love them.'

'But I don't like to see animals locked up.'

'We're all locked up in our own way, Kat.'

She looked at him then, curiously. It was the second time she'd seen vulnerability exposed in his face.

The baboons behaved very badly, regurgitating their food and scratching their bright-orange bottoms with long, bony fingers. The gorillas pulled in the largest crowd. Encouraged by the stream of apple cores, chips and nuts that reached the edge of the cage, the male found himself a stick and used it to scrape food inside. The crowd was impressed and showed its approval by throwing more food. The female attempted to eat some of the stray nuts but the male angrily shoved her away and scoffed the lot. Feeling sorry for her, the crowd distracted the male and managed to get an apple to the female. When the male realised he'd been duped he made a terrible noise and beat his fists against his chest. Bored with the game moments later, he yawned loudly and went into the corner to sulk.

'I know a male model a bit like that,' Kate said, giggling.

'What do you do now the *prêt à porter* is over?'

'Castings mostly. There's usually something going on, commercials, advertising jobs. Mind you, it won't be long before the *couture.*'

'Do you have favourite designers?' Roe stuffed Kate's gloveless hand into his coat pocket to keep it warm.

'I like some of the less well-known names. Léger's a favourite, you can always rely on him to bring out a strong collection, but most of what goes down the runway these days is unwearable!'

'Like they're running out of ideas?'

'Exactly. So we models end up having to flash bottoms and breasts. Unimaginative but provocative – it keeps their name in print.'

'You don't like that?'

'No, but that's not the point. It's my job to make anything they give me look good.'

'You'd look good in a sack. Still, my impression is that

women haven't stopped spending despite the quality of the clothes,' argued Roe. 'They'll still fight over a $30 thousand *couture* gown.'

'Only a handful and even they're beginning to feel the pressure. Times are changing, not just in fashion. There's the environment, the Third World, animal rights. Most of my friends, given the choice between a Christian Lacroix or a down payment on a one-bedroom flat, would opt for the latter. Except maybe Bea.'

She smiled at him, enjoying this rapid, intellectual exchange.

'What about Vaubelle?' asked Roe carefully. They passed a harassed mother trying to discipline a boy for emptying a bag of cheese and onion crisps into his sister's pram. He looked thoroughly pleased as he tried to cram pieces into her wailing mouth.

'This was my first Vaubelle show. Beautifully-made clothes, but it's all been done before. Claude seems to have gone the other way and played safe to the point of dullness. I hear they are having financial problems.'

'They're not alone. One of Britain's biggest fashion names went into receivership last week. They'd been going seventy years. That's one hell of a long time.'

Kate looked at him curiously. 'Why all the interest?'

'Hey, I'm interested in everything,' Roe shrugged evasively. 'Remind me to have you on my side in an argument.'

The boy, having been given a resounding whack, held an indignant hand over his sore bottom. Glaring at his mother he weighed up the chances of another slap. His sister's pram throbbed with interest.

As they made their way to the cafeteria Kate got her heel caught in a grid. Roe bent down to help her free it.

'My, what big feet you have!'

'I do not!' she said in a tight, hot voice which indicated that it was a sensitive subject.

They drank tea out of polystyrene cups and Kate took the afternoon vitamins she kept in her bag. A pretty young woman writing postcards at a table nearby was staring at Roe. Her interest was unmistakable but Roe seemed not to notice. Kate was beginning to sober up and had the beginnings of a headache. Roe, noticing her shiver, took off his coat and wrapped it round her shoulders. A sudden wind blew her hair away from her face, revealing her white forehead. Roe impulsively kissed it. Kate shyly dropped her head against his shoulder.

'C'm on, beautiful one,' he said tenderly, 'it's getting late.'

Yah-boo, sucks to you, thought Kate as they left the postcard-writer behind, chewing on the end of her Pentel.

The loud B52s accompanied them home. Kate would have preferred Mozart or Eric Satie, but she could only find rock. The roads were slushy and folds of cloud clustered above them. From her window she watched stray people huddle in their coats, blowing their hands to keep warm. The car warmed up. Headlights went on. Kate closed her eyes and stretched her legs in the now familiar front seat, suddenly tired. She wanted to be alone so that she could think about Roe and their day together, make it all real. As the car pulled up outside her block, Roe switched off the engine and undid his seat belt.

'I won't be able to see you for a while. I'm leaving Tuesday on business.'

Kate's eyes tightened. It had been too good to be true.

'Where are you going?'

Roe was surprised by the anxiety in her husky voice. 'LA. What have you got planned for the weekend of the 19th?'

That was three weeks away and he wasn't leaving for two days. He can't be that keen if he's prepared to wait so long, Kate reflected. Probably wants to see Jody minus that rotten fur coat.

'I'm supposed to be going to London,' she lied.

'Break it.'

'I don't know if I can.'

'I want you to come skiing. A group of us are going. Should be a blast.'

Kate studied her hands, her heart skipping, and paused just long enough to get him worried. When she looked up her eyes were shining.

'I've never skied before. Probably won't even manage to stand up!'

Roe laughed. 'I'll call you nearer the time, but promise to keep the weekend free! I'll provide all the entertainment.'

Kate tapped in the security code and pulled back the heavy front door of her apartment building. With a sudden burst of energy she raced furiously up the three flights of stairs and from the landing window she watched the black Porsche weave its way through the traffic. She couldn't stop smiling.

7

Claude Vaubelle, clutching a mobile phone, framed himself in the doorway of Roe's office. His childish, unlined face looked set and petulant. Roe stood by the open window looking down on the rue du Faubourg Saint Honoré. It was only nine o'clock but he'd already been at his desk for three hours. The room hummed with traffic sounds.

Claude spoke first. 'You wanted to see me?'

'Yes. Come in. Take a seat.'

'I don't have time. Madame le Penn's waiting for a fitting.' He hovered by the door as if he couldn't bear to come right in.

'Suit yourself.'

Roe slammed the window shut, bringing an immediate hush to the room and returned to his desk.

He said, in a businesslike tone, 'I want your resignation.'

'*Comment?* You are joking!'

'Last year you lost Vaubelle $8 million. I don't find that anything to joke about. You're out, Claude. I've had it with your airs and graces, chauffeur-driven cars and three-hour lunch breaks that this house can ill afford.'

Claude gave a disparaging smirk. 'You obviously haven't read the small print in our contract. You can't threaten me!'

'This isn't a threat.' The American voice was very soft.

'Well, it certainly sounds like one. What do you know about making clothes anyway! You think you can just come over here and change a century of tradition overnight. Are you crazy? You'll never sell your cheap American cosmetics simply by attaching our name to them. This *maison* has been built on foundations of tradition and quality. It has taken many decades to get where we are.' Although he sounded confident, Claude's body was tense, an angry heat-rash forming on his neck.

'You said it! Vaubelle's been living off its reputation for the last ten years. Times have changed. You're just not coming up with the goods any more.' Roe opened a side drawer in his desk. He pulled out a handful of receipts and dropped them lightly on to the desk. 'Did you approve these expense receipts from Jean-Marc?'

'Where did you get them? These documents are kept in my personal bureau. You can be arrested for trespassing.' Claude glared at Roe for a moment then added, 'Did Nicole give them to you? I'll have that girl sacked!'

'She has nothing to do with this. Don't blame her for your own carelessness.'

'Please, get to the point.' Claude was finding it hard to control his anger.

'For a start I want to know why Jean-Marc has such an inflated salary. According to his four-figure expense account he's on the same perks as you.'

Claude suddenly looked flustered and stared at the pile of receipts on the desk as if they might hold the answer. Very slowly, his eyes came back to Roe.

'You were in Aspen for three weeks last November,' Roe continued. 'Jean-Marc, who had only recently joined the company, was staying at the same hotel, while your wife checked into hospital in Paris with an infected ovary. Odd you didn't return from your vacation. Mind you, if she were to see this shot of you and Jean-Marc I have here, I'm sure she'd understand. You were obviously having a ball!' Roe held up a photograph of the two men.

Claude's face turned ashen and the small Napoleon slumped into the chair he had rejected only five minutes ago. Roe studied the man's swollen, pitted nose in distaste. An alcoholic's nose.

'I know how much you crave publicity, but think about the headlines,' Roe continued nastily. 'Claude Vaubelle, the man behind the Vaubelle name, shocks Paris with current male lover, thirty years his junior . . . shall I go on?'

'You make an impressive speech, Monsieur.'

'You should see me with slides.'

'I can't believe you would do this. You have no one but me to finish the collection. You cannot possibly find a replacement so late in the day.'

Claude said it bravely, but he was clearly worried. Should he call his lawyer? Roe's mouth curled. He flicked a phone switch.

'Monsieur?'

'Nicole, bring in those papers I had you type up, would you?' Then to Claude, 'Look, you've had a good run for your money. You shouldn't feel bad about this. In a way I'm doing you a favour. No one goes on for ever. Not in this fickle business. Why not take up gardening or something? That's what people of your age usually do.' He did nothing to hide his contempt.

'But my clients. The press? I'm in the middle of a collection. Surely you expect me to finish it?'

There was a tap at the door and Nicole walked in. She handed Roe a file then retreated, without once looking at Claude.

'I want you out by the end of the week,' Roe continued icily. 'I have these papers for you to sign which relinquish your rights as designer and active participant in the house. You will of course be paid a retainer, but your services to the company are at an end.'

'May I know who my replacement will be?' Claude seemed robbed of all his dignity.

Roe hesitated for a second. 'There will be a press release on Monday when Vaubelle's new designer begins work. Your resignation will be announced at the same time. The remaining details don't concern you. Meanwhile until next week I expect you to keep this delicate matter to yourself. For my part I will return the favour. Jean-Marc will be kept on to avoid suspicion, but things certainly won't be as cushy around here for him. I intend making him put in some extra work. He owes the company.'

'I see.' Claude's voice dragged. 'You've done your home-work, Monsieur Lewis. I underestimated you. A grave error as I must comply with your wishes.' Claude's voice was so soft Roe could hardly hear him. But his pale eyes radiated hatred. 'But I warn you now. Be careful. Many times people have tried unsuccessfully to change this company. You won't be an exception. As you say, no one goes on for ever and your turn will come. Of that I am certain!'

'In the circumstances your threat carries little weight. You know your way out.'

As soon as Claude left the room, Roe picked up the telephone. 'Nicole, have everyone in the boardroom for a five o'clock meeting. No exceptions. I'm going to make an announcement.

At 10 a.m. Bea was still in bed watching a pop video and eating cold baked beans out of a can. She couldn't decide how bad her hangover was. An hour ago she'd struggled, half-asleep, to the bathroom for a shower, and had then meant to write to her parents and pay a few bills, but the chill of the top-floor flat had sent her diving straight back under the duvet. Kate was always banging on about global warming, but there was nothing warm about this spring. She yawned tiredly. No more lovely nicotine to accompany my morning coffee, she thought gloomily, scooping up the last of the baked beans. Clothes and dirty underwear were scattered all over the floor. On the wall behind her bed was the poster she'd shot for Clairol, her laughing face in profile. Next to it was the small, favoured Fragonard landscape her grandmother had bequeathed to her and by the bed was a framed photograph of her parents, staring self-consciously into the camera. It was ages since her last visit. Maybe she'd call them instead.

Bea yawned again. Ten more minutes and she'd get up. Inspecting a new mole on her left breast she allowed her thoughts to stray to Ray Marks. During their torrid affair sex had always been competitive, the bedroom a sexual battle-field. But three nights ago at his flat Ray had gone too far. They'd drunk their way through three bottles of South African wine and ended up in bed. As Bea was just about to climax, Ray had thrust a small bottle of chloralhydrate under her nose. Far from the desired effect – a synchronised

108

multiple orgasm – Bea launched into a ten-minute sneezing fit. Still wildly excited, Ray then took her from behind, with Bea bent double and hanging on to the edge of the curtain for dear life. Just at the point of orgasm, he withdrew and peed over her back, while gasping something in Danish (he always came in Danish). Angry and humiliated, Bea had stormed off home.

Reporting all to a shocked Kate at breakfast, Bea had calmly put Ray through the emotional shredder.

'It would never have worked,' she had said philosophically, 'he could only come if I massaged his prostate gland and he was hopeless at oral sex. Guess that's why he was always so kinky.'

Kate, whose sexual education had quadrupled since living with Bea, refrained from asking where the prostate gland was.

The phone shrieked. Naked, Bea hauled herself out of bed, grabbed the damp towel and picked up the extension in the kitchen.

'Hallo?' Her voice was guarded. She couldn't deal with Ray while feeling so appalling. It was Evelyne, her agent.

'You're working at two. Kevin Cassini's booked you for a jewellery brochure for Japan.'

Bea glanced at the kitchen clock. 'Hell! I'm testing with Gunther for my new composite card at twelve. It's been a nightmare trying to tie him down.' On the other hand she couldn't afford to turn down work. Like the majority of models she was always chronically broke.

'Don't worry. I'll call Kevin and let him know you're coming from another job. You don't need to bring anything, just clean hair and face. Oh, and remind Kate she has that Vaubelle casting tomorrow before her fitting.'

With the towel now wrapped around her belly, Bea kicked the kitchen door closed to keep the heat in. She sat down with a cup of black coffee (they'd run out of milk) and a copy of Kate's English *Marie Claire*. She skimmed through it, toying with the idea of doing the crossword, but discarded it; the answers were on the bottom and she knew she'd cheat. Instead she turned to the horoscopes on the back page: 'This has not been an easy month for Geminis. You must back off from too many arguments and uncooperative people. You should also concentrate on finding solutions to long-running ailments which you have possibly ignored and you need to sort out your finances.'

Nothing like a positive start to the day. Bea examined her face in her powder compact and resolved to stop drinking. Why couldn't she be more like Kate? In the beginning she had hoped that some of Kate's discipline might rub off. But it didn't. Like it or not she wasn't Kate and never would be. Smoothing a creamy Shiseido foundation on to her pale, translucent skin, Bea lingered on a thin blue vein on her temple. Some had begun to show up on her chest and she studied them resignedly. Nothing she could do. Her mother was riddled with them. Her eyelashes needed tinting again. More money! Thank heaven for this job. She owed Amex £800 and that dress she'd bought last week had been a terrible extravagance. It was highly unlikely she'd ever wear it again. Somewhere near the hem was a mud stain. Could she get away with taking it back?

Evelyne called back to say Monteau wanted her in for a quick fitting before tomorrow's private showing. Could she make it before her shoot with Gunther? Time to get the skates on. She dressed with lightning speed, throwing clothes, accessories and make-up into a large, sky-blue sports bag.

More bells. Madame Couris, the concierge, stood outside the front door, flushed and stooping slightly, catching her breath from climbing three flights of stairs. Throwing a guilty look at the state of the apartment, Bea grabbed her coat and car keys.

'*Pardon, madame*, I must run. Help yourself to whatever you like in the *salle à manger*. The washing's in the bedroom and could I possibly settle up with you next week. *A tout à l'heure.*'

The day, as Bea's horoscope had predicted, was a disaster. Wearing Kate's new sweater and smelling of Kate's almond and honey hair shampoo, Bea arrived at Monteau's studio to find everyone in a panic. He was in a bad mood, so

Bea was hurriedly undressed and ushered into his studio. Staff scuttled silently about their duties, terrified of putting a foot wrong. They put Bea into a short black gazar dress, with the neckline slashed to the waist. You had to be flat chested to get away with it. Still, it felt looser than last time.

'*Qu'est-ce que c'est?*' Monteau asked the seamstress.

'Monsieur, the dress is too big around the 'ips.'

'Weren't you fitted for this two weeks ago?' he said to Bea.

'Yes.' God, she *had* lost weight.

'Measure the width,' Monteau instructed, folding his arms. The seamstress told him. '*Alors, prenez le tour des hanches.*'

'*Quatre-vingt douze, monsieur. Elle a maigrit.*'

Everyone looked at Bea.

'What's the matter,' she asked, surveying their glum faces, 'Has World War Three been announced?'

'You've lost almost three centimetres from your hips!' Monteau said accusingly, 'This dress doesn't fit you.'

Three? Oh, lord. That's torn it, thought Bea, feeling her armpits go damp. 'I just gave up smoking. My body's probably gone into temporary shock.'

'Then you'd better start again, *chérie*,' said Monteau, only half-joking, 'or my dress will be in shock when you wear it on the runway!'

Bea stomped moodily back to her car. Bloody cheek! Wish he'd make up his mind. He usually complained the models were too fat. Five minutes after she left the studio Monteau phoned the agency and cancelled her £500 booking.

Gunther was in a complete state when she arrived at his studio. It transpired his beautiful Dutch model wife had left him for a West Indian gynaecologist. They got some shots done, but his mind wasn't on the job so in the end they sat drinking cheap Beaujolais, with Bea feasting on all the gory details. When the phone rang her watch showed an offensive two forty-five. She'd completely forgotten her job with Kevin. Outside it was raining and she had to make a dash for the Beetle parked miles away. Ripping off a parking ticket from the window screen, Bea chucked it in the glove box with all the others. At the red lights she examined her face and clothes. Hell! She was soaked and now there was no time to go home and change. An irate driver behind her tooted impatiently as the lights changed.

'Bugger off!' she yelled, crashing the car into first gear as a shocked pink face in a business suit sped off to the left.

At Kevin's studio, on the fourth floor of an undistinguished warehouse, Bea passed an immaculate brunette clutching a portfolio. The young girl's mouth curled into a smile but her eyes were looking for competition. Bea noticed irritably that there wasn't a single crease in her Irish-green suit. The clock in the hall said three twenty. Kevin, who was covered in hair and had a weight problem, raised a ginger eyebrow.

'Glad you could make it!' he said sarcastically, inspecting her appearance. 'Lucky we're not in New York or you'd be billed for everyone's time here.'

'Sorry,' said Bea sheepishly pulling off her coat and wiping raindrops from her brow. 'Didn't the agency call?'

'Make-up's in the back. Come on, I'll take you.'

The Japanese clients, drinking Pepsi, didn't look overly impressed with Bea's appearance, and launched into Japanese, hands bobbing up and down like two footballs at the FA cup.

The make-up girl, Christiana, supporting a mobile between her ear and shoulder, was perched on a high stool smoking a cigarette. She pressed the 'end' button on the phone as they entered. On the table was an impressive layout of brushes, sponges, bottles of foundation, lip-liners, eye-liners, powder-puffs, tissues and make-up containers that looked like children's paintboxes.

'I'll leave you girls to it,' muttered Kevin, closing the door behind him.

'Don't think I'm very popular,' said Bea in a whisper.

'If you can take your top off I'll get going,' Christiana said rudely. She stubbed out her cigarette and exhaled a stream of menthol smoke, then immediately picked up a hair band and used it to pull Bea's hair off her face.

Washing your nicotine-stained hands before you apply them to my face would be nice, thought Bea, squeezing her head through the snug polo neck. They both looked mournfully at her grey bra. Unthinkingly, Bea had thrown a new pair

112

of black jeans into the wash, ruining three of Kate's bras and two of her own. The studio was freezing. Bea yawned, already regretting the wine.

When Christiana picked up a bottle of hair mousse, Bea said, 'Can you not use that? Someone tried it recently on a job and I came out in hives.'

'I've never had any problems with it before,' said Christiana, bristling, 'you must have reacted to something else.'

All the same, she put the bottle down and inspected Bea's skin. 'You've got a spot coming up on your chin.' She opened a tin to reveal eight shades of concealer cream and began mixing three of the colours on the back of her hand with a tiny brush. 'Right, I'll do your make-up.'

Friendliness obviously wasn't one of Christiana's strong points. Sitting on the high stool Bea offered her face to the lights and Christiana's magic skills. She worked deftly and in silence, first cleaning Bea's face then carefully adding foundation. Her touch had an edge to it and once or twice she carelessly scratched or rubbed Bea's delicate skin too hard. Bea studied the faint dark hairs above Christiana's top lip.

In her rush to catch up on time and not having studied Bea's face properly, Christiana applied too much make-up round her lovely eyes, and back-combed Bea's hair into a fifties bouffant. It made her look a middle-aged frump, and all the healthy shine had been flattened. At least no one will recognise me, reflected Bea, careful not to move her hands in case she smudged the newly applied varnish. After a while she stopped looking in the mirror and closed her eyes to the room and Christiana's aggressive mood, finding sanctuary in a daydream of John Malkovich. Christiana sprayed Bea's hair, then squirted a little hair spray on to a small bristle brush which she used to keep Bea's eyebrows in place. Kate wouldn't like you at all, Bea thought, closing her mouth against another onslaught of CFCs. Very environmentally unfriendly.

Out in the studio Kevin was pacing up and down checking lights, issuing instructions to his French assistant. A Margaret Urlich tape was playing. Kevin took a packet of cigarettes from his trouser pocket and lit one. Bea, in jeans and a white towel held at the back with a large metal clamp, contemplated asking him for a puff.

At least the Japanese clients seemed happy with her appearance. Bea was handed a rather gaudy pair of earrings, matching ring and bracelet, then took a seat behind two massive styrofoam walls propped up against wooden stands. In front of her on the table were two silver reflectors which Kevin's assistant shifted around.

'Light reading,' ordered Kevin. Agnes, his assistant, held a tiny meter against Bea's face.

'Would you like me to say a few words?' Bea joked, trying to ignore a sudden icy draught. The two girls smiled at each other conspiratorially.

A light blinked. 'Eight-point-six.'

'Flick that backflash, Agnes. I'm getting a kick off that ring.'

Bea waited patiently while the clients hovered in the background making suggestions, pointing towards her, generally getting in the way. For the most part Kevin ignored them, except to ask them to move to one side. Then at last, after four polaroids and much fiddling about with the lights, he began to shoot.

Click! 'Nice.' Click. 'No, not so much of a smile. Chin down. Yes. Right a bit.' Click. 'Good. A little more. No, too much.' Click! Oops. She had blinked. 'Left a bit. Yup, more of that. Good.' Click. 'Now back the other way. Okay, yes. That's nice. Now look away, over here where my hand is.'

Kevin, standing on an upside down milk crate, waved his left hand away from his body. Bea dutifully studied the pale, freckly skin covered in wiry red hair but soon got bored and instead followed the line of cable wires lying on the floor and the rows of multi-coloured background paper supported in rolls and on wall brackets.

Click!

'Now hold your hand up closer to your face,' Kevin's voice was muffled, head buried in his camera like an ostrich. 'And rub your arms, sweetheart, I'm getting goose bumps showing. Christiana!' he yelled. 'Can you do something about these goose bumps?'

A heater might help! Bea tilted her head demurely to one side with a smile.

'Yeah, that's it. Now twist your finger so I can see the ring, more . . . no . . . yes, like that. Christ!'

Now what! The ring was too big for her finger and kept slipping so they couldn't see the stone. This meant a further delay while they stuck it down with double-sided tape. Christiana hovered with the menacing bottle of hair spray, most of which had ended up in Bea's ear. The clients stood on the sidelines looking for problems. A dull throbbing was now working its way up Bea's spine. She rubbed her temples.

'Careful! Don't smudge your make-up,' warned Christiana.

Catching Agnes's eye Bea realised she wasn't the only one who wanted to punch Christiana on the nose. Ready to go again, Bea summoned a smile and thought of brandy and log fires and John Malkovitch's mouth trailing her body.

'How's that?' she asked, forty minutes later. Her back was so arched it was screaming at her.

'Good. No, further down, that's too low now. And smile more, your eyes look flat.'

'I'm not bloody surprised,' muttered Bea, now on automatic pilot. The rate Kevin was going she could run an entire marathon between frames! Her mind wandered – they needed fresh milk and loo paper and some stuff to descale the kettle – she'd meant to do it weeks ago. Oh, and she mustn't forget to pick up the dry cleaning on the way home. She'd absolutely promised Kate.

'New roll, please.'

Agnes dutifully slipped a new film into the camera, wound it on, then carefully wrote down the job number on the used roll. She did another light reading and mouthed, 'You okay?' Bea nodded gratefully. 'I'll get you some coffee in the next break.'

'It looks better when you raise your hands above your head, sweetheart, I can't quite get it all in,' mumbled Kevin into his lens.

Bea snapped to attention. Oh no! Her hairy armpits! She'd forgotten to shave them this morning. She looked beseechingly at Christiana who came over to powder her

115

nose and reeked of fresh nicotine.

'What is it?'

'Have you got a pair of tweezers?'

'There's some in my bag. Why?'

'An emergency!'

Sitting on the loo seat moments later, Bea inspected her armpits, which actually weren't too bad after all. She plucked them out, one by one, then pinched a bit of face cream from the make-up room to sooth the redness.

'When you're ready, Belinda,' said Kevin as she returned.

Ready, you sarcastic overweight baboon!

As she struggled with the clutch in her car three hours later, Bea wondered if the four thousand francs she'd just made had been worth it. God, she was tired. Forget the parties, the limos, the first-class restaurants, men with fat wallets and tiny dicks. All I want is a nice hot bath and bed! Zooming off up the road the exhaust pipe coughed out thick black smoke, witnessed by the car behind. The driver, a pinched-faced housewife, waved an indignant hand in front of her face, and made a mental note of Bea's number plate to report to the environmental authorities.

On Thursday Vaubelle's top-floor studio was full of activity. The casting for the new house model had begun at ten. Now, at almost four, everyone was getting bored because they hadn't seen anyone they liked. Rachel Winger, sitting at the head of the table making constant notes, was the exception. This was the end of her second week at Vaubelle and time had flown! Claude's retirement had caused a tremendous stir in the press; not only was it sudden and unexpected, but a girl less than half his age had taken his place. Vaubelle, suddenly newsworthy, had made the front page of *Le Monde* for the first time in years. Several magazines had been quick to approach Rachel for interviews; little was known of her except what had already been written in *Harpers and Queen*. Mercifully, Roe had been a tower of strength.

'Rachel's talent lies in her designs,' he had stressed firmly to a barrage of cameras outside Vaubelle on her first day, 'not in entertaining you guys.'

The fabric samples Claude had ordered for the *prêt à porter* had left Rachel uninspired. She had tried to work with what she had, conscious of waste, but having spoken to Roe about her own quickly formulating ideas, he had told her to buy whatever new fabric she needed.

'I'll call the fabric department and let them know, but if you have problems of any kind, and I mean any kind,' Roe had told her, 'you bring them to me, OK?'

Thus armed, she had arranged to fly to Italy with Richard to visit the great Italian showrooms, after first inspecting the local factories where fabrics were exhibited to buyers just the same as designers showing their collections.

In between taking care of business and getting to know the staff Rachel was constantly drawing doll-size sketches on a stationery pad she carried at all times. Almost everyone had been very nice to her, but she was sensitive to Sebastian Vaubelle's hostility and to the more senior staff who showed strong loyalty to Claude. She was determined to win them over and make her first collection a success. Her future depended on it. Roe had warned her about personal sacrifices but she was used to her life being disrupted. Leaving her life in Argentina so that she could be closer to her father had been a terrible wrench, but designing meant everything to her. Nothing else mattered.

Sometimes she thought about the man with the odd-coloured eyes. She felt a twinge of regret. After all it was the first time in years someone had expressed interest in her. At night she allowed herself to fantasise over what might have happened had she gone to his party. But with all the exciting changes she'd lost his address, and she was insecure enough to think her absence would go unnoticed. No doubt he had dozens of glamorous girlfriends.

She had on the same tortoiseshell John Lennon glasses she'd been wearing the day Toby had spotted her (fast becoming a trademark), and had her dark hair tied back in a high pony tail. But she had balked at Claude's white overalls, preferring leggings and over-size sweaters, and the staff had quickly followed her lead. Nicole brought in a tray of steaming pots of coffee with tiny *langues de chat* and chocolate-covered Florentines and put it on the table. Rachel began sifting through a thick pile of model cards, writing comments on the back.

A stunning blonde with flicked-up hair collected her book from Richard, and walked self-consciously out of the room. No one paid her any attention. In the corridor outside a long line of bored-looking models flicked through magazines, checked their make-up and exchanged gossip while they awaited their turn. New girls stuck out a mile and gazed at the more seasoned models with respect. They, in turn, were regarded with some suspicion. Nicole sat at her desk trying to deal with their endless demands of 'Will they be long? Can I go first as I have to be somewhere else in five minutes' and 'Can I use the phone to check in?' All models spoke to their agents at least once a day to find out about castings and bookings coming up.

The hunt for the Vaubelle face was proving fruitless. No one could agree. Joni had wanted Christie Turlington but she had extended her contract with Calvin Klein so was unavailable and, anyway, much too expensive. Richard had suggested two internationally acclaimed models but Roe wanted an unknown. Richard, already tense because his hairline, which he measured every morning, had receded by half an inch, glared at Roe. He was torn between helpless admiration and a desire to kill him for being so fucking sanctimonious. After all he'd been with Vaubelle longer than anyone else in the room (with the exception of Nicole – he didn't count her).

'OK,' Roe stood up, 'what we're looking for here is someone unique. A woman that appeals to women but also to men. Someone like Cindy Crawford who says it's OK to be voluptuous.'

'Not available,' said Marie-Claire quickly. 'She's back in Tibet with Richard and anyway her agent says she wants to concentrate her career on television.'

'What about Eva?' suggested Brigette, thinking of the Russian beauty whose looks had earned her instant fame.

'No!' said Roe. 'She's over-exposed and looks like a

118

stick-insect. I hate this skinny, flat-chested look that's always dominated the Parisian runway. At last some real-looking women are starting to emerge, girls with sex appeal.'

All eyes were glued to Roe, pacing up and down the room. There was an undeniable energy about him.

'We've got to recognise what women want to identify with, and it isn't Grunge, the anorexic or glorified clothes-horse. We well and truly fucked up with our last advertising campaign and all of us know who was responsible for that.'

Brigette, who'd heard the rumours, glanced briefly at Jean-Marc, but if he was feeling Claude's absence he was doing a good job of not showing it.

'I agree,' said Rachel, 'and I'd like to see someone with some character. Most of the runway models are so intent on not blinking for the video and having their picture taken, they forget to project their personalities to the audience.'

Richard nodded. 'You're right. I can't think of one girl who's been able to do that since Inès.'

'Wasn't she great,' gushed Brigette. 'She'd light a cigarette, bring on her dog, flirt, anything to camp up the act and the audience loved her for it.'

Rachel opened one of several art history books she'd taken out of the library for ideas and stopped at a picture by Dante Gabriel Rossetti. It was of a full-figured woman with huge bow-shaped lips, enormous green eyes and a cloud of cork-screw red hair. She was wearing a heavy medieval robe and holding a flower.

'We need something to market besides clothes,' continued Roe. 'Today's cult of supermodels is a smart revival of the Hollywood star. Look how successful Lancôme have been with Isabella Rossellini or Revlon with Cindy Crawford – both, incidentally, big girls. We have to sell a lifestyle to women. The *couture* gown on the runway sells the *couture* and ready to wear, the glossy magazines sell status, but the supermodel sells the lot!' He paused and downed his fourth glass of water. 'Now, while we've got a minute, what's the latest on the make-up?'

Brigette cleared her throat, inviting a glance from Roe. 'The samples arrived late last night.'

'I'd like to have a look at them,' said Roe.

Nicole appeared with an American model and was dispatched to get the make-up.

The model gave her book and best smile to Jean-Marc, thinking he was the designer. She had eaten nothing all day and she glanced longingly at the plate of biscuits on the table. Richard skimmed through her book, having already decided that she wasn't right. Everyone else around the table, in turn, looked at the portfolio, with Rachel taking the longest. She stopped to point out shots that she liked then handed it back. The model, smelling rejection, smiled professionally and left the room.

'How many more?' Roe asked as Nicole reappeared with the make-up display and another model in tow.

'About fifteen. One model's just arrived and asked if she could be seen straight away as she has a fitting in half an hour. Shall I send her in?'

Roe nodded. 'Just hold on five minutes.'

The make-up samples sat in the middle of the table and were passed around for everyone to examine.

'*J'adore les couleurs,*' said Marie-Claire admiring one of the neat black compacts with a large silver V in the centre, which were rimmed in the same colour. She tried out the plum, russet and saffron, emerald-green, soft magenta, rose and Prussian-blue on the back of her hand.

'We haven't solved the problem of the model yet,' said Richard petulantly. He had an appointment in less than an hour to discuss a hair transplant. No way was he missing that!

Roe looked up coldly. 'Suggest something then.'

'What we need is a redhead,' Rachel suddenly announced. She'd been formulating her ideas for a collection and now she saw it clearly.

Exactly on cue Kate walked into the studio wrapped in a long petrol-blue cashmere coat, belted tightly at the waist. Her hair, freshly washed, hung in tight curls down her back and seemed to light up the room. Her white skin gleamed and the green eyes flashed around the table. Her appearance was dramatic and effective. Kate was unaware of how still the room had become or of Roe standing in one corner with his back to the light. She stood confidently for a moment before approaching the table. Kate handed her book to Rachel who smiled warmly at her. That's her, Rachel thought triumphantly, she's the one.

Underneath Kate's apparently calm exterior, she was a bag of nerves. Contracts like this were usually snapped up by top editorial girls who regularly appeared on the cover of *Vogue*. Kate's six-year career had been steadily climbing but she had secured nothing spectacular enough to justify all her hard work. Casting a professional eye around the table, she looked for signs that they liked her. She was dying to go to the loo. She'd only been just two minutes ago to make sure her tummy was flat. Now she needed to go again. Rotten timing as usual. Was her make-up too heavy? Should she have tied her hair back? Maybe they wanted to see her legs? And if so, should she remove her coat or wait to be asked? No one spoke. The balding man in the baggy designer suit who she remembered from the Vaubelle show seemed engrossed in her book. So Kate waited, a monitored smile on her face, and glanced curiously around the room.

Marie-Claire chewed the top of her Pentel; what a lovely-looking girl. Brigette, looking up briefly from Kate's portfolio, was thinking she would kill to have hair like that. Richard now recognised her from the press show and kicked himself for not having thought of her. Only Jean-Marc had doubts. He loathed redheads.

'Have you done any recent cosmetic work?' said a male voice from the window.

'I shot a commercial for Shiseido about a month ago, but that had restricted marketing and is only being shown in Japan. I've also got a Pond's commercial running in England.' Kate couldn't make out who the owner of the voice was. He sounded American.

'How old are you?' Richard asked.

'Twenty-five.'

'Too old,' muttered Jean-Marc, which Kate heard.

'And you're planning to stay in Paris permanently?' asked the voice.

'Well, that's hard to say. I get quite a few trips abroad.' She didn't want to sound too available.

'You realise this casting is for an exclusive contract, which would tie you to Vaubelle for a minimum of six months?' The voice again.

'Yes. I do.' Kate sensed irritation. Had she said the wrong thing? 'Of course, if I got the job I'd stay.'

'Where was this picture taken?' Rachel asked, pointing to a photograph of Kate walking in pink hills with a collection of mongrel dogs. Her hair blazed in the sunlight.

'Scotland. Beautiful isn't it? That was taken in September on the west coast when all the heather was out.'

'I know it well,' said Rachel.

'Could you try something on?'

Richard got up from the table and walked across the room to a side door. Kate followed him and re-emerged five minutes later in the green suit that Bea had worn in the Vaubelle show. It was slightly snug and Kate willed her hips to shrink as she modelled it for them. As she turned, a fat white cloud temporarily blocked the bright sunlight streaming through the window. Kate, recognising Roe for the first time, gave a small, startled gasp. Rachel and Brigette glanced at him curiously.

'What is your availability from 1 May?' continued Roe calmly.

'I'm not sure.' What the hell was Roe playing at? 'I'd need to check with my agency.'

Rachel said she'd like to take some measurements. As she pulled the tape measure over Kate, Brigette jotted them down. Kate then went off to change back into her own clothes. She tried to eavesdrop but all she could hear were muffled voices. Please make them like me, she silently prayed.

When she returned Roe politely thanked her for her time and handed her back her book. Two of Kate's composite cards had been taken from it and placed on top of several other model cards. How many girls had they seen, Kate wondered, suddenly discouraged. Rachel had written several comments on the front of hers, but Kate couldn't make out what it said.

As she left Roe said, 'We've obviously got more girls to see, but we should have an answer for the agency by tomorrow.'

Outside the other models besieged her with questions. Why had she been in for so long? Had she tried anything on? What did they say about the job? What was the new designer like? Was she very young? And Roe Lewis, the American hunk who had taken over the running of the company, was he as good-looking as everyone said? Kate, desperate to get away and already late for her next appointment, had to fob them off. In the back of the taxi she studied her flushed face with care. The compact jogged up and down as the driver, leaning forward now, urging his cab to overtake a Mercedes, whizzed round the place de la Concorde – or was it her hands shaking? They passed an aggressive Iranian demonstration and she twice botched up her lipstick. She felt cheated, humiliated! So that's why he was so interested in fashion. And I thought he was a merchant banker. Fool! I'm going to be away for three weeks, he'd said, but when I get back . . . That had been almost a month ago and not one call. No doubt they were all having a good laugh at her expense. Well, to hell with him. He could keep his rotten job.

At the fitting she paid the driver but didn't tip him – he'd more than justified the rumours that all French taxi drivers were appallingly rude.

The following morning two surprises were in store for her. The first was an anonymous bouquet of flowers – she had to use every vase and a milk jug, there were so many. The second was a call from her agent, Evelyne, telling her that she'd got the Vaubelle contract.

'There wasn't even any competition,' gushed Evelyne, 'they decided the moment you walked through the door.'

'Are you absolutely sure? Has it really been confirmed?'

'I've got your contract right here, *ma biche*. All you need to do is come in and sign it.'

The phone rang the minute she hung up. Kate picked it up in a daze.

'Still angry with me, sweetheart? Or has this morning's news helped to soften the blow?' Roe's unmistakable voice grinned down the phone at her. 'Listen, I'm about to go into another meeting, but I'll be done by twelve. Does that give you enough time to get ready?'

'For what?' Kate asked, her head spinning.

'The snow. We're flying up to Val d'Isère this afternoon. Remember? It's the long weekend. I'll pick you up at twelve thirty. Oh, and congratulations. We're very lucky to have you on board.'

'Did you send me some flowers today?' Her voice was soft and husky.

'Hope you liked them. Look, I must go. They're calling me. Bye, beautiful.'

After she'd called Bea at work to tell her the news, walked round the flat four times and checked and re-checked her appearance in the bathroom mirror, Kate stood in the middle of the drawing-room and gave a great shriek of delight.

Madame Couris, the concierge, four floors down, heard it and dropped her nicely risen soufflé on to the kitchen floor.

8

Leo Schofield's ten-seater private jet landed smoothly at Val d'Isère. Its six passengers piled into the waiting hired Land Rover and Kate snuggled further into her parka. She was squashed next to Julian Kainz, the Dutch actor currently taking Paris by storm with the release of his new film. On her other side was Leo, a wizard accountant with a string of computer companies, who worked for Cortes in London. Julian's wife Natalie, a Louise Brooks look-alike, who was French *Vogue*'s deputy fashion editor, sat chain-smoking on Chris Berkin's lap in the front. She'd hardly said a word all morning. Chris was a professional skier, known as 'The Pigeon' because his toes turned in and for his ability to fly down black runs. Roe, looking relaxed in a light-brown suede jacket, black turtleneck and jeans, was driving.

As they climbed the steep road the landscape changed, leaving behind great avenues of poplars, patchwork fields, small towns draped in billboards advertising hot chocolate, Bonne Maman confiture and Renault cars, and moving into a smooth, white world of mountains, impressive and dangerous-looking. As the road became more treacherous they passed several drivers attaching wheel chains to their cars. Normally Kate would have felt daunted by going off for a weekend with such an élite group but she was feeling too happy to take much in. While the others caught up on city gossip she daydreamed about her Vaubelle contract and being with Roe for two whole days. My life's changing, she thought, smiling at her ghostly reflection in the window, something wonderful's finally happening to me. On her right hand was a small, perfect cluster of emeralds. It winked expensively as she moved it against the sun. Roe had given it to her when he'd collected her that morning.

'Roe, it's beautiful!' She couldn't believe it was real.

'You're beautiful! The others are waiting in the car but I think we've got time for a morning kiss.'

He had pinned her then against the bathroom wall and very deliberately kissed her until her knees gave way. If Julian Kainz hadn't rung the doorbell that very second to find out what was keeping them, she wouldn't have been able to hold him off.

They arrived at the hotel in a chaotic whirl, scattering snow all over the lobby floor. Leo dashed to the bar and ordered large drinks for everyone, while Roe organised the rooms.

'Nat, you and Julian are in 406, Leo can bunk with Pigeon in 407, which I guess leaves 405 for you and me, baby,' he said smiling at Kate.

'I hope it's not going to be one of your fitness weekends, Roe,' Natalie said, lighting another Marlboro and inhaling deeply, 'or Jules and I won't get any sleep. Remember the thin walls?'

Kate sized Natalie up. She was probably in her late twenties but she already had a pair of dark crescent moons etched below her brown eyes and tiny smoker's lines above her full, taut mouth. Attractive but brittle-edged and quite unfriendly. Perhaps she'd relax over the weekend. Kate hoped so. Natalie wrapped herself around Julian and announced that she was starving. Kate's stomach growled in agreement so they made their way to the packed dining-room. The window ran the length of the room, revealing the range of mountains beyond, slopes parted with lines of ski lifts and dotted with hundreds of Day-glo enthusiasts. They were all drinking whisky, except Roe, who drank vodka, and Kate who was on Aqua Libra.

'What a week!' said Natalie. 'Two re-shoots, a model who refused to go topless and a suicidal photographer who's just cracked up with his wife.'

'Split up, darling, and remember your promise not to talk shop.'

Natalie pouted prettily at her husband.

'Have you two worked together?' asked Leo, who had a flushed and cheerful face.

'No, I think Katie more often does shows. At *Vogue* we like to stick to the younger editorial girls.'

Kate bit back a retort.

'What, that bunch of plastic-looking schoolgirls?' mocked Pigeon, chucking his gloves and room key on the table. 'Give me a real woman any day.' Kate smiled at him gratefully. 'Someone order me a hamburger or something. I'm going to call Carey.' He took his drink with him as he left.

'Saw your film last week, Jules,' said Leo. 'Best thing you've done in years. Been meaning to ask you about the blonde bird who cops it in the end. Don't suppose there's any chance of getting her number?'

Julian broke a cashew nut with very white teeth. 'Forget it. She's a teetotaller, votes for the Social Democrats and only sleeps with women.'

Roe smiled. 'What are you working on now?'

'An American comedy set in Mexico. I play a newsreel cameraman who's crazy about Marx and older women. Promises to be a rather odd set – all very hush-hush, with half the crew in the dark about what they're doing, including me. We start shooting in a week. Did you pack my script, darling?' he added to Natalie.

'In the green bag with your diary.'

Julian tilted the back of his seat and stretched his long legs out. 'So, Kate, I gather this is your first time skiing?'

'Yes,' she said, anxiously watching matchstick people flying down the slopes like cars at Silverstone. 'I suppose you're very good?'

'Only because I've been skiing since I was five. I'm a complete sportaholic; riding, athletics, racing, tennis . . .'

'And soccer!' Natalie made that disparaging noise the French make, a sort of noiseless explosion of breath. 'Stupid sport with grown-up men playing with a tiny little ball.'

'Hey!' said Julian, laughing. 'Less of the little, darling. I've got my reputation to think of.'

'You blew that years ago,' said Roe smiling.

Leo choked on his whisky. 'Jesus H. Christ. Have a look at that!'

A voluptuous woman entered the restaurant, majestic breasts preceding her by a foot. Her dyed-blonde hair had been so thoroughly back-combed that it would have held back an avalanche. Her black and gold track suit was embroidered with a sequined eagle and 'I love LA' sewn on to the back. Clearly waiting for someone, she fiddled with her designer sunglasses, displaying long, shocking-pink finger-nails. Her pot-bellied and middle-aged companion arrived seconds later; sweating profusely, he didn't look capable of climbing the lobby stairs let alone the slopes.

'Here for the *après-ski*,' Roe explained, following Leo's gaze. 'Not likely to get much exercise outside but plenty in the bedroom.' He placed a warm hand on Kate's thigh under the table.

'I'll say! Talk about Twin Peaks!' Leo looked beside himself with excitement.

Pigeon returned and said the line was busy. A pretty waitress with ash-blonde hair pulled back off her face with a black Alice band took their order. She look flushed and overwhelmed by the sudden rush of lunchers. Kate smiled kindly at her.

'Can I get you anything else?'

Roe glanced briefly at the girl. 'Just the check, thanks, honey.'

'Must say the waitresses here are definitely prettier than last year,' said Pigeon.

'How come Carey's not with you?'

'Her father collapsed in the House of Commons last week. Massive coronary.' Pigeon, chewing on a liberally-buttered roll, sprayed the table with fine bits of bread as he talked. 'No one knows if he'll pull through but when I spoke to her last night she seemed more optimistic.'

'Well, I'm going up to change,' said Natalie, stubbing out her cigarette. 'I want to try the black run while the weather's good.'

'Relax, Kat,' said Roe, noticing her alarm. 'I'll take you on ahead and teach you the basics.'

'All right, but don't say I didn't warn you when I go careering into the nearest tree.'

'Not with legs like yours.'

But it proved even harder than Kate expected. The boots, designed with futuristic, space-age technology (and they still hurt), were extremely difficult to walk in. She felt like an oversized Michelin man squeezed into several layers of Bea's ski wear, and found her hat hot and itchy. English tourists decorated the slopes. They wore colourful woollies and unsightly white lip-gloss. Stuffed into bright C & A anoraks and reflector glasses, they looked like ads for *Terminator Two*. Outside, Roe helped her into the bindings and, holding hands, they shuffled over to the ski-lift.

'Tuck the bar under your bottom as it comes up behind you and hold your poles in your left hand. Don't worry, you won't fall off. Just keep the skis pointed in a straight line.'

With only thirty seconds to get into position as the T-bar shot round, Kate very nearly had them both down as she struggled to keep her skis together. At the top of the nursery slope skiers raced down the side of the mountain, jumping high into the air over bumps and hurtling in between the flag poles. Kate got so caught up watching one exceptional skier that she lost her balance and landed on her bottom. Roe laughed and helped her up.

'I forgot to tell you to keep your eye on the road. You're doing fine. Now, I'm going to put my arms around you and ski us down together. You don't have to do a thing, just try and get used to the motion. And relax.'

'Now I know how Bambi must have felt,' muttered Kate, slipping again. 'Abandon me any time you like. I'm hazardous!'

Wrapping his arms around her, with Kate's legs tucked between his, Roe pushed them off down hill. Kate held her breath. Surely they'd collide with the criss-cross traffic of skiers. But they reached the bottom easily and Roe very patiently began to teach her the ground rules.

Natalie appeared with Julian whose eyes were hidden by beetle-blue wrap-around glasses. By the intimate glances Kate saw them exchange, it was obvious they'd just got out of bed.

'Nice outfit,' said Roe to Natalie, admiring her fluorescent, blue and pink suit and reflector goggles.

'Guaranteed to be out of fashion next season,' said Julian, remembering how much it had cost. He stepped expertly into his skis. 'We're not waiting for Leo. He's crying off from a hangover!'

'And Pigeon?'

'Already gone up. I think he's pissed off about Carey not being here. They haven't seen much of one another lately.'

The men shuffled towards the snow buggy.

Kate hesitated.

'Coming?' asked Natalie.

'You bet she is,' said Roe, grabbing Kate's gloved hand. His pupils had darkened and enlarged, suggesting much more than a quick, terrifying plunge down the side of a mountain. Kate slunk backwards.

'You go on. I'll stick to the nursery slopes, practise a bit before I get more adventurous.' No bloody way was she going to show herself up in front of Natalie.

'You sure, baby?' Kate nodded vigorously as Roe withdrew his hand.

'Well, don't break anything or Roe will be impossible for the rest of the weekend.'

'Cut it out, Nat,' snapped Roe.

Natalie arched her eyebrows innocently. 'Will you be okay on your own?'

'I'll be fine. Really. Have fun.'

All the same Kate felt depressed as she watched them go. If only she could ski brilliantly like Natalie and impress Roe. So far the only thing she'd done consistently was collide into solid objects; her ski tips were notorious for catching in the snow – usually in front of several sniggering fellow-skiers. Getting up was the worst bit. She stayed out for a couple of hours but it was bitterly cold and had resumed snowing. Frigid wind whipped snow into her face. Finally, when she couldn't feel her hands or feet any more, she gave up and made her way back to her hotel. Passing an attractive young woman in bright-red ski boots, Kate recognised her as the blonde waitress at lunch.

'Hope you're better at this than me,' she said, bending down to release her skis.

'Your first time, is it?' the girl asked sympathetically. 'No, hang on, let me help. You'll never get out of them that way.' And she showed Kate how to unclip her skis.

'Thanks.'

'It's easy once you've done it a couple of times. My name's Joelle, by the way.'

'Thanks, Joelle. I'm Kate. I feel as if I'm the only novice.'

'Believe me, you're not.' Joelle pointed to a couple near the ski chair. The girl had just fallen over and the man, very awkwardly, was trying to help her up. Seconds later he went down too.

Both girls laughed.

'Where are your friends?'

'Somewhere at the top of that end piste. Too good for me. My boyfriend gave me a lesson earlier on, but I finally shooed him away. Didn't want to completely disillusion him so soon into the relationship.'

'The American?' Kate nodded proudly. 'Lucky you. He's real cute. Well, I'd better get moving before the light goes.' She waved a piece of paper in the air and grinned. 'My map of the ski runs. Best way to get lost. Enjoy your evening.'

Back in her room Kate had a shower, locking the bedroom door in case Roe made an impromptu return. Putting on a simple but very effective navy-blue cashmere dress, she felt in control (and warm) once more. Here at last was one area she could compete with Natalie. She found Leo in the bar downstairs.

'Roe always manages to pull the prettiest girls.'

Like the restaurant, the bar window had a spectacular view of the slopes. The mountains were bathed in a pink light. The sun lingered at the top as if it was glued there, then slipped behind a black sea of mountains. The cosy bar was decorated with celebrity caricature prints. A large, noisy German family sat devouring doorstep sandwiches, and four young men were playing cards at the bar watched by a disgruntled au pair who had been stuck indoors all day looking after baby twins.

Leo ordered a large pot of tea and a generous plate of

cholesterol-loaded cakes, sagging under an avalanche of whipped cream and crumbling flaked chocolate. Kate had meant to be good, but all the mountain air had made her ravenous and anyway she must have burnt off a million calories.

'How's the head?' Kate asked gently.

'Legs are still a little shaky.'

Leo looked sheepish. He had a habit of holding his arms redundantly against his side as if he didn't know what to do with them. Kate wondered if he was conscious of doing it. He had a small, egg-shaped head with sharp, blue eyes, pale skin and no jaw. The overall effect was not unattractive and he had an infectious smile.

'Slightly overdid it last week so I've only myself to blame. What happened to Roe?'

'Still intent on killing himself out there with Julian and Natalie.'

'Mmm,' said Leo thoughtfully. 'Natalie does like to monopolise the boys. She won't like your being here, I'm afraid. You're much too pretty.'

'Rubbish!' said Kate, flattered all the same, 'It's obvious Julian's mad about her.'

'Julian's not the problem, Roe is. They went out for a while and she's still carrying a torch for him. All his exes seem to,' he said tactlessly, then noticing Kate's face drop, tried to make amends. 'But I'm sure you'll be the making of him.'

'Have you known him long?' she was longing for more information.

'Ever since I joined Cortes, which is about five years. Roe's a funny bloke. Try to put your finger on him and you touch dust. I know no more about him now than I did when we first met.'

'I'm not doing much better. Perhaps that's part of his attraction?'

Leo looked at her curiously. 'How long have you been in Paris? Can't understand how we missed meeting you until now.'

'Funny, that's what Roe said to me the night we met.'

They both studied the tray for a moment, lost in thought.

Outside the sky brewed. It looked as though they were in for a storm. The bar was beginning to fill; glamorous couples and divorcees on the lookout for spare men replaced fraught parents and staff on afternoon shifts. Kate transferred her weight, already regretting the cakes. She could feel them making their way down to her thighs. She suddenly felt fat and anxious. What was keeping Roe?

By seven, when the quartet finally turned up, she was frantic. She had checked three times at reception. They arrived, glowing from the fresh air, Pigeon and Julian arguing affably, Roe devastating in a black polo neck and a tan suede jacket, and Natalie inappropriately dressed in tiny shorts and a scarlet bodice, the small brown eyes dramatised with kohl. Her efforts were rewarded with several raised eyebrows.

'What have you done with Kat?' Roe asked, signalling to the waiter.

'Gone to the loo,' said Leo, his skin puckered and bright like a tangerine. 'I must say we have had a very enjoyable, relaxing afternoon.'

'Well, you're not skiving off tomorrow,' said Pigeon, pulling out a chair, 'so easy on the hard stuff, old man, or you'll end up alongside Carey's dad in casualty.' He gave a sudden low whistle as he spotted Kate walking towards them. 'Bloody hell, Roe! How do you keep on pulling birds that look like that?'

The dark-navy cashmere dress hugged her like a second skin, revealing soft curves. The flaming hair fanned around her white shoulders. She looked very pale. All the men gazed as Kate crossed the room. Natalie glowered, not liking to be upstaged one bit.

'I thought you'd had an accident,' said Kate both relieved and resentful because he'd been gone so long.

Roe laughed. 'We very nearly did. Julian should wear a government health warning – he's goddam lethal out there!'

'What are you complaining about? You won, didn't you?' said Julian, good-humouredly. He put an arm round Natalie and said to the hovering waiter, 'I'll have a double whisky, a packet of pretzels and a Bloody Mary for my good woman here.'

'With lots of ice,' added Natalie, lighting up a cigarette.

Someone sitting at a table alone on the far side of the room briskly clicked his fingers at the waiter.

'*Garçon!* If you don't mind, I've been waiting to order a drink for over ten minutes.'

'I'm sorry, monsieur. We're very busy tonight.'

'So I see,' the man said, glaring at the noisy table the waiter had just left. 'Bring me a bottle of Sancerre and a White Russian on ice.'

'*Tout de suite, monsieur.*'

Sebastian Vaubelle tried to concentrate on the sporting magazine he held but the words kept blurring. He glanced back at Roe's table, resentful of the easy command the American had of his friends, the obvious devotion of that redhead hanging on to his every word. Blind fools! Just his luck they had picked this resort. He looked impatiently at his watch. What the hell was keeping her? It infuriated him the way she was always late. *Merde!* He suddenly felt irritated with everything. And the whole point of coming had been to relax, take his mind off work. Unconsciously Sebastian began to attack the side of his thumb with his teeth, contemplating going back to his room. He needed his pills.

Cassy Peck arrived five minutes after their drinks.

'It's blowing a right old state outside. Hope it calms down by tomorrah.' She slipped into the opposite seat. 'We've hardly done any skiing together, babes.'

'You're late!' he snapped, still thinking about Roe.

'Sorry, but there weren't no hot water. I had to get housekeeping up to sort it out. Have you ordered some grub?'

'No. We're not eating here.'

'But I thought you'd made reservations?'

'I had, but now I've changed my mind!'

'All right. Keep your bleedin' hair on. What's eating you all of a sudden?'

'Nothing. I just don't like to be kept waiting and you manage to make an occupation out of it. Come on, Cas, are you going to drink that?' he asked, pointing to her White Russian.

'Well, it's paid for, innit?'

After four hours of skiing Cassy was shattered and had been looking forward to a nice relaxing drink. If Sebastian was in such a sodding hurry, he could effing-well go on his own. Defiantly she scanned the room for unattached attractive men.

Roe was still revelling in the rush of his afternoon run, hurtling spectacularly down the icy slopes, once narrowly missing a tree as he and Julian battled for first place. He pulled Kate down on his lap and kissed her, making it clear to everyone whom she belonged to. She was his trophy. Kate, dizzy with love, thought how relaxed and happy he looked and hoped she'd contributed to his good mood. He smelt of cold and hotel soap.

Ruffling her hair tenderly, he said, 'It suits you down. You should wear it like that more often.' Kate immediately forgave him his absence. 'How did you get on?'

'Oh, I fell down several hundred times, but I made sure I took a few victims. You should see the bruises!'

'I intend to. Sorry we were gone so long, baby, but I promise you have my undivided attention now.'

Natalie was eavesdropping. 'Roe, *chérie*, why not get Kate an instructor? You know how bored you get teaching novices.'

'Don't be such a cow!' Julian muttered under his breath to Natalie.

Roe was still gazing at Kate. 'That depends on what I'm teaching.'

Kate took a hasty slug of wine.

'Where did you meet Roe, Katie?' Natalie asked, ignoring her prawn salad and rudely blowing cigarette smoke over everyone's food.

'At a club. I was being grilled on the dance floor and Roe came to my rescue.'

Roe's hand casually rubbed the back of her neck.

'How sweet. Let me guess. Castelle's?'

'Shut up, Nat,' warned Roe.

'Why? Isn't that where you meet most of your women friends?'

Roe's arm stiffened.

'Ignore my wife, Kate,' said Julian in a deceptively light voice. 'One Bloody Mary and she's bloody to everyone.'

He speared several of Natalie's prawns with his fork and popped them greedily into his mouth.

'Time for another drink, I think. Any offers?' Leo's blue eyes, under bushy eyebrows, darted around the table.

Kate nodded, not trusting herself to speak. How dare Natalie be so bloody patronising? Was it jealousy or did they all know something she didn't? What on earth was going on? Kate suddenly felt out of her depth. And having spent the whole day wanting Roe to herself, she was now dreading it. She was also worried because she hadn't gone back on the pill and felt reluctant to tackle the subject of contraception with him. Typical! After all her sensible advice to girlfriends about condoms and safe sex. She rose from her seat.

'Back in a sec.'

'*Moi aussi*,' said Natalie, following her.

Natalie went straight to the mirror and started combing her hair. The bob fell obediently into place and shone like a conker under the tungsten lights.

'You haven't known Roe long?' she mumbled, applying scarlet lipstick to stretched lips.

'Not very.'

'That look of his won't last, not once you've been to bed with him.'

'Not that it's any of your business.'

'Don't be so defensive, Katie.' God, the way she said 'Cat-ee' was really getting on Kate's nerves. 'I'm just warning you not to get involved with Roe.'

'Why? Are you hoping to win him back? Must rather cramp your style having a husband here.' Unsure of her ground, Kate washed her hands for something to do. Don't let her get to you.

'You're just not his type. He needs someone much tougher with a lot of experience.' There was no apology in Natalie's voice.

'Like you, you mean!' snapped Kate furiously. 'Christ, you make Roe sound as if he orders girlfriends from a catalogue!'

136

Natalie, quite unperturbed, fished out a cigarette from her bag. 'He's a bit like that. Easy come, easy go.'

'You obviously think you know him very well.'

'Better than you,' said Natalie, professionally snapping shut her lighter. Smoke seeped through her nose, reminding Kate of a sea serpent. 'And you're taking this conversation the wrong way. All I'm saying is take care.'

'You don't like me, do you?'

'I really don't have an opinion. But you're wrong about me wanting Roe back. I'm not a masochist.'

The blonde lady with the 'I love LA' T-shirt sailed in on a cloud of Lauder's White Linen and Kate was forced to swallow her retort. Natalie picked up her bag and walked out. Moments later a loo flushed and Cassy Peck emerged buttoning up her jeans.

'Hi, babes. Whatcha doing here?'

'Good question,' muttered Kate, glaring at the door.

'Couldn't help over'earing some of that. Mate of yours, is she?'

'Hardly.' But Kate didn't want to talk about it. 'I saw your Renault commercial. It's wonderful.'

'So's the bread. Went and whacked a deposit down on a flat in Les Halles last week. I'd love you to bring Bea round once I get meself sorted. We could have a girls' night out with the Chips.'

'Chips?' Kate repeated dumbly.

'You know who I mean, the Chippendales. I used to date one of them. 'Course, I went and jacked him in right before he got famous. Nothing like getting your timing right!'

'Is Sebastian with you?'

Cassy's face clouded. 'Old misery-guts. We're eating out tonight or else I'd suggest having a drink.' She glanced at her watch, 'Shit. I'd better leg it or I'll get even more stick from his lordship. Don't know what's got into him tonight. But if he keeps it up I'll be looking for some excitement elsewhere. Know what I mean?' She smiled wickedly and kissed Kate's cheek. 'Might catch up with you tomorrah.'

Back at the table Leo, in a croaky voice, was describing his weekly local rugby match in Battersea.

'Most of the office lads take a break from the brandy and cigars for a bit of fun, but our opponents are all incredibly fit, black and under eighteen. Your life flashes before you when you see one of them racing across the field crying "Get the posh cunt". Particularly when you realise he's pointing at you.' Leo drained his glass and looked around for the waitress. 'Anyone for another drink?'

Natalie put a warm, manicured hand on Julian's thigh and announced she was going to bed. Kate, still shaken by their earlier conversation, ignored her good night. Not bothering to cover up a gargantuan yawn Roe grabbed her hand.

'Bed,' he said firmly.

Kate trailed behind as they climbed the stairs, faintly excited at being told what to do, yet at the same time filled with dread. She could always say she had the curse or was feeling tired. No. That was too lame. As if reading her thoughts, Roe's hand tightened around hers.

'Don't think that I'm going to let you escape tonight. I've been waiting for this for a long time,' he whispered.

They all exchanged good nights in the corridor. Roe locked the door behind Kate and threw the key on a chair.

'Christ, I never realise how much I miss it until I'm back.'

For the upteenth time that day, Kate wished she could ski so that she could share his euphoria. As she clutched her bag, her coppery-green eyes grew solemn.

'Hey, don't go quiet on me, baby. Come here. I won't bite.'

She was suddenly very nervous and with as much confidence as an actor about to perform his first night. She caught her reflection in the mirror above Roe. Her eyes glimmered from too much alcohol. Whisky eyes, she thought. Roe put on a tape of Van Morrison's *Poetic Champions*.

'Roe, I thought I was going to have my own room.'

'Well, that could prove tricky. I've never had telepathic sex before.'

'I hardly know you.'

'I hardly know you but I'm willing to risk it.' He moved towards hers, 'I haven't been able to stop thinking about you since I first saw you.'

'Could I have a drink?' said Kate, stalling for time.

'Sure.'

Kate had experienced her first sexual relationship at eighteen. He was six years older and an actor. One glance at his broody face and she was hooked; dark-haired, dark-eyed and exotic. He wore a black leather jacket and cowboy boots which reminded her vaguely of Heathcliff (Cathy had been a favourite heroine). From all the romantic novels she'd read Kate had expected to rise from her lover's bed like Botticelli's Venus, her name written in fireworks, a full-scale orchestra, applause. But the event had been an appalling anticlimax in every sense: one day in late September she had lost her virginity in a caravan (the actor later confessed that he'd been on the dole for a year) and on a damp mattress. While he had asked for reassurance on his performance, his breath heavy as he pumped in and out, Kate lay in uncomfortable silence. Words seemed so inadequate, unnecessary somehow. She was embarrassed by some of the things he had said, the urgent shouting at the point of orgasm, and felt all the time like a voyeur, divorced from the body he fondled. When he'd finished he had fallen asleep on her pillowy breasts, snoring gently, while Kate gazed unseeingly at the ceiling, wondering why she didn't feel the warm glow of womanhood promised by all the magazines. It had all started off so well. She had never heard from him again.

After that Kate simply couldn't believe men found her desirable. In her mind she was still the fat schoolgirl who stuttered and got hot flushes. Alone in her own bed she could orgasm in under a minute, but with a partner, hours of clumsy foreplay only increased her anxiety. She insisted on making love in the dark, eventually faking orgasm as they rubbed her angry clitoris with an enthusiastic if somewhat inexperienced hand. Each lover, sensing her unease, came quickly and rolled off to sleep, leaving Kate twitching and unfulfilled by their side. As a result none of her men had lasted for long; feeling inadequate, they left Kate convinced that the quickest way to lose a man was to go to bed with him.

'Kat?' Roe was holding out her drink. 'You've got that far away look again.'

'Sorry. It's a bad habit.'

They both sipped their drinks experimentally.

'Why didn't you tell me about Natalie?'

'So that's what this is all about?'

'Well, it's a bit rich inviting me along for the weekend only to flaunt your ex under my nose. She's still carrying a torch for you, you know.'

'So she did hassle you in the john. Look. Sure, we had a brief fling but that was months ago, before she got married. I had no idea she was coming until Friday afternoon. She's very happy with Julian.'

'Could have fooled me. She's been insufferable all day.'

'I agree,' he said evenly, 'but that's only because she's jealous of the attention you've been getting. Under all that aggressive behaviour is a deeply insecure woman. Believe me, she's no threat to you.'

Kate slipped out of her shoes and tucked her legs under her. Roe noted the defensive gesture and laced his fingers thoughtfully under his chin. She was like a tight golden spool. That lovely guarded body of hers was crying out to be unravelled. Roe couldn't resist it.

'What are you running away from? We both know why you're here.'

'I wanted to get to know you better.'

'So it's my mind you're after. I'm devastated!'

Kate coloured and looked down at her drink.

'Must you always treat everything as a joke?' she said bitterly.

'Sometimes it helps. What's wrong with opening yourself up to your feelings?' said Roe, switching tactics. 'Do you expect to go through life putting up impenetrable walls, then expect people to pull them down? I'm not a mind reader, you know.'

'That's unfair. I just don't like to rush into things.'

'Who's rushing? We've got all night.'

'But I don't know how you feel,' wailed Kate.

Roe moved suddenly across the room, took her free hand and placed it on his groin. His erection was rock hard.

'This is how I feel about you.'

140

'Don't!' She snatched her hand away and backed towards the door.

'If you leave now, Kat, it's over between us.'

Kate's hand hovered on the door-knob. Turning, like a rabbit transfixed by headlights, she stood motionless as Roe moved towards her.

'I can't,' she sobbed, terrified of losing him. He was so close. Aware only of his smell, his power over her she felt stifled, overwhelmed by fear and lust. She couldn't move.

'It's okay, baby. There's nothing to be afraid of.'

And suddenly he touched her. Kate gasped, letting out the air she'd unconsciously held in. He caught the back of her neck with his right hand and pulled her face up to his. The kiss locked them together, swaying until she pulled her chin back, gulping air. Roe's mouth came down mercilessly on hers and suddenly she was swept up into his arms and carried across the room. Reaching the bedroom, he stumbled and they fell on to the bed. As she lay spread out before him, her white skin flushed from his touch, Roe expertly undid the row of navy buttons and slipped his hand inside.

Kate automatically pulled her stomach in. Her hands struggled to stop him even though her body moved like warm dough in his hands. Shouldn't they discuss condoms, or something?

'Roe, I . . .'

'No!' he said in a voice that held no room for argument. 'No more waiting.' His voice was coarse and fevered, and clasping both her hands above her head, he pulled the dress free. Overwhelmed by her senses, Kate stopped fighting.

In his dream that night Roe walked through a sprawling empty hall with walls covered in crimson feathers. He found himself drawn towards a tiny room at the far end which was full of laughing, naked women. Gazing at their Pre-Raphaelite beauty he was surprised to find none of them had pubic hair. He mingled among their beckoning smiles and it dawned on him suddenly that he could do whatever he liked, fulfil his ultimate sexual fantasies. Touching a coffee-coloured breast, he sampled the nipple with his tongue and felt safe and happy.

141

No one was going to leave or make empty promises to him the way his mother had. There was no conversation in the room.

The women were all mutes.

Kate lay listening to the distant sounds of early risers and a room service trolley rattling in the corridor. She was dying to go to the loo but Roe's arm was wrapped possessively round her waist and she didn't want to wake him up. She ran her free hand experimentally through the dark forest of chest hair which was both tantalising and dangerous territory. Last night came drifting back and she reddened, remembering the things Roe had done to her. After they had made love Roe, still lying on top of her, had taken her face in his hands.

'Do you ever come?' he asked, watching her.

Kate was embarrassed by the question and studied an eyelash on his right cheek. She contemplated removing it.

'Kat?'

'Are you disappointed?' she said in a small voice.

'It can be much, much better, you know.' Roe stroked her right nipple. 'Have you ever had an orgasm with a man?'

'No.' Kate dropped her head, snuggling against him for comfort. She felt ashamed.

'Then it's time you did,' said Roe, inching down the bed.

'You're wasting your time,' squealed Kate. 'I've never been able to grasp the technique of sex.'

'Sex isn't like working a computer, and there's nothing wrong with your body. It responds beautifully to my touch. The only block is in your head. We've just got to connect it to this,' he pointed to her ginger bush. 'You've obviously never had a man who was patient enough to teach you.'

The large green eyes watched him like an anxious child. Roe began to kiss her very slowly, murmuring soft endearments as his mouth moved along her neck, down to her breasts, teasing the pale pink nipples with his tongue until he felt them stiffen. Taking his time, he used his mouth to trace the groove of her ribs, the curve of her waist, the milky white skin, planting kisses as he went, feeling her body relax under his touch until he moved down to her belly.

142

'You're so beautiful, Kat.' His voice was like honey as his tongue moved lower down.

Kate instinctively stiffened. 'Please!' she panicked, grabbing his head.

Firmly he removed her hands. 'Stop fighting me,' he said gently, 'I want to.'

And after his tongue had gone to work for a while she did relax. His mouth moved back up to hers as his hand moved down, oh so slowly, circling the pubic hair, his fingers moving against her clitoris with increasing pressure, until she was in a fever, then he entered her and her whole body started to shudder and she was gasping his name.

Roe stirred and Kate nestled against the curve of his taut olive body. Roe stroked her hair and placed a series of playful bites along her neck. Oh, how she loved him doing that, shivering with pleasure, and squeezing her long feet together like a stretching cat.

'Morning.'

'Mmm, you smell so good!' murmured Roe, burying himself in her arms.

'You know you've ruined me for anyone else.'

'I don't want anyone else to have you.'

'What's this?' she asked dreamily, tracing a nasty scar on Roe's left buttock with her finger.

'An orphanage I once checked into believed a regular beating kept your soul clean. Sometimes they got carried away.' A careful veil had dropped down over his eyes as he spoke.

Kate's smile evaporated. 'That's appalling!'

'That's reality. Happens all over the world.' He ran a tongue along the side of her neck. 'Christ, Kat, I can't keep my hands off you.'

'Must just go to the loo.' She leapt up. Unused to morning intimacy, she wanted to wash her face, clean her teeth. When Roe appeared in the doorway looking for her a few minutes later, he caught Kate swallowing some pills.

'What are you taking?'

'Nothing,' she mumbled.

'Come on,' he persisted, moving further into the bathroom, 'I know you're hiding something behind your back.'

'It's nothing, honestly. Just some vitamins.'

'In that case . . .' catching her off guard, he sprang forward and snatched the bottle from her hand, 'you won't mind me taking a look.' There was a pause while he read the label. 'Antibiotics. Kat, why're you taking this stuff?'

'It's OK. It's only a small dose,' she said, reddening. 'I won't bore you with the details.'

'Oh yes you will. How long have you been taking it?'

Kate looked away in shame. 'A few years. I had this mild acne and a doctor prescribed a three-months supply. When I tried coming off them my skin went mad. It's been a vicious circle ever since.'

'Are you crazy! This stuff can screw up your immune system. There's nothing wrong with your skin!'

'Roe, don't . . .' she tried to stop him but it was too late. Roe had emptied the contents of the bottle into the loo which he then flushed.

'There. No more pills. I want you healthy. Now,' he continued, his voice softening as he pulled her back into the bedroom and on to the bed, 'where were we?' Kate's hair fell silkily over his face like a curtain and Roe's tongue probed greedily in her mouth.

The phone rang. Kate, on top, was nearest and picked it up.

'It's Julian,' she said breathlessly, holding the phone out to Roe. 'I think they've just had a row.'

'We have had a bloody row,' said Julian to Roe, 'don't ever marry a sodding Frenchwoman. They're hell!'

Roe laughed. 'What's she done now?'

'Pinched my new script, without asking permission, I might add. Reckons I lied about the sex scenes. Next thing I know she's packed her bags and practically inside a cab until I managed to talk her out of it. It was four in the morning before we got to bed!'

'What time is it now?'

'Ten. We lost an hour because the clocks went forward last night.'

Drowsily, half-listening next to him, Kate put a hand on

Roe's large penis lying half-hard on his thigh. Immediately it stiffened.

'So what's the plan?' Roe yawned, stroking her hair.

'Well, Nat's sleeping off her hangover and Pigeon's the only soul to surface. I fancied a couple of runs before breakfast. Are you up for it?'

'Hang on, I'll ask Kat,' Roe said, putting his hand over the receiver. 'Feel like some more exercise, baby?'

Kate's pupils swelled and darkened. Roe knew that look on a woman. His eyes travelled down to her full white breasts partly revealed by the rumpled sheets. Immediately his penis shot up like a Scud missile.

'Sorry pal. Something big's just come up. Catch up with you downstairs in an hour.' He hung up and plunged straight into a soaking Kate, who was quivering with expectation.

They joined the others for breakfast an hour later and found a red-faced Leo being teased. Julian explained.

'Our friend's been bed-hopping.'

Roe raised an eyebrow, 'This I'd like to hear.'

'Seems like the stacked blonde here for the *après-ski* had an argument with her boyfriend and turned to Leo for a bit of moonlit sympathy. He was still spitting out pubic hair at breakfast.'

'Give it a rest, Pigeon,' snapped Leo, flushing an even deeper red. 'We just had a couple of drinks. No harm in that.'

'None at all, but it looks like you missed some hair,' said Julian, sniggering. 'You'd better shave your teeth.'

Everyone rolled around laughing except for Natalie, who despite a bath, half a pot of black coffee and three Alka Seltzers, was feeling terrible. Enjoy it while you can, she thought, watching Kate's glowing face, because it won't last for long.

Back in Paris Kate walked on air for a week. Roe had asked her to move in with him and although she'd tried not to take his offer too seriously, they'd been practically living out of each other's pockets ever since they returned, so in the end she had agreed. Bea, giving her a hand to pack, was amazed by her friend's transformation. She had never seen Kate so radiant, so softened with love. Often she'd caught her staring into space or grinning stupidly.

'Are you sure about this?' she asked, as Kate rushed energetically around the room, pulling clothes from cupboards and drawers, chucking rubbish into the bin.

'Far from it,' said Kate, inspecting a shirt that had a stain on the front. 'I only know that it's unbearable when I'm not with him. Will you stop biting your nails?'

'Another nasty little habit I've picked up from you, Katherine. It's just it's all so sudden. You're normally so cautious when it comes to men.'

Kate laughed. 'Yes, but I've never been in love before. Oh Bea!' She consigned the stained shirt to the bin before rushing over to hug her friend. 'Be happy for me. I'm so nervous about seeing him again I can't even eat!'

Bea gave her a week to settle in, then called her from a Speedo shoot.

'I've memorised your number. Aren't you impressed!' Bea never announced herself. 'How are you, darling? It's beastly outside!'

'Is it?' said Kate dreamily. She had spent the entire morning in bed, ignoring the seething grey rain-clouds. 'I dropped the mobile phone in the bath, and it's been sulking ever since. Roe will be furious.'

Bea chuckled. It was good to hear Kate sounding so carefree. 'Well, it's horrid not having you at home. The flat's like a morgue. I miss your noise. I'm almost tempted to move Sam in now that he's back.'

'Who's he?' Honestly, it was impossible trying to keep up with Bea's sex life.

'A stockbroker I met at La Capole. Didn't I mention him? Sam's the sort who puts romantic dinners down as expenses and wears a suit on Sunday. His mobile phone went off in the cinema last night and caused a terrible fuss. But he's got heaps of loot and has one of the fastest tongues in northern France. An irresistible combination.'

Indeed, reflected Kate, thinking of all the unmentionable things Roe had done to her in bed that morning.

'The reason I'm calling is that you've got an invite from

some actor called Julian Kainz, some sort of promotion for his new film. Ring any bells?'

'He was with us at Val d'Isère,' said Kate, switching the phone to the other ear. 'Nice man and very attractive, but his wife's awful. She's one of Roe's exes. We didn't get on at all.'

'Who is she?'

'Natalie Kainz. *Vogue*'s deputy fashion editor.'

'Well, that explains it. Natalie's got quite a reputation at *Vogue*, doesn't like to be upstaged. Don't you remember she spear-headed that cattle call I went to last month? Didn't get the job, of course.' Bea pulled on the long telephone flex and used it to beat the surface of the kitchen table. 'Anyway, this party's a week on Saturday. Do you want to go?'

'Yes, just have to check with Roe what his plans are. We might be going away. Why don't you come?'

'So it's we already. Things are moving fast.'

Kate laughed. 'Bring Sam. I'm sure Julian won't mind.'

'Mmm. If Julian's as scrummy as you say I'd rather come alone.'

'Up to you. Hell, I'd better go or I'll be late for the gynaecologist. I'm being fitted for a diaphragm. Makes a change from dresses.'

Bea laughed. 'You've become so exclusive, darling, your diaphragm will probably be engraved with Vaubelle's logo!'

9

The inspiration that had struck Rachel while searching for the house model continued and she used the Pre-Raphaelites as the theme for her collection. She had produced a series of designs based on the works of the painter Edward Burne-Jones, an admirer of the Italian Renaissance. For her day dresses, she chose a selection of smoky cashmeres, sketching fitted jackets on the midriff with dozens of tiny buttons running down the front. The collars were scooped to reveal the neck and clavicle, and braided with fabric to match the buttons. Her chiffon and muslin blouses were draped in natural folds with invisible fasteners and she lengthened the skirts to below the knee.

Her evening sketches evoked the later Pre-Raphaelite period. Using warm colours there were long medieval dresses in sumptuous velvets and silk taffetas, and trumpet sleeves that revealed a finer second sleeve of organza underneath, intricate lattice detail on the cuffs and neckline and braided chains around the waist.

Italy had been tremendous fun and Rachel had particularly enjoyed inspecting the great showrooms, although she was careful not to exceed her budget. Material was the single biggest expense in a collection, which meant if she overestimated how much she needed the fabric would have to be put into storage and sold at cost later on. If she underestimated her stock, orders had to be rejected which lost the house valuable business.

Soon after Rachel's return, samples of cashmere and wool jersey, silks from the Orient in vibrant greens and plum, and chiffons in magenta and duck blue arrived. The main delivery, however, often took seven to nine weeks and would reach them by June, which would leave Rachel, already working at a disadvantage as it was her first collection, with only about a month to get her designs made up. But this was a problem that affected all designers working to a deadline. The responsibility for chasing up problems lay with the fabric department, situated next door to Colette and Monique's atelier and run by Madame del Roy. It was here that the fabric was delivered and immediately inspected for flaws by being run on rollers over fluorescent light. Bolts of taffeta, linen, organza, all carefully labelled, were stacked on metal shelves running from floor to ceiling.

Kate's feet were murdering her. She'd been standing in front of the studio mirror for five hours, helping bring to life the fabrics Rachel draped against her. The room was so hot and stuffy. Couldn't someone open a window? She'd skipped lunch for the third time that week and was feeling light-headed – they'd been eating out so much lately and it showed on the bathroom scales. Her eyes stole a look at the studio clock. Not long now. Kate bent her knees slightly to stretch the back of her calves.

After a dress or blouse had been pinned, Colette and Monique returned to their downstairs studios and started working on it in calico or muslin. This way, if one of Rachel's ideas did not work, expensive fabrics were saved. Since most of the collection was being made on Kate, her measurements had been taken and a fitting dummy was padded to match. This enabled them to work when Kate wasn't available for fittings.

Brigette, her face like a suet-pudding because she had viral flu, sat at a table cocooned in a pile of germs, propped up on her elbows. Her short-cropped hair stuck up like a porcupine because she hadn't bothered to wash it and it was still thick with gel. With her were Jean-Marc, sketching ideas for shoes, and Richard, in a black and cream striped T-shirt, matching socks, and black trousers held up with braces, cutting out sample swatches. Brigette thought he looked like a Licorice Allsort. In front of her were some tissues and a box of lemon-flavoured Strepsils.

'I love that,' enthused Brigette, sniffing as she flicked

through some of Rachel's designs. 'Are you going to use the dropped waistline in the day wear?'

'No. It works better full-length. If we used it as part of a suit it would create too much emphasis on the hips and then no one would buy it.'

Richard helped Rachel pin yellow chiffon to Kate's arm to create a sleeve.

'How many pieces haf we got?' asked Brigette, referring to the outfits in the show.

'We've thirty-five on the board,' counted Richard. 'We need another forty-five.'

'What's the length on the skirt, Colette?' Rachel asked, her mind on the dress she was creating.

'*Vingt-trois centimètres, mademoiselle.*'

'Let's lower it by three.'

Rachel rolled up the sleeves of her sweater and knelt in front of Kate. Satisfied with the results, she unpinned Kate and handed the fabric to Monique hovering next to her. She pulled out another roll.

'What was this used for?' she asked, unravelling green silk taffeta.

'Nothing,' said Richard. 'Claude ended up never using it. Shame, because I really like it.'

'I like it too. See if we can get some more. I could use it in the cocktail story.'

She demonstrated her idea, letting the roller drop to the floor and pulling the fabric tightly over Kate's midriff and arms. Then she draped it into a short skirt in minuscule folds of fabric while Colette held the back together. Kate dutifully threw her hips forward, and put her hands on her waist, holding the fabric in place as if posing for a shot.

Nicole poked her head around the door.

'*Mademoiselle, Monsieur Abrahms de Bastien à l'appareil.* Have you made a decision about the embroidery for the wedding dress? He needs to know. I also have the jewellery man who's arrived early for his appointment.'

'Oh, good. Show him in and tell Abrahms that I promise to have an answer for them first thing tomorrow. On second thoughts, let me have a quick word now.' She took off her

151

glasses and as she left the studio rubbing her eyes said, 'Brigette, can you sketch that quickly for me, please?'

Brigette blew her nose and threw her tissue into an almost full bin, which was worrying Richard in case he picked up her germs. She pulled a black Magic Marker from a box in front of her and began drawing, guiding the marker with wide, confident strokes. Kate shifted her pose to make it easier for Brigette to sketch. Once Brigette had finished she walked over to the fabric roll and cut a small piece off which she stapled to her design.

'Do you want a Strepsil to keep you going?' she asked Kate. Now that she'd got over her looks, Brigette was able to talk to her.

'How about a gin and tonic?'

'Well, at least Rachel's aware of the time. Claude was always so inconsiderate. Didn't matter if you had a date with Matt Dillon. Sometimes he made us stay till midnight!' Then she lowered her voice in case the men overheard, 'Are the rumours true?'

'What rumours?'

'About Monsieur Vaubelle being a homosexual. They say he has the AIDS virus and that is why he left.'

Kate didn't get a chance to answer. Walking confidentially back into the studio, followed by the jewellery man, Rachel pounced on two of the four recently arrived fabrics Richard had unearthed. Taking the navy-blue chiffon and a georgette over to the window, she put on her glasses and held them up to the light.

'These are wonderful!' said Richard excitedly, joining her. 'We can use the chiffon for blouses with the cashmere story.'

'The colours are perfect for what we want. Oh, and I made a decision to go ahead with that embroidered grosgrain after all. Abrahms have promised to deliver by the end of April,' said Rachel, looking delightedly at her discovery.

She walked over to Kate and resumed pinning. Her eyebrows bunched together in concentration as she worked. Funny how terrifying the thought of socialising with strangers was, yet when it came to work her confidence rarely faltered. When she inadvertently scratched Kate with a pin, Rachel was very apologetic and got Colette to take over. It occurred to Kate that without the pin, a tiny worthless piece of metal, *haute couture* simply wouldn't exist.

'How are you coping?' Rachel asked sympathetically later.

'I'm fine,' lied Kate. Her back was killing her.

'Well, if you can bear it a little longer we'll push on. We should be done in an hour.'

Something was going on outside the studio. Kate could hear an angry male voice arguing with Nicole. She exchanged a puzzled look with Brigette.

'Mais monsieur, vous ne pouvez pas entrer!' said Nicole, protesting.

With a bang the door to the studio suddenly opened to reveal Claude Vaubelle's squat frame. He reminded Kate of a demented bull. A distressed Nicole pushed past him, followed by a snuffling Louis who seemed unperturbed by the sudden chilly atmosphere.

'Désolée, mademoiselle,' she apologised, her voice high, 'I couldn't stop him.'

'That's all right,' Rachel said soothingly, 'you can go back to your desk. Monsieur Vaubelle, you wanted to see me?'

'Shut up!' Claude sneered, obviously drunk. 'A girl like you, young enough to be my daughter. It's an insult!' He spat out the words, and banged his fists against the wall in a rage. 'You have no right to be here, snooping around my studio, stealing my creations!' He walked around the room glaring at all the changes. Everyone stood rooted to the spot. 'And look at this! It's like a pigsty in 'ere!'

Kate glanced apprehensively at Rachel. Two dark red spots had appeared on her cheeks but her voice was calm when she spoke.

'I understand you are upset, Monsieur Vaubelle, but you should discuss any problems with Roe Lewis, not me.'

'A problem!' snapped Claude, as if Rachel had suggested he'd farted or had syphilis. He took a threatening step forward.

'Look, if you're going to make a scene, I'll have to . . .'

He stopped her, flicking a contemptuous hand. *'Ça suffit,* you stupid girl! You forget who you are talking to. My family built this company long before your grandparents were born. You're not fit to sweep the floors!'

Rachel pressed the intercom button connected to Nicole's desk and spoke calmly into the machine. 'Nicole, see if Mr Lewis is in the building and ask him to come up to the studio, please.'

Rachel's apparently calm demeanour seemed to incense Claude further. Swiftly he crossed the room, and picking up the intercom yanked it from its socket and threw it across the room. It smashed against the wall near Kate who jumped nervously out of the way, losing the roll of fabric that she was attached to. Louis pitched in and started an enthusiastic barking which ricocheted around the walls. Richard, who had been standing in shock, now stepped forward and grabbed Claude's arm.

'Monsieur Vaubelle, I think you had better . . .'

Claude, looking for a victim to vent his rage on, turned on him furiously. '*Laissez-moi!*' he roared, yanking his arm away. Then recognising Richard, he lowered his voice to a contemptible sneer, 'So, they were stupid enough to keep you on.'

Richard sniffed indignantly. 'There's no call for that kind of talk, Monsieur.'

Louis revealed his gums in a nasty snarl, then sailed straight at Richard and sank his fangs into a fleshy calf.

'Shit! Get your wretched dog off me!' Richard screamed.

Kate looked on horrified. Where was security, for God's sake?

'You don't understand! None of you understand!' Claude's voice had climbed to such a hysterical crescendo that Kate feared he'd have a heart attack. 'You don't have talent. What could any of you possibly know about designing. Look at you! It is because of me, my work,' he spat, jabbing a fleshy finger at Richard's chest, 'that this company is where it is today.'

'Correct.' A deceptively quiet voice came from the door, 'I reckon we can hold you entirely responsible for the mess things are in. If you had invested as much time in your work as you do on your stomach you wouldn't now find yourself in the ranks of the unemployed, Monsieur Vaubelle!'

Kate watched Roe stride into the room, dark and

154

menacing. Taking care of problem number one, he gave Louis a sharp kick in the ribs. Whimpering, the dog skulked behind Claude to lick his wounds.

'Thanks,' mumbled Richard checking his ankle for teeth-marks. The wretched dog had bitten right through his ruinously expensive designer trousers.

Roe spotted the wrecked intercom and looked at Claude. His features were hard and set.

'I see you're being your usual charming self.' His voice was heavy with sarcasm. 'Don't you think this is all rather pathetic?'

Claude looked at the floor.

'You guys OK?'

Roe looked first at Rachel then at Kate. Both nodded gratefully.

'This only goes to prove what I've always thought. You're washed up, Claude. Finished! No one wants to know you any more. Salvage what little dignity you have left and go home.'

They all looked at Claude except for Jean-Marc who had retreated behind the fabric corner. Slumped like a popped balloon, Claude seemed to have aged suddenly, tears pouring down his face. Poor man. How sad. No longer frightened, Kate wanted to do something to comfort him, but Rachel moved first.

'Come on, sir, let me help you. I'll get someone to take you home.'

'Don't!' snapped Claude, backing away as if he couldn't bear to be touched. 'I don't want your help!' He was shaking, his face alarmingly white. 'Just wait. Your turn will come. And when the critics have destroyed you, I shall return and claim what is rightfully mine.'

Rachel looked close to tears.

'Get out of here! Go on,' Roe ordered, 'before I get security up here. And if you ever show your face round here again I'll have you arrested on the spot!'

As he frog-marched Claude out of the studio, he turned to say to Rachel, 'Don't worry, sweetheart. This won't happen again. I'll be back to check on you later.'

'No harm done,' she said bravely.

Brigette, Kate noticed, watched Roe leave with dog-like devotion.

After Claude's scene it was impossible for anyone to work, so Rachel let Kate go. Back in the *cabine*, which was cold because of an open window, Madame Geneviève's portable radio was singing *You must remember this*. Kate changed gratefully back into her own warm clothes. All she wanted was to get back to Roe's place and have a bath. About to pack her things into her bag, she spotted a note from Roe which he must have slipped in earlier. It said he'd pick her up from the flat at nine as he wouldn't be able to make dinner. Obviously sorting out Claude Vaubelle once and for all, Kate decided, but said nothing to Geneviève who was a frightful old gossip. Now, what on earth was she going to wear for Julian's party tonight?

Richard buzzed down on Nicole's intercom asking Geneviève to cart up eight prototypes. Making a quick escape in case Rachel had decided to do another fitting, Kate closed the *cabine* door humming *Woman needs man, man must have his mate*. She broke off uncertainly in the middle of the next sentence, forgetting the words, then caught up with *the world will always welcome lovers, as times goes by*.

In Bea's car Kate rummaged for a cassette but Bea's collection was mostly rock, so she got a favourite Mozart tape from her bag and slipped it into the player. Bea, who hadn't worked for a week, had offered Kate the use of the Beetle. One look at Bea's anaemic face when Kate had turned up to collect the keys and she correctly guessed that her friend had got the curse. Bea's irregular seven-week cycle induced horrific cramps. Kate had never known anyone bleed so heavily. Waving off Bea's plans to work through the pain in the gym, Kate had ordered her to bed, tucked her up with a hot water bottle, a box of Feminax, hot home-made soup, a couple of unputdownable novels, the TV, which she carried in from the living-room, and a box of nut clusters.

'And try to eat something sensible today.'

'I am, I am,' said Bea, savouring the taste of nuts and caramel in her mouth.

Kate pulled on her coat. 'Are you sure you're feeling up to

tonight?' Bea's face was bleached and puffy. 'You don't have to come.'

'Oh, but I want to. Don't fuss. I haven't been man-hunting for ages!'

'But I thought you and Sam . . .?'

Bea managed a faint smile. 'I wasn't actually thinking about Sam. I adore him to bits but it's the same old routine each week. Dinner out, back to his flat for a bonk, races on Saturday, golf on Sunday. Besides which we've nothing in common. It was never going to be serious.'

Kate had heard that before. 'That's not the impression I got. I'm sure Sam would get very serious, given half a chance.'

Bea put up a dramatic hand. 'Don't! He's already talking about life insurance, pension plans and which school we're going to send the children to. Not the sort of future I thrill towards, as you know.'

Two days earlier Bea's stockbroker boyfriend had taken them both out for a slap-up lunch. Although he wasn't the usual type Bea went for (clean-cut, a bit humourless and a small nose – Bea liked big noses) Kate had liked his generous and considerate manner. But from the moment he'd picked them up Bea had walked all over him, getting him to stop at a chemist for aspirin, sending him back to the car for her glasses, and so on. Oh, Bea had smiled warmly at him all the evening but Kate had recognised the signs. It wouldn't last.

Thank God for the car, she thought now. Parking was hell but after standing all day she couldn't have faced the Métro. Mozart's *Requiem in D Minor* soothed some of her tension. Flicking the indicator, Kate joined the home-going traffic. The full moon hung like a naked light bulb against an ink-black sky, spotlighting the early evening commuters streaming out of Paris for the weekend. Outside the multi-cinema complexes street entertainers took advantage of the long queues and regular supply of new tourists. One man pulling faces followed unsuspecting pedestrians on his hands. Kate had seen him many times before but his act still made her laugh.

A dark-green Mercedes pulled up next to the Volkswagen at the traffic lights. Its driver, talking on his car phone, glanced idly in Kate's direction, his fine patrician profile unmistakable. Kate nodded to Sebastian Vaubelle, sending a dim wattage smile. He smiled back with recognition, but the smile somehow never reached his pale eyes. He had a girl in the car with him but it wasn't Cassy Peck. An unease flickered inside Kate and she looked away. Relieved to see the traffic lights change to green, she put her foot down and Bea's car leapt forward, unable, however, to compete with the powerful engine of Sebastian's Mercedes, which roared past her.

Kate watched him disappear into the night and shivered.

10

'I thought this was going to be a quiet bash,' whispered Kate as Roe guided her towards the noise.

'Not when Julian's got anything to do with it.'

It was a little after nine and the rented loft was already packed. The hall was jammed with glistening, scented female guests kissing air and their escorts rigorously shaking hands. Lots of kissy-kisses and loud *'Chéries!'* and 'Have you met my new man? Inside, the dimly-lit pale-grey walls had been adorned by a local artist with a frieze of female breasts. The room was full of thin, expensively-dressed women wearing public smiles and YSL earrings. Black was the dominant colour. The exhaustion of constant smoking and dieting showed on their faces: their eyes sized up the competition. Some glared enviously at Kate's strapless yellow fringe-dress, designed by Rachel to show off her sensational legs. Her red hair was swept back in a thick hairband to reveal star-shaped earrings which matched her dress. And there were a few raised eyebrows as a young woman made her entrance in a dress cut out at the back to reveal her bottom. Was this one of Julian's publicity stunts? Out of work actors looking like James Dean clones circled the room with steaming jugs of sake.

Looking around Kate was impressed by the number of celebrities. Michael Hutchence from INXS had flown in to be with his model girlfriend Helena Christiansen. Only a super-model, thought Kate glancing at Helena's blue jeans and clean face, could get away with such casual attire. Keanu Reeves, looking even better than he did on the screen, was deep in conversation with two young men. Both seemed familiar but Kate couldn't quite place them.

'But come on,' persisted a young producer who hoped to do a documentary on Rachel Winger, 'I can understand you drawing the line with your private life, but a little background information would make the programme so much more intimate and therefore more interesting to the viewers.'

Julian Kainz, relaxed and completely at home as host, lounged on a leather art deco sofa having his picture taken for *Hommes* magazine. His right arm was draped round a black girl with long frizzy hair.

'And we're just good friends,' he finished, winking at one of the press photographers. Everyone laughed.

Honestly, thought Kate, she looked young enough to be his daughter. Roe disappeared to get drinks, and for a moment Kate stood alone. Then a smooth, familiar voice behind her said, 'How are the best-looking ski legs in Paris?' Pigeon, handsome and almost unrecognisable in a tuxedo, kissed her on both cheeks.

'Both intact, which is more than I can say for you. Have you recovered?'

'Much, but I won't be skiing horizontally again in a hurry,' he ruefully patted his bulky right leg. 'Missed a couple of tournaments but the plaster comes off in a week. I'll have to get you to sign it.'

'I see Julian's glued to someone about half Natalie's age. Where is Miss Cheerful, anyway?'

'She was supposed to be in Fiji but ended up in the Canary Islands for a re-shoot, which isn't half as glam. Bitched all the way to the airport according to Julian, who had to get up at four to take her. Rather him than me. But never mind Natalie, how are things working out between you two? Roe shouldn't leave you alone dressed like that. Someone's bound to devour you.'

'Well, start off by devouring this.' Roe had returned with two enormous drinks. Kate took a sip and almost choked. It was neat vodka.

'Sorry, baby. It was all I could lay my hands on.'

'Look, mate, five minutes alone with your bird isn't much to ask. Can't you go away again?' Pigeon squeezed Kate into his shoulder.

'You've got ten minutes,' said Roe, grinning at her. 'I want to catch Julian while he's still sober.'

Lingering female glances followed Roe across the room and Kate felt a twinge of jealousy. Did they always have to make it so obvious they fancied him? Handing her vodka to one of the waiters, she swapped it for a glass of wine. If only we could have stayed in tonight, she thought wistfully. Lately Roe had been so wrapped up with work, they'd hardly had a moment alone. Trying to talk him out of coming earlier on had been a waste of time.

'It's good for business,' Roe had said, zipping her up slowly, 'and you should be seen more. We've both got to do our bit for Vaubelle.'

'Just promise me the moment I get stuck between two crashing bores and start sending you signals, we can go home.'

'Deal.' He had grabbed her suddenly.

'Oh Roe!' murmured Kate, melting in his arms. 'You know I'm wild about you!'

'Wild, eh? I've yet to see that side of you.'

With one eye on the clock, Roe patted her bottom, 'C'mon, move it or we'll be late.'

The colourful sushi had been expertly arranged and Kate helped herself to a California roll. Bea's familiar shock of blonde hair gleamed fleetingly across the room, then disappeared into the clutches of a tanned hunk with slick black hair and flawless skin. He looked like an ad for furniture polish. Sam was at the bar discussing the share index with Leo Schofield. With one eye on Bea, he looked about as cheerful as a cow heading for the abattoir. Poor thing, thought Kate. Another one of Miss Parker's victims. A thin, sulky-looking girl in a singing-yellow jacket sidled over. Her short skirt, matchbox-size quilted bag, and gold chain belt all screamed Chanel.

'Carey, my darling!' said Pigeon, handing her his drink. 'Come and meet Kate Temple.'

Carey looked hostile. Removing a cigarette from a silver engraved case, she lit it and blew the smoke out through her nostrils.

'Do you smoke?' she asked as an afterthought, offering the case to Kate.

'No thanks.'

'Kate came skiing with us in Val d'Isère.'

'On my bottom mostly,' admitted Kate.

'Kate's Roe's discovery. Though what she sees in him defeats me.'

Carey threw Kate a slightly more accommodating look. 'Well, that's brave of you. I'd be terrified of leaving him alone for more than a second, in case someone snapped him up.'

'Are you insinuating, darling, that I'm less good-looking than Roe?' Pigeon feigned a martyred look. 'Any more cheek from you, Miss, and I'll trade you in for a younger model.'

'And if you go bald, darling, I'll take a much younger lover!' She winked at Kate.

'Oh, I'll be off long before that with a floozy on each arm!' threatened Pigeon.

They looked adoringly at one another.

'I'm sorry you weren't able to make Val d'Isère. Pigeon told us about your father. Is he better?' Kate asked Carey.

'Driving my mother mad!' Her voice was distinctively upper class. 'Five minutes after surfacing from the bypass, Daddy was chatting up all the pretty nurses with a large Scotch and ice.'

An emaciated giant with huge cloudy eyes and puffed up hair swooped down on them. Dressed from top to toe in black, she kissed everyone including Kate.

'I thought I'd never make it! Donald's bloody jet broke down in Monaco so we had to take the chopper. Have you seen Billy? I desperately need to talk to him about tickets to his new concert.'

'Tess!' said Pigeon. 'Have you just come from a funeral?'

The girl's face clouded over. 'God, nobody important died while we were away, did they?'

'Billy who?' said Carey removing scarlet lipstick from Pigeon's cheek with a tissue.

'Honestly, Carey, you are a tease! Thought you two were going to join us in Stuttgart?' The girl took a sip of Pigeon's champagne. 'Well, I do hope you're coming to Sting's do on Sunday?'

Carey leaned sideways and whispered loudly, 'Tess only has famous friends.'

Kate giggled, warming to her.

A photographer hovered. 'Squeeze in a bit. Yes, that's great. Just like that,' he instructed, pushing Kate against Pigeon.

'Just as well she's off duty, mate,' said Pigeon, 'that shot could have cost you a thousand francs.' The photographer made a note of Kate's name.

Julian lumbered over with his co-star, a waif-like beauty in a chiffon dress over hot pants. While making introductions he slipped an arm around Kate.

'You smell delicious,' he whispered, grabbing a tray of drinks from a passing waiter and handing one to her. Kate found herself drinking a rather sweet wine. 'This party needs some class.'

'I heard that, Julian!'

'Ah, Tess! you look lovely too.'

Kate leant towards him. 'Have you spotted Roe? He said he was going to look for you.'

'Might still be in the pool room. Don't let him forget he owes me fifty quid and I'm not going to be palmed off with any cheques.'

'You must be very good if you beat him.'

Julian's eyes briefly travelled across her body. 'I'm very good at lots of things, Kate.'

Julian's bald and chubby agent rushed over in a state of excitement, demanding his immediate attention; an American director had shown interest in using Julian on his next picture and the agent wanted to clinch a deal before the man sobered up.

'Don't run away,' Julian whispered to Kate. 'Got to do my bit with the press but I'll be back.'

As she watched him go, Kate caught a tall man with straw-coloured hair staring at her from across the room. How rude!

Bea, wearing wicked-purple platform shoes and still on Mr

Sheen's lap, was doing her casting couch routine. The recently arrived model lived in black 501s and white T-shirts but had been rejected by Milan and was now pinning his hopes on Paris. For half an hour he had been quizzing Bea about Parisian model agencies.

'And what was it like working for Saint Laurent?' His Sicilian eyes trailed celebrities round the room.

'Rather sweet,' said Bea, who thought he talked a lot of crap but was admiring his moulded torso and eyes like milk chocolates. 'He's a recluse, hardly speaks these days but never stingy with the bubbly. One girl got so drunk during last season's show she passed out backstage.'

'You must show me some of this beautiful city,' said the model, deciding that Bea must have made it if she had worked for Saint Laurent. 'Tell me, what do you like doing?'

Bea grinned. 'Eating, sleeping and fucking.'

From the other side of the room Sam punched in another long-distance number on his mobile phone, which had already shrieked four times, nearly giving Leo heart failure. Glaring at Mr Sheen, Sam said something to Leo, busy tackling his third packet of potato crisps, then beckoned over a couple of young black models.

'Hello Kate.'

Kate recognised the young waitress she'd met on the Val d'Isère slopes. She looked glorious in a pale pink taffeta dress, her blonde hair framing coltish features. She'd lost weight. A lot of weight. At least a stone. It made her look more fragile than Kate remembered. Pigeon went off in search of more drinks.

'It's Joelle, isn't it? We met at Val d'Isère.'

The girl smiled nervously. 'I very nearly didn't come. I get very shy around all you celebrities, but Roe can be very persuasive.'

Kate's smile drained away. Roe. Since when did she know Roe? 'Elusive too,' she said guardedly. 'How's work?'

'The season's over at Val d'Isère so I've been shopping around for more work here. I've always wanted to live in Paris but there's not much available in the way of jobs. But I have been short-listed for a job as cook-general during the polo season in Palm Beach, so fingers crossed.'

'Julian's going to be up for child molesting if he's not careful,' said Roe, miraculously appearing with more drinks, 'that girl he's been mauling is only fifteen. Hi, Jo,' he kissed her cheek and handed her a drink. 'You look great.'

All of a sudden it was Jo. Kate noticed her blush. What the hell was going on?

'Darling,' she said, concealing her sudden anxiousness, 'you've been gone ages.'

Pigeon grinned. 'Partying is such sweet sorrow.'

Someone turned up the music and a bald-headed man with sleepy brown eyes and very broad shoulders asked Kate to dance. Oh, why not? He was a good four inches shorter than herself, but rather attractive and she was longing to dance. Conscious of Roe's eyes following her round the floor Kate began distributing smiles like strewn confetti. Gradually she relaxed and let the music wash over her. Under the soft, tungsten lights her red hair seemed to ignite. Catching the admiration in her partner's eye, she moved erotically to the music. Funny how her inhibitions evaporated the minute she stepped on a dance floor. Another quick look at Roe, but his head was bent, deep in conversation with the distressingly thin Joelle. Warning bells clanged in Kate's head.

Pigeon and Carey were dancing nearby. Carey, unsteady from too many glasses of wine and ludicrously high heels, clung on to Pigeon, both of them hooting with laughter at Carey's comments on neighbouring dancers.

After six tracks Kate returned to the table, catching Roe's eye.

'Having fun?' he mouthed over Joelle's head.

Kate shrugged. She'd be having more fun dancing with him but pride prevented her from saying anything. The tall, straw-haired man she had caught staring at her lurched forward. His jeans were deplorably tight and smoke curled like wispy cotton wool from his joint as he offered her a glass.

'Thought you might need one of these. Where did you learn to dance like that? You're amazing!'

'Thanks.'

She accepted the gin and tonic. Shouldn't really mix my

165

drinks, she thought, straining to hear Roe's conversation with Joelle. Then unthinkingly drained her glass.

'Virgo, am I right?'

'Wrong end of the zodiac. I've got hoofs.'

The man looked pleased. 'Very nice ones at that. Capricorn, huh? An earth sign. Even better. I'm a Gemini which makes us very compatible.'

'What for? Tennis?'

He laughed and casually stubbed his joint out on the carpet, which made a horrible smell. From the corner of one eye Kate jealously watched Roe propel Joelle on to the dance floor as Phoebe Snow began singing *Let someone touch your soul*.

'You could have modelled for some of the paintings here,' the Gemini was gazing at her breasts. 'I'm getting good vibes from you.'

'Speakers, probably. They've just turned up the volume.' She wished he'd go away so that Roe would ask her to dance.

Jack Winger, Scotland's current star golfer, in Paris for twenty-four hours, was leaning against the fireplace with an arm round Rachel. So that was her famous father. Roe had mentioned he'd be here tonight. Not that he had needed to. The family resemblance was obvious. Kate could hear him entertaining a captive audience with a hilarious tale; Lee Trevino, it seemed, was travelling in a lift after a successful pro-am tournament. In the lift was a rather well-endowed lady whose bosom Lee had accidentally bumped with his elbow.

' "I'm so very sorry, madam," ' said Jack, trying to mimic the American in his thick Edinburgh accent, ' "but I know that if your heart is as soft as your bosom, you'll forgive me."

' "If the rest of your body is as hard as your elbow," responded the lady with a glint in her eye, "my room number is 317." '

Rachel, who was not used to drinking, couldn't work out if her head was reeling from all the excitement at Vaubelle or because of the two glasses of champagne she'd allowed herself. She just felt very, very happy. And with Jack here, everything was perfect.

'Have I told you how very proud I am of you?' said Jack. 'You really did it, didn't you?'

'I haven't done anything yet, Dad. I've still got to produce a collection. Even now there hardly seems time to get it all done.'

'Are you setting aside some time for a social life?'

'Not really,' mumbled Rachel, dropping her head. 'I did meet someone recently but it never got off the ground: we sort of lost touch.'

'Well, just don't go using work as an excuse not to get out a bit. You always did that, even as a little girl.'

'I rang Mum to tell her the news,' Rachel said hastily. She felt uncomfortable talking to her father about her sex life, or rather her lack of it.

'How is Margarita?'

Jack hadn't seen his first wife in years. Despite the fact that they had both remarried, he would have liked to have kept in touch. But his second wife was so pathologically jealous that Jack's only means of contact was through Rachel.

'She's so busy running the farm these days I don't think she has time to miss me. Besides, Santiago makes her very happy.'

I'm sure he does, thought Jack with a stab of jealousy. He'd seen pictures of the proud Argentine polo player with the flashing black eyes and the kind of gleaming olive body that put his own to shame. It further dented Jack's ego that the Argentine was eight years younger than his ex-wife.

'Why don't you come up to Scotland for a break? Olivia and Fergus would adore to see you,' said Jack.

'Maybe this summer.'

Kate was still trapped by the man with bloodshot eyes.

'Then my wife left me for another woman and joined the United Nations,' he was saying. 'She was a Cancer. Should have realised then that we were doomed. But that was before I'd got into spiritualism and the zodiac. Now I read palms for a living. I'll do yours if you like.'

'You'd be better off asking my friend,' Kate said nodding in Bea's direction. 'She'll believe anything you tell her as long as you hum a bit and produce a glass ball.'

167

Bored with holding an empty glass, she looked around for someone to fill it. Why was the room so hot!

'You're too pretty to be a cynic,' he said, grabbing her free hand. He turned her palm upwards, 'Ah, but you have an interesting hand!'

I have? Kate peered at it for some visible sign of confirmation but all she could see was dry skin.

'And a strong lifeline, but this line cutting across, see it? This indicates an upheaval. Not good for Cappys. You need roots and stability to grow.'

'And watering three times a day, I suppose.'

Honestly, who wrote his lines? Next he'd start telling her about a tall, dark stranger entering her life. Roe entered her every day. She giggled as the man ran a thumb across the fleshy part of her palm. It tickled.

'Money's important,' he said seriously. 'To you it represents security but of course it doesn't really. Your past line shows an older man in an authoritative position who has brought a lot of pain.'

'Sounds like Bea's bank manager.'

He squinted closer at her hand. 'There's a great deal of activity going on. Movement could mean a career change or travel. My guess is a move abroad. Somehow that's all tied in with a second man. He'll be a powerful force in your life. Oh, and animals. Something to do with animals. Horses perhaps?'

Not very likely, thought Kate, who had fallen off the last time she rode and broken her collar bone.

'See this?' her companion excitedly traced a deep groove, 'that's Uranus crossing his path which probably means this man has extraordinary creative powers. Don't lose him.'

'I already have, about ten minutes ago,' said Kate, searching the room for Roe. 'Although one prediction out of three isn't bad,' she said more kindly.

The man hesitated. 'What sign is this man?'

'Scorpio.' Kate looked up. Someone had dimmed the lights. 'Don't you think it's hot in here?'

'*Your lonely nights of conquest will never make you whole . . .*' sang Phoebe Snow.

He shook his head. 'Scorpions. Charming but deadly. And

they always sting. Can't help it. It's in their nature.' His eyes dropped back to her hand. 'There's something else. Something . . .' he looked at Kate suddenly, his eyes uneasy. And then he smiled, rather too earnestly, she thought. 'Time's up.' He dropped her hand. 'No charge for the insight but how about another drink?'

What? What was he about to say? Kate's eyes scanned the room, now very dark. Suddenly she froze. Two figures were locked together on the dance floor. The man whispered something in the girl's ear and Joelle tilted her head, laughing up at him. He put a hand up to her chin, tilting it and she stopped laughing.

'Don't squander your body. Let someone touch your soul . . .' sang Phoebe Snow.

They gazed solemnly into each other's eyes and Roe lowered his mouth.

'Lucky cow,' whispered a passing blonde, eyeing Roe wistfully. 'I've been dying for that man to notice me. He's gorgeous!'

'I thought he was going out with a red-headed model?' said her friend.

'That was last month.'

Kate's confidence collapsed. She fled from the room, ignoring the cries from her astrologer, up the stairs and past a group smoking pot. Through her sobs she could hear someone say, 'Hey gorgeous, you all right?'

Locking herself in the loo, Kate was almost overwhelmed by the smell of asparagus pee. Trembling, she sat on the seat. Men were not to be trusted, not even Roe. Hadn't it been proved to her time and again, first with her feckless father, then with . . . No, don't think about that. She'd pack her bags the minute she got home and move straight back to Bea, ignoring his calls, his desperate pleas for her to come back. She would be merciless, make him get down on his knees and beg her. Or even better, she would kill herself and Roe would suddenly realise how blind he'd been about this beautiful misunderstood woman. God. Calm down, Kate. Don't be so dramatic. It was only a kiss. It didn't mean anything. Hands shaking, she blew her nose on the last piece of loo paper, then got up, washed her face in cold water, and tried to repair the damage to her make-up. I look a mess. Who'd want me looking like this? Someone banged on the door.

'Come on, for fuck's sake! I've been waiting hours. If you don't get a move on I'm going to puke all over the carpet.'

Opening the door, Kate was practically mowed down by the black schoolgirl last seen on Julian's knee. Sounds of vomiting diminished as she closed the door behind her. She found Julian in the hall.

'Can't seem to take her drink,' he said sheepishly. 'Why Kate! What's all this? I can't allow tears at my party.' Suddenly he was the picture of concern. Putting a gentle arm round her shoulders, he guided her solicitously into a bedroom. The bed was littered with coats. Julian cleared a corner and sat Kate down.

'Don't move an inch,' he ordered, darting out of the door.

'Sorry.' Kate was still clutching the soggy piece of loo paper when he returned moments later with some champagne.

'This should help.' He handed her a glass. Kate mopped her eyes.

'Period?'

'Aspirin's not going to work on Roe.'

'But it all seemed to be going so well.'

'Not any more. He's busy devouring someone I thought he didn't even know,' she wiped her nose on her hand.

Since when did that ever stop us, thought Julian with an uncharacteristic pang of guilt. 'Oh dear, did you catch Roe in bed with someone?'

'Not exactly.'

'Well, that's a relief. Here, use this.' Julian produced a grubby-looking handkerchief from his pocket, then said kindly, 'It's hard being a woman, isn't it.'

'I should have realised this would happen.'

'Look, he's probably just had one too many and got a little carried away. You know what little boys we are. It's easy to be insecure in a new relationship, but it takes time to work it through. You have to remember that Roe's led a pretty active sex life and it's not easy for him to change overnight.'

'Obviously.'

'Come on. You two haven't been out of one another's sight for a second.'

'Maybe that's the problem. I'm becoming too dependent and I don't like that. Makes me feel insecure.'

'Darling girl, you're the last person who should be feeling insecure. Don't you know that we're all secretly lusting after you behind Roe's back. If it wasn't for him, you and I would have had the most outrageous affair.'

'But what about Natalie?'

'What about her?'

'Well, you married her. You must have loved her very deeply.'

'Deeply,' said Julian meaningfully, 'and don't change the subject.' God, she looked sweet when she smiled. 'Do you have any idea how jealous I was of Roe at Val d'Isère? Seeing you two snuggling together in the back as we drove to the airport. I dreamt about you for nights.'

Kate was beginning to cheer up. Julian, who seemed suddenly a tower of strength, leaned forward and kissed her brow and her cheek until suddenly things were getting out of hand. Julian's lips felt soft and warm tracing her neck. As they travelled down to her breasts, Kate pulled back suddenly and put her hand up against his mouth.

'We mustn't,' she whispered, giggling.

'Oh, but we must,' Julian breathed and started kissing her fingers. 'What is that perfume you're wearing? It's driving me mad.'

'You're only kissing me because I'm miserable.'

'I'm kissing you because you are sensational.'

The door barged open making them both jump and a very drunk couple rolled in to collect their coats. She recognised the astrologer man immediately.

'Ah! The Capricorn lady! I thought I'd lost you.'

Julian stood up. 'You did, friend.'

Giggling, the girl had managed to find her coat and was staring curiously at Julian.

'Haven't I seen you somewhere before?' she slurred.

171

'I expect so,' and he gently but firmly guided them out of the door. Kate made some attempt to fix her face then started rummaging through the pile of coats for her wrap.

'I'm going home. I couldn't face Roe right now. Will you tell him I've gone back to the flat?'

'You're more than welcome to stay at my hotel if it helps,' Julian offered. 'No one will bother you.'

With her heels on Kate was slightly taller than him.

'I'll be fine. I'll call a taxi.'

'No you won't! I'll take you.'

'But this is your party.'

'Doesn't mean I have to like it.'

They pushed their way through the river of bodies in the hallway, now thick with smoke, sweat and freshly applied perfume. They got outside, with Julian's arm still round Kate, and walked to his car parked on the pavement. The cold air was refreshing after the stuffy interior and Kate took great gulps of it as she gazed up at the full moon and myriad of stars.

She sighed. 'What a beautiful night! Why is it we forget to look at the sky?'

'Too many beautiful things down here to admire,' said Julian, watching her. Kate hugged him gratefully and for a moment they looked in companionable silence at the deserted road.

'Hey, buddy,' called a familiar, husky voice. Kate's heart jumped to her throat and thumped nervously. They turned towards the sound.

'Going somewhere?' Roe was standing a few yards away and spoke in his usual lazy drawl, but his eyes were like steel.

'I said I'd give Kate a lift.'

'She's coming home with me, Julian. Thanks for the offer.' Roe didn't look remotely grateful.

Kate could feel Julian tensing, his arm still wrapped protectively round her. Then he shrugged and smiled.

'No problem. Give me a call next week.'

Roe drove home with jaw clenched. He jumped several red lights and narrowly missed hitting a car as it pulled out of a drive. He swore viciously at the surprised driver and gunned

172

the car down a sleepy avenue. A muscle was twitching on his left jaw and his pupils looked huge. God only knew how much he'd had to drink. Kate gripped the sides of her seat and concentrated on breathing. Why was he so angry? She was the one who should be feeling cross.

'Roe, can't you slow down a little? You're frightening me.' She touched his thigh, a peace offering.

But Roe's eyes remained fixed on the road and Kate withdrew her hand. The tension in the car was suffocating. By the time they got back to the flat, Kate had built herself up to a rage. She threw her coat on the sofa and followed Roe, stony-faced, into the kitchen.

'When I want a ride on the bumper cars I'll buy a ticket at a funfair. That was bloody irresponsible. You could have killed us!'

Ignoring her, Roe removed the leftovers of Kate's pasta salad from the fridge. He hadn't spoken a word since they left the party.

'I don't see why I should get the cold-shoulder treatment. You were the one all over Joelle like a hot rash.'

That wasn't quite the cool way she'd meant to bring it up, but all those drinks had loosened her tongue.

'What exactly is that supposed to mean?'

'Just what I said. People were getting the impression that Joelle was your girlfriend, not me.'

Roe shoved the pasta and some leftover bread into the microwave, his voice dangerously quiet. 'Don't start what you can't finish, Kat. Nothing happened, so drop it, okay?'

'No, it's not okay. I wasn't aware you two had ever met.'

'There was a possibility of my getting her a job. We exchanged numbers. Nothing more sinister.'

'Then why were you kissing her?' she said, fighting the urge to throw something at him.

'Didn't know you had exclusive rights.'

That stung. 'For someone after a job she provided you with a very lengthy c.v. Are you sleeping with her?'

'No, of course I'm not sleeping with her. But she's been having a rough time and I was trying to give her back some self-esteem.'

173

'What, by kissing her?' said Kate sarcastically, jumping as the microwave pinged. Roe removed the pasta dish, wishing he had another hit of coke, then turned on Kate.

'As it happens, yes. The kid's had a rough ride, I wanted to . . .' he seemed to check himself suddenly. 'Look, let's get something straight right now. You want to continue living here, then you do it on my terms. I don't hassle you about where you go or who you see, so don't start with me, Kat. You're not my goddam wife!'

Kate was speechless. This Roe was a complete stranger. He took his food into the sitting-room and switched on the television. It was the late night news. Slouched on the sofa, his long legs stretched out, he stared grimly at the set. There had been an earthquake in California, another bomb had gone off in Belfast and the forecast threatened storms. Kate gazed unseeingly, her eyes hot with tears. I won't be insulted like this, she thought furiously, hovering in the doorway. Roe glanced up, the amber eyes like marble.

'Either leave or come and sit down, but don't just stand there. You're not impressing anyone with your Little Orphan Annie act.'

He might as well have hit her.

'Bastard!'

Stumbling blindly into the hall and slamming the front door behind her, she was only aware of the awful thumping in her ears, and the icy chill in her veins. Outside she searched urgently for a taxi but the street was empty. She didn't want him to find her here after such an undignified exit. A feeling of outrage was immediately followed by a hefty dose of self-pity. Kate sat on the cold steps and began to sob. She heard a distant clock chime midnight and cars drive past. All of a sudden her happy life looked unbearably bleak. Hoping to find solace, Kate gazed up at the moon which seemed to be watching her sympathetically.

She froze at the sound of her name. Roe stood above her in the doorway. He appeared gaunt under the street light, his handsome face unusually harsh.

'Go away! Bloody well leave me alone,' snapped Kate turning her head away so he couldn't see her tear-stained face. 'I've gone right off Americans!'

Roe sat down next to her and pulled her stiff body into his arms.

'Come here, baby,' he murmured, stroking her hair. 'You're far too sensitive. You know I didn't mean any of that.'

'You convinced me,' mumbled Kate. She felt reluctant to give up her huff. 'You were hateful.'

'Sometimes I go too far and I forget you can't take it. Listen, baby, you've got to believe me about Joelle. The girl's about to crack. I just made her feel like someone cared. Don't let's argue.' He turned her towards him and Kate nestled into his neck. 'You know how crazy I am about you.'

'Do I?' The argument still hung in the air but Kate's anger was replaced by a sudden wave of lust. It was scary this power he had over her. 'You don't deserve me.'

'Can't argue with that.'

And because Roe smiled so rarely, when he did, like now, it had devastating consequences. Kate was drawn irresistibly to his light. She felt his warmth and love flowing back into her, in waves and waves of relief. She slumped against him, clinging fiercely like a child. She could have stayed like that for ever but he suddenly pulled her to her feet.

'Let's go.'

With one deft movement she was lifted into his arms and swept back into the flat, Joelle and the quarrel erased with an impassioned kiss. He muttered something but Kate was only aware of the delicious shivers rippling through her, as Roe's mouth furrowed into her neck, her brow, her lips. In a blur they climbed the stairs, past the front door, the hall, and into the kitchen with Roe's half-eaten pasta by the sink. The telephone began to ring.

'Shouldn't we answer the phone?'

Roe was lowering her to the wooden floor. 'Ignore it.'

'But it's late. It might be important.'

It was a feeble protest. Roe had impatiently pushed the fringe-dress up to her waist.

'Baby, nothing's more important than this.' A draught from the door fanned across her stomach and the kitchen floor was cold against her bare skin. Kate didn't care. She was intoxicated, her bruised mind assuaged by his touch, his syrupy voice, arching towards him, sinking against his maleness.

'I love you, Roe,' she whispered as he entered her, and his eyes and mouth replied wordlessly, his hands warm.

In the weeks that followed Kate went through the effects of an emotional whirlwind. Life with Roe was difficult and it was hard not to blame herself for moving into his flat so quickly. It was as if he resented her being there, invading his space, although she made great efforts not to. Instead of a wife she felt like a guest. Kate found herself reacting to his moods like a barometer. One minute idyllically happy, the next plunged into despair. With one small gesture Roe could make her feel as if she were the most important thing in his life, but, unable to anticipate his frame of mind, Kate lived in a perpetual state of insecurity.

After the first ecstatic throes of love Kate had realised they had little in common. Roe was ruthless about money whereas Kate, although careful with her savings, was for ever handing out money to charities and friends who'd fallen on hard times. She played Mozart and Telemann but Roe wouldn't be swayed from his rock. Not a natural sportswoman, she valiantly joined Roe, bleary-eyed, on his daily eight-kilometre jog. But after she had hyperventilated on three consecutive mornings, Roe left her dozing strenuously between snooze alarms. Swimming was much more enjoyable. Roe continued to practise Tai Chi but stopped doing it at home when she said it reminded her of her school ballet classes (Sophie had always wanted her to be a dancer, but her weight and height had put a stop to it). Kate devoured mainstream novels, poetry and glossy magazines. Roe, when he had the time, read biographies of important men and the pink bits of newspapers. His energy was phenomenal. Roe seemed able to burn the candle at both ends; he liked clubbing until one or two in the morning but Kate longed to spend a few intimate evenings in. There never seemed to be time to do her nails, wax her legs or watch the box. It was always rush, rush, hiding the Jolen Bleach, her stash of sweets or the sex manual at the bottom of her underwear

176

drawer. She needed her eight hours' sleep. The late nights were beginning to show under her eyes.

The days Roe returned from work blackly depressed became more frequent. His enormous sexual appetite waned and because sex had been the foundation of their relationship it was not long before the cracks started to show. Finding she had returned to her old doubt about her sexual desirability, along with everything else, Kate began to crave the contact sex provided. They seemed to have learned each other too well. Instead of staying up half the night to make love they took short-cuts, quickies, only coming together uncon- sciously in sleep. Their frequent arguments (usually about Roe's refusal to make more of a commitment to their relationship) ended with him stomping off into the night and Kate in tears. She never knew where he spent those hours.

One evening when she was least expecting it, Roe had tried getting her to open up, but instead of explaining her fears and doubts Kate had been prickly and defensive and they'd ended up quarrelling about Bea.

'Well, I can see his point,' Bea had said when they discussed it over lunch the next day, 'I mean, he's probably jealous. Lots of men get like that when their girlfriend has a close relationship with another woman. Makes them feel alienated.'

'It's just that it's so much easier talking to you.'

'Of course it is. But then you're not sleeping with me!' Bea reached for the sugar bowl and added three spoonfuls to her hot chocolate. 'Look, you wouldn't feel so dependent on him if you spent more time with your own friends.'

She chose her words carefully, knowing full well that if she agreed that he was a rat Kate would defend him, and that if she sided with Roe Kate would say she didn't understand her. Bea had long since decided that, although people thought they wanted advice, they rarely followed it when it was given to them. What they really wanted was sympathy.

'He says I'm a flirt.'

'Well, you are, Kate.'

'Only because I feel insecure. If he paid me more attention I wouldn't need to. I just wish I didn't think about him the

177

whole time. It's like one of those wretched commercial jingles you hate but can't stop humming. He got to something inside me that no other man has ever reached.'

'Your G spot?'

'Not everything's to do with sex, Bea!'

'There you go,' said Bea, looking pleased. 'Now why can't you show some of that spark with your American! No, sex isn't everything but it's a large part of a relationship, particularly a new one, and you need to keep the upper hand. Look, I adore men, but you must learn to play them at their own game. Enjoy them but don't get too serious. Not unless you're very sure they feel the same way about you.'

'You sound so callous.'

'Just a little more experienced, darling. What you need is to take back some of the control. Have you thought about getting away for a few days?'

'I have got some London bookings that had already been confirmed before signing with Vaubelle. I could still do them, but I'm loath to leave him.'

'Do them, Kate. You need a break from one another. Honestly, it might help to put things in perspective, and you know what they say about absence . . .'

'Perhaps you're right,' said Kate, cheering up suddenly because someone else had made the decision for her. 'I'll ring the agency first thing tomorrow. Five days isn't such a long time.' Impulsively, she leaned over and embraced her friend. 'And just so you know, this pep talk alone has done me the power of good.'

Noticing the dark shadows under Kate's eyes, the washed-out complexion resulting from too many nights crying herself to sleep, Bea decided Roe Lewis was doing her friend about as much good as a course of heroin. If only she wasn't off to Indonesia in a week. Now, if ever, Kate needed allies.

At 1 a.m. Kate lay awake in bed. An old Gérard Depardieu film starring the popular Natalie Baye silently flickered on the TV. She wasn't watching. Her mind spat out angry, resentful thoughts because their latest row had been resolved in bed. She glanced glumly at the screen. Gérard Depardieu had removed his clothes and was shouting at someone from the bathroom, brandishing a toothbrush furiously in the air. You're not the only one, she thought, realising how obsessed she was becoming with this relationship. She told herself she was worth more but she didn't feel it. She glanced down at Roe. His love-making tonight had been wonderful. Instinctively he knew how to turn her on. Who taught him our secrets, she wondered, what woman had made him so skilful? He'd obviously had masses of lovers but had there been someone in his life he had really loved? Kate felt a stab of jealousy as she fantasised about her adversary, and regretted the intimacy they had just shared because he knew too much about her and she felt short-changed.

Through the gloom she gazed at his face, the predatory nose, the indecently long eyelashes that cast shadows across his cheeks, the dark lion's mane of hair that needed a trim. She desperately wanted to talk but he was sleeping soundly. How could he, after all the hurtful things they'd said to one another? She looked at him, this man she had lived with and loved for eight weeks, and felt empty and let down as she realised she still knew nothing about him. A wave of misery descended on her. A single tear escaped and splashed against her hand. Roe grunted next to her and rolled back into his dream.

'Your arse is getting bigger,' he had said earlier, his voice soft and warm from their love-making.

'It's all these late night meals you insist we go out to. I don't have a chance to work it off.'

'Then get up early and come running with me.'

Kate had pulled a face. 'I almost killed myself trying that. I'd much rather get my exercise with you in bed. If you'd only allow yourself the odd lie in. Couldn't we forget about work for a day and call in sick?'

For a moment he had studied her, then he said, 'Don't expect too much, Kat.'

'Now, what's that supposed to mean?'

'Just don't expect too much of me.'

'For God's sake's, Roe.'

But he didn't respond. After a few moments his breathing

179

had deepened and Kate realised that he had gone to sleep.

She reached for the remote control and flicked off the television. For a moment she lay watching the moonlight which filled the curtainless room. It always made her slightly uneasy, this lack of privacy. Surely people in the opposite building could see them? It didn't seem to bother Roe. He liked the openness, the fresh air, even at sub-zero temperatures. Silently Kate eased herself out of the warm bed and retrieved her abandoned T-shirt. She negotiated the armchair and a pile of Roe's washing to the left of the bed and padded stealthily into the kitchen. She opened the fridge door. Light plunged across the dark floor like a flag. The fruit *pâtisserie* she'd bought at Bouchon looked inviting and she cut herself a large slice. She couldn't be bothered about getting a plate and fork, so she sat on the floor, eating from the box, surprised to see how quickly she wolfed it down. Still feeling hungry, she cut herself some more, until somehow she'd eaten the lot. It was only because she'd missed supper.

Returning to the fridge she gorged herself on the rest of its contents, eating with frantic haste and without enjoyment: a whole baguette with a quarter of a pound of butter, half a barbecued chicken, three croissants, a pint of milk and a packet of Chèvre cheese. Kate kept expecting Roe to materialise in the doorway, disgust on his face, but she remained alone with her guilty binge.

Eventually she tip-toed into the bathroom in her white T-shirt and examined her distended stomach in the mirror. Her reflection stared back in shame. Oh, God. She looked obese, grotesque. How could she have done it? She must have gained pounds! She sat on the cold floor and peered into the loo anticipating weeks and weeks of gruelling workouts. Then, after reaching a decision, she stuck two fingers harshly down her throat. Nothing happened. Heavy strands of hair kept getting in the way, so she pulled it savagely back into a knot. She pushed harder and felt herself gag. Tears came to her eyes. She spat into the loo bowl and watched the phlegm swim in circles. Damn. Maybe she should drink warm salt water. She forced herself to think of images that would revolt her, and gave one final prod with her fingers. She heaved violently and the food she had just eaten came up still undigested. A few bits landed on the floor. When there was nothing left inside her, Kate flushed the loo with the lid down in case it woke Roe, brushed her teeth and went shakily back to bed.

Her whole body ached, her throat was sore and her nose tingled painfully where some food had come up. She was appalled by what she had done, having thought that at last she'd put all that behind her. She would never, ever, do it again! All the same she felt empty and relieved.

In the dark stillness of the room, Kate ran a hand across her belly. Its flatness was comforting because, in less than six hours, she had fittings at Vaubelle.

11

Marble Arch looked greyer and shabbier than Kate remembered as she emerged from the congested Underground. The late May air was sharp, the pale, clotted sky unwelcoming. Bolshy commuters rudely pushed past her, homing in like radar towards their over-heated offices and morning fix of Nescafé and McVities.

Kate joined the crowd waiting to cross Baker Street, trying not to breathe the exhaust fumes as she battled to the front. She hated standing at the back. It made her feel vaguely neglected and as if she were missing something important. Cars swarmed past. The lights changed and Kate stepped unthinkingly off the pavement, narrowly missing a black Porsche driven by a lunatic. Instinctively she checked the number plate as it nipped in front of a Ford Estate and stopped briefly to pick up a girl in thigh-length boots and dangly earrings. The Ford honked angrily. Fool, she told herself crossly, as her heartbeat went into over-drive. What would Roe be doing in London? She reached the other side of the road and weaved between strangers, passing dull shops pleading rock-bottom prices, organic ant-killer, smoke-free zones and rain sticks from the South American rain forest. It seemed that one window in three carried a notice saying 'For lease. For sale.'. A depressing sign of the times.

It was Friday, her third day in London and still no word from Roe. Bea's eldest brother, Justin, had lent Kate his bachelor flat in Holland Park. It was on the top floor of a Georgian house whose peeling white paint exposed bald patches of brick on either side of the front door, but it had a very pretty communal garden. Mrs Tate, the landlady and local busybody, lived in the basement with her large family of hard-bitten tabby cats. The first thing you noticed inside was the smell of cats' pee mingling with Mrs Tate's enthusiastic but tuneless singing, and the hiss of her kettle. No one escaped the mandatory cup of tea.

A small catwalk had been set up on the first floor of Marks and Spencer, running between racks of separates. It was flanked by grey plastic chairs all occupied this morning by cheerful housewives with red-faced, shrieking babies and bursting carrier bags. They seemed happy to be resting their shop-worn feet.

Kate got back from lunch with five minutes to spare, but nobody seemed unduly concerned. Cathy Step, the choreographer, wearing a Comme des Garçons T-shirt, black platforms and a large stop-watch round her neck, was checking the music changes with the technician. The room hummed with gossip. Kate's enormously fat dresser, Carol, was dishing out Jaffa cakes and salt and vinegar crisps. The girls, already in their first outfits, were admiring shots of her three-month-old granddaughter. The two male models stood silently to one side, inspecting their suits in the mirror.

Cathy approached Kate's rail with the M & S marketing manager as Kate slipped on two pairs of tights to save time on changes.

'Kate, love. Can you wear a flesh-coloured bra in the lingerie scene? They're worried about you revealing too much for the afternoon show.'

'Personally I thought it was the highlight of the morning's show,' said the marketing manager, winking at Kate.

That's original, she thought irritably. Tucking her hair back behind one ear, Roe's ring, which she had moved earlier, flashed on the engagement finger.

Some of the seats were still empty but once the music started customers stopped for a better look and soon a large crowd had gathered. A group of teenagers and four old biddies who had been waiting for half an hour sat hogging the front row. One of the biddies reached out and tugged Caroline's skirt as she moved down the catwalk.

''Ave a feel of this, Dot. Lovely cloth! 'Ow much, luv?' she asked, addressing Caroline as if she were a sales assistant.

Caroline smiled disdainfully. She was used to the OAPs chatting during the show as if they were at home watching the television. Yanking the skirt free, she did a quick full turn and sailed off.

'Those wretched geriatrics are back,' she hissed as she passed Kate and Garry, 'almost had my skirt off.'

Garry released Kate's arm so that he could remove his jacket. At the sight of his huge, rippling torso six teenage hearts fell instantly in love.

'Isn't he gorgeous!' whispered a spotty brunette to her friend.

'Your Bill would look a treat in that,' said another gravelly voice from the front row as a second male model appeared.

'Go on, I double-dare you to ask for his number after the show.'

'You ask him!'

'Ooh, Dot, look! Bill's favourite colour an' all. Bet it must be ever so expensive.'

Cathy, peering through the backdrop, noticed that Caroline was coming off too soon. She checked her stop watch. How irritating! Now the music would be mucked up.

'Coming to tea after the show?' a strawberry blonde asked an exquisite beanpole wrestling with a catsuit.

'Can't. I'm seeing Keith tonight and have to lose ten pounds by eight thirty.' She grabbed a baseball cap and some pink sunglasses from her chair then raced over to Cathy.

'You're wearing the wrong shoes!' shrieked her dresser. 'Those ones don't fit.'

'Come on, love, it's only for a couple of minutes.'

'That's what they all say,' grumbled the model, whose feet, after years of wearing ill-fitting shoes, were covered in bunions.

'Love this album,' said Garry, coming off and casually throwing his jacket at his dresser. 'Any chance of getting a copy, Cath?'

'Possibly, if you stop trying to corrupt my models. You're getting yourself a reputation.' Garry smirked. 'Get your skates on, this is a quick change for you.'

Cathy could see Kate posing at the top of the runway,

185

which meant she was about to come off. 'Jane!' she hissed, 'I need you now! Oh, never mind the gloves. You can carry them. Just get on!'

Dragging the beanpole away from the mirror, Cathy straightened her collar and shoved her on stage.

'Shit!' the model muttered, stumbling through the backstage gloom, 'Should be modelling bruises not sportswear.'

After the last show Kate and Caroline grumbled about the hassle of living in London over tea. Kate, afflicted by dreadful pre-menstrual tension, ordered scones with clotted cream, while Caroline, who ended up eating most of them, admitted problems with her boyfriend who was storing a stolen Saab in her garage. Kate urged her to give him an ultimatum to move the car out or move himself out.

As they left the coffee shop someone yelled her name and Kate looked round to see Julian Kainz loping towards her. She hadn't remembered his hair being that blond and he'd grown a goatee. For once his Dutch roots showed through.

'How's my very favourite redhead?' Julian's teeth gleamed brilliant white against the beard. He kissed her on the mouth.

'I thought I'd left you in the arms of the adoring French public?' said Kate, pleased.

'Yes, but it wasn't the same without you.' Another grin. 'The Beeb's roped me into doing a couple of chat shows, so I'm in town until the end of the week. I'm plugging the new film on Wogan tonight, then I'm going to a post-production party at the director's house. Why don't you come with me?'

'You're forgetting your wife and I don't exactly get on.'

Julian scooped her arm into his. 'Ah, but we do, and tonight, angel, I'm footloose and fancy free.' Kate laughed and introduced a blushing Caroline. She was a terrific fan and was making it obvious by staring at Julian. If only I'd worn my new pretty River Island dress and not been caught in this dreary track suit, she thought crossly, he might have suggested I came along too.

'So, Kate, how about it? There'll be loads of celebs and you'll like the director. You never know, he might give you a part in his next film.'

'Why not?' She'd only spend the evening at home moping about Roe.

Jotting down her address he said, 'I'll pick you up at nine pronto. Bye, beautiful. Oh, and nice meeting you,' he said as an after-thought to Caroline.

Julian drove along the Brompton Road with the roof down. The warm evening air smelt sweet, and stars dotted across the sky blazed like sparklers. Kate had spent most of the day hoping for a message from Roe. By eight she told herself he just wasn't missing her. So when, just before nine, the phone did ring, Kate was thrown into such a panic she switched on the answer machine and listened greedily to his message. She replayed it three times before retreating to the bedroom. Should she call him back? In the end she decided to wait. Julian might arrive at any moment and it would do Roe good to wonder what she was up to for a change.

'What's this man Davenport like?'

Not that she was really interested, but it was less of an effort to let Julian do the talking. Kate studied his blond profile as he pushed in the cigarette lighter. His long curls had been slicked back with a thick suede scrunchy and he wore tight black jeans.

'You'll like him. Skander went into television as a young nobody and made it big overnight. Directs commercials mostly, but bloody good and can pick hits. Now he's making films. Family's loaded so I guess he can finance his own ideas.' Julian paused as the lighter snapped out of its case and brought it up to his cigarette. Smoke curled in the car and Kate unwound her window. 'He works hard, plays hard. Never known a guy to pick up so many women with such ease.'

'He sounds exhausting,' Kate said, her green eyes narrowing to thin slits in the light of an oncoming car.

Having spent the last two nights in front of the box, Kate was determined to enjoy herself and had gone to some lengths over her appearance. And from the approving looks she'd been receiving from Julian, the emerald-green body and short, clinging black skirt were a success. But she was

187

concerned about her rapidly swelling stomach. Kate's hands rested on it as if to conceal it. That was the trouble with PMT, she reflected moodily, no sense of timing. Not only water retention (she hoped), you spent your whole time thinking about food and when you weren't thinking about it, you were eating it.

'Is he a close friend?'

'Skander? Not close exactly. I only worked with him for three months, but Natalie adores him.'

Hardly a recommendation, Kate mused, adjusting the back of her seat.

The car pulled up in front of a terrace of large, newly done-up Victorian houses off Kensington Church Street. Skander Davenport's was the end one. Engraved on a plaque above the navy-blue door was 'Woollahra'. A young woman with a glorious mane of silver-blonde hair and a body to rival Linda Evangelista's opened the door. Oh. Suddenly nervous, Kate sucked in her stomach and forced a five-star smile.

'Hello there,' the woman said, flashing Julian a toothy grin. 'Everyone's upstairs, come on up. Sorry about the mess. We've had people staying so it's all a bit chaotic.'

They followed the rampant noise and smoke to the first-floor landing, where guests had moved from the living-room to get some space. The party was well under way and Kate spotted several well-known faces. Immediately, a thick-set man with straggling blond hair waved at them. He outdid all the men in height.

'Julian!' he shouted over the din, raising one hand holding a cigarette in acknowledgement. 'Brilliant of you to make it!' He fought his way through the crowd as they entered the room, glancing curiously at Kate. 'Caught the last ten minutes of Wogan. Nice combination of plugging and laughs. Natalie isn't with you?'

Kate thought that was pretty obvious.

'She sent her love and apologies but got bogged down with work – she's joining me at the end of the week. So instead I've brought along the girl I told you about on the phone. Skander, this is Kate. Isn't she gorgeous?'

Kate wasn't feeling at all gorgeous. 'Like all actors, Julian tends to exaggerate,' she half-apologised to her host.

'Oh, I don't know. Just this once I'm inclined to agree with him. How do you two know one another?'

'Skiing in Val d'Isère,' said Kate. 'My first time and I completely let the side down. Next time I'll stick to tobogganing.'

Skander grinned. Under the bold gaze of his blue eyes Kate wished she'd worn something a little less revealing. His voice was deep and sounded English, but there was a hint of something else. She couldn't quite place it.

'Kate spends half her time gracing billboards or swanning off to Palm Springs to sell fur coats,' Julian explained. 'She's just signed up as the new face for Vaubelle. And don't believe a word about the skiing. She was flying down pistes on her first day.'

'Then you should have been awarded the Nobel Piste Prize for bravery. I never did get the hang of skis. Don't suppose you can cook as well?' he added hopefully. 'My housekeeper's got the flu.'

'Perhaps you overwork her?' said Kate drily, not sure if she was being teased. Skander laughed and took her arm.

'Come and grab a drink before these scavengers completely demolish the bar.'

Kate inspected the bright, crowded room. It was decorated with huge, rich Kilims, abstract paintings on bright-yellow walls and scattered oriental cushions. There were no curtains but the view was so pretty it didn't seem to matter. Plants, leaning towards the window, looked in need of attention. Some of the leaves were beginning to go brown. Shelves sagged under rows of well-used books; a strange assortment, she could see, of novels and film scripts. Under the window, ignoring the noise, an Irish terrier lay snoring on a shabby sofa. None of the furniture matched but the house had a chaotic charm about it. To the right of the room, through a door left slightly ajar, the Linda Evangelista blonde was on the phone. She was leaning against a large desk piled with books, papers and an Apple computer. Above her head was a shelf layered with rows of marked video tapes. Peering in, Kate recognised some of the commercials. Well, he was obviously very successful. On the wall was a large pinboard covered with postcards from exotic places, scribbled notes and photos of two large giggling baby boys in various stages of undress.

'Not mine,' said Skander, following her gaze. 'The twins belong to my sister and that's Liz, my PA. Keeps my chaos under control and makes wonderful coffee.'

'A useful qualification,' said Kate as he handed her an enormous drink. 'Could I just have a mineral water?'

'Have anything you like. Julian can have yours.' Julian, anxious to promote himself, looked ready to bolt. 'Liz, love, where did you put the Perrier?'

'Try the balcony.'

'We're not completely barking,' Skander explained. 'The fridge has just packed up and there was nowhere else to put it.'

'Back in a sec,' Julian squeezed her arm as he prepared to slip away. 'Keep an eye on her for me, Skander, she's rather special.'

'Are you pleased with your film?' she asked politely a few minutes later when the Perrier, having been finally tracked to the bath, was served up with a dubious-looking piece of lime. She glanced at a bronze trophy of a racing car engraved with the words 'Hans Decker, Silverstone 1962'.

'You know what this business is like.' He shrugged light-heartedly and stubbed out his cigarette. 'No director's ever really satisfied and I'm still learning. Still, it's getting good ratings. Julian's certainly made an impact.'

He waved to a departing guest who looked suspiciously like Tony Slattery.

'Yes. His picture's plastered all over Paris.'

It *was* Tony Slattery. A telephone shrilled in the background.

'Are you married?' Now where did that come from? 'The ring,' Skander gestured towards her engagement finger. She'd forgotten to swap it back to her other hand.

'Oh, that's to ward off lechers,' said Kate unthinkingly, then at once realised how rude that must have sounded. She glanced quickly at Skander, but he was wearing one of the quirky, lopsided smiles she was already beginning to associate with him. Grabbing a plate of thick, smoked salmon sandwiches, he offered her one. Kate declined and waited for the inevitable remark about saving her figure. It didn't come. Skander helped himself to three.

'Skander!' a voice shrieked. 'I've got Sue from Taurus on the phone. She's calling from the States and wants to know if you'll shoot Schkolind for them next week?'

'No, I bloody well won't!' he growled, making no attempt to lower his voice, 'I'm snowed under and I've already told Sue I'm not doing any more beer commercials, not after the last talent drank his way through a week's supply and wrecked the set. That set us back ten grand.' He winked at Kate, pushing back an unruly strand of blond hair.

'Wasn't that a slight exaggeration?' said Kate.

Skander smiled. 'A bit, but it's a lousy product and I do try to keep some integrity – hard to do when the whole advertising industry is based on lies. To me the biggest sin in life is wasting time, and I see too much of that going on around me. One good thing about getting older is that you sort out your priorities. You reach out and grab the things you might have let pass before.'

Kate, preoccupied by her nagging uterus, was only half-listening. 'Like what?' she said, scrunching up her face in pain.

He smiled. 'Maybe I shouldn't answer that, Kate. I don't know you well enough.'

'Eats, anyone?' Liz, armed with a bowl of Twiglets, was doing the rounds. Even though she was starving Kate declined, conscious of her bloated stomach.

'We're about to run out of booze, Skander. Nick's offered to go out and replenish the stock.'

'Thanks, love. Use the petty cash.'

They both watched Liz glide off.

'So Kate, what's lured you away from the Paris catwalk?'

'I needed a break. My London agent had some work lined up so I accepted.'

'Are you escaping from a man?' He gave her a penetrating look.

'No.' It was said too quickly.

There was an awkward pause. Skander wondered why such a gorgeous woman had nails bitten down to the quick. Her concentration was wandering as if she had something on her mind, and when at last she bothered to look at him, her expression was faintly hostile. Definitely the uptight sort. She was fumbling for something in her bag and had pulled out a tiny silver object that looked like a snuff-box. Her amazing hair reminded him of crisp autumn mornings and a distant college romance. He caught a faint whiff of her sweet, almondy perfume but couldn't identify it. She turned her head slightly and slipped something into her mouth – was she on drugs? He'd seen that slightly haughty, don't-touch look on a lot of models. It invariably stemmed from insecurity, and it usually bored him rigid. But he read intelligence in Kate's face and suppressed sensuality in her movements. Something about the carefully veiled eyes made him want to behave rashly, make her react. Instead he raised his glass to his mouth and drained the contents.

'What does the Woollahra sign over your front door mean?'

'It's a suburb of east Sydney where I went to school.' That would explain the accent. 'Have you ever been to Australia?'

'No, but friends of mine rave about it.'

'My parents have a stud farm in the north. I get out there three or four times a year, more when I have the time. Fantastic place. Out there I stop thinking about the grottiness and expense of London and I don't smoke half as much, which is another good reason for getting away.'

'My girlfriend used to say the same about smoking. She gave up recently because she couldn't afford it but now spends twice as much on chocolate.'

Skander laughed and patted his thickening waistline. 'I know the feeling.'

'Oh, don't get me wrong,' said Kate, quick to defend her friend, 'Bea's as thin as a rake and glorious-looking. She's lucky like that. Have you ever tried to give up?'

'Countless times. I even tried hypnosis, but I'm so foul to everyone it never lasts.' He removed a box of Camel cigarettes from his trouser pocket and offered her one. 'I take it you don't?'

'No thanks.'

'Don't smoke, don't drink. What else don't you do, Kate?' He struck a match, his startling blue eyes igniting at the same time. Their expression was ironic.

A vision in gold organza wearing half a bottle of Giorgio descended on them. The voluptuous female wrapped herself around Skander, a frail wing of organza floating across his face.

'Dar-ling!' she shrieked, marking his cheek with orange frosted lipstick. 'I've been trying to pin you down all evening.'

She was certainly doing a good job now, clinging to his neck like a stubborn vine.

'Sorry,' the woman said, not looking sorry at all. In fact the look she sent Kate was decidedly cool. 'But I'm going to steal him away for one teeny sec. Skander, I want you to meet an actor friend. He's frighteningly good. Bill's thinking of using him for the new Channel Four series. I'll bring him right back.'

The brunette tucked a golden arm firmly into Skander's and whisked him off.

'Won't be long,' Skander mouthed before disappearing into a crowd of people.

Kate nodded half-heartedly, then searched the room in vain for Julian's blond ponytail. Not exactly your run-of-the-mill director. All that stuff about the advertising industry being based on a pack of lies. Weren't most things? The American presidential elections had stirred up enough scandal to keep Danielle Steel in business for the next twenty years. Kate's smile strained along with her stomach. She was getting tired of sucking it in. Hopefully the two Feminax she'd just taken would start working their magic soon. And some-one should tell Skander not to stare. It was rude and disconcerting. Strange man.

Someone changed the tape and put on Van Morrison. Abandoning her drink on a shelf, Kate studied a collection of mounted photos, mostly of actors thanking Skander with flashy, illegible signatures. She spotted him in one of them looking very young. He was sitting behind a ravishing blonde girl with his arms locked around her shoulders. Kate studied the photo more closely. He looked a good two stone lighter.

The room was full of smoke. Someone laughed and Kate's eye caught a young couple fooling around on a large armchair. She felt a sudden wave of Roe-sickness. Why am I here, choking in this foul cigarette smoke from people I don't even know? She thought of leaving but the prospect of going home to Justin's empty flat alone was too depressing for words. She caught Skander's eye, now trapped between two blondes. He shruggged apologetically. Kate's eyes focused on the telephone. How she itched to call Roe. But what if he wasn't there? What if Joelle or some other woman picked up the phone? Was she being irrational? Hormones betraying her? Where was Bea when she needed her? She missed those safe, warm hours with her friend, snuggling up under the duvet after a hard day while they pondered over her deceptive self-confidence, Sophie's ability to reduce her to tears, laughed about Bea's latest conquest, worried about the rise in rent, the drop in work. They dissected all their problems through amicable arguments and careful support, and Kate always went to bed feeling better about the world, as if she had expressed herself and been fully understood.

Julian was pushing his way through the crowd towards her.

'Darling one! Sorry I abandoned you for so long but I might just have landed myself four weeks' work. I s'pose Skander made a play for you? Never could resist a pretty face. You haven't gone and fallen for him?'

'Julian, let's go somewhere we can be a little more private.'

'Now I like the sound of that!'

Together they made their way to the landing and slipped through a door on the right. They found themselves in what was obviously the master bedroom. It smelt male – musky with traces of cigar smoke. There was a television on a chest of drawers, two bedroom chairs, and a small table with several paperbacks piled on top, but the huge bed dominated the room. From the open window came a smell of fresh rain and cut grass.

'*There's a dream where the contents are visible. Where the poetic champions compose,*' sang Van Morrison. '*Will you breathe not a word of this secrecy, and will you be my special rose?*'

'I need a hug.' Thinking of Roe, Kate slid into the warm, dark comfort of Julian's arms. He murmured something into her hair, then kissed her firmly on the mouth. He smelt soapy, his beard was unexpectedly soft and she could taste the mixture of nicotine and red wine on his breath. Kate snuggled against him and, encouraged, Julian pushed his tongue further into her mouth.

'Christ, Katie, you must know how I feel about you?'

'I'm certainly feeling you now.' The almond-shaped eyes widened seductively.

'I'd like to peel all your clothes off right now and ruffle you up on that absurd bed.'

A slight giggle. 'It is very absurd.'

'Come on, Kate. Are we going to keep on having dress rehearsals or shall we make this a first night?'

He was trying to find a way of undoing her top but wasn't having much luck.

'Julian, we can't! You have a wife.'

'Yes, but absolutely no principles. Kate, you're driving me crazy.'

Julian was now tackling the buttons of her skirt. She could feel his cock pressing against her stomach. He wants me, she thought, panicking, he really wants me.

'We'll only regret it afterwards.'

She tried breaking away but Julian had her trapped.

'I'm willing to take my chance.'

'Don't you think you're a bit old to be rehearsing Romeo and Juliet?' said a deep voice from the door.

They spun round, appalled to find Skander towering in the doorway. By his side was the Irish terrier last seen snoring on the living-room sofa. How much of the conversation had he overheard?

'Kate's got the most frightful headache, haven't you, love? Thought being away from the noise would help.'

Julian had switched with remarkable ease to the role of

concerned chaperon. It was unfortunate that he was wearing most of Kate's lipstick.

'Then we'd better get her some aspirin. The bathroom's next door.'

Feeling like a naughty schoolgirl who'd been caught in the wrong dormitory after lights out, Kate meekly followed him into the hall.

A woman emerged from the bathroom and smiled at Skander as she slipped past. He began rummaging through a cupboard under the sink until he found a packet of Anadin. Kate noticed for the first time what huge hands he had.

'Here,' he said handing them to her. 'You'd better take two.'

She didn't want any but there wasn't much else she could do. He was so big and tall standing there in the enclosed space of the loo. He looked quite capable of forcing them down her throat. So she obediently took the pills and swallowed them, sucking tap water from her cupped hand. The water left a nasty taste of chlorine in her mouth and she began to repair her face hoping he'd get bored and leave.

For a moment he stood watching her in the mirror then he said, 'You can tell me it's none of my business but you'll only get your fingers burnt mucking around with married men.'

'I'm not mucking around with anyone married. Julian's just a friend.'

Skander raised an eyebrow. 'Do you treat all your friends so affectionately?'

She put down her lipstick and gave him a cool look. 'I need to use the loo. Are you going to watch me do that too?'

He shrugged, putting a hand on the door. 'No, I'll leave you in peace, but take some well-meant advice, Kate. Julian uses girls like you to feed his ego.'

'What makes you such an expert?'

'I know the type.'

Julian stuck his head around the door. 'It's bloody rude leaving so early,' he said lightly, 'but I should take Kate home.'

Downstairs a late arrival with fine bones and skin the colour of peanut butter was talking to Liz. From the understated way she was dressed, Kate could tell she was a model.

'Vickie! What a nice surprise,' Skander warmly embraced her. 'Let me just show some friends to the door then I'll get you a drink.' He turned to Julian, 'I'll be abroad for two weeks from Monday. Why not bring Natalie round for a drink on Saturday?'

'I'll do that! Thanks again, mate.'

The door shut behind them with a thud and Kate shuddered, suddenly chilled. She was glad to see the last of him!

'You all right?' Julian put his arm round her.

'Fine. But I don't think much of your director friend.'

'Probably gave you a hard time about Nat. They go back a long way and he sometimes gets a little over-protective.'

'Suffocating, more like. How can you bear to work with him?'

'Don't be catty. It doesn't suit you. Skander's a good bloke. You know where you are with him.' Julian opened her side of the car then climbed into the driver's seat. 'By the way, I meant to ask, are you still seeing Roe?'

'Yes.' But she didn't want to talk about it.

'Just wondered if some of the American gloss had worn off? Roe's a good mate but the man lives entirely for his work. You need someone who really knows how to appreciate a beautiful woman.'

She suddenly realised that half her attraction was that she belonged to another man. Why was it that men were so turned on by rivalry, pinching a friend's girl just to prove they could? She had no illusions about herself, perhaps she was just another conquest. But, honestly, if anyone's gloss was wearing thin it was Julian's.

'Julian, I'm sorry to be such a wimp but I'm really bushed. All I want to do is flop into bed.'

'Sure you don't want to flop into mine? I even changed the sheets.'

'I bet you did! The answer's still no. So are you going to see me safely home or watch me get murdered?'

He grinned. 'OK. I'll be nice but not without a goodnight kiss.'

Conciliatorily she turned her face up to his and felt him seal his lips against hers. His mouth tasted stale and held none of its earlier promise. Repulsed, she tried to push him off.

'What's the matter? You liked me kissing you earlier.'

'Sorry. I'm just not in the mood.'

Suddenly Julian's wet lips and tongue were thrusting against her mouth and clenched teeth, his hands urgently kneading her breasts, which were swollen and sensitive.

'Julian . . . don't!'

But he seemed out of control. She jerked her head violently away, pushing against his chest. In the ensuing struggle she must have whacked his nose with her chin because he let her go suddenly, clutching his nose in his hands. When he looked up at her his expression was so furious Kate became frightened. Grappling with the car door all fingers and thumbs, her heart pounding because she was afraid he'd try and stop her, Kate somehow got it to open. She was out in a flash. She took off down the street at full speed, rubbing her mouth with the back of her hand. She glanced back nervously to see if Julian was following her and caught Skander, showing someone out, watching from the front door. Go on then, gloat, you sanctimonious pig! All the same an unease gripped her as she vanished into the gloom.

The alarm was set for seven, but when Roe called sunlight was pouring through the curtains. Kate hauled herself upright, thick with sleep.

'Did I wake you?' Roe sounded bright and energetic.

'I had to get up. What time is it?'

'About nine your end.'

She glanced at a series of scribbled bits of paper next to the bed. Failing to find a free taxi after her near miss with Julian, she had walked through the deserted Holland Park neighbourhood and started composing a poem in her head. At the flat she scribbled it down on the back of an envelope, unaware of time, then, as it developed, swapped the envelope for an A4 pad. It wasn't until three, and a sixth draft, that she had finally got to bed.

Stifling a yawn she said, 'How are you surviving without me?'

'Guess you didn't catch the news. They had a nasty tremor in LA last night, registered seven on the Richter. The site I've been working on with Carl collapsed.'

She was instantly awake. 'God, that's awful! Was anyone hurt?'

'A couple of our guys are in intensive, but they'll pull through. Bad news for Carl though. It was one of his biggest investments. Thank Christ for the insurance. It could have cost him millions!'

'Will the insurance company take long to settle?'

'Don't they always? Look, it's too complicated to explain on the phone, baby, but it's the kind of problem I can do without.'

'I'm so sorry. I suppose you'll be flying out to help?'

'Not until Tuesday. I've got meetings coming out of my ears this end. Hang on, baby, one sec.' Kate could hear mumbling in the background as Roe put his hand over the receiver. She imagined him in his masculine fifth-floor office, effortlessly dealing with international faxes and documents flooding his desk. Roe's voice came back,

'I called you last night. Did you get my message?'

'Yes. I was out. Thought it a bit late to call back.' Why was it with Roe she could never come right out and say what she meant, ask for what she wanted?

'Sounds like you made a night of it. When does your flight get in?'

So he wasn't going to ask where she'd been.

'Eight thirty.'

'I should be done by seven. I'll pick you up.'

That was a good sign. The bedside clock was flashing angrily at her. 'Roe, darling, I should go. I'm late.'

'Busy day?'

'Errands, then lunch with my mother. Can't say I'm looking forward to it.'

'That bad?'

'Don't ask.'

'While I remember, Leo Schofield's having a dinner party on Wednesday. He's flying a few of us up to Deauville in his chopper so keep it free, will you? Hang on.' Again muffled background sounds, then Roe's voice came back.

'Baby, I've got to take this call. I'll see you tonight.'

The faint click of the phone echoed down the line. Why was it he was always the one to end the conversation?

She spent the rest of the morning catching up. Mrs Tate came up for a chat, bearing tea and assorted biscuits. While Kate packed Mrs Tate sat on the bed with Lottie, an overweight tabby, grumbling about the flies in her kitchen and the price of cat food. Luckily she was so busy talking and eating all the biscuits, she hardly noticed Kate's preoccupied gaze.

Promising to keep in touch, Kate left a bunch of freesias and a hastily scribbled thank-you card for Justin. With her poem, which she felt enormously pleased with, safely in her bag, she left, clutching a list as long as her arm, consisting mostly of things Bea had asked her to get from Boots, and a rented video to be dropped off.

Sophie's house in Onslow Gardens, a generous pay-off from her second husband, was formal, with stiff, brocaded curtains and expensive furniture that said 'please do not touch'. Sophie had shared it with a concert pianist for six years and showed every sign of finally staying put. There was a lot to be said for Derek who, ten years Sophie's junior, showed remarkable maturity and was heralded as a young genius. Sophie, wildly in love, had at last settled down and was taking an active role in her lover's career.

Maria, the maid, who lived in the basement, opened the door to Kate and burst into a fluent stream of Spanish. Ruskin joined in the frenzy, frantically barking and jumping up and down like a yoyo.

'Oh, and I've missed you too!' Kate nuzzled the excited spaniel affectionately.

Sophie emerged. Smelling faintly of Madame Rochas, she kissed her daughter lightly on both cheeks. She snapped at Ruskin to get down and disappeared back into the kitchen.

'Come on through, darling. Fay stopped by for coffee and we lost track of the time, so I'm a bit behind with lunch. Can you do with a sandwich?' she said, her voice sounding soft and musical. She's lost weight, Kate thought, inspecting her mother's neat slender form, but then Sophie had always been thin. A tray holding used coffee cups and some half-eaten biscuits was on a walnut table near the French windows. A favourite old armchair had been re-upholstered in an expensive-looking chintz. Kate preferred it the old way.

'What's the occasion?' Kate asked, spotting a basket of glossy green gooseberries and a bowl of home-made custard.

'Dinner for some of Derek's business friends. Usual last-minute because I had absolutely no warning. But I think the panic's now over. You look tired, darling,' Sophie said looking properly at her daughter for the first time. 'Working too hard, I suppose?'

Sophie, on the other hand, looked wonderful. She always did. She was wearing navy culottes and a white, short-sleeved jacket with shoulder pads. Her hair had been cut fashionably short, like an early Audrey Hepburn, framing her oval-shaped face. It was still a rich, dark brown and made her grass-green eyes look huge. There were a few new lines around the eyes and mouth, but she still looked much younger than her forty-eight years.

'You've cut your hair. Makes you look years younger.'

Sophie looked pleased. 'It was Derek's idea. I got it done by a chap in Walton Street.'

'Grantly's?'

'How did you know?'

'I've worked with them on loads of shoots.'

'Now what's this I hear about Vaubelle bringing in a new designer? She seems very young to be taking on such a responsible job.'

'She may be young but she's really good. I think Rachel's going to make quite a name for herself on the Paris runway.'

'Shopping in Paris.' Sophie's looked suddenly wistful. 'I'm desperately bored with London fashion. All those ugly plat-form shoes and short pleated skirts.' Sophie glanced suspiciously at Kate's floral dress. 'That looks like silk. How much did that set you back?'

'Seventy pounds,' lied Kate, who had paid a hundred and sixty for it. 'Do you like it?'

'They must be paying you well. Oh, careful, darling! Don't

sit on the table, it's too delicate. Use one of the chairs.'

That was another thing about Sophie. She had always managed to make Kate feel like a clumsy, overweight teenager. She slithered off the table and on to a chair. Ruskin settled himself on the floor with his hind legs splayed out on either side.

'I wrote something last night.'

'Mmm?' Sophie was carefully measuring coffee beans into the grinder.

'Can I read it? It's only short.'

'Show it to me after lunch.' The grinder screamed into action. 'I think that's everything. We just need some coffee cups. They're on your left in the grey cupboard.'

While Kate got them down Sophie removed the cellophane from two Marks and Spencer sandwiches and placed them neatly on white china plates.

'I got a selection. You're not dieting or anything silly, are you?'

Kate shook her head, patting Ruskin. One of the sandwiches was ham and pickle. No point in saying anything. Kate had given up reminding Sophie she was a vegetarian. 'How are things with Derek?'

'Wonderful. I just wish he didn't have to travel so much. I miss him. He'a always off giving charity performances instead of making money, and the more he takes on, the more he's offered. Still, I'm hoping the new house in France will keep me busy.'

'I didn't even know you'd bought a place,' Kate said in surprise.

'Oh, darling, I'm sure I told you. All the rooms need to be furnished, which suits me of course. You know how I like browsing in antique shops. On a more serious note, George has been playing up again. Apparently he walked into some-one's room in the middle of the night and started yelling orders. The poor old thing keeled over and died. Sister told me he's started hearing voices again. Thinks there are bugs under the carpet in his room. He refuses to sleep in it. Thinks they'll give away trade secrets to the enemy!'

Kate giggled. She adored her grandfather but he was

certainly difficult. He made a point of stirring up the staff.

Sophie opened the fridge and removed some milk. 'Do you want your milk heated?' Kate shook her head. 'I mean, I do love George but he can be exasperating. He forgets that his wife has been dead for twelve years, that I'm in my forties with a grown-up daughter and that he no longer has a job.'

'It'll probably happen to us all.'

Sophie looked appalled. 'Over my dead body. He's going to have to start behaving or the home will throw him out. Goodness knows where we'd find somewhere for him if that happened.'

'Couldn't he come and live with you? Maria wouldn't mind helping.'

'It's all very well saying that, but you haven't had to deal with it all. It's out of the question having him here. He wets the bed, can't hold a knife and fork, he can't even make it up the stairs. We'd need a full-time nurse and a chairlift. I've had to go up to the home twice in the last week to see him. Sister's been awfully good about the whole thing, but I do find it most embarrassing.'

'Derek's got stacks of money.'

'Out of the question. Besides, now we're thinking of spending the summers in France.'

Sophie hated the country! Helping herself to a sandwich, Kate studied her mother's *retroussé* nose while Sophie flicked an invisible piece of dust from her trouser leg.

After a few minutes Kate said, 'Then what about Aunt Rose?'

'It wouldn't work. They live too far from the city and Robert can't afford it. So like you, Katherine, to shirk your responsibilities for months then come back and try rearranging everything. You can be just like your father.'

There was an uncomfortable pause. Kate knew her father, during the short time he'd been around, had been neglectful and unloving but she didn't want to be reminded of it the whole time. Sophie hadn't exactly been Mother Earth herself. Sometimes Kate felt her childhood was a terrible wound which had never really healed.

'Derek and I had a talk about you last night. We think it's time you settled down.'

We? Kate thought, feeling herself grow brittle and suspicious.

'I mean, you're not getting any younger. I'd been married for three years at your age.'

And you've been divorced twice, thought Kate bitterly.

'I just think you should think about what you're going to do. The modelling won't last for ever, darling. Have you got a man?'

'Yes. An American. You'd like him, Sophie.'

'Well, I hope he's an improvement on the last one. I thought he was a very casual young man. He practically lived off you. He was going to whisk you off on some wonderful holiday then just disappeared without so much as a call.' Sophie conveniently forgot her own abortive pass at the twenty-two-year-old. 'What does this one do?'

Kate couldn't help boasting. 'He's Vaubelle's managing director.'

Her mother considered. 'Not very professional of him to mix business with pleasure, surely? I thought that sort of thing was against the rules?'

Kate's pride was dampened. 'We're very discreet.'

'At least he's got money. That's something in his favour. Just be careful. I don't want to see you get hurt again. You keep letting men walk all over you. Be tougher with them, darling. Have you given any thought to what you might do when you stop?'

'No, but at least I'll be in a financially secure enough position to choose.' Kate took a bite of her sandwich.

'Derek thinks you should move back to England, settle down a bit.'

Why was it the conversation always turned to Derek? Kate looked at her mother delicately chewing her crust and suddenly felt an enormous weight. Why couldn't it be easy between them, just for once. She already regretted the visit and having mentioned the poem she'd written, because it made her feel childish and demanding. She wouldn't stay long. Another half an hour, that's all. Mind you, nothing felt less appealing than the prospect of having to get herself to sterile, glaring Heathrow. Thank God Roe had said he'd meet her the other end.

Ruskin, deciding he wasn't getting enough attention, leapt up suddenly and gave chase to an annoying bluebottle buzzing round the kitchen. Jaws snapping against the air, he knocked over the coffee tray which sent everything crashing to the floor. Squealing like a piglet, he fled from the room.

After Kate had gone, the unread poem still in her bag, Sophie stacked the washing-up machine and fed Ruskin, who'd been spanked and was now trailing her with martyred eyes. Sophie meandered around the drawing-room, checking for dust on the furniture. Everything had to be perfect for tonight, she decided, reminding herself to iron the Whistles skirt. Derek's friends were in for a treat: baked salmon, avocado and walnut salad and warm brioches. She found a pile of soot under the rug by the fire. Lazy Maria had obviously hoovered around it. Really, that girl had her head in the clouds half the time. Too many Mills and Boons. Pausing by a grand piano which was covered in silver-framed photographs, Sophie picked up one of herself in a pretty duck-blue silk dress, taken almost twenty years ago. She'd been wearing it the day René had proposed to her. What had happened to it? Surely she hadn't given it away? She thought of the pretty dress Kate had been wearing today, of her high-powered American and of the glamorous life she now had in Paris.

Across the bright, sunlit room, Sophie caught her reflection in the huge seventeenth-century mirror and thought, when did I start growing old?

The following Thursday, having spent most of last week's American trip fighting lawyers, Roe had worked off his stress at the gym. Unfortunately he'd pulled a back muscle and had been forced to take a couple of days off from work. Now, soaking in his swimming-pool-size bath, he had fallen into a punishing silence. Tactfully Kate had retreated to the bedroom and was lying crosswise on their bed reading a novel.

Roe took a call from Nicole on the mobile phone. It was

supposed to have been her day off, but since Roe had given Nicole a salary rise and organised a part-time housekeeper to help with her children, she had happily taken on the extra work.

Hanging up, Roe placed a call to Carl in Los Angeles, then to Leo Schofield in London.

'Kat!' he yelled, when he'd finished.

She walked into the bathroom wearing sludgy-green silk pyjamas. 'What's the matter?'

Using a plastic clip she tied back her washed hair and sat on the loo.

'I'm trying to reschedule a loan with the banks but they're making it so fucking tough. Can you believe it! I put forward a proposal that could make these guys rich and all I get is talk about the loopholes they've found – nothing but negativity! That's the trouble with the French. They're just not willing to take risks.' He ran a weary hand through his wet hair. 'Look, I'm really sorry, baby, but I've got to chair a meeting at one. And I'm going to have to spend most of tomorrow on the phone.'

Kate tried not to look too disappointed. They had planned to spend the day looking for things to furnish Roe's flat. She'd been on at him about it for ages but, apart from the addition of her own things, nothing had altered. Kate found the starkness unsettling.

'If you must, you must. How's your back?'

'Still twingeing but that oil you used really helped. I might get you to put some more on. Oh, by the way, Nicole's stopping by with some documents I need for this meeting.'

'Then I'll go and change.' Kate bent over her knees to inspect a toe. Her pyjama top fell open revealing a full white breast.

'I like you the way you are,' said Roe, suddenly horny. 'Come and join me in the tub.'

'But you just said Nicole's on her way.'

'Yeah, but she won't get here for a good half-hour and I can't think of a better way to spend the time. Get your little butt over here.'

She was worried about his back. 'I've just dried my hair.'

'So live dangerously.'

The next minute Roe leaped out of the bath in a great soapy wave, splashing water everywhere and lunged towards Kate. Squealing with pleasure, Kate fled to the bedroom before he caught up with her and pulled her to the ground.

'Ouch! Darling, careful,' she laughed, landing heavily on her shoulder, 'I'm soaking wet!'

'Wet and hot,' Roe muttered, pushing his index finger roughly inside her. 'You smell of sex. Christ, I've never wanted a woman as much as you!'

And suddenly the giggles evaporated. Kate opened her lips to meet with his blinding, unashamed love. 'Oh, Roe!'

He came very quickly. Mounting her like a horse, legs pushed impatiently to the side, he entered her with fast short stabs, his head buried against Kate's neck. Afterwards they lay on the bedroom floor, sweaty and breathing deeply. The curtains puffed out from the light breeze and she could hear the occasional passing car, the low roar of engines sounding like waves landing on the shore. It was almost warm enough not to bother with clothes. Kate made leisurely circles with a finger along his hairy chest, taking advantage of his five-minute slumber to study him. She was careful not to make any sudden moves even though the circulation in her left arm which Roe's head rested on had gone to sleep. Roe's shrivelled penis twitched as her free hand reached his groin. She longed to make love again. But Roe caught her wrists and held them, the curious honey eyes now green, blinking.

'Hold that thought.'

Disappointment. 'Why?'

'Because you deserve more than a quick screw and that's all I've got time for. Look, why don't I take you somewhere special tonight?'

'Promise?' she stroked his forehead. 'Just the two of us?'

Roe frowned. 'Shit. I've got dinner with Gary Mart.'

'Can't you cancel it?' She kissed the side of his neck, then began to nibble his earlobe.

'I would, baby, but he's flying back to New York in the morning. We'll do it tomorrow.'

Kate rolled away. 'I won't hold my breath. Another VIP'll

fly into town for twenty-four hours and demand your undivided attention.'

'The only thing I'm going to give my undivided attention to is this great ass of yours.'

'Forget it, matey. You've blown it.'

'Goddam!'

And suddenly they were both smiling. Briefly kissing both her breasts, Roe got up and walked into the bathroom. He washed his penis in the sink.

'Do you really have to go now?' Kate pleaded.

'I must. Got to get this thing with Claude sorted.'

'Can he make trouble?' Kate curled her naked form round a cushion, wishing for some of his cavalier attitude towards sex.

'He's trying to reinstate himself with the company. But he doesn't have a leg to stand on. Our lawyers know what they're doing! Just wish I didn't have that little shit Sebastian breathing down my neck the whole time.'

Roe walked naked to the cupboard and pulled out the ubiquitous black suit. Kate stared moodily at his neat bottom. How nice if, just for once, they could spend the day in bed and talk. Why was it that after every time they made love Roe was compelled to distance himself from her?

Dressed, Roe made another call. Then the doorbell rang. Slipping on a robe, Kate answered it. Nicole, looking immaculate in a recently purchased Anne Klein, was clutching a briefcase. All at once she seemed potentially menacing. Roe replaced the phone in the bedroom and joined them. In his suit he looked every inch the business man, ready to get going.

'Thanks for bringing these round,' he said taking the case from Nicole. 'Don't bother coming back to the office. I'll call you at home if there are any problems.'

'Would you like some coffee?' Kate asked, pulling her dressing-gown closer around her body. Nicole was the only person at Vaubelle who knew about their affair.

Nicole, who'd been up since six and hadn't had time for breakfast, nodded gratefully. 'D'accord.'

'Right. Gotta make a move.' Roe's manner was formal now

208

that Nicole had arrived. Grabbing his keys from the hall desk he kissed Kate lightly on the mouth. 'Call you later.'

Kate moved into the living-room with Nicole, feeling the distance pull between herself and Roe, their intimacy left on the bedroom floor as he briskly closed the door behind him, his mind already elsewhere.

Hugging her arms to her chest, Kate fingered a bruise that was already forming on her shoulder, then, with a deep breath, produced her brightest smile for Nicole and reached for the kettle.

12

Sebastian Vaubelle sat at his desk staring at the blinking cursor on a screen filled with figures. A cigarette burned in the ashtray. What a morning! Some bastard had smashed and broken the side window of his car. Not that he cared about the CDs or the digital pull-out stereo he'd bought only last week. What tormented him was the missing cigarette lighter he'd inherited from his great-grandmother. It bore her silver initials on one side and was his talisman, brought him luck. Used to fiddling with the smooth cold block, he drummed the fingers of his right hand on the desk, brooding over his loss. His eyes paused on a redundancy memo Roe Lewis had sent up earlier that day, and he flicked it irritably away. It seemed as if he was being robbed of everything he cared about. How dare the American dismiss his concerns with such arrogance. He, Sebastian, a Vaubelle and next in line to his father's company. The man's insensitivity was intolerable. No one ordered him around. No one!

Like his father, Sebastian was ambitious and enjoyed reaping the benefits the Vaubelle name gave him. He had felt an immediate loathing towards Roe Lewis, first for the insulting manner in which his father had been dismissed – in the ensuing weeks Sebastian had watched his father age ten years – then he found himself demoted to nominal director. Nominal director! A meaningless title. He might just as well be a cleaner for the shred of responsibility it left him. These days all he did was sit in on board meetings and watch Roe's cronies make a mess of his father's company. His financial talents were being wasted. And now he'd been forced into a meeting which would prevent Claude, once and for all, from ever having access to Vaubelle again.

As a child Sebastian's hair, almost white, had had an obstinate little cowlick. But over the years it had grown darker, like his moods, and now he wore it in a fashionable mousy bob down to his chin and curtaining his face, which was fine-featured like his mother's. The cold, unusual aquamarine eyes belonged to Claude.

The son of France's most respected fashion family, Sebastian had had his choice of an endless supply of pretty girls who walked the Paris runway. Despite rumours which suggested he had a sadistic streak in bed and belittled women, he was always seen escorting the most recent beauty in town. Since he had just celebrated his thirty-first birthday at Maxim's, his adoring mother hoped to see him settle down soon and give her the grandchild she yearned for.

His parents had always thought he would follow in Claude's footsteps, but Sebastian showed none of his father's flair for design. He was, however, brilliant with figures and possessed a quick, logical mind which could solve the most complicated mathematical problems. This was why he was the youngest employee ever to be put in charge of Vaubelle's accounts.

Angrily he picked up a glass of water and gazed at it, tilting the sides so that the clear, heavy liquid climbed to its brim. Sebastian was afraid of the sea. It smelt of death to him. As a young boy his parents had taken him sailing in the Mediterranean. They had been staying on a tiny island midway between Sicily and Malta, and had joined some close friends on their yacht. For three days they had drifted under the deliciously hot, melodic sun, caught fish and watched their skin turn brown. But on the last day John Skittles, Claude's childhood friend, had made a fatal error and ignored a weather forecast warning boats of threatening storms. He would regret the decision for the rest of his life.

They managed to radio for help minutes before the awesome wave hit them. The boat, unable to take the strain, capsized immediately, casting all it's occupants unceremoniously into the sea. Claude somehow grabbed his wife Isabella and kept the two of them afloat by clinging to a small inflated dinghy. John Skittles, a strong swimmer, managed to hang on

212

until help came. But his wife wasn't so lucky. As she was thrown overboard she had hit her head on the bow of the boat. The impact smashed her skull, killing her instantly. Sebastian's blue-white body was found washed up on shore six hours later. Though still breathing, he was rushed to hospital heavily concussed and suffering from shock. The doctors didn't expect him to pull through.

Sometimes when Sebastian was close to the sea he would stand transfixed for hours watching the sunlight splinter like glass on the water's surface. He pictured himself caught up in dark tangles of weed pulling him down into its black hidden depths, afraid that the icy water would embrace and suffocate him. He had never learnt to swim and he carried this fear coiled inside like a twisted piece of string – too ashamed to tell anyone or do anything about it.

Sebastian opened his desk drawer abruptly. From it he removed a small box divided into ten sections. He counted a battery of pills and coloured capsules which he carefully laid out on the table. Then he poured himself some more Badoit, crammed the pills in his mouth and swallowed. Glancing again at Roe's hated memo, he returned the glass to the desk but his hand remained gripped around its edges. Lewis carried all the trump cards. But one day, he thought angrily, his hand tightening, the American would slip up. Lewis was a risk taker. All he had to do was wait his chance. The phone gave a shrill and Sebastian felt a sudden sharp pain. Curiously, he looked down at the broken glass and the thick, clean blood dribbling from his hand.

Upstairs Rachel was in a panic. Some velvet she had needed to complete a design had failed to arrive, and now, because the factory had over-sold, they were unable to meet her order. Still determined to use the half-made dress, she had sent Richard down to the fabric studio in search of a replacement.

Kate stood patiently in front of the mirror wearing a plum chiffon tube yoke, designed to be fitted to a top dress in the missing velvet. Colette, kneeling on the floor, was altering the hemline.

Richard, recovering from a thumping hangover, returned carrying several rolls. 'I found some silk taffeta I think you might like,' he said, dropping the rolls to the floor with a thud, 'and there's no problem getting more of it.'

Rachel picked up a roll of cerulean blue taffeta. 'This might work,' she said unravelling it.

Brigette, who had toned down her punky image with stirrup pants and a long navy cardigan in the hope that Roe might take more notice of her, looked on doubtfully from her desk. Rachel pulled the taffeta across Kate's bust to the end point of each shoulder. She then wound the fabric tightly round Kate's arms down to the elbow.

'I want to see the chiffon sleeve underneath at this point, so fan it out from here,' she explained to Colette, holding the material in place at Kate's elbow. 'Let's keep it as part of the medieval story.'

Sweeping the fabric from the waistline, Rachel created a full second skirt, concealing the chiffon underneath. In a moment of fatigue she removed her glasses and Kate noticed that she was really quite pretty. Her Latin skin was flawless and needed no make-up.

'Brigette, can you get me the gold brocade in the corner, please?'

Brigette unravelled a couple of yards before handing it to Rachel. Rachel pinned about a foot of brocade around the hem of the skirt. When she'd completed this, she stepped back to inspect her work. She was beginning to feel excited. She always did when she was on the point of creating something really good.

'It's fabulous!' said Richard admiringly. 'Somehow the taffeta works better than the velvet.'

Rachel approached Kate again, frowning, 'Something's not quite right. Let's lower the neckline.' With Colette's help they dropped the neckline so that it scooped off the shoulder. 'Now put a three-inch slit in the centre, so that we see the plum chiffon underneath,' Rachel instructed. 'No, that's too much. Make it two inches. Yes, that's better.' She squinted at the dress, pleating her fingers together under her chin.

'It's still not working. What do you think, Richard?'

'The neckline needs some detail. It makes the hemline look bottom heavy now that you've used the brocade.'

'Okay. Colette, reduce the height of the brocade around the hem by four inches . . . too much. Yes, that's right. Just there.'

'That helps,' Richard said feebly once she'd finished pinning. He was having hot flushes and felt sick. No more Sunday drinking binges. It just wasn't worth it.

'Why don't we use the gold embroidery we have on the bustline?' suggested Brigette. 'It would lift the eye and balance the dress.'

'Try it,' said Rachel, cleaning her glasses on her sweater before replacing them on her nose.

Nicole stuck her head round the door. 'Mademoiselle, I can't get Linda or Diane for the show. The American models won't do the European collections because of the terrorist bombs.'

'Oh, lord! I hadn't thought of that. Find out who's available in London. What about Karen Mulger or Yasmin?'

'She's pregnant again,' said Brigette who was a big fan of Duran Duran and avidly read all the tabloid stories, 'not doing the collections this season either. We could get Yasmeen Ghauri.'

'And Naomi?' suggested Richard.

'No,' said Rachel decisively, 'she's lovely but quite wrong for this collection. Ring up all the agencies and get cards on all available girls in town. We'd better organise a casting.'

Nicole nodded and left.

Brigette had pinned the gold emboidery to the dress bustier, and was puffing out the skirt from underneath.

'Sorry,' she mumbled to Kate as her head reappeared from under the skirt.

'Thought we'd lost you for a moment,' said Kate wryly. The two girls exchanged smiles.

'That's it! I adore it,' exclaimed Rachel with her back to the mirror, 'we've finally got a dress I'm happy with. Edouard,' she called, looking round. 'What's happened to Edouard? He should have been here twenty minutes ago with a list of the designs. Brigette, that can go up now.'

Brigette pinned the sketch of the dress with its attached fabric sample to the board in the order the designs would be appearing in the *couture* show. The style number of each dress was written on the bottom of each sketch. So far very few of the eighty-five designs had been actually made up.

Kate, beginning to sweat and afraid of staining the fabric, rushed to the loo. The tiny airless room reeked of urine and cigarette smoke so she opened a window. Since Roe had banned smoking everywhere, the loo was the only place the staff could sneak a quiet puff. On the wall someone had crudely written in French, 'I'd swap a year of sex for one night with Roe Lewis'. Underneath in lipstick was written, 'Join the queue!'

Kate turned on the tap, waiting for the water to heat up, and dreamed back to last Friday when Roe had whisked her away for a surprise weekend – to make up for the disappointing previous weekend. Three days. Three blissful days together. No interruptions, no unexpected ex-girlfriends popping up, no phones, no early morning jogs, no work. Driving north with no planned destination, they had stopped in Long Pont, a sleepy village famous for its crumbling abbey and medieval luxurious hotel. They had explored the surrounding countryside holding hands, made love in the afternoon, got bitten by hotel fleas, allowed the patron to suggest dishes for them which they ate outside under the stars from each other's plates. Even the weather had been perfect.

The tap gave a sudden burst, vomiting scalding water over Kate's hand.

'Ouch!' she yelped, snatching back her hand and quickly adding some cold. When she'd got the right temperature she washed under her arms.

What an incredible weekend. Just when she was beginning to have real doubts about their relationship, she'd fallen in love with Roe all over again. He had been so attentive, so warm, so . . . unexpected! Like the afternoon they'd carried a picnic basket the hotel had made up for them into a secluded field. Roe had opened the champagne while Kate unwrapped the waxed-paper parcels and laid out a feast of black olives, two kinds of runny cheese, home-grown tomatoes, a warm

crusty loaf, a smoked chicken stuffed with mushroom pâté
and a bag of yellow peaches. Afterwards, drunk from sun and
champagne, they had gone off exploring the ruined abbey.

'It's so dark! I can't see a thing,' she had whispered.

'Take my hand. I'll lead you.'

Through the ecclesiastical darkness they reached the altar.
'Gosh. This must be the archbishop.' Kate ran a hand over
the cold marble tomb, her voice hushed. 'What a small chap
he was.'

'Poor diet and lack of sex probably. Why don't you take
your clothes off?'

'What here? We can't, Roe. Not in a church. It's . . .
sacrilegious!'

'My soul's already been black-listed. Come on, Kat, you
can lie on my jacket.'

'I feel wicked,' she murmured weakly as Roe pulled off her
T-shirt.

'That, baby, is the whole point.' And he gently guided her
head down between his thighs.

They'd made love slap-bang in front of the altar. As the
marble archbishop looking on disapprovingly, Kate was terrified someone would catch them at it but she had to admit it
had made the experience wonderfully exciting. Afterwards,
exhausted and glowing and still inside her, Roe had murmured,

'I could stay like this for the rest of my life.'

For a while they dozed, then Roe woke her up and refused
to let her go until she'd sung the whole of *I've got you under
my skin*. Kate felt as if she were walking inside a charmed
circle; nothing, no one could spoil her ecstatic mood.

Back in the studio the missing Edouard was handing out a
typed list of the collection so far, containing the style number
of each outfit and a description of the design.

'See your picture in *Vogue*?' Richard asked, proffering Kate
a copy of the magazine. It was an awful picture of her and Roe
taken at a fund-raising cocktail party. The caption read,
'American Roe Lewis turning tables at Vaubelle with house
model, Kate Temple.'

Brigette had already studied the picture for twenty

minutes during her lunch break but peered over Kate's shoulder. Kate was ravishing in a simple burgundy dress, her hair swept into a French pleat. Roe, dark and brooding at her side, but with a territorial arm around her waist, looked every inch a movie star. It simply wasn't fair. Glancing down at her sketchpad, she found she'd doodled Brigette Lewis several times.

'Kate,' said Rachel, hanging up the phone, 'Joni's got the details of your commercial trip. I gather you're shooting in Tuscany, lucky thing. You'd better pop down now as we've finished with you for today. Thanks for being so patient. Tomorrow at nine thirty?'

But by the time Kate got down to the Attaché de Presse Joni had already left, leaving Kate's ticket and schedule with her secretary. The details she'd been given stated only that they were going to Camaiore, a two-hour drive south of Pisa. As she made her way downstairs to change Kate wondered idly who the director and crew would be.

'I'll get it,' yelled Jack Winger, picking up the phone extension in his study. 'Strachur 814.'

'Daddy, you're in.'

'Rachel! What a lovely surprise. I was beginning to think you'd become far too famous to bother with the likes of us,' he teased. 'We haven't heard from you in ages.'

'Didn't you get my message? I rang last week and spoke to Lorna.'

'She probably forgot,' he said, knowing full well that his wife hadn't. 'How's it all going?'

Rachel let out a weary sigh. 'Exhausting! We're having to work really hard, partly due to my being new and having to learn so much, but I'm loving every minute. Still can't believe I'm really here.'

'I suppose this means a second professional golfer in the family is now out of the question?' They both laughed.

'The reason I'm calling, Dad, is I want to invite you to the press show in July. I so hope you'll be able to come. It will make all the difference.'

'Try and stop me. When is the big day?'

She gave him the date. 'What about Lorna? Do you think she'll come?'

'I'm sure she will,' he soothed, making a note of the show in his diary. 'Now is there anything that we can get you?'

'Yes. A forty-eight-hour day. The weeks just seem to evaporate. I don't even cook any more – no, I tell a lie, I did have a girlfriend over for dinner last week, which made a nice change, but usually I end up grabbing something after work, then go straight home to bed. Sounds very boring, my life, doesn't it?'

'You sound dedicated, darling, which doesn't surprise me one bit.'

Jack could hear another line ringing in the background.

'I'm sure the main reason I keep working so hard is because it stops me thinking about how nervous I am. Daddy, the other line's going and I've got my next appointment waiting for me downstairs. I'd much rather carry on chatting to you, I'm dying to hear all your news, but I promise I'll get the invites off to you today. Give a big hug to the kids. I really miss them.'

After hanging up, Jack turned towards the window and skimmed the breathtaking Argyll view of Loch Fyne. It was evening. The surrounding west-coast hills had turned a deep mauve and the still loch looked like a sheet of glass. God, he loved this place.

On his desk a bundle of unopened letters awaited his attention. He ignored the bills except for the builder's invoice half-way down the pile which, out of curiosity, he investigated: £56 thousand. Jesus Christ! And it didn't even cover the new swimming-pool. He'd have to talk to Lorna. Her extravagance was getting out of hand.

He found his wife upstairs in their bedroom, sitting in front of the dressing-table mirror. She was wearing a black velvet jacket and matching trousers and was back-combing her dark hair into a fashionably messy look. A gin and tonic sat among the cosmetics, imprinted with orange lipstick on one side. Smiling briefly at him, she glanced anxiously at her small, diamond-studded Piaget watch.

'Jack,' she said, pecking his bent cheek, 'I thought I heard

219

you come in. I was beginning to worry.'

'Sorry. I got stuck on the M1.'

'Well, you'd better get a move on. We're going to be awfully late.'

'I want to talk to you about this.' He placed the bill in front of her. 'Why do we have to have another bathroom, when we've already got two?' He looked suspiciously at her outfit. 'And where did that come from?'

'Country Casuals two years ago,' she lied. 'Not that you ever notice what I wear.' Jack's frown deepened. 'Oh darling, don't pout. We don't have time for this now.'

Lorna studied her husband's set face and sighed. She had been so looking forward to tonight's party. They hardly ever went out and now Jack had to go and spoil it. As for the bathroom, they'd already discussed it, for goodness' sake, and he'd agreed with her. Oh, she knew the building work had set them back a bit, but Jack had already won three golf tournaments this year. They had never been short. All the same she guiltily tucked the £400 sales receipt into her bag. What Jack didn't know wouldn't hurt him.

'You don't really expect guests to keep on using the children's bathroom. They certainly can't share ours.'

'Why not? It never bothered you before,' argued Jack, opening his dressing-table drawer where he kept glasses, cufflinks and a wad of twenty-pound notes. Lorna crossed her fingers so that he wouldn't notice the dwindling pile.

'Would you like me to make you a drink while you shower? We've got twenty minutes.'

'Before what?' Jack pulled off his shoes.

'Robert's new exhibition. I mentioned it last week. Remember? The opening's tonight and then a few of us are going on for drinks at Barry's.'

'That old poof! I thought he'd run off to London with a schoolboy.'

Lorna pulled a face in the mirror. She slipped on a pair of treasured diamanté sling-backs.

'You know people spend a lot of money on his paintings,' she said pompously.

'People spend a lot of money on clothes, but it doesn't mean they have good taste.'

'Is that some kind of dig at me?'

'No,' sighed Jack, refusing to be drawn into an argument. 'Do I have any messages?'

'They're on the blackboard. Nothing urgent. By the way, who was that on the phone?'

'Rachel wanting to know if we can make it to her show. She especially asked if you'd be there.'

'It depends on when it is. There's an awful lot happening over the next few weeks.' Lorna pulled a tissue from its cardboard box and used it to blot her lipstick. 'Come on, Jack, ple-ease. Tonight's very important to me.'

'Honestly, love, I've had an exhausting two days in London. I'm shattered.'

'But what will everybody think? They're expecting us. Barry called less than an hour ago to confirm,' wailed Lorna, dropping a Lancôme lipstick into her bag, which she snapped shut.

'Go then. You don't need me tagging along. You're the one that likes all that stuff.' Jack collapsed on the bed. 'I'm all in, I'd only spoil your fun.'

You can say that again, thought Lorna, glaring at him. She got up and marched into the bathroom. Robert had warned her an old flame would be at the exhibition and she was desperate to show Jack off. What excuse could she make? Inspecting her face in the mirror, she erased a thin line of eye shadow that had collected in the crease of her eyelids. God, I could do with a facial, she thought. Running a hand over her voluptuous curves, she realised she could afford to lose a stone and fill in the brackets round her mouth with a bucket of collagen, but the boobs were still good – large and firm despite suckling two babies. She cupped them in her hands and tried to remember the last time she'd had sex with her husband. The night of Olivia's birthday, almost three weeks ago, and even then she'd masturbated while Jack was in the shower. Had it been that long? Did he no longer find her attractive? In the old days they'd been at it like a couple of rabbits. Not any more. Other men she met at parties seemed to find her attractive but she rarely reciprocated. She realised she was bored with her life, bored with only ever being seen as a mother, a golfing celebrity's wife. She'd given her best years to Jack, raising his children, supporting him from the sidelines, accommodating one golf match after another which kept her husband away for hours, sometimes days, without really taking into account her own needs. But what really shocked her was how much she'd grown to hate the game.

For a few minutes Jack could hear running water, then it stopped and Lorna re-emerged, drying her hands.

'How are the kids?'

'Fergus is teething and Olivia got sent home from school yesterday for picking a fight.'

'Did she win?'

'Jack, you mustn't encourage her. If she thinks it's clever she'll start doing it all the time. You could make more of an effort with our relationship. All you ever think about is golf. I understand it's work, but I don't think it's too much to ask you to escort me to one measly exhibition down the road! You flew all the way to Paris to see Rachel.'

'That's not fair and not the same thing at all. You know how much Rachel wanted our support. The poor little duck was terrified. So would I have been, faced with all those press people.'

'Don't be silly. You've had a lifetime of the press,' snapped Lorna.

Jack closed his eyes for a moment then opened them again. 'Why can't you be a little more understanding? She is my daughter.'

'And I'm your wife. You could try taking my side for once,' she said bitterly.

'This isn't a bloody competition!' barked Jack, losing his temper.

'Ever since that precious girl arrived back from Argentina she's been trying to take you away from me. It's not surprising I turned elsewhere for comfort.'

'Jesus! Why bring that up all of a sudden?'

'Because he worshipped the ground I walked on and you hardly know I exist,' she shrieked. Then, afraid she might have gone too far, 'A little affection from the man I love wouldn't go astray.'

'I don't need to come home to this. I'm going down the pub for a bit o' peace.'

Lorna was on the verge of tears. 'What about supper?'

'I'll get my own!' he snapped, grabbing his jacket on his way out.

'Do that!' Lorna hurled, banging her glass down on the table. 'But don't expect me here when you return!'

She heard the door slam downstairs, and in another room Fergus, her three-year-old son, began to wail. She went into his room and found him standing in the dark with all his toys, tidied up half an hour ago, strewn all over the floor.

'Come on, darling. It's time to go to sleep now.'

'Want Daddy,' said Fergus with a trembling lip. He always got upset when his parents argued.

'Daddy'll come in to see you later and give you a kiss goodnight, but he has to work for a bit. Now, will you be a good boy for Mummy?' Lorna glanced at her watch. She must hurry or she'd be late.

Fergus, deciding he was rather tired, dutifully lay down and stuck two fingers in his mouth. He watched his mother with wide, cautious eyes.

Downstairs eight-year-old Olivia Winger walked into the kitchen dragging a blond Labrador by his lead. Mrs Brodie, the Wingers' housekeeper, was cutting up a Victoria sponge she'd just made, and arranging the slices on a china plate which had a crack down the middle. Olivia immediately grabbed a piece.

'Can you no' take your coat off first and wash your hands, pet?' said Mrs Brodie gently.

'I'll only get them dirty again,' said Olivia logically, cramming cake into her mouth. She flicked the television remote control and found a channel showing *Blind Date*. 'Goody. My favourite.'

'Toast, Olivia?'

The little girl nodded enthusiastically without once taking her eyes off the screen.

'Daddy said he might buy me a piano. Have you got a piano, Mrs B?'

Toast smothered in peanut butter was put in front of her.

'Oh look, how sweet. Dickens wants some too.'

'He's already eaten, so don't you go feeding him. What did you do at school?'

Mrs Brodie added Winalot, cling-film, baking-powder and bin-liners to the kitchen blackboard.

'History. Why did Henry VIII have so many wives? He had a big tummy and cut everyone's heads off. My daddy's only been married twice and he's much nicer. I like drama best. Mrs Garrett says I can play Camille in next term's play because I'm pretty.'

Mrs Brodie removed a pint of milk out of the fridge, only half-listening.

Lorna, still furious with Jack, walked briskly into the kitchen. She had her coat on.

'Mummy, Mummy!' Olivia shrieked, jumping up to greet her mother. 'I can do a handstand. Watch!'

'Not now, darling. And don't put jammy fingers on Mummy's expensive coat,' she said, moving hastily away. 'I'm going out for the evening, Mrs Brodie. Jack shouldn't be long.'

'Will I put you something in the oven?'

'Don't bother. I'll pick something up while I'm out.' Lorna glanced briefly at her appearance in the corner mirror and inspected her teeth for lipstick. She thought she should say something about the television programme. Jack forbade Olivia to watch such rubbish and Lorna was inclined to agree, but why should she look like the spoilsport?

Mrs Brodie took off her apron. 'While I remember, Mrs W, Farmer Peck's been on the phone complaining about the dog. Said he caught him chasing his sheep again. He didna sound very friendly.'

Lorna immediately looked at her daughter. 'Olivia, have you been letting Dickens off his lead?'

Olivia pretended not to hear. 'Are you going to another party, Mummy?' Used to seeing her mother all dolled up to go out, she no longer got upset. 'Will you watch *Blind Date* with me before you go?'

'I can't tonight, darling. Mummy's already very late, and don't change the subject. You know perfectly well how much Mr Peck hates having his sheep disturbed. If you're going to let him off the lead, then do it here. Otherwise I'll have to forbid your taking him out on your own. Now, I've put Fergus down. He shouldn't be any trouble. Just look in on him later on.'

Mrs Brodie nodded.

'Can I have a packet of cheese and onion crisps?' asked Olivia, sensing weakness.

'You'll not eat your supper, hen.'

'Ple-ease, Mummy!' Her voice was high and urgent.

'Just one then, Mrs Brodie, but no chocolate tonight. You eat far too much sugar.' Olivia pulled a face. 'Must dash or I'll be late.'

She kissed her daughter's blonde head briefly, and left in a cloud of Coco Chanel.

'Daddy slammed the front door too,' smirked Olivia, inspecting her face in the mirror just as her mother had done a few moments ago. 'Whenever Mummy puts on too much make-up they have a row.'

13

Bea Parker was on the ten o'clock express to Gatwick Airport. She was one of twelve models flying to Jakarta to perform a gala charity show raising money towards building a hospital for polio victims. For weeks their agencies had haggled over the rotten fees, but every model in town had wanted to go. In these recessionary times trips abroad were coveted.

Returning from the buffet bar Bea spotted a man deep in a paperback; thirty-fourish, single, a city type, judging by the pin-stripe suit and briefcase on the table. Not earth-shattering exactly, she thought, squinting because she couldn't see properly, but with distinct possibilities. Bea stared, wishing he'd look up from his wretched book. She crossed her legs, clicked open her coke can and coughed, receiving raised eyebrows from the woman opposite, but Adonis remained obstinately glued to his book. Finally he got up and loped along to the loo. The right side of his face was bruised and he wore a large plaster over one hazel eye, which slightly spoiled his beauty. Bea bit thoughtfully into her king-size Mars bar, watching the occupied sign lit up above the door. He was gone an awfully long time. Some of his attraction diminished.

The Guruda flight was a nightmare. Though promised club class seats, the models were put in economy, which was chock-a-block. The ever resourceful Cassy, however, had managed to get herself up-graded to club class.

'Tell me what I've been doing wrong all these years,' Bea asked in admiration as they were boarding.

'Told 'em I'd just had a commercial released and that I didn't want to be mauled by me fans.'

227

At Singapore they had to wait three hours for their connecting flight, with a further delay re-boarding when the endless zips on Cassy's leather jacket set off three airport alarms. Eight hours later the dishevelled group stumbled off the plane into a crowd of Indonesian press photographers.

'Fucking hell!' muttered Martin, shoving on Ray-Bans to cover his bloodshot eyes. 'They could have bloody warned us!' With a commanding nose and a small scar that ran between his handsome eyebrows, thirty-three-year-old Martin Tulloch was Jean-Paul Gaultier's latest muse.

Their waiting coach set off through a green, overcast landscape. Paddy fields unravelled like flat sheets of glass. Coconut trees and Asian billboards, advertising cigarettes and fashions long superseded in Europe, flanked the terracotta road. They passed rudimentary homes made of tin, bleached clay and wood, and hundreds of tents. Between the scruffy buildings were empty petrol drums used as cooking fires. Filthy children played in nearby mud, while their mothers sat in the shade paring vegetables.

The traffic, as they reached the city centre, was appalling; far worse than the rush hour at Etoile, Bea thought, as a bus-load of police cruised by. Brown-faced drivers honked and flashed one another irritably and showed little compassion for the street beggars in their path, some with horrific deformities. Bea was surprised to see so many four-wheel drives. This was supposed to be a Third World country.

The city centre hotel was a pleasant surprise. Expecting a dump after their exhausting flight, Bea cheered up at the sight of the splendid five-star Sahmadid Jaka. Eye-catching porters in sky-blue silk tunics, scarlet balloon trousers, batik cummerbunds and fixed smiles flanked the porticoed entrance. Heat hit the models like thick velvet as they stepped off the coach. They entered the huge, glitzy, air-conditioned lobby and flopped on to the white sofas while their guide signed them in.

'*He's* nice,' said one model, as a pretty Indonesian walked past.

'Don't bother having an oriental, Sharma,' Martin advised.

'Their dicks are so small you wouldn't know they were inside you!'

Twelve pairs of curious eyes returned to the unsuspecting Indonesian, but as he was wearing baggy trousers it was hard to tell. Bea found herself on the fourth floor sharing a room with Cassy, who immediately rang room service.

Although they were high up, the industrial view was disappointing. Bea turned up the air-conditioning and flopped on the bed. All she wanted to do was sleep. Cassy, lighting a cigarette, stripped down to her bra and pants and unpacked her YSL luggage. Within minutes the room was littered with expensive clothes, black silk lingerie, several CDs, a magnum of duty-free champagne, a half-eaten king-size bar of fruit and nut, two packets of extra-fine condoms, chewing-gum, hair dye (for her pubes, as Bea later found out), three Jackie Collins paperbacks, dried prunes and a box of laxatives.

'Divine, ain't they?' said Cassy gleefully, as Bea admired a skimpy set of crotchless knickers and push-up bra. 'Now that I've got tits I can't pass a lingerie shop without using me Amex card.'

'That's what's different! You *are* brave. When did you get them done? They look fantastic!'

Cassy proudly whipped off her bra and inspected her splendid breasts in the mirror. 'Feel them if you like.'

'Did it hurt?' Bea prodded them gently. They felt firm but quite real. Gosh, maybe she'd get hers done too.

Someone knocked on the door. Cassy opened it in only her knickers. A pink-faced porter with carefully averted eyes handed over two pillows, a hair-drier, a box of tissues and a towelling dressing-gown.

'That'll give the staff something to talk about,' Cassy smiled impishly, shutting the door with her foot. 'Me boy-friend used to say he had to shake me around in the shower to get wet, I was so skinny. So in the end he got me to see this doctor in LA. Oh, he could afford it. Owns half of Docklands.' She laughed, sucking her cigarette down to the butt; Bea wondered if Cassy's incessant smoking would get on her nerves.

'What happened to Sebastian? I thought you were a match made in heaven.'

A flicker of anger crossed Cassy's face, 'Hell, more like. Right bastard that one! All that money and flashy talk was just show, weren' it. Wouldn't let me out of his sight, not for a second. I liked the attention in the beginning, all right, but then he started slagging me off, accusing me of sleeping around and everything changed. He used to hit me. Oh yeah,' she said, seeing Bea's shocked face, 'they weren't just rumours. I'm well out of it. I've got meself someone who really loves me now.'

The show wasn't until Friday and for the next two days there was little to do. Tired of sunbathing, Bea decided to investigate the hotel gym. For ten minutes she had the modestly equipped room to herself, then was joined by two men laughing at a shared joke. The skinny Indonesian was in a blinding outfit of tartan shorts, lime-green Aertex shirt and pink and orange socks. She recognised the other at once. It was Adonis with the bruised face, last seen disappearing into British Rail's loo.

The Indonesian warmed up next to her with all the seriousness of an Olympic competitor. He made a lot of blowing sounds, flapping his arms like windmills. Bea, trying not to laugh, concentrated on the treadmill. Then she started doing lunges.

'Let me get those for you,' offered a gruff voice, handing her the hand weights she had bent to pick up. Her thighs already felt ready to ignite.

Glancing up, Bea found herself gazing into glimmering hazel eyes. The grubby plaster was still stuck to his forehead, he had deep circles under his eyes and his navy track-suit bottoms had shrunk in the wash. Close up, she could see he was on the heavy side but he was undeniably magnetic. The hazel eyes flashed at her, held her, dared her to look away. She couldn't.

'Got any tips on how to end up with a body like yours?'

Bea laughed, wiping faint beads of sweat from her brow. 'Your friend's certainly enthusiastic.' Bea nodded towards the Indonesian thrashing away on the rowing-machine.

'Oh, Kastan!' old brown eyes laughed. 'Don't let that rig fool you, he's got one of the sharpest minds in town.'

'I'll take your word for it.'

'Just my word?' he raised a dark eyebrow.

'I've had it, Cameron, my friend,' wheezed a scarlet Kastan, staggering off the machine and approaching Bea with a rueful smile. 'For God's sake, don't let him talk you into a game of squash. He's a menace when he gets hold of a racquet. I, however, play like a gentleman.'

'Sorry mate, but I got here first.'

'Okay, okay,' Kastan laughed. 'I know when to give in gracefully. A quick word about tomorrow and I'll leave you two to it.'

'I should be getting back to my programme anyway, before my muscles cool down,' said Bea, retreating. She could feel Cameron appraising her.

Half an hour later Cameron had disappeared. Bea, wondering if she was losing her touch, trounced off to the steam room. Accepting a paper gown and unattractive flip-flops, she offered herself up to a female masseuse with more muscles than Sly Stallone. Far from the relaxing experience the hotel literature had promised, Bea spent the next twenty minutes having her body pummelled on a wooden catafalque, a session rounded off by a bucket of icy water thrown over her to wash away the soap lather. Bracing stuff, she thought, getting dressed, but she had to admit she felt fully restored. Cameron was waiting outside.

'Now I know what it feels like to be a steak tartare. You should try the massage. It's quite an experience!'

'I already did. You forgot something.' He dangled her gold Rolex in one hand.

'Oh, brilliant,' she said gratefully, 'I'm always doing that. I'd forget my head if it wasn't attached to me.'

'But it's such an unforgettable head.'

Bea giggled. 'Talking of heads, what happened to yours? I mean, you look as if you were hit by a truck.'

'Try a carefully aimed fist,' he said, getting up. 'Come and have a drink and I'll tell you about it.'

'I have a six o'clock appointment.'

231

Cameron glanced at his watch. 'Then we'll have to drink fast.'

They drifted out into the sapping heat. The air was filled with exotic smells; a mixture of honey and someone's coconut lotion. A hot wind brewed, tugging at the sun umbrellas which flapped loudly above their heads. The monsoon must be about to start, thought Bea, trying not to stare at Cameron's long, powerful legs. Her short hair was dry in no time.

'What are you doing in Jakarta?' she asked removing a chunk of pineapple from her drink.

'I'm covering a story for my paper. Kastan, the guy you met in the gym, is my local contact and I could be on to something big.' He knocked back his drink and signalled to the pool waiter. 'I got this,' he said pointing ruefully to his bruised face, 'by asking too many questions. Cigarette?'

'I've just given up. Sounds as if you move in dangerous circles.'

Bea was unable to curb the low-voltage current tingling along her skin. She hadn't felt this excited about a man in ages. Must be all the spicy food.

'Oh, it has its moments. I seem to spend most of my time propped up in bars writing stories about snatched handbags or the misbehaviour of married politicians. I'm ambitious and if this tip comes off it'll re-launch my career. Then it's goodbye Fleet Street, grannies and royal visits, hello Uncle Sam.'

'So you've set your cap at America?'

'Well, it's where the money is, sweetheart, and I'm ready to spend it. I'm sick of tinned coffee and cardboard sandwiches. I'm after the finer things in life.'

'I don't doubt you'll get them.' They gazed at one another. 'You've got to be a model with a body like that.'

'You're joking! That work-out practically killed me. Too much food and sitting around.'

'You must have been too thin before.'

'Flattery, darling,' the china-blue eyes flashing wickedly, 'will get you everywhere with me.'

'Are you famous?'

WALTER WILLSON 038
COCKERMOUTH

RETAILER ID   01041661
TERMINAL ID   017521784
EFT NUMBER   6176
                   5902

28-02-96   13:10

SWITCH   07-98 1
4903401803911112317

GOODS   £6.78
SALE TOTAL   £6.78

Please debit my account
with the total sale
value shown

Sign: *Donald Ferguson*

Transaction Confirmed

Please Keep This Copy

Thank You

K	B
42	267
	335
49	463
90	473
121	
133	
142	
169	
196	
313	
476	

'Infamous.'

'Then let's have another drink to celebrate.'

'You know, it might be fun doing a piece on fashion models abroad,' mused Cameron a little later, 'see how differently you behave away from home.'

'Shedding our British hangups and all that kind of thing?' Bea bit provocatively into her glacé cherry. 'Do you have to get to know your subject very well?'

'Intimately.' Cameron held her with his kernel eyes. 'Would you be embarrassed if I kissed you in a public place?'

'I'd be embarrassed if you kissed me in a private place in front of all these people,' Bea said, giggling.

She picked up her second Margarita and gazed at him through a purple umbrella, and a maze of fruit. The alcohol had already begun to take effect. She took a messy sip, spilling a few drops on to her small, partially-clad breasts.

Cameron leaned over and picked up the edge of her towel. 'I'll do that,' he said, wiping them off. He cupped her half-protesting hand in his and methodically kissed the tips of her fingers. Bea pretended not to notice, as if the hand being kissed was not hers, as if the nerve endings weren't respons-ible for the exquisite tingling between her legs. Fortunately or unfortunately, Bea wasn't sure which, the small convoy of models descended on them, clutching shoes, books, suntan lotion and damp towels slung over their shoulders.

'Belinda!' snapped Michelle, a prim brunette. 'Don't you think you had better change? Mandrick's going to be furious if you're late.' As a teetotaller she eyed the half-empty Marga-rita glass with distaste.

'Oh, hell. Hang on, I'll come with you.' Bea leapt up from the sun-bed. 'Maybe I'll see you later on?'

'Don't worry,' said Cameron warmly, 'I won't let you escape that easily.'

'Where'd you find the Jack Nicholson look-alike? He's a bit of a dish,' whispered Sharma as they walked away.

Bea was feeling so highly charged, she didn't think she could make it to the lift door. She hooked an arm into Sharma's for support.

'The man needs a bloody government health warning!' she

muttered faintly. 'My blood pressure's reached boiling point and I've only known him an hour!'

Later, the fittings over, Bea felt too keyed up to go to bed. She'd caught the sun on her legs and they burned gently, making her feel wanton and exotic. She wandered down to the bar hoping to run into Cameron, and instead found some of the others on their way out.

'We're going shopping at the Pasorya. Don't tell me Cassy's being a party pooper?' said Martin.

Bea nodded. 'She's already been out and bought half of Jakarta and is recovering in the tub.'

'A likely story. She's probably smuggled one of these gorgeous blokes under her bed.' He beamed at a chocolate-skinned porter who was holding open a taxi door.

They asked the driver to take them the long way round so they could see more of the city. The taxi seats were covered in shaggy lambswool and a pair of rubber dice swung from the mirror. It was uncomfortably hot and there was no air-conditioning. From her back seat window Bea watched the city sweat and wilt; so many families living in squalor. Their driver wore blue shorts and a T-shirt with ripped-off sleeves. He was chewing gum and turned up the radio which blared scatchy music, more US west coast than South-East Asia. They drove past the vibrant patchwork of old and new Jakarta, weaving through its profusion of markets and small bric-à-brac stores. They passed shanty towns, the Merdeka Palace, the Fatahilla Square surrounding a great spurting fountain, and two sprawling parks in the middle of the city. They finally pulled up outside Pasorya, a large, unprepossessing shopping mall, and the driver honked the horn, drawing attention to them as if they were VIPs.

The first two floors, frigidly air-conditioned, looked much like any European store but the top three floors were an Aladdin's cavern of silks, hand-woven rugs, batik tablecloths, wall hangings, exotic cushion covers, garish puppets that Bea had seen among Cassy's purchases, intricate brass and silverware, the short traditional daggers called 'keris', and basketware, Chinese ceramics, carved wooden statues of birds and dancing Indonesian women. With cries of delight

234

they seized armfuls of silks, tossing them about and preening in front of the mirror, to the bewilderment of the staff. They laid carpet after carpet out on the floor, but surrounded with such a glut of colour it was impossible to choose.

Picking up a phallic-looking statue which looked like her vibrator, Bea absentmindedly rubbed the smooth surface. She jumped when a voice said,

'Thinking of anyone in particular?'

Cameron was watching her from the corner of one gypsy eye. Picking up a statue of a naked woman, he examined it with his firm, strong hands. His broad shoulders strained the back seam of his pale blue jacket and a few black curls had edged over his shirt collar. She licked her lips nervously.

'Shouldn't you be interviewing locals or something?'

'I should, but I find you much more interesting.' He put back the statue, tracing the line of each wooden breast with his index finger. 'All this eastern magic does strange things to a man. Is it having the same effect on you?'

Bea realised she was holding her breath. 'It is rather erotic,' she babbled, unconsciously picking up the statue Cameron had just held. 'Do you think this would make someone a nice gift?'

'Well, that depends on who you give it to – these symbols are powerful stuff.' He took her arm.

'I must say I do find you very disturbing,' Bea admitted, not quite meeting his eye.

'Good,' Cameron moved closer, 'because I've wanted you from the moment I first clapped eyes on you on British Rail.' His hand was running over her back. Delicious shivers raced down her spine.

'So you did notice me! You seemed so engrossed in your horrid book.'

Taking her arm, Cameron firmly steered her past a blur of Indonesian silks and hand-painted gift boxes. A thin partition wall jutted out as a display extension from the main wall. Bea found herself pulled behind it and pinned to the wall. There was a thud as her bag dropped to the floor.

'You want this as much as I do. Don't try to deny it,' he muttered, covering her mouth with his.

'I'm not exactly struggling,' responded Bea, kissing him back with all the strength she could muster.

His hands were pulling at her skirt which had already inched up the sides of her thighs of its own accord. Bea battled with her conscience, aware that she should try to stop him, but she was so excited she could hardly stand. I'm a lost cause, she thought fleetingly as Cameron's hands grappled with the buttons of her skirt, no self-control, that's my problem. Thank God for the pill! She could hear the high, jangling department-store music, which sounded like an Iraqi funeral, and the low-pitched chatter of shoppers. Cameron's mouth was now finally clasped to her right nipple. Bea ran her hands through his thick mane of hair and moaned. Grabbing on to both buttocks, Cameron pulled Bea against him, rubbing his concrete erection against her bush. God only knows where my knickers are, she thought, then gasped as Cameron bit gently into her neck. A young, olive-skinned face appeared around the wall.

'Jesus!' shrieked Bea, trapped behind Cameron.

'Would madam be wanting a servicing?' the male shop assistant asked politely.

'Thanks awfully,' Bea said faintly, as Cameron's hidden hand probed between her legs, 'but I'm already being seen to.'

The man's face dissolved and Bea's legs gave way. With Cameron supporting her she clasped her legs around his waist. His cock was the size of a marrow, but she was so excited it slipped in easily. Their mouths banged together in a frenzy of saliva and tongue as Cameron rocked her furiously back and forth.

'Talk about Bucking Bronco!' she muttered afterwards. 'My back's going to be covered in bruises tomorrow.'

Bea emerged dishevelled from the partition wall. Cameron followed, pulling down the back of her skirt, hastening from the scene of the crime and the scandalised whispers of the staff.

'There you are, darling!' yelled Martin, staggering towards her under a mound of shopping bags. 'I've got one more pressie to get downstairs, then I'm done. What are you

236

giggling about? You look as if you've just seen the Second Coming.'

'That's one way of putting it,' Bea smirked.

The following morning the models assembled in the hotel ballroom at six, tired and yawning. Because of technical problems the air-conditioning had been turned off, exacerbating everyone's lethargy. The huge stage had taken three days to build and consisted of three runways running from backstage in straight lines. These connected to a runway at the end, which ran parallel with the back stage. A huge polystyrene model of the Arc de Triomphe rose like a giant squat frog, flanked on either side by two screens projecting images of Paris. The ballroom had been done up in white, with the exception of the domed ceiling, elaborately painted in bright Asian colours, and coiled gold serpents. From the ceiling's centre hung one of the most ostentatious chandeliers Bea had ever seen.

Cassy turned up half an hour late in leggings and an orange lycra body, which immediately drew everyone's attention to her plunging cleavage. She was clutching a steaming cappuccino, two chocolate éclairs and a box of tissues. Martin swanned in twenty minutes later, straight out of *Bonanza*, wearing black cowboy boots, slashed denim shirt and a silver-studded belt in his jeans. They both received stern looks from Mandrick, the producer.

Mandrick was worried. According to Keith several light sockets were faulty and they didn't have enough back-up power. No head sets had arrived for Jane and Simon, the production assistants, which meant that Mandrick, watching the show from out front, had no way of telling them when to send out the models.

'Okay, can you all stop talking, please. We've lots to do so I need your concentration.' He waited patiently for the noise to subside, 'That means not interrupting,' he said, looking pointedly at Martin, 'no disappearing to get food or trips to the loo without telling either myself, Jane or Simon. Lunch has been organised, so you will be fed.'

'That's a weight off my mind,' hissed Martin. Someone sniggered near by.

'If all goes well, we'll break at one. At one forty-five I want everyone backstage in their first garments for a dress rehearsal. We're working under difficult conditions, so bear with me and we'll get through this. The show's at nine, and hair and make-up's available from six o'clock.'

'Not going to have much time for anything else,' grumbled Bea, thinking of her planned rendezvous with Cameron after the show.

In the opening scene Martin, Bea, Rufus and Sharma wrote down their steps on the printed stage plans Mandrick had given them. The choreography seemed simple enough, but with twelve scenes to follow it would be easy to forget scene one by the time you got to scene nine. A staff member handed Mandrick a small packet.

'Can I have group B on stage, please,' Mandrick said over the mike as the lights flickered off and then came on again. Cassy and five Asian models struggled on to the high stage for the next scene. Martin nicked her seat and polished off the second éclair.

'Bea!' yelled Mandrick reading from the package. 'This is for you.' He gave it to Martin to pass along.

'How fab. A pressie! Do let's see what's inside.'

Martin rummaged through thick layers of pink tissue paper and to Bea's horror held up a pair of edible panties which he gaily waved above his head. There was a card attached.

'Look forward to eating my way through these. Signed C,' Martin read, unabashed. 'Looks like our Belinda's shagging someone.'

Cassy blew her nose. 'I ain't tried that brand before.'

'Strawberry,' said Rufus, expertly sniffing the panties. 'My favourite.'

'Give it back!' Bea howled, whipping them from under his nose.

'I think it's disgusting,' muttered Michelle. 'No wonder models get such a bad name.'

Martin unfortunately overheard. 'I agree. You give us a very bad name,' he sneered, 'you're so brittle, dear, you'd chip if anyone so much as touched you.' He turned back to Bea, 'What's C stand for?'

'Climax,' said Bea sweetly.

'If it's not too much trouble,' said Mandrick in a deceptively light voice, 'I'd like everyone back on stage.'

The dress rehearsal, following lunch, went less smoothly. Mandrick was unable to hear himself speak over the technicians, banging and drilling the set into place. Time was running out and the already tired models were not concentrating. He was beginning to wonder if he'd ever get this show together. Running a frustrated hand over his face, Mandrick replaced the glasses which magnified his intelligent brown eyes.

The lighting technician was having a private fit with the lights which kept shutting down, and studied the maze of buttons on his electrical board in despair. He stuffed another cigarette in his mouth. Some bugger had wired the bloody keyboard incorrectly and Mandrick kept asking for more smoke to create stage mood. If he wasn't careful, thought Keith nervously, they'd run out before the show.

At nine thirty everyone was backstage sweating in their first outfits. The show should have started an hour ago but the champagne cocktails had gone on far too long, and the audience were only just starting to tuck into great plates of gingered beef. Much to the chef's horror the mint sorbet, dished up in the kitchen to save time, was melting. Sounds of cutlery and glasses chinking swelled around the great ballroom, while backstage the air crackled with excitement and nerves. Simon, wearing a baseball cap and furiously chain-smoking, was attempting to get everyone into their running order.

Martin was doing his utmost to talk one of the waiters into getting him a double vodka. Michelle, looking pea-green, had a case of the runs and kept dashing off to the loo. Please god, she prayed, as another crampy wave gripped her, let me make it through the show. Bea was playing travel backgammon with Rufus on the floor. Cassy, pale but very beautiful, had knocked back three black coffees and was on her second pack of cigarettes in an attempt to go to the loo, but still hadn't had any success. Sharma, tired of standing in four-inch stilettos, inelegantly hitched up her taffeta skirt and sat on a prop.

'Keep the noise down!' snapped Simon. 'They can hear you out there.'

Fifteen minutes later the show began. There was a lot of shooshing backstage, while the President of Indonesia made a painfully long token speech, thanking everyone for their contributions and proudly announcing how much the event had raised. Unfortunately, one of the technicians' concentration wavered. He hit the music switch by mistake and the end of the President's speech was drowned out by Madonna's punchy *Vogue* track.

Martin, waiting in the audience with a camera, took his music cue and leapt on to the front runway in a black Jean-Paul Gaultier suit. Click, click, click went his camera as Bea stormed down the runway in a slinky fuchsia catsuit, black satin gloves and ludicrously high heels which exaggerated her long, skinny legs. Her blonde hair shone under the lights, *'Pose!'* echoed Madonna's throaty voice, and Bea threw her arms in the air like Marilyn Monroe, both flirting and teasing Martin, who was making his way backwards and crouched down so low he was practically doing the splits.

'C'mon baby,' he mouthed encouragingly as Bea pouted. 'Fab! Gimmie more!'

The crowd loved it too and broke into thunderous applause.

The music changed, smoke hissed dramatically on stage and for a moment the audience was unable to distinguish the emerging ghostly figures. The stage was suddenly flooded with light and models appeared through slits in the screens as if the film had come to life. They filled the three runways in an array of orange, green and purple-printed leggings, worn with matching jackets and chain belts.

Cassy charged back from her next change looking furious.

'What's up?' Bea asked.

'Me fucking dresser keeps sloping off to watch the show. I might as well dress meself.'

'Say something to Simon.'

'What's the point? She can't even speak English.'

For the last scene the models wore stiff satin gowns. Holding champagne glasses, they were elevated on a central platform with images of the French Resistance flashing on screens behind them. The audience clapped approvingly as the male models, dressed in tuxedos, emerged from seats in the audience and clambered up on stage. Martin was first up and marked Michelle with his eyes, posing demurely, centre stage, in a powdery-blue halter neck dress, the ends of her hair flicked up. With his back safely to the audience, Martin ran a casual hand over her breast then leaned closer. Unable to move Michelle turned a dull red, her cornflower-blue eyes widening as Martin stuck his tongue in her ear and whispered,

'Bet you wish it was my cock.'

An Indonesian waiter was supposed to carry a tray on stage and collect the models' champagne glasses. This was their cue to start down the runway. Unfortunately the young waiter, who'd been marvellous during rehearsals, got a bad case of stage fright. On stage, rigor mortis set in. He walked off without taking a single glass and no amount of cajoling from Simon or Jane could get him back on. As the tenor in *Madame Butterfly* bellowed arias over the speakers, Bea realised something was horribly wrong. No one had collected her glass but according to the music she should be half-way down the runway by now.

'Somebody move, for Christ's sake,' hissed Mandrick into the mouthpiece, 'and get that bloody waiter back on stage, they look like a Dubonnet ad!'

'Lift,' muttered Cassy at Bea's side, 'lift!'

It was obvious no one was going to move, so Bea bravely sailed down the runway with the full glass in hand, elegantly twirling in her Christian Lacroix. To her horror most of the champagne landed in the President's lap. As she turned back, Bea's heart sank. No one had moved. Come on Cassy, her eyes pleaded. As she reached her, Bea hissed, 'For God's sake, someone go! We must look ridiculous!'

'I can't,' said Cassy the ventriloquist in despair, 'me fuckin' dress is stuck!'

By now Mandrick was epileptic. 'Move, Cassy!' he bellowed into his mouthpiece, making both Jane and Simon jump. 'Somebody, anybody, get a bloody move on!'

In desperation, Cassy gave a final tug at her skirt. The trapped £25 thousand dress ripped from the floor partition and she drifted off down the same path as Bea, followed by the other girls. At the bottom Cassy toasted the President, recovered from his soaking, and took a sip from her glass. The charmed President thought it was part of the show and clapped loudly. Mandrick released the breath he'd been holding for five minutes and muttered a prayer of thanks to the chandelier.

Later a celebratory party organised by the charity committee went on until five in the morning. All the models went, with the exception of Cassy, who had disappeared. Bea, in her room to change into something more comfortable to dance in, found a note from Cameron. He apologised but something had come up and he had to cancel their meeting. It also said that she wasn't to be cross with him for letting her down. He had a surprise for her, and would take her to the airport the following day. Bea spent the rest of the evening dying of curiosity.

'Would you like something to drink before lunch, sir?'

'How about some champagne?' suggested Cameron, lighting a much-needed cigarette now that the 'no smoking' sign had been switched off. Bea, sitting next to him, nodded, indicating she'd like the same.

'What are we celebrating?' she asked once Cameron had paid and the stewardess had moved on to the next aisle where most of the other models were sitting.

'Whatever you like, sexy. Your trip, my story, our . . . meeting.' Cameron's eyes slanted against his cigarette smoke, and glanced appreciatively at Bea's tanned legs. 'The colour suits you.'

'Won't last long. Tans have a deplorable habit of fading the day you get home. At least mine do. Cheers!'

They both took a thirsty sip of their chilled drinks.

'When you said you'd be taking me to the airport, I never dreamt you meant Heathrow.'

'I promised you a surprise, didn't I?'

'And it's a lovely one,' said Bea warmly. 'But I thought you said you were going to stay in Jakarta for another week. Why are you coming back to England?'

'The paper want me to cover a much bigger story. I've no complaints. I wasn't having much luck with my lead, things were moving too slowly. Maybe the humid weather has something to do with it.' He paused briefly to gaze into her eyes. 'Mind you, I wouldn't exactly call Jakarta a wasted trip.'

Bea grinned impishly. She took another gulp of champagne, put her plastic glass on to the spare seat's table, then put her hands behind her head and stretched her back as far as it would go. 'Ooh, golly, I'm still so sore from that workout.'

Cameron slipped a warm hand between her thighs, 'Anywhere in particular?' his deep voice warm as he began nibbling her ear, 'I'm very good at making things better.'

His hand had found its way under her skirt and slowly, tantalisingly, Cameron slid a finger inside her. Fortunately the aisle seat belonging to their row was empty and Cameron had covered their laps with a blanket, but Bea, biting down on her lip, glanced furtively around the cabin to see if anyone was watching.

'Christ, Cameron, don't! Not here anyway. I'm going to come!'

'Well, I'd hate to think I was losing my touch.'

Bea tried to fight it but Cameron's finger was sending her out of control. Somewhere in the back of her mind she remembered Sam saying he'd pick her up from Heathrow. She had visions of herself arm in arm with Cameron as they exited customs, of Sam, the spurned lover furiously waving his mobile phone in a jealous rage. Oh, God. That's all she needed. She'd have to find some way of getting rid of Cameron without making it too obvious. She didn't want to hurt Sam's feelings. It was just a harmless fling after all, only she wished Cameron would stop doing the things he was doing to her because she couldn't think straight. The complications of life, she thought, shivering deliciously.

The plane started bobbing up and down like a yoyo as they hit some turbulence. The seat belt and no smoking signs pinged on and stewardesses came round to check everyone's belt, but Cameron carried on. Bea giggled, clinging on to the arm-rests as her excitement reached fever pitch, all guilty thoughts about Sam temporarily abandoned.

'You are a dangerous man to be around,' she said with a wicked glint in her eyes a few minutes later. 'Tell me something. Have you ever tried it in one of the loos?'

14

Limmonara, once an Etruscan settlement, sat perched in the Tuscan hills almost a thousand feet above the shimmering Mediterranean Sea. The owner, a middle-aged sculptress with alarming orange nails and gold-plated front teeth, had bought and renovated it ten years ago as a retreat for culture-loving tourists.

The steep road to the hotel was dreadful. For the last kilometre it thinned into a narrow, tortuous track permitting access only to the smallest cars. Rash drivers of Mercedes often found themselves stuck half-way up and many got lost in neighbouring hilltop villages, remembering too late the local advice to stick to Fiats and first gear. The Vaubelle crew was no exception. After abandoning their location van half a mile down the road they had lugged the expensive equipment up to the hotel. It was a slow job made harder by the heat, and they were all sweaty and gasping by the time they had finished. Finally, with everything safely installed, the crew piled into the cool, inviting shade of the terrace bar.

Kate, however, had gone straight to her room, which was sparsely furnished and had a shower which administered hot water for about two minutes then packed up, a sink with a leaky tap and a cracked mirror. The view from the terrace was magnificent. Kate could see for miles. The rolling hills were covered in dense cypress and olive trees, the June sun burned against the horizon and she could just make out the small town of Camaiore. This was a land to intoxicate the senses.

Despite all this, Kate had never felt more depressed. Roe was spending more and more time at work and she was beginning to fear that he had lost interest in her. Attempting to make their last evening together special, she had spent hours preparing the perfect meal; the eggs for the ambitious lobster soufflé had curdled twice but she had got it right eventually. She pored longingly over tantalising pictures in her cookery book, vowing to make the lemon *brûlée* tart on her return from Italy for Bea, who would certainly appreciate the effort, but as Roe never touched sugar Kate had prepared slices of fresh mango and mint. Labouring until the cookery book was stained and soggy from the ingredients, Kate had spent an hour cleaning up the mess. Inspecting the spanking-clean room, she had felt very pleased with her efforts.

At eight thirty she had poured herself a glass of wine and checked the nicely rising soufflé. At a quarter to nine, having eaten nothing since lunch and already feeling the effects of the wine, she cut herself a slice of white bread – never mind the flat stomach. It had a powdery crust and was crying out to be smeared with some of the velvety Dolcelatte, which was sitting on top of the fridge so it would be ripe and gooey for supper. She was on her second slice when she heard the sound of Roe's key in the door. Her heart thumped. Even after all these weeks he reduced her to a nervous wreck. Please be in a good mood, she prayed. She glanced at her watch. He was an hour late. They'd have to eat right away. Chucking the half-eaten bread into the bin, she briefly checked her appearance in the hall mirror and clicked off Mozart's *Twenty-First Piano Concerto*. Her smile was wiped away the minute the door opened. Roe wasn't alone.

Standing in the doorway behind him was a stocky man with strawberry-blond hair whom Kate judged to be in his forties. He had deep grooves beneath a pair of faded-blue eyes and his tan creased like paper under the Machiavellian smile. In front of him were two women; a tiny bottle-blonde with hard-blue eyes and a guitar-shaped figure, who, Kate noticed jealousy, was clutching Roe's arm as if she'd been doing it all her life. The other woman had a mane of heavy, ink-black hair that reached her bottom and was dripping in gold jewellery. Her long fake fingernails, which matched her plum lipstick, played with a cigarette.

'Nice dress,' Roe said approvingly, 'I hope that's for me.'

'Darling, you said you'd call. I've been waiting hours!'

'My fault,' explained the strange man, displaying nicotine-stained teeth. 'I resorted to kidnapping. Only way to stop your boyfriend from working.'

'Honey, this is Schneider Brink,' said Roe, laughing. 'Don't believe a thing he says. And this is his wife, Narvelle. Lucinda – ' he said, indicating the blonde, 'well, let's just say we met somewhere across the Atlantic.'

The blonde woman giggled.

'Hello,' Kate managed, her heart sinking.

'We thought we'd get a bite somewhere then hit a few clubs. Schneider and I haven't seen one another for months and I wanted to show you off. Do you want to grab a bag or something?'

'But I've just made dinner. Everything's ready,' Kate said plaintively, feeling excluded from their high spirits. 'It's my last night.'

The Morticia Addams clone turned to the blonde and shrugged.

'All the more reason to go out,' said Roe, with a slight edge to his voice.

Schneider was watching her from the doorway with a half-smile on his face. He thinks this is funny, thought Kate, disliking the man. Roe checked the answer machine.

'Can I have a private word?' Kate's voice was strained.

'Don't mind us,' said Schneider puffing on a cigarette, as they disappeared into the bedroom.

Roe, after a two-hour drinking session with Schneider, was feeling mildly, pleasantly tight. He looked at Kate with her faint air of martyrdom and thought, now what? He'd been on edge all week trying to sort out Vaubelle's chaos. Claude's army of lawyers, still trying to get him reinstated, were really pushing things and interfering with Roe's busy schedule. Meanwhile there was the Vaubelle cosmetics marketing campaign to worry about. The products would hit the shops in under two months but they didn't have an ad to run. He'd been uninspired by both advertising companies. And all the empty advertising space they'd reserved. He'd have to make a decision soon or it was going to cost them a fucking fortune. Not that Carl was being much help. Cortes Western American restaurant chain, which had begun so well ten years ago, had been hit hard by the recession and the losses it had been clocking up could no longer be ignored. Carl should be focusing his attention on salvaging the company, reflected Roe, and getting in the insurance money before things got out of hand. But Carl was also caught up in an ugly divorce; his fourth wife was cleaning him out.

'I'm getting it from both ends here, kiddo,' Carl had growled down the phone. 'Can't even afford to take a leak these days. Not only is my attorney taking up all my time, he's costing me a grand an hour.'

'D'you need me there?' Roe's voice was cautious.

'Nah. Nothing I can't take care of. Call me Tuesday. I'll be in better shape by then.' The line had clicked in his ear.

Kate, watching Roe from the bed, was trying to curb her frustration. Why had it suddenly become so hard? During those first weeks they'd always made time for each other. It would have been unthinkable to have spent a last night with other people. Why then, did their timing always seem to clash these days? And what had been the point of making the soufflé when no one was going to eat it. I should have gone to Bea's birthday party, she thought, suddenly depressed.

'Roe, you've had to work every night this week and I leave for Italy tomorrow. Can't you see these people some other time?'

'I could but they're here now and I don't feel like being stuck in the flat all evening. Come on, baby, these guys are fun.' They didn't look like fun. 'It'll do you good to get out for a change.' Roe's voice dropped and he ran a leisurely hand down her back, 'Hey. Are you wearing any underwear?'

'Yes,' said Kate faintly.

'Well, ditch it. I want to fantasise about what I'm going to do to you while we're out.'

Kate trembled with excitement. 'I can't afford another late night. I haven't even packed.'

Roe switched tactics. 'Then I'll help you. C'me here, baby.'

He kissed her very soundly. 'Mmm. You taste cheesy. What have you been cooking?'

'Lobster soufflé and it's no good looking like that,' she said unsympathetically, at Roe's sudden hungry expression. 'It sank ten minutes ago!'

'Yeah, but look what's risen.' They both glanced down at the bulge in his trousers. 'Maybe I'm not in such a hurry to go out after all.' The next minute they were on the bed and because he hadn't been near her for days Kate was like putty in his hands.

'Roe,' she whispered, shaking him gently a few minutes later. 'You're friends are still waiting for us?'

'Mmm,' he said, slowly opening his eyes. 'Yeah, you're right. We'll just go for a couple of hours. Okay?'

'Okay,' she agreed, feeling suddenly that her world had been righted. After all, what was the harm in a couple of drinks?

But it didn't turn out like that. They had ended up at L'Escargot Montorgueil in Les Halles, the former market-place once called 'the belly of Paris', now a trendy shopping haunt for the young. The restaurant, stuffed with erotic fin-de-siècle paintings of fornicating couples, had the air of a nineteenth-century brothel.

'Didn't think anyone was allowed to do that sort of thing back then,' giggled Lucinda, inspecting them closely, 'this one's very rude.'

The waiters, who could easily have been cast from a Fellini film, hovered around the half-dark interior of faded-red chairs, enormous cut-glass mirrors, tulip chandeliers and red banquettes. Schneider ordered snails in mint, curry fennel, passion fruit, ice-cream with ginger snaps, and champagne served in a carafe. Kate hated it all. She tried edging away from Schneider who was wedged beside her but there wasn't much room. His cologne was giving her a headache. The scent reminded her of someone but she couldn't remember who.

'Why's it called passion fruit?' asked Lucinda.

'Because it looks like a woman's vagina,' said Schneider, nonchalantly gouging out snails from their shells and then soaking up the sauce with French bread. Some of the sauce ran down his chin.

Narvelle was as restless as a thoroughbred horse. She hardly touched her food so Schneider ended up eating hers as well as his own. No wonder she's so thin, Kate reflected, watching her. She was both fascinated and repelled by Narvelle, whose exotic sexuality seemed to be affecting the whole table. With the exception of Kate they all seemed determined to drink as much as possible.

While they ate, with Schneider and Roe doing most of the talking, Kate learned that the Brinks had twice travelled the world. Schneider had been in jail for three years for embezzlement and there was talk of him having smuggled cocaine from Pakistan. They seemed an unlikely pair of friends for Roe. Kate wondered what the attraction was.

'It must be such a cushy life being a model,' said Lucinda tactlessly as a woman walked past their table wearing glasses the size of compact discs. 'All that money you get, all those lovely trips, and free designer clothes.'

Kate looked at her coldly. 'I wouldn't exactly describe modelling as "cushy".'

'It just seems a bit unfair when us mortals have to work so hard just because we weren't blessed with good looks.'

'Stop fishing, Lucinda,' warned Roe.

'You do have an exclusive contract with Vaubelle, though?'

'For the moment,' Kate glanced briefly at Roe, 'but nothing's for ever and there are always younger and prettier girls waiting in the wings.'

Later on Kate found herself swept off to a nightclub which was so crowded they left after half an hour. They tried getting into Les Bains but the doorman didn't like the look of Schneider so in the end they headed for Schneider's apartment.

Kate reluctantly tagged along, concerned about the late hour and all the things she had to do before her morning flight. A taxi cruised by and her hand went out involuntarily to stop it. But Roe, holding firmly on to her arm, pulled her in the opposite direction towards Schneider's parked BMW. Casting him a sideways glance, she wondered why he bothered to stop her going home. He's hardly said two words to me all evening, she thought, and it's obvious I'm not enjoying myself. What the hell's bugging him?

Schneider's rented flat had Narvelle's touch stamped all over it. There was a large collection of Indian vases, and thirty or more oriental cushions were scattered across the floor. Incense burned from the mantelpiece and fine silk shawls had been draped over the lamps. A wave of musk filled Kate's nostrils. She was feeling more and more uneasy. Narvelle put on Leonard Cohen and lit dozens of candles around the room. It instantly warmed up and looked very intimate, cosy even. A den of iniquity. Kate decided to wait ten minutes then politely make her excuses and get Roe to take her home.

'My wife's addicted to chaos, as you can see,' said Schneider, grinning. 'Let's all have a drink.'

After a couple of drinks Narvelle produced a heavy oak cigar-box which she placed on the coffee table. Kate had hinted on three occasions about how late it was getting, but Roe had deliberately ignored her. Narvelle's box revealed cocaine. She placed a small mirror on a cushion on the floor and carefully poured out some of the white powder. Using a razor blade, she chopped it into a finer powder, then divided it into five thin lines. Schneider passed her a thousand-franc note from his pocket.

'Got to do it in style,' he said, before lighting a cigarette, 'this stuff'll blow your mind.'

Narvelle rolled the note into the shape of a thin cigarette. Placing one end into her nostril, she snorted up a line of coke. Schneider went next, followed by Lucinda and Roe. Kate, curled defensively in the Jacobean chair, refused her turn.

'Try it, baby. It's good stuff.'

But Kate was adamant so Roe snorted the last line. Schneider laughed at something Lucinda was saying. They were looking in her direction. Don't be so paranoid, Kate told herself sternly. All the same, she hated Schneider's laugh, which came out in short, slow rasps. When he talked his head moved up and down like a bobbing dog in the back of a car. Sitting cross-legged on the floor at his feet, Narvelle absently caressed her tiny breasts while she talked, her voice soft and low. The coke was already taking effect. Her slanting blue eyes gazed dreamily into space. Kate sipped the warm Sambuca Schneider had given her, hoping it would make her feel more relaxed. But, ironically, the more she drank the more sober she felt. Roe sat back against the sofa, his head raised to the ceiling. His eyes had gone very dark.

'Roe, darling, we should be going soon. I've got a very early start.'

'You're young enough to get away with it, dear,' said Schneider, emphasising the 'dear'. Sophie always called her that when she was angry.

Schneider was smoking the tail-end of a joint. Stubbing it out in a bronze ashtray shaped like a cupped hand, he moved over to his wife on the floor and started kissing her. Kate was unable to tear her eyes away as his hands reached inside the black fabric and fondled his wife's breasts. Narvelle rested her head against Roe's knees, arching her back as Schneider's mouth pulled the tiny buttons of her dress free. Her white breasts exposed, the huge dark nipples grew hard with excitement. Kate glanced anxiously at Roe who was watching in fascination.

What followed happened so quickly that Kate wondered later if it had really happened at all. Removing her dress, and wearing nothing underneath, Narvelle swivelled round so that she was facing Roe. Schneider, fondling his wife from behind, was grinding his erection into her back. Slowly, not taking her eyes from Roe's face, Narvelle undid his flies and released his rock-hard penis which shot up against his shirt. Just for a second Navelle turned and looked at Kate. Her thin, plum lips smiled victoriously, then with those same lips she took Roe's penis into her mouth. Roe groaned, holding her head down, pushing deeper into her mouth. Schneider was now wildly excited and released his own surprisingly small penis, entering his wife from behind. Her skinny bottom writhed pleasurably against him while her hands gripped on to Roe's thighs.

Lucinda walked over and stroked Kate's hair. Kate flinched.

'What's the matter, darling?' she giggled. 'Don't tell me

you're shy? I used to room with a model and, boy, did she open up my eyes to sex!'

Her hands travelled along the edge of Kate's face and neck. Kate pulled away, repelled. Roe, having extracted himself from Narvelle's mouth, was watching them.

'Come here,' he commanded. 'Let's shed some of those English inhibitions.'

Kate, too shocked to move, remained glued to her chair. Suddenly, horribly, everyone's attention was on her. Lucinda was caressing her bare shoulders. Kate yanked herself away.

'Take your revolting hands off me!' she spat.

This couldn't be happening. Suddenly Roe was by her side. Before she had time to react he grabbed either side of her dress and yanked it down to reveal her amazing breasts.

'Sweet Jesus!' murmured Schneider in awe. Narvelle eyed her husband territorially.

'Beautiful, aren't they?' said Roe proudly as Kate squirmed unsuccessfully to free herself. He caressed each nipple with his thumb. 'Come on, Kat, just go with it. Lucinda knows what she's doing.'

. His words brought Kate back to reality. She felt as if she'd been watching a film in slow motion and now the lights were on, bringing everything back into sharp focus. I must get out! Giving Lucinda a vicious push she jumped to her feet, clutching the torn dress against her breasts. The green eyes, now huge, darted to the door looking for escape but Roe was too quick for her, catching her wrist.

'No, you don't,' he hissed cruelly, 'you're not going to ruin it for everyone. The fun's only just started. Come here, Narvelle. Show her how the grown-ups play.'

'You're mad. Let me go!' Kate struggled furiously against him.

Wearing a slightly contemptuous look, Narvelle hauled herself up from the floor. While Roe held Kate down, Narvelle put her mouth over one of Kate's nipples, teasing it with her serpent-like tongue. Kate gave a desperate moan and bit down on her lip so hard she drew blood. If she kept very still she'd wake up from this nightmare. A sudden wave of Schneider's cologne rising from Narvelle pulled Kate back

253

to her childhood. Everything started to get muddled. Roe was screaming at her, only it wasn't Roe. Why was he so angry? She must have done something unforgivable, so terrible that it had never been spoken about again.

'Please!' she whimpered, 'I'm sorry.'

Roe finally turned his head to look into Kate's eyes and saw the damage he had done.

Someone dived into the pool and Kate's attention returned to the present. Looking out over the serene Tuscan country-side, basking her skin in warm sun, last night seemed a lifetime away. She wished more than anything that it hadn't happened. Why had everything gone wrong? What had she done to make him behave so destructively? She closed her eyes. Would she ever understand him? More important, could they repair the ravages of last night?

Once home, Kate had waited in vain for Roe. Trying to shake off her depression as she threw lightweight clothes into her suitcase, she was gripped with the same uneasy dread she used to get when going back to school for a new term. She had a bath, then, finding comfort in food, cleaned out the fridge, until her belly felt stretched and sore. Wracked with guilt and self-loathing, she brought up the lot, then swallowed half a packet of laxatives. The purging made her feel better, a sense of control restored. But she knew it would happen again, driven by some madness. One of the three outfits wardrobe had got her to try for the commercial was a tailored Caroline Charles suit. Its snugness had been niggling away at her and she'd vowed to lose five pounds.

Finally, her packing done, Kate had applied an eye mask, unplugged the phone and flopped down on the crumpled bed, which looked empty without Roe. She fell into an exhausted sleep, dreaming of Narvelle's wild face swooping down on her like a great black eagle. She woke in the morning to a thin strip of sunlight seeping through the curtains. Her first feeling was of happiness, as if she'd been sleeping for days. Then she noticed her packed suitcase, the silent flat, the empty space beside her, and her stomach turned over. Roe had been gone all night and there were no prizes for guessing who he'd spent it with. She rolled over on to her side and buried her face in the pillow. I've lost him. All these weeks together, all the intimate, late night talks under the duvet that should have reassured her. But then, hadn't she been right to feel insecure! Hadn't he just proved it to her! It seemed she had felt like that for her entire life. Even those school holiday plans her mother had failed to keep, shunting her off to darling Aunt Rose or a holiday camp while she stole away with her latest lover on the pretext of work. Lies. Always awful lies!

By nine it was obvious Roe wasn't coming. Deciding that self-pity would get her nowhere, Kate collected her heavy suitcase and strugggled down the four flights of stairs. She regretted wearing the navy blazer and cotton slacks as soon as she stepped outside; the sun was glaring down like a thousand-watt bulb and made her feel instantly crumpled and weary. But there was no time to change. She was supposed to be at Charles de Gaulle at ten. Outside the apartment building she waited for a taxi, but the ones that flew by were full so she dragged her suitcase to the roundabout, and sat on it. The heavy Friday morning traffic glittered and flashed. Kate sagged against her case. Already exhausted, she dreaded the trip and the demands it would make: to be strong, bright, funny, professional. Nothing today felt beautiful. A whippet-thin woman strolled by in a tight lycra dress with a ratty dog tucked under one arm. Four sets of male eyes followed her. Kate instantly felt fat, vowing to diet for the next week. No taxis appeared and in the end she was forced to take the Métro. Her shoulder burned under the strain of her suitcase and by now she was gibbering with rage, snapping at anyone who inadvertently brushed against her.

Arriving an hour later at Charles de Gaulle, the details of last night were already becoming hazy. She caught sight of herself in the Tie Rack mirror. Terrific! I look as if I've done eight rounds with George Foreman.

Kate was about to get her second shock in twenty-four hours. Searching numbly for the Air France terminal, she was quite unprepared to see the figure of Skander Davenport

255

looming towards her. He was fiddling with a cigarette and looked as if he'd been up all night. Kate, only too aware of her own scruffy appearance, pulled the Jackie O glasses from her head, and hastily shoved them on her nose.

'You're late!' He took her heavy bag and put it on to the conveyer belt. 'I've been hanging around waiting for you. The others boarded twenty minutes ago.'

'Then they've been on the plane twenty minutes too long, haven't they! Anyway, why are you here?' She rubbed her sore shoulder, glad she'd seen the last of her wretched suitcase.

'I've got a commercial to shoot, that is,' he said pointedly, 'if I can get everyone to the location. Got your ticket?'

Had she? God, where had she put it? Kate scrambled around in her bag. It was here somewhere.

Skander glanced briefly at his watch. 'Now's not a good time to tell me you've left it behind.'

'Here it is.'

He handed the ticket with a wide smile to the stewardess. 'Quick as you can, love.' He dropped his cigarette and stubbed it out with his foot. 'Why were you so late?'

'I couldn't find a taxi,' Kate mumbled, looking away.

'That's not good enough. Everyone else managed to make it on time.'

'And no doubt you'll give them all Brownie points.' Kate gritted her teeth. The prospect of five days in Tuscany was beginning to look intolerable.

After upgrading her to club class from economy, Skander frog-marched her to the terminal gate. Boarding the plane, Kate recognised a couple of familiar faces. She'd worked with the art director on two other commercials, and Neil Hunter, London's top hair and make-up artist, she'd known ever since she'd started modelling. His handsome blond head emerged from a fat airport novel and the large cornflower-blue eyes grinned mischievously at her. 'See you when we land,' he mouthed, before returning to Jackie Collins. He was coming to a juicy bit. Kate settled into her seat and watched with a sinking heart as Skander sat down beside her.

'I thought you were a smoker?' she said ungraciously.

'I'm also a childminder.' He glanced up at a passing hostess. 'Do your belt up.'

'When I want a parent, I'll ask for one,' she said tartly.

Infuriatingly, he smiled at her. 'You're not in a position to choose. Hungry?'

Kate sat with her back to him and stared moodily out of the window. Someone's got it in for me out there, she decided, thinking that it was all too much, then realised she was about to cry. Oh no you don't! Not in front of him. Glaring at the seat-back pocket in front of her, Kate hoped to find something she could pretend to read. She didn't feel remotely like making idle chat but all she could find was a card illustrating emergency procedures.

'Glad to see you're taking this in,' said Skander pushing his seat back.

Rotten bully. He's probably going to recite the Ten Commandments to me next. But after knocking back both their meals (Kate wasn't hungry), a large Bloody Mary, and three cups of extra strong black coffee (she lost count of how many sugars he had added) Skander was quietly snoring at her side.

Neil, dressed in new Reeboks and a tangy-orange singlet, sauntered into Kate's bedroom. A veteran of working trips, he was permanently tanned. With his golden boy looks people often mistook him for a model, which appealed to his vanity. In recessionary times, clients found him cost-effective because he was able to double up as a make-up artist and hairdresser. When he wasn't working on shoots he and his boyfriend were busy running a successful hair salon in Walcot Street.

'Dah-ling! We're miles from the others so we can be as wild and as wicked as we like!'

'Just don't get fresh, OK,' said Kate, grinning.

Neil hugged her affectionately and glanced briefly round the room. 'I see we share the same interior decorator. You must come and see my bathroom. The Jacuzzi's big enough to swim laps in! Let's have a look at you.' The cornflower eyes narrowed slightly as he sized up her appearance. 'Oh, oh. Boyfriend trouble. I can always spot the signs. I'd better take you for a very large drink and you can tell me all about it.'

The last thing Kate wanted to do was talk but Neil was one of those rare breeds who listened without judging. Impossible to shock. Thank God for a friend, she thought, suddenly relieved to have him on the shoot. Someone she could trust. These trips were always a gamble. With the right people they could be memorable, but often personalities clashed, tempers flared. And then there was the inevitable bed-hopping. All the same, even Neil's feathers got a little ruffled ten minutes later when, dunking Cantuccini biscuits into cups of tea, Kate told him about her ordeal.

'They're all bastards,' said Neil sanctimoniously, 'ruled by their cocks. You can't trust any of them, I should know. Love 'em and leave 'em, that's my motto. You'll get over him, darling,' he said consolingly. 'It's just a matter of time.'

'Think so?' The greengage eyes looked suddenly very young and vulnerable. 'I still can't believe it happened. Those awful people he called friends. I guess love really does make you blind,' she laughed bitterly. 'At least you and Grant are happy.'

'Happy, yes, but Grant and I stopped sleeping together years ago. Nothing's quite what it seems. You should pop by and see him at the salon. I'm sure he'd love to cut your hair.' He picked up a curl and inspected it. 'Hmm, it could do with a bit of a trim, darling. Lucky for you I brought my scissors.'

Their attention wandered to a far table where some of the crew had grouped. Skander was sitting with the art director, the cameraman, the assistant director and Joni d'Akouri, who'd flown in the day before. Joni was looking very pretty. Gone was the severe look she adopted for Vaubelle. The heavy, dark-brown hair framed her face in a soft cloud and she was wearing only a hint of make-up. She'd caught some sun too. Kate wondered if there was anything going on with Skander. She was aware of his sardonic appraising eyes watching their table as he lit a cigarette, his gaze briefly resting on Neil. Probably thinks I'm trying to convert Neil now, Kate thought mutinously, as he turned back to Joni and suddenly roared with laughter.

'Have you worked for him before?' she asked, nodding curtly in Skander's direction.

'A couple of times. Now there's a man. Shame he doesn't swing both ways. I've had the hots for him for years. Funny, I thought he'd stopped doing commercials. I mean, it's not like he needs the dosh or anything. Family owns a stud farm or something in Australia. You're lucky to be working with him.'

About as lucky as Salman Rushdie. They traded news about mutual friends and gradually she stopped thinking about Roe. Neil's energy and good humour were contagious and Paris seemed a long way off. On the way back to their rooms Colin, the assistant director, gave them their schedule.

'We're eating at seven thirty if you want to join us. Five o'clock morning call for you both, I'm afraid. Skander wants to start shooting at seven. Worried it might rain in the afternoon. I'll have Joni bring the make-up samples to your room later on.'

'Right.' Neil glanced at Kate. 'Fancy a quick plunge?'

'Love to. I'll just go and change. Meet you at the pool.'

'And no brooding, darling,' he warned. 'He's simply not worth it.'

Back in her room, however, Kate's resolve collapsed. Why had Roe suddenly let her go? Was he now having second thoughts? Did he regret what had happened? If only she could understand his mind. She sighed, anxious again. I must stop this. Somehow she had to get through the next five days and put her personal life on hold. One of the worst things about modelling was you couldn't turn up for work with a hangover or look dreadful because you had the curse or a bust up with your boyfriend. Your job was to smile and look wonderful twenty-four hours a day. Nobody gave two hoots about your private tortures.

Pulling herself together, she grabbed a new blue and white stripy swimming costume from her case, and stopped abruptly. Kate glanced at the fabric in her hand suddenly overwhelmed by a memory. She was in a garden; below her, lovely green slopes unfolded down to the sea. Her stepfather was hosing the grass and Kate was running through the spray shrieking with excitement. Stretched out on a nearby rug was Sophie. She looked incredibly glamorous in a pink bikini, sixties glasses and a yellow pudding-bowl hat. Kate frowned, trying to remember more, but it was like looking at a damaged film revealing a pin-prick of light. Why this childhood amnesia? Try as she might the first eight years of her life seemed filled with an infinite amount of nothing, a black hole that had been covered with made-up things. It filled Kate with panic that she was unable to distinguish between what was real and what was imaginary. She often felt she was walking the middle of a tightrope, never able to reach the other side. The stripy costume fell forgotten to the floor. Suddenly weary, Kate lay down on the bed. Tears ran backwards down her face into her hair.

The first two days were so full, Kate had little time to dwell on her personal life. Up each morning at five, she stumbled into the shower then made her way through half-closed eyes next door. Neil's room was littered with clothes and make-up, the ubiquitous television flickering by the window. By six Kate, in curlers and full make-up (her foundation carefully mixed with sun block), sat chatting to Neil in the trailer while the rest of the crew appeared for their fix of sweet coffee and microwaved breakfast. It was hard getting up so early but the dawn drive through the Tuscan hills to their location spot was reward enough for the effort.

By ten it was already too hot for clothes and most of the crew lolled around in shorts, roasting their English backs a warm chestnut. Because they needed the energy for their equipment there was no air-conditioning in the trailer and the line of light bulbs framing the make-up mirror was making Kate and Neil sweat. Kate picked up an Evian bottle and sipped from a straw so she wouldn't ruin Neil's carefully drawn lips.

To pass the time they amused themselves with light-weight novels and gossip about the royals; Neil occasionally cut the Princess of Wales's hair and was privy to inside news. His stories caused a tremendous stir among the crew. Only a few years ago, like many gay make-up artists and hairdressers, he would have regaled the others with details of his own outrageous sexual exploits, but in this image-conscious business where AIDS had taken more than its fair share of victims he now found it prudent to stick to other people's tales. Kate, who wasn't sleeping well, had dark circles under her eyes. But he said nothing and she was grateful. Occasionally passers-by stopped to watch, hoping to see some action. One man had watched from a discreet distance all morning, then came back after lunch with a camera and his entire family.

On their third day, after a marathon lunch, Kate returned to the trailer to change. Good. She had the van to herself. Stepping out of her sweaty clothes she inspected the minuscule swimsuit the stylist had left out for her. Kate's heart sank. I'll never get into that. There was a warped mirror on the loo wall. She slipped the costume on but when she glanced at her reflection she didn't see how the avocado green matched her eyes or how its clever line flattered her hour-glass figure. All she noticed was her distended stomach. The pasta had been a big mistake. Why on earth hadn't she stuck to salad? Because you were fed up to your eye-teeth with salad, said a voice in her head, and now you've blown a week's dieting. The image of her stomach took on new proportions. She suddenly looked huge. Just look at those thighs! Like two blancmange puddings and riddled with cellulite! Why hadn't Neil told her she was putting on weight?

Suddenly irritated with everything, Kate viciously yanked down the shoulder straps to her waist, gulped two glasses of water then stuck her fingers down her throat. Head buried into the loo bowl, she had just about brought up the last of her lunch when the door to the van suddenly opened. Kate froze.

'I'm sorry,' said a voice after a pregnant pause, his frame blocking the light in the doorway. 'I didn't think anyone was here. I'll come back later.' He closed the door softly behind him.

For a full sixty seconds Kate was too shocked to move. Eyes fastened on the aluminium door handle, she listened to the sound of his diminishing footsteps, and her thumping heartbeat. Had he seen? What must he think? God! She'd always been so careful. Maybe she could say she had food

261

poisoning. He'd have to believe that. Only yesterday one of the crew members had got sick from tinned salmon and had been up all night with the trots. She became aware of her nakedness. Hauling up the costume straps, she tied a sarong around her waist, grabbed her sunglasses and stepped out into the sun. No sign of him. Okay, calm down. There was nothing to be ashamed of. She hadn't committed a crime. But for some reason, Skander catching her off guard like this had left her feeling horribly vulnerable.

They had two days to shoot the second of two half-minute commercials. Skander was crossing his fingers they wouldn't go over schedule. The filming involved several close-ups of Kate's face. For the first time Kate appeared with no make-up (though, in fact, she was wearing a subtle application of foundation, powder, blusher, mascara and a pale lipstick), starting off with a blank expression, then changing to surprise, impishness, cool, sexy, confident as another layer of Vaubelle make-up was applied (though much of what Neil used were other brands).

Later they had her jumping down from a chopper, which caused endless problems for Skander. The pilot couldn't speak a word of English and kept landing on the wrong spot so the whole scene had to be repeated. Every time Kate made a graceful dash from the whizzing, whirring blades her carefully set hair had to be redone. Skander was going spare because they were rapidly losing the light.

The lighting man moved around Kate with a silver reflector trying to catch the right light, his jaw working overtime on his gum as he concentrated. The director lent Kate his baseball hat to wear in between shots to help protect her from the punishing sun. As her hands were often in frame Neil had to make them up. She had bitten her nails so badly, he had to fix on false ones. Now veins were showing up in the heat. This meant she had to hold her hands in the air for the blood to drain until they were ready to shoot. On set Skander bullied her, worked her hard, barking at anyone who dared leave without his permission, but, though she didn't like to, she had to admit he was good at his job and was one of the fastest directors she'd ever worked with. Not once did he mention the incident in the van. For that she was grateful and by noon the second of three variations for the last commercial was in the bag.

'Break for lunch, everyone!' yelled Colin, running around with a walkie-talkie. 'I want you all back by four thirty. No excuses. Kate, you're back at three thirty for make-up. OK,' he said, clapping his hands, 'let's go!'

'Obviously thinks he's still in Hollywood,' muttered Neil.

Kate collapsed under a tree. 'God! I can't wait to get this stuff off my face. The thought of a swim is what's been keeping me going.'

'Lucky bag. I've got to meet Skander and Joni to check the footage. See that we've done a good enough job on you.'

Kate escaped to the pool with a couple of books and some overdue postcards. After nabbing a bed she ordered a mineral water from the waiter. It was insufferably hot and sweat dripped down the back of her neck and under her arms. She pulled off the baseball cap and wiped her brow. Littered around the pool guests with fair complexions were drenching themselves in cooking oil. Crazy fools. A hungry-looking Italian approached her for a cigarette, then wouldn't move when she said she didn't smoke. Irritable and tired, Kate snapped at him to go away. Some of the Tuscan charm was beginning to fade. Kate's stomach grumbled as she sipped her drink. Having thrown up all her lunch she was hungry again. The sight of her neat, flat stomach, however, pleased her.

Ignoring her BBC Italian phrase book and a sizzling airport novel Bea had lent her about an ambitious woman who clawed her way to the top of her career while secretly yearning for Mr Right to stride into her life, Kate began to write, images of Roe filtering into her mind.

'You dip into dark corners of women, unannounced like a winter swallow, offering tastes of undiscovered love, promises wrapped in lace and drawn towards you, women unseam secrets and offer themselves like lonely bending swans. You peel me with your persistent hands. I, your little plum, so partial to your eyes, your greedy lips, forgive and soften like a cat . . .'

The sun was making her drowsy. For a second night she had hardly slept, muffling sobs into her pillow in case Neil heard her next door. A khaki-green world faded in and out of Kate's half-closed eyes. Her mind turned down the volume of guests splashing in the pool, the constant swish of the gardener's brush sweeping dirt. Within minutes she was asleep.

She awoke with a start. Someone was shaking her. Skander looked furious.

'What the hell do you think you're doing!'

'What does it look like. Giving birth?' Kate snapped, struggling to sit up. She glanced at her watch but she'd given it to Neil while they had been shooting. 'It can't be three thirty already.'

'Ever heard of a thing called continuity? We're shooting cosmetics, not a commercial for ketchup?' He looked really angry.

Appalled, Kate brought her hands to her face. He was right, her cheeks were burning. Skander ran a frustrated hand through his hair.

'Look. We can't shoot you looking like that. You'd better go to your room and cool down. Just my luck to have you catch sunstroke on the very day some Vaubelle VIP decides to drop in for a sneak preview. I should have booked you a minder!'

'Oh God! I'm sorry.'

'I'll have some water sent up to your room and for Christ's sake, Kate, put some clothes on before you fry.'

Mortified, Kate got dressed, shoving her hat and towel in her bag, then looked around for her writing-pad. Skander had picked it up.

'Can I have that back, please?' she said curtly.

The dark-blue eyes had a deplorable way of unsettling her when she was off guard. He read out her poem. 'But think me not some frail camellia to pluck and discard with ease, I have stained you with my scent, rubbed my pollen on your lips, you cannot forget me. I, who arrived deliberate as morning will stand public like a jewel, watch you descend from your last migration and come home at last to me.'

Skander lowered the notepad. 'Still dreaming about Julian, I see. What's your problem, Kate, can't you get your kicks from single men?'

'Oh, just get off my back!' she hurled at him, using one of Roe's expressions.

'What about your front then, darling?' someone yelled out.

Snatching the poem she turned furiously towards the hotel. When she got to her room, which had been immaculately cleaned but left dark and cold, the shutters having been closed against the sun, a savage-looking Red Indian scowled back at her in the mirror. She rushed to the bathroom and splashed cold water on her face. Neil was going to hit the roof! Somewhere among her things she retrieved a small bottle of Aloe Vera gel some of which she rubbed into her skin. Kate groaned, overcome suddenly by a dizzy spell. She sat down on her bed, the room spinning around her, and closed her eyes. When she opened them again she could see red and gold spangled amoebas mixing together like oil on the ceiling. Sunstroke! How could she have been so stupid!

Someone knocked on the door. A waiter had brought her a bottle of Evian, some grapes, a packet of aspirins and ice. She noticed Skander had signed the chit with his room number. Well, that was nice of him, she thought grudgingly. After having rubbed more Aloe Vera into her skin she drank three glasses of water. Two new freckles had appeared on her nose and her forehead was looking almost as angry as Skander's expression. Why was it that whenever that bloody man was around she ended up looking the fool? The end of the week couldn't come soon enough as far as she was concerned. She'd be glad to see the back of him. Spotting a defenceless mosquito she clapped her hands, squashing it, then immediately felt guilty. The phone rang. Now what. Probably Skander ringing in for another lecture.

'Yes?' she snapped.

'Hi.' The unmistakable voice caressed her ear and Kate's heart started to do mad things. Roe!

'Were you asleep?'

'No. I . . . I was about to run a bath.' She fiddled with the mosquito coil. Why now? Five days ago she had been ready for him, fuelled by a burning sense of outrage. But caught off guard like this. It just wasn't fair!

'Don't.'

'What?'

'Save the bath. I must see you.' No may I or can I. A command.

Kate squashed a large piece of wax running down the side of a candle. 'Where are you calling from?' she asked guardedly.

'Reception. Come down.'

There was a pause. She yanked more wax from the top of the candle.

'Kat. We've got to talk.'

'I know we have. But . . .' Her mind was blank. Where were all her carefully rehearsed words? 'All right, I'll be down in a minute.'

Hanging up Kate looked down at her hand. Her index finger was in the flame. She snatched it away and sucked on it. The room throbbed in sympathy.

15

Bea slammed the front door and dropped her suitcase in a fury. Hell and damnation! How could she have been so stupid! Dashing to the loo, she cried out at the burning between her legs. Peeing was excruciating. It had been like this ever since her return from Indonesia. On the third morning at her parents' house in Kent she had woken up to a blinding pain. Stalling Sam's garlicky kiss and an erection out-doing the Leaning Tower of Pisa, Bea had barricaded herself in the loo. Sitting on the floor, she used her magnified make-up mirror to inspect herself. Her vagina looked angry, the labia horribly swollen. What dreadful thing had she picked up?

After half an hour Sam had knocked on the door. '*Chérie*, are you okay?'

'I'm fine,' lied Bea, her eyes fastened to the mirror.

All thoughts of Sam swamped her with guilt and shame. It was God's revenge on her for being so wayward, she decided, as another wave of pain gripped her. Who could she confide in? Not her mother, who thought that VD was a computer program. It would mean a discreet visit to a doctor but she couldn't go to the family GP. She might just as well announce it in the local paper. Perhaps TCP would help.

With elbows resting on her knees, Bea studied the floor tiles. She'd always been so lucky with sex. Of course she'd been through the usual cystitis and thrush and administered endless sensible advice to girlfriends with similar problems. But this! Maybe it was some incurable Indonesian disease. The prognosis was growing worse. Pain ripped inside her. Bea howled and lowered a tentative hand to dab her vagina. If only she could stop the burning.

She limped back to the hall and picked up a pile of mail on

the mat. The ones for Kate she put to one side. The bills went straight into the bin. Opening the rest, Bea played back her messages; three urgent ones from the agency – was it possible someone wanted to book her? She must remember to collect her cheque. Amex had sent her a letter saying she had been pre-approved for a gold card. What a joke! As far as she knew she was grossly overdrawn. One deceptively light letter from Kate asking to be collected from the airport. Kate's letters were normally full of amusing anecdotes – the kind you put aside to keep. But there was no humour in this one. Was she all right? The answer machine gave another bleep; four messages from Sam wanting to meet her for dinner. The thought depressed her. After all she'd only just seen him. Maybe she'd say she was sick. It wasn't exactly a lie. Let him down gradually.

Bea looked at her watch. Six o'clock. Too late to call her gynaecologist. She'd have to wait until tomorrow. She rummaged through the rest of the post. Justin had sent a dirty postcard from Munich, which made her laugh, and there were a couple of agency statements. A letter from the American Clinic in Clichy caught her attention. Opening it, she threw the envelope to the floor. The short letter explained that Louis Prevet (whom she'd never heard of) had contracted HIV. He had apparently admitted to having had sexual relations with Ray Marks. Bea's name had been linked with Mr Marks and although there was no cause for alarm they strongly urged her to contact the clinic for tests.

Strongly urged! She re-read the letter three times, convinced that they'd made a mistake. An administrative idiot had confused her with someone else. But Ray's name glared accusingly at her in black and white. Oh, God. She had AIDS! Her hands were trembling. Yellow spots appeared before her eyes. The room spun as she struggled to remember how many times they had used a condom? Devastated, Bea sank to her knees, all thoughts of vaginal pain forgotten. She couldn't think what to do. Call someone. Kate was the obvious choice but she was in Italy and Bea didn't know which hotel she was staying at. She couldn't call her parents. The shock would probably kill her father. Sam? No. He'd only panic. Another appalling thought occurred to her: If I'm in danger, then so is he. Had Sam been sent a letter too?

Gradually, as the enormity of her situation dawned on her, she worked herself into a rage. How could Ray have been so fucking irresponsible! Everyone knew how rampant AIDS was. Why hadn't he told her he was bi-sexual. He must have known the risks. They'd used condoms most of the time, of course, but occasionally, around her period, they hadn't bothered. And what about Cameron? Guilt pounced again. Okay, he was a rat for slinking off at the airport without so much as a goodbye kiss, thank you very much. But now . . . In her top-floor flat, clutching the letter, Bea walked to the phone and with a trembling hand dialled the clinic's number.

Roe sat in Limmonara's downstairs bar nursing a vodka. He had meant to reach the hotel by lunch, but Pierre had caught him half-way out of the door with urgent papers to sign. Still, he'd had a chance to look over the rushes and the director seemed to know what he was doing. Joni had assured him that Davenport was the best in his field. He'd mulled over the company figures Leo had faxed through that morning from London. Vaubellle shares were up by 3p. Promising but not as much as he'd hoped. So much depended on Rachel's collection. Another concern was the news that Carl's insurance company had come up with a contract loophole and were refusing to pay up for the damaged Wilshire Tower block. With $200 million at stake the situation looked as though it might blow up in court.

Two technicians walked through the lobby carrying extension leads. Their clean sweat filled his nostrils. Roe's thoughts turned to Kat. After their disastrous last evening he'd found consolation with the all-too-willing Lucinda. Not prepared to analyse his own turbulent feelings, he'd taken Lucy on to another club then back to her hotel. Buxom, fleshy, uninhibited Lucy. Part of her attraction was that she made so few demands. The freedom he felt with her only magnified the claustrophobia he felt with Kat. It was never really going to work. Natalie had been right when she'd said they were worlds apart. And yet . . . He felt a twinge of regret. Initially it had all been so uncomplicated. Kat had been a refreshing change to the sexually aggressive women he usually went for, even surprised him by how quickly she'd responded in bed. His face softened as he remembered their early days together.

Kat! Luxurious, classy, irresistible. And discreet. Thank God she'd never let their relationship interfere with work. Sebastian could make things pretty difficult if he ever found out. Should he end it? Before things got too serious? Nothing was for keeps. Hadn't he learned that the day his mother had walked out. Oh, with tears and love and fierce promises to come back for him once she'd got settled. But as time passed, with his father drinking himself into a grave, the grim years at the orphanage and not one word. After that he'd vowed never to get close to a woman again. And, if he was honest, the fun had long since gone out of their relationship. They hardly made love any more, which proved once again that passion in a monogamous relationship couldn't be sustained for long. It angered him that Kat was on his mind so much, a sure sign of attachment. No way was he going through that shit again.

Kate walked into the bar wearing jeans and a green and white gingham halter neck. The moment he saw her Roe knew he must have her again. Without a scrap of make-up she was still the most stunning woman he'd ever seen. Automatically he felt a stirring in his groin. Kate walked towards him, her face set. She avoided Roe's attempt to kiss her.

'Drink?'

'I don't have much time.'

'Let's go over there. It's more private.'

He took her arm, guiding them to a booth near the fireplace. Kate sat stiffly opposite him.

'So you're the VIP I've been hearing about.'

Roe ignored the sarcasm in her voice. 'I wanted to straighten things out. You didn't leave us on the best of terms.'

'That's hardly surprising.'

The waiter brought over their drinks. Kate picked hers up

270

and rolled the chilled glass against her forehead, wishing she smoked, just for something to do.

Finally Roe spoke. 'I missed you.'

'Oh? I'm surprised you found the time.'

'If it makes any difference, Lucinda was posted back to LA four days ago.'

'That's a weight off my mind.' She glared at the mole on his left cheek.

'I'd hoped you weren't going to make this into a big deal.'

'Then you thought wrong. The other night . . .' Inevitably her guard slipped. 'God, Roe, I've never felt so humiliated in my life!'

'Come on, nobody got hurt,' he reasoned calmly, 'you and I never discussed monogamy and I'd be a goddam hypocrite if I'd promised never to look at another woman.'

'Looking and fucking are two different things.' She knew she sounded crude, but that's how he'd made her feel.

'I do care about you, Kat.'

'Well, you've a funny way of showing it!'

Disconcerted, Kate pushed a damp hotel coaster back and forth with her finger. Roe watched her then covered her hands with his own. They sat for a long time saying nothing in the hot, stuffy bar. A fly zigzagged its way across the table and stopped to feast on a grain of sugar. They contemplated it in dismal silence. This was getting them nowhere, thought Roe. What the hell was he really trying to say?

'Look, I still find you beautiful and mysterious but I need my space. Guess that's why I've always been a loner. Try to understand that my work has to come first.'

'We're not discussing your work!' Kate snapped, unable to keep the bitterness from her voice.

'No, but we're talking about a commitment I'm not able to make and whether you can handle that.'

She was floundering. 'I can't win, can I?'

'Maybe that's been the problem. You try too hard.'

Kate looked down to hide the hurt. 'You just won't let me get close.'

Roe smiled suddenly, winningly. 'I'll get as close to you as you like.'

She looked into his eyes, saw herself reflected in the black, swollen pupils, but they gave nothing away. There seemed such a gap between them she could hardly bear it. She wanted to open him up, get inside and feel what it was like to be him, just once.

Skander Davenport, escaping the unforgiving sun, was having a quiet drink at the other end of the bar as he worked out how to shoot their next outdoor frame. Glancing at his watch he realised he should get back to the set. They still had three hours of shooting and he wanted to go over tomorrow's layout. Gathering up his things, he signed the hotel chit, and stubbed out his fifth cigarette. On his way out he caught sight of the two intimate figures and recognised the smooth 'Milk Tray' client introduced to him earlier by Joni. He'd taken an instant dislike to the man, blindly, instinctively. Nothing he could put his finger on, Roe had been open and direct during their meeting. Just something about his roving eyes. Skander's mouth tightened as he looked at Kate. There was always one on every trip. Waving to the bartender, he had to pass their table to get to the door. The man had his back to Skander, but Kate glanced up briefly and saw him. At least she had the grace to look embarrassed, thought Skander, wincing against the afternoon glare as he stepped outside and slipped on a pair of sunglasses.

Kate picked up her room key. 'I've got to go. They're expecting me back on set. Are you staying tonight?'

'No need. The shots look great and I've got a stack of work back in Paris. I was going to catch the eight o'clock flight, unless . . .' he flashed her a sudden devastating smile, flooring her, 'unless you felt like some company.'

'It's not that easy, Roe. You can't just turn up like this and expect everything to go back to the way it was. Not after what happened.'

Roe's face betrayed nothing. 'So what are you saying?'

'Just that I need some time alone to think. Plus I have a job to get through. Having you here would only distract me.'

There, it was said. She squeezed her hands tightly between her legs waiting for his reaction. Roe studied the contents of his glass then frowned into space, a muscle

272

throbbing in his neck. Why did it always have to be so complicated when they obviously both wanted the same thing? He contemplated dragging her up to bed and screwing her stupid. Some instinct told him she wouldn't put up too much of a fight. But then what?

'Okay, baby. You obviously need some space. Let's talk about it when you get back to Paris.'

He placed some lira on the table, then picked up the beautiful jacket he had flung casually over the back of a chair. Kate's courage faltered. Her new feeling of power was already slipping. She sat helplessly as he crossed the room, fighting a panicky urge to run after him and tell him she'd changed her mind. Instead she watched the door close against her, against them.

The handsome barman, whistling, strutted over to collect their untouched glasses. He'd been watching the foreigners while washing up. Such a handsome couple. They were obviously very much in love. He waited until the dark-haired man had left, then went over to collect the money and wipe the table. It was with astonishment that he found the beautiful redhead's face wet with tears.

Much later on Kate piled into a taxi with some of the others and went to nearby Viareggio. The restaurant wafting out strong garlic smells had a marvellous view. It was still light, and from the balcony bar they watched the tomato sun sink into the phosphorescent sea. The interior was covered in grape vines and lit with candles inside red glass hats. Someone was playing the guitar. Kate took a seat between the art director and Neil, both dressed from head to toe in white.

'You two look like a Persil ad,' she joked, determined to enjoy the evening.

'That's me,' said Neil, methodically scanning the room. 'Squeaky clean on the outside, but inside just waiting for someone to give me a spin!'

Skander, sitting opposite, had ordered several bottles of Chianti and was deep in conversation with Joni.

'How was the Shiseido commercial? I never did see the final results.'

'Restricted to Switzerland, Kate, but the clients loved you,' said Tim, the art director, enthusiastically. 'Remind me to send you a copy.'

Beautiful waiters with warm skins and roving eyes hovered round their table, looking for a glass to fill, an ashtray to replace, a plate to whisk away. Business had been slack since the recession. Neil eyed them up greedily.

'Looks like Christmas has come early this year,' he said, twisting prawned angel hair round his fork, 'and I know just what I want in my stocking.'

'Everything to your liking, signore?' asked the *maître d'*, coming round with the Parmesan.

'Delicious, *grazie!*' Neil gave him a smouldering look. 'I couldn't persuade you to wrap one of your equally delicious waiters for me to take home?'

Kate kicked him under the table but the cornflower-blue eyes remained quite unabashed. Sometimes, like now, Kate thought, Neil reminded her so much of Bea. They could easily have passed for brother and sister, not only in looks but in their stoic, irrepressible good humour, a yearning for adventure and damn the consequences! Skander, pouring chilli olive oil on to thick chunks of Italian bread, was discussing Julian's new film with Joni. Unable to resist, Kate eavesdropped on their conversation.

'The Americans can't get enough of him,' enthused Joni. 'They're calling him the Englishman's Jeff Bridges. MGM's thinking of signing him up. I heard all the gos from Natalie over the phone last Monday.'

'How trying for you,' Kate muttered.

The red wine was rough and oaky and left traces of iron in her mouth. Everything was heavily laced with garlic and she was having difficulty getting through her pasta. Must be sunstroke.

'How is she?'

'Radiant. You know she's pregnant?'

Skander glanced briefly at Kate.

'The signorina is not happy with her food?' The waiter was glancing worriedly at Kate's untouched plate.

'No, it's fine, thank you. I'm just a slow eater.'

'How far gone is Natalie?' Tim asked politely.

'Almost twelve weeks. Hardly shows – you know how slim she is. Julian's so over the moon he's taking her to the West Indies for a second honeymoon.'

'That's good to hear,' said Skander topping up Joni's wine glass. 'Let's hope they work it out.'

Kate pushed her food to one side. She just wasn't hungry.

'If you don't want it, Kate,' said Skander who had polished off his fish. He grabbed her untouched plate. 'Waste not, want not.'

It was swelteringly hot. Everyone fanned themselves furiously with menus while Colin recounted a catalogue trip to the Canary Islands. Due to continually bad weather, one evening the crew had entered the make-up artist in the hotel's fancy dress competition.

'Having been left in his room with a bottle of whisky and a four-day shadow he emerged an hour later as an incredibly sexy blonde,' Colin said. 'Had us all fooled. Turned out he used to be a professional drag queen. You should have seen the security guard as Simon waltzed by. Poor bloke didn't know whether to bow or go for his gun!'

Neil leaned towards Kate. 'I do find closet queens tedious. They give us such a bad name.'

'Was he arrested?' asked Joni.

'Bloody won! Announced his room number in case anyone wanted personal servicing. The other contestants never stood a chance.'

The waiter returned to clear the plates and asked if they wanted coffee. Kate ordered camomile tea. Neil asked to see the sweet trolley.

'Better save the figure,' he said finally, having agonised over the calorific selection, 'none of it looks quite decadent enough. Just coffee for me, darling.' The waiter collected up the menus.

As they were leaving the restaurant Skander caught Kate's arm and pulled her to one side. Neil winked at her as he squeezed past.

'Listen, I'm sorry you had to find out like that, but I tried to warn you. Julian's a nice enough bloke but he'll never change.'

'As you seem so chummy with Julian, you'll know we met last week. He told me everything.'

'Oh.' Skander sounded surprised.

'Can't imagine Natalie as a mother. Poor thing's bound to grow up a mess.'

'Like you, Kate?' Skander drew her towards him as people squeezed past. 'Happy people don't normally go around vomiting up their food.'

Kate's mouth dropped. 'That's a dreadful thing to say!'

'I agree. It makes me wonder what demons you're fighting in there?' He pointed to her chest. His closeness, the sheer size of him unnerved her. She tried sliding towards the door but Skander blocked her way. She could smell garlic on his breath – enough to bring a Roman army to its knees. 'Listen, Kate . . .'

She averted her head. 'I can't very well do anything else!'

'Nat's had a pretty rough couple of years though she hides it well. She's already been through one marriage. Think how you'd feel in her position.'

'Why should I? She's only ever been bloody to me.'

'You can be a bit of a pain yourself.'

'Ooh!' The green eyes flashed with fury. 'You think you're so much better than the rest of us, up there on your high moral horse, everyone telling you how wonderful you are! Well, I'm neither intimidated nor impressed by you. In fact I find you arrogantly smug and this job can't end soon enough!'

Out of the corner of one eye she saw Neil flagging a taxi. Please don't go without me.

'Look, will you let go of my arm? We're holding everyone up.'

'Not yet. Why did you lie about Julian? You didn't see him last week because he's been filming in Germany for the last three weeks. I took him to the airport myself.'

Kate glared at a leaving customer, avoiding his eyes.

'The problem with you, Kate, is that you're bitter. Somewhere along the line you got hurt by a man and now you're hell bent on revenge, playing on your looks instead of using your brain. Which is a shame, because I suspect it's rather a good one.' Kate flinched. 'Oh, have I touched a raw nerve? You'll never find Mr Right if you carry on like this. The rich ones will chase you because you make them look good – like their flash cars and flash jobs – but they won't make you happy.' He paused for a second, studying her. When he spoke again his voice was dangerously soft. 'Maybe that's how you like it. No feelings, just the kudos and men to adore you from a safe distance. I can just imagine what you'd be like if a man over-stepped the mark. You're afraid of anything intimate, Kate. You play games with men, manipulating them with that wonderful body of yours, then you run a mile. Deep down you're just plain scared.'

Her heart was thumping wildly but she couldn't think of anything cutting to say. Trapped by this monstrous bully she glanced helplessly at the others getting into a third taxi. Skander put a hand to her chin and gently tilted it upwards.

'Why aren't you sleeping?'

'I never sleep well on trips,' she said mutinously, thrown by the sudden kindness in his voice. She felt cornered, as if he was inspecting her under a microscope, and studied the floor in embarrassment.

'I don't believe that. All the same, you should rest properly. We've got three more days of shooting and they're mostly close-ups. At least your skin has calmed down. I'll give you a couple of sleeping pills when we get back to the hotel. They're strong enough to knock out an elephant.'

'Charming!'

'Kate. You don't have to . . .'

'Can I go now,' she hissed, gritting her teeth, 'or must I endure another chapter of your Penguin Freud?'

Skander immediately released her arm and looked at her with disappointment. 'I can see why you get on so well with Neil.'

'Why?'

'Because as a male he presents absolutely no threat to you.'

Kate stumbled to the taxi, half-expecting one of his great arms to grab her and yank her back against him.

16

Toby Wilmot-Smith woke at eight to the gentle snoring of his girlfriend. The cream duvet cover they'd bought in the Conran shop was wrapped around her tiny hips, displaying small but perfect breasts, her heavy blonde hair sprawled over the pillow. Toby turned his thoughts back to last night. He'd known the minute they'd arrived it had been a mistake to come. It wasn't his kind of party and as a result he'd had too much to drink. Mostly because he was bored watching Tanya spend the whole evening twisted around an HTV executive producer. He vaguely remembered someone accusing him of being an alcoholic. Well, the booze had run out so he'd gone searching for cooking sherry in the kitchen. Personally he thought it had shown great initiative.

It wasn't that he didn't care about Tanya but sometimes he felt that he did all the giving. He was tired of accompanying her on trips, of her endless, demanding friends, and sick of footing the bills she ran up. Not that he begrudged spending the money, but did everything always have to be in three figures? And why the hell couldn't she occasionally tidy up after herself, he thought irritably, inspecting the clothes strewn across the floor. They'd stay like that too unless either he or the daily picked them up for her. What about this play she was supposed to be rehearsing? It didn't seem to be getting very far. All Tanya seemed interested in was television. Toby yawned. Rubbing his eyes he considered today's game of golf. He was meeting Yarnton at his club at twelve for lunch, followed by a round of golf. They had a wager of £500. Toby smirked. He'd dropped his handicap by a further two points and Yarnton didn't know.

Tanya stirred and opened one grey eye. 'Hello, Tiger.' She

stretched like a Persian cat. Her voice was warm and husky, 'I was dreaming about you. D'you want to know what we were doing?'

Toby pulled back his side of the duvet. 'Sorry, angel, but I've got to get up. I'm meeting Yarnton in an hour.'

'That's the third time this week. Anyone would think you've found yourself another lover.' She smiled seductively. 'Couldn't we have a teeny weeny bit of breakfast in bed before you go?'

'Eleven thirty's hardly breakfast, Tanya.'

Her eyes grew smoky. She slipped a small hand out of the covers and touched his cock. 'Come on, Tiger,' she urged, triumphant as he swelled in her hand, 'come back to bed.'

That was the problem, Toby reflected on his way to meet Yarnton. Their relationship was based entirely on sex. But he couldn't resist her. Going to bed with Tanya Cook was rather like a Weight-Watcher gorging on a box of beautifully-wrapped chocolates, then bitterly regretting it.

'You're thirty-two,' Yarnton said pointedly over lunch, 'you should be married with a good job. Roots are what matter, m' boy. You've been at a loose end for too long. I'd had both my boys at your age.'

'I'm not sure babies are quite Tanya's thing.'

'Rubbish!' Yarnton waved a dismissive hand. He cut a sliver of Stilton to go with his port and Bartholomew biscuit. 'It's just the sort of thing to settle a girl. You've just got to be firm. Do have some of this cheese, it's really excellent. There's some Dutch if the Stilton's too strong.'

'No thanks,' said Toby, reaching instead for the port, 'I'll stick to Dutch courage.'

'You'll need it on the golf course, my boy. I feel lucky today!'

'While we're on the subject, Yarnton. About my handi-cap . . .'

Riding a victory cloud four hours later, Toby broached the subject at home. Tanya, who was supposed to be rehearsing in Battersea, had called in sick and spent the day in bed nursing her hangover. Now, sitting in the drawing-room wrapped in a mint-green Nina Ricci dressing-gown, scoffing

Toblerone, she had made a miraculous recovery.

'Babies!' she squealed. 'Honestly, darling, you are a scream. What would we do with a baby?'

'Well, I just thought, now that we've been living together for . . .'

Another shriek. 'We've oodles of time for that, darling, and I've got my career to think of. Clive wants to put me up for a mini series Central are thinking of doing. I know I'm perfect for the part. And you know how much my work means to me. Besides, a baby would mean I'd have less time to spend with you.' She knelt beside his chair and stroked his thigh. 'On the other hand, there's nothing to stop us from practising.'

'Babies are supposed to bring us closer together,' said Toby feebly.

'Think of all those four o'clock in the morning feeds, ghastly nappy changes, hunting for last-minute baby-sitters, sick everywhere,' she said, warming to her subject. 'Our lives would be turned upside down.'

'How long is your play going to run for?' asked Toby, sorry he'd brought the subject up.

'Six weeks, then I'm all yours. Don't forget the cast party tonight. Clive especially asked me to bring you.' I bet he did, Toby thought with a shudder. 'Should be a wondrous night. I thought I'd wear my new Alistair Blair. What do you think?'

'Depends on how much I had to pay for it.'

The phone rang and Tanya sprang up to get it. 'That'll be Patricia. She's just back from New York and I'm dying to hear about the new man. She's calling collect. I said you wouldn't mind, darling. I'll take it upstairs so I won't disturb you.'

Flicking moodily through the *Sunday Times*, Toby decided the last thing he wanted was to go to another wretched party, particularly one of bloody Clive's. All Tanya ever talked about was Clive this, Clive that. After weeks of hearing his name Toby hadn't liked the man any better in person. And his dreadful boyfriend who name-dropped the whole time. What was it about the man that so impressed Tanya? Clive's action-packed films included about ten minutes of monosyllables and B-rated actors hoping to shed their soap images. He turned to the TV section. Celebrity golf was on at seven.

281

Another one for the video. Toby clicked the remote control and let Maria Callas drown out his frustrations. He rubbed his itching eyes. Bloody hayfever had been playing up all week.

In the colour supplement Toby found himself staring at a girl with amazing brown eyes. Crikey, it was his elusive date! The photographer had caught her unawares and a tall, fierce-looking man with dark-brown hair had his arm around her shoulders to ward off the press. Boyfriend? Toby hoped not. He was disgustingly good-looking. Far from the small-time world of waitressing, she was being heralded as the new fashion queen of Paris. She looked marvellous. There were two more pictures taken inside the Vaubelle studio, and an editorial which Toby carefully read. Afterwards he sat think-ing for a long time, as howls of excited laughter filtered from their upstairs bedroom. Hearing the ping of the bedroom phone, Toby picked up the receiver and dialled a friend in Paris. He was making a second call when Tanya exploded through the door. She had changed into the Alistair Blair, what there was of it.

'Tiger! Patricia's getting married. Can you believe it! The most amazing man took her up in a hot-air balloon somewhere over New Mexico and proposed to her. Desperately roman-tic.'

'Good. Maybe he'll start paying for her calls from now on.'

Tanya pulled a face. 'Who are you calling?'

Toby held a finger up to his mouth to silence her. 'Reservations please. Yes . . . Paris.'

Tanya smirked. She knew he couldn't have been really serious about babies. She had been a teeny bit difficult lately, but it was ghastly nerves. Television commercials were so much easier and there was never any question of fluffing your lines. The opening was in a week and, as the lead, she so wanted to do well. I'll make it up to him, she promised herself. Toby hung up.

'Tiger, I haven't been shopping in Paris for an age! You are wicked. When do we go?'

'*I'm* leaving tomorrow morning.'

'But what about me?'

'*You*, darling,' said Toby firmly, 'are not going anywhere.

282

You're what's now called an employee. And with your play about to open, I know you'll want to spend every second preparing for it. As for tonight, I'm afraid you'll have to go to the party alone. I've already made commitments. I'm going to the opera.'

'But, darling! I love the opera.'

'The only opera you've ever expressed interest in was *Tommy* and you saw that on video. Give Clive my best!'

Feeling a great deal better than he had in months, Toby went upstairs to change.

In the Vaubelle camp tension was palpable and tempers increasingly short. Neither Rachel nor her staff were getting enough sleep. They were working morning and night on a mind-numbing amount of detail before the *couture*, now only two weeks away. A photographer from *Elle* trailed Rachel round the studio, clicking furiously as she fussed with fabric on Kate's stand-in.

Brigette, meanwhile, was busy rushing up and down the stairs with half-finished dresses. 'I must haf lost half a stone,' she wheezed, climbing the stairs for the umpteenth time.

By next week the sixteen booked models would start filtering in for their fittings. Any alterations would have to be done on the spot, as most of them would be flying on for further fittings in London.

The *Elle* photographer took a shot of Rachel making a quick sketch change, while the journalist asked her what she thought about taking on such a responsible job. Having agreed to the interview a month ago, Rachel was now regretting it. The photographer's presence was adding to the general tension because everyone was trying to look and act normally in front of him.

Nicole stuck her head round the door. 'Both Tatjana Patitz and Yasmeen's agents have confirmed their bookings, Mademoiselle.'

'How's Linda wearing her hair at the moment?' asked Richard, drinking his fourth glass of Badoit. 'Is she still red?'

'Jet-black, twenties style, but she had it blonde for *Vogue* last month so it doesn't much matter,' said Brigette. 'We can

283

always use a vig. Do you want to see the model now?'

Rachel nodded. They still needed three models for the press show. 'Which dress did we decide for Gina?'

'The russet with the ruched sleeves.'

'What about the embroidery for the wedding dress? That should have arrived a fortnight ago. Jean-Marc urgently needs some to match the shoes.'

'I've already checked,' said Jean-Marc. 'Should be in this afternoon.'

An exquisite Danish model was ushered into the studio. Richard went out to give her a dress to try on. He came back five minutes later saying ruefully, 'Hips are too big but I like her look. Perhaps if we put her in less fitted skirts?'

'Let's have her in,' said Rachel.

The model appeared wearing one of the dresses. She glided self-consciously to the front of the studio, constantly checking her appearance in the mirror.

'Could you turn round, please.' Rachel frowned slightly. The zip was undone at the back.

'We couldn't get it done up,' said the model apologetically. She'd been starving herself for a week.

'I'm sorry,' said Rachel, indicating that she couldn't book the girl. 'Thank you for coming.'

The intercom buzzed in the studio. Brigette, coming back, answered it.

'Call for you on line one, Rachel.'

Glancing at her watch to see how they were doing for time, Rachel flicked a switch in front of her and picked up the extension. 'Hello?' she said, signalling for Richard to lower the skirt hemline he was pinning on the model. The girl was good but she'd be glad to have Kate back. The photographer's camera clicked. 'Who is this?' she asked, then putting her hand over the receiver, she mouthed, 'Richard, no. That's too much. Take it back up an inch.'

She listened for a few moments, then turned pink.

Oh no, Brigette thought, watching her, don't tell me Claude Vaubelle's causing more problems.

'Of course I remember,' Rachel was saying, 'how on earth did you find me? . . . Oh, I see.' She went pinker. 'Opera?

Well, just a minute, I'll have to put you on hold.'

The journalist, pen poised, looked at her keenly.

Rachel buzzed Nicole on the intercom. 'Nicole, what am I doing late Wednesday afternoon?'

'You've a meeting with Textiles at three. An 'air appointment at five with Monsieur Alexandre; he cancelled someone else to fit you in, and a dinner appointment with Marc Frazer from *Paris-Match*.'

'Thank you,' said Rachel, before switching back to line one. 'Four o'clock would be lovely. I've got nothing planned.'

Brigette and Richard looked at one another in astonishment. The *Elle* journalist wrote in her notebook: Personal call. Date Wednesday, 4 p.m. Possibly opera?

After that the morning took on a distinctly lighter note. Rachel hummed softly while she worked, arousing no end of curiosity in her staff. The photographer took advantage of the change of mood and managed to cajole her into posing for a few shots. Rachel even failed to notice a dress which had been wrongly corrected. Brigette took it back down to Colette herself and explained the mistake.

Returning from lunch, Rachel received several raised eyebrows.

'What's your secret?' said Marie-Claire, rushing by with some documents she had to fax for Joni, still in Italy. 'Things like that never happen to me.'

'I thought for a moment you'd taken up gardening,' said Roe on his way to the bank.

Was she imagining it or had Eric, the doorman, winked at her? Opening the door to the studio, Rachel thought, I do hope nothing's wrong. She stopped in her tracks. The room was filled with flamingo-pink roses. There must have been over a hundred of them.

'Nicole . . .' she called in a faltering voice.

'*Oui, mademoiselle.*' Nicole rose from her desk.

'Where on earth did all these flowers come from?'

'*Elles sont jolies, n'est-ce pas?* There is a card addressed to you.'

Rachel opened the envelope. The bold handwriting was loopy and practically illegible, 'Call me a cautious chap but I'm a firm believer in insurance policies. I thought that if I bought enough flowers you'd feel too guilty to stand me up a second time. Can't wait till Wednesday. Toby Wilmot-Smith.'

Turning an even deeper pink than the roses, Rachel sat down in a daze.

'Is anything wrong, Mademoiselle?' Nicole asked.

'No, Nicole,' said Rachel smiling suddenly, 'everything is wonderful, really wonderful!'

He picked her up from work in a chauffeured limousine. They drank champagne in the back of the car as it made its way to the place de l'Opéra. Toby had managed to get tickets for *The Marriage of Figaro*, the hottest production in town. Rachel was captivated by the music and inspired by the costumes that had been made on such a grand scale. After that the limousine ferried them to the Seine at the Pont de l'Alma. They boarded one of the Bateaux Mouches for a candlelight-dinner cruise. Rachel, never having taken the cruise, was unaware that Toby had hired the entire boat for the evening so that they could be alone.

'Why did you stand me up?' he asked, once the champagne was poured and their orders had been taken. 'It's been on my mind all these weeks.'

'I didn't. That is, the Vaubelle offer came out of the blue and I had to drop everything. It all happened so fast there was no time to explain, and I'd lost your address so there was no way of getting in touch with you. I'm sorry.' He could see she meant it.

'So will I be if you tell me you're now madly in love with a Frog.'

Rachel laughed and shook her head. The small amber earrings she wore twinkled in the candlelight, complementing her russet dress. 'I've had no time for romance.'

'Well, I hope you'll have time for me.'

He was fascinated by the way her dark eyebrows met. Her mesmeric eyes, unadorned by make-up, were so well defined they looked as if they had been outlined. She appeared much more confident. The self-deprecation was still there, but she seemed older, more in charge of herself, which he found enormously sexy.

'Tell me how it's all going,' he asked. 'The collections must be quite soon.'

'Horribly soon! There's still so much to do. I haven't got all my designs finished yet and only thirty per cent of the dresses are made.' She sighed and fiddled with her glass. 'I'm in danger of becoming a bore about it all. I've even begun sketching in my sleep.'

'What happens once the collection's over?'

'That depends on how it's received by the press. If it's good I'll be offered another contract, if it's bad then it's back to waitressing,' Rachel said philosophically.

'Surely not?'

She smiled. 'Perhaps I'm exaggerating slightly. I hope one day to have my own fashion house. Nothing grand like Vaubelle, that would be beyond even my wildest dreams, but I'd like control over my designs. That way if I made mistakes I'd have only myself to blame. It's really daunting being held responsible for someone else's money. This is very good champagne.'

Toby beamed. 'I'm glad you like it. This is *your* night.'

Rachel blushed.

'You know I envy you.' He was suddenly serious.

'Me!' said Rachel in surprise.

'You're talented and ambitious. You have something that motivates and excites you every day.' Toby paused and stared into his drink. 'I had that once.'

'What did you do?'

'Worked for my father's bank. Nothing glamorous like you, but I enjoyed the challenge of making numbers work for me. That's all merchant banking is, really. Numbers. If you thought about the millions in terms of money you'd go mad.'

'Then if you were so good, why did you stop?'

For a split second he hesitated. 'Because I messed up an important deal and it was my fault.'

'We're all allowed to make mistakes,' Rachel said pragmatically, 'so why are you so hard on yourself?'

Toby studied his glass. 'I was drunk at the time and it cost the bank millions.'

When he finally glanced at Rachel he expected her to look

shocked, but all she said was, 'I bet you were really good.'

'I had my moments. I came top in most things. Everyone used to say "That boy will go far. He's destined for a brilliant future." ' He paused again then spoke almost to himself, 'I wonder what happened to him?' Then he pulled himself together. 'God, this must be boring! The last thing I wanted to do was talk about myself. Women are always complaining we monopolise the conversation, and they're right.'

He poured out more champagne.

But Rachel wasn't deterred. 'You must have hobbies. Music, travel, sport?'

'Ah. Now golf's quite a different matter. I confess to being a complete addict!'

'What's your handicap?'

Toby's eyes lit up like a traffic light. 'You play?'

'A little,' said Rachel cautiously.

He was suddenly a ten-year-old, bursting with enthusiasm as he talked about his favourite subject.

'I once dreamed of becoming a pro. Used to spend hours at our summer house whacking white balls into the sea practising my swing. Drove my mother mad. I might have made it but I slipped a disc and after that had to face up to the fact that I'd never make a serious contender. I play as much as I can and keep up with all my idols, Faldo, Trevino, Winger, Nicklaus. They probably don't mean much to you though, if you don't follow the game.'

Rachel smiled into her glass but some instinct stopped her from coming clean. She was still a little overwhelmed by Toby's interest and didn't want her father's identity to influence him in any way. At least not yet. She caught him watching her in the same eager, secret way he had the first time they'd met, and all thoughts of Jack evaporated. She was back on that high wire of excitement.

The kitchen staff had drawn lots to see who got to serve the Englishman. No one, in all the years the *maître d'* had worked on the Bateaux Mouches, had ever made such an extravagant gesture for a lady. Why, it put the French to shame! Despite bursting with curiosity the waiter refrained from more than a quick formal glance at the young couple. He could watch them from the kitchen porthole once they'd finished eating.

'Escargots with garlic cream and fresh artichokes!' announced a waiter with a flourish.

'That's for me,' said Toby, nodding towards the plate. 'I'd like to have another look at the wine list.'

'*Tout de suite, monsieur,*' said the waiter, briskly clicking his fingers in the air as a second waiter placed Rachel's meal before her. '*Et voilà,* the grilled red mullet with pimento for madame.'

A third waiter came rushing forward. While Toby deliberated over the wine list Rachel studied him under her long eyelashes. He looked so English in his check jacket, an Irish-green cardigan done up over a striped shirt and YSL tie, which had got twisted and was showing the label. She studied his long, artistic fingers. The soft, unlined hands could have belonged to a woman. Maybe it's his feminine qualities that I'm attracted to. She took another pleasurable sip of icy champagne.

Toby selected a wine and handed back the list. A lock of grey hair flopped over one of his eyes. His ears stuck out sharply on either side of his patrician head and a tiny piece of bread was stuck to the edge of his mouth. Rachel, unable to help herself, brought up her right hand and swept the bread crumb off his face. Instinctively, Toby trapped her hand in his own, catching a whiff of her musk perfume which made his senses reel.

'Sorry. I didn't mean to do that.' Rachel felt embarrassed.

'Don't be,' said Toby, kissing the back of her hand. 'I wish you'd do it more often.'

'What happened to your hair?'

'I get it dyed at huge expense in Bond Street. But if you don't like it, I'll go back to being blond.'

Rachel giggled. Toby drained his glass.

'When I was nineteen my parents were killed in a car crash. I was at Oxford at the time studying not terribly hard for my prelims. When I heard the news I went into a bit of a decline; got into the wrong crowd, drank too much and spent a lot of money. Bit irresponsible, I'm afraid. Have I shattered your illusions?'

Rachel, who had imagined Toby coming from a large, happy family in the country, was horrified. She covered his hand with her own.

'On my twenty-first birthday my girlfriend of three years walked off with my best friend. Had it coming really. I was drinking too much of this stuff,' Toby tapped the side of his champagne glass, 'and I suppose I hadn't been all that decent. But we were going to get married. I somehow never thought . . .' Toby faltered. Why the hell was he telling her all this? 'Don't remember much but I'm told I went a bit loopy. Overnight my hair turned grey. Shock, apparently. I've got used to it now.'

'I love grey hair,' said Rachel passionately.

'I still can't believe I found you, after all this time.'

Despite the late hour, Wednesday night in Paris was a circus. In order to avoid the congested Champs Elysées, the hired limousine weaved its way through the narrow back streets to Rachel's smart, tree-lined, leafy road. Toby instructed the driver to wait while he escorted Rachel to the front door.

'I won't insist you ask me up for coffee, although it's an attractive thought,' said Toby, standing almost a foot taller than Rachel. 'I know you've got to be up early.'

'How long will you be in Paris?' Rachel fished out her key.

'As long as it takes me to win you over. I've nothing to rush back to. Can I see you again tomorrow night?'

'I can't.' Toby was relieved to see Rachel looked as disappointed as he felt. 'I've got a meeting at eight after work and they tend to run on a bit.'

'I see. Playing hard to get, are we? Well, let's get one thing straight,' he said, pulling the green shawl over her shoulders. 'If that's a ploy to get me more interested, my sweet, there's no need. I'm already hooked. See me Friday.'

'Yes,' said Rachel in a whisper. 'Thank you for your lovely flowers and for tonight. You've no idea how much I've enjoyed it.'

A sudden blinding flash went off in her face. For a moment

Rachel blinked, clinging on to Toby's arm. As her vision cleared she could see a man with a camera scuttling off into the darkness.

'What was that?'

'Bloody press!' snapped Toby, watching the man go. 'Want me to get him back?'

'No. Let him go.'

'Probably followed us from Vaubelle. I keep forgetting I'm in the company of a celebrity.' Toby tilted her chin. 'And I shouldn't.' Rachel relaxed against him. 'Don't worry, angel. He won't come back. Now get inside and . . . dream of me a little tonight.'

When Toby bent and kissed her, Rachel's heart hammered as loudly as the bells of Notre Dame. What is happening to me, she wondered dizzily, putting her key in the lock.

As she closed the door, Toby was left with the warm dark and Rachel's lingering perfume. He smiled as he walked back to the waiting car.

Claude Vaubelle could hear his wife calling to him from downstairs. *Dieu!* What now? Couldn't he be left alone in peace. Naked, except for a pair of silk pyjama bottoms, he ran a hand over his little Buddha belly, gave a wide yawn then opened the window. In the last two months everything about him seemed to have grown heavier and weaker. He shouldn't have gone last night. His second visit this week. Too risky. The steam baths were notorious. And yet he hadn't been able to resist that pretty creature with the wide-set eyes and clever hands. Such persistence in someone so young. He'd never have dared been so bold at that age. Madness! Before saying goodbye last night they'd arranged another illicit meeting. But by the time he'd got home he had resolved not to go. The risk was too great. If Isabella ever found out!

He glanced at his sacred office walls which were covered in sketches from collections he'd worked on. Some dated back almost twenty years. He looked at them fondly and tongued the tip of his cigar, savouring old triumphs, the days when the press had called him the king of fashion. This morning's paper was spread over his desk, open at an article predicting the revolutionary changes at Vaubelle. In a copy of the latest *Elle* there was a picture of Rachel pinning a dress on a model. The model's arms were held in the air, her head bent to watch what Rachel was doing. Claude's eyes hardened. No revenge was too great for what she'd done to him. He, Claude Vaubelle, could no longer show his face in public. They were all laughing at him behind his back. His enemies. They thought he was washed up, finished. Fools! They were wrong. He just had to sit back and wait. Rachel Winger's collection would be a disaster, Claude was quite certain of it. So certain that he'd prepared a series of new sketches for the spring/summer collections. Let Roe Lewis come crawling back on his filthy American knees and apologise. Claude could hardly wait. Three weeks. Only three more weeks and he'd be back where he belonged.

17

Up and down the avenue Montaigne, home of the French *couturier*, pre-collection tension and excitement continued to build. The humidity generated bad temper and people were melting like ice-cream. For Rachel the few days leading up to the show passed in a blur. There was still a staggering amount of work to do, so many last-minute hitches to sort out at Vaubelle that she hardly gave Toby a thought. But when she did her eyes glazed over, her pulse quickened and concentration went out of the window. He had called three times yesterday and only this morning more flowers had arrived. They'd had to be put in Nicole's office as there was no more space in the studio, which already looked like a garden centre. She knew that everyone was talking about her 'mystery man', but she did not care. She was seeing him again tonight. Throwing another look at the studio clock, she thought she would burst from frustration. The hand hadn't budged.

'Mademoiselle?' Monique was fitting Kate into an evening dress.

'Didn't we alter that before you left?' Rachel said, scratching her head. 'It seems awfully big suddenly.'

Monique glanced quickly at Kate. 'Colette took it in an inch, Mademoiselle.'

Richard checked the back of the dress. 'Well, it's gaping. Don't tell me you've been dieting, dear.'

Rachel pushed her specs further up her nose. 'You do look thinner, Kate. I can't believe they didn't feed you properly in Italy. All that cheese and pasta!'

'I'm just a bit under the weather,' said Kate feebly. 'There's a nasty flu virus going round.'

Richard took a hasty step backwards.

'Well, you must take something for it,' said Rachel worriedly. Kate was looking unusually pale. 'I don't want you getting sick just before the show.'

Nor did Richard, who was fretting about his dodgy lungs. 'Powdered vitamin C and raw garlic three times a day should do the trick.'

Nicole deposited a series of photocopied designs on Rachel's desk.

'Monsieur Lewis is leaving for Los Angeles in an hour and wants to see you in his office.'

At the mention of Roe's name Kate was instantly alert. She hadn't seen or heard from him since her return. Now, after almost a week, the cold reality was beginning to sink in. He hadn't called because he hadn't wanted to.

Rachel removed her glasses which had left two angry marks and rubbed the bridge of her nose.

'Take the shirt in a further inch round the hips and send Tatiana up for her fitting. Kate, when Monique's finished, have a rest. Why not pop out and get something for your cold? I shouldn't be too long.'

As Rachel left, Monique fiddled with the back of Kate's dress. Kate found the occasional pressure on her sensitive skin irritating. God, her throat was killing her. Her glands were swollen into a lump the size of a golf ball making it hard for her to swallow. Maybe she *was* getting the flu? Ever since Bea had collected her from Charles de Gaulle she hadn't been herself.

Stuffed in the cramped Volkswagen hurtling back to the city, Kate's luggage stamped 'Pisa Airport' in the back alongside a bottle of duty-free Amaretto, Bea had explained to her what had happened during her trip to Italy.

'You're joking!' snapped Kate. She had her feet tucked up against the dashboard.

'Well, it was as much of a shock for me, darling, him arriving out of the blue like that with all your things.' Bea checked the rear mirror, shoving the car down into third gear as she neared some lights, then into neutral. 'I have to say he was perfectly nice. Not a word against you. Stayed for two cups of coffee and you know what my coffee's like.'

Kate glared out of her window at a Renault factory. Even her best friend seemed to have fallen for his charm.

'What did he say?' Not that she cared. She refused to care.

'The beast skirted most of my questions and I'm usually so good at getting people to talk. The men's Wimbledon final was on at the time so we ended up watching that – so exciting when Max Carter won. Roe just said you'd discussed it and the decision to move back had been yours. Oh Kate, darling, I'm so sorry. But he wasn't making you happy. He may have been exciting and sexy, but what you need is someone you can depend on.'

'Bea, for God's sake keep your eye on the road!'

'Whoops!' Bea had almost ploughed into the side of a transit van boasting several GB stickers on the back window. Rucksacks had been tied to the roofrack and Kate could see thugs inside.

'Stew-pid fucking cunt!' one of them yelled, his shaved head sticking out of the window, leering at them.

'Your wit and intellect astound me!' Kate shouted back with sudden fury, ignoring the violent V-signs. 'And I suppose you made that up all by yourself!'

Bea calmly retrieved a Twix from the glove box and handed half to Kate.

'Men!' Kate said contemptuously. 'They're not bloody worth it!'

I agree, reflected Bea, picking bits of caramel from her teeth. Her swollen vagina was itching like mad.

Kate recounted her trip to Tuscany. The commercial had looked wonderful and everyone seemed pleased. They'd finished ahead of schedule, which meant they were able to squeeze in some sight-seeing. Neil (Bea laughed at this point) had apparently run off with a very pretty Sicilian actor, while Kate, it seemed, had clashed with the director whom she described as a bully with a huge chip on his shoulder. Skander, Kate thought sullenly, had given her little more than a perfunctory nod before she left.

Bea, only half-listening, was preoccupied with her own problems. Arriving limp with nerves for her appointment at the AIDS clinic, she had had to endure an hour's counselling. The room was full of lurid posters warning her of the depressing HIV statistics and someone had given her a medical pamphlet outlining the effects of the disease (such a sensitive and well-thought-out gift). The counsellor could have been an AIDS victim himself, she thought grimly, as the pale, emaciated man warned her of what would happen if she tested positive. Be prepared for the worst was the general message.

Next she saw an Algerian doctor she had great difficulty in understanding. His thick accent came out like congealed grease as he began by getting her to fill out an alarming white form with 'confidential' stamped in red over the top. This he studied as if it were the Official Secrets Act. Then he asked her some embarrassing questions about Ray.

'It says here you last had sex with Mr Marks four months ago. Has there been anyone since?' the doctor muttered, lowering his Moorish nose over some notes.

'There's my boyfriend Sam. But there's no need to worry about him. He's an absolute sticker for condoms.'

A starched nurse was sterilising alarmingly sharp knives in the background. The doctor mumbled something then scribbled on a form which Bea strained her neck to read. She soon gave up. Like most doctors' writing it was illegible to her and might just as well have been written in Chinese.

'Mmm,' he muttered. 'Anyone else?'

'Just one,' admitted Bea, thinking of Cameron. She hoped she wouldn't have to go into too much detail.

'But no other partners?'

'No, that's it.'

The doctor looked disappointed. Surely three in the last two months was enough for any self-respecting girl.

'Oral?' the doctor questioned. 'Anal?'

'I'm afraid so,' Bea whispered, hoping the nurse couldn't hear. She leaned forward in her chair. 'There is one other thing.' The doctor's nose twitched with interest. 'It might not be related but I think I might have picked up something nasty in Indonesia. I have a terrible burning sensation and it seems to be getting worse.'

'I see,' he said, managing to get three syllables out of see. Obviously on to something. 'I'd better examine you, then. Please remove your lower garments and jump up on the bed.'

Bea fixed her eyes on a particularly interesting part of the ceiling as her legs were pulled apart and thrust into iron stirrups by the nurse who gave her hand a reassuring squeeze. Bea smiled apologetically as the Asian head disappeared between her legs and grunted. Well it can't be all that bad, surely? Bea tensed as she felt his hand prod inside her followed by a terrifying metal clamp which he used to hold her open. Honestly. He might have warmed it up first. She was told to relax and closed her eyes while foreign things moved inside her, trying to take her mind off the pain.

Let's see, she thought, she had three people coming over for dinner on Saturday night. What pre-made food could she pass off as her own? And could she afford to splash out on some good plonk? No. But what did it matter. Wasn't she about to be told she had a month to live? I could write a note to my bank manager, something really profound and apologising for not being able to carry on shouldering the burden of my overdraft, she thought, cheering up. That would get that power-suited, sanctimonious, grey little man feeling really guilty.

There was a bang and Bea opened her eyes as the door barged open. A second nurse appeared, followed by a young man. Now what!

'Don't worry, *ma biche*. He's a nurse,' the nurse said reassuringly.

Oh, well that's absolutely fine! Why not bring in the receptionist too? I'm sure he'd like a peek.

Old Doc Hussein was clearly having no luck. Depositing a scraping from her womb on to a glass slide, he snapped off his soiled prophylactic gloves and tossed them into the bin.

'You can get up now,' he said briskly. 'I'll take a quick blood sample then the nurse will show you where to go.'

'But what's wrong with me?' Bea squeaked, alarmed by the

size of the syringe. Was it necessary to take quite so much blood?

'Herpes.'

Did he have to look so disappointed.

'Herpes!' Bea shrieked, forgetting that the student nurse was hovering close by.

'Oh, I wouldn't worry too much. The first attack's usually the worst.'

'You mean I'm going to get this again!'

'Only if you allow yourself to get run down and over-stressed. For a great majority of people, however, the attacks grow weaker and more infrequent. You'll find that if they do come back it usually occurs around your period. Now, nurse will take you to the dispensary and give you something to help clear the sore up. As for the blood test, you'll get the result in about a week.'

'You must be joking!' Bea exclaimed to the nurse, once they were safely out of earshot. 'I can't possibly wait that long.'

'I'm afraid you'll have to, mademoiselle,' said the nurse as she wrote the name and reference number carefully on the back of her sample. 'You're lucky. Most people have to wait up to a month.'

They walked back through the waiting-room where a fraught mother was smacking a small baby. The child opened its mouth and howled. Bea felt like doing the same.

'But what should I do in the meantime? I'll be sick with worry!'

The nurse looked sympathetic. 'Look, you really have a very good chance of not being HIV positive. Despite what you read it's still quite hard to catch unless you fit in the high risk bracket. You can try calling us a couple of days earlier in case the result has come in, if that helps.'

Seven days, brooded Bea, eyeing the anonymous brown bag stuffed with Lysine pills, vaginal creams and half a ton of suppositories beside Kate's feet in the front of the car. Well, one thing was certain. No matter how much she fancied someone, there was no way she was going to bed with them unless he came with a guaranteed complete, up-to-date

298

medical. And references! Kate was right. They absolutely weren't worth the trouble. It might be the hardest thing she ever did, but she had managed it with smoking and she'd do it with sex, if she had to wear a bloody chastity belt and throw away the key!

The hôtel d'Angleterre, set back from the busy shopping area of Saint Germain, had once been the British Embassy. Rumour had it that Benjamin Franklin had refused to enter the place to sign the US Declaration of Independence because he considered it to be British soil. Rachel Winger, however, had no such misgivings at being there, ensconced on a sofa with Toby in the Ambassador's suite which was inappropriately done up in pink satin. Half-empty coffee cups and a plate of untouched *petits fours* were laid out on a footstool in front of her.

It had been another gloriously romantic evening. Their seventh, reflected Rachel dreamily, beginning with dinner at Maxim's, a barefoot stroll on the grass in the forbidden grounds of the Luxembourg Palace, where they'd smoked marijuana, which she had never done before, and talked about books they'd read and places they wanted to visit. Later they had ventured on to a smoky jazz club, something else she'd never done before. All those evenings she'd spent with books and fabrics and solitude – what an awful thought! Two nights ago, feeling brave enough to ask Toby in for a nightcap, she had played him some Argentine music, translating a famous tango love song, *El día que me quieras, The day you might have loved me*. They had talked till sunrise.

'This is pretty,' he said now, inspecting the silver crucifix necklace she always wore.

'My mother gave it to me for my sixteenth birthday. I never take it off.'

'You must miss home.'

'I miss my family and El Refugio, our farm in Lobos.' Rachel's eyes softened. 'You can't imagine how lovely it is. I used to lie outside at night and watch the sky. The stars seemed so big and close you felt you could reach up and pluck one out.'

'What about your friends?'

'I left home so young I don't really have any. My closest friends moved to South Africa six years ago. We keep in touch. But the distance makes it hard.'

Toby tenderly folded her against him. 'We'll go there together.'

Inevitably Rachel's thoughts returned to the collection. She was worried about the wedding dress. Despite constant pleading the embroidery still hadn't arrived, and having seen the half-finished *toile* on Kate she was now having second thoughts about the design. Did she dare change it so close to the show?

'Penny for them,' mumbled Toby, nuzzling her neck.

'What? Oh, I was just thinking about work. There's still so much to do and I'm scared to death. What if I let everyone down?'

'You won't. I've the greatest faith in your skills. But you're not to think of work when you're with me. If you're to design efficiently, you've got to give those lovely batteries of yours time to re-charge.'

Rachel smiled. 'You're right. I'm sorry.'

'What are you doing for Christmas?'

'Toby, it's only July. I don't usually think that far ahead.'

'I do and I'd like to take you somewhere warm. It'll make a nice change from skiing and electric blankets. We'll lie on the beach all day drinking Pina Coladas and toast ourselves until we pass for natives. I want time to learn about you, every delicious corner.'

Rachel thought she must have done something very good to have deserved Toby.

'Why don't we take the rest of the week off and just spend it in bed? I'll call down to reception.'

'I have to work!' A pause, then, 'Toby?'

'Mmm?'

'Do you ever think about going back into banking?' No response. 'It just seems a waste, not having something to motivate you.'

'You do that.'

'That's not the same thing. I know you went through a

300

difficult time and you may say that none of this is any of my business but you were obviously very good.'

' "Were" being the operative word.'

'Well, will you think about it?'

'I'll think about it.'

'Promise?'

'Promise.' His breath tickled her neck. 'Do you really have to go?'

Rachel hastily sat up. 'I . . . Toby, I have a confession to make.' She knotted her hands together in her lap. 'About you, I mean.'

'This sounds interesting,' said Toby, fishing for a compliment. Really, she had the most delightful ears. He could go on nibbling them for hours.

'This is the first time I've been alone in a strange man's room.'

'But you're not alone, darling. You're with me.' He snuggled against her soft bosom.

'I didn't mean that.' Rachel looked at the floor. 'I've never been to bed with a man.'

Toby, immediately the picture of concern, was stunned.

'God, darling! I'm so sorry. I had no idea.' He sat up. 'And here I am mauling you like a thug. What must you think!'

It was not the reaction Rachel had been expecting.

'You mean . . . you don't mind? It doesn't put you off?'

'Mind! I'm completely knocked out by you.' He rose suddenly. 'Now, I suggest we get you home. You're too much of a temptation on this sofa and I'm only human, after all.' He kissed her. 'Shall I get your coat?'

Rachel gazed wonderingly at him for several moments. Then, with just a trace of hesitation, she reached for his hand. She suddenly knew what to do.

'Where's the bedroom? I haven't had the full conducted tour.'

'Are you sure?' asked Toby nervously a few minutes later, as they lay down on the bed. He'd dreamt of this moment for so long, he didn't want to spoil it by rushing things.

'Are you?' Her voice, like the rest of her, was soft.

'Didn't I say, darling?' Toby tentatively caressed Rachel's

face as if he were afraid she would break. 'I've been waiting for you all my life.'

He did nothing but kiss her for a full half an hour until he felt sure she was completely relaxed. Rachel was aware of buttons being undone and Toby's hands struggling with her bra. He was breathing deeply, murmuring into her ear and she gave herself up to his tender kisses. This was heaven and she didn't feel at all nervous. Nothing about Toby made her nervous. Bells were ringing in her head. No doubt celebrating the end of my virginity, she thought with a giggle. Her hands burrowed their way into Toby's thick, floppy hair. She discovered an earlobe and gave it an experimental nibble, then grew bolder, encouraged by Toby's pleasurable moan, pushing her tongue inside his ear. Maybe I have gone to heaven, she thought hazily, as the bells grew more insistent. But she soon realised the ringing wasn't coming from her head but from the phone. Cursing under her breath, Toby rolled over and picked it up.

'Wilmot-Smith,' he snapped irritably. He listened for a few moments then glanced quickly at Rachel. 'How did you get my number? Oh I see. Yes,' he paused, then his expression changed. He looked really worried. 'How did it happen? Are you all right? Oh my God, yes of course, I'll catch the first flight back. Now don't worry. Everything's going to be all right. I'll be there as soon as I can.'

He replaced the receiver.

'Trouble?' said Rachel, hitching up a bra strap.

''Fraid so. Apparently there was a gas-leak in my kitchen and it exploded this morning. I have a friend staying there and I think she's hurt. I'm really sorry, darling. I've got to go back.'

'Of course you have.' She understood. She really did. It was just hard hiding her disappointment.

'Hey, now wait a minute,' Toby pulled Rachel back against him, devouring her with kisses, 'this is to be continued. And no more disappearing acts, do you hear. Another six months of waiting for you and never mind grey hair. I'll go bald!'

At ten o'clock the following evening Rachel was sitting on the floor with Richard trying to piece together the running order of the collection. They were both extremely tired. Two models had cancelled at the last moment, which meant a re-jig with the outfits. What made it so complicated was that the new models were different sizes and it was too late to fly them back from London for a fitting. They'd just have to risk it. As they worked Brigette swapped sketches around on the board.

'Colette wants to bring up the wedding dress,' said Nicole, wrapped around the studio door. 'She seems to be having a few problems with it. Can I send her up?'

Rachel nodded enthusiastically. She was eager to get it finished. Ten minutes later she lay down on the floor staring up at the ceiling. It was hopeless. The dress was a disaster. The priceless embroidery had finally arrived yesterday after-noon and had been sewn to the dress (Colette had worked on it most of the night), but the effect was awful. Rachel's concern wasn't in rescuing the embroidery – that could always be put to use on another collection – no, it was the time they didn't have to make up a new one. The show was only seventeen hours away. Kate walked up and down trying to bring some life to the dress, but Rachel clearly wasn't happy, and glancing at her reflection in the huge studio mirror, Kate could understand why.

'What can we do?' said Richard in despair. 'There's no time to start again, not unless we make a variation on last season's.'

'It didn't sell,' said Brigette flatly.

Rachel groaned, 'Oh, God, I'm so tired I can't think straight any more. When did we last eat?'

Nicole buzzed through.

'I'll get it,' said Richard.

'Trion Videos need to know what time you want them tomorrow?'

'Eight thirty at the latest,' Richard spoke into the intercom. 'I don't want them setting up in the middle of hair and make-up. We're going to carry on working, Nicole. Could you organise something to eat? Café Rouge do take-aways. Sandwiches, drinks, anything they've got.'

'And can we have something vegetarian for Kate,' said Brigette kindly, who had started playing around with some bronze organza. Rachel watched wearily from the floor. Why couldn't they have had this problem a week ago? She could have faced it then. But now, so close to the show and with all of them so tired, she couldn't think straight. Her head was splitting. Kate, ever professional and chatting to Brigette in low whispers, held the fabric against her body. Poor girl, thought Rachel, she looked all in. Come to think of it she hadn't been herself since Italy. About to tell them both to have a rest, Rachel suddenly sprang up, all evidence of fatigue disappearing.

'Wait a minute, Brigette! Put that back. No, just as you had it. That's it!' She had an idea. 'Kate, take that dress off. It doesn't work and we're only wasting time with it.' Both girls looked slightly alarmed. 'Richard, can you get me the gold-embroidered border we looked at this morning. Oh, and four large gold and ivory buttons. We've been missing the point completely! It's too busy, too much going on. That's where Claude went wrong, going over the top with all his designs. Women today are afraid of anything too ostentatious, that's why the likes of Armani and Ralph Lauren are doing so well. Clients want luxurious fabrics but clean simple lines. Hand me some pins, would you, Brigette?'

She began to work frantically, unwinding yards and yards of bronze organza against Kate's white skin.

'I want this to be very feminine, see? Big sleeves like this,' she explained, bunching sheer, floating fabric round Kate's arm, 'and we must see plenty of skin.'

'I've got the embroidery,' puffed Richard, trying to get his breath back after racing up and down three flights of stairs. 'This is all we have left.'

'But we can get more?' Rachel asked.

'Oh, yes, No problem.'

'Good. I want it for the waistband. Oh, this fabric looks wonderful on you, Kate! With your hair loose and masses of jewels around your neck. Oh, I just know it will work!' She clapped her hands in excitement. 'Colette, can you do it?'

'The *toile*, mademoiselle,' she said, meaning the calico

version, 'will take at least two hours.'

'That's too long. Forget the *toile*. Just go ahead and make it up. We'll have to risk it.'

Rachel's mind was racing, thinking the running order through. Brigette quickly duplicated the design on paper.

'There's a problem,' contributed Richard, 'we don't have Kate as the bride.'

'Damn. Who do we have?'

'Karen.'

'No, I want Kate. The bride's got to be a redhead. Does that muck the running order up?'

'Slightly, but we can get round it. It'll just mean Kate will have a very fast change.'

'Then make a note that we must have extra dressers standing by. Any ideas for accessories, Jean-Marc, since our luck seems to have taken a turn for the better?'

Jean-Marc was already rifling through a box. 'These would look superb!' he said, pulling out a pair of sheer tights that had a slight shimmer.

'And shoes? Nothing too heavy,' Rachel warned as Jean-Marc fished out a pair of black satin sling-backs. 'I'd prefer them to match. Do we have anything else?'

'I've got these,' he said waving a pair of gold sandals, used in the last show. '*Quelle taille*, Kate?'

'Forty-one.'

He looked disappointed. 'I don't have her size.'

'Me and my big feet,' said Kate ruefully. 'I've got some gold sandals at home that would do.'

'Will you bring them, just in case?' Rachel removed her glasses. 'Oh, I'm so relieved. It just goes to show accidents do sometimes work. Well done, Brigette, for jogging my silly brain.'

Ten hours later, as the last of the outfits were still being pressed, less than a mile down the road the Vaubelle black and silver logo was being hung on the rear stage wall. Several hundred glossy brochures outlining the collection, and tiny samples of make-up were being placed on chairs. The runway had miraculously taken shape while lights were hung, speakers tested for power. Barriers were being set up outside the entrances where soon an army of security guards would appear, carefully inspecting each invitation.

Rachel and her team had kept going through the night, coordinating each scene until they were completely satisfied. The wedding dress was finished at 6 a.m., but without Kate (who had finally staggered home at 2 a.m.) they had no way of knowing if it worked until she arrived for the show. Wearily everyone had then gone home to shower and change. Now, pale and absolutely shattered, they raced around backstage checking that everything had arrived.

Roe Lewis, back late last night from Los Angeles, looked fit and energetic. Rachel, dressed in a long navy wrapover skirt and a crisp white shirt, couldn't remember a time when she'd seen him look any other way.

'How are you?' he asked warmly. He'd had a good trip.

'Ask me that in three hours. Right now I'm feeling terrified!'

'Don't be. From what I've seen of the collection I'd say the best investment I ever made was to take you out for that lunch.'

Rachel was so flattered that she blushed.

'Mademoiselle!' a plaintive voice cried. 'Can we have you backstage? *Vogue* wants to photograph you with Kate.'

Rachel started wringing her hands nervously. 'God, I've been absolutely dreading this bit.'

'Hey,' said Roe, putting a reassuring arm around her, 'this is your big moment. You've worked damn hard. Make the most of it.'

'Wish me luck then.'

'You won't need it, honey. They're going to love you.'

Smiling gratefully, Rachel pulled herself up to her full five foot six and walked towards the frantic, scrambling assistants, the noise and the terrifyingly élite audience that was about to make or break her career.

18

Rachel woke to an insistent buzzing. She reached out blindly and grappled for the alarm but the ringing continued. Fumbling for her glasses, she climbed out of her single bed and threw on a dressing-gown. Her brain wobbled inside her head. So this was what a hangover felt like, she thought dolefully. A blurred delivery man was standing outside. The morning paper and four letters lay at her feet. Rachel picked them up.

'Mademoiselle Winger?'

'*Oui, c'est moi.*'

The postman extended his arm and offered her a cage. A tiny lovebird fluttered nervously inside. Oh, how wonderful! It had to be from Toby. Beaming at the postman, she signed the registered post form and closed the door. At last! It had been a week since he'd left Paris and she hadn't received a single word. Mind you, with all the excitement from the show she hadn't had time to worry. But having bombarded her with so much attention his silence had been unsettling. Placing the cage on the kitchen table she gave the lovebird some water, then ran herself a bath. Back in the kitchen she studied the card but found it impossible to read between the lines – it was curiously formal and his handwriting was diabolical. Perhaps he was shy on paper. If only he were here to share her success.

Rachel allowed herself a few minutes to gloat over the rave reviews which had followed the show two days ago. 'Vaubelle's new girl is the toast of Paris,' wrote one; 'At last, clothes we can wear,' wrote another; and from *Vogue*, 'Rachel realises that women no longer need the power suits of the eighties! Her clothes give you freedom and choice.'

There had been endless celebrations and calls of congratulations. Jack, as a surprise, had turned up backstage – Lorna had called off sick – with a huge bunch of sweet peas and an amber bracelet. Then last night, after the collection had been heralded as a look forward compared with an abundance of retro, and her wedding dress was immortalised on the front page of *Women's Wear Daily*, Roe had whisked her off to a champagne supper. She must call her mother in Buenos Aires tonight and tell her the good news. The sound of running water filtered into the room.

'The bath!'

Rushing into the bathroom she yanked out the plug until enough water had drained away, then put it in again. Drifting back to the kitchen she made coffee and swallowed two paracetamols, hugging the thought of seeing Toby again. She glanced hopefully at the phone. Please, please call me! He'd left in such a tearing hurry she hadn't thought to ask for his number. She giggled at the memory of their last evening together. And now, with the success of the show . . . She felt so happy she could burst!

Picking up the paper Rachel wondered if there might be some more reviews. She was curious to know if there was anything in the English tabloids. An unflattering picture of Claude Vaubelle glared at her from the front page of *Le Monde*. Unfolding the paper, she started to read, her face draining of colour. She was so shocked that her coffee crashed to the floor, splashing scalding liquid against her legs. She felt nothing. She was too busy digesting the screaming headlines:

CLAUDE VAUBELLE FOUND DEAD,
SUSPECTED SUICIDE.

Somewhere in another room a phone began to ring.

Roe double-parked the Porsche, grabbed his leather briefcase and stormed towards the Vaubelle building. Having been up most of the night he was in a filthy mood and scowled at the fleet of journalists and television cameras clustered outside.

'Hey, that's him!' one of the journalists shrieked excitedly, brandishing an alarmingly large microphone. 'Mr Lewis. One moment, please! Could we get a statement from you.'

'I have nothing to say!' snapped Roe, striding through the front door, which Eric, the doorman, purposefully shut against the cameras.

Ignoring the waiting lift Roe climbed the five flights to his office taking the stairs two at a time. He passed Richard in the corridor, and Joni, who hastily stubbed out her cigarette. A white-faced Nicole was standing by the fax machine. She opened her mouth to say something.

'No calls, Nicole! I don't want to be disturbed. Get Pierre up here. Now!'

He banged his briefcase on the desk and threw his jacket over the back of the chair. Fuck! Why now? Right after the collections! Claude had always been an attention-seeking little runt, but suicide! Christ! The story was splashed all over the front page of every major French paper. Roe thought gloomily of the press camped downstairs. They'd be looking for someone to blame, a scapegoat to use as headlines for the next week. And to make matters worse he now had Carl on his back. Yet again, he went over their earlier phone conversation.

'I've just heard. What the hell's going on?' Carl began. 'Dungeons, transvestites and bondage gear! What was this guy, some kind of sex freak?'

Roe, immediately awake, had jammed the receiver between his ear and hunched shoulder. He had never told Carl the exact circumstances in which he had ousted Claude Vaubelle and now certainly wasn't the time.

'I was going to call you at the office once I'd got a few more details. We had no idea how close to the edge he was. From what I've heard Claude's tried the suicide stunt before – he was what's known as a manic depressive. Even his wife made him see a shrink. All we know so far is that last week he got caught in a compromising position with a rubber-clad youth. Christ knows who leaked the story to the press, but the police think that's what sent him over the edge.'

'Jesus, Roe!'

'Shit happens.'

'Not to me, it doesn't.'

'Hang on. By next week someone else's problems will be making headlines. People have short memories here. It'll blow over.' Roe peered at the digital clock. Four in the morning!

'It'd better, kiddo. I've got enough aggravation this side of the Atlantic to last a lifetime.'

'How d'you find out anyway?'

'News reporter, how else? All looking for a piece of dirt, the bloodsuckers.'

'Yeah. What's happening with the insurance company?'

'They've a strong case and they're going to stretch it out for as long as they can. I've hired a hot-shot lawyer from New York. He reckons we'll win but it's not going to be cut and dried. They might call you in to testify, but that could be months from now. There's no telling. How are the figures looking your end?'

'Last week's report showed our shares are up to 65 cents. They may have dropped a little over the weekend but they'll pick up again once all this has died down. With a conservative gross figure of $1.5 million by the end of the year, we'll be looking at doubling our profits in less than two years. Have you seen the reviews of the collection I faxed you?'

'Yesterday.' There was caution in Carl's voice. 'Guess your hunch about that girl paid off. She's good, kiddo.'

And worth every penny we're paying her, thought Roe, but Carl wasn't known for his excessive compliments. Roe pictured him leaning back in his chair and sighing into a huge cloud of smoke.

'When's the funeral?'

'Friday at the Père Lachaise cemetery. They're going to bury him next to Oscar Wilde and Marcel Proust in honour of the Vaubelle name. Talk about letting sleeping queers lie.'

Carl allowed himself a laugh. 'They certainly dug up the dirt on him. The guy had kids too.'

Hardly kids, thought Roe. 'Look, things will calm down. I'll make sure I'm at the funeral so that we give the right impression. Oh, and I've been working on the idea of bringing out our own perfume. If you go for it we could be looking at a launch a year from next spring.' He stifled a hiccupy yawn. 'We're starting work on the ready to wear in a couple of weeks. It's all coming together. Trust me.'

'That's usually my line. Just make me happy, kiddo, and get the press off our backs.' The phone clicked in Roe's ear.

He ignored the tap on his office door. Carl had borrowed a fortune against the Wilshire project. If he lost the case it could bankrupt him. And where would that leave Roe? Should he be concerned? Roe began to question his own judgment, to wonder if he might have been wrong about Carl all along. On the other hand, it wasn't the first time Carl had run into trouble.

Claude Vaubelle glared at him from the front page. Roe covered the picture with his briefcase, unable to bear the sight of him.

Pierre's tentative head appeared around the door. 'Monsieur, I heard you were here and wanted to know if I could be of any help?' He was clutching a copy of Roe's newspaper.

'Yeah. Come on in. I don't want this getting out of hand. I'm going to issue a press statement. Can you fix one for this afternoon?'

The phone screamed at them. Roe grabbed it and snapped, 'I said no calls, Nicole! Oh,' he paused, running a frustrated hand through his dark hair, 'sure. Put her on. Rachel . . . Yes, I've seen them. Definitely suicide. Look, hon, don't worry. It looks worse than it is. What? . . . No, I want you out of the way until some of this blows over. Just for a couple of days. Don't be surprised if the press start hounding you. But for Chrissake don't talk to them. They're likely to print anything. I'll be in touch.' Roe hung up.

'What else can I do?' Pierre asked nervously.

'Get me Leo Schofield in London. I have a feeling we're going to need him to work out some new figures.'

Pierre half got up, poised like a sprinter for the door.

'One more thing, Pierre. Check out how Claude's shares are to be divided. Before the press get hold of it.'

Roe's hunch was that they would be split between the two children and if Carl really was having financial problems Roe would need to secure part of the company for himself. If, that

311

was, he could find enough funds to do it. But after almost six months of hard slog he had begun to think of Vaubelle as his baby. No way was he about to relinquish his paternal role. Picking up the phone he punched in his stockbroker's long-distance number as Pierre closed the door behind him. Now that Roe was thinking more clearly he had some homework to do.

After his conversation with Roe, Carl scribbled some figures on to the pad in front of him. He had some real estate lying redundant in Tokyo which would bring in a quick $20 million. He could dump thirty per cent of Vaubelle. That had to be worth close to $50 million and would still leave him with a sizeable stake in the company. It would also keep the banks off his back for a while. Goddam banks. They were making his life a misery.

He drained his glass then picked up the phone and placed a call to Tom Glover in New York. Tom was a formidably successful merchant banker with Citibank, dealing mainly with Europe. His secretary put the call straight through.

'Carl! I was meaning to call you. Great lunch last week. We should get you over here next time you're in town.' He paused momentarily. 'I heard about Cindy. I'm sorry things didn't work out. She was a wonderful girl.'

'Still is. But hey, after four marriages, people would start to worry if one of them actually worked. Why break old habits?'

Tom laughed. 'So what gives?'

'Wanted to let you in on a tip. I've just had some news in on that designer company you showed some interest in. Well, watch that space. Looks like it's going to sail all the way to the top. And we're talking major bucks here.'

'Are you looking to off-load?'

'There's room for negotiation. Can I count on your discretion, Tom?'

'You got it.'

Carl hung up, pursing his lips together in a conspiratorial smile. The news would be round the network within the hour. If there was one thing you could rely on Tom Glover

312

for, it was not for keeping his mouth shut.

'Bea, it's Kate. Are you busy?'

'Not at all. What's up?'

'Nothing. I need to talk to you, but not on the phone. I'm at the Café Costas. Can you meet me here?'

'Come home. I've got my booker round who's just spent a fortune at Fauchon and we're stuffing our faces in front of the video. You must be shattered after doing fittings all day. I'll put the kettle on and save a piece of this orgasmic chocolate cake for you. That is,' she said giggling, 'if I can stop both of us from finishing it.'

'I'd rather see you on your own.' Kate's voice sounded strained.

'Is everything all right?'

'Yes. No . . . Just please come.'

'I'm on my way.'

It was seven weeks since her last period. Kate had checked her diary six times in which she had scribbled a capital P, appropriately in red ink, to remind her when she was due. That was ten days after the night Roe had brought back his horrible friends to the flat, and that girl, Lucinda! She stamped on the memory. I'm not going to think about it, she told herself sternly. Her periods had always been as regular as clockwork. Of course it was always possible to make a mistake, which was why she'd gone and bought a home pregnancy kit. She wasn't going to wake up to another anxious, nail-biting day. Having peed in a plastic cup and poured a third of the contents into the test tube provided, Kate had waited an agonising hour to see if it changed colour. Mortified, she found that it had. Blue. Baby blue. Did that mean it was going to be a boy? For one brief afternoon she had fantasised about having it. She would tell Roe and he would change because he would suddenly realise how much he loved her. A real person was growing inside her womb. The thought made her feel proud, secretive, superior. She pictured herself in bright smocks and leggings, Roe at her side, warding off careless passers-by, evenings in with him rubbing her tummy with scented oils. The fantasy didn't last very long. Kate's insecure boundaries shut back with a clang. Real life simply didn't work that way. So she went back to the crying and nail-biting which, she reflected, examining her chewed fingers, was getting worse.

At first she didn't believe it. But after the early days of flu and loss of appetite, Kate had grown suspicious of tingling, enlarged breasts at the beginning of her cycle. Then there had been the morning sickness. She even lost her appetite – that alarmed her. Then to her horror her waist shot up to twenty-eight inches. Thank heavens the show was over. She'd never have been able to hide her stomach from Vaubelle. Rachel knew her body almost as well as she did herself.

She couldn't bring herself to tell her mother – history repeating itself. Furthermore Sophie would only want to take over, or even worse insist they got married. Instinctively she turned to Bea.

'Does he know?'

Kate shook her head violently. 'And I don't want him to.'

'But it might change things.'

'I've already made my decision. He'd just feel hemmed in. Roe only likes other people's children. He once told me he didn't want commitments in his life.'

'It's fear of the unknown. All men say that.'

'Yes, but some of them mean it.'

Bea sighed heavily. 'It's because he's so attractive. That's where you went wrong. One of life's ironies is that the nice, reliable men who can never do too much for a girl are always odd-looking. The sort who sweat a lot and have gorilla hair down the back of their necks.' At least she made Kate laugh. 'You know he's seeing someone else.'

Kate couldn't keep the surprise out of her voice. 'He didn't waste much time. Who is it?'

'It's only a fling, Kate.'

Kate, stabbing at the sugar bowl with her teaspoon, said, 'Who cares.'

'Let me come to London with you, darling. You shouldn't be on your own.'

'Why? It's not the end of the world. Thousands of women

have abortions. Most are back at work the next day.'

'Darling, you don't have to be brave.'

'I'm not,' she said, fighting back the tears, 'I'm being practical.'

After the show she'd told everyone she was going into hospital for a minor operation and would be off for three days. Now, at the abortion clinic in Twickenham, she gave her name to the receptionist, a thin, unsmiling girl with dark skin and yellowish-blonde hair. An inch of dark brown hair was sprouting from the roots.

'Age please, Miss Temple,' the girl said, glancing briefly at Kate as she punched letters into the computer. Kate wondered if she imagined the girl putting emphasis on the Miss.

'Twenty-five.'

'Have you been to this clinic before?'

'No.'

With the morning sickness hurdle out of the way, Kate was now worried about feeling hungry all the time. She shouldn't be thinking of food. The doctor had warned her not to eat or drink after midnight – some patients reacted badly to the anaesthetic. But this morning while waiting for a taxi she could practically have murdered some poor girl eating a McDonald's on a bench. She'd watched her like a slavering dog while the girl had crammed matchstick French fries into her mouth, oozing dollops of ketchup. Why was it the minute you were denied something you immediately craved it?

On a glass-topped coffee table was a mottled plant and some magazines, most of which were nine months out of date. I'm perverse, Kate thought glumly, spotting a spectacles ad she'd done in one of them. How could they have published such a dreadful shot? She was desperate for a drink. Greedily she eyed the Seven-Up tin sitting next to the receptionist's telephone. The waistband of her trousers felt horribly tight, a reminder of her fat, unhappy childhood. She caught the receptionist looking at her impatiently.

'I said that's £300.'

Kate nodded, wondering illogically why the receptionist didn't bleach her upper lip which sprouted a patch of fine back hairs.

'How would you like to pay?'

'Sorry?'

'Cash or cheque?'

'Cheque.'

Miss Sourpuss resumed punching letters, her chipped fingernails working efficiently on the keyboard. Why couldn't this secretary be more friendly, more sympathetic to the distress in the room? Maybe she'd become immune to endless women with thickening waistlines and reluctant cheque books. Her blank face and gloomy voice seemed more suited to a funeral parlour.

A very pretty Chinese girl with ink-black hair and a big bottom sat grimly on one of the pine waiting-room chairs. Her mother sat by her side scoffing crisps. Kate wrote out a cheque. Another woman sat clutching her boyfriend's arm. He was talking soothingly to her and stroking her hair. Bea was right. I shouldn't be on my own. Roe should be here with me.

'Would you like a receipt for that?' the receptionist asked.

A flicker of distaste crossed Kate's face. Certainly I'd like a receipt. My accountant can claim it as part of my expenses!

'Take a seat over there. It shouldn't be too long. You're due in at three o'clock. Someone'll be along shortly to take you to your room.'

Ten minutes after Kate had sat down another woman arrived. She was in her early forties, brandishing a large shopping basket. She went through the formalities quickly then sat down next to Kate. The four female strangers sat waiting, bonded by the four unwanted lives growing inside them.

When the nurse came for them, they followed her in a polite, orderly line. How English we are, Kate reflected, climbing the stairs. They were shown into a small dormitory which housed eight beds, each with a small bedside table. Light flooded through the bay window with a large cherry tree standing proud and blooming outside. The furniture bore traces of defeat and the light showed up a patched hole on the south wall. The window was open, letting in a light breeze. Such a warm, perfect July day. Gales and frigid rain would

316

have been more appropriate, Kate thought bleakly.

Once they were undressed, a nurse came by to ask them their medical history and to check their blood pressure. Kate was third on her list and while she answered the nurse's questions her attention moved to the Chinese girl sobbing on the bed next to hers. The nurse went over and talked to her. Ten minutes later the girl got up and left. According to the nurse this sort of thing happened all the time.

Kate wondered for the hundredth time if she was doing the right thing. The three women began to talk to one another, each of them glad of the company. Their presence was mutually comforting.

Sally, the young girl, worked on the till at British Home Stores. Her boyfriend, she'd explained, had been made redundant three weeks ago and they'd only been going out for a couple of months, which was why she was having an abortion. The woman with the basket was very sympathetic and full of well-meant advice. A married woman with three children, this was her third abortion. Her husband simply couldn't afford to support another mouth and the risks of having a child at her age were too great.

'What do you do, Kate?' Sally asked curiously.

'I model.' Shouldn't have said that. Fatal!

'Really! I've never met a real model before. Are you in *Vogue* and all that stuff or do you do the shows?'

Embarrassed now. 'A bit of both.'

'You lucky thing. Sounds so glamorous, all that travelling, meeting famous people. Bet you make loads of money.'

'Well, come on love,' coaxed the older woman who'd stopped reading her book. 'Have we seen you on the box?'

Me and my big mouth. 'I did one for Ambassador chocolates.'

'The one with the cheetah?' Her voice incredulous. Kate nodded.

'That was you! Gosh, that ran ages,' Sally exclaimed, looking really impressed. 'Just wait till I tell Tony.'

They both studied Kate more closely, trying to reconcile the pale, freckled girl by the window with the stunning redhead in the bronze sheath dress they remembered seeing

317

on their TV screens. Joan spoke first.

'My youngest has always wanted to be a model. Bit on the heavy side but lovely-looking and nice and tall like you. Perhaps you could help her to get into an agency?'

How many times had Kate heard that before?

'Perhaps.'

At twenty past three the tension in the room mounted as Sally was wheeled out. It was worst for Kate who was to go last. Having watched Joan go next, she saw Sally brought back in. Although still under general anaesthetic, she was writhing from side to side and sobbing. Poor little thing! When the nurse came for Kate she kept on repeating to herself, there is nothing more I can do. It is beyond my control. Christ, she sounded like John Malkovich at the end of *Les Liaisons Dangereuses*. She knew she was babbling as she was wheeled along the stark, brightly-lit corridor, but the nurse seemed preoccupied. Try it from my end, Kate thought, as she was wheeled into the anaesthetic room. I'm about to be knocked out, my legs sprawled in the air so that some strange man can poke around inside and destroy a tiny life. Oh Roe, why couldn't things have been different?

She could just make out the operating theatre beyond two plastic swinging doors. A nurse was in green overalls and wore a mask. Kate could smell her own panic. Her palms felt damp.

'Will this hurt?' she asked, her voice small. What she wanted to say was, please get me through this. Make them take care, do it properly. The nurse produced a huge syringe. Kate shrank from it. The action was involuntary.

'OK, Miss Temple, just take a deep breath, that's a good girl,' the nurse encouraged as she turned Kate's inner right arm towards her. The skin was white and translucent. Kate tried to make a joke.

'At least you won't have any difficulty finding my veins,' all the problems they'd caused for poor Neil in Tuscany, 'I'm like a map.' The joke fell to the floor with a sad plop as the needle pierced her skin without resistance.

The nurse said efficiently, 'That's right. Now count to ten for me. Good girl . . .'

★ ★ ★

She was in a bar stinking of stale beer and smoke watching a blonde woman scream at Roe. He was slumped against a pillar at the far end of the room. The blonde was goading a group of alcoholics with red crucifixes round their necks. One of them started punching Roe in the stomach but no one took any notice. Kate ran over and pulled the man away, screaming at him to leave Roe alone. The people faded and Kate was cradling Roe in her arms. He lifted up his shirt and showed her his stomach. She saw a huge gaping hole and what looked like a brick protruding from inside. It was covered in blood. He said in a child's voice, 'See, Kat! This is nothing compared with what they've done to me. I can take this pain.' He looked at her in despair. She was overwhelmed with a need to comfort him.

She woke up vomiting. A nurse was calling her name and far away Kate could hear a clanging; a sound of metal against metal. Was it over? It felt as if she'd only just closed her eyes, which felt gluey. She couldn't open them. The need to sleep was overwhelming, pulling her back, down into a dark pit. Then blackness. When she floated up through the anaesthetic the second time she was crying; because this time she could feel the gnawing pain and realised part of her had been neatly disposed off. She cried and some of her tears fell with relief because in the back of her mind Kate had expected to die with her baby on the operating table.

Sally and Joan were sitting up in opposite beds calling to her, but Kate was still too dopey from the anaesthetic. Gripped by a terrible gnawing in her uterus she moaned, curling up on her side. A nurse appeared. Kate asked for some pain-killers.

'I can't give you anything for an hour,' the nurse said sympathetically, 'we have to make sure that there are no side effects from the operation. I'll bring you a cup of tea in a little while. The pain will go away soon, dear. You'll see.'

And amazingly it did. Just over an hour later they were all, somewhat haphazardly, sitting up in bed drinking tea and eating digestive biscuits. Kat believed the worst was over.

Back in Paris the next day she followed Bea wearily upstairs to their flat feeling as if she'd survived a plane crash. Why was it that everyone she knew lived on the top floor? God, the place looked so bright and cheerful. Her feet throbbed from the heat, a July sun streaming through the windows. Kate felt misplaced, as if she'd been gone for a very long time. Light flooded through the skylight, catching an explosive bunch of anemones on the kitchen table.

'Have we given Madame Couris a rise?'

'No,' said Bea proudly, 'I did it myself.' She dumped Kate's bag outside her room.

'Coffee or tea? Only we've run out of coffee.'

Bea had promised herself she wouldn't mention the abortion unless Kate did first. Kate collapsed on the sofa and rummaged through her bag for some Feminax.

'Vaubelle want to extend my contract,' she said.

'Oh Kate, that's absolutely wonderful!'

Bea dumped several tea bags into the pot. When it had brewed she quickly fished out the bags and flicked them at the sink. One of them missed and landed on the floor with a splat. She ignored it, adding milk and three spoonfuls of sugar to her cup. She left Kate's black but produced a plate of biscuits.

'It's hot. Careful.'

'I've told the agency to turn the offer down.'

Bea's mouth dropped in astonishment. 'You're joking! Tell me you're joking.'

Kate looked resolute.

'Is it because of Roe?'

'Partly. Mostly, if I'm honest. Too much has happened and now all this publicity over Claude Vaubelle. I just know I can't go on working there.'

'But you were earning so much money. Another year at Vaubelle and you'd be practically a millionairess!'

'I'd rather keep my peace of mind.'

'You're not going to give up modelling, surely?'

'No. But now that I've got some financial security I'm in a position to choose. I've had time to think about my life in Paris these past two days,' Kate swallowed two Feminax.

320

'Everyone rabbits on about how wonderful it must be living here that you eventually come to believe it yourself. It's time for a change, so I'm going back to London.'

'But to chuck in a contract most girls would give their eye teeth for! Don't you think you might be feeling this way because of what's happened? You've made a life for yourself here. If you went back to London you'd have to start all over again, find a flat, build up new clients. And life in the fast lane wouldn't be the same without me or the Beetle.'

For a second Kate smiled. 'You won't be here for ever. Anyway I spoke to Nigel at Prime last week and he's already lined up a catalogue trip to LA. You're the only thing I'll miss.'

Bea settled back into the sofa and sighed. 'Well, this is a bit of a blow. What shall I do without you? I don't get on with the French models. They're so humourless and are always trying to knock you off the catwalk. Oh, bugger the tea. Let's have a drink!'

While Bea riffled through a cupboard for the whisky bottle, Kate went to the window and looked down glumly at the avenue de la Grande Armée. The café where she and Bea had spent so much time looked busy; waiters, in their skirt-like white aprons, hurried out to the pavement tables carrying round trays, professionally flicking crumbs with their napkins, adding notes to their already bulging wallets. A Great Dane was trying to copulate with a poodle, much to the embarrassment of its elegantly-dressed owner who was pulling fiercely on its lead. A girl, in a stripy top and bell-bottoms, stamped on her cigarette stub then slowly wiggled her way towards the traffic lights, enjoying the lustful stares of three lads who had just parked their mopeds. Funny, Kate thought nostalgically, but now that she was going, she would miss it.

'Do you ever think about having children?' Her voice was so quiet, Bea had to strain her ears.

'Not if I can help it.' Bea poured whisky straight into her mug.

'Pregnancy's a strange thing. All these hormones flying around your body quite intent on doing their own thing. I realise now I want the sort of home I never knew as a child.

321

Why did I have to go and fall for a high-powered over-achiever?'

'I know it doesn't seem possible now, but you will forget, darling. We always love the things that are taken away from us the most but time is a great healer. Here, have one of these biscuits,' offered Bea, helping herself to four. 'Madame Couris made them especially.'

'That's the one good thing about all this. I seem to have lost my appetite.'

Not that Kate needed to, Bea noticed. She'd lost so much weight her shoulder blades were sticking out.

Suddenly Bea put down her cup and leaned forward, elbows on her knees, and stared down at the carpet. 'Three years ago I was living with this artist chap. I met him when I was on holiday in Spain. Completely bowled over the minute I clapped eyes on him. Anyway, we began an affair and I got pregnant. There was a lot of parental pressure to give it up; Mum thought that at seventeen I was far too young, but I decided to keep it.'

Bea's eyes darted briefly to Kate, listening intently.

'John, that was his name, got wildly excited and came up with some crazy plan about sharing a house with three other couples. We would work and support one another as one big family, at least that's what he said. We stayed with his parents for a few days during my third month. They had a lovely house in Wiltshire and I felt so loved, so content. One evening I took a swim in this great big heated pool they had. I suddenly got an awful pain in my abdomen. I thought it was cramp but I saw that the water was red and that I was swimming in my own blood. At some stage I must have passed out because I don't remember anything about being in hospital or recovering from the miscarriage but I was left with infected Fallopian tubes, which is why my periods are always so heavy. Unfortunately I can't ever have children.'

Kate was appalled. 'Bea. That's awful!'

'Not really. Running true to form I'd have been making the most frightful passes at my daughter's boyfriends.'

She made a joke out of it, but Kate sensed her friend's

322

deep loss. Bea loved children, would have done anything to be able to have one.

'The reason I'm telling you all this is that at the time I didn't think I could bear to go on living. Needless to say, John left and I felt ripped to pieces. But time does help. You don't forget exactly but you get stronger and you know that whatever comes up next will never be as bad. You must believe that.'

Bea glanced at Kate. She had not moved from the sofa corner. 'Kate?' Kate raised her eyes so that Bea could see the pain in them. 'Oh sweetheart. Please don't.'

'I miss him, Bea. I miss him so very much.'

19

Toby, plugged into Sony's new portable CD Walkman, walked out of Mothercare clutching five carrier bags. His car was parked at the bottom of Wright's Lane, which was littered with shoppers. Looking dolefully at his purchases, he collided with a black teenager wearing sweat pants, a purple singlet and Reeboks.

'Hey, man,' he yelled, 'mind where you're goin' now!'

'Sorry?'

'You got ears or wot? I said mind where you're fuckin' goin'!'

Toby, feeling disorientated, switched off *La Bohème*. He had a terrible pain in his stomach. It was the same recurring thing, bloatedness, loss of appetite, the need to be sick. He could handle it when the attacks had lasted only a few hours, but this had been going on for weeks and he was really worried. Maybe he had stomach cancer. The last chap he'd been to see about it had said it was a parasite and had given him homoeopathic tablets to take. And they'd actually worked. He'd been so relieved at the time. Now it was back and the pills weren't doing a blind bit of good.

Another wave of nausea gripped him. He received one or two odd looks from passing shoppers as he bent forward in pain. What on earth was wrong with him and what were all these people doing in the middle of the afternoon, for God's sake? Shouldn't they be at work? And why had he bought all these things? It was madness! They wouldn't know its sex for months. It was just that by going out and buying something he'd felt it would make it real somehow.

Toby's mind veered inevitably back to Rachel. He missed her. Did she ever think of him or did she hate him so much she had put him out of her mind altogether? Not that he could blame her. You don't send someone a lovebird then not call, not after the two weeks they'd had together. He'd gone over and over what to say, but in the end it seemed pointless making promises he couldn't keep. Somewhere, in the unconscious depths of Toby's mind, lurked an anger. He wasn't aware of it but he did feel the injustice of the situation. When he'd followed her that day he had been unable to articulate why he'd done it. He had made the decision instinctively and only later, much later, given it meaning. He was in love. And yet, all he'd wanted to do was to browse through bookshops and art galleries with her, sharing coffee and humour, and past secrets; to be with her without guilt, without recrimination. Too late for that now. He wondered if she was feeling as lonely as he was.

His Mercedes Sports was parked on a meter. Some wretched warden had given him a ticket. He always got bloody tickets and he was only five minutes over the time. Not my bloody month, he thought moodily, chucking the shopping bags into the boot. Tanya was organising a dinner party for tonight. She'd told him not to worry about a thing and had sent him off on a shopping errand, forbidding him to return before six. He glanced at his watch. Ten past four. Now what? He sat in the driver's seat staring into space. That was the problem. He had nothing to do, and whereas in the past that had seemed not to have mattered, it did now, very much. What did his life amount to? No responsibilities, no career, no one to look after. Tanya certainly didn't need him, though she claimed she did now that she was going to have a baby. His baby!

The news still hadn't sunk in. Arriving back in London he had found his kitchen looking remarkably clean, but no explosion, no crater on the wall, no demolition sight or mutilated body. Tanya, uncharacteristically, had looked dreadful. Her eyes were puffy and swollen from crying, her blonde greasy hair pulled back in an aggressive knot. The gas explosion had been no more than a ploy to get him back from Paris after she'd found out about Rachel. He'd tried denying it but Tanya had produced a tabloid showing Rachel and him together outside Rachel's apartment. His incriminating arm was around her and their expressions left little to the imagination.

'I didn't think you read rubbish like that,' he said defensively.

'I didn't know you were a two-timing bloody hypocrite!'

There followed a further fit of insults with expensive Harvey Nichols plates and cups skilfully hurled across the room along with a treasured golf trophy he had won in 1986. Then Tanya shot upstairs, collapsing on their bed in a hysterical fit of sobs.

Rocking her in his arms minutes later, the truth finally came out. The play, which had opened three nights ago, had been hammered by the critics and Tanya, five weeks pregnant, had walked out.

'I didn't want this to happen,' she had choked. 'I wanted to be a star. I wanted people to take me seriously. Now I'm going to be fat and ugly and no one will want me.'

Toby made soothing sounds and stroked her blonde hair. 'There, there. Hush now. Everything's going to be all right.' He tried not to notice the appalling state the room was in, or the fact that his favourite suit, which had just come back from the cleaners, was now lying strewn across the floor with the sleeves rolled up.

'When I saw you in that paper with that . . .' she couldn't find an adequate word. 'I can't tell you what the past week's been like. Not knowing what to do, how you'd react.' Sniff. 'I thought I'd have to get rid of it.' She screwed up her face. 'I knew I couldn't go through with it on my own. You do want the baby, don't you, Tiger? You won't leave me?' She looked very young suddenly.

'No, darling,' he had whispered, giving her the sleeve of his shirt to blow her nose on. 'Hush now. I won't leave you. I promise. It's all going to be just fine.'

When Tanya fell into an exhausted slumber, Toby glanced hopelessly out of the window and thought of Paris.

She woke up sweating. The room was dark and she could hear ringing, loud and insistent. Kate grappled for the phone.

'Hello?'

'How'd you like to go to Australia?'

'Who is this?' Defensive, guilty-sounding.

'Who'd you think it is, busting a gut to keep you girls in work?' The voice sounded offended.

'Nigel. Sorry. You sound different.'

'It's called the flu. I'm riddled with the damn thing. Three days of LemSip and antibiotics seem to have made me worse.'

When had she dozed off? 'What time is it?'

'Ten o'clock and I may have just clinched you a brilliant deal.' Someone outside popped opened a bottle of champagne.

It was a crisp evening, a noticeable temperature drop and Kate was lying on her old bed in Onslow Gardens. She glanced at Ruskin stretched out on the floor. From time to time he twitched in his sleep or snapped at some invisible bug crawling around his fur. Sophie was away in France and Kate had agreed to dog-sit having not yet found a place of her own – quite honestly she wasn't physically up to it. One window had been left open and music and excited chatter drifted up from a neighbour's barbecue.

'Benton Sackville's been invited to Sydney to launch the opening of some shopping mall and suggested you as his model. I've just been on the phone to the client, negotiating, which is why I'm still stuck in the office. They want you out there for a week to do a gala show, press interviews, TV, that sort of thing. I've no idea what sort of a budget they're on so I took a gamble and asked for £15,000 cash.'

'Do you think you'll get it?'

'Doesn't cost anything to say no, sugar, and they seem very keen. Benton must have raved about you to them. With any luck they should be faxing me through the details in the morning.'

'Sounds as if they're in a hurry.'

A phone rang in the background.

'Yes, well, don't get too excited. You can't go until November because your catalogue trip to LA has been confirmed. Hang on. Prime modelling agencya' A pause.

328

'Yup, Greg, I'm going to have to call you back, I'm on the other line. Where are you, Milan? Yup. Got the number right here.' Nigel hung up on the other phone. 'Why clients can't call me during office hours, I don't know. Look, sweetheart, I know you need your beauty sleep. Ring me in the morning and I'll have more news. I also need your voucher for the Harvey Nics show.'

'Oh God, I completely forgot.'

'Well, the sooner it's in the sooner you get paid. You can collect your flight details at the same time.'

Before hanging up they arranged to meet for lunch on Thursday. He'd take her to Langans, of course. That's where he took all his favourite models. So she was off first to Los Angeles then Australia. Well, she had wanted to escape, hadn't she? Why not to the other side of the world. Anything to get her out of this pit.

Back in London for almost two months and still she couldn't shake off this awful, sluggish state. Initially, with Sophie's permission, she'd set about redecorating the spare bedroom. The challenge of practical manual work appealed to her and it was a good excuse for staying at home. Subconsciously she was using the house to make a nest.

And then she hid in it.

Maybe it was something about the start of autumn, the dying season; rationed days, empty trees, dark, dreary nights, everything going underground in preparation for winter. In a way she envied them. All she seemed to do was sleep or cry, which was silly because she never knew what she was crying about. It would catch her unawares; lunchtime when the chores were done and she realised there was nothing to fill the rest of the day; or when she was feeling let down because of a last-minute cancellation from a friend she was meeting for coffee. Silly, really, but even five minutes of *Anneka's Challenge* had her bawling her eyes out. Sentimental fool! She hadn't told Nigel about the abortion but he must have realised something was up because he had been uncharacteristically nice of late, only making her do the important castings.

She suffered acute pangs of loneliness. Sometimes she

went two or three days without seeing anyone. Didn't want to risk it, not in her fragile state. What if she broke down? No. She couldn't allow friends to see her this way. Then there was the question of finding herself a flat. She obviously couldn't stay at Sophie's for ever. But somehow the effort involved was too much. So she kept putting it off. When she got desperate she would wade through the fallen leaves, pulling Ruskin (who wanted to go to the park in the opposite direction) down to the local shops, stopping to chat to the paperman who, through a cloud of Benson and Hedges, always had a kind word for her, or to the girls in the health food shop who kept an eye out for her face in magazines. That way, if she did suddenly feel the need to be alone, she could race back home. Perhaps that was why she was so tired. This morning she had made a couple of phone calls, piled up the washing machine which she forgot to turn on, then tried writing her thoughts down. For years when she'd been at her most frightened and alone, she'd felt the urge to write. Now, it seemed, was no exception.

Another pop from a champagne bottle and several drunken cries of 'hooray'. The party was clearly under way. Kate's hand moved across her body, enjoying the sensuous feel of silk from her robe, then on to skin which was warm. She was aware of every hair, every pore, the smell of Fenjal on her skin from her bath. Roe always used to get turned on by the sweet, oily smell. She'd promised herself she wouldn't think about him, but that was as impossible as not eating or breathing. Her eyes travelled across the room and rested on Lottie, an old doll Sophie had given her. She'd forgotten all about Lottie. Why had she kept it all these years?

'Naughty, Lottie! Bad, bad girl! I'm not letting you have any pudding tonight. Mummy says you're too fat!' Slap, slap. 'And don't start crying because I don't like you any more.'

Kate closed her eyes and determined to take Lottie down to the charity shop in the morning. What is the matter with me, she thought, why am I feeling so tired! Her index finger probed into her belly button and she tried to imagine it having once been attached to Sophie. Unthinkingly her hand strayed further down and she touched herself.

330

In her fantasy Roe was with her in the room and she was watching him undress by the window. There was nothing rushed or self-conscious in his movements. He took time to fold his clothes but his eyes never once left hers. Naked, he walked over to the bed and climbed on top of her. He was fully erect and Kate closed her eyes as he pushed her legs roughly apart, driving into her. Her breathing quickened. His roughness excited her, she could almost smell the faint traces of Fahrenheit, the shape of his small, tight buttocks, the inverted muscle line of his back against her hands. Her fingers moved faster until she was making tiny little gasps. The orgasm was intense and over very quickly. She lay there, eyes closed until the sweet waves subsided. She could still feel Roe inside her, hear his hot, velvety moan against her neck, 'I could stay like this for the rest of my life.' More excited shrieks from outside, this time children's voices. 'Again, Daddy! Do it again!' Kate's face suddenly crumbled. She couldn't bear it any more. The bed shook from her tight, choked sobs.

The Kitchen Jolly catering company Toby had hired for his engagement party had excelled itself. On this bright but chilly September afternoon his Holland Park home was full of happy, inebriated guests tucking into an elaborate buffet. Tanya, in a yellow Anthony Price suit, was encouraging some boisterous children to play in the garden. Watching her, Toby felt a twinge of guilt because he knew the thing he'd remember most about today was that his idol, Jack Winger, was one of the guests. Not wishing to analyse his troubled feelings he went and answered the door.

'Darling! You made it!'

Bea Parker, intent on something going on at the end of the street, had her back to the door. Her blue eyes were hidden by dark glasses.

'I know, I'm horribly late but there was a bomb scare at South Kensington and I couldn't remember your number. Then I got mowed down by a lorry driver who called me a "stupid posh cunt", so I hit him. There was the most frightful scene!' She raised her eyes and sighed, then gave him one of her famous smiles. 'Can I come in and have an enormous drink?'

Beneath the nonchalant manner Toby could see that she was upset. Her hand trembled as he ushered her in.

'You shouldn't be allowed out alone, darling. The British simply aren't up to you. There's some very good wine floating around. Or would you like something stronger?'

'Vodka, if you still keep a bottle in the freezer.'

'Come viz me, mein Schatzlein.'

They passed Tanya coming down from the loo, reeking of Poison. She looked to Bea like someone who had just got out of bed.

'I believe congratulations are in order,' said Bea politely.

'Darling!' Tanya squealed, kissing air on either side of Bea's cheeks. 'It's so lovely of you to come. That jacket's delicious. How would you describe the colour? Green doesn't do it justice.'

'Grassy?'

Tanya laughed. 'How's work?'

'Don't ask. I spent most of yesterday sucking up to my bank manager.'

'But, darling, Toby's always telling me how well you're doing.'

'That's because Toby's a love. The truth is the recession's shrunk the market so much that what little work's around is going to the top editorial girls not wrinklies like me.'

'That's ridiculous and damned unfair!' Toby said angrily.

'Imagine what it must be like for the young girls starting out. It's so competitive these days.' Bea glanced at Tanya's stomach. 'I was expecting lumps but you don't show at all.'

'Not at this stage. I haven't even had the teeniest bit of morning sickness. I'm terribly lucky.'

'Well, Bea wasn't. She had to take on half of Hell's Angels to get here.'

'Clever old you!' cooed Tanya. 'You didn't bring your glamorous friend?'

'Kate, if I'm not mistaken, is now half-way across the Atlantic on her way to Los Angeles. Poor darling. The press really hounded her. She hardly knew Claude Vaubelle but because she left about the time it all happened the press got suspicious.'

'Well, it was quite a story,' admitted Toby, 'male prostitutes, S&M, cocaine and leather-bonding.'

'I thought leather was out of fashion?' said Tanya.

Toby ignored her. 'Why'd he do it, kill himself, I mean?'

'From what Kate has said, he just couldn't bear the fact that the company was doing so well without him. Vaubelle was his life. Sad, isn't it?'

'Well, it's good having you back in England and I'm dying to catch up on all your news.' Tanya gave a proprietary glance at her guests in the living-room. 'We must have a girly gossip once lunch is out of the way.'

And she hurried over to talk to Lady Trollope, Toby's bossy Aunt Maud, a heavily made-up woman with a large voice and chest to match. Chairwoman of the Women's Institute for twenty years, mother of seven children, grandmother of twenty-one, she was a matriarch to be reckoned with. Tanya was very pretty, Maud reflected, tucking into her gooseberry trout, but the girl was so dizzy! Would she really make a suitable wife for Toby? It had all been so sudden. Lady Trollope paused to admire some pink and white Dutch double tulips acting as centrepiece on the table. After her brother's death Toby had gone into such a decline. Such a shame about the grey hair but it did make him look rather dignified. All that money – well, it simply couldn't compensate for a parent's love. Maybe now, with a child on the way, he'd start to settle down. She devoutly hoped so.

After two glasses of neat vodka and a snoop around the house, sunny and glossy after an expensive refurb with Colefax and Fowler, Bea's mood brightened. She helped herself to a plate at the buffet table. Two overweight women watched, green with envy at Bea's slender frame.

'It simply isn't fair!' one of them said, sipping Kenco coffee with two Hermesetas as Bea piled up her plate. 'I spend the whole week counting calories, yet I couldn't look like that in a million years.'

'Yes, but she's a model, Sheila, dear! It's her job to look that way,' the second woman reasoned, nonplussed all the same as Bea crammed the liberally-buttered potatoes into her mouth.

'I thought models didn't eat,' Sheila muttered crossly, watching Bea add Kenya beans, glazed carrots and two chunks of French bread to her plate. 'They're supposed to live on water biscuits and celery sticks, and look at her!' Perhaps she shouldn't have had the pavlova, the other thought guiltily. It would mean sacrificing her evening meal. Weight Watchers' weigh-in was only three days away.

Toby wheeled his way across the room towards Bea.

'Enjoying that?'

Her mouth full, Bea gave an enthusiastic nod.

'Now tell me,' Toby propped himself on the edge of her chair, 'if work's so tough here, why did you leave Paris?'

Bea shrugged resignedly. 'Because my agency was bought out by a big league PR company. They wanted to re-vamp their image and the 'older' models were asked to leave.'

'That must have been a blow.'

'Only for a second. I'd already done my stint in Paris and I missed Kate. Not something I like having to admit but I'm no good living on my own.'

Nor am I, thought Toby, who was becoming increasingly aware of the personal sacrifices involved.

'Would you like some wine, miss?' A young man stood over Bea poised with a bottle of Chardonnay.

'Lovely. But I seem to have lost my glass.'

'I'll get you one,' said the lad and dashed off to the kitchen. Toby, catching sight of Tanya, who was holding the phone receiver towards him, excused himself. As the waiter returned to pour the wine a large dog hurtled past pursuing a shrieking child and half the glass's contents slopped over Bea's trousers. Hell! She'd just had them dry-cleaned.

'Oh, Christ, I'm sorry!' groaned the waiter. 'Let me get a cloth.'

'Don't worry. I'll go and rinse them.'

'Are you sure?' He looked anxious.

'Honestly, it'll come out. Just lucky it wasn't red wine.'

The party was now in full swing. Guests, discovering other guests with similar backgrounds, careers, children and fashion labels came together in small groups. Bea retreated in search of a bathroom and slipped up to the first floor to avoid the downstairs queue. There was no lock on the door but luckily nobody was about. The room was a surprise. Unlike the rest of the house it had been wallpapered with sheets of music which, on closer inspection, turned out to be extracts from operas. Toby had always been an opera buff. In the old days when he was going out with her school chum Camilla, Bea used to tease him about it. While most boys had fantasies about Marilyn Monroe or Sophia Loren, Toby's dreams were filled with images of Dame Joan Sutherland and Maria Callas.

She rinsed the soiled trousers and draped them on the radiator to dry. Then she rearranged the shoulder pads stuck into her Marks and Spencer vest. In the garden below she could see a beautiful blond child, who couldn't have been more than three, trying to feed a squirrel. A young girl, obviously his elder sister, was trying to mount a Labrador, whom she recognised as the wine culprit. Snapping his hand back suddenly the boy started to cry. His sister ignored him, dragging the reluctant Labrador towards a cherry tree. A few minutes later, a young woman appeared from the kitchen, scooping up the tearful boy. Thumb plugged back into his mouth, the other hand clinging on to the woman's pony-tail, he was returned to the kitchen.

Bea grabbed a favourite Dickens novel from a nearby stool and settled herself on the loo. Her new shoes were pinching so she kicked them off. She was just at the bit when David Copperfield comes home to find that Dora has ruined his supper, when a fair-haired, bearded man opened the bathroom door.

'Fucking hell!' Bea yelled, hastily covering herself with Dickens. 'Can't you see it's busy! Get out, get out!'

'Sorry!'

The man hastily retreated, closing the door behind him. Bea leapt off the loo and jammed the door with a chair. Doesn't anyone knock any more?

'Here she is,' cried Toby when she returned to the drawing-room. 'I couldn't find you.'

'I was having a nose upstairs.'

He introduced her to an attractive brunette whose hair had been layered and highlighted expensively. She had the sort of prettiness that was already starting to fade, accelerated by sun and too much booze; she had curvy, even lips and sharp brown eyes that sloped down at the corners and appraised her warily. Bea recognised the Armani suit from last season's show. It had looked better on someone with more height. Definitely a man's woman, thought Bea, who felt like the Jolly Green Giant standing next to her. Talking a few feet away was Toby's solicitor friend, Yarnton Miller. Bea liked his warm voice and the smart brown eyes that matched his corduroy trousers. She imagined him with lots of grandchildren.

'I caught the end of that round,' Yarnton was saying. 'Jack's really back on form. I've never seen him play so well.'

'Well, I'll be putting my money on him for the Ryder Cup, that's for sure,' enthused Toby.

'Who's this?' Bea's eyes, along with those of the two Weight Watchers, darted to the pavlova remains being cleared away.

'My husband,' said the brunette. 'But if you're not a golf fanatic Jack Winger probably won't mean anything to you.'

'Angel, you must have heard of the Mole!' said Toby proudly. 'He's the best golfer this country has.'

Bea nodded uncertainly. Come to think of it, the name did sound vaguely familiar.

The small girl with bright-green eyes and blonde bob Bea had watched playing in the garden appeared, holding a bottle. She had grass on her skirt and gooseberry sauce on her chin. Lorna wiped it off and took away the Moët.

'Livi, what have you done with your poor brother?'

'Eating chocolate cake in the kitchen.' Olivia threw a cautious look over Bea who was smiling at her. 'I'm saving mine for the journey home.'

'Did you come across Daddy, anywhere?'

A naughty smirk came over Olivia's face as her mother took the heavy bottle from her. 'I saw him talking to a woman wearing dangling earrings and big bosoms.'

'Well, tell him that I want to speak to him, and don't let Fergus eat any more cake,' she instructed as Olivia rushed off clutching the sides of her skirt, 'or he'll be sick in the car.'

'You have ravishing children,' said Bea enviously. Out of one eye she watched Tanya sweep across the room to greet a late arrival.

Lorna looked smug. 'I am sorry, Toby. They've probably pulled up most of your garden by now. God knows what Jack's up to?'

'He's in the study playing backgammon with Sir Giles,' said Yarnton, who was an old friend of Lorna's parents and had invited the Wingers to the party. 'It all looked incredibly serious when I popped my head round.'

'Which means we'll be here all night,' said Lorna tactlessly. She had been hoping to leave early. They were going out for dinner and she was still nursing last night's hangover.

'Are you staying up?' Yarnton asked Lorna.

'At the Savoy tonight. Then I take the children back to Argyll – Jack's staying on for work.'

'How's the house?'

Lorna sighed. 'We're being driven mad by a convoy of builders and the summer midges. Jack's managed to avoid it all because he's been away so much. But it's beginning to look heavenly and we've at last got a pool. You and Dorothy should come up for the Ryder Cup.'

'We'd adore it. The Turnberry course has always been a favourite of ours.'

'Sounds like a pudding,' said Bea.

Yarnton glanced at his watch. 'I'm afraid we'll have to be on our way. Dorothy's asked some of her bridge friends over for dinner.'

'What's all this about leaving?'

'Jack! Everyone's been looking for you!'

The first thing Bea noticed about the man were his brilliant green eyes. He had fine, blond hair which was thinning on top, and a pale blue shirt. His powerful, square shoulders, weather-beaten face and mottled skin, half-hidden behind his beard, betrayed a lifetime outdoors.

337

He grinned. 'I was just giving Giles a few pointers in backgammon.'

'Thanks to your husband, Mrs Winger, I'm down £200,' said Sir Giles good-naturedly. 'He's got the luck of the devil! A winner at everything. No doubt that's why he married you.'

Bea winced. Dear old Sir Giles – corny as ever! Lorna, however, took in the upright, military stance, the immaculate pin-stripe suit, the clipped Etonian voice, the faint traces of expensive aftershave, and liked what she saw. Mmm. There was just a hint of Dirk Bogarde about the man.

'Darling, I'm worried Olivia has developed a liking for champagne.'

'Moët, I think. Your daughter has expensive tastes, Jack,' teased Yarnton. 'And this is Bea Parker, who I'm told comes with a title.'

'My darling girl,' said Sir Giles, kissing Bea's cheek, 'how is that mother of yours? First-class woman, Lady P. Should have married her when I had the chance.'

Lorna threw Bea a slightly more accommodating glance. Mind you, she thought, she didn't look like a lord's daughter. The clothes were all wrong and dark green definitely wasn't her colour. Only accentuated her paleness. Striking, in an unusual way, but too thin and, Lorna noted with some relief, flat-chested.

'I have a feeling you played in the celebrity tournament with my father last year,' said Bea with uncharacteristic shyness.

'I did. He played very well that day.' Amused apple-green eyes focused on Bea's flustered face.

'Have you two already met?' asked Lorna.

'Only briefly. Don't we share a love of Dickens?'

Suddenly twigging, Bea looked at the carpet, from which a waiter was scraping squashed courgette. How horribly embarrassing! Sir Giles was asking Lorna about Rachel's job with Vaubelle.

Jack turned to Bea, lowering his voice. 'Why are you wearing glasses? The sun went down half an hour ago.'

'I've got a hangover,' lied Bea, still pink with shame.

'Of course, we're absolutely thrilled for her,' Lorna

gushed, her accent shifting up a class to match Sir Giles's. 'It was all so unexpected! But then I attribute her talent to Jack's genes. We've just bought Olivia a piano. She's really good. Might have another Mozart in our midst.'

'More like Mike Tyson,' muttered Jack, and winced as Olivia wrestled her baby brother to the ground. 'Christ knows where she gets it from. I've never been that energetic.'

'No, Olivia, don't do that! You'll break something.' And Lorna rushed off to unscramble her children.

'What is it about golf that makes it so compulsive?' Bea asked, recovering her composure.

Jack was instantly serious. 'The game has three intrinsic merits! No two courses in the world are ever the same. The handicap system allows players of all standards to play together and it's the only sport where you can chatter and socialise while you play. Have you ever given it a try?'

Bea shook her head. 'Golf's one game I haven't tackled.'

'Then you must come and play at the club.'

'I warn you, Jack!' Sir Giles squeezed Bea's arm. 'This one's like her mother. Mighty competitive.'

'Good. I like a bit of spirit.'

Lorna, back with Toby after saving a priceless vase from being knocked over, sent Bea a thinly-disguised look of hate.

'Darling, we should get going. The children are tired.'

'I should go too,' said Bea, 'I've got exactly half an hour to get to Paddington.'

'Then we'll give you a lift,' said Jack lightly. 'The station's on our way.'

No, it bloody isn't, thought Lorna crossly. She picked up her bag, scrabbling for paracetamol. 'I'll go and find the children.'

Now that people were leaving the rush was on for coats. Most were upstairs camouflaging Toby's bed. The catering staff, swigging the leftover champagne, were washing up and throwing fish bones into large dustbin bags.

'And steer well away from anything in a leather-studded jacket,' said Toby walking Bea to the door. 'I want you home in one piece.'

339

'Are they happy?' Bea asked, as Jack and Lorna helped their children into coats.

'Who knows? They've been together for ever. I believe Jack was married briefly once before but I only know this from the few things Yarnton's let slip. There was a sticky patch a few years back when Lorna ran off with Jack's best friend, but that's common news.'

'Mmm,' said Bea thoughtfully, 'she's a bit uptight, don't you think?'

'Never used to be,' interrupted Yarnton, coming back with his coat. 'They were very much in love. The problem started when Jack began to make money. Lorna got herself into new social circles. Gave up all her old friends, which I think she now regrets.'

'And Jack?'

'He won't leave her because of the children. He learnt his lesson doing that with Rachel.'

Toby's ears pricked up. 'Rachel?'

'Jack's daughter from his first marriage,' Yarnton explained. 'You must have heard of her. Jack's always singing her praises. The English designer who's all the rage in Paris; had a brilliant first collection.'

'Of course!' said Bea. 'She's Kate's ex-boss. The one regret Kate had about leaving Vaubelle.'

During the confusion of people in search of lost children and handbags, neither Yarnton nor Bea noticed the appalled expression on Toby's face. He knew her surname was Winger but he'd never made the connection. God, and all those stupid things he'd said about wanting to be a golf player!

Outside in the hall kisses and thank yous were being exchanged. Tanya had finally surfaced and was arranging to have lunch with Lorna. Jack, having helped the children into their coats, handed Bea a slip of paper.

'My agent's office number. He knows more about what I'm doing than I do. The offer still stands. I'll be around until the end of the month, then I'll be back in Scotland.'

'That's really kind of you.' Bea looked at him properly for the first time. It struck her suddenly how attractive Jack was.

Stuffed in the back of the Wingers' Land Rover ten minutes

later, with Dickens the golden retriever, a collection of golf clubs, picnic baskets and a filthy dog blanket, a sleepy Fergus sat on Bea's lap chewing his thumb. Olivia, who had just started biology at school, eagerly described trees, in between singing *Insey Winsey Spider*. While Lorna applied powder to her face she gushed about Sir Giles and how much she was looking forward to dining at the Manor. From time to time Bea caught Jack's eye in the driving mirror, her right hand holding on to the back of his seat. His shoulder was so close, so tempting. She wanted to touch it.

'Thick!' said Fergus, looking green.

'I'm not surprised.' Lorna's tilted head looked quite unsympathetic as she applied fresh coral lipstick in the flap mirror. 'Bloody Toby let you eat half the chocolate cake! He's so irresponsible.'

'I like him,' said Jack. Ditto, thought Bea.

A Sainsbury's lorry suddenly pulled out in front of them as they reached Shepherd's Bush roundabout. Jack threw an automatic arm across Lorna, who wasn't wearing her seat belt, and slammed on the brakes, bringing the car to a screeching halt. There was a moment's silence. Then a thud and the sound of broken glass as the Land Rover jolted forward. Shocked, Bea twisted round and saw that a Ford Fiesta had gone into the back of them.

'Great!' yelled Jack, angrily waving his fist at the lorry turning off towards Hammersmith. 'Fucking great! Didn't even bother to stop!' He got out of the car and checked the damage, ignoring angry hooting. The driver of the other car got out and approached him. Fergus started crying.

'For God's sake! What now?' muttered Lorna in the front.

'Mummy, Dickens trod on me!'

'Shh, Livie. I can't hear what Daddy's saying.'

As she tried to calm both Dickens and the children Bea watched Jack talking to the man. He glanced over from time to time at the Land Rover then after a few minutes bits of paper were exchanged and Jack returned to the car.

'Everyone okay?' he asked slamming his door.

'Fine in the back,' said Bea.

'I hurt my hand, Daddy,' Olivia wailed. 'Will you make it

341

better?' Jack inspected his daughter's hand then kissed the tiny palm.

'Naughty Dickens,' she said, appeased.

Finding a forgotten Opal fruit in her coat pocket, Bea popped it into Fergus's mouth, then prodded him with her index finger until he collapsed into rapturous giggles.

'I want a sweetie too,' begged Olivia.

'Wait until you're offered one,' said Jack, switching on the ignition. 'Can you believe it! That chap was a priest! Pissed as a newt. Said he was late for mass or something. I couldn't understand a word he said. He was too busy guzzling Mintos to disguise the alcohol fumes.'

'Will the car be all right?' asked Bea.

'Just a scratch. His took the brunt of it, being such a small car. Smashed both his front lights, and took quite a nasty dent on the bonnet.'

Lorna had spilt her brand new Chanel powder all over the car floor.

'Honestly, darling, look at this mess!'

'You're lucky it wasn't your face,' Jack said grimly, 'now, will you do your seat belt up?' He glanced at his watch. 'You should still make your train.'

Bea nodded gratefully in the back.

'Will you come and visit us at the Manse?' Olivia tugged Bea's arm. 'And bring some photos of your modelling?'

'Of course, sweetheart.'

Lorna, still irritated with Jack for showing her up in front of Bea, scooped powder back into its pot. 'I can't do this if you keep jerking the car.'

Jack crunched the car down into second gear.

'Fucking,' said Olivia.

'Thick,' said Fergus.

At Paddington the children made a lot of noise about Bea having to leave. Olivia thought Bea had played I-spy better than her friends and decided that she wanted to look like her when she grew up. Lorna waved politely, then relaxed back into her seat and yawned. She might just have time to wash her hair before drinks with Gary Player and his wife. Then on to dinner at San Lorenzo's, her favourite London

342

restaurant. She wanted to look her best.

Bea watched the children wave to her from the back window as Jack reversed the car, and thought, if he turns and looks at me I'll go to bed with him. She was more than a little miffed when he didn't.

Bea had forgotten all about Jack when, after several uneventful days marked only by the steady growth of her overdraft, she came across his scribbled number while hunting through her coat pockets for a favourite lipstick. She almost threw it away, then changed her mind. Why not? Serve that dragon wife of his right. Wrapped in a bath towel, she tweezered a few blonde stubbly hairs from her legs while the number rang. After a long time a man with a high-pitched voice answered.

'St Patrick's Church.'

'Oh, I must have got the wrong number.'

She could hear giggling in the background, then a different, more formal voice came on the line.

'Who did you wish to speak to?' asked the voice, slightly muffled.

'Jack Winger.'

'Who's calling?'

'Bea Parker.' Bea stopped plucking. She was getting cold feet.

'Hang on.'

There was a lot of clattering and fumbling with the receiver. A door squeaked open and she could hear her name yelled and the man saying not very quietly, 'Shall I say you're out?'

Bea contemplated hanging up. Then a deep, gruff voice said, 'Jack Winger.'

'Oh,' she stammered, 'you probably won't remember me. We met at Toby Wilmot-Smith's party a couple of weeks ago and you suggested . . .'

'I do indeed. I promised you a game of golf. I hope you don't want to play now, it's bucketing down.'

She was flattered he remembered her so quickly. 'No. I mean, any time really. Work's desperately quiet at the moment. Whenever suits you.'

There was a pause and a rustling of paper. 'How about next Tuesday afternoon?'

Bea checked the depressingly blank pages in her diary. 'Tuesday's fine. Where should I go?'

'Come to my club,' he gave her the address, 'I'll meet you in the lobby, at say, two?'

'Okay.'

'You'd better give me your number in case I need to contact you.'

In case you change your mind, she thought cynically.

'Should I bring anything?' she asked, wondering if she was supposed to wear a pair of those awful check trousers.

'I think we'll be able to rustle up the odd club for you. See you Tuesday.'

And that was that.

It took Bea exactly ten minutes to work out she wasn't a natural golfer. Despite sensible pointers from Jack (wearing reassuringly plain blue slacks and a yellow Fred Perry shirt), all she seemed to hit were chunks of expensive emerald-green turf. She spent most of her time surreptitiously patting the earth back into the ground. Once only, she gave the ball a resounding whack and watched smugly as it sailed off towards the horizon. But the smile was soon wiped from her face as the ball flew across a nearby road, landing on a passing car.

'Stop trying so hard and keep your eye on the ball,' advised Jack, after he'd caught her secretly dropping an extra ball in place of her lost one.

An even more humiliating moment was at the fifth hole, when they had to make way for some impatient OAPs who had started an hour after them and had already caught up. Bea tried to be gracious, but being naturally competitive, she was furious with herself for being so bad. One of the OAPs recognised Jack who obligingly scribbled his name with a biro on the back of a score card.

'I won't be losing this in a hurry,' the happy fan exclaimed. 'We saw you win the British Open. Can't tell you how proud we all were. And may I say that's a mighty fine lassie you've got there. You've got your father's looks, deary!' he said to

Bea who was desperately trying not to laugh. 'And best o' luck at Turnberry.'

'Now I really feel my age,' said Jack ruefully.

He took her for tea in the local village teashop. It was one of those rare September afternoons when the sun put in a gutsy performance, giving them a brief reminder of what summer was all about. As a result the small shop was packed with hungry customers awaiting cakes and pastries. Flushed waitresses in Laura Ashley dresses and frilly aprons rushed to and from the kitchen scribbling orders. Absolutely famished, they sat outside and ordered cheese and tomato dampers, followed by warm scones with cream and home-made strawberry jam. Jack was pleased to see a girl with such a healthy appetite. Lorna usually pecked at her food. Bea poured the tea. A waitress asked for Jack's autograph.

'When is the Ryder Cup?' asked Bea curiously. It seemed to be all anyone was talking about these days.

'Next week. It's a tournament that takes place every other year between the United States and Europe. The Yanks have held on to the Cup for so long you can understand why it's so important for us to win it back.'

'What do you think your chances are?'

'Fair,' he said modestly.

'Don't you ever get tired of all the attention? So many people wanting a piece of you?' Bea spoke with her mouth full. She wasn't remotely starstruck – over the years she'd met loads of famous people – but there was something dazzling about Jack.

'It's largely thanks to their loyalty to the sport that I'm where I am now. The poor buggers pay a lot of money to see very little. They're out in the pouring rain most days scrambling over sandhills. They'll pay five quid for a steak sandwich, which is mostly gristle, then trek to some distant car park only to find their car stuck fast in mud. And for what? Half of them don't even get to see the ball!'

'What made you become a golfer? Or is that a silly question?'

'It was that or go to dancing school. With three older brothers I'd never have lived it down and I didn't look good in

345

a tutu.' He grinned. 'Actually I was more interested in soccer, cricket and cycling until I watched Arnold Palmer on the box. From that moment I was hooked and my cricket bat and bike disappeared to the garage. How d'you know Toby?'

'Still can't get over him getting married. He used to go out with an old schoolfriend of mine. Camilla often invited me to their parties, which were pretty outrageous. Nice girl but wild and completely batty. She finally left him for an Indian millionaire's son who played polo and lived off chocolate ice-cream.'

She pointed to the last scone. 'Do you want that?'

Jack shook his head.

'Of course that didn't work out either. Two weeks after the Argentine Open he sent Camilla home having arranged for another girlfriend to arrive the same day. The flights unfortunately overlapped and in a frantic last-minute panic he'd had to put the girl in another hotel. Camilla found out anyway and gave him hell. Talk about wanting your chocolate cake and eating it too!' Bea giggled and scraped the last of the clotted cream on to her scone. 'I lost touch with her years ago but kept up with Toby. Now he's going to marry Tanya, who's quite wrong for him. She'll never make a real home for him because she's basically a five-star gypsy.'

She blew on her tea then explained, 'Tanya likes room service and spending other people's money. No disrespect to Toby, but he needs a homebody.'

'Anything wrong with that?' asked Jack, stretching out his legs.

'Not at all if you like that sort of thing.' Bea hastily scooped four spoonfuls of sugar into her tea.

'But not you?'

'Oh, I adore children and everything, I just don't think I'm the kind to settle down. Besides,' she said half-jokingly, 'no one would put up with me!'

'Well, you certainly made a hit with my two. Olivia's talked of nothing else since she met you. She now wants to be a model.'

'Every little girl dreams of being famous. She'll grow out of it.'

Walking back to the car afterwards, they passed a cricket game on the green and stopped to watch. A few villagers stood watching near by. Despite the earlier promising sun it now looked as if it might rain.

'I think it's very rude the way they rub the ball against themselves like that. Their white trousers get awfully dirty,' said Bea.

'The rubbing smooths one side of the ball so that it spins,' explained Jack, taking her arm.

'I'm sure it does.' She almost stepped in some dog's mess but Jack steered her away. 'I wasn't very good today, was I?'

Jack smiled kindly at her. 'Come on, now, don't say that on your first go. We pros make it look easy but it takes years of practice. I was a disaster the first time I tried golf. My father took me out when I was four. I remember him saying my swing looked like a polo player without a horse. I was so mortified it took him six months to get me to play again.'

'If I'd played another ten minutes they'd have had to plant a new course. It looked like a mole invasion!'

Jack laughed. 'I don't think anyone will mind. You're by far the most attractive player we've had in years.'

Bea was thinking how nice Jack was. Most successful men would have already mentioned their thirty-foot yacht, their Manhattan penthouse with a three-hundred-degree view of Central Park, the Porsche they'd just up-graded. Not forgetting the obligatory name-dropping. She wondered if she could add Jack to her 'spot the celeb' list. Probably not. Kate would say he didn't count because they'd become friends.

The green Land Rover was parked in a private lane. Jack fumbled for the keys in his trouser pocket and opened the passenger door for her – he had excellent manners. As he climbed in the other side Bea removed a yellow golf ball from her seat and examined it.

'Keep it as a souvenir.'

'Can I?' said Bea, with childish delight. 'Hard to believe this small innocent-looking object can cause golfers to seek psychiatric help! I'll display it at home with "Here lies one of Jack Winger's balls" as a caption.'

Jack raised an 'I'm not sure that's such a good idea'

eyebrow. As he shifted the car into drive, Bea put out a hand to stop him.

'Do we have to go back now? I've had such a lovely afternoon.'

'I don't think we'll get any more play. It's going to pour.'

Exactly on cue the heavens opened, slamming a warm river of rain on the car window. Blurry cricketers made a dash for cover. It's now or never, decided Bea. She took a deep breath.

'I had something a little more intimate in mind.'

The car was suddenly very hushed. Jack turned on the window wipers, watching them interrupt the rain. Bea waited. It seemed as if he was searching for something behind her curved smile, the impish face, the wide swimming-pool eyes that made him want to dive right in. It had been a long time since he'd felt such a strong sexual attraction to a woman. It would be so easy!

'Don't you think a girl like you should be out having fun with people your own age?'

Bea's confidence soared. 'I stopped being a girl a long time ago,' she murmured, placing a bold hand on his upper thigh.

Jack gently removed it. 'Don't.'

'Why? Don't you like me doing that?'

'Bea, I'm forty-three. I'm too old for games.'

'I thought that was how you made a living.'

'Don't be bloody facetious and don't look at me like that.'

Like a kicked dog, with large reproachful eyes. He could still feel his leg burning from her touch. He tried again. 'Listen. I won't deny I'm attracted to you. But I'm a married man. You should find a boy your own age, someone to have kids with.'

This was harder than he had thought it would be.

'You're patronising me, Jack,' Bea snapped, her vanity bruised. 'I'm old enough to make my own decisions.'

'Yes,' he said slowly, 'which is precisely why I'm taking you home.'

She sat in a sulk while Jack drove, wallowing in rejection. I must be losing my touch. Married men were normally so grateful! Perhaps she'd come on too strong. Jack might prefer his women submissive, like to make the first move. Maybe he had a thing about big-breasted women. She glanced down forlornly at her chest. Bee stings, Justin used to call them, the rat. Lorna's, however, could rival Dolly Parton's! Perhaps, she thought glumly, he just didn't fancy her. The Land Rover pulled up outside Justin's flat.

'Thanks for tea.' Bea fumbled at the door handle.

'It's automatic locking,' said Jack gently, 'I do it for the kids without thinking.'

'And you've made it very clear you put me in the same bracket. No,' she raised a hand, 'don't say anything. I've embarrassed both of us and ruined what was otherwise a lovely day.'

She just wanted to get out, she felt so humiliated.

'You didn't ruin anything.' Jack put a hand on her arm. 'I'm sorry if you thought I was being patronising. I haven't had much practice at this sort of thing. Look, I'm very, very flattered, but I don't like to start something I can't finish.'

He obviously felt sorry for her. How cringingly awful. If there is a God, Bea prayed, take five minutes off from Croatia or Somalia and get me out of this. Even worse, he was wearing one of those indulgent smiles. She looked down at her lap in shame.

'Are you going to be all right?'

'Perfectly! I haven't been shot or gang-raped or told I have an incurable disease, for God's sake. Now, will you please open this door. It's time I went back to kindergarten.'

Jack bit back a smile. 'I'll see you at Toby's wedding in the new year.'

'If I'm still here,' she said bitterly.

At last the door opened. Bea sprang from the car and hurtled up to the house. She wouldn't turn round. She absolutely wouldn't. She refused to let him see her furious tears.

20

Kate stepped out of the heat, closed the door of her motel room, dumped her key and the Vons brown paper carrier bag on the table, and flopped exhaustedly on to the double bed. Thank God that was over. What a week! And they still had four more shooting days to go. She closed her eyes and inhaled air-conditioned air through her nose, pushing it right down into her stomach. She held it there for as long as it was bearable, then very slowly let it out again with a whooshing sound. She felt instantly better.

The catalogue trip had been frenetic right from the start. Having arrived at Los Angeles airport late last Tuesday, Kate and two other models were up at five the following morning for hair and make-up. Normally the first day of long trips was called a rest day, giving the models time to get over their jet-lag, but as the clients had rashly brought out twice the number of garments originally chosen the models had had little time to themselves. They were, however, compensated by the weather, which had been spectacular. Bleak and shivering England seemed a distant memory.

The first few days were spent taking shots around town using the familiar backdrops of Beverly Hills, Rodeo Drive, the Chinese Theatre, Melrose Avenue – good for shops – and the infamous Venice Beach. On their third afternoon when the brown smog was so thick they couldn't even see the Hollywood Hills they stopped to shoot eight dresses downtown. Kate was shocked to see Carl Elliot's headquarters and gazed up at the flashing neon 'Cortes' sign which, from its commanding skyscraper height, seemed to taunt her. Was Roe in Los Angeles too?

By Saturday the clients asked the photographer for a

change of scene. The location vehicle headed south to a unique studio complex which boasted two outdoor carousels. The complex was half an hour from San Bernardino and civilisation. Surrounded by a flat, arid desert, the semi-circle carousels, standing sixteen feet and rotated in either direction at the push of a button, were used as backdrops. For three days the models endured the punishing heat in a seemingly endless battery of hideous winter garments. Unlike some shoots which stopped for a long lunch while the sun was at its highest, the girls were made to keep going through the day. One white polo neck used for many of the outfits was soon wringing with sweat.

Kate found she had little in common with the other two models, both much younger than her, and spent most of her time between shots reading and writing. She was still very low and worried about her constant need for sleep. Dragging herself out of bed in the morning was the hardest part of her day. She had genuinely tried to get into the team's light-hearted mood, joining them for dinner at local restaurants. But Kate was finding it increasingly hard to be bright and receptive when she simply did not feel it, and on the fourth night she cried off. From then on she stocked up on food from the local supermarket, which she took back to her hotel room. After removing her make-up and having a quick shower, she ate in front of the TV, switching mindlessly from one cable station to another. At least it enabled her to blot out the world and her problems for a few hours. Her life seemed to be a perpetual treadmill of planes, taxis, trains, tickets, suitcases and strange beds. She longed to stop.

Not that it was all bad. She had, at last, found an adorable two-bed flat in Cranley Gardens – actually Bea had found it for her. The rooms were small but it had a west-facing garden (a cultivated wilderness, Bea had called it) and the rooms were bright and sunny. It was the light that clinched the sale. The Vaubelle money Kate had saved more than covered the asking price and left her with enough cash to make improvements. She moved in and for the first time in weeks began to feel her spirits lift. She threw herself into making it hers, ruthlessly stripping down cupboards, filling and painting. Bea helped. The girls spent many happy breaks eating take-aways on the floor, their hands splattered with paint, their bodies aching. But as Kate's trip to the United States loomed, she found herself growing anxious again and withdrew.

Neil Hunter called the night before her flight.

'Darling! I couldn't let you go without saying goodbye. Just remember to take lots of condoms.'

'I'm only going for two weeks, Neil, I'm not going to have time for men.' Nor did she want to.

'Don't give me that, darling. I know what you girls are like. One glance at those tight California bums on Venice Beach and your ovaries will be going into a frenzy!'

Good old Neil. He always cheered her up.

The motel phone purred next to her bed. Pressing the remote control's mute button, Kate reached out and picked it up.

'Kate.' It was one of the models calling from the reception lobby. 'There's some gig on at Griffith Park tonight and we wondered if you'd like to come. Should be fun.'

'Oh, that's really sweet of you, but I couldn't move if my life depended on it. All I want is an early night.'

'Well, okay. If you're sure.'

'Really. Any idea what my call time is for tomorrow?'

'Four thirty. Poor you. So you're wise to stay in. We'll probably look like dogs tomorrow but I don't want to waste a moment of being here. See you bright and early.'

Four thirty! Kate glanced at her watch then realised she'd given it to the make-up artist to hold while she was shooting. Damn. She was always doing that. And now she'd spend the rest of the evening fretting about not getting enough sleep. Hauling herself off the bed, she switched on the TV, riffled through the Vons bag, pulled out an economy-size bag of corn chips and set about devouring it.

After several weeks of unemployment, Bea was confirmed for a five-day booking with *Woman's Journal*. At the crack of dawn, yawning strenuously, she and seven other models boarded an air-conditioned luxury coach which was to transport them to Scotland.

Rosterary's tenth incumbent heir, Lord Henry Macdonald, was an authentic sixties figure; he sported long, silvery hair, open-neck shirt, flared trousers and enough jewellery to rival Liberace. His aristocratic voice echoed round the great hall as he gave the girls a brief potted history of the place and apologised for the cramped changing room, one floor up from the ballroom.

'I'm not a bloody Olympic runner,' one model complained, 'it's miles away from the catwalk. And have you seen the size of that staircase? It looks like something from *Gone with the Wind*!'

'Well, just imagine you've got Rhett Butler waiting for you at the top,' said another drily.

They raced through the rehearsal, grateful to the producer who let the girls make up their own routine. It saved much time and heartache. Choreography, a hated word among models, evoked paranoia; frantic last-minute glances at notes (which often went missing backstage); hoping the girl thundering towards you would miraculously veer off to the side, while at the same time wondering if you were somewhere you shouldn't be; or, even worse, being stuck on the runway until the next model (usually slow with her changes) was ready to replace you. At no time was the stage to be left empty.

At eight o'clock they returned to the hotel and then sloped off to their rooms. No one stayed up late. It had been a long day and the country air acted as a soporific.

At ten the next morning Bea, already in her first outfit, stole a look at the *Journal* readers from the minstrels' gallery. From the panelled walls Irish elk antlers jutted rudely into an atmosphere rich with clashing perfumes. Excited voices rose around the crystal chandelier while trays of smoked salmon and complimentary champagne (the cheap stuff, Bea noted) were handed round.

'Belinda! Your mother mentioned you'd be here, dear,' Lady Trollope boomed, interrupting her conversation with Lord Henry and stretching her pale, fleshy neck towards the balcony. Several curious eyes followed her gaze. 'Toby and I wondered if you'd like to join us for lunch at Turnberry. It's the last day of the Ryder Cup, and for once we're in with a chance.'

The Ryder Cup!

'I'd love to,' said Bea, quickly calculating her day. The show finished in an hour, which left her free until six when she had to be ready for the evening show. She glanced dubiously at the leggings and suede-fringe jacket hanging on the back of her chair, but there wouldn't be time to go back to the hotel and change. Oh well, it would just have to do.

Tessa, the make-up artist, a Yoga teacher in her spare time, grabbed Bea's arm. 'I can't stand all this perfume. We need some air.'

'Five minutes, Bea,' warned the designer, trailing them with grey eyes. 'You're in the first group.'

'Cassy Peck's been had up on drug charges,' said Tessa, calmly lighting a cigarette. They'd raised themselves on to a low wall and dangled their legs over a field sprinkled with cowslips and dandelions. Bea, who'd snagged her tights, was sitting on her hands to keep them warm.

'What! I only worked with her a few weeks ago.'

'Well, I don't know all the details, just what I've heard from the other girls, but she's apparently been hanging around some shady Chilean polo player. He was using her to carry stuff through customs and on her way back from Peru she got caught.'

'Lord!' Bea's mouth dropped. 'I can't believe it!'

'It's not as bad as it sounds. One of her high-powered boyfriends twisted a few arms and got her out on bail. But if you ask me Cassy's bloody lucky. She could have landed a nasty sentence. Customs are really clamping down on that sort of thing.'

Tessa exhaled smoke through her nose. Bea resisted asking her for a puff.

'Anyway, now she's getting married. Dempster did a write-up about it last week with a photo. Didn't you see it?'

Bea hardly looked at a paper these days. 'Not that appalling Sebastian Vaubelle?'

'No. She dumped him weeks ago. Some art dealer called Jean-François. Used to be a tremendous club owl in Paris and has now set up shop in New York. Something like that, but doing very well. 'Course, he'd have to be. Cassy's blown all her earnings, and as we all know, she's used to an expensive lifestyle.'

'Well, well, well,' giggled Bea. 'What a tiny old world it is.'

'Do you know him?'

'Let's just say they're a match made in heaven.'

Tessa drew on her cigarette and threw it to the ground. They both watched the abandoned stub glow in the grass.

Bea's hands and feet were like ice but she quickly warmed up on stage twenty minutes later; four neat lines of chairs flanked each side of the runway, a raised white platform trimmed in pink rosettes. Bea counted at least nine hats as she waited for the magazine's resident photographer to take her picture. Her shoes were huge and had been stuffed in a last-minute panic with tissue paper. It was like walking in flip-flops. Still, she liked the orange cotton piqué coat and struck a second pose, click! A thank-you wink from the photographer and she was off. More cameras, mostly Instamatics with noisy zoom lenses from Boots, snapped like a pack of hungry dogs along the front row, where stripes and Technicolor spotted outfits heavily competed with one another. Cecil Beaton would have had a field day, thought Bea, expertly undoing gold buttons. She smiled at a woman in the front row, who hastily looked away. Hell. Did she have spinach in her teeth?

Someone had arrived late. Head bowed, body hunched with embarrassment, the woman tip-toed cartoon-like across the room to a vacant seat. Bea waited patiently for her to pass then continued up the runway to the sounds of appreciative oohs and ahs. A couple of neat full turns and Bea removed her emerald-green coat. Unfortunately the coat got stuck on one sleeve. Willing it off her arm the smile on Bea's face took on a distinctly fixed glaze. Help was at hand in the form of Stephanie, a pretty brunette with masses of long curls, who emerged in a cream shantung jacket, satin-back silk crêpe skirt, and ludicrously high silk shoes with thin suede straps. She dazzled the audience with her fuchsia smile, aware of how good she looked. While attention was diverted, Bea grabbed her chance, tugging at the obstinate sleeve to reveal a violet chiffon dress. A delighted gasp from the audience, a professional smile, one final turn, and she was gone.

'I'm famished!' she squeaked, hurtling past steaming aluminium dishes full of food. 'What are they getting for lunch?'

She'd already unzipped most of her dress.

'Ch-ch-chicken breasts,' stuttered the spotty caterer in a white baseball cap, trailing her with wide eyes.

Bea wondered if she'd survive until lunch with Lady Trollope. She legged it along the oak corridor under the stern gaze of Lord Macdonald's ancestors, pulling the silk dress over her head. The sweeping mahogany staircase was the final hurdle back to the changing-room. Already sweating, Bea sprinted upstairs two at a time, trying to ignore the American party who had at that very moment assembled on the landing to admire the priceless grandfather clock. Much to the annoyance of their female guide, all male eyes were glued to Bea's minuscule pink G-string.

'Excuse me,' she beamed, diving behind the changing-room screen.

'Back already, luv!' said her dresser as Bea chucked the coat and dress to the floor. She'd only just finished picking up the clothes from the last change. Already dripping with sweat, Bea packed some fresh powder on to her nose. 'Blue dress next. Change your tights again, oh, and don't forget your bust pads. This dress is huge on you.'

Two men in suits were standing by the door trying to look as though they belonged to the frenzied chaos.

'Who are they?' whispered Bea as she struggled into a shirt.

'No idea,' replied her dresser. 'Want me to find out, luv?'

'No. I'll deal with them.' Bea marched across the room managing to look controlled and indignant in only her tights and a flimsy shirt.

'If you want a thrill I suggest you go down to the local newsagents and buy yourself a copy of *Playboy*. We're not paid to give you creeps a free show. So bugger off!'

The men hastily retreated.

'Way to go, Bea,' praised an American voice from the back of the room.

'You bloody tell 'em!' chirped another.

For the finale the models filed out in their evening dresses, spraying a new, cloying perfume one of the sponsors was eager to promote on to the unsuspecting readers. Afterwards they all lined up at the back of the stage while the raffle winner was announced. Bea could have curled up and died when the sponsor's managing director climbed up and joined them to make a speech. She immediately recognised him as one of the 'creeps' she'd yelled at earlier on.

Walking off, one old woman caught Bea's hand, 'You were my favourite, dear. Lovely smile, really lovely!' leaving Bea feeling as if she'd just received her very own modelling award. Moments like that, she reflected, walking back to the changing-room, made it all worthwhile.

It was one of those cold but beautiful Scottish September afternoons. Pink heather, abundant and sprawling, set off the electric red and ginger leaves at their most vibrant now that their seasonal life was drawing to a close.

Toby picked them up in the Mercedes Sports. Braving it with the top down, Tanya hopped in the back with Bea, making room for Lady Trollope, resplendent in tweeds. Tanya too looked gorgeous in a toffee wool-gabardine trouser suit. It was clear she saw Bea's leggings and suede-fringe jacket as quite inappropriate.

'Darling! That outfit's too killing. All you need now is a lasso and we can enter you for the rodeo!'

Cow!

Running along some of the most scenic stretches of West Scotland the Ailsa course at Turnberry is also one of the most demanding and is named after Ailsa Craig, the volcanic plug that dominates the seascape which stretches off the Argyll-shire coastline. As the last Ryder Cup championship had been held in South Carolina, it was Europe's turn to play host.

'If you can see Ailsa Craig,' explained Toby pointing out to sea, 'it's going to rain. And if you can't, then it already is! At least so the local saying goes.'

The golf course was huge. Ailsa's green and faded-yellow slopes were already showing signs of a packed season with the beautiful Firth of Clyde beyond it glinting blue, the sweeping banks flanked by blue rope to stop spectators walking on to the fairway. Bea was surprised by the large turn-out; it seemed as if every Scot had brought his family to watch the final. Obviously a hugely popular sport. She got some pretty odd glances as they settled down to have their picnic lunch and one man winked at her when his wife wasn't looking. Maybe my outfit isn't such a disaster after all, she thought, her hand going straight for the spicy chicken wings that Tanya had bought from Sainsbury's and was trying to pass off as her own.

At first she couldn't see a thing, the crowd was thick and there were a great many hats, but half an hour later Toby managed to find a gap at the front and Bea squeezed her tall frame in behind him. Tanya, milking her pregnancy to the hilt, had been given a chair next to Lady Trollope and was thumbing through the programme looking for people she knew in the social pages.

'Okay, Toby, explain the rules, please,' instructed Bea. 'I'm the novice here.'

'So am I,' said Tanya.

'Basically, you have twelve players on each side. For the first two days each team works in pairs which is called foursomes in the morning and fourballs in the afternoon.' And presumably foreplay in the evening once the victors got home, thought Bea to herself. 'Today they're playing singles. The winning team will be the one that makes the most points.'

'I see,' said Bea, not sure she saw at all, and watched a very tanned player miss a hole by a hair's breadth.

'Oh, very bad luck!' boomed Lady Trollope, whose face had turned an unfortunate lobster-red. She'd been drinking since ten that morning.

'There's the American Tom Watson,' Toby said, pointing out a sandy-haired man in a green polo shirt and white shoes.

'He's one to watch out for, played really well yesterday. But our side's holding on. Anything's likely to happen in this game.

Bea wasn't really paying much attention. After an hour's standing around she was starting to freeze. Maybe she could slip off and get a cup of tea. She watched Tom what's-his-name hit the ball with a thwack, then play a third clever shot on to the green, bringing him up to three under par (as explained by Toby). The American made it look so easy. Maybe she'd take lessons. Still feeling hungry, she pulled out a couple of Bourbon biscuits she'd pinched from her hotel room and popped them into her mouth. Just watching the game wasn't much fun but already Bea could see why so many players got hooked.

There was a sudden ripple of applause as a white ball plopped on to the green, rolled down a shaved bank, finally coming to a stop about eight feet from the flat post. A few minutes later another ball came sailing through the air and hit a nearby tree, bounced back on to the fairway and landed in the sand bunker. Judging by the sympathetic murmurs the invisible player had got himself in a spot of bother. Two women dressed in white sweat pants and crinkly wind-cheaters went over and stood by each of the balls, holding up signs identifying each player's ball. Four figures appeared over a distant hill, two weighed down by golf bags. Binoculars trailed them as they approached, but without her contact lenses, the figures were just a blur to Bea.

'Look!' Toby said excitedly. 'There's Jack!'

'Jack Winger?' Surely not.

'And that's Fred Couples behind him. They're on the eleventh tee, which means Jack has two choices; he's got a fifty-fifty chance with the long shot to the flag or he can play carefully out of the sand on to the fairway. It's a gamble either way. If he mucks it up, it could lose us the championship.'

Bea followed his gaze; her eyes skidded to a halt as they focused on the tall blond figure. My god, he's shaved off his beard! The effect shocked her like the unexpected sight of pubic hair, but it took years off him. Bea couldn't tear her gaze away and because of the red sweater he wore and his powerful build he stuck out from the rest. She had to admire his composure as he prowled around the ball (which looked firmly entrenched in the sand). He bent down to test the ground level while his caddie did the same on the other side of the hole, trying to judge the distance and his best manoeuvre. She could hear two women behind her whispering. By the things they were saying about the players it was obvious they weren't here for the golf. Couples watched Jack anxiously from a discreet distance.

'Must be awfully hard for them to concentrate with the television cameras trailing their every move,' Bea said anxiously.

'Most of them have played professionally for years. They're used to it. Incidentally, I hear Jack took you out for a round. Lucky girl.'

'News travels fast.'

'It does in this circle. How'd you two get on?'

Bea evaded the question. 'Fine, except that I spent most of the time hitting the golf tee further than the ball. Jack was very patient.'

'He's like that.' Toby shaded his eyes with his hand as he squinted at Bea. 'Shame you have to work tonight. Lorna's invited us all back to the Manse for dinner. She always provides lots of eligible young men. You would have enjoyed it.'

'You're assuming Lorna would have invited me.'

'Why on earth wouldn't she?'

Careful, Bea. 'Do they live close by?'

Eyes still on Jack, she hoped her voice sounded neutral. Why, oh why did she have to work tonight!

'About three miles down the road. Lovely secluded spot. They've spent a fortune doing the house up. We'll go another time.' Toby paled suddenly. 'Christ, Jack's picked the four-iron. He's going for the long shot.'

Bea hadn't a clue what Toby meant by a four-iron, but it sounded serious and she followed Jack with anxious eyes.

'No cameras, please.' Jack's caddie snapped in a low, stern voice. The blonde ponytail was the only indication that she was female. Jack held the club as if it were his most revered possession and Bea admired the power of his physique. He shuffled his feet, adjusting the position of his body, the forehead knotted in concentration, eyes darting frequently from the ball to the flag post and back again. There was a hush. Bea could feel the crowd willing him on. It was so cold she longed for a hot drink, somewhere to warm her hands. But she waited like everyone else for Jack to take his shot. Suddenly the club swept up behind him, the iron head flashing in the sunlight like an executioner's axe. It whipped down through the air and gave the ball a ruthless whack. Golden sand sprayed and the ball soared on to the green, rolling closer and closer to the flag. At one point it seemed to veer off to the left, then amazingly rolled back and slipped neatly into the hole.

'Awesome!' shrieked an American voice.

'He's done it with a birdie!' cried Toby.

The crowd went mad. There was no doubt who their favourite today was.

Bea, wondering what birds had to do with anything, was tugging on Toby's arm, her heart pounding.

'Does that mean he's won?'

'No, but it's put the two teams level at five points each. Fred will pot this next shot, then they've only got two holes left. Skill no longer comes into it. It's now a game of nerves.'

Bea's stomach muscles tightened again with anxiety as she willed him on, along with an entire golfing continent, but after Jack's remarkable come-back Fred Couples's game went to pieces. To everyone's amazement the American missed the easy putt and never fully recovered his game. Jack, as captain, coolly holed the final putt, winning the victory point his team had only dreamt of for so long. Although bitterly disappointed, Couples graciously accepted Jack's extended hand.

'You deserve it. You played real well today, buddy. Well done!'

The players and caddies all shook hands while Seve Ballesteros, who had partnered Jack for the first two days, was less restrained, and embraced his friend. After that a

362

great deal of champagne was consumed by everyone except Tanya.

'Better not,' she said, opting for a glass of Perrier, 'you know what the doctor said.'

Bea, who remembered Tanya knocking back two bottles of Lanson at the engagement party, thought she was slightly overdoing the mother earth bit. If only Toby would take her over to meet Jack! She was dying to talk to him, wanted a chance to apologise for the way she had behaved. But Jack, already the winner of this year's British Open, was absolutely swamped with fans and press, showering him with congratulations like confetti, all wanting to get a shot of him and the team with the Cup. His presence was magnetic. Bea felt turned on by the glory and Jack's superiority to the rest of the players. And I know him, she thought with just a trace of smugness, wanting to share her secret with everyone.

Her euphoria was short-lived. Lorna, looking absurdly young, appeared from nowhere with both children in tow. She threw herself into Jack's arms, timing it perfectly for the BBC to capture the moment for the nine o'clock news. The picture would make the front page of every sports section the following day.

'Nice to see a celebrity making a success of his marriage,' said a fan.

'They say he's planning to take her on a second honeymoon to celebrate their fifteenth wedding anniversary.'

'Isn't he dreamy!'

Bea felt sick. 'Toby. Could you possibly take me back to the hotel?'

'Angel!' Toby looked concerned. 'What's the matter? You've gone awfully pale.'

'I'm just cold. Don't let's make a fuss. You can say goodbye to the others for me.'

As they walked back to the car, Bea couldn't resist one last peek at Jack. The sun had lost its glare and was casting long, loopy shadows across the grass. Olivia and Fergus had clambered on to his broad, powerful shoulders, Lorna was holding his hand, smiling up at him. They looked like a page out of *Hello* magazine; all smiles and neat poses. The model family. A repulsive brown beetle crawled up a blade of grass, then back down again, carrying a prized crumb of pizza on its back. As it paused, contemplating its next route, Bea raised her foot and stamped on it.

Rachel hovered in the doorway of Roe's office and watched him scribble something on a black leather-bound pad.

'May I come in?' she asked tentatively.

'Of course,' he smiled, rising immediately from his seat. 'These can wait until later. Come and sit down. I'll get you a drink.'

'Just something soft,' she said, as he slid open the door to a walnut cabinet which housed a small fridge.

'Orange juice okay?' Rachel nodded. 'Brigette was showing me some of your sketches for the summer *prêt à porter*. They're good. Here, no ice, I'm afraid, but it's fresh.'

'Thank you.' Rachel took the glass. 'Yes, I'm really excited about this one. I'm obviously much more confident now that we've got the first collection out of the way. I picked up lots of ideas while I was in Morocco.'

'I heard you'd been away but somehow we keep on missing one another. Did you have a good break?'

'Wonderful! I slept all day in the sun and ate my way through the hotel's entire food supply.'

Roe grinned. 'Good for you. The reason I got you in here was because I see your contract with us comes up for renewal after the *prêt* in October. I wanted to discuss it with you.'

Rachel, suddenly apprehensive, wished now that she'd asked for something alcoholic but gulped down her orange juice anyway.

'And don't look so worried. Sales are up, everyone's pleased, particularly me as I know the kind of pressure you've been working under. No, this is good news, at least I hope it is. Vaubelle would like to extend your contract for another year.'

'Oh golly, I wasn't sure. I mean, I know the press liked the collection and everything, but . . . That's wonderful!'

'Of course, we'll need to renegotiate terms and put you on

a higher salary, but we can go through that with Sebastian nearer the time.'

Roe, who was concerned not to be late for his next appointment, checked his watch. 'Who have you got now in the *cabine*?'

'A French girl. She's very young but a similar shape to Kate and fits the winter collection, which makes it easier for the ateliers.'

'Good.' He stood up and shuffled together some papers, indicating that their meeting was at an end. 'Perhaps after the *prêt* we can think about getting you a more permanent replacement.'

Rachel would have liked to have asked more about why Kate had left so abruptly, but something about Roe's expression stopped her. At the door she suddenly turned round.

'I probably shouldn't mention this, but I've listened to what's being said about Mr Elliot's financial problems and I don't believe a word of it.'

Roe put up a hand to stop her. 'It's okay. I know what's being said and I know exactly who's been saying it.' His voice had a very slight edge to it. 'But you have nothing to worry about. Vaubelle's going from strength to strength. Trust me on that.'

'I do.'

Remonstrating with herself for having doubted him for even a minute, Rachel slipped out of the room and made her way back to the studio. A roll of hot-orange chiffon had arrived earlier and she was dying to put it to use.

'Coming?' said Tessa.

It was the last day in Rosterary and with only one show left some of the models wanted to go into town and browse through the tartans.

Bea shook her head. 'Don't have any money. Thought I'd take a walk as it's stopped raining. We'll be cooped up inside all evening.'

The flattened heather glistened from last night's storm. The still, glassy Argyll lochs mirrored the bleached sky and stray birds dipped and lolled playfully above Bea's head.

Judging by the map the hotel had drawn for her, she was about two and a half miles from her destination. She shouldn't go, of course, but curiosity had always been her downfall and at the moment she felt driven, out of control.

It only took her half an hour. Following a steep, private road which she almost missed because the turn-off was partially hidden from the main road, Bea glimpsed a large grey-sandstone house which rose out of a band of pine trees. She followed the steep, curved gravel drive, leading up to the Manse. The picturesque view of the house was slightly spoiled by the sight of a bright-yellow skip overflowing with rubbish and crowned by a scruffy-looking toilet. The front gate was locked so she climbed over it. At this point her nerve gave way and she paused. What was her reason for being here? What if Lorna was home and answered the door? What the hell could she say? Oh God. She shouldn't have come.

Bea climbed the four steps. There was no bell. With a trembling hand, she lifted the antique door-knocker and let it fall with a loud thud. Somewhere in the background a dog started to bark. God. When no one answered she banged the knocker again. Perhaps no one was home. Peering through the letter-box she could see a wide hall with a staircase leading upstairs on the right wall. A child's bike was on its side next to some golf clubs, and several toys and a pair of tennis shoes lay scattered across the floor.

'Anyone at home?' she called half-heartedly through the box.

Silence. She rang again, waited for about a minute then turned, feeling a mixture of relief and disappointment. She had just reached the bottom step when a deep male voice yelled through the door, 'Hang on, for Christ's sake, I'm coming!'

Jack Winger opened the door, towering above her like a great Saxon warrior. He was tying an emerald-green terry bathrobe at the waist, his blond hair wet as if he'd just had a shower. For a moment they stared at one another. Bea spoke first.

'I probably shouldn't have come. I wasn't sure if anyone

would be in but I'm working down the road,' she stammered nervously. 'I saw you play in the final on Sunday and just wanted to say that I thought you were magnificent . . .'

Before she could say anything else, Jack pulled her inside, slamming the door shut with his bare foot and crushed her against him. Without his shoes on Bea was a good two inches taller. Somehow he had removed half her clothes and manoeuvred the distance between the corridor and sitting-room. The dog was still barking energetically in the back.

'Shut up, Dickens!' he snapped, struggling with the zip of Bea's trousers.

Bea thought she was drowning as Jack pulled her to the floor and removed her underwear with an urgent hand, his tongue tracing the firm lines of her body. I don't believe this, she thought incredulously as all rules evaporated. God, it had been so long! This was what she'd come for. His flesh was moist and smelt of talcum powder. His hands and mouth were everywhere and when his tongue pushed between her legs, Bea felt as though she'd been electrocuted. Moaning, she called to him urgently. She could feel the tip of his rock-hard penis beating like a pulse against her belly. As his mouth travelled back up to hers, she gripped him fiercely with her legs and rolled over so that she was on top. Straddling him, Bea slipped his wide cock inside her and moved her strong, slim body back and forth, gaining momentum.

'Is that nice? Do you like that?' she asked breathlessly, bobbing up and down.

'Relax. Stop trying so hard.'

Jack pulled her down and sucked greedily on a nipple while Bea pushed her tongue in Jack's ear. They rolled again, with Jack on top this time. Bea clenched her vagina muscles holding him tighter, then slid a hand between his legs and gently rubbed his balls. She was so involved in what she was doing that it took her a few moments to realise that Jack had stopped moving. Pulling at the sides of her hair, he lowered his head and gently kissed her.

'Easy, my beauty. Stop competing with me! You don't have to prove anything. Let's try it another way.'

As she relaxed Jack very slowly picked up the rhythm, her

367

legs up around his ears. Bea's excitement mounted until she was screaming with frustration but Jack continued to hold back until he was sure she was ready. Then, with a tremendous thrust, they climaxed together.

'Don't pull out!' She pressed him to her. 'Stay inside me!'

'I don't believe this!' Jack could feel himself grow hard again.

'Now let me get on top.'

He gasped as Bea rolled over, his cock still inside her. Her clitoris was on fire. On top now she began rocking backwards and forwards, all the time watching Jack. He was so close to coming she could see the veins straining along his neck. His hands held on to her bottom, trying to control the rhythm.

'Wait!' Bea gasped, 'don't come yet.'

Jack was grinning. 'I'm not sure I can last the course . . .'

'Don't laugh, it'll slip out.' Bea's own giggle turned into a sharp cry as her second orgasm rolled over her in a delicious wave. Jack came almost immediately after.

Gazing into each other's eyes, Jack announced, 'You are truly amazing! I haven't had sex like that for years.'

He lay back exhausted on the floor with his arms stretched out behind his head. Bea nestled on his damp chest, her hands touching, caressing the irresistible wiry hair that was beginning to show signs of grey.

'You're in very good shape,' she said admiringly and bent to kiss an old scar she found on his shoulder.

Jack's mouth twitched. 'For a man of my age, you mean. I guess I should apologise for hauling you in like that. But you've been on my mind so much, seeing you there my instincts took over.'

'I like your instincts. I just can't believe I'm actually here like this with you. What happened to the beard?'

Jack grinned. 'It was hiding my good looks. You took a risk turning up at the house unannounced. Why did you come?'

'You have a very persuasive tongue.'

Jack tweaked her ear affectionately.

'You have a very experienced one, young lady.'

Plummeting down to earth, Bea's smile turned to a frown. 'Now what's that for?'

'Nothing,' she muttered, 'only I'm a bit worried that we didn't use a condom. I know men hate the wretched things and I do too but I had a bit of a scare recently and I promised myself I wouldn't take any more risks.'

'If it eases your mind, I had to have an AIDS test last month for insurance purposes. I'm in the clear.'

Bea's sigh of relief was audible.

'Where is everyone?' she asked, settling back happily against him. Any minute she was going to wake up.

'Gone to visit Lorna's mother in Aberdeen for the day. We don't exactly get on, so I made excuses. I like having the place to myself. Especially with you here.' He stroked her hair.

Bea glanced at her watch. Four o'clock. 'Oh hell. I have to go soon.'

'I'll drive you. It's going to rain any minute and I don't want you getting soaked.' He ran an admiring hand over her breasts.

'They're not in Lorna's league. Are you disappointed?'

'If I die today, I can die happy.'

Bea, feeling something unexpectedly close to love, rolled on top to kiss him and farted. She looked so mortified that Jack began to laugh. He blew a loud raspberry in the centre of Bea's tummy until she began shrieking with laughter too. The dog was whining piteously from the kitchen, obviously feeling left out. Jack opened the back door and the affectionate but independent golden retriever padded in.

'Get down, Dickens!' ordered Jack, returning with a box of tissues. He handed Bea a tissue, before wiping himself.

'You're bleeding,' he said, inspecting his cock.

'God, I'm hopeless with dates. I hope I haven't made a mess of your carpet?'

'No matter. I can always blame it on the dog. He's forever getting into fights. Either that, or chasing female dogs.'

Dickens was trying to examine Bea's crotch.

'Don't be rude, Dickens,' she pushed him off. 'We haven't been formally introduced.'

Picking up a trail of scattered clothes, she chuckled, 'Look at this place. It looks like the first day of Harrods' Christmas

369

sale!' She stopped to examine a stack of CDs which appeared to consist mostly of Andrew Lloyd Webber musicals and Kylie Minogue.

'Afraid I don't know the first thing when it comes to music. Lorna's the musical freak and Olivia's just discovered a group called Wet Wet Wet. Sounds pornographic to me.'

'They're actually pretty tame.'

Jack looked at his watch. 'We'd better get going. What time's your show?'

'Six.' She threw her arms around his neck. 'Tell me again that I didn't just dream this.'

'No dream, beauty. This is real flesh and blood. I just wish I could come along and see you do your stuff.' Bea began counting the sea of freckles on his face. 'Next time we'll do this properly.' He kissed her very firmly.

Yippee! He'd said next time. 'What will you tell Lorna?'

'I don't know. Maybe nothing. This is new to me,' he put a finger on Bea's mouth, which was about to protest. 'It's not my way,' he said firmly, 'let's just see what happens, okay?'

Bea nodded silently. She felt very young with Jack.

He dropped her at the gates of Rosterary. Two locals walked by with their dog who barked excitedly at the sight of Dickens in the back of the car. Recognising Jack, the couple stopped to wave, so they were careful to make their goodbye formal. Bea didn't watch him drive off. She ran back up the path with a feeling of happiness and expectation she hadn't felt for a very long time. Glowing from the firm kisses he'd given her, and safe in the knowledge that her home number was tucked in his coat pocket, she rushed across the hall towards hair and make-up.

Behind her the dark sky rumbled and finally released the rain it had been storing up all day.

'I want my old job back,' Toby said bluntly, after he'd given his order to the waiter, surprising Yarnton with his request for Perrier.

Yarnton looked stunned. 'What brought this on?'

'Tanya and the baby, I suppose. But I've been thinking about it for a while now. For too long I've been afraid to go

370

back to work, afraid of failing. I've got to give it a try.'

'You've been out of the business for six years, Toby. You won't be able to pick up just where you left off.'

'I'm aware of that.'

'You were damned good.'

'I appreciate the vote of confidence. But I'd only be fooling myself if I thought it would be easy. I have let people down.'

'It's one of the hazards of living. We all do it, especially in this business. I, for one, will back you up to the hilt.'

Toby looked away, not wanting the old man to see the emotion in his eyes. He'd behaved pretty irresponsibly over the years but Yarnton had always been there for him, never let him down.

'When are you two going to tie the knot?'

'We fixed a date for December. Can't do it before because Tanya's parents don't get back from Africa until then and she understandably wants them to be there. She won't show much.'

'Oh, in this day and age I don't think anyone will mind,' said Yarnton, gazing greedily at the lamb chops the waiter had brought. 'Incidentally, you must try the apple crumble. Don't ever tell her I said this, for God's sake, but it's even better than Dorothy's!'

'What have you done to yourself?'

George Temple explored the corners of his mouth with his tongue for stray bits of shepherd's pie as his granddaughter bent to kiss his frail grey head. Plugged into the CD Walkman she'd given him for Christmas, he had the volume up too loud and shouted, 'You look peaky!'

'There's no need to shout. I heard you the first time.'

Kate gently removed the ear plugs, noticing the food stain on his shirt and that he'd lost a shoe. He was sitting on a red velvet sofa in front of a magi-log fire and the room was stiflingly hot. Kate longed to open a window.

'Hope you haven't brought your mother with you,' George glanced anxiously behind her for Sophie.

'Mum's in France, darling, visiting friends.'

'Spending money, more like.' Kate settled herself into a

chair. 'Still having problems with René? Thought I told her to get rid of him.'

'I can see you're in a good mood. They divorced years ago, remember?'

George looked indignant. 'Nothing wrong with my memory. What's the time? You'll stay for tea?'

'Depends how civil you are.'

Kate was slowly adjusting to the smell of urine. The two exchanged smiles and George relaxed against the back of his sofa trying not to look too pleased that it was his granddaughter visiting him and not his irritating daughter Sophie.

Kate was admiring the view from the pair of sash windows in the visiting room of Laurel's Home for the elderly. Beyond it lay the tapestry of fields and meadows which melted into the hazy Wiltshire countryside. The roomy Georgian house, once used to entertain royal guests and foreign diplomats, now accommodated sixty crumbling old folk, some of whom were slumped despondently in front of a large television set. The closest any of these had got to royalty was watching the Queen's speech on Christmas Day.

'I've brought you some things.'

Kate ferreted around in a smart black and tan leather bag and produced a camel cashmere scarf, a box of French truffles, individually chosen, and a bottle of George's favourite whisky which he immediately grabbed.

'Ah!' he muttered. 'Well done, Kate! I'll sneak this under my mattress away from Sister's clutches. All your mother ever brings me is underwear with name tapes sewn in, as if I haven't enough of the damn things already.'

He glanced contemptuously at the other residents as if it was their fault.

'Mum means well,' said Kate, rearranging the tartan rug more firmly around his legs. 'Now, what's all this about your new room-mate? Sister said you'd had a bit of a set-to last week.'

'Don't talk to me about that Fascist! Caught him trying to send a message to the enemy over the radio. Well, I soon put a stop to that. Oh yes. Buried it in the garden.'

'You buried his television, George,' said Kate, curbing a

smile, 'and he's not a Fascist, he's a lonely Yorkshireman who got so upset by your bad behaviour that he had to be moved to another room. You can't be such a bully.'

It was because he was bored, of course, as much as anything else. Blind in one eye and with bad arthritis, there wasn't much for George to do. Since his second wife's death eight years ago, George's one real joy was gardening. Digging, pruning, mulching, he was often seen working in the small patch he'd been given and he guarded it with ferocity. His roses were a triumph and much admired among the staff.

A nurse wheeled in a tea trolley, unceremoniously plonking two plastic cups of luke-warm tea and a plate of pink iced-buns on their table. George scowled at the nurse then picked up one of the buns.

'Probably poisoned,' he said, taking a suspicious bite.

'Hush,' said Kate gently.

'Do you want to go to the toilet, George?' asked the nurse.

'Mind your own business!' he snapped.

The nurse turned to Kate with a smile. 'If he wants to go to the toilet give me a shout and I'll take him.'

'I'm going to Australia in a couple of weeks,' Kate announced after the nurse had gone. Following her grandfather's lead, she tested the tea with a tiny sip but found it wasn't too bad. An old lady nearby was singing tunelessly, her gums flapping as saliva dripped down her chin. She was rocking from side to side as if in pain, but no one took any notice.

'Australia!' George looked incredulous, as if she'd said Siberia or the IRA headquarters in Belfast. 'I know someone in Australia.'

Having finished his bun, he now picked up Kate's.

'Who do you know?' she asked in surprise.

'Remember Beth?' his voice wistful and suddenly young. 'That lovely young widow I was going to marry,' he frowned, 'or was it your mother I had this conversation with? Ended up running off with some chap, what was his name . . . Lonsdale, that's it. Swept her off to Queensland. Better looking than me.'

'Nonsense!' said Kate crossly, aware that George was

flattered by her reaction. 'Why have you never mentioned her before?'

'Because it happened a few years before you were born. Oh, she was a beauty, that Beth. No make-up for her and bright as a button. Wouldn't put up with any nonsense. Had all the men running circles round her, me included. Always did have a weakness for navy-blue eyes. You must look her up for me.'

His faded gaze held Kate's for the first time that afternoon.

'George, Australia's a big place.'

'Oh, but I still have her letters. You can take them with you. No harm in trying, eh?'

The *Neighbours* signature tune blared from the television. Eleven shrunken heads stared mindlessly at the screen, the room echoing the sounds of the old woman's ramblings. The whole place reeked of death.

She glanced at her grandfather, once a proud, handsome man who'd battled through his long life with the same courage he'd displayed during the war. And what was left to show for it all? Loneliness, senility, humiliation. Don't ever let me end up this way, she prayed. Allow me my dignity.

George, now flicking through an out of date *Sporting Life*, drained his cup and grimaced, 'D'you think you could persuade that old boot of a nurse to bring us a few more buns?'

Lorna arrived back at the Manse from her bridge party at four o'clock. She found Mrs Brodie sitting in the kitchen rocking-chair clutching a tear-stained Fergus to her matronly bosom. Fergus, who was sucking a dummy, pulled it out of his mouth and offered it to his mother like a prize.

'Daddy,' he said gravely, 'Daddy.'

'Hello, my darling,' she murmured, lowering her head to kiss him. 'I'm sorry I'm late. I got stuck in traffic. Has he been very bad?'

Mrs Brodie rose. 'I'm afraid I've a bit o' bad news, Mrs W. Something awful's happened. I didnay know what to do.'

The next moment Olivia, tearing downstairs dressed as Catwoman and wearing fluffy, red Mickey Mouse slippers, sent Lorna flying.

'Oh Mummy, Mummy!' she cried in a shrill voice. 'He shot Dickens. That nasty, horrible, beastly man shot our Dickens!' And she burst into a fit of hysterical tears.

'What!' Lorna looked shocked while Olivia gripped firmly on to her leg. Fergus, copying his sister, immediately began to cry.

'Mrs Brodie?'

'Olivia took Dickens for a walk this morning. He must have slipped his collar and disappeared. She came rushing back to the house and I went out looking for him with her.'

'We searched for a whole hour, Mummy,' sniffed Olivia, wiping her runny nose on her sleeve.

'Here pet, take this,' said Mrs Brodie offering her some kitchen paper. 'Shortly before two, I heard the sound of a car and a wee noise out the front so I went to have a look. Thought it might have been Mr Winger, but it was old Farmer Peck. He pulled open the boot of the car and took out Dickens' poor wee body, dumping him on the doorstep, cold as ice. He said, "I warned you to keep that dog off my land," then drove off, with never another word.'

'Do you mean to tell me that awful man killed Dickens?'

Lorna was appalled. Mrs Brodie nodded, too upset to speak further.

Lorna lowered her voice, 'Where have you put the body?'

'I had one of the boys put him in the back shed. I didnay know what else to do.'

'You did the right thing, Mrs B. What an awful thing to happen. We'll just have to wait for Jack to get home. He'll know what to do. You put Fergus down and I'll stay with Olivia.'

Olivia clung tearfully to her mother's skirt. 'My tooth is hurting again, Mummy. Can I have some chocolate buttons to make it better?'

By the time Jack got home both children were in bed. Olivia had taken the longer to settle, gazing mournfully up at the luminous stars and half-moons stuck to her bedroom ceiling. When Jack, after taking Mrs Brodie home, came downstairs from checking on them, Lorna put her arms round him.

'Oh, darling, what are we going to do?'

'There's nothing we can do. It's just terribly sad.'

After a polite pause he disengaged himself and walked into the drawing-room. Lorna, now wearing a comfortable Viyella skirt and an on-its-last-legs rust cardigan, followed, moving towards the fire, which was crackling and spitting new wood.

'Shouldn't we at least call the police?'

'If Dickens was on his land, Peck was within his rights to shoot. He was only protecting his sheep.'

'But that dog never hurt a fly.'

'Of course not. We all know what a sadistic bastard Dan Peck is, but I'm afraid we haven't a leg to stand on. Poor little Livi. She adored that dog.'

'It's been a horrible shock for us all,' said Lorna, hoping for another hug.

'We're best putting it behind us. I'll go and see Angus tomorrow. See if he'll spare us one of the new litter.'

He picked up the post and a list of phone messages, 'Don't think I could face any of this now.'

'Then let's go to bed, darling. You've got an early start tomorrow.'

Skipping the ominous brown envelopes, Jack stopped at a postcard and flipped it over.

'Ian Woosnam's pulling out. Buggered up his neck at Wentworth last week. I can't believe it!'

'That narrows the odds a bit for you, at least.'

'I'll call him in the morning.'

Lorna studied her husband, head bent against the mantelpiece as he poked the fire, gazing intently into the flames. It wasn't fair. He had changed far less than she had, if anything the added years had improved his looks. His body was still in great shape. He had lost a bit of hair on top but it was still fair, still natural. Hers had started going grey four years ago, only a sprinkling at first, but being a brunette they stood out, broadcasting the fact that she was getting old! All these years of Jack lapping up the glory. By rights it was her turn. She felt betrayed by her own body.

'Jack. Are you coming to bed?'

'Mmm? You go on. I'll be up in a bit.'

'Don't start working now. It's so late!'

'I just need to unwind a bit on my own.'

Like you did last night and the night before. She bit her lip to stop the fear.

'What's happening to us, Jack? Your daughter's not the only one who could do with a bit of comforting around here. Sometimes I think you forget you're married. We never do things together, you don't talk to me any more.'

'Lorna . . . Not now, please.'

'No. Now's never a good time, is it? Whenever I try to get close you just fob me off. Look at me, Jack. I'm your wife, I'm special. Don't I matter to you?'

'Of course you matter! It's just been a long day, I'm tired and I don't need this from you of all people.'

Lorna's face hardened. 'Fine. Do whatever you like then, you usually do, but I warn you I'm getting tired of sleeping on my own. I won't bother to wait up!'

Setting their grievances aside they buried Dickens at the bottom of the garden under the spreading cherry tree, next to Pea the gerbil, two goldfish and a white mouse Olivia had adopted called Squeaks. The children decorated his coffin with photographs of the family, a red and green tartan blanket which Dickens had lain on for twelve years and two bones in case he got hungry on his way to heaven. The children watched Jack with wet, crinkled eyes as he covered the box with earth and planted the cross Olivia had made. On it she'd carefully painted 'DIKINS'.

'Do you think God took Dickens away from us because I smacked Alice Lumpkin at school, Daddy?' she snivelled.

'No, my sweet. This was Dickens's time to go. We all have to eventually.'

'I won't have to go for a long time, will I?'

Jack picked his daughter up and hugged her. 'You've got a whole life ahead of you.'

Over the top of Olivia's blonde head Jack caught his wife's eye and thought of Bea. He felt guilty because he'd always thought he was the sort of man who was above infidelity and yet he couldn't get her out of his mind. The funny, sexy, lovable creature, bursting with beauty and energy had given him a new lease of life. He didn't want to hurt his wife, whom he cared for, but it troubled him that he couldn't remember when he'd stopped being in love with her.

21

Coochin Coochin was a typical old Queensland house. It stood on stilts on a hill overlooking the lazy curves of a creek and the oddly-shaped mountains across the broad valley, the slopes richly swathed in rain forest. A wooden veranda flanked the house on three sides and a large jacaranda tree graced the front of the property, littering the ground with mauve petals like strewn confetti. Close by were two flame trees, and a magnolia which accounted for the sweet smell in the air. Dylan Lonsdale, still an impressive figure at fifty-nine, opened Kate's side of the car, then removed her bags from the boot. Rising over six foot four, he had a leathery face that was covered in a sea of freckles, and grey-streaked sandy hair.

'Beth should be around somewhere,' he said, 'probably spoiling our latest acquisition down at the stables.'

Barks were coming from inside the house. As Dylan locked the car the front door opened and a large black and tan Dobermann came bursting out, followed by a tall, elegant woman wearing gardening gloves. She had a smudge on her nose.

'You've arrived! Do excuse me, I must look a mess but I can't seem to pass a flowerbed without spotting a weed, and once I get started there's no end to it.'

The woman gave a musical laugh.

'Oh, and do look!' she pointed gaily, as the Dobermann sniffed Kate's luggage. 'Prince matches your bag exactly. I'm Beth. Come on in and have an enormous drink. You must be exhausted in this heat. Dylan, darling, will you take Prince with you when you check on the mare. He needs a pee.'

Prince shot off after Dylan, and Kate followed Beth

through a welcoming drawing-room and into a bright, cheerful kitchen. A heavy, oval glass table stood on a base covered in a rich Kilim. What a clever idea, Kate thought, admiring the unusual arrangement. On the table was a very old Siamese cat and bowls brimming with custard apples, paw-paws, guavas, macadamia nuts, pungent frangipanis. The cat briefly opened one sardonic blue eye at Kate before resuming its arduous task of snoozing. Sophie would never have allowed that! Kate guessed Beth was quite a lot younger than George, but the years had been kind. Her eyes (which were indeed navy) were set in by a tawny-gold face, framed by a sleek, blonde bob which had been swept to one side with a pin. She was a tall woman, but gave the impression of being much smaller because she was so slim and had angular, delicate bones. For some reason Kate felt as if they had already met.

'Let's take our drinks on to the veranda. It's such a glorious day,' said Beth, handing Kate a huge glass of wine and a bowl of olives. 'You must be starving.'

The outside wall was dripping with scarlet bougainvillea and there were terracotta pots full of Busy Lizzies, pansies and a miniature tree which Kate didn't recognise. She thought it might be Japanese.

'Bonsai,' said Beth, following her gaze. 'We've even got a couple of coffee trees out the back.'

'What a lovely house,' said Kate, her head reeling from the cacophony of cicadas and the scent of frangipani. They sat on rusting chairs and Beth immediately passed her a cushion.

'Hope it's not damp. We had a heavy storm last night.'

'In the middle of summer?'

'Looks idyllic, doesn't it,' said Beth, inspecting the view, 'but this country can be deceptive – floods, droughts, fires, you name it we've had them all!'

Tilting her black Ray-Bans to the sun, Kate skimmed the view before her, finding it hard to believe that somewhere so beautiful could be anything but peaceful. The sky was smudged with neat, baby-blue and lemon clouds. The fields it surveyed lay back to back like a great patchwork quilt, scattered with cattle and wattle trees, their coats of gold and green swaying like the national flag. She could feel poems exploding in her head, looked forward to solitary hours when she could write them down and explore her creative side, so neglected these days. The sounds of unfamiliar birds, distant horsy activities, even the growl of a tractor ploughing in river flats mesmerised her. She had only been in Australia two weeks but her visit to George now seemed a world away. After a couple of false starts she had finally tracked down Beth Lonsdale in Melbourne and was promptly invited up to their property in Queensland.

'But you must!' Beth had sounded delighted to have news of such an old boyfriend and brushed aside Kate's protests over the phone. 'You can't be in a hurry to get back to work. I would have thought it was a blessed relief away from such an artificial environment.'

She was nothing if not blunt, thought Kate, listening.

'You've come all this way. Enjoy it. Besides, last night's news said that the whole of Europe had ground to a halt with snow blizzards!'

'You're sure it's not inconvenient?'

'We're flying up tomorrow. Got a new Arab stud being delivered, but if you let me know what day you finish your job I'll arrange a ticket for you. Dylan can pick you up from the airport. No trouble at all.'

So, defiantly, Kate had faxed Prime in London instructing them to book her out until the end of the month. Nigel, away for a break, would hit the roof, of course, but she needed the holiday and Australia's warm touch was already doing her a power of good. Kate felt herself relax away from city pressures and work. The countryside always had that effect, made her feel calm, grounded. No one fussing with her hair or face, no one expecting her to look perfect, no dictatorial directors, no Roe to hurt her. She took great gulps of clean, pure air, obliterating London and Paris from her mind. Here in this wild, exciting country across the world she was invisible. Safe.

Unravelling like a spool under the northern sun she sat listening to Beth explaining the mechanics of Coochin.

Macduff, the cat, grazed her legs, his sharp grey head turned upwards, miaowing hungrily with increasing urgency each time Kate stroked him.

'The arable land is share-cropped with the Freemans, our neighbours,' explained Beth. 'They live across the creek, real, true blue Queenslanders. Matthew Freeman's an old friend and runs it with his two boys, though at sixty-eight the dear man really should be thinking about retiring. I envy him having his sons so close.' Beth's face was suddenly wistful.

'George told me you were widowed but I didn't realise you had children.'

'Two from my first marriage. Alexander's the elder. My daughter Naomi lives with her husband in Bath. She was working for a publishing company but gave it up after she got pregnant.'

'Are you close?'

'Very, but it's hard when your offspring live on the other side of the world. The twins make travelling difficult for Naomi, we're so far away. Alexander's usually bogged down with some new project but he visits when he can.'

Beth used her fingers to jiggle the ice in her drink. 'And tell me, I'm dying to know. How is George, the old codger? The last time we met he was teaching at Bristol University. All us mature students were mad for him. He was so clever and terribly handsome.'

'Still is,' said Kate with a smile, 'but a bit forgetful these days.' Macduff had jumped up on her lap and was circling himself into a comfortable position.

'Just push him away if he bothers you. Macduff's like oil. You can never get him off.'

'Oh, but I love animals. My first job was working for a dog's home. George, I'm afraid, had to be put in a home himself four years ago. He hates it but it's hard to know what else to do. He needs constant supervision and no one's got the time to give it to him. You left quite an impression on him, by the way. Talked of nothing else when I visited him.'

Beth chuckled.

'I did write to him for a while, but you know how it is when you don't see someone on a regular basis, and this place keeps us so busy. It still seems like only yesterday we were making eyes at one another down at the Devonshire Arms. I was so English then, all peaches and cream, long flowing skirts, afternoon teas. Now look at me!'

Kate admired Beth's beautiful face, unadorned by cosmetics.

'Is my wife fishing for compliments again?' teased Dylan as he came through the French windows, his intelligent, Oxford-blue eyes ridging at the corners.

'We were just reminiscing about England, darling. I must say it's lovely having someone to do that with. You're so terribly colonial these days.'

'How do you manage this place? It's huge!' Kate asked Dylan who collapsed in a chair next to Beth.

'My wife runs most of it but we also have a constant stream of temporary help: visiting Brits, Argentinians, South Africans, the odd Yank, even horse-mad young Aussies. The places around here all have Aboriginal names but sadly we haven't many Aboriginal stockmen left. There's still so much prejudice.' He smiled sadly at Kate.

'How do they survive?'

'With difficulty. The unemployment figures are forever on the up, though contrary to popular belief fewer blacks receive social services than whites, despite having ten times more unemployment. Which is why most Abos spend their time drinking. Well,' he said noticing Kate's surprise, 'it's the constant frustration of not being able to change their lives that makes many of them give up hope.'

'Drinking,' said Beth, 'at least provides a form of release from an otherwise intolerable situation. I do some voluntary work at the Abo art and craft centre when I have time, but they don't make it easy to get close. Can't honestly say I blame them. Anyway, my poor child, here we are thoughtlessly rambling on when you look absolutely washed out. I'll take you to your room so you can unpack, rest and have a shower. No formal programme at all. I run a very relaxed house, as you can see.'

'I've put Kate's things in the yellow room,' said Dylan.

'Then you can stay and have your drink, darling. I'll take her up.'

Prince, who'd been asleep under the table, sprang to his feet and ignoring Macduff's whiny complaints ambled after the women along an enormous corridor made of Australian cedar. She was shown into a small yellow and green room with a huge brass bed half-hidden by a knotted mosquito net. It looked romantic. On the bedside table was a mosquito coil in a metal saucer and a box of matches. A splash of bougainvillea had wiggled its way up the French shutters, concealing the fact that they needed a good lick of paint. Outside the heat haze shimmered. Kate, looking up at the sky, remembered a Gerard Manley Hopkins poem she had learned at school:

> The glassy peartree leaves and blooms, they brush
> The descending blue; that blue is all in a rush
> With richness . . .

'Oh!' she said and beamed at Beth.

'Everyone seems to like this room.' Beth breezed through checking that everything had been done according to her instructions. 'If you feel like it later, why not join me for a swim. We've a pool round the back of the house.'

'Sounds blissful.'

'While I remember, we have a little green frog who lives in your bathroom. He's a family pet and may occasionally plop into your bath, but don't worry. He's very sweet and absolutely harmless.'

Kate giggled, wondering what other surprises were in store for her.

It was almost midnight when Skander Davenport pulled up in his E-type Jaguar alongside the old estate wagon his parents used. He felt absolutely shattered after the long drive from Sydney, having already spent several hours in a meeting to raise money for a new film he hoped to make. Discussions with a hugely successful property developer had gone well, but the developer was hard to pin down and Skander, who liked to work quickly and effectively, had found it hard to curb his irritation. The whole month had been exhausting, waking up at the crack of dawn to make calls to London, plus two fruitless trips to Los Angeles. He'd hardly slept at all over the past three days.

Getting rid of Charlotte hadn't been easy either. Damn, he thought, as he switched off the engine and listened to the sudden hush, he should never have gone to bed with her. But three weeks ago at the opening of a friend's club in the Cross, looking gloriously wanton in a plunging black dress which stopped half-way up her thighs, she'd seemed a desirable proposition. Besides, it had been a while and he wasn't made of stone. On Saturday night he'd taken her back to his room at the Sebel Townhouse Hotel in Elizabeth Bay. By Monday morning the novelty of champagne and staying up all night had worn off and Skander had turned up for his meeting in a thoroughly bad mood.

He brushed back the dirty-blond mane from his face, knots in his brow unwinding as he locked the car door and stopped for a second to breathe in the warm, gum-scented air. It was extraordinary the effect this place had on him. Why had he left it so long this time? In the distance he could hear an owl hooting. Looking up he saw a group of flying foxes swooping past. Home at last. It felt good. Grabbing his luggage, he walked briskly to the front door.

Kate, at the other end of the house, couldn't sleep. A possum had been crashing around on the roof above her room. It didn't seem possible that something so small could make such a racket. Bloody animal! Having tossed and turned for an hour she finally gave up trying and was now staring up at the tent-like mosquito net, hanging around her in the warm air like mist. In spite of its protection and the glowing end of the mosquito coil, she'd been savagely bitten. The itchiness was driving her crazy! She turned on the light to read but could not concentrate. It was too hot and the Chardonnay they'd had at supper was making her feel thirsty. Kate walked naked from the bed and threw on a T-shirt which smelt faintly of Fenjal. It was dark in the corridor, and she paused so that her eyes could adjust. As she neared the kitchen Kate could see light spilling out into the hall. Funny, she was certain she'd turned off all the lights, and Beth and Dylan had been in bed for hours. Perhaps they had an intruder, she thought nervously. Then Prince emerged from the kitchen wagging his tail. Some guard dog you are! Something *was* burning. God, what if they had a fire. Then a familiar deep voice behind her spoke.

'I don't remember anyone saying we had guests.'

Caught completely unawares,' Kate backed into a pair of powerful, denim-clad arms. Turning round, her eyes slowly travelled up along the huge shoulders, the tanned neck, up to Beth's unmistakable navy-blue eyes.

'God! You frightened the life out of me!'

If he shared her surprise, however, he hid it well. Smoke from his cigarette oozed between them.

'You do turn up in the most unexpected places,' he said calmly.

'Speak for yourself. We weren't expecting you.'

'Clearly.' Skander looked amused, his eyes taking in her extreme state of undress. 'Do you usually parade around my parents' house dressed like that?'

Kate blushed and pulled the inadequate T-shirt over her bottom.

'Oh, come on, Kate, don't start playing the prude. I've seen you with a lot less on than that. How have you been?'

'A bit tired,' she admitted, 'but you were right about this place. It's magical.'

'You've lost weight.'

'I've been on a health kick,' she said, creeping further away.

'It doesn't suit you.'

'Thanks. I'd forgotten how liberal you are with compliments!'

Honestly, did he have to stare at her like that? She was at a distinct disadvantage. They were silent for a moment.

'I heard you'd moved back to London. What happened? Were you hoping to see more of Julian or is Roe Lewis the cause of your sleepless nights these days?' Skander said perceptively.

'Leave his name out of this . . .'

A smile. 'Okay.'

' . . . because I could do without another of your bloody sermons at two o'clock in the morning!'

'I said okay. Calm down.'

'I'm perfectly calm!'

Skander suddenly laughed.

'What's so bloody funny?'

'It's just that I came here for some peace and quiet, and found you, of all people, on my own doorstep. It's somewhat ironic.'

Kate yawned.

'Your manners haven't improved much.'

'You don't exactly bring out my best side and, if you don't mind, now that I know you're not a burglar I'm going back to bed!'

Somewhere a door slammed, then there were low voices talking. Kate peered at the digital clock through heavy eyes, the green dots beating like tiny hearts. Eleven already! Memories of last night filtered through her mind. Skander, short for Alexander, was the son Beth had been raving about all this time. She should have twigged.

Throwing on a pair of stone-coloured slacks and a white linen shirt, Kate swept her newly-washed hair off her face with a tortoiseshell comb and added a touch of coral to her lips. Casting a critical look over her appearance she decided she could do with a bit of sun. She was looking pasty. One of the temporary stable hands passing her on the way to the dining-room would happily have argued the point, admiring how the copper cloud of hair set off her English complexion. Not like the daggy girls round here, he thought ruefully. They all had skins like leather, spending their lives outdoors and giving little if any attention to their appearance.

The dining-room was empty. Anticipating a quiet breakfast she helped herself to some cereal and a newspaper and settled herself at the end of the table. She was just finishing a front-page article about more atrocities in Northern Ireland when Beth popped her head round the door.

'You're here! Alexander arrived late last night without telling a soul. Isn't it wonderful!'

'Wonderful,' Kate replied flatly.

Beth removed from the window seat a sleeping Macduff who miaowed crossly then skulked off to find a more secluded spot.

'Then this morning Dylan got a call from the office. They want him in eastern Europe to set up some financial deals and I'm being allowed to go with him.' She looked apprehensively at Kate. 'I feel awful about leaving you.'

Kate's smile wavered. 'When are you off?'

'First thing tomorrow. I know you haven't had much time to settle in so I've invited a few friends for dinner as a sort of farewell. It will give you an opportunity to meet our neighbours.'

'Perhaps it's time I went back to England. I don't want to be a burden.' She didn't want Skander on her back.

'I won't hear of it! You must promise to stay. Alexander's more your age and he'll love having a pretty face around.'

Hardly! Perhaps she could invent a job back in London. But then there was the business of changing her flight again, which had already caused no end of problems. After Beth had gone Kate flicked through the rest of the paper, pausing to read her horoscope. Automatically she read Scorpio, featured at the top of the page. It was 14 November! Today was Roe's birthday: 'Out with the old, in with the new. Saturn is in your opposite sign, attracting dozens of beautiful and intelligent partners, giving you ample outlets for your passions and desires.' She threw the paper aside in disgust. Rising signs, Jupiter in Uranus. It was all a big con.

After breakfast Beth took her to see the horses. The morning was beginning to throb with the gathering heat and Kate could feel sweat trickling down the inside of her arms. The stables, which looked like a hospital, they were so clean, ran off the east side of the property and they passed rows and rows of curious, hungry heads. Nut, Coochin's resident Blue Heeler, ran on ahead. He looked like a Boeing 747, his loopy ears flying out on either side as he tried to catch a small lizard he'd spotted. Resting on a log stump in the stable yard, Kate watched Beth move from stall to stall, talking to the horses and hired hands with easy familiarity, pausing finally at the end stable.

'Come and meet our pride and joy, Goliath!' she announced proudly.

Even with her limited experience with horses, Kate had to admit he was an impressive animal, with a gleaming coat that looked as if it had been dipped in Golden Syrup. Kate wondered if it was safe to enter the box as he stamped and fidgeted on his long legs, much like some highly-strung fashion models she had known.

'He's gorgeous,' she said in awe, watching the expert way Beth handled him. 'I wonder if he'd ever behave like that with me?'

'He's a temperamental beast and doesn't trust many people,' said Beth, 'you'd have to be pretty good with horses to ride him. We'll get you up on Ghanum for a ride. She's a more gentle mount.'

Kate was enchanted with Ghanum. Her ginger ears pricked up in interest as they entered her box. Kate put a hand up to the soft, hairy chin, enjoying the way Ghanum snorted through her fingers, hoping for food. Her lovely marmalade forehead was marked with a white star and she had a white sock on her offside hind leg.

'She's got a great heart and is very even-tempered. I think the two of you will get on fine.'

After some pointers from Beth, they mounted the horses and set off for a tour of the property. Goliath curvetted across the stable yard, eager for a gallop, but eventually settled down to Ghanum's more staid pace. A cloud of bush flies settled on to the riders.

'Take no notice,' said Beth, 'it's a feature of bush life. Quite inescapable, but they're not dirty, just irritating. They say that's why Aussies don't move their lips when they speak, too busy keeping the flies out.'

They certainly didn't bother Beth as she told stories of how Coochin had been miraculously saved from a bush fire after the wind had changed direction within fifty metres of the house; of a station hand who'd been an opal miner at Coober

Pedy and still polished gems as a hobby; and of the horrors of the spreading cane toad epidemic. Kate loathed toads.

'Don't believe that life in the bush is easy,' Beth went on, 'but it's a great place to have a holiday. Loosen your reins a little and try not to keep moving your hands, Ghanum's got such a soft mouth; you can't even feel her teeth. That's it, Kate. You look like a natural horsewoman. We'll have you rounding up cattle yet!'

Laughing, they broke into a gentle canter. Passing the river as they returned to the stables, they spotted a black horse tethered to a nearby tree. Stretched out on a group of rocks was Skander. His eyes were shut and one arm was flung out in abandon above his head. He'd been swimming and Kate couldn't help but notice his semi-naked form as he bathed in the sun, the round belly, his smooth skin turning a warm olive which contrasted with the unruly blond hair. His face had softened in sleep and his full mouth was slightly open as if waiting for a bunch of grapes. Beth put a finger to her lips as a sign not to disturb him and their horses passed by unnoticed.

'My son,' Beth whispered proudly. 'You'll meet him properly later. Poor lamb's absolutely exhausted.'

Probably been working overtime on ways to be insufferable, Kate thought viciously. She kicked Ghanum on, wanting to put as much distance between them as possible.

She spent the rest of the afternoon successfully avoiding Skander. After tea, or 'smoko' as the locals called it, she escaped to her room and brought her diary up to date. Somewhere outside the light chinking of a clay mobile indicated a rise in wind. It was now too hot to sit outside and at some stage she must have dozed off. When she awoke it was seven. Time to get ready for dinner. She ran a bath, searching for her elusive green friend, but so far the frog had stayed out of sight.

Kate decided to take particular care with her appearance. War paint, she thought grimly, as she applied the last touches of make-up to her face, and staring back at her reflection decided that she quite fancied herself tonight. The plum-coloured Azzadine Alaia suited her slim figure. It was cut low at the back and accentuated her soft curves. She wondered if it was too short for provincial Queenslanders? Oh, to hell with it. Beth was extremely liberated. She paused outside the drawing-room. She could hear people laughing. Good. Always nice to make an entrance. She took a deep breath, pulled back the doors and walked in.

There were seven people in the drawing-room, which had a fireplace and was stuffed with books and pictures. Dylan, looking tanned and relaxed, was pouring drinks for everyone. Beth, radiant in a gold-embroidered full-length jacket and a silk knitted polo-neck, was laughing with a distinguished-looking gentleman; he stood ramrod-straight despite, Kate guessed, being almost seventy. That must be the neighbour Matthew Freeman. Close by a young man was talking to a couple on a large faded sofa. His brown hair flopped forward over his eyes and just for a second Kate was reminded of Roe. They were less frequent now, these rushes of longing. They just caught her at odd moments; made her feel dizzy, slightly sick. Then the feeling passed. In fact when the man raised his head she could see there was little resemblance. By the window, lounging casually with a glass in his hand, was Skander. He gave her an appraising glance and raised a blond eyebrow at her short skirt. Good, she thought, that will get his holier-than-thou hackles rising. Prince, acting territorially, went around the room sniffing everyone's crotches.

'Here she is!' cried Beth, spotting Kate. 'You look stunning! Come and meet everyone. Dylan will get you a glass of champagne.'

Propelling her into the room, Beth made the introductions. 'And you're not to worry if you don't get everyone's name right. It's taken me years.'

'She introduced me as Gregory only last weekend,' Dylan chuckled.

The couple on the sofa were from Melbourne. Old friends of the Freemans, they had flown up to Queensland for a break. Lizzie Cooger was pregnant, with merry brown eyes, big breasts and a mane of dyed-blonde hair which Kate noticed needed touching up. Her husband Brian, a thin, laconic barrister, looked owlish and had a nervous habit of pushing his horn-rimmed spectacles back on to his nose when he spoke. The young man turned out to be Matthew's nephew, Paul Lambert, who had caused a tremendous stir by landing his own Cessna plane in a nearby field. He was gazing at Kate's legs.

Beth pulled her son across the room. 'It's about time I got you two together.'

'Kate and I have already met.'

'Oh, but why didn't you say so?'

Kate threw Skander a dirty look. 'We worked briefly together last summer. I'm afraid I didn't make the connection. I make so many trips.'

'Well, Alexander's just back from California,' said Dylan, passing round a tray of nibbles. 'He's been telling us how appalling it was. Cat psychiatrists, re-birthing and four taxis for the entire city that you spend half your life waiting for!'

'LA's not known for public transport, but I really enjoyed it there,' said Kate, feeling argumentative.

'And what about all those fabulous Venice Beach girls?' Paul contributed.

'LA girls are like chemically-sprayed fruit,' Skander looked pointedly at Kate, 'very pretty skins but no taste when you bite into them.'

'I've always wanted to go to Hollywood,' squealed Lizzie from the sofa. Macduff, nestled in her lap, had the same concentrated expression one wore on the loo. 'We caught your film last week. I must say we really enjoyed it, didn't we darling?'

Brian nodded. 'Where did you shoot the final scene? I had a bet with Lizzie it was North America.'

'No,' said Skander, 'Ireland. We needed rain.'

'You're a model, Kate. You must have met masses of beautiful film stars in LA?'

'Some. Gene Hackman was the nicest. But one actor's much like another. Happiest when they're talking about themselves.'

'To themselves, most of the time,' said Skander.

'Do you really think it's true that we're going back to a

more womanly look?' Lizzie asked hopefully, digging into the chilli olives.

'Yes, but it won't last long. Fashion's about as consistent as British Rail.'

'But, strewth, look at you,' said Paul. 'You're tiny!'

Lizzie paused on her sixth olive and regarded Kate's figure enviously.

'Come on, Kate, you know as well as I do most models are skin and bone,' argued Skander. 'Did it never occur to you that their shape is dictated by homosexual designers? They've made women look like young men and they're still getting away with it.'

Beth nodded. 'I quite agree. I find it sickening how far women will go to conform to an ideal. I recently read a survey in which eighty per cent of American women said their greatest wish was to be slim. Not healthy, happy or rich, just slim.'

Kate could feel Skander watching her contemplatively.

'When's the baby due?' she said, quickly changing the subject.

Lizzie brightened. 'Two months.' She smiled, displaying a piece of black olive lodged in her front tooth. 'I had a scan done and actually saw its head, its feet and legs. I even saw its penis. Oops!' Lizzie brought a hand to her mouth. 'I've let the cat out of the bag. And I wasn't supposed to tell. Darling,' she said turning to her husband as a phone shrilled in the background, 'does its sex really matter to you?'

'It does now that I know it has a penis.'

Realising he'd just made a joke, Brian started to laugh, the glasses slipping down his nose. Just for a second Kate caught Skander's eye.

Beth rose. 'I'm going to check on supper. Answer the phone, will you, darling. It could be Robyn calling about those tickets we wanted.'

Paul poured more champagne into Kate's glass. 'How long are you here? Because I'd like to take you out to dinner one evening.'

He didn't waste much time.

'I'd like that.' Kate smiled, glad to have made such a quick conquest. She cupped her chin in one hand. 'Did you really arrive in your own plane?'

'I'll take you up for a ride while you're here.'

'Only if you promise not to go too high. I'm terrified of heights.'

'Then I'll graze the tree tops.' He gazed at the emerald ring on her right hand which matched the colour of her eyes perfectly. Panther eyes. 'Nice ring.'

Kate's hand dropped involuntarily. 'It was a gift.'

'Someone has good taste.'

Beth came out in an apron, waving everyone in for supper with a buttery wooden spoon. Kate was irritated to find herself seated next to Skander, but her mood improved when Paul Freeman was placed on her right.

'That was Steve Finch,' said Dylan, hanging up, 'he's pulling out of the Mount Bowan trip.'

'Quite right too.' Beth pushed the fringe off her eyes with the back of one hand. 'It's not every day your wife has a baby.'

'Poor bloke lost his last two,' Dylan said sympathetically.

'So who does that leave?' asked Matthew.

'Four of us including Skander.' Paul was watching Beth dish out steaming bowls of thick Jerusalem artichoke soup. 'There's a slim chance Virginia might come. I spoke to her last week.'

'Forewarned is forestalled,' said Skander enigmatically.

'Now you mustn't give Kate the wrong impression, darling. Virginia's my step-niece. Very pretty but quite a handful. She's had a crush on Alexander for years. Wasn't there some talk about her going to work for Packer at Channel Nine? It's been years since we last saw her.'

'I hope she's changed,' said Skander, 'she behaved very badly the last time we met.' He took a final drag from his cigarette, blew a neat smoke ring towards the ceiling, then stubbed it out in the ashtray.

'Well if Virginia's going why don't you take Kate?' suggested Dylan.

'Oh, but I . . .'

'Nonsense, Kate, you'll love it, you really will,' insisted

Beth. 'It's your chance to see proper outback.'

'What exactly is involved?'

'A six-day trek on horseback through the rain forest,' Paul explained. 'We do it every year. Beth's right. There's nothing quite like it.'

'Just don't expect a five-star hotel,' said Skander ominously.

'Insinuating . . .?' Kate gave him a wintry look.

'Just that we'll be on horseback for six days pitching our tents in the rain forest. The only bed partners you'll get out there will be snakes, mosquitoes and fruit bats and you'll have to leave the hair-drier behind.'

'Does this have a happy ending?' said Kate drily.

Lizzie's fascinated gaze darted from one to the other like a spectator at Wimbledon.

'I'll get the lamb,' said Beth quickly. 'The boys can help. Dylan, darling, Matthew's glass is empty. You're in a house with big meat-eaters, I'm afraid, Kate, but I had Sharon make you a cuttlefish risotto. It's one of her specialities.'

Lizzie gave another black-olive smile. 'How long have you been a vegetarian, Kate?'

'About five years.'

Skander shook his head, smiling.

'And I don't see anything wrong with that,' Kate snapped at him defensively.

'Nothing at all except your children will only grow to be two-foot-seven grown-ups. You just have to glance inside a health food shop to see a bunch of people looking like they've been struck down with yellow fever. I've yet to see a fanciable vegetarian. Present company excepted, of course.'

'You can't generalise like that . . .'

'I can, having lived with one for three years,' said Skander smoothly.

At that moment Beth wheeled in a large rack of roast lamb, thus preventing Kate from delivering a crushing reply.

'Dylan, will you carve?'

Kate, refusing to look at Skander, carefully placed three new potatoes the size of marbles on to her plate. Matthew Freeman turned to Beth.

'When are you going to be persuaded to sell me that fine horse of yours?'

'Which horse?' asked Dylan.

'Goliath. Now, Matthew, dear, we've discussed this. He's not mine to sell any more. You'll have to talk to Alexander.'

'I'd give you a good price for him, Skander.'

'It's not a question of money. Sorry, Mat. I'm keeping him.'

'You'll be riding him on the trek?'

'No, too risky. Putting a stallion with mares is like giving a drink to an alcoholic. I'm taking Eblis.'

'And Kate?' prompted Beth.

'That's up to her.'

'Yes, say you'll come?' begged Paul.

'When is it?' Kate's fork hovered in mid-air.

'Saturday.'

Skander guessed her thoughts. 'Changed your mind already?'

'That's wishful thinking.'

'I hear the Starks bought themselves a very fine bull last week,' said Matthew receiving anxious signals from Beth with her eyebrows.

'That should make a few cows happy!' Kate retorted, spearing peas viciously with her fork. 'And I'm definitely coming.'

Paul beamed. 'Great!'

'Brian. Do help yourself to some more. It all needs eating up,' said Beth.

Kate had hardly touched her food and was now feeling quite drunk. Studiously ignoring Skander on her left, she went over the top with Paul, laughing at all his jokes and amusing him with anecdotes from Paris. When the coffee had been poured, Paul offered Kate a cigarette. She declined.

'Do you mind if I do?' he asked politely.

'Not at all. It's cigars I can't stand!'

Paul glanced uncomfortably at Skander who was puffing meditatively on a large one.

Later on, in the huge, cool drawing-room with the net

396

blinds pulled down over the veranda doors, obstructing the plague of mosquitoes, moths and other nocturnal bugs, they played Trivial Pursuit. Kate might have enjoyed it more if she hadn't kept landing on orange squares. How the hell was she supposed to know who won the FA cup in 1953. Even more annoying was that Skander seemed to know the answers to everything.

At midnight everyone said their goodbyes. Beth and Dylan had to be up at the crack of dawn in order to catch their flight and they still had some last-minute packing to do. Skander had offered to take them to the airport. Hugging them both in turn and wishing them a safe trip, Kate made her excuses and because she was still angry with Skander, allowed Paul to kiss her goodnight.

'Now don't forget you promised to let me take you to dinner when we get back from the trek.'

'Or your offer to take me flying,' she said, gaily waving him off. 'See you Saturday.'

Kate's headache in the morning was as powerful as a runaway articulated lorry. Her eyes were firmly stuck together and she could hear the thin, shrill sounds of birds, cicadas throbbing, and a raucous croak which sounded suspiciously like her green bath companion. Staggering to the window she opened the curtains only to recoil from the dazzling sunlight. Oh dear, her reflection scowled, that'll teach me to drink on an empty stomach.

Slightly improved after a bracingly cold needle-spray shower she dressed and went in search of some much needed tea. The idea of food made her stomach heave. She found Skander with his feet up on the table drinking black coffee, papers sprawled out in front of him, the breakfast things cleared away. Feeling in no condition to deal with him, Kate made a hasty retreat.

The pounding in her head clashed with the frantic noise of cicadas and hot sun. Maybe a quick dip in the pool would help. But then she got distracted by the breathtaking view. The day was so clear that she could see the dramatic peaks of Mount Bowen across the valley. Lost in her thoughts she lay down on the grass, shielding her eyes with one hand. Her head began to swim.

It was almost lunchtime when she returned to the house. She found Skander lolling in the doorway, clad in boxer shorts. He'd been swimming and was clutching a drink. Nut panted furiously at his side.

'Good morning,' he said cheerfully.

'What's good about it?'

'Don't tell me you're still sulking about last night?'

'I'm not sulking,' she said sulkily, 'I feel sick.'

'Serves you bloody well right. You'd better come and have something to soak up some of that alcohol you consumed.'

'I couldn't eat a thing!'

'Well that's not very gracious considering the efforts I've made with lunch.'

At that moment a delicious aroma of garlic and herbs practically knocked her sideways. She glanced at the table. On it were two settings, a bowl of pasta covered in lashings of butter, smoked salmon, black mushrooms and Parmesan, an enormous salad of tomatoes, avocado and fresh basil, a slab of smelly, runny cheese, blackberry muffins and a bottle of red wine. She was suddenly ravenous.

'Beth believes all men should be cooks. She had me making omelettes at the age of seven.'

'No doubt you'll make someone a wonderful mother!' she said scathingly. 'Is there no end to your talents?'

'Try me.'

I left myself wide open for that, she thought, giving him a withering look. 'No thanks. You're not my type.'

'Oh, that's right, I was forgetting the kind of man you go for. They have to be either married or fucked up but definitely unavailable for commitment. Talk about complicating things for yourself.'

'How come I always end up stuck with you! I mean, what did I do in my previous life that was so foul?'

'I don't know but you're doing a pretty good job in this one.'

He was laughing at her now.

'Shut up!'

'Don't like it, do you, Kate, not being able to manipulate

me the way you do everyone else, or the fact that I've seen a part of you you prefer to keep hidden.'

He was now leaning up against the wall, his huge hands on either side of her. She could smell the chlorine on his skin. Her eyes grew shifty, looking for escape.

'When are you going to stop retreating inside yourself? I know it feels safe and secure but you've got to start taking risks, open yourself up.'

'I'm not going to sleep with you,' she hissed.

'I haven't asked you yet.'

He was very close, too close. She felt the cloying warmth of the room and suddenly the smell of tobacco, coffee and the sweet smell of sweat was unbearable.

'I want to go to my room. I'm going to be sick.'

'No, you're not. You're going to sit down and eat what I've cooked you. Then, if you decide you still want to continue your sulk, you can go back to your room.'

He took her face in his hands and studied her. Accustomed now to her sudden explosive outbursts he was giving her a few seconds to calm down. Kate however felt the hot shock of contact and for a terrible moment thought he might try to kiss her. It was a huge relief when he merely took her arm and sat her down at the table. What might have been a pleasurable lunch turned out to be a strained and silent forty minutes. Kate, absolutely burning with rage, refused the wine Skander offered her and picked at her food. He made her stay until she had finished what was on her plate and had digested it, every now and then taking a long, contemplative drag from a cigarette. The rat obviously didn't trust her to keep it down.

Much later, hearing the front door slam, Kate sneaked back unobserved to the kitchen. She was still choking on her rage at being treated like a child. Her eyes fell eagerly on the remains of the pasta and she wolfed down the lot. Even cold it was delicious. She had to admit Skander really knew how to cook, which surprised her. The men she'd grown up with only ever appeared in the kitchen to ask how long supper was going to be. And Roe. She couldn't remember ever having seen him make so much as a cup of coffee.

Having polished off the salad, she was in the middle of demolishing the tail-end of the bread and cheese when to her horror she heard the sound of footsteps and a door slam. When Skander opened the kitchen door in search of the riding whip he'd left behind, he found a scarlet Kate frantically swallowing the food in her mouth. He threw an astonished look at the now empty plates.

'I see your appetite's returned. Looks like you've saved me the job of washing up. I've never seen the crockery look so clean! Well done, Kate.'

He stubbed out his cigarette in the sink, where it sizzled and was gone.

I hate him, I hate him, I hate him! Choking back the tears of humiliation, she avoided him for the rest of the afternoon but even thirty laps in the pool couldn't diminish her anger.

22

Bea shot round her brother's Holland Park flat in a complete state. There were a million things to organise but she had spent the last half an hour running in circles. The phone rang. Panic! Jack had changed his mind after all and was cancelling their rendezvous. She answered in a strained voice, but it was only Dennis from the agency chasing her up for not having sent in a job voucher. Bea went weak with relief.

'Hope it goes well today,' he said.

'Hope what does?'

'Your doctor's appointment, silly. Just hope you haven't gone and got yourself stitched up.'

If only you knew, she thought, as she hung up and immediately began hunting for a clean pair of knickers. After a fruitless search she hand-washed the one pair that hadn't gone pink in the wash and dried them with the hair-drier. The bow on the front looked silly, so she ripped it off with her teeth – she couldn't find any scissors. She'd chosen a tight-fitting dress in what she hoped was a subtle shade of yellow and coaxed her reluctant hair into neatish curls. Then there was the inevitable hunt for the car keys, which turned up inside the bread bin. There was no time for breakfast so she grabbed two bananas from the kitchen to eat *en route*. Useful for practising oral sex, she thought wickedly, chucking the morning's post unopened on to the passenger seat. Then she had to go back because she'd forgotten to put the answer machine on.

She was driving too fast. The bright yellow Beetle, which she swore she'd get cleaned first thing in the morning, hurtled down the motorway with Radio Four blaring. She lost the frequency once she turned on to the A27, and swivelled

the dial to a local programme, whose guest was an American
health nut talking about colonic irrigation. Definitely one for
Kate.

Bea's mind raced with the car. This was crazy! Rule
number one was, you never got involved with married men.
Sleep with them but never get involved. She rolled down the
window to get rid of the condensation and to cool her flushed
face. What did she think she was doing! Separated from Jack
often for days at a time, she spent hours having wild dreams
about him, touching him in her mind. The relationship was
new, not only because it was continuing with such intensity;
they made love with urgency and passion and Jack was
certainly the most unselfish lover she'd ever had; but what
really made if different was having a man as a friend, someone
to depend on. Most men saw her as a fun night out but not
someone to take seriously – her own fault, when she thought
about it. She gave out all the wrong signals.

She could smell sulphur. The uneasy odour clung to the
inside of the car. Just her luck if the Beetle packed up now.
Bea checked the choke (she'd once left it out, flooding the
engine) but it was tightly pressed against its socket. After a
few minutes she forgot about the car, rushing on in her head
as she anticipated her meeting with Jack. Well, hardly a
meeting! The excitement of seeing him again was so great
she almost collided with a passing car. In Scotland Tessa had
taught her breathing exercises which were supposed to quell
your nerves. She tried them now but it made her so dizzy she
gave up and ate both bananas instead. A metallic grey
Mercedes zoomed by in the fast lane so Bea put her foot on
the accelerator and followed it, checking the rear mirror for
police. They'd caught her two weeks ago without tax or
registration and fined her on the spot. Oh, bugger it. The
cheque would probably bounce anyway.

She turned off the motorway and followed the signs to the
village. The dashboard flashed to indicate she was low on
petrol but she didn't want to stop. She'd fill up on her way
home. She spotted the tiny church and the red garage with
the For Sale sign, just as he'd explained. Take the first left,
follow the low cobbled wall past the fountain. Road bends to

the left and the hotel was on the second right. Pulling into the short driveway, Bea glanced at her watch. She'd made it in an hour. She turned off the ignition.

Stillness.

The exquisite medieval manor, Popjoy, sat in a tranquil pocket of Sussex farmland, enclosing a square courtyard. Not far from the house was a tiny restored Norman chapel now occasionally used as a private theatre. Popjoy's southern wing faced the unspoiled coastline, merely a hundred yards away. What a ravishing place, thought Bea, as she walked towards the wide oak front door, which dwarfed the Gothic mullioned windows, half-hidden by trailing ivy.

Jack, who had arrived early, was in the bar hunched over a whisky. Poor angel! He looked tense and very tired. Curbing a desire to rush over and hug him, she went straight to reception and asked to be shown to their room. Jack had already signed them in. The porter led her through the main hall with its beautiful, moulded oak ceiling and up the creaking staircase into a cool, pretty room. There was a huge four-poster bed, a walk-in wardrobe behind a secret panel, two large Victorian baths with clawed feet, side by side, a stone fireplace with a lit fire which was spitting out bits of newly-chopped wood, and low black beams running across the ceiling which Bea promptly whacked her head on.

'You want to watch that,' the porter said earnestly, 'our last guest needed twelve stitches.'

'That's a comforting thought.'

The door closed silently. Bea picked up the phone and dialled reception.

When Jack appeared five minutes later he was astonished to find Bea in front of a roaring fire brandishing one of his golf clubs. Apart from a gleaming pearl choker around her neck, she had nothing on.

'I needed some help on my strokes and I'm told you're the local expert.'

Jack laughed. 'I don't think that was quite the reception Dora would have given Copperfield. She was much too much of a prude. But I like it. Come here, you gorgeous woman.'

Bea, realising suddenly how anxious she'd been, rushed gratefully into his arms.

Later, after they'd ordered room service and demolished a bottle of Sancerre, Bea got up and put on Jack's denim shirt. Her pale skin glowed in the firelight.

'It smells of you. I won't ever take it off.'

She padded into the bathroom and bent over the bath to run some water. Jack followed her.

'Now that's what I call a view,' he said, admiring her bottom. 'Never mind the bath. Let's have a shower.'

The denim shirt got soaked as Jack pulled her under the fierce jets of water. He began soaping her back, her breasts, between her legs until Bea grew excited again. They were soon a mass of slippery limbs, exploring and rolling together like two mud wrestlers. Bea came very quickly, shuddering against Jack's skilful, attentive hands. He instinctively knew all the right buttons to press. Afterwards they lay on the carpeted floor and Bea kneaded the skin on his belly.

'When I was nine I was going to be an astronaut,' she said.

'You were never nine.'

Jack smiled, his eyes shut. Bea gazed at the deep grooves on either side of his mouth and the dark pouches under his eyes. He looked tired. Gently, she kissed each eyelid then ran her tongue down his cheek to his mouth which automatically responded to her kiss.

'I was deadly serious at the time. I used to practise holding my breath in the bath. Two minutes was my record. Then I was going to be a professional skier but I never pursued it. There was always something to distract me. Modelling came out of the blue. I've stuck it out this long because of the money, but sometimes I want to scream with boredom.'

'Then why don't you give up?'

'What else could I do? I'm not exactly career-orientated. I like my freedom too much. It's not easy breaking out on your own after years of having an agent organise everything for you; they tell you where to go, what to wear, how much you're being paid, what you need to bring on a job. That's not to belittle what we do. It just becomes difficult to make decisions for yourself. I did once think of taking a year off to go to art school.'

'Art school?' Jack interrupted. 'So there's a creative side to you as well as everything else.'

'Not a side I get to exploit much,' Bea admitted. 'Anyway it would have made it hard for me to get back on the fashion ladder and I don't know of any other job where you can earn in a day what most people make in a month. It's like a drug. Weeks of checking in with your agency, your heart sinking when you hear "nothing for you today", but you keep on thinking, just one more year, one more go at the jackpot, and then I'll get out while I'm still flavour of the month. Unfortunately for most of us, that never comes.'

She smiled resignedly, remembering how close she'd got.

'What about you? Was it always golf or did you have other ambitions?'

'Only to meet beautiful girls like you. Growing up with three brothers fuels the imagination. I wanted to do my share of sowing wild oats.'

'And your family? I still know so little about you.'

'My mother died of cancer not long after the birth of my youngest brother. There're four of us. My father's a retired naval officer who still thinks I should get a proper job.'

'That's ridiculous. You're a complete star!' She smothered him in urgent kisses then said, 'Jack . . . I need to know. Am I just a fling to you?'

He was surprised by the urgency in her voice. He opened one eye, looked at her and closed it again.

'You're no more a fling than you are plain, nice or ordinary. I'm just not sure how to handle you.'

'You seemed to be doing all right just now.'

'I'd like to make you promises, Bea, but I can't. It's true that my relationship with Lorna has been steadily going downhill, but I daren't risk hurting the children. Can you understand that?'

'Yes.' Bea's voice was small and fragile.

'Besides which I'm old enough to be your bloody father.'

'You've already used that excuse. We're both responsible adults, we know what we're doing.' She removed an eyelash from his cheek and kissed each corner of his mouth. 'Funny,' she said, 'I never usually like this part. But for some reason I don't want to let you go.'

'Who said anything about going?'

'All right then, how about coming?'

She ran her tongue along his neck, tracing the salty line down to his belly button, then lower still. Jack closed his eyes and sighed. Whatever he had to face later on, he owed himself this little bit of heaven.

After he'd gone Bea ordered herself tea and opened her post, which included a lengthy, uproariously funny letter from Kate. Her friend sounded much more like her old self and had included a rather good sketch of the place she was staying at. Coochin Coochin. Funny name for a house. Bea then ran a bath, adding both bottles of Popjoy's luxurious bubble bath. Jack's shirt, which had been too wet for him to wear, was draped over the bedroom radiator – fortunately he was carrying a spare. She climbed into the bath with a copy of the *Mail*, submerging herself in jasmine-scented bubbles. In the colour supplement there was a picture of herself advertising a truly frightful pink bed-jacket – the sort only your grandmother would wear. Definitely not one for the portfolio but at the time the shoot had made Bea a much-needed £500.

Bea felt lazy and unhurried. Go with the flow, she advised herself, forget about the future, which at the moment consisted of a Lloyds overdraft and a blank diary. Instead she lingered over thoughts of Jack's farewell kiss.

'Behave yourself while I'm gone!'

'Must I?' she'd replied, joining in with the game.

'And don't drive home like a maniac. That car of yours looks as if it's on its last legs. I want you back in one piece.'

She submerged her body deeper so only her head was out, stretched like a tortoise. Jack. Jack Winger. Bea Winger. Mrs Jack Winger. No. Mustn't think along those lines. It was forbidden territory, which, of course, was precisely why she was doing it. She settled her attention back on the *Mail* and was soon lost in an article about sex in the nineties, which claimed that the size of a man's penis did in fact matter very much.

The phone rang in the next room, but Bea couldn't be bothered to get out of the bath. No one except Jack knew she was there and he was more than likely half-way down the M4 by now. Probably reception wondering what time she was checking out. They could wait. The room had cost Jack a fortune and she planned to use every penny's worth. She trailed a hand along the top of the water, dispersing bubbles.

The chrome-plated bath tap dribbled. Bea was just debating on whether to add some more hot water, as it was getting tepid, when she paused. Was someone next door? She listened, careful not to splash: there it was again, that sound. Someone was moving around in her bedroom.

She froze. Who could it be? Surely they weren't cleaning the room. It was only five o'clock and she could have sworn Jack had left a 'do not disturb' sign on the door. Slowly Bea eased herself out of the bath, leaving the plug in so as not to make any noise. She'd left the hotel robe on the bed so she had to make do with a towel which barely covered her bottom. She padded across the bathroom in her bare feet and opened the door.

On the little bedroom chair lay a fur coat and a Mulberry handbag. Lorna Winger was standing by the bed clutching Jack's still damp shirt.

'Washing away your sins?' she said in a politely wrapped voice.

'What are you doing here?' said Bea dumbly. Lorna sat down on the edge of the bed.

'I might ask you the same thing. I believe this belongs to my husband.' She held Jack's shirt out at arm's length as if it exuded some terrible smell.

What do you say when you've been caught with your hand in the till?

'I thought this might happen. You're the sort of girl who has no scruples whatsoever about jumping into bed with someone else's husband.'

Bea decided to brazen it out. 'How did you find me?'

'Jack shouldn't leave hotel literature lying around. I knew he wasn't playing today, so I pretended to go to see a friend

407

in London and instead followed him here. I saw you arrive from my car but you were in too much of a hurry to get your greedy hands on my husband to notice.'

'It's not what you think,' Bea's throat was dry, 'we just played a game of golf.'

'In your underwear, I suppose?' She glanced disdainfully over Bea's boyish frame and despite herself, Bea blushed.

'I'm so sorry. You were never supposed to find out.'

'Didn't stop you thought, did it?'

Bea shifted her weight from one leg to another, disadvantaged by her state of undress. There seemed nothing to say.

'Just what exactly do you expect to gain? If it's Jack's money you're after, he hasn't got any. Most of it's tied up in trust funds for the children.'

Bea reddened. 'I'm not that calculating.'

To hell with it, why should I let her intimidate me? She dropped the towel and calmly pulled on her knickers.

Lorna withdrew her eyes and walked round the room, inspecting items dismissively. 'I hear you're a model. You obviously don't work much or you wouldn't be taking baths in the middle of the afternoon. Might I have seen you in anything other than your underwear?'

'All right. I probably deserved that,' Bea said, pulling on the rest of her clothes. 'I'd feel the same way if I were in your position. I could swear I'll never see your husband again but I'd be lying. He's told me your marriage has been in difficulty for a while.'

The idea that Jack had been discussing their intimate life in bed with this leggy tramp infuriated Lorna.

'How dare you! How dare you think you can just waltz in and break up fifteen years of marriage. I know my husband better than you ever will. He's not going to leave me.'

'It was never my intention to break up your marriage,' said Bea hotly.

'No, you just didn't think. You may not like hearing this but all you are to Jack is a distraction. After a tournament he likes to let off steam, prove his masculinity. I've seen several like you come and go. Always the same; swept away by the glamour and fame. It never lasts.'

'I don't believe you.' Bea hoped she sounded more confident than she felt.

'I think you do.'

This was a nightmare! Did she have to stand there looking so very much in control in her herringbone suit? Probably a Paul Costello rip-off, Bea thought spitefully. If only she would go.

'You can't have him,' said Lorna, examining one of her neat, yellow suede shoes. 'Do you understand what I'm saying?'

'That's for Jack to decide.' What was she doing talking to this woman? She was only making things worse.

'You know, I almost feel sorry for you. At your age and with your background you could have your pick, but you choose a man who already has a family. It's really quite pathetic!' Lorna's eyes narrowed like those of a small malicious animal and she played her trump card. 'Jack has a very public image. You wouldn't be very popular trying to break us up. Whatever attraction you hold for him now is nothing compared to his love for his children. Remember that.'

Bea clenched her hands.

'I've worked hard at this marriage. I love my husband and I'm not about to give him up. Not to you or anyone else. Think about what I've said today. Save yourself the embarrassment of Jack ending it first, because he will. And if I ever see you around my family again . . .'

'I know the speech.'

'As I said, you're that sort of girl.'

Lorna didn't even bother to close the door, leaving in a sickly wake of Chanel's Coco. Bea unclenched her hands and saw that her nails had made deep crescents in the fleshy part of her hand. Jack's blue shirt lay abandoned on the bed. Lorna had either forgotten to take it or didn't want the unpleasant reminders it would evoke. Picking it up she pressed it to her face, identified Jack's comforting bitter-sweet smell. Sam had always smelt like a department store. Jack had a smell of his own. Salty, sexy, male. Stuffing it in with her things, she went through the motion of drying her hair, made a call to the agency, collected her bag and checked out.

409

As she descended the steps she caught her foot and tripped on the hem of her trousers. She crashed on to the hard cement drive. For a second she just lay there in a daze, then a porter came out to help her.

'You all right, Miss? You took a nasty fall.'

Bea looked down at her ripped trouser-leg, which already revealed a nasty open gash on her knee. She felt sick, registering the dull pain for the first time.

'I'll be fine.' Her voice sounded faint and she leaned against the wall for support. 'I just need to rest for a minute.'

As the man rushed off to get the first aid kit, Bea began to shake. In that instant she knew she was in love with Jack. No! She was being irrational. Probably just good old PMT. Only it wasn't that time. Aghast, she brought her trembling hands to her hot face. She *was* in love with him! Jack wasn't a quick fling. She wanted more. Much more. And it was all hopeless because bloody Lorna would use the children to keep him. Oh, for a cigarette! Had someone offered her one, she would gladly have smoked the whole packet.

She didn't wait for the man to return, terrified in case Lorna was still around. I can't let her see me in this state, I won't give her the satisfaction. Flushed, with damp hair and her blouse buttoned all wrong, Bea hobbled across to the Beetle, her cut knee burning and throbbing. After placing her model bag in the boot she turned on the ignition. It wouldn't start. Even with the choke right out and the accelerator to the floor the only thing that showed signs of life was the flickering 'low on petrol' sign. Feeling as if everything was suddenly against her, Bea did what any sensible woman with such frayed emotions would do; she collapsed against the steering wheel and sobbed.

23

They set off two days later. By eight it was already sweleringly hot so everyone wore hats. Determined to look the part, Kate appeared in tight designer breeches tucked into shiny-brown boots, a riding hat, and an expensive cream silk shirt. Two of the grooms working nearby wolf-whistled loudly as she passed.

'Where on earth do you think you're going dressed like that?' Skander said, as he walked over to help her mount. 'This isn't a point to point, you know.'

Deliberately ignoring the hand he offered her, Kate hauled herself on to Ghanum. Then she trotted over to Angus, a thick-set cattleman in his forties on a sleek, sixteen-hand bay. Angus gave the impression of someone who knew exactly what they were doing, exuding the bandy-legged confidence of a man accustomed to dealing with animals.

'That's a good-looking stallion you're riding,' she said warmly.

'He's a sheila, mate.'

'Sorry. I'm not in the saddle enough to tell males and females apart.'

'Could have fooled me,' said Skander, overhearing.

Kate scowled. Hunting for allies her gaze rested on Paul Lambert talking to a ravishingly pretty girl. He looked far less glamorous than he had at the party, in torn-off jeans and a crumpled shirt. Glancing round he caught her eye and waved.

Kate coaxed Ghanum on to walk. But the horse wouldn't budge. She kicked her more firmly. 'Come on, girl.'

'I wouldn't do that, Kate,' Skander advised as he tightened Eblis's girth.

'I'm not staying like this all day,' she said tartly, then

turned a dull red when Ghanum suddenly let out a tremendous fart and deposited a pile of steaming dung on to the road.

Paul rode over on a mean-looking chestnut which was swishing its tail. Kate didn't like the look it gave Ghanum. 'G'day,' he said. 'You're the first person I've seen who really looks tops in jodhpurs!'

'Thanks,' said Kate *sotto voce*, 'but appearances can be deceptive. I'm still wearing L plates.'

'Oh, you don't want to worry about that. Ghanum's very steady.' The chestnut bared its teeth.

'I hope the same applies to your horse. Who's that pretty girl you were talking to?'

'Ginny. I mentioned her the other night.'

'Oh yes. Skander's wayward cousin.'

'Wayward step-cousin,' corrected Ginny, joining them, 'and none of the stories are true.'

'I thought you sounded fun,' said Kate as Ghanum's coat quivered against the flies.

'Then I take it all back. I'm the bloody scandal of Queensland!'

Ginny's blonde hair was cut in a neat Purdie bob. She wore jeans and a green and red gingham shirt tied at the waist. Her skin was the colour of pale coffee. Kate·felt anaemic in comparison.

'Alice, luv, you got the food supplies all packed?' called Angus to his stocky English wife, who was wrestling with her saddlebag.

'We've enough to feed an army,' she said cheerfully, brushing away flies, 'even lemingtons. I only hope I put the hard-boiled eggs on top, or we'll be having them scrambled this arvo! God, this bag's a bugger to do up.'

Skander gave her a hand.

In the soporific haze they set off in pairs, with Ginny and Skander coming up from the rear. Eblis snorted and bounced haughtily, pulling on his chinking bit, but Skander calmly kept the horse under control, his eyes enjoying Kate's bottom bouncing up and down in her saddle. The sky was a deep blue and completely clear. The sun shone glowing colour on to the golden-hued sandstone rocks and Kate, beginning to enjoy herself, breathed in the heady smell of eucalyptus. A group of rainbow lorikeets, wild with excitement, chased one another and somewhere in the distance she could hear the sound of a braying jackass.

Gradually they made their way down the steep, winding track into the valley and for a while Kate allowed her horse to drift along with the others, enjoying Paul's company while he pointed out things of interest and continued to flatter her. They stopped briefly by a small stream to water the horses and eat. It was sweltering hot and Kate's silk shirt, which had seemed such a good idea that morning, was now crumpled and her hair mutinied in sticky wisps. Lying down under the trees, they spread out their lunch. Alice's hard-boiled eggs had survived after all.

'Bearing up okay?' Paul asked, passing her a bottle of water.

'I will be if I can just take these boots off for a while,' she said, stretching out on the bank. 'My legs are so stiff I feel like John Wayne swaggering down the street of the OK Corral.'

Paul's hazel eyes closed for a second as he flopped down next to her. 'You'll get used to it after a day or two. I have to admit I was worried you might have a thing going with Skander, but after the other night at the Lonsdales' it's obvious you hate each other's guts.'

Kate took a greedy swig from the bottle. 'I don't hate him exactly. We just don't get on.'

'Well, that's ripe. Skander's usually so popular with the girls.'

'Is he?' said Kate drily.

'You know, something about you reminds me of Alex.'

'And who's Alex?'

'Skander's long-term girlfriend. We all fancied her like mad. Gorgeous-looking and smart, fair dinkum. Things lightened up when she was around you. She'd already had two books published when they were planning to get married, then Alex caught the ME virus – got real crook. Skander nursed and supported her but back then nobody knew much about the disease. Then one day she just took off with this doctor bloke. He left his wife, two kids and practice to be with her. What made it so awful was that his wife was about to have another baby. It destroyed Skander at the time.'

Kate digested this piece of information. Skander's strong principles and family priorities suddenly began to make sense. That night Julian had taken her round to Skander's flat, she vaguely remembered seeing a photo of a beautiful girl hugging Skander. Had that been Alex?

'How am I like her?'

'Physically you've nothing in common; Alex had that Scandinavian, almost albino hair and very pale-blue eyes. No, it's more your personality; she had the same cool self-control I see in you. Every now and then she'd let her guard down and this funny, warm woman would emerge. I don't know . . . there's something about you. Maybe when I get to know you better.'

'Can we move into the shade? I'm melting.'

The unrelenting southern sun, stretched across the sky, looked almost bleached. It was suffocatingly hot and Kate was being driven mad by the ubiquitous Australian fly. Damn things. She longed to swim but Skander was already way ahead and she had a nasty feeling he might leave her behind. Pulling her hair off her face, Kate fastened it into a casual knot, replaced her hat and kicked Ghanum on, swiping at a particularly irritating fly trying to park itself on her head.

By the time they set up camp it was almost six. The sky was a burning orange, the clouds a deep mauve, shaped like fat pillows. In the distance Kate watched an unusual flock of birds winging their way across the spectacular mango backdrop. When she pointed them out to Paul she was told they were black fruit bats. Kate loathed bats, and was always afraid one would get caught up in her hair. This evening she was too tired to care. When Kate almost fell off her horse, Paul caught her and held her slightly longer than necessary. His constant staring was beginning to make her feel uncomfortable. Her legs and shoulders had seized up with stiffness and her head throbbed from the sun.

They were all allocated tasks – it would be dark soon and

414

fires had to be made, tents put up. Kate's job was to gather firewood and she trotted off dutifully to find some, taking great gulps of the sweet warm air. Skander and Paul, having tethered the horses, were busy hammering in tent pegs and the others had unpacked most of the provisions by the time she returned. Angus lit the fire and they sat around enjoying steaming mugs of tea, while Alice made supper, which came out of a packet and was served with boiled rice.

Kate watched as Alice bent over the fire, displaying a wide stretch of blue-jeaned bottom. Her fine, brown hair kept on flopping into her eyes and she made several failed attempts to push it away. The food looked about as appetising as a three-day-old curry but tasted surprisingly good and anyway Kate was so hungry she didn't really care.

'We'll take the north trail to Paradise Mountain past Tindley's Creek,' explained Angus, leaning over a well-thumbed and earmarked map. 'It's not as steep for the horses and we'll be able to stock up on fresh water supplies. It means a longer route but a ripper and I reckon no one's in a hurry to get back, right?'

Kate half raised her hand but let it fall, immediately guilty for not being more enthusiastic. She gazed briefly at Skander, trying to imagine him nursing his Scandinavian ice queen while she browsed through intellectual hardbacks, but the image didn't come easily. Yawning for the fourth time she made her excuses to everyone and tripped through the black gloom to her tent.

She had never slept so soundly.

The long ride, hot sun and fresh country air had worked more effectively than any sleeping pill, and now that it was dark, she could enjoy the luxurious cool of the night. Struggling with the zip of her sleeping bag, she tested the ground beneath her. Not very comfortable, but at least the base protected her from ants. Paul had warned her that a bull ant bite could be nasty so it was important to protect her sleeping area. She undressed quickly and used the last of her energy to rub insect-repellent cream on to exposed skin. Without bothering to place the lid back on to the tube, she closed her eyes and was asleep in seconds.

When a rude hand disturbed her the next morning Kate had difficulty dragging herself awake. She'd been dreaming about Bob Peck doing unmentionable things and was just getting to the good bit. Peering out of one eye, she found Skander looming over her. Oh, no. Not him again.

'Morning.' With a cigarette dangling from his mouth, he was wearing his lopsided grin, looking at her with amused and lascivious pleasure. 'I thought you might be a little sore, so I brought you a peace-making cup of tea.'

'What time is it?' she muttered, still half-asleep.

'Six.'

'Oh God. It's the middle of the night. Go away.'

'Charming! And no, you can't go back to sleep,' he warned as Kate rolled away from him, 'it's a long walk home.'

'You wouldn't!' Kate struggled to sit up.

'Listen to me. We've got six days to get through, it'll be a lot easier if you and I aren't jumping down each other's throats every five minutes. And . . .' his eyes dropped to her breasts, 'if you don't plan on inviting anyone into your bed on this trip, I suggest you wear a little more clothing.'

Kate pulled the sleeping bag up further. 'What's that supposed to mean?'

'Just be careful. I've seen the way Paul looks at you. You don't want to bite off more than you can chew.'

'Oh, of course I was forgetting my man-eating role. No doubt you think I've got my evil eye on Angus too. Well, I think you're disgusting!' Grabbing her washing things she fled through the tent opening with Skander's hateful voice following her out.

'You should have been an actress, Kate. You'd have been wonderful!'

Kate stormed off in the direction of the stream. She must pull herself together. He was only doing it to get a reaction.

It was already sweltering hot. The small stream was shrouded with thick, short gum trees, which from a distance looked deep blue. She bent down, cupped some water in her hand and splashed her face. A sudden sound startled her.

'What's eating you?' said a voice. 'You look very cross.'

Ginny, without a stitch of clothing, was bathing in the stream.

'I didn't realise anyone was there,' said Kate. 'You were so quiet.'

'Come on in. The water's to bloody die for.'

Kate hesitated, fingering the fresh crop of stubble on her legs.

'Oh, none of the blokes can see us. They're all too busy playing Tarzan.'

Kate giggled. 'You're on.'

'Skander was telling me that you're a top model in Paris.'

'Hard to believe, isn't it?' Kate was floating on her back looking dreamily up at the sky, all thoughts of hairy legs forgotten. 'And I can't imagine Skander having anything nice to say about me!'

'He didn't. Say much, I mean. It's impossible prising information out of him. Always has been. You must have an amazing life. Have you really worked with all those big French names?'

'Some,' said Kate modestly. 'But it's not all it's made out to be. The glamorous image is only a small part.'

'Do you get to keep the clothes?'

'It depends on how much the designer likes you.'

'Skander mentioned that you two had met in Italy.'

'We shot a commercial together. Meeting here was a complete fluke.'

'You mean he didn't invite you?'

'God, no, his parents did. I had no idea they were related.'

'I wish I wasn't related to him. He refuses to take me seriously,' Ginny said wistfully. She had the Australian habit of lifting the end of each sentence which made it sound like a question. 'I was hoping to snare him on this trek but with you around I don't stand a chance.'

'Oh, but you're wrong, Ginny. Skander's not interested in me.'

'You're not just saying that?' There was such hope in her young, open face.

'If only you knew!' Kate inspected an angry mark on her

417

arm. 'Do you have anything for mosquito bites? I'm covered in them.'

'You're really nice,' Ginny said suddenly. 'I was miserable when Paul said you were joining us. Models are supposed to be stuck up and full of themselves but you're nothing like I imagined.'

'I think I'll take that as a compliment.'

Then a little later, 'Don't you fancy him at all?'

Kate was getting used to Ginny constantly changing the subject.

'I wish I never had to clap eyes on him again!'

'I'm afraid that's one wish I can't grant you, Kate,' said an odiously familiar voice above them. 'All those wearing red ankle bands, your swimming time's up!'

'Skander, you devil! How long have you been eavesdropping?'

Kate noticed that Ginny made no attempt to cover herself.

'Long enough to know my name's been taken in vain. You girls have five minutes to get dressed and then we're leaving.'

Kate, blushing furiously, withdrew under some trailing branches.

The clear sky they had enjoyed yesterday was now filled by large, ominous-looking clouds, although the forecast hadn't mentioned rain. As they started to climb, the path narrowed and they followed its curve towards the mountains. Already the landscape was changing. Coachwood trees towered on either side and now out of direct sunlight they could enjoy the cooler air. Finally they reached the daunting canopy of the rain forest. All Kate could see was a jungle, masses of towering trees and vegetation, like a frame from *The African Queen*. She half expected Tarzan to come flying through the treetops hollering for Jane.

As the afternoon moved on, the sky looked more and more ominous and they all watched anxiously for rain. Kate rode with Alice and asked her how she had come to live in Australia. Alice, from Cirencester, had met Angus, her sheep-farming husband, while visiting a great-aunt. Finding him refreshingly different from the boring boyfriends she'd left back in England, the couple embarked on a frenzied two-week romp in bed and an impulsive marriage. It had been hard for Alice to adjust and she missed England dreadfully, but she'd grown to love Australia as much as she had Angus.

That night Paul produced a bottle of whisky round the camp fire and they all got slightly tipsy. Ginny, Kate noticed, had taken her at her word and was flirting outrageously with Skander. So when Paul invited her to go for a walk, she accepted. Anyway, it was too hot by the fire.

'Take the torch,' instructed Skander as they got up to leave, 'and watch out for snakes.'

The trace of irony in his voice was clearly for her benefit. Away from the crackling flames it was pitch black and their eyes took a few minutes to adjust. The cicadas were making a terrific noise and things kept jumping up from the ground which unnerved Kate who was still thinking about snakes. She tied her cardigan around her waist and stumbled on a twig. Paul steadied her.

'Careful.'

They had been walking around for half an hour and were nearing camp when Paul came to an abrupt halt. He looked pale under the moon as he turned to Kate.

'Something wrong?'

'No.' A pause. 'At least, I hope not.' He looked down at his feet and shifted awkwardly. 'Look, Kate, this may not be the right time but as you've probably already guessed I've quite fallen for you and I need to know if the feeling's reciprocated?'

The cicadas would choose this particular moment to shut up. Oh, God. That awful squirming moment when someone you didn't fancy admitted they'd spent sleepless nights thinking about you. Kate wished herself anywhere but here. Beam me up, Scottie. Stupid fool! Why had she allowed herself to be alone with him. She should have read the signs.

'Paul, you hardly know me.'

'I know enough.'

'After only three days? Bet you say that to lots of girls.'

He looked offended. 'No way. It's rare to find a beautiful woman who's also smart. With you I feel I've found a kindred spirit. We've shared a lot of the same experiences, we're

419

both travellers. I feel something special between us and I think you feel it too.'

He could have been reciting from a Mills and Boon. She didn't want to upset him but she hadn't been prepared for this awful sentimentality. Neither did she believe one word. It was all too soon, too rushed. His hand, firm but damp with sweat, started to knead the back of her neck and she wished he would take it away. Instead she gazed up at the vast sky which was studded with so many stars it didn't seem possible to fit any more in. A group of fruit bats flew across the sinister inky canvas and involuntarily, Kate took a fearful step back against Paul. Misconstruing the gesture, he took it as a sign of encouragement.

'A bloke couldn't ask for a more romantic setting. I know I'm moving fast, but we only have a few days, then you'll be off back to England. I'm afraid of losing you.'

He pulled her into his arms.

'Paul, I'm flattered, really I am, but . . .' Kate found her nose squashed sideways against his chest as he murmured hotly into her hair.

'A man could go crazy about a girl like you.' He was now trying to kiss her.

'Paul! For heaven's sake, let me go.'

'All you girls like a bit of a struggle.'

'Not this one. Now stop that. I said no!' Fear turned the 'no' into a shriek. She could smell whisky fumes on his breath. Suddenly his hands were everywhere, clumsily grabbing at her breasts, her bottom.

'C'mon Kate, don't fight it. Tell me what turns you on?'

'Paul, you're drunk! You don't know what you're doing. We'll both regret this tomorrow.'

She tried to swivel away but his grip was too strong. Paul messily covered her mouth with his hand.

'Help!'

'Shhh,' he murmured. 'Mustn't wake up the others.'

'Take your hands off her. Now!' They both turned towards a voice that was so deathly quiet Kate wondered if she had imagined it. Skander was standing less than three feet away. With one stride he grabbed Paul and hit him squarely on the nose. Paul went flying.

'Go on!' he yelled furiously. 'Go and sleep it off, for Christ's sake, and don't ever touch her again!'

'Strewth, what the bloody hell was that for?'

Paul's bewildered face twisted suddenly in the moonlight and for a moment he looked quite ugly. Clutching his right eye as if he were afraid it was going to fall out, he managed to pull himself to his feet and scuttled off into the dark.

'And as for you!' bellowed Skander, venting his anger on Kate. 'Running true to bloody form, I see.'

'Don't shout at me! He started it. It's not my fault he can't control himself!'

Skander's face was a thundercloud. 'Ch-rrr-ist, Kate, grow up! He only tried it on because you've been throwing yourself at him from the moment he arrived.'

'Oh, and I suppose that makes attempted rape all right in your book!' she snapped defensively.

'You're bloody lucky I decided to come out for a cigarette. Who knows where this might have led?'

'Well, another five minutes and you'd have found out, wouldn't you!'

'I'm beginning to think I should have given *you* the hiding, not Paul. Maybe you should take a look at your own screwed-up sexuality before casting disparaging stones.'

For a moment they glared at one another, then Skander made the fatal mistake of laughing, and when Skander laughed it bounced off walls, echoing for miles. Kate saw red. In a blinding, furious rage she sprang forward, hurling herself against his chest.

'Don't you dare laugh at me! You want a fight? Go on then, show me how big and strong and tough you really are because I hate you, do you hear! I hate you!' she screamed, lashing out at him with her fists.

Off guard for a second, Skander caught a stinging slap to the side of his jaw. The laughter immediately drained from his face.

'That's enough, Kate.' He caught her hands in his, but still she struggled, fuelled by a rage that had been gradually building over the months. Now it finally boiled to the surface.

'You're a monster! You're so bloody charming to everyone except me. You pretend to care but it's lies, all bloody lies! You men always stick together in the end. Well, I've had enough!'

'Will you just listen to yourself!'

'Take your flaming hands off me!'

'What's going on?' For a moment they froze, then turned guiltily towards the voice.

'Ginny! You shouldn't be out here on your own.'

'I heard voices. I was worried.'

She looked very young, hovering uncertainly in the gloom.

'We're just sorting out a few things.' His voice was comforting suddenly, full of concern. Bloody hypocrite. 'Nothing to worry about. Go back to camp. We'll be along shortly.'

'Well, okay,' she said dubiously, deflated. 'Sorry again. I didn't mean to interrupt.'

Brilliant, thought Kate, now she'll think I've been lying about Skander all along. Still, it must have looked pretty incriminating the two of them out here in the dark clamped together like a sealed envelope. Skander had her in a vice-like grip, her wrists were screaming in pain. In a desperate effort to escape Kate opened her mouth to call Ginny back but Skander anticipated this, covering it with a hand. Ouch!

'Shut up! You've caused enough trouble for one night.' His voice was cold again, sarcastic. 'Now, madame, you're going to behave because I'm not taking my hand away until you do and I don't care how much it hurts.' For a moment she struggled then realised it was useless. He was much too strong for her. Defeated, she let her body go limp.

'That's better.' He let her go. 'No, just bloody calm down. You're not in Paris now.'

'I wish I bloody was!' And she fled sobbing back to her tent.

Later, having tossed and turned for hours, her itchy bites driving her mad, Kate finally fell into an uneasy sleep and had a dreadful nightmare. She was still screaming blue murder when Skander found her.

'Hey, hey!' he whispered, taking her drenched, trembling

422

body into his arms. 'Hush now. You were having a bad dream, that's all.'

'Don't let him. Please! I'm afraid.' She seemed to be in a trance. 'I won't! I won't! It isn't my fault!' she cried, hardly aware of who she was clinging to. 'Ple-ease help me!' It was a desperate plea.

'I'm here now. I'll make the bad go away.'

She could feel the warmth from his body, his hands stroking her soaking hair, and she relaxed against him, reassured by his strength and comforting voice. Her words started coming out in short, furious gasps.

'I had Sophie to myself for three years but all that time I dreaded her remarrying. I suppose I was afraid of losing her. Then René came along with his good looks and houses in Europe. He was much older and set in his ways but that didn't seem to matter. He was nice to me, and Sophie was impressed with his lifestyle and friends – I think she really loved him. We used to spend the summer holidays in his French villa, which overlooked the sea. He'd take me swimming and I grew to love him, but he was a difficult man to get close to. He analysed everything, very controlling . . .' A mosquito whined around her ears.

'Go on, little one, you're doing fine.'

'We had planned a picnic. René had just got back from a trip and I remember I wore a blue and white stripy costume. While Sophie went off to the village René said he had something to show me upstairs. I thought he was going to give me a present; he always brought me something back from trips.' Kate wiped her nose on her arm. Her voice had taken on a child-like quality.

'Up in his room he sat me on his knee and stroked my hair, kept telling me how pretty I was, how much I meant to him. I couldn't believe my luck. He never spent time with me like that.' Warm tears splashed on her hands. 'You don't know what it was to have his full attention. He was so rarely with us, so many endless business trips. All I wanted was for the moment to continue for ever. When he held me close and kissed me I felt loved. I wasn't aware of us doing anything wrong. He was my new daddy and all I cared about was pleasing him. He didn't hurt me, not really . . .' She scrubbed her eyes, trying to get the words past her sobs.

'I didn't understand! It was my birthday, don't you see? Nothing bad happens on your birthday. But when I saw Sophie watching us from the doorway like a ghostly, white statue . . . I'll never forget it. That's when I knew I'd done something unforgivable. They had a terrible row then she told René to get out of the house and for me to take a hot bath.'

'That's all she said?'

Kate attempted to nod inside his embrace. 'She refused to discuss it. Once René had gone it was as if he had never been part of our lives. I never saw him after that day.'

Kate's face flooded with colour as the full enormity of what she'd just admitted started to sink in. Oh, God. It couldn't be true. It couldn't! And why was she remembering now? Devastated, she no longer tried to cover up her tears, but let them fall openly.

'You poor little duck.' Skander pulled her fiercely to him. Such a simple thing really, a hug.

'I was so fat at school. I hated being that way. I would have done anything to make myself pretty.'

'Perhaps the fat was a form of protection?' suggested Skander. 'Making yourself unattractive was a way of being sure nothing like that would ever happen again.'

'Except that I went and chose modelling of all things as a career!' Kate sniffed loudly. 'Have you got a tissue?'

'Let me look.' Skander searched his pockets. 'Maybe Paul did you a favour after all,' he said, wiping her tear-stained face with his sleeve. 'He's just bloody lucky I didn't kill him!'

'Sorry. It probably was my fault.'

'An apology from you, Kate!' Skander looked astonished. 'I wish I had a tape recorder. No one will believe me!'

'Well, it's only because you've been nice to me for once.' He'd withdrawn the warmth of his arms and the relief Kate felt from her confession was beginning to turn rancid in her stomach. Already she regretted exposing that dark part of herself. Pulling her knees to her chest, binding them with her arms, she tried to hide her face – couldn't bear him to see her so damaged, so vulnerable, so ugly! She suddenly noticed her unshaven legs and hastily shoved them back in the sleeping bag.

The first time Skander had seen Kate, at his Kensington flat, she had resembled a ballerina. There had been an ethereal quality about her, all that pale skin and red hair, those green eyes that tilted up at the corner and slightly overwhelmed the rest of her features, but he remembered her face had been expressionless, her mouth hard because of the unnecessary, dark lipstick. She looked younger without make-up and after four days in the bush she'd caught the sun, bringing out more freckles – they looked adorable – and a few faint lines around her eyes. Her face seemed to have grown into itself, now looked more defined, more interesting. And he now knew her better.

'You are a surprise, I thought you'd hate all this but you've really mucked in. Everyone's quite taken with you.'

Kate dropped her eyes. Something was changing between them.

'Do I detect a blush? What brought that on, I wonder?' She studied her hands in confusion. 'Well, I'll take it as a compliment. Now try and get some sleep. I won't be far if you need me.'

He left her feeling shattered and slightly dizzy. Could the horror of what she'd just admitted really have happened? All these years and not once had Sophie uttered so much as a word. Things could have been so different between them if only they'd been able to talk about it. But now . . . how was she ever going to face her mother again? She was appalled that she'd told such intimate details of her life to Skander, of all people. What must he think of her now! Yet he hadn't appeared shocked or disgusted. He'd only acted with kindness. Kate stared at the tent flap long after he'd gone, listening to the low, rumbling sky.

It was all Ginny's fault: she had been boasting about how quickly they'd been making ground, when suddenly, at about noon the next day, the sky turned an ominous, coppery-yellow. There was a flicker of lightning which made Kate jump eight inches and then it began to rain, spearing down on them like fired bullets. Skander leapt off Eblis and yelled at everyone to make camp. Throwing on drizabones they shot about frantically, rigging up a shelter. Help, thought Kate, who was terrified of storms and had never seen anything so explosively dramatic. Another flash cut across the sky, which had now turned purply-black.

Skander was trying to calm down the frightened horses while thunder and lightning battled it out above them. Kate, already soaked, quelled her nerves by helping Alice look for dry twigs and moss to light the fire. Half an hour later they had things under control and sat huddled under the shelter. Wonderful, Kate thought, squashed uncomfortably between Angus and Alice.

'Anyone for tennis?' she said feebly.

'Tropical storms seem fierce, mate.' Angus called everyone mate. 'But don't worry, they stop as dramatically as they start. Just as if someone pulled a switch.'

Paul, suffering from a bruised ego and a black eye which, tactfully, no one mentioned, passed round the whisky.

The rain was vomiting down like great gobs of phlegm. The noise was awesome and the ground was littered with fallen leaves dancing violently under the enormous pressure from the sky. Skander wondered how he'd missed the signs.

'Is there a short-cut we can take?' he asked Angus.

'Sure, mate. We could head south through the hills which would bring us out to that little creek we stopped at. It would cut our journey home by a day.'

'OK,' said Skander, shaking water from his blond hair. 'Let's give it an hour, then if it hasn't let up we'll push on.'

'He's joking, surely?' whispered Kate, trying to calm her churning fear. She hadn't been able to look Skander in the eye all day.

'No, he's not,' muttered Ginny. 'The rain could go on for days. And if we stay here the camp will soon be a mud bath. Kate . . .' she lowered her voice so none of the others could hear, 'you could have bloody told me. I felt a right prat last night.'

'I know what it must have looked like but it's not what you think. Really. Paul made a pass and Skander intervened.'

'And from what I could see he was carrying on where Paul left off.' Ginny couldn't keep the bitterness out of her voice.

'No. We were having a row. I've you to thank for stopping it. You must have heard us shouting?'

'That's what woke me up. Guess this weather's making me tetchy. I got the curse last night. Sorry. I just thought . . .'

'Forget it.'

Skander shrugged unselfconsciously out of his sodden denim shirt and was drying his body with a towel. Kate, trying not to stare, noticed the powerful chest and how smooth and brown his skin was. She was reminded of Roe's slim body, dangerously male, covered in all that dark, wiry hair. Did he ever think of her? There was a leak in the tent and Kate could feel rain trickling down her neck and inside her clothes. Skander had slipped on a T-shirt and was pulling on a large black sweater which made his blue eyes look very dark. He caught her watching him and smiled. Feeling ridiculously shy, she averted her head and gazed back at the storm.

Two hours later the group were back on horseback, slowly retracing their steps. Heads bowed, the drenched figures braced themselves against the sharp sting of the rain as they stumbled along. Kate's hands were already numb and she took turns in warming them under her arms. Ginny was right. The ground beneath them was a mud bath. The horses frequently slipped and on either side contorted tree trunks and roots obstructed their way. It was difficult following the path as the dark, monstrous trees blocked out most of the daylight. There was a strong smell of fresh wood and mud, wet moss hung down and touched her like slimy limbs. Kate shuddered, clinging on to Ghanum who followed the rest of the horses in single file.

'You okay?' Paul had fallen in beside her. It was the first time he'd spoken to Kate since the previous night.

'Nothing a hot fire and a good meal wouldn't mend,' she said, smiling ruefully. 'How's your head?'

'Not half as sore as my ego. Look, I'm sorry about last night. I was out of order.'

'I'm the one who should be sorry. I have the feeling I egged you on.'

'Bloody oath, Skander's a lucky bloke.'

'Oh, don't you start!' said Kate, feeling herself go hot.

'Only a jealous man would have gone for me the way he did last night and you're much too defensive about him to be indifferent.'

'Rubbish!'

'Oh, yes? Methinks the lady doth protest too much.' He coaxed his horse on to a slow trot, followed reluctantly by Kate.

After that it was difficult to hear themselves speak, which was just as well. Feeling slightly depressed, Kate wasn't prepared to work out the turmoil of confusing emotions she was feeling. The rain was like a dull roar and above them was the rumbling of distant thunder. Kate watched a blade of lightning split the sky and held on more firmly. Ghanum's ginger ears were flattened.

'It's all right. Good girl.'

Angus led the way up a steep trail followed by Alice, then Ginny, Paul, Kate and finally Skander at her rear. Through the rain Kate watched a loin-toed frog leaping for safety, croaking its disapproval as it landed. By now, they had reached the densest part of the forest and the enormous trees acted like a canopy, shielding them from the rain which was coming down in thick warm sheets, but they had to duck constantly or push aside branches and tangled thickets that got in their way. A giant liana vine hung in twisted contortions from a host tree looking like an enormous snake. Skander had pointed one out to her earlier which she'd reacted to with some alarm. Now, imitating Paul, Kate steered Ghanum around it without fear.

She was day-dreaming about having a bath and washing her hair. Oh, to feel clean again; wax her legs, do her nails. A proper bed to sleep in. Maybe treat herself to a facial. There was a small liana vine directly in front of her. While she was planning her four course menu she unthinkingly brushed it aside. To her horror it moved. She screamed and in the confusion Ghanum, already shaken by the noise of the storm, reared up, carting Kate into nearby trees before fleeing into the gloom. Paul fled after the bolted horse.

Skander was off Eblis and at her side in a second. Even against the pounding rain, his navy eyes blazed down at her.

'For God's sake, Kate! What is it with you? There are easier ways of killing yourself.'

'It was a snake! A horrible, slimy snake!' Kate, sprawled in a muddy heap, was on the verge of tears. 'How the hell did I know beastly Ghanum was going to start practising loop the bloody loop!'

Skander suppressed a smile. Kate's face was streaked with mud and the ravishing red hair, now wringing wet, hung like weeds around her face. The only discernible features were the green eyes, which were glaring at him.

'You never, ever take your horse for granted! Especially not out here. Is that understood? Come on, let's get you up.'

Kate winced as he took her arm. 'Careful,' he said supporting her. 'Shoulder hurt?'

'I'm fine,' said Kate miserably, who felt as ungainly as a newly-born foal. 'Where's Ghanum?'

'Probably half-way home by now. Here, lean against me.'

'You okay, Kate, luv?' yelled Alice, who'd dismounted.

'She'll live.'

'No sign of the horse, Skander,' shouted Paul, emerging with Angus from the gloom.

'Oh God,' sighed Kate helplessly. All her things were tied to the saddlebag.

'You'll have to ride with me.'

Eblis was standing patiently where Skander had left him. He bounced his head up and down to shake the rain out of his eyes then looked at Skander as if to say, 'What's all the fuss about?'

On they rode, Eblis making valiant attempts to keep the speed up but the ground had become so muddy, it was like walking in treacle and Eblis's hooves made loud sucking noises as he pulled them out. It seemed as though they'd been riding for ever. Kate was exhausted and very hungry. She'd attempted to strike up a conversation, but Skander only answered in monosyllables, which meant he didn't want to talk and anyway the noise of the rain made talking impossible. At least she was warmer. Kate wrapped her arms self-consciously around Skander's waist, snuggling up against the broad back, her eyes shut tight against the rain.

An hour after the cloudy daylight faded, the hidden moon above them began to claw its way across the night sky. They made camp in a small clearing a little way from the path. The ground fell quite steeply and was about a hundred yards from a small waterfall, which was busily competing with the heavy rain. Their campsite was far enough away to avoid moisture from the waterfall seeping into the ground. Above them the dense ash trees rose over a hundred feet. Angus and Skander fastened the last of the tent ropes.

'That should do it,' said Angus firmly, wiping rain from his face. 'Storm seems to be letting up.'

'Yes, but for how long?' moaned Paul. 'I don't fancy drowning in my sleep.'

'Not much chance of anyone sleeping with this racket going on,' said Skander, planting himself down next to Kate and lighting up a cigarette. 'How's your shoulder?'

'Better, thanks,' she said shyly, not quite meeting his eye. She huddled inside the blanket Paul had given her. 'Ginny told me you have Austrian blood in you.'

Skander helped himself to some coffee Alice had just brewed and looked at her through a fine haze of smoke. 'Only on my father's side. Obsessed with cars right from the start. His first job was in my grandfather's firm working as an apprentice mechanic. At twenty-five hc was offered a job with Lotus in England. From there he became a circuit driver. Got a reputation for taking risks so people started calling him the Gambler.

'Strewth! I remember him,' said Angus, who had been listening. 'Hans Decker. Bloody oath, the bloke was as big as Nigel Mansell in his day. Fancy him being your dad.'

Skander laughed and took a drag on his cigarette. 'I can see my stature is rapidly rising in your eyes, Angus. Always knew I was in the wrong job.'

Kate was greedy to know more. 'When did Beth meet him?'

'At the peak of his career. She was a photojournalist covering a race at Silverstone. Dad took one look at her and knew he'd marry her. He had everything: fame, money, respect from his peers. My grandparents had already died so the only thing missing was a family of his own. They married three months later in Bath, Beth's birthplace. Naomi, my sister, lives there with her family.'

'You are a dark horse, Skander. I never knew any of this.' Alice was sitting in between her husband's legs with his arms wrapped around her ample waist. 'What happened next?'

'Formula One commitments kept us moving for several years before we finally settled down. I was about six when Dad was killed. Ironically it happened in a little village lane, not the racing circuit. The press went overboard with the whole thing, so we went into hiding and Beth went back to using her maiden name. I've stuck with Davenport ever since.'

Poor thing. For Kate who had never paid the slightest attention to sport, it suddenly seemed crucial to learn everything there was to know about circuit racing.

'I'm sorry,' she said, meaning it.

'Don't be. I've had a bloody happy upbringing. The move to Australia was an easy adjustment and all that outdoor life was a great way to bring up kids.'

For a moment they were both reminded of last night's conversation.

'Give me London or Paris any day,' said Ginny wistfully, 'I'm sick of this daggy place.'

'Not me. I'd move back like a shot if it wasn't for work and if I wasn't constantly hassled about bringing home a pregnant wife,' Skander said with a touch of irony. 'Beth's dying to have more grandchildren.'

'What about the vegetarian?' Kate couldn't resist fishing. 'You mentioned you'd lived with one for three years.'

'She's now got three beautiful kids – not from me – and runs a very successful health farm in Devon with her husband. He's a doctor.' So he did still keep in touch with Alex. 'Now, much as I'm enjoying this trip down memory lane, we should get some sleep. We've got an early start.'

431

By noon the next day they had reached the edge of the rain forest. Out of its protective coat of leaves, the rain fell with more force, but the air felt warmer and Kate raised her head to take in her surroundings. She hardly recognised the creek she had bathed in with Ginny only two days ago. The heavy rain and flooded creek mingled together in a steamy haze and it was impossible to see to the other side. Skander and Angus dismounted.

'Hold the reins,' Skander ordered Kate.

He followed Angus to the creek's edge. Angus stopped to pick up a stick about five feet long and two inches thick. He tested the water depth with it then walked over to a thick plank sticking out of the water.

'The causeway's gone,' he yelled. 'About a yard over the level post. We'll have to wade across.'

'Anyone bring their cossie?' said Ginny, trying to still her nervous horse.

Kate inspected the creek in front of her. Despite the rain she could see a strong current building in the centre. No way was she setting one foot in that! Alice obviously shared her fears.

'The current will pull us downstream in minutes.'

'No choice, I'm afraid,' said Skander bluntly.

Ginny threw up her arms. 'Great. Who fancies going first?'

'We will,' Skander said decisively.

Kate's head snapped round.

'Don't worry. You'll be fine. Eblis can't take both our weights. Not in this current. You get on and I'll lead you in. Come on, Monkey,' his face softening, 'I won't let anything happen to you. The rest of you stay where you are until we're safely across.'

'What if Eblis stumbles?'

'I'll catch you.'

'What if you fall?'

'I won't.'

'Be careful,' Angus yelled as they waded in.

'I don't like this,' Ginny said to Paul, 'I don't like it one bit.'

Eblis bravely entered the churning water but he was very

432

shaken. Skander, already waist-deep, had to pull firmly on the bridle to move him on.

'Come on, fella,' he coaxed as the horse stumbled on unseen rocks and stones.

Kate clung on, blinking back the rain. Glancing behind her she saw a blur of anxious faces. Skander was in up to his shoulders and finding it hard to place the stick in front of him. Something's wrong, she thought worriedly. Angus had said the water level was three feet above the causeway. So why the hell was he going so deep? Skander was so busy concentrating that he didn't see the fallen tree speeding towards him. Kate shouted something and he turned just as the log hit him head on. Knocked off balance he yanked the reins, taking Eblis down with him and suddenly they were all in the water caught up in the churning current. As Skander went under, the weight of the log crashed over his head. Struggling against the menacing current Skander started to flail his huge arms, gasping for air spasmodically and sinking further as he did so.

Fighting panic, Kate struggled against the current but it was too strong and pulled her downstream. She saw brief flashes of Eblis in front of her, heard him squealing in fright as the current pulled her under and back up again. Oh, poor, poor Eblis! Dragged along and struggling for air, she shouted Skander's name. The long drizabone coat was twisted round her legs, restricting her movements. She pulled her arms from the sleeves and kicked it from her. Realising it was useless to fight the current, Kate concentrated on swimming on a gradual diagonal towards the river bank, fighting out of the current until she was clear. Desperately, she made another left-handed turn and headed back towards some trailing branches at the edge. It was her only hope. Arm outstretched, she grabbed blindly at them and came to an abrupt halt. She pulled herself out of the stream on to the muddy bank. The laps she'd religiously swum each week in Porte Dauphin had paid off, after all.

She lay there panting, then staggered to her feet. Her head spun and she could feel a large bump above her right temple. The bank they'd left the others on was a blur but she could see Eblis caught downstream. Stumbling in the mud, her soaking clothes now like weights, Kate called to the shaken horse. His reins had got caught up in the trees and he had somehow managed to get a footing on the bank. Kate undid them and coaxed him away from the creek. For a while she just stood stroking his mane, ignoring the punishing rain, and gradually the trembling horse calmed down. Where the hell was Skander? Her eyes darted wildly looking for him. Then just when she was beginning to lose hope she spotted him.

He was lying on his back about a hundred yards down from the spot she'd found Eblis. When she reached him she thought he was dead. He didn't move. There was a large gash on the back of his head, blood pouring from the wound and his arms were badly scratched. Her mind spun as she tried to remember how to give the kiss of life. She knew that you had to clear all obstructions from the mouth. Turning Skander on to his left side, she pulled his left arm above his head. Kneeling behind him, she started to massage his stomach and watched as water began to dribble from his lips. She prised open his mouth and gingerly placed her fingers inside to check for any blockages. There were none. She had to move quickly. If more than four minutes passed Skander would have permanent brain damage.

Rolling him on to his back Kate tilted his limp head backwards to open the airway to the lungs. She pulled his slack jaw open and pinched his nose to close the nostrils, rain slamming down on her back. Her head was splitting. Concentrate! Skander's life depended on her. She bent forward and placed her mouth over his, breathing oxygen into his body. She released her mouth and emptied the air in his lungs with several short jerks on his chest. Again she breathed air into his mouth as she watched his chest rise. She repeated this several times, growing more and more alarmed. If only this was just some horrible dream. She felt a longing to be safely back home with blankets pulled up round her ears, and someone to remove this terrible responsibility and look after her. What if he died? Suddenly Skander retched. Turning him quickly on to his side so that he wouldn't choke, Kate waited for him to stop and gently wiped his mouth. Her whole body started to shake with relief.

I must get him out quickly! She tried dragging him out of the water but he was too heavy. This is useless, she thought after her third attempt. The rope still attached to the saddle gave her an idea. After first cushioning his head with her shirt, Kate slipped the rope around Skander's waist, knotting it as she worked. The other end she fastened to the saddle and, coaxing Eblis on to a walk, watched anxiously as Skander's limp heavy body was slowly pulled out of the water. She kept Eblis moving until they were back under the trees and had some protection from the rain. Quickly she felt for Skander's pulse. God, so faint!

They only had about an hour of daylight left. She'd have to work fast to get them shelter. If only she had paid more attention as a Brownie. It was so cold, her clothes clung to her like a leaden skin, her fingers frozen and clumsy. The tent and most of their food supplies had been lost in the creek, but Skander's saddlebag and drizabone were mercifully still intact.

Kate searched for four large sturdy branches, two Y-shaped. Using the tin mug she found in the kit bag, she dug a small draining ditch in the shape of a square and pushed the four branches into each corner. Grabbing the drizabone, she draped it over the four branches, using rope to secure it. Underneath the shelter she scattered armfuls of damp leaves on to the ground. Removing Eblis's saddle, she placed his under-blanket on top of the leaves and the saddle which at least offered them some protection.

Then she dragged Skander's body under the shelter. The gash glowed angrily at her and Kate did her best to clean it. Funny how you took things like cotton wool and disinfectant for granted. Her silk shirt would have to do. As she worked, she thought of all the terrible things she'd admitted. How it had felt to be in his arms – was it only last night? She'd expected him of all people to be judgmental. Instead he'd offered only comfort, displayed unusual tenderness in a man. Getting up abruptly, she refused to analyse her feelings. There were other things to worry about. Like food. All she could find was one tin of soup. No fire. No dry clothes. And now Skander had started to shake. Great! Kate wasn't sure if he was in shock but knew he had to be kept warm. She removed his wet clothes, taking care to avoid his gash as she passed the sweater over his head. There was a nasty bruise on his lower rib and one on his upper thigh. She tried not to notice his penis (circumcised), which lay bud-like in its bed of unexpectedly dark pubic hair. He was shivering violently. Not the time to be bashful. Shared body heat was the only thing that would keep them warm. It was only when she had pulled off her own clothes that she noticed the cluster of black leeches fixed to her ankles. Fighting an urge to vomit, Kate grabbed the kit bag. Salt. She remembered watching a wildlife programme which said that rubbing salt got them off. No salt. Damn. She went through Skander's pockets looking for cigarettes but the packet was empty. Her eyes steered fearfully back to the slimy slugs feasting on her blood. Yeuck! OK, keep calm. She picked up Skander's yellow lighter and flicked it several times. When, finally, it ignited, she held the flame against the leeches, biting her lip against the searing pain. One by one they feebly dropped off and Kate flicked them away with revulsion. Naked, she wrapped her arms around Skander, trying not to think too much about what she was doing or how soft his skin felt against her own.

With Skander muttering incoherently, Kate pulled his body closer to her own, drawing comfort from his heat. Exhausted, she finally drifted into a light sleep, by now immune to the hammering storm above them. If Skander stirred or tried to scratch his bandaged head, Kate instantly woke, gently pulling his hand away. They couldn't afford to let it get infected.

By morning the rain had stopped as suddenly as it started. Skander opened his eyes groggily then snapped them shut against the bright sunlight. For a second he had no idea where or who he was. Bringing a stiff hand to his head he winced. Christ! He must have had one hell of a night. He groped into his short-term memory for a clue. A great log hurtled towards him then an explosion went off in his head. Something moved against him. His eyes opened.

'Hello,' he said ruefully.

'I thought you said you wouldn't let anything happen to us.'

Skander grinned ruefully. 'I lied.'

'How are you feeling?'

'Better, I think. At least I am now.' The blue eyes dropped to her naked breasts. 'The last nurse I had didn't give me this sort of treatment. You're obviously not with the National Health.'

Kate blushed scarlet, searching for something to cover herself with.

'No. Don't move,' he said holding her against him. They both became aware of his erection at the same time. She shifted her weight and tried to wriggle free.

Skander laughed. 'That's only making it worse.' Then more seriously, 'Come on, Kate, stop fighting me.'

Green eyes glared into blue, trying to adjust to the sudden shift in their relationship. It's going to happen. Somehow she'd always known it would. She suddenly resented him for what he represented; his male body, male superiority, male aggression disguised as kindness. At that moment Kate relived all the hurt that had been done to her by the men in her life and felt sick and ashamed for having allowed it.

Skander held her with his gaze, waiting, then very gently said, 'I'd give a lot to know what's going on in your mind.'

'Why?' How defensive she sounded.

'Because I care about you and I don't think many people in your life have.'

Just when she thought him predictable he went and surprised her by saying something like that. For some reason it made her want to cry. She tried to turn away, fighting back the tears but he took her head between his hands and guided her lips to his. His mouth felt strange, experimental. Kate watched him, almost with fear, removed her mind so that she wouldn't feel anything, made herself immune to intimacy.

For a while she just lay there passively. Then it happened. Something suppressed deep within her snapped and she was kissing him back like a starving animal. Half-fainting, she closed her eyes and relinquished control to his lips which followed the line of her neck and down to her breasts. Shifting her body downwards so that he was more comfortable, Skander's lips fastened on to her nipples, now hard as bullets. She moaned softly and his hand tightened against her hair, the other explored her body, moving urgently between her legs. Kate wrapped herself around him and for a second he winced.

'I don't know where to touch you,' she said hesitating. 'Does it hurt?'

'No. Yes. I don't care. Nothing could stop me from making love to you now.' Skander pushed his tongue in her ear which sent delicious shivers down her spine.

Then later. 'What are we doing? This is madness!'

'This is good, Kate. Stop fighting.'

And his lips came down on hers, crushing any further doubts from her mind. They rolled over so that he was on top. Skander's hand searched for her clitoris. She was so wet, he was afraid he'd come before he had a chance to enter her. Locked together they were oblivious to the beauty of the forest around them, releasing the tension of the last few days.

When they finally surfaced the land was transformed. The morning sun had lightened first to primrose then to flame as it heaved itself over the horizon. All around them wet leaves and vegetation glistened in the sunlight. The air was so still, hushed and solemn, that Kate felt as though she were standing in a cathedral. And then, quite suddenly, the air exploded into noise as black cockatoos, double-eyed fig parrots, willy wagtails and pied currawongs made their presence known. The storm was over. All around were great pools of water and young treetops emerging from the water's surface as if gasping for air.

'Camping's taken on a whole new meaning,' said Skander, standing behind Kate, his arms hugging her. Her face felt angry and sore from the roughness of his four-day-old stubble, but she didn't care. Nothing mattered now except for this moment. For the first time in her life she felt light, buoyant and at peace with herself.

They stood and surveyed the scene before them, their damp clothes steaming under the hot sun.

24

The early morning wind whipped Roe's face as he emerged from Leonora Vaubelle's luxury apartment. He fumbled for his car keys as snow melted against his exposed skin. Jesus, it was freezing! The weather forecast had been a change for the better but this was like stepping into *Lost Horizon*! Roe loathed snow, hated the interminably long European winters which had everyone diving for bed at the first sniff of dark. Should have spent Christmas in the States, he thought, wrapping his Armani cashmere coat round himself more firmly. But though the idea had been an attractive one, escaping for a couple of weeks had been out of the question. Too many problems to sort out this end. Roe unlocked the car door, then scraped what snow he could with his hands from the windows. The heating would do the rest. The car engine broke the morning stillness and Roe pointed the Porsche back up the Champs Elysées. He wanted to make a head start.

Feeling angry and betrayed by Carl's decision to sell off shares without consulting him first, he had confided his plans to three people earlier that week. One of them was Leo Schofield whose support Roe had to secure if he was going to pull this deal off. Leo knew all the numbers, and was as intimate with the financial health of Carl's companies as anyone they were liable to come up against. At least, that's what Roe hoped. Besides, if there was anything that smelt like trouble Leo would spot it.

'I don't know, Roe. It doesn't seem right. Carl and I go back a long way.'

'And we don't? Listen, I owe him everything I have, but I won't be doing Carl any favours by letting the proverbial ship go down. It's not as if I'm asking you to do anything illegal.'

'No, but you're going to buy stock from Carl without telling him.'

'Only if I can raise the funds,' Roe sighed wearily, tired of never having anyone fighting in his corner. 'Shit, Leo, I was working for the guy twelve years before he sent me here! He knows how much this company means to me. How do you think I feel, knowing he's been trying to off-load company stock on the quiet?'

There was silence down the phone, then, 'I'm still not sure.'

'Leo, someone's got to make a bid. Word about the shares is going to hit the streets any minute now. All I'm trying to do is avoid a stampede and unless I get a head start Vaubelle doesn't stand a chance. Can't you understand, I'm trying to save the goddam company!'

'What personal collateral do you have?'

That sounded more encouraging. 'There's my Manhattan flat. That's got to be worth four hundred thou.'

'It's a start. But it won't buy you a big enough slice of the pie to make you overall shareholder or convince the banks to take us seriously.'

'So what do I do?'

'It would really help if you already had some shares.'

Roe grinned for the first time. 'I've thought of that.'

After Claude Vaubelle's funeral his shares, worth forty-nine per cent of the company, had been divided between his two children with Sebastian getting twenty-five per cent and Leonora the remaining twenty-four. Realising his only hope was with Leonora, Roe had asked her out to dinner on the pretext of discussing company politics. As she was flying to the Bahamas the next day they had to delay their rendezvous for two weeks but that just gave Roe more time to prepare.

He took her to a popular restaurant in the Boulevard Suchet near the Etoile, an elegant place with diffused lighting, pale-pink tablecloths and a sensational view of the Bois de Boulogne. Not that Leonora paid much attention. She was too eager to chat about the latest fashions and her trip to the Bahamas with a string of male models in tow. It appeared fag hags ran in the family. She didn't seem remotely career-orientated when probed but revealed a strong egotistical streak, and like most children of famous parents Leonora was suspicious of newcomers, determined to be liked for her own merits. Roe was banking on that. Several times she asked his opinion of mainstream designers, who was in and who was on the way out. In particular she wanted to know who were his favourite models. Roe wondered if she was fishing for information about Kate. In spite of the circumstances, he felt sure no one at work had found out about their affair and Nicole had been sworn to strict secrecy.

Considering Leonora flatteringly across the table, Roe erased her father's unkind nose, moved the grey-green eyes further apart and lopped about five inches off the manufactured-blonde hair. Not that the body needed any improvements. It was fantastic. Reminded him of Steffi Graf smashing her way through the Wimbledon final. For a moment he wondered what Leonora would be like in bed then tuned his ear back to what she was saying.

'I've got this thing for Italy. Daddy bought a villa in the south.' She drunkenly waved her glass of Rose Laurent Perrier, then looked directly into his eyes. 'Maybe you'd like to come and visit it some time?'

'Maybe I would,' Roe said guardedly. 'Did your father leave the house to you?'

'No. I got the flat in Paris and some shares, of all things. The house was left for all of us to use. Most of the money is tied up in trust funds until we reach thirty.'

'You could always sell.'

'Sell what?' said Leonora irritably, who would much rather have been talking about more romantic things. 'The house?'

'The shares. As you say, they're no use to you.'

'Oh, my brother wouldn't like that. Seb thinks the family should stick together, see that Daddy's precious company isn't split up. Mind you, it would serve Seb right if I did. He's becoming boringly pedantic.'

'They might be worth a bit.'

The thought obviously hadn't occurred to her. 'You really think so?'

He had her full attention now.

'Well, you'd have to be very careful. With such a small company, selling a percentage of that size could be a disaster. You don't want to just offer them on an open market and have a bunch of cowboys running the company. My advice would be to go for a single buyer.'

'Would you know of one?'

Good. She'd taken the bait.

'I could shop around for you,' he said non-committally.

Roe tipped the champagne remains into her glass then wisely changed the subject. 'Actually I had ulterior motives for asking you out tonight. I have a proposition to make.'

'I love propositions!' Leonora leaned forward on to her arms so Roe could get a good look at her marvellously brown tits. 'What exactly did you have in mind?'

'Vaubelle needs a new face and a new angle. I thought of using you.'

Having expected him to make a pass, Leonora attempted to bring her surprised face to order.

'You want me to model for you?'

'Why not? You've got the right credentials, and just think of the publicity we'd get with you coming from one of France's most respected families, and one that still owns, in part, its own fashion house.'

'I don't have any experience,' she said, warming to the idea.

'Nor did Princess Stephanie. She still made *Vogue* in her first month.'

'Do you really think so?'

Roe wished she'd stop repeating herself. It was starting to irritate him.

The rest had been easy. Leonora had invited him back to her flat and dispensing with the preliminaries, stripped off in front of the fire. She had been so eager to get into his pants, throwing herself on to him like a bitch on heat that Roe didn't think he'd be able to get it up. But in the end he didn't have to worry. Leonora, out to please, gave him one of the best blow

442

jobs of his life (and her career). Afterwards, ecstatic and high, she rabbited on about how they'd leak the news to the press, what her new image was going to be, how he was going to realise what a good investment she was. It was about the last thing Roe remembered before finally drifting off.

At 3 a.m. on the other side of the channel, Toby Wilmot-Smith was still wide awake. Accustomed to the dark, he turned to his fiancée asleep beside him and stared suspiciously at her stomach. At four months she still hardly showed. Mind you, he'd read stories of women who'd gone right to labour without even realising they were pregnant! They'd been making so many plans: the upstairs spare bedroom was transformed into a nursery, already stuffed with gifts. There was even talk of school enrolment and it was barely sixteen weeks conceived. Toby couldn't get used to the idea. Nothing made any sense to him. And yet, hadn't this been what he wanted? A family of his own? Maybe he wasn't ready to be a father. They were finding it almost impossible organising their own wedding, let alone a baby! They'd postponed the date twice, first because Tanya's parents had extended their South African trip, then because a fire had destroyed half the appointed church, which meant a second location change. Everything seemed against this marriage.

He still ached for Rachel, thought longingly of a trip to Chile he'd contemplated during the summer, and of his misspent youth. It all seemed out of his grasp for ever. He could feel the door to his independence slamming with a menacing clang and wondered if he'd ever be able to breathe properly again. What if it didn't work out? What if he messed things up the way he always did? He gazed at the ceiling, the room momentarily flooded with light from a passing car, feeling the sudden weight of responsibility. Trapped!

Thank God for work. In a way Rachel had been responsible for that, encouraging him very subtly to go back. And Yarnton. Unfailing Yarnton who once told him that information was the most useful commodity he knew. Backing him up to the hilt despite everything. How many people retired at the grand old age of twenty-five? Crazy what a bit of drink could do to a fellow. He knew how many strings Yarnton must have pulled to get him back in. These days old standing meant very little in the city. It was the new, pushy players that counted and Toby didn't feel particularly new or pushy. Nor was he pulling in the big deals with his old aplomb. Not yet anyway. For the moment he was a back-room boy, but playing for high stakes. It took time building up credibility – you're only as good as your last deal. But slowly, very slowly people were beginning to sit up and take notice of his name. His biggest sense of achievement was that he hadn't touched a drink for three months.

He mulled over a chance conversation he'd overheard at this morning's board meeting between two colleagues.

'This guy's got some shares he's looking to off-load. Got them mostly tied up with European companies. Could be worth looking into. I reckon we could pick up several shares for next to nothing. It's a bargain basement deal because he's in trouble.'

'Elliot's smarter than that. He's never been one for handouts.'

'Don't think he's got any choice. If he loses his insurance case it'll set him back $200 million. Word has it the banks are chomping at his heels.'

One of the men was skimming through the Cortes annual report.

'What's this one in Paris? Shares seem to be on the up.

'Vaubelle. Shares have doubled since the launch of their cosmetics and the fashion has made a come-back since it's takeover last year. Tom Glover's been making interested noises about it.'

'The trouble with Tom,' said the other disparagingly, 'is that so much of what he says is hot air. You can never tell when he's being legit.'

A junior investment banker put his head around the door, interrupting them. 'Chairman wants to see you both in his office.'

'Shit. On our way.'

In their haste they forgot the list of Carl's companies lying abandoned on the table. Very casually Toby had picked it up and slipped it unnoticed into his briefcase.

The bedside digital clock clicked forward to 4.25 a.m. In less than two hours he had to be up. If only he could sleep. Toby sighed against the dark, oppressive room, wishing there was some way to switch off his brain. His stomach was playing up. Maybe he'd try that acupuncturist Bea had mentioned. Nothing else had worked. Doctors just put it down to stress. His bowels grumbled. He got up to go to the loo.

'Can't you sleep, Tiger?'

Why did her saying the obvious make him feel so angry?

'Go back to sleep.'

By the time he got back from the bathroom Tanya was dead to the world. Slipping back under the duvet he realised sadly that he had to forget Rachel. It was time he woke up to reality and got his life sorted out. He had to face up to himself, face where his responsibilities lay. He reached for the woman he'd spent the last two years of his life with, the woman he doubted, felt guilty about because he'd come to resent her, when in fact he should be grateful for what they had together, and folded himself around the small of her back.

'Stud,' she murmured in her sleep. Her flesh felt warm and comforting.

Tanya Cook had been suffering from a series of headaches. Her masseur said it was stress-related and he was probably right. Such a perceptive little man. This secret that she'd been carrying around for the last five weeks had been a tremendous strain and she was desperate to tell someone about it. She had to or go mad! At first she'd been very nervous about phoning him. She wasn't sure he'd take her call, not after she'd let him down by walking out on the play and everything. She had even thought of hanging up as she waited for his stand-offish secretary to put her through. But as it turned out Clive had been very nice and they'd arranged to meet for lunch the following week.

445

Tanya smoothed down her blonde mane and Jasper Conran chiffon dress, checking her face in the lobby mirror. Her skin was her best feature. Its creamy flawlessness made her look much younger than her thirty-five years. Well, her passport claimed she was twenty-eight. She'd altered her age one night after overhearing how one of her actress friends had done so to get a job. When they'd first met, Tanya had told Toby she was twenty-six, afraid he'd be put off by the age gap. As she was blessed with a youthful face and he'd never said anything she saw no reason to disillusion him. Over tea at Simpson's yesterday a girlfriend had brought along her one-year-old baby and Tanya had been shocked by her appearance. She had ballooned up to twelve stone during pregnancy and still hadn't managed to shift it and her thick legs revealed varicose veins. As the waiter brought over their hot scones, the friend casually mentioned she was saving up to have the veins stripped. Tanya found the whole thing repugnant.

She saw him first, wearing his favourite grey Prince of Wales check suit and reading a copy of *Vanity Fair*, which he'd propped up against the salt and pepper mill. His right hand absently fondled a gin and tonic. As she crossed the room, passing huge spotlit vases of flushed-pink gladioli and water-colours on creamy walls, Tanya pretended not to notice the appreciative glances she got from neighbouring tables. Vivaldi's ubiquitous *Four Seasons* blotted out the light tap-tap of her shoes against the marble floor. Clive Barlow pulled back his chair and kissed her cheek.

'You look radiant, dear. Pregnancy suits you.'

'And you've lost pounds. The diet's obviously working.'

Clive looked pleased. 'Seen this month's issue?' he waved the *Vanity Fair* in the air. 'I must say there's a rather flattering picture of me set against the Hollywood Hills. Mind you, I'm baffled why they refer to me as the new Michael Winner. I don't look like him, do I?'

'Well, maybe something about the eyes.' She smiled quickly to show she was teasing and shrugged out of her matching pink jacket, which she gave to a hovering waiter. 'How much time have we got?'

'As long as you like. I've just swung a brilliant deal with the Yanks so I don't have to be back at the office until four.'

'Then let's get a bottle.'

Clive looked surprised. 'At this time of the day, darling. I thought drinking was taboo with pregnant gals?'

'You sound just like Toby.'

'Oh dear. I detect a slight edge to your voice when you say the T word. You'd better tell me all about it. I'll order.'

So she did and it was such a relief. At first the words came out slowly because she wasn't sure how Clive was going to react. But once she'd started Tanya found she couldn't stop. Clive nodded sympathetically as she described her most recent check up with Doctor Clinch at the private clinic (in her book the best because he was the most expensive one she could find), and her initial horror when she discovered she wasn't pregnant, quickly followed by relief.

'Seems a bit inappropriate to be drinking champagne,' she said with a twinge of guilt as a bottle of Lanson was brought to the table and poured into tulip-shaped glasses with a strawberry in the bottom.

'Not at all. We're celebrating my new partnership with the Yanks. Go on.'

'Apparently it's called a phantom pregnancy. Some women develop symptoms the full term simply because they're so desperate to have a baby.'

'And were you desperate?'

'No. Just confused.'

'Then why the hell didn't you tell Toby when you found out?'

Tanya stalled by taking a delicate sip of champagne. 'I meant to. I really did. But then I panicked. He has been seeing this girl in Paris, you see. Oh, I don't think it was anything serious,' she said quickly, catching the surprised look on Clive's face. 'Toby doesn't have it in him. But I thought he might think I'd tricked him into staying.'

'But you did trick him, Tanya.'

'Not at the time.' Sensing disapproval, Tanya's lovely grey eyes suddenly filled with tears. 'Oh God, Clive, it's all such a horrible mess. Perhaps I shouldn't have called but I didn't know who else to turn to and you've always been such a friend in the past. I'm reaching breaking point!'

'Now, now. There's no need for that. Here, take my hanky.' Clive glanced quickly round the room to see if anyone was watching. He had an aversion to drama unless it was in its rightful place up on the screen. 'My advice would be to tell Toby. He's going to find out anyway but it should come from you.' Clive refilled their glasses. 'Did you want this baby?'

Tanya had her emotions under control again. 'No I didn't! Toby is the keen one, at least he was. I'm not so sure now.'

'And do you love him?'

'No.'

It was the first time she had admitted it to herself, let alone anyone else. The relationship had been going steadily downhill for months. They'd both changed and the prospect of a baby was the only thing that had kept them together. That and Tanya's fear of being left without financial security. Clive was right. She couldn't go on living a lie. Toby had to be told and then she'd leave him.

'What am I going to say? I don't think I could bear to spend another night at that house but I can't turn to my friends. They all know Toby.'

Not now, she thought dreading a confrontation.

'Then you'd better come with me to California. That deal I mentioned earlier, they want me to produce an Anglo-American soap. Casting starts in two weeks and we'll be looking for several new faces. I'm not promising anything, dear, they've already got Lysette Anthony in mind but you're a better actress and they'll love all that blonde hair.'

Tanya's stomach did somersaults. She was afraid to say something in case she broke this unexpected new course her life was suddenly taking. What an incredible stroke of luck!

'Do you really mean it?'

'I don't say anything I don't mean,' said Clive pompously. 'What's Toby doing now?'

'Holding some beastly meeting at the bank, I think. Shouldn't be back before seven.'

'Then if you're really serious about leaving him I suggest

448

we hop in a cab back to Campden Hill and grab your things. You can camp at my place until we leave.'

Tanya couldn't believe her ears! Her mother had always said she had the luck of the gods.

'What about Simon?'

'Oh lord, he won't mind, dear. The Royal Opera House has promoted him to Artistic Director. He's hardly ever home these days. I think he's sulking because I won't take him with me to the States. Silly boy.'

A slow Vivien Leigh smile spread over Tanya's face and she leaned across the table to kiss him. 'Well then. As you seem to have the whole thing so brilliantly worked out, Clive darling, let's get the bill. I've got this sudden urge to move!'

When Toby pulled up outside the house it was almost ten o'clock. Campden Hill Square was quiet and he was surprised to see no lights on at home. Funny, he couldn't remember Tanya saying she was going out. As he approached the house the outside light automatically floodlit the garden. Dropping his keys on to the hall table, he switched off the alarm then went into the drawing-room and checked the answer machine. Nine people had called but most of them hadn't bothered to leave messages, which irritated him. There were two calls from Yarnton sounding unusually harassed and an invitation from Guy to a dinner party next Tuesday. He wouldn't go. Guy's wild nights of sex, drugs and rock and roll were starting to wear thin. And his stomach was playing up too much to risk it.

He was just debating whether or not he was hungry when he spotted Tanya's note propped up against the television. A sixth sense told him what it contained. With a slightly trembling hand he opened it and skimmed through the scribbled lines – obviously written in haste. Then he read it again. This time more slowly.

'Saw my GP today, Tiger – false alarm, after all. Obviously not destined for motherhood. I'm cutting my losses, lover, off to play the lead in Clive's new American mini-series. Sorry I'm being such a wimp telling you like this, but it really wasn't working for us and in a way I'm doing you a favour – leaving the romantic path back to Paris free. It's for the best.'

She'd signed the bottom with a large squiggly T and three kisses. Was there any significance in three kisses? Why not four kisses or two? For ages Toby just stared at the note then he slowly tore it up and threw the bits into the fireplace. He took off his jacket, loosened his tie and lay down on the sofa, listening to Bach's *Concerto for violin and oboe in C minor* with the stereophonic earphones – he didn't want to disturb his neighbours. A fly buzzed lethargically around the room then landed on his hand. Toby couldn't be bothered to flick it off. In another few hours it would be dead anyway. He just lay there, thinking. Tanya wasn't pregnant. No baby. The whole thing had been a mistake. Some mistake! Not that he'd ever really felt connected to the idea.

The music stopped as the tape clicked to auto-reverse, then his ears filled with violins taking over in the second movement. He felt light-headed, as if someone had lifted the lid from his brain and scraped off the dull residue of depression. Everything was suddenly quite clear. He'd been given a second chance. Life was no longer black and white but glorious Technicolor!

He no longer felt afraid.

At three o'clock on Thursday Leonora Vaubelle had just signed her contract as house model and was in Roe's office. So that they'd have complete privacy Roe had ordered lunch in. An empty bottle of Moët was propped up against the sofa, and sprawled across the large desk, her lengthy, coffee-coloured legs in the air, was Leonora. Experiencing her third orgasm in half an hour she let out a feverish cry of pleasure. To her astonishment (such fantastic stamina) Roe was still stiff. He lifted her to her feet and propped her up against the wall. Trying to do it standing up wasn't easy and she had to hook her legs around his waist to steady herself. They were both bathed in sweat, concentrating on the rhythm. In out, in out, their bodies thrashing together while Roe muttered angrily, 'Come on baby, come on, faster!'

There was a knock at the door.

'What the hell?' snapped Roe, his words none too steady.

'I've got Mr Schofield on line one. Shall I get him to call back?'

'No,' he ran an unsteady hand across his forehead, then calmer, 'no, hang on, Nicole, I'll take it.' Leonora felt herself slip to the floor.

'Leo. What's up?'

'Bad news, I'm afraid. Word just came in that Carl's sold off thirty per cent.'

'Who to?'

'Haven't got a clue. It's an anonymous buyer but it's definite.'

'Shit!'

She could hear the phone ringing and fumbled with the key in the lock. Come on. Come on. Stupid door. It was always jamming. Justin had promised to get it fixed. She dropped her model bag to the floor so that both hands were free. The lock sprang open. At last! Bea rushed breathlessly to the phone.

'Justin? I thought I'd missed you.'

'No it's not Justin, it's me. Either you've been having a very active social life, young lady, or you've been screening your calls. I've been trying to get hold of you for days!'

'Jack!' She chucked the keys on to the sofa, which missed and fell to the floor. Never mind. She'd pick them up later.

'Yes, Jack, the man you've been sleeping with for two months, the man you haven't seen for six days. Have you been avoiding me?'

It was a shock hearing his voice sounding so warm and pleased to talk to her. She sat on the sofa, kicked off her shoes and brought her knees to her chest. There was nothing for it, she'd just have to tell him.

'Your wife came to see me.' She held her breath.

'My Lorna. You saw Lorna?'

'Yes. Your Lorna.'

'When?'

'At Popjoys. She followed you there. Can't say it's an experience I wish to repeat.'

'Oh, Christ, no. What did she say?'

'I got a brief run-down on all the affairs you'd had and was

451

then told I was a fool to think I meant anything to you.'

'Obviously you believed her?'

No answer.

'Well, not a word of it's true. In all our married years you're the only other woman I've slept with. Finding out about you probably frightened the life out of her.'

A flicker of hope. 'Really?'

'Yes. Really!' Now he sounded angry. 'Come on, Bea, what do you think this is? It's me you're talking to. You know how I feel about infidelity.'

'I'm sorry. I should have given you a chance to explain.'

'Lorna can be pretty convincing when she wants to be.'

'You're telling me. She should have been a barrister. Not that I can really blame her. She was only trying to protect her turf. And then there are your children. I've thought so much about them. All of a sudden I've developed a conscience.'

'Bea. You aren't responsible for my marriage not working. If it hadn't been you it would have been someone else eventually. I've been holding this marriage together because I thought it was the best for my children. If anyone's got to carry the guilt, it's me. Do you have any idea what hell I've been through wondering why you wouldn't see me?'

Bea chewed the inside of her cheek. She'd agonised all week over how she was going to tell him.

'Jack. I don't want to be the cause of your marriage breaking up and then find that one day you wake up and realise it was all a ghastly mistake.'

'You're much more likely to do that than me.'

'Things have changed. Your wife's visit really shocked me. Up until then I could pretend your family didn't really exist, but they do. They're part of your life.'

'This sounds ominous. You think we should stop seeing one another?' There was fear in his voice.

'You know Lorna will fight you in court for the children. Are you really prepared for that?'

'Hang on,' Bea could hear a door squeaking in the background, then, 'Livi, not now. I'm on the phone.' Jack lowered his voice, 'Look Bea, I don't want to lose you. Can't we just give it some time?'

'Jack, I . . .'

'Don't. Come on, don't cry. This is killing me.'

'I can't help it. I feel so miserable.'

'I must see you!'

Just as she felt herself weaken, Bea suddenly heard Lorna's voice, 'Darling, you've been on that phone for hours! Aren't you going to join us?'

'Look, I have to go. Can I call you at home tomorrow?'

'It's better you don't. I'm sorry, Jack. Goodbye.' And she hung up.

The click of the phone in Jack's ear made him feel as if his connection to life itself had been severed.

'Who was that?' asked Lorna curiously, as Olivia barged back into the study clutching a Jack Russell puppy, the Manse's newest acquisition.

'Daddy, Arthur wants to say hello.'

'Harry Barnfield. He wants me to play in Florida at Christmas.' Jack regarded the telephone.

'Terrific! I absolutely love their house. I hope Mary brings the kids this time.'

'Can Arthur sleep on my bed tonight?'

'No, he stays in the kitchen. You know the rules. Go and put him back in his basket,' snapped Jack, still studying the phone as Olivia skipped unperturbed from the room. Then to Lorna, 'I might have to go by myself.'

'Oh.' Lorna's heart dropped. Her. He'd been talking to her. 'Darling, everything is all right, isn't it?'

'Mmm. What? I'm sorry. I've just got some things on my mind.'

He seemed to shake himself out of his trance and rose from the desk. Putting an arm around his wife he walked her to the door.

'C'mon, let's go and eat before our two start World War Three and destroy that new kitchen of yours!'

'Basil! Come here you bloody animal.'

Lady Parker's strident voice rose above the noise of barking dogs back from their morning walk and woke Kate from a deep sleep. Tree branches tapped like bony fingers against her bedroom window and she could hear the clatter of horses' hoofs in Campion's drive. It reminded her instantly of Coochin Coochin. She closed her eyes, stretched her hands above her head and yawned. It was Christmas morning and her birthday!

Opening them again she glanced around her. It was still dark and the room was cast in shadow. The small window-panes were covered in morning frost and her nose was cold. Kate leant across the bed and switched on the side lamp. Colour jumped at her. The walls were a pale peach, with chintz curtains and a huge dressing-table under the window. Facing the bed was a heavy Victorian wardrobe with a full-length mirror. Kate studied her reflection. The wonderful red hair, newly washed, fanned across her shoulders. She looked lost in the enormous sixteenth-century four-poster bed where, it was claimed, Cromwell had spent the night before King Charles's execution. Kate snuggled further down to keep warm and found the hot water bottle Lady Parker had given her. Since it was no longer warm, she kicked it away.

Oh, the bliss of not having to worry about work! No more castings until early January! Sophie, by now, would be floating somewhere off Mauritius with Derek and a week-old suntan. Her own tan was fading fast. Was it really only two weeks since she left Australia? Sometimes she felt as if she'd dreamed the whole crazy thing. Bits of conversation with Skander stuck in her mind. She kept going over the things he'd got her to admit, trying to work out her turbulent feelings. After Roe, she had convinced herself that she would never again allow a man to hurt her. Was she mad to put her trust in a man who knew all her secrets? And what now was the extent of her feelings for him?

Matthew Freeman and two of his stable hands had been unable to conceal their shock when they stumbled across them while out inspecting the storm damage to his land. They had found Skander, still suffering from concussion and alarmingly weak, riding Eblis, while Kate, her delicate skin burnt and peeling but otherwise unhurt, led the exhausted horse. Both were filthy. A search party, quickly alerted, had picked up the rest of the group unharmed a few miles from the creek.

The return to Coochin Coochin had been a shock too. The storm had ripped up thirty per cent of the trees, which lay prostrate around the house resembling dead bodies; one had collapsed through the kitchen window, scattering glass everywhere. The roof tiles had been blown off, letting the rain into the house, and all the carpets would have to be replaced. Skander, after a proper meal and a good night's sleep, ignoring both Kate's and the doctor's advice, was up next day mending the roof. Only the bandage on his head served as a reminder of his near-miss encounter with death. For the next week Skander and his men lay siege to the damage. Kate did what she could to help, sweeping away the debris, rescuing precious books and pictures, hanging Kilims in the sun to dry them out, fixing endless meals while listening to Skander singing off-key. She got a nasty shock when in the early part of the second afternoon he collapsed from exhaustion. Sounding furious, in order to hide how worried she was, Kate ordered him back to bed. The men supported her, and Skander was feeling too weak to argue. So many things needed her attention, and in a funny way she enjoyed rushing around with little time or regard for herself or her appearance; she only looked in the mirror when she cleaned her teeth in the morning and, even then, she hardly recognised herself.

456

She'd put off calling the agency. Nigel had expected her back a week ago but she couldn't bear to leave. Not yet! Australia was weaving its magic and she was shedding the old Kate and her old habits with surprising ease. While she was there, she didn't have to think about her unhappy life in England. Skander, though definitely on the mend, continued to tire easily and still dragged his left leg, which had taken the full brunt of the log. In the end, though, Nigel tracked her down and used a Harrods brochure booking to woo her back. She almost refused, almost made Nigel find a replacement, but it was Skander who persuaded her to leave.

'You know as well as I do you can't afford to get yourself a bad name in this business. And maybe it'll help you to put us in perspective.'

'But who's going to look after you?'

'Just possibly me! I have managed for thirty-four years,' he smiled wryly. 'And Dylan and Beth get back tomorrow.'

At the airport Kate had clung to his neck in a sudden panic. Was she mad to go back?

'It's only for a month. You'll be too busy with work and Christmas to give me a moment's thought.'

'You don't want me to stay,' she said flatly.

''Course I do. You've already shown remarkable dexterity and I'm proud of you. I really mean that. But to be honest the men will work faster without you as a distraction. I found Thomas the other day cutting your picture out of a magazine!'

Kate blushed scarlet. None of the men had said more than a couple of words to her. She hadn't realised she'd been noticed.

'Now, if you need anything, just call. You know the number. I'll be back on the thirteenth.'

'You'll miss my birthday,' she wailed. She realised she sounded like a four-year-old!

'We'll do something about that when I return. Now, can I have my neck back? Unless we hurry you're not going to make your flight.'

She missed him the minute she boarded the plane. Missed the pressure of his hand, the rich, chocolaty-sound of his voice, his six-foot-three oarsman frame which made her feel small and feminine, his bullying, his great happy smile, even the faint smell of nicotine which lingered in his hair. Was she running away again? As the plane ate up the distance between Skander's protection and her mother shores, Kate's anxiety returned.

She couldn't get used to being back in London. After a month of sun, virgin sand and space, the city tension was unbearable. Wrapped in layers of socks and sweaters to combat the cold, Kate gazed at the swell of commuters with new eyes: armies of worried men and women plunged aggressively along the grey pavements, relentlessly searching for better jobs, better relationships, faster ways to make money and spend it. The sheer speed of London exhausted her. Kate forgot that she'd once been one of them, lugging her bag from one camera to another runway, avoiding eye contact with beggars, lost tourists, the relentless traffic roar. Instead she day-dreamed of the Queensland rain forest, the singing birds, the bloodshot skies, the sun splintering through the coachwood trees like laser beams, the creek where Skander had found her bathing with Ginny and where they'd nearly drowned.

Nigel, relieved to have one of his best earners back, hit the roof when he saw the state her skin was in.

'Bloody hell, Kate! I can't send you out on castings looking like that. You're supposed to be the pale and interesting type, not sodding Tropicana! I'm calling Sassoon right now. You need a haircut.'

'It's good to see you too, Nigel.'

Actually the client had been very nice, and the make-up artist so skilful that her tan hardly showed. Kate made Nigel eat his words when the client put more option dates on her for February. At least she got some nice pictures out of it! The rest of December flew by. Then Sophie, running true to form, told Kate her plans at the last moment. Which meant that but for Bea's invitation to stay at her parents' estate in Gloucestershire, Kate would have spent Christmas alone.

There were footsteps on the gravel outside, then voices; the sharp slam of a door, then silence. Minutes later Bea burst into the bedroom, clutching a king-size pink elephant. Trailing behind her was Basil, the Parkers' Irish red setter.

'Morning, birthday girl! Is it ghastly being twenty-six?'

The elephant, dwarfing Bea, had a pale-pink trunk, wide powdery-blue eyes and huge satin ears. Basil wasn't about to be left out and jumped on the bed. He had swiped the cat's tuna at breakfast and his breath smelt terrible.

'Oh Bea, he's adorable! But how the hell am I going to get him back to London?'

'Justin's driving us back in the Range Rover. He said he wanted to watch you open your presents, but trying to wake my brother is like trying to raise the dead!' Bea put a large pile on Kate's lap. 'You're a popular girl. Oh, and someone called for you early this morning but you were asleep.'

'Did they leave a name?' she asked with greedy curiosity.

'No, but Daddy said it was long distance. Sounds like your dishy Australian, if you ask me. I can't believe you don't have a single picture of him!'

Charlie, Lord and Lady Parker's six-year-old grandson, shot into the room wearing new Batman pyjamas and yelling, 'Pow! Zap! Pow! Zap!' Behind him came twenty-nine-year-old Justin, looking a little the worse for wear after too many Christmas parties. Wearing a towel around his slim waist, he had a bottle of champagne tucked under one arm and was eating Frosties out of a mug.

'Who's responsible for waking me at such an ungodly hour?' he said, heading straight for the bed. 'Gangway!'

'I got a Terminator Two set in my stocking!' shrieked Charlie excitedly.

'And guess what I've found in mine?' said Justin climbing in next to Kate. 'Shove off, Basil! There's only room for one man in this woman's life.'

Kate giggled and Justin opened the champagne. He had impressive dark circles under sky-blue eyes and very straight, blond hair. Basil sulkily moved to the bottom of the bed and studied Justin with grievous eyes.

'Oh, look! Poor Basil.'

'Should have gone on stage, bloody dog. Don't be taken in for a moment. Can I play join the dot with your new freckles?'

'Who wants to play Terminator Two with me?' said Charlie, bouncing up and down on the bed. 'Pow! Whap!'

Justin gazed at Kate. 'What about Doctors and Nurses?'

'Boring!

How come you're so brown?' Kate asked.

'Skiing in Switzerland with my uncle, lucky bugger,' mumbled Bea, who was now eating Justin's Frosties. 'I'm going next time.'

'Charlie, be a sport and stop jumping, there's a good chap,' said Justin, closing his eyes. 'I like to be stirred, not shaken. Why don't you make yourself useful and get us some glasses. There's a good chap. One can't drink Moët out of mugs.'

They guzzled the champagne while Kate opened her cards and presents in amazement. Such lovely gifts. She was so used to Sophie forgetting. Even the agency had sent her a home-made card signed by everyone and a beautiful Hermès scarf. Charlie had bought her a golfing cap from his father's club, Bea a pretty silk body from Christian Dior and a T-shirt emblazoned with the slogan 'Today's Pigs Tomorrow's Bacon'. Justin had given her a Butler and Wilson clasp for her hair.

'I don't know what to say. How absolutely lovely of you all.'

'Slip this on – just to see if it fits,' Justin suggested, waving the silk body.

'Wait. You've forgotten one,' said Charlie, rescuing a card that had fallen to the floor.

Kate glanced at the cream envelope with the familiar bold scrawl and froze.

'Oh, that came in the post about a week ago,' said Bea. 'I assumed it was a birthday card. Didn't recognise the hand-writing.'

Kate's hands shook as she opened the envelope. An exquisite pair of emerald studs in the shape of cats fell on to the eiderdown. In a daze she read the accompanying card.

'Don't leave it too long, Kat, I miss you.'

'Looks like I have stiff competition,' said Justin, reading the card. 'What's this mystery writer have that I don't, apart from being loaded?'

The card bore no signature but only one person called her Kat. She frantically searched the envelope for more information but it was empty.

Bea grabbed the card. 'Oh Kate, you lucky, lucky thing! Put them on.'

Lady Parker walked briskly into the room holding a whip. A tall, handsome woman in her fifties, she was wearing riding boots and breeches several sizes too small. On closer inspection Kate could see traces of Bea's features – the china-blue eyes, the translucent skin, the neat upturned nose, the same energy too.

'Darlings, Mrs Warmbath has breakfast ready downstairs. Do go down before it gets cold. And don't forget morning service at eleven. Kate dear, Basil's not allowed on the bed.'

The deep, clipped school-matron voice camouflaged one of the softest hearts in Kent.

But Kate wasn't listening. She was still gazing at the tiny emeralds in the small of her palm. God! He wanted her back!

'Mummy, it's Kate's birthday,' said Bea, 'do relax for five minutes and have a glass of champagne.'

'Congratulations, dear. Rotten luck having it on Christmas Day. Couldn't your mother have held out another twenty-four hours?'

'Eighteen hours of labour practically killed her.'

'Goodness! Your poor mother.'

'Yes,' said Kate with a trace of bitterness.

'I've just had Arabella on the phone to say they can't make it. Family crisis, so it'll just be your friend, Jus, and the Pratts. Mont Pratt is the Master of Foxhounds,' she explained to Kate as if she were describing royalty. 'Can I get you a dressing-gown?'

Justin pulled Kate closer. 'She's fine as she is, Mum. Are you going riding again today?'

'Once lunch is out of the way,' Lady Parker said, retrieving their empty glasses. 'Goodness! Look at the time. I must get on.'

Bea rolled her eyes in despair at Kate. 'Ever since Henrietta Pratt died from breast cancer three years ago, Mum's been inviting Mont and his frightful daughter, Fiona,

461

to everything. I'd just like you to know I have nothing to do with it.'

Someone had turned on the Christmas tree lights in the great hall and they paused on the staircase to admire it. The shiny, waxed floorboards were covered in cheerful old rugs, frayed from generations of feet. Beneath the Christmas tree were brightly-wrapped parcels, and Mendelssohn, the resident parrot, squawked his approval from his stripy cage near by. In a shabby dog's basket by the hall fire was a large marmalade cat with half a dozen tiny kittens firmly attached to her teats. Their bodies swelled and drained of air in rapid movements like tiny bellows. Another one had escaped from the basket and with its tail pointing towards the ceiling was swanking across the floor, full of purpose.

'That kitten has a future,' giggled Bea, 'walks just like me!'

In the dining-room Lord Parker sat at the head of the table buried in yesterday's paper. He sported his favourite paisley dressing-gown, and his left leg, encased in plaster of Paris and a large tartan sock, was propped up on a stool. He was large, like his wife, but without her energy he appeared smaller, his complexion pasty and his small brown eyes lost behind rimmed spectacles. He seemed to Kate gentle, withdrawn and preoccupied and wearing the permanently puzzled expression of someone trying to remember where they'd put the car keys. The room was full of cigar smoke and Lady Parker went straight to the window and opened it.

Lord Parker's spectacles rose above the newspaper, smiling at his wife.

'Nice ride, dear?' he asked automatically.

'Now you shouldn't be smoking those things at breakfast. Doctor Pokey would have a fit! And aren't you going to dress for church?'

'I think I'll give it a miss,' he said, reluctantly stubbing out the cigar, 'awful lot of writing to do over the weekend. Ah, and here's the birthday girl,' quickly changing the subject. 'Did you get the phone message? Couldn't quite catch his name but he said he'd call back later.'

'I did, thank you.' And because she was feeling so happy Kate impulsively bent down to kiss him.

462

With breakfast over, everyone donned coats, boots, scarves and gloves and shovelled snow off the drive. Then they piled into the Range Rover and drove to the morning service. The church was packed and bitterly cold. No one removed their coats except Lady Parker, who was already sweating from her active morning and the struggle to get in and out of the car. 'Hellos' and 'Happy Christmases' were exchanged. The Parkers knew absolutely everyone. Kate glanced sideways at Bea who was off in another daydream. She hadn't been herself for ages. But if something was troubling her she was hiding it behind jokes and a deceptively light mood. Kate thought she'd suggest the two of them slipped off together for a few days. It would be her treat and maybe cheer her friend up.

After church and lunch they went for a blowy walk joined by Lady P, who'd elected not to ride a second time. The pearl-grey sky hovered broodingly over the land, the snow crunched under their boots. They climbed the steep, winding road to the top of Campion's drive, passing the pond, now frozen, over the stile and up into the hills. At the top they looked down at the powdery sea of meadows, just making out the L-shaped house, its brick walls now completely buried in snow. Kate exhaled and watched the fine mist evaporate into the wind. Bea ducked behind a bush for a pee and emerged howling with pain having sat on some frosted stinging-nettles.

They reached home just before dark and the snowstorm which had threatened all day. The wind whistled and sang about the eaves and the handsome old windows trembled in their frames like loose teeth. Everyone thawed out with tea and home-made crumpets by the drawing-room fire, although Kate would have preferred the cosiness and romance of the kitchen, her back pressed against the warm Aga. At five they opened their Christmas presents.

The guests were expected at seven, so, leaving the ecstatic animals deep in paper and tinsel, everyone collected their gifts and disappeared upstairs to get ready. Sounds of baths being run mingled with the clinking of cutlery as Mrs Warmbath laid the table downstairs.

'Bea!' yelled Justin, appearing on the upstairs landing in

odd socks and a pair of boxer shorts decorated with purple pigs. 'Have you been at my hair gel again?'

'No, I bloody haven't. The last time I used that horrid stuff it took me a week to wash it out!'

Lady Parker sat in front of her dressing-table mirror and studied her reflection. Removing several bobby pins, she brushed her hair for a few moments as she thought about her children. Despite her bullying she adored them all and took great pride in their achievements. After a six-month stint in Germany Justin had finally committed himself to London and seemed to be enjoying his new publishing job. Harry, her eldest, was making a terrifically successful political career for himself, but had been so caught up in the last election his marriage had suffered. Thank goodness they were both prepared to work it out and were having a second honeymoon over the Christmas break. And dear Charlie, her only grandson. He was growing more like his father every day. Bea worried her though. She had noticed how absent-minded her daughter had been lately. Not her usual bubbly self. And much too thin.

Basil waddled into the room with a dead bird in his mouth, his tail swinging wildly. He dropped it at her feet, panting with pride.

'Warmbath!' Lady Parker boomed, putting down her eye-shadow with a crash. Basil's tail waved then started up again with more energy as she rose. Perhaps he'd get a second walk?

'Madam?' Mrs Warmbath, whose pink face appeared in the bedroom door, was rubbing her hands on a white frilly apron.

'Could you please take this beastly dog downstairs and put him in the back garden. The guests are due any minute now and I can't have him disrupting dinner. Has Lord P organised the wine?'

'Yes, madam,' she bobbed nervously. 'The champagne's cooling and I've lit the fire in the dining-room. Miss Bea asked me to tell you that she's running a bit late 'cause she's waiting for the water to heat up again.'

'Which reminds me. There's a trail of scanty-looking knickers on all the house radiators. Will you kindly ask her to remove them before the guests arrive. Where's Katherine?'

'Down in the library playing pool with Master Justin.'

'Well, do get them to help with things downstairs or we'll be entertaining everyone in the bath!' Lady Parker muttered, now rummaging in her wardrobe for a pair of evening shoes. 'I suppose that wretched dog ate my last good pair?' she asked, deep in the cupboard.

After a frantic search they finally turned up under the bed and Mrs Warmbath dashed back to the kitchen to check the turkey and to bury the dead bird. She crossed Lord Parker hobbling up the stairs, helped along by a walking stick.

'What's that you've got there?' he asked, peering through his spectacles.

'It's a bird, sir.'

'Won't feed nine of us,' he said.

'Don't be silly, dear,' called Lady Parker from the top of the stairs, 'that's Basil's.'

The doorbell rang.

'I'll get it,' yelled Justin, coming out of the library. 'Basil! Will you bloody well shut up for five minutes!'

For some perverse reason Kate had decided to wear the emerald earrings. They flashed importantly against the bright, flickering fire.

Enter the Pratts: Mont, in his early fifties, sported startlingly red hair and a foxy moustache. He was a tall, slim man and had a beaky nose which had once been broken in three places from a fall. Kate had an uneasy feeling she'd seen him before, but couldn't place him. Fiona, his only daughter, wore a short, bottle-green velvet dress, flat patent pumps and several rows of real-looking pearls.

'We're not late, I hope?' She handed Jasper an expensive-looking coat. 'It's still snowing and half the roads are blocked!'

Lady Parker sailed in like a cruise liner, with her one painted eye doing a good impersonation of a bruise. She'd forgotten to do the other one in all the confusion. Mont, who'd secretly been in love with her for years, presented her with a large bunch of orange roses.

'Oh, you are clever!' she said, burying her nose in the flowers. 'They even have a scent.'

'More than I can say for the hounds yesterday. Not a fox to be seen!'

'We've met,' said Fiona, giving Kate a limp handshake.

'I don't think so.'

'Are you sure? Not one of Henrietta's lot, are you?'

'God, don't inflict that dreadful girl on Kate.' Lord Parker had appeared looking stiff and uncomfortable in black tie. 'Henrietta organises balls for a lot of excruciating young people. If you know what's good for you, keep well away. What's your fancy, old boy?'

'A drop of Scotch, if you'd be so kind,' said Mont.

'Darling, do have a sniff of Mont's lovely roses.'

'Fiona?'

'Have you got any Perrier? My Candida diet expressly forbids alcohol.'

'Oh dear,' said Algie Parker, who liked his drink and disapproved strongly of diets, 'how about a Schweppes tonic? I think we have some that hasn't gone flat.'

Justin sat on the arm of Kate's chair and lowered his voice, 'Don't worry. All's not lost. I've invited a friend from the office. Casper's a lark and very attractive but committed to a lady fifteen years his senior. Of course she would be the managing director's wife. Office scandal. But Casper's so good at his job the editor daren't sack him. He speaks three languages and picks best-sellers as fast as my sister collects parking tickets.' Justin admired Kate's slinky black dress. Her hair was swept back in a high knot, displaying her long white neck. She knew how to play backgammon too.

A pink-faced Bea emerged from her bath, wearing a black see-through chiffon shirt tucked into tight black jeans and thigh-length suede boots. Around her neck was a huge bronze crucifix. She made straight for the fire. One of the kittens shot in behind her giving chase to an invisible insect.

'Hell, this room's absolutely freezing! Can't we turn the heating up?'

'It might help if you wore more clothes, darling.'

'Hello, Fi,' said Bea, squatting in front of the fire. Her father handed her a glass of champagne. 'Still getting everyone to toe the line?'

'Belinda and I went to the same school,' Fiona explained to Kate, adjusting the velvet hairband more securely on her sleek blonde head. 'For my sins I was made head girl while Belinda was always doing dreadful things like getting caught in bed with boys. We were all secretly in awe of her. I never thought for a moment she'd become a model.'

Bea glanced sardonically at Kate. 'Green and red check blazers never brought out the best in me. I hear you're working at the Armani Emporium in Knightsbridge. Can you get us stuff at cost?'

'You can't even buy a pair of socks there for under fifty quid,' muttered Justin. One of the kittens shot up the back of Kate's chair and landed on her lap. Kate gently extracted its tiny claws from her dress and cupped it in her hand.

Fiona stared at Kate. 'Are you sure we haven't met?'

'You probably recognise her as the Vaubelle face,' said Bea smugly.

'Of course! I've just been reading all about them in this month's *Vogue*. Terrific goings on. You got a mention. I suppose you know they're having all sorts of internal problems.'

'No, I didn't.' Kate glanced at Bea.

'But their last collection sounded brilliant!'

'Oh, absolutely, Lady P. They've got a terribly clever girl designing for them. But their American backer's just lost a fortune. Something to do with a bogus insurance policy. I don't really know. But I do feel sorry for the chap left in charge. He single-handedly got that company back on its feet.'

'Are you talking about Roe Lewis?' Bea asked curiously.

Kate started fiddling with an earring.

'If he's six foot and frightfully good-looking, I am. There's a picture *Vogue* took of him in his office.'

'Which I suppose you've got pinned up on your wall,' said Justin, winking at Kate.

'I thought George Michael was all the rage these days,' Mont remarked, feeling left out of the conversation.

Fiona, studying Kate, took a thoughtful sip of tonic. 'So what do you think of your replacement?'

'What replacement?' Since leaving, Kate had deliberately avoided all publicity on Vaubelle. It evoked too many painful memories.

'Oh, I thought you knew. They're using Vaubelle's daughter. What's her name?'

'Leonora?' Kate was shocked. 'She's not Rachel's type at all!'

'No, but she seems to be Lewis's. Word at Armani has it that their relationship is rather more than just professional.'

Kate's face fell. What the hell was he doing sending her earrings? The bastard!

Charlie rushed into the room with Basil. 'Gran, Warmbath wants everyone to sit down right away or the plum pudding will be spoiled. And Justin's friend got his car stuck in the snow. He's getting changed in my room because Basil's been sick in Justin's and it stinks.'

'Great!' muttered Justin.

'Can I have some champagne?' begged Charlie.

'No, you can't. There's orange juice in the fridge.'

Bea leaned across to Charlie and whispered, 'You can have some of mine at dinner.'

The kitten, who was getting bored, jumped off Kate's lap and latched on to Basil's tail in a frenzy.

'I don't think we'll wait for your friend any longer,' said Lady Parker, placing her empty glass on the mantelpiece. 'Let's go on through, shall we?'

There was a general shuffle as they all made their way to the dining-room. Bea caught Kate's arm.

'Isn't Fi priceless? She spent a year at Lucie Clayton's where you learn all the social graces, so that when you marry you're able to do the flower arranging, direct the cook in fluent French and run an enormous household single-handed. All she ever actually learnt was how to get in and out of her boyfriend's sports car. She's only doing the Armani job to meet loads of eligible men.'

A great delicious wave of turkey filled the air. The fifteenth-century dining-room looked beautiful, lit festively with huge Gothic candles Bea had bought as a gift, which stood six feet on wrought-iron stands. On the thick, oak-panelled walls hung sombre ancestral portraits, for once relieved of their twentieth-century picture lights. To the right of the room alongside the table blazed an impressive log fire flanked on both sides by enormous baskets of wood. Mrs Warmbath was unloading hot plates from the trolley.

'You come and sit here next to me, Mont, and Justin, you can sit on my left,' commanded Lady Parker.

As she spoke an outstandingly good-looking man with shoulder-length hair and a ruby mouth that looked as if it was made expressly for kissing walked into the room. His hair was still damp with snowflakes and Kate smelt Fahrenheit on him. Why did everything have to remind her of Roe?

'I'm terribly sorry for holding you up, Lady Parker, you must think me very rude.' He took her hand and gave her a devastating smile.

So this was Casper. Kate had expected someone much older. Lucky managing director's wife!

'Let me get you a drink,' offered Lord Parker.

'I won't actually, thanks. I'm on antibiotics and I've got to drive on to Gloucester later tonight.'

Kate wondered if the managing director's wife lived in Gloucester.

'I hear your car broke down,' said Lady Parker.

'Just a flat tyre and old age. I've been trying to sell it.'

Another lethal smile. Lady Parker was melting fast.

'Well, we can always lend you one of ours. There are plenty around. Justin, I think after all we'll put you on the other side of Kate. Algie dear, you'll get Casper a tonic or something, won't you? Do sit down.'

She patted the seat on her left. Lord Parker sat at the head and opened his linen napkin with a loud crack. Mrs Warmbath dished out baked shrimps with sour cream on to white bone china edged with gold.

Fiona began quizzing Algie Parker about some land she was thinking of selling, while Lady Parker kept Casper's attention firmly in her direction by asking lots of questions about publishing. Kate chatted to Justin about the latest films they'd been to see, but in the back of her mind she kept trying to work out Roe's motives. Was he really seeing

Leonora? He had always been so rude about her. And why go to the trouble of sending her emeralds? It couldn't be true. Algie, perhaps to escape the dreadful Fiona's advice on avoiding high cholesterol, got up to cut the turkey, resplendent with crispy bacon, chipolata sausages, roast potatoes, Yorkshire pudding and bright, crunchy vegetables.

'Breast or leg?'

'Kate's got plenty of both,' said Justin, helping himself to Brussel sprouts with chestnuts, creamed onions and nutmeg from a china bowl. Lord Parker's heavily-jowled great-grandfather on the wall scowled at them under his floury wig. When Lady Parker got up to supervise, Casper was able to spend a few minutes chatting to Kate.

'I hear you're a top model. Lady P's been telling me all about your stint with Vaubelle. Sounds fascinating.'

'I'm quite glad to be shot of it all.'

Casper nodded. 'I read the *Vogue* piece. Were you there when that designer killed himself?'

'Yes. It was awful. Happened right after the collection. I left a week later.'

Casper leant back in his chair while Mrs Warmbath came round with the vegetables. 'But why? From all accounts you had yourself a top-notch job.'

'All good things come to an end. You should know that,' she said drily. The truth was she'd broken the oldest rule in the book and slept with the boss.

'Gravy, miss?'

'No thanks.'

'This boss of yours. The American. What's his name?'

'Roe Lewis.'

'He sounds like quite a character.'

'Never a dull moment when that man was around,' said Bea enigmatically.

Casper was thinking. 'You know,' he said, 'this would make a fantastic book. You've got all the ingredients: Paris fashion house rescued by American entrepreneur; designer who kills himself when his homosexuality is discovered; top model who mysteriously leaves the company. Then a take-over bid and I'm sure that's not half of it.'

'Start everyone, before it gets cold!'

Bea, who had been listening, poured thick, creamy bread sauce over her turkey. 'Sounds like Jackie Collins could have some competition!'

'And why not? I think Kate's experiences at Vaubelle could make a best-seller.'

'Oh, come on, Casper!' Kate looked at them both in disbelief.

'It's a great idea,' chimed in Justin. 'Then when you've cornered the market and are making pots of loot, you can make an honest man of me.'

Charlie stuck his hand in his mouth and blew loudly against it.

'That will do, Charlie!' warned Lady Parker.

'But I have absolutely no writing experience!'

'Yes, you have,' Bea gushed. 'What about all those poems and the school prize you won for English? You write brilliant letters. I've kept them all.'

Kate laughed. 'Not quite the credentials for writing a book.'

'It's more than most authors have,' said Casper pragmatically.

'Just make sure there's plenty of sex,' said Justin, feigning bashfulness as he raised his napkin over his face so that only his eyes showed. 'I'll help you research.'

Lady Parker, who was listening, said, 'As I keep telling Bea, beautiful as you girls are, modelling can't go on for ever. This could be your second career.'

'You wouldn't have to make anything up. It's all there.'

'But that would mean all sorts of libel suits, surely?' Mont pointed out.

'Not if it was fictionalised,' argued Casper. 'Change the names and appearances etc. Nothing to it.'

'Enough!' giggled Kate. 'I'm really quite happy modelling.'

'Up to you. But take my card in case you change your mind.'

Mrs Warmbath came in to clear the main plates and while they waited for the Christmas pudding they all changed places, pulled crackers and laughed at the dreadful jokes.

471

Charlie put on a purple hat and terrified Fiona by dropping a plastic spider in her wine glass. Then she pulled a cracker with Mont and won a mini-paintbox. Basil had managed to sneak in and was running around the room chasing cracker debris. Lord Parker sat meditatively drawing lines on the tablecloth with his fork. Mont started talking about fox-hunting to Kate, insisting that there was nothing cruel about such a thoroughly English sport. Kate, still thinking about Roe, agreed because to say anything else would have been a waste of breath, and quickly turned the conversation to a play she had seen in London. In no time at all they were back to fox-hunting, and remained there for the next fifteen minutes.

Rescue appeared in the shape of Mrs Warmbath, who returned with the flaming pudding, to gasps of approval.

'Scuse me, madam, there's an overseas call for Miss Kate.'

'Why don't you take it in the library, dear? You'll have more privacy there,' suggested Lady Parker as Kate sprang up.

'Thank you, Warmbath,' said Lord Parker, getting up slowly and coughing again. 'Will you all excuse me. I've some papers to go through in my study.'

Bea watched her father limp from the room. He was a good man, in her heart she knew that, but weak, a shadow of the man her mother had once fallen in love with. Not once had she ever seen him stand up to her mother or make an important decision. Jack, however, and her stomach turned to liquid just thinking about him, represented everything she ever wanted in a man and more. They had so much in common. Was he missing her? Lorna was a fool not to see what she had in Jack. Had she been mad to give him up? Was she destined to pine the rest of her life for a man she couldn't have? She scoured the sporting pages every day, hungry for crumbs of information about him. Last thing she'd heard he was playing in Florida. The only thing that had cheered her up was that he'd gone without Lorna.

Mrs Warmbath, making her way round the debris of nuts, crackers and wine with the pudding, stopped at Fiona.

'Do you have any organic fruit?'

'We've got some muesli, miss.'

As Kate returned to the dining-room she bumped into Bea on her way back from the loo.

'Well, was it him?' Bea asked eagerly.

'Who, Roe?'

Bea raised an eyebrow.

'Well, that was a colossal Freudian slip. I actually meant the Australian. Remember? The man of your dreams?'

She linked an arm into Kate's and about-turned her in the opposite direction, back to the library.

'Come on. Let's sneak off for a quiet glass of champers. You can tell me all about it. Sounds like, yet again, you're in need of my superior insight on the male sex! Which reminds me, did I ever tell you about the time I got stuck in a skiing lift with Yehudi Bareyar? Russian ballet dancers have got the most incredible muscle control!'

26

'We regret the late arrival of flight BA 219. Passengers will disembark at gate 14,' intoned a robotic voice. 'British Airways apologises for any inconvenience this delay might have caused.'

About bloody time! Kate had been waiting at Heathrow for three and a half hours and her nerves were in shreds. To relieve the boredom she had flicked through some airport novels and magazines on display (she found herself in two of them), consumed three cups of tea – the kind that put holes in your stomach – a Danish pastry, a bag of Maltesers and a packet of Opal Fruits.

She felt fat.

'Careful!' she snapped, as an Arab woman almost ran into her with a trolley.

Skander had called at three in the morning while his plane had stopped to refuel at Bangkok. It was a terrible line and she could hardly make out what he was saying. Because she was still only half-awake, Kate had suggested meeting him – Sophie, away in France, had lent her the BMW. He started to say something else, but then they got cut off. She had spent the rest of the night dreaming of trapped elephants and being on a navy-blue airplane which Sophie and Jean-François were trying to land in Sloane Square.

She should never have got out of bed! The weather was predictably atrocious; a bad-tempered hailstorm hurling itself at the windows like uncooked rice accompanied by a distant, ominous rumbling. Somehow during the night Ruskin, who was staying at her flat, had got hold of Kate's new Russell and Bromley shoes, now mangled and unrecognisable, then woke Kate up by being sick on the bedroom floor. Lunch with Bea carried through into tea after she admitted being in love with a married man, further complicated by the fact that he was a celebrity with two young children. Going to the loo (and they say bad things come in threes), Kate found that she'd started her period. Depressed, she had set off early in Sophie's BMW, hoping to avoid the rush hour. She had gnawing cramps and a blinding headache.

A small Chinese lady with bow legs, an orange mouth and an Air-Lingus travel bag pushed in front of her for a better view of the arrival gate. What was it about airports that always depressed and fatigued you, and gave you instant jet-lag! She was getting horribly itchy feet. Wouldn't it have been better to have met for dinner when Skander had had a chance to catch up on some sleep? It might turn out to be an awful anti-climax. Situations like this happened all the time: meeting someone, a mutual attraction which involved a few drinks, a couple of dates. Then they got keen and suddenly the magic was gone; your attention homed in on their irritating eating habits, the embarrassing amount of time they spent over the restaurant bill, the ready compliments they paid to every woman but you, the fact that they wore grey shoes, or even worse plastic shoes. And suddenly you wondered what you ever saw in them. Was it possible she had gone off Skander? No. That was unfair. How much could someone change in a month? He won't have grown an extra head or put on three stone. Nor was it likely he'd be frothing at the mouth when he greeted her. But for some reason these grotesque images stayed in her mind so that when the arrival gates opened half of her expected to see a monster.

She had to wait five more minutes before he emerged. For a monster Skander was looking remarkably normal, wearing faded jeans and a large shoulder bag strapped across one shoulder. In fact she had to admit he looked wonderful. His weathered, handsome face was tanned to a warm olive, his hair bleached from the sun. The navy-blue eyes seemed even more brilliant against their dark backdrop. He certainly didn't give the impression of someone who'd spent the last twenty-four hours on a plane. Nor were there any tell-tale injury signs. Immediately every other passenger looked a little ill-kempt, a little slouched, a little diminished. She waved awkwardly, but it hadn't been necessary. He'd already spotted her.

They didn't get off to a good start. One of Skander's cases holding half his photographic equipment failed to turn up and they had to hang around filling out complicated forms at customs. Having sorted that out, Kate had to empty the contents of her bag on to the floor to find her parking ticket; novel, Lilets, uncashed cheques, tissues (used), pill box, keys, the morning's post, an incriminating chocolate bar, but alas, no ticket. To make matters worse she couldn't remember which floor she'd left the car on. They spent a further twenty minutes searching for it, which did nothing to improve Skander's mood.

'Sorry,' she mumbled for the third time when they drew a blank on level four. 'It must be the next one down.'

They almost missed it, squeezed between a dark-blue Range Rover and a filthy transit van with an 'If you've come this close then show us yer tits' sticker on the back.

'Here, let me,' said Skander, taking the keys.

At the ticket office they had to pay the twenty-four-hour rate to get out. Saying nothing, Skander found a Miles Davis tape which he slipped into the cassette player and put the heating on full blast. In an attempt to quell her nerves, Kate told him about Christmas with the Parkers. Skander sat lazily beside her, driving with one hand on the wheel. When she thought she couldn't bear the tension any longer, he suddenly reached across and folded her hand in his.

'You look gorgeous. I've missed you.'

She almost said thank you, she was so relieved. Only then did she realise how afraid she'd been that he might be the one to get cold feet. She brought his left hand up to her mouth, which bore the mark of a recent burn and kissed it.

'Poor hand,' she murmured tenderly.

In the dark interior of the car they exchanged smiles.

The earlier heavy rain had dwindled to a fine, persistent drizzle. Two juggernauts swept past in the opposite lane, their bright headlights intrusive. Kate lowered the back of her seat and studied Skander through the safe gloom of the car. Dylan and Beth, back from a packed trip to Prague and Budapest, had sent their love and a birthday gift stored in Skander's bag. Work at Coochin was still going on and they'd put in a massive insurance claim – Matthew had been enormously generous both with his time and men, who were busy erecting new fences. Kate wasn't really listening. She was too busy gazing at the floppy blond hair, the navy eyes, animated and warm as he talked about his cherished home. His voice, a gentle hum, carried through her body affecting her like wine. Why had it taken her this long to notice how attractive he was? As she relaxed her eyelids grew heavy. At last the pills were beginning to take effect. She lay down across his lap using his jacket to cushion the sharp edges of the hand brake, her head turned upwards so that she could watch him through half-closed lids. Bunching together a few strands of red hair Skander brushed her forehead and nose with it like a paintbrush. It tickled.

Some time later, when she'd slept a while, Kate lifted her head and squinted out at the string of red tail-lights.

'Where are we? We've been driving ages.'

'Ran into a bit of traffic but it's cleared up now. Go back to sleep, Monkey. We've still a little way.'

She yawned, arching her back, which felt stiff, but at least the pain in her uterus had dwindled to a dull ache. 'Would you like me to drive for a bit?'

'Not with your eyes closed. Feeling better?'

'Mmm,' she yawned again. 'Those pills are strong. Have you really missed me?'

'That's a trick question, surely?'

'Silly! Are we going to your place?'

'Yes. Do you mind? I need to check my machine.'

'Fine by me.'

'Can't say what state it'll be in. I had to leave in such a hurry, and there'll be nothing to eat but we can stop for something on the way if you're hungry.'

'No, not at all. I ate enough at the airport to keep me going a week!' she admitted. 'Have you got much work on?'

'Masses. I'm probably going to have to fly out to Paris next weekend.'

But he'd only just got back. Kate tried to hide her disappointment. 'How long will you be gone?'

'About a week. Do you want to come?'

'Gosh, I'd love to. I'll call Nigel in the morning and check my bookings.'

Another yawn. 'Sorry, there's so much I want to talk to you about but I can't seem to shake this off.'

'There's no rush, little one. Why don't you go back to sleep? I'll wake you when we're there.'

Obediently she lay down in his lap and closed her eyes. The gentle rocking movement of the car soon put her back to sleep. Skander's left hand stroked her hair, tracing the outline of her fine neck and jaw bone, while he kept his eyes firmly on the road. He'd packed so much into the last four weeks that it wasn't until he saw her again that he realised just how much he had missed her.

Tired as he was, he felt the familiar tension descend on him as they approached London. His intense dislike of the city was always exacerbated after a stint back home. He should have stayed on longer. There was so much to do and it didn't seem fair lumbering Dylan and Beth with it all. But he had to get this film under way. He lived for the day he could move out to Australia and concentrate on the things that really mattered to him.

He glanced at the car clock. Almost ten. He'd give his sister a call once they got home and check up on Barrington – the dog loved it on the farm near Bath. It was great walking country and Naomi and the twins spoilt him rotten. Naomi had once threatened to keep Barrington the last time he came back from a six-week trip. Skander glanced down at Kate. Maybe he'd take her down to the farm for a weekend. She'd like it there. Stirring in his lap she gave a little moan. Were the pills wearing off? She'd been sleeping for almost twenty minutes. Funny little thing. His dark, sun-kissed arm seemed almost black against her paleness; she looked so trusting, so childlike with her long, bony stockinged feet up against the passenger door, one hand tucked pillow-like under her head. No trace of the explosive, angry girl who'd spent so much time fighting him. He smiled suddenly, remembering a few lines he'd once learned from *The Taming of the Shrew*:

> . . . you are called plain Kate
> And Bonny Kate, and sometimes Kate the curst;
> But Kate, the prettiest Kate in Christendom,
> Kate of Kate-Hall, my super-dainty Kate,
> For dainties are all Kates, and therefore, Kate,
> Take this of me, Kate of my consolation.

Why did she stir such feelings of protectiveness within him? God knows she wasn't easy – all those years of carefully laid walls to keep out men. He felt a sudden, powerful urge to break them down, one by one, because having glimpsed what was underneath, he felt the rewards would be great. Kate was capable of great courage and kindness. But her trust in him was so tenuous, the slightest thing could make her bolt.

Careful not to wake her, he gently spread one huge hand over her stomach and kept it pressed there like a hot water bottle.

Jack escaped the noisy celebrations of Olivia's surprise birthday party and slipped upstairs to the bedroom. Christ! If he heard one more word about how 'marvellously wee Angus swings his club' and 'what a natural putter young Jimmy is' and 'would it be possible to get that handsome Nick Faldo's autograph for my young Ian?' Young Ian, my foot! For some extraordinary reason people seemed to think that because you'd niched yourself a reasonably successful sporting career in golf you wanted to spend your whole time discussing the game. Thank God for Yarnton Miller. At least he'd had someone sane to talk to. Why did Lorna bother wasting her energies on such time-wasters? He walked over to the bay window and rested his head on the glass pane, which was straining against the harsh westerly wind. No, that wasn't fair. He knew exactly why she bothered. Lorna was making an effort with their marriage but the same couldn't be said for him.

Last week, coming home from an exhausting second round

480

against Fred Couples, he had been anything but pleased to find their bedroom transformed into a church – Lorna had lit hundreds of candles to create a romantic atmosphere in which, no doubt, she had hoped to seduce him. The whole thing had been completely over the top and it was all he could do to get his feet up, let alone anything else, he was so whacked, but even to his own ears his excuses had sounded lame and tinny. The truth was the more Lorna clung to him the further she pushed him away. If only he could snap out of these moods. He'd become so withdrawn and that wasn't like him. It affected the children.

He'd hoped the break from home while he was in America might improve things. Indeed, by the time Lorna and the kids had flown out and joined him for the Christmas week he was feeling relaxed and fit. Lorna had always loved Christmas and had pulled out all the stops to make this one the best ever. She succeeded. On Christmas morning they'd made love for the first time in weeks and for a while things were good again.

A door banged somewhere along the corridor followed by running and excited young screams.

'Give it back! It's mine. It's mine!'

'Mummy said we should share it.'

The shrieks receded. Jack glanced at a pile of mostly golf magazines on a nearby table. Any editorial that was about him had been carefully earmarked. Frustrated but reluctant to rejoin the party downstairs, Jack idly flicked through a copy of *Woman's Journal*, Christmas issue. Lorna had circled a piece about health farms which sounded tortuous. Why on earth would anyone pay good money to go on a Third World diet? Come to think of it, hadn't Lorna mentioned something about going to Champneys this month? On the next page was an article with the caption 'The Golfing Habit'. It seemed as if that had been done months ago, when in fact it was only last September when the building work was still going on and the house had been in chaos. There were shots of Jack playing throughout his career, one with the family, and a sweet one of Olivia showing off a new dress Rachel had made for her. Nice journalist, he thought, remembering the prettty but intensely shy woman who'd come to interview him. What she'd written was certainly very complimentary, heralding him as the best golfer in Britain today.

Skimming through the rest of the magazine Jack almost missed the photographs highlighting the fashion tour. His eyes focused on a flawless beauty caught smiling in a half-turn. He gazed at the picture, studying the girl's face as if he wanted to memorise every tiny pore.

'Jack? Jack, darling!' yelled Lorna. 'Are you upstairs? Livi's going to open her presents.'

'I'll be right down.'

Tucking the magazine into the bottom of his dressing-table drawer, Jack left the room and made his way downstairs, back to his wife and party guests, images of Bea Parker burning in his mind.

'Oh, not again!'

Rachel bit down on her bottom lip to curb her anger. It wasn't fair to take it out on Brigette.

'When did she say she would be back?'

'Some time this afternoon. I'm sorry I can't be more specific.'

'This is ridiculous! That's the third time this week she's let us down. How are we supposed to make a collection with no model?'

'Shall I call her home?' suggested Brigette.

'No. Try Glamour Agency and see if they can get us a model to fit for today. And put an option on her for the rest of the week. I'll speak to Mr Lewis about this later.'

Leonora Vaubelle had stepped into Kate's position as house model three weeks ago and was already proving unreliable. Unless she had an inkling of Roe being around (and even then she was late), she made absolutely no effort with her appearance, turning up with unwashed hair and alcohol-induced bags under her eyes. Rachel could see why he'd brought her in – the publicity had been marvellous – but Leonora was allowed to get away with murder and Rachel, trying to find inspiration for her new collection, felt her patience was being stretched to the limit.

Lately she always felt tired. The very success of her last

two collections put tremendous pressure on her to come up with a third. She'd lost her inspiration. Oh, it wasn't just Leonora, though the girl was an absolute pain. Other things bothered her: Claude's suicide, Kate's leaving so abruptly and Roe's cagey explanation, the continuing rumours that Carl Elliot was withdrawing his support from the company. Rachel sensed that a lot was going on behind her back and it made her uneasy. Another mainstream fashion house had recently approached her, offering a higher salary and additional perks, but Rachel had turned them down. In the end designing wasn't about money. At least not to her. She believed in Vaubelle, believed in the integrity of her job and, yes, a loyalty to Roe, who despite the spiteful things that were being said by more senior staff had only been good and kind to her. Then there was the recent success of the company. It made her feel incredibly proud to know that part of it was because of her work. And she wasn't about to give it up. Whatever! She liked to think it was one of the things she had in common with her father. Stubbornness!

Her eyes dropped to the pad she had been working on. The sketch of a man's face was rough but instantly recognisable. Toby! She had a whole collection of them in her drawer. Glumly she looked at the veins of rain against the window. Oh Toby! All those promises you made. Were they just lies? She had tried so hard to blot him out. She kept on telling herself she didn't care. Her work, after all, was her life. And yet she'd kept the love-bird (how could she not?). It sang to her at breakfast and kept her awake at night, its wings fluttering against the side of the cage, calling to her through the dark like a whisper. In a bedroom drawer was a blurred picture of Toby and Tanya taken by *Vogue* shortly after their engagement party: Tanya the actress, soon to be the mother of Toby's child, in a flattering blue and white halter-neck dress and matching shoes which showed off her fine ankles; her own chubby ones couldn't compare. It wasn't a very good shot of Toby, his eyes were closed, but it was the only one she had and for some perverse reason Rachel hadn't cut Tanya out. On paper, Tanya remained a gleaming, radiant, enviable animal unsuitable for these winter days.

Richard put down the phone. 'Regina's on her way over. We've got her all week if we need her.'

'Thank goodness!' Rachel snapped out of her mood and rolled up her sleeves. 'Well then, I suggest we get on. Let's have a look at that silk dress Colette's been working on.'

Roe had put up everything he owned as collateral to secure the loan for Leonora's stake in the company. The whole thing had been done through a broker under a bogus name, to cover up his identity – he was afraid that if Carl found out he might try and stop him. Having completed the final negotiations (the exchange had gone through last Tuesday), Roe had been trying to find a way of appropriating Carl's remaining twenty-one per cent, which along with Leonora's twenty-four per cent would mean he'd just need a further six per cent to make him controller of Vaubelle. And Roe knew that, sooner or later, Sebastian would sell. According to Leo it was just a matter of weeks before Carl put his shares on the open market – and still no word from the great man himself.

These were frustrating times for Roe. He still hadn't managed to find out the identity of Carl's mystery purchaser and now he was having a hassle with the banks. No sooner had one carefully laid deal been agreed than it fell through. Roe was baffled. Who was trying to sabotage his takeover? It had to be someone with inside information. Who else could move so fast? Roe had racked his brains trying to work it out but he couldn't get anything out of the banks. One of the first things he'd done was to check out Sebastian, but he didn't have the necessary liquid assets.

Nicole stuck her head round the door, 'Mademoiselle Vaubelle's on the phone.'

'I'll have to call her back. Take a message, will you?'

'She was very insistent she speaks to you.'

Roe took a deep breath and picked up the phone. 'Hi.'

'I know. It's not a good time because you're up to your ears in some high-powered business meeting. Just didn't want you to forget Saturday.'

Saturday? What the hell was happening Saturday?

'Leonora, aren't you supposed to be working?' he said, stalling for time.

'I had a doctor's appointment – don't worry. Rachel got a replacement.'

That was the third time this week. Roe glanced at his week-in-a-day diary: Saturday 2.30 p.m. Meeting with Leo Schofield – check figures.

'We're having dinner with your mother?'

'There, you see!' she said triumphantly. 'I knew you'd forgotten! You're supposed to be taking me to the *Vogue* do. Everyone's going.'

'Sweetheart, I've a company to run. I can't afford the time.'

'But you promised!' she whined. 'You spend far too much time at your desk, Roe. You're in danger of becoming boring.'

'Well, we wouldn't want that, would we?' he said drily. 'What time should we be there?'

Appeased, Leonora's voice softened, 'Seven. But we can always turn up late.'

'Seven's fine, but I'll have to slip off early.'

'OK. Can you stop over tonight?'

'I'm meeting my lawyers at six. Could go on until late.'

'That's OK. I'll wait up for you.'

God, the woman was pushy! But until he had the company in the bag he couldn't afford to get her back up, not when he was so close – she'd run straight to big brother Sebastian and tell him who she'd sold her shares to. If servicing her in bed meant keeping her happy (and her mouth shut), he'd do it.

Sebastian Vaubelle shut the door to his office and sat down in a cold rage. He didn't know who to be more angry with, his sister for betraying the family or that snake Roe Lewis for corrupting her – he had absolutely no doubt Roe had been using his sister from the moment he'd arrived. Now, after this telephone call, his suspicions had been confirmed; Leonora had sold out and the silly bitch hadn't even had the guts to tell him.

Right from the start, Sebastian believed he would eventually win back his father's company – inheriting half his father's shares had done a lot to raise his hopes – but today that hope had been irrevocably squashed with one phone call. At first he'd been angry with the man who told him, had accused him of being no better than Roe. No one was to be trusted. He'd learnt that the hard way. Now, having had time to think it through, he thought perhaps he had hung up a little hastily. The future of Vaubelle was out of his grasp but within Roe's, which was dangerous. Sebastian had been reckless with his money and debts were starting to mount up. If Carl Elliot really had sold thirty per cent of Vaubelle and was thinking of selling the rest, he might help Sebastian stop Roe. But at what personal cost? And who was to say someone else would be any better than Roe? Perhaps he should get out? Accept that he'd been beaten. Certainly, staying on to endure any more of Lewis's dictatorial authority was out of the question. He could go and live abroad for a while, maybe try the States – he liked American girls. Good clean, strong bodies. French-women were so unhygienic – all that superfluous body hair.

Sebastian drew a large circle round the man's number in front of him. Five o'clock in London. He'd leave it ten more minutes then call him back. After all, one informal meeting wouldn't commit him to anything. He began formulating a plan, which, the more he thought about, the more he liked. After buzzing his secretary to ask for some coffee he opened the top drawer of his desk and pulled out his black pill box. The day, he decided as he leaned back in his chair and threaded his hands together at the back of his neck, was turning out to be rather a good one.

Number 8 Blenheim Crescent had been given a lick of paint since last spring and was now a smart Pompeiian red. It had been easy to find but, because there were no free spaces, Jack had parked fifteen yards down the road. He told a jubilant Olivia to wait for him in the car then walked back to the house. He was just checking the names under the bell when someone from the basement shouted.

'Can I help you, love?'

The scratchy voice belonged to a beefy woman whose kind, rosy face was besieged with curlers. She was support-ing an angry-looking tabby cat under one arm.

'I'm looking for Bea Parker.'

'Ah, she's on the top floor. Hardly ever there though. I'm forever having to let the gas and electricity men in to read the meter. Press the bell that says Turner. Don't ask me why but they never bothered to change the name.' They? thought Jack as the cat hissed at him. That unsettled him.

'Thank you.' He rang the bell then glanced back at the Land Rover, waving reassuringly to his daughter. Seconds later the door was opened by a very tall, skinny man wearing torn jeans and a grubby white shirt with the sleeves rolled up. Jack's heart sank. For despite his slightly ravaged appearance the man was exceedingly good-looking.

'Yes?' he said unhelpfully.

'I was hoping to speak to Bea.'

'She's not here.' The man looked annoyed.

'Are you expecting her back soon?'

'I bloody well hope so. She borrowed my car this morning and promised to be back by twelve.'

Both men glanced at their watches. It was one thirty.

'Sorry. I'm being very rude. We had a bit of a wild night and both overslept.'

Jack's heart sank even further. What had he expected?

'Do you want to leave her a message?'

'No. It was just one of those spur of the moment things. I'll give her a call later in the week.'

The young man watched him go back to the car, wondering why the man's face seemed so familiar. Further down the road a little girl stuck her head out of a car window.

'Is she coming, Daddy?'

'She wasn't home, darling. You'll just have to make do with me.'

Jack was about to get in when there was a terrific noise of a car exploding down the street. He turned just in time to see a silver Golf GTI come to a screaming halt outside the house. A leggy blonde wearing outrageously bright, floral-printed leggings, a man's blazer and a suspiciously familiar denim shirt stepped out of the car. Olivia let out a shriek of excitement.

'It's Bea! It's Bea!'

'Where the bloody hell have you been?' yelled the young

487

man, padding out to the car in his bare feet. 'You were supposed to be back over an hour ago!'

Bea kissed him and shoved the car keys into the front pocket of his jeans.

'Calm down, darling. The client had me try on half his collection, then insisted on taking loads of polaroids. As it's ninety per cent sure I'll get the job I filled your car up with petrol. Wasn't that nice of me? So stop scowling or you'll spoil your beauty and Georgie won't want to see you any more.'

The man looked appeased. 'You have a visitor.'

'How nice, who?'

He gestured towards Jack standing by the Land Rover. Even without her contact lenses, Bea recognised him instantly. Her knees buckled. Jack! Here in the flesh! She couldn't believe it!

'I should have called first but it seemed easier to drop in,' Jack said, walking towards her cautiously.

'I'm so glad you did.'

'Right. I'm off. I'll leave you two to it,' said the young man, racing back to the flat for a pair of shoes. 'Thanks for the petrol, Sis.'

'That's your brother?'

'Hard to believe, I know. Justin's the heart-throb of Holland Park and, as you can see, takes his role very seriously. I can't believe you're here.'

Goodness, he looked wonderful!

'I should have come sooner. Have you any plans for this afternoon?'

'Not now you're here.'

She'd have cancelled lunch with Harrison Ford.

'Friends have loaned us their flat for the night, I'm practising in East Sussex and wondered if you wanted to join us?' He dropped his voice, 'Lorna's away so there's just Olivia and me. She's waiting in the car.'

Olivia's little face was pressed up against the rear window watching them anxiously. Bea immediately rushed over to greet her.

'What are you doing hiding in the car? Come and hug me immediately, you little duck.' Olivia scrambled out and threw

488

her arms around Bea's tiny waist. It gave Bea a chance to regain her composure. 'I believe you and I have a date on the golf course,' she said to the small blonde head, stretched up to gaze at her.

'We've got a picnic and everything!' Olivia said excitedly. 'And then we're going to the cinema to see *Lethal Weapon Three*. Daddy said I could have an ice-cream. Please say you'll come. I'm sure he'll let you have an ice-cream too.'

Bea caught Jack's eye.

'Well, I'm not going to pass up an opportunity to ogle Mel Gibson. Have I got time to grab some things?'

Jack grinned. 'We'll wait for you in the car.'

They got back to the borrowed Chelsea flat at seven thirty. After Mel Gibson, two chocolate ice-creams, a full cream tea and several hours racing round the golf course in a fever of excitement, Olivia had fallen into a deep slumber in the back of the car. They had put her to bed in the spare room and when they were certain she was asleep they tip-toed back along the hall. Alone for the first time that day, they stood in the warmth of the kitchen and gazed at one another.

'I thought I'd never see you again,' said Jack, dazzled by the oceanic blue eyes. He pulled her into his arms, pushing her hair back from her forehead. 'When Lorna said she was going away and I got offered this tournament, I only accepted because it meant I had a chance to see you. I was afraid that if I phoned I'd get your answer machine again.'

'Oh Jack,' mumbled Bea, her voice breaking, 'I really missed you. Nobody warned me that loving someone could hurt so much!' She buried her face in his sweater, the same moth-eaten sweater he'd worn the first day they had met.

'Hang on a minute,' Jack said, pulling her away from him so that he could see her expression. 'Did you just say you loved me?'

Bea looked up at him, her eyes shining. 'Totally and utterly. I'm a lost cause.'

'It's funny,' he said later, when they were wrapped up together in bed, 'I can't remember when I first started to love you. It hit me today but I think you had me snared the day

489

you so politely asked me to fuck off out of Toby Wilmot-Smith's bathroom.'

Bea blushed scarlet. 'Don't remind me! That was the most embarrassing moment of my life!'

For a moment they lay in silence, then Bea asked the question neither of them had dared ask.

'Jack. What are we going to do?'

'What we should have done weeks ago. You were wrong, you know, when you said that I'd regret walking out on Lorna. It's something I should have done a long time ago. I don't love her. At least, not any more.' He raised a hand to Bea's mouth. 'No darling, wait. Hear me out. I've had a lot of time to think, taken a really good honest look at my life and in the end I kept arriving at the same conclusion; that I can't live without you. Even if it means risking everything I've got, I only know I've got to keep you in my life.'

'She'll do everything she can to keep the children.'

'Let her. Views on infidelity have changed a great deal. Anyhow, she can't stop me from seeing them. I've been a bloody good father. Lorna will come round in the end.'

'Do the kids know?' Bea's voice trembled with emotion.

'They're not stupid. Olivia's school work is beginning to suffer and Fergus has started wetting the bed again.' He ran an absent-minded finger along Bea's arm. 'Lorna's out most of the time. She's afraid of growing old and thinks to avoid it by living in the fast lane. But it catches up with us all in the end.'

Bea pulled herself up on to one elbow and looked Jack in the eye.

'Before this goes any further, there's something I've got to tell you.'

'You've already got a string of husbands around the globe. Okay, sorry. I'm listening.' His finger had become a hand and was massaging the back of her neck.

Without attempting to embellish the facts Bea told him about John and her pregnancy, about the miscarriage and how she could no longer have children. She searched his face anxiously for signs of disappointment but it showed only love and compassion.

490

'You have had a rough time, haven't you, my brave darling. Well, you're about to inherit my two. Lorna can't keep them with her the whole time. There'll be plenty of school holidays we'll get to have them for. And we could always adopt. Have you thought about that?' Bea put a finger on his mouth, her eyes full of love. She had her answer.

'No more talk. Not now. I want to make the most of us being alone, before I hand you back to your public.'

'Everything I do from here on will be to keep us together.'

For the sixth time that evening, they made love. It was Jack's record.

27

Both girls, for reasons of their own, had worried about Tuesday's get together but in fact dinner with Jack and Skander had gone rather well. It had been Bea's idea. For three weeks she and Jack had kept a low profile, avoiding friends and family until some of the furore from the press had died down, but she was dying to talk to someone. Impulsively she had rung Kate and asked them round to their new flat, south of the river in Barnes, with a spectacular view.

'It's just until things are a bit more organised,' she had said breathlessly. 'I raided the Conran shop today – hordes of tourists and I had my new umbrella pinched but at least we'll have four chairs to sit on. Just wait till you see the wonderful fireplace! We've used it every night. Come about eight and for God's sake don't dress up, Kate. We'll be in jeans.'

They were in the kitchen doing the washing up, their empty wine glasses parked on the windowsill. The men had offered (which earned them both Brownie points) but it was a rare chance for the girls to be alone. Kate's hands were submerged in warm soapy water, while Bea dried. They could hear animated male conversation next door.

'What a difference!'

'What?' asked Kate, handing Bea a plate.

'Well, he's so . . . I don't know, right for you. I wasn't sure what to expect. You've been so cagey about him all this time. But I really like him and the way he is with you.'

Kate ran more hot water, picking up Skander's voice then more laughter. She wondered what they were talking about.

'I like your Jack too.'

'We're thinking of going away. Just until things have died down a bit.'

'All this must be hard for you.'

'The press bit is. I honestly don't know how Jack deals with it all so calmly. Most of what they write are lies. Then in yesterday's tabloids they dug up all the dirt about Lorna's affair with Jack's best friend. But what can you do? I still worry about how it will affect his children – they're awfully young. But being with Jack feels so completely right. Sometimes, at night, lying next to him I watch him while he sleeps and wonder how I managed to get this far without having him in my life.'

Bea opened a cupboard door and stacked the clean plates inside.

'Have you told your parents yet?'

'Mum's been wonderful about the whole thing and she won't let on how much a strain it's been coping with Daddy.'

'How is he now?'

'Getting better by the day. As heart attacks go it was a pretty mild one, but he's going to have to give up the booze and cigars. Mum'll make sure of that.'

'Your mother is amazing! Is she worried about Jack being so much older than you?'

'Don't think so. She obviously twigged something was going on at Christmas. I was so miserable. We all spent last weekend together and I told her then. Justin didn't bat an eyelid but Mum thought we should wait and tell Daddy when he's a bit stronger.'

The tea towel Bea was using was sodden so she draped it over the radiator and pulled out a clean one from a drawer.

'So, when are you going to move in with Skander?'

A champagne cork popped in the other room.

'It's a bit early to think about that,' said Kate cheerfully. 'He's only been back a month.'

'Oh, Kate! Cautious to the end! What are we going to do with you?'

'I just don't want to make the same mistake twice.'

'You won't,' Bea said confidently.

494

'Did I mention that Casper called again? He's still very keen on doing this book.'

'Well, it's a great idea. What did you say?'

'Told him I'd think about it. D'you want some more wine?'

'Yes please. Just don't think about it too much. You have a knack for talking yourself out of anything that has a hint of risk.'

Jack poked his head around the door. 'What's so exciting about a bowl of dishwater that you have to spend all night in here with it?'

'We're coming, darling, just drying the last plate.'

They exchanged secret smiles.

'Well, we're about to embark on a backgammon tournament. I said I'd come and ask if you wanted to join in but Skander said neither of you were competitive enough. Particularly you, Kate.' Jack's mouth curled, impudently.

'Oh, did he indeed?' she said, pulling off the yellow gloves with determination. 'Well, tell him from me we'll be right there!'

It seemed as if the whole world had turned up to celebrate *Vogue*. A bevy of stars, fashion editors, supermodels and designers had come to pay homage to the queen of magazines, which had put on the lavish party in Paris in gratitude for the millions of advertising dollars which kept the magazine alive.

There were many familiar faces, some Kate hadn't seen in six months – had it been that long already since she'd left Vaubelle? Natalie Kainz, her pregnancy now well into its seventh month, was at the door welcoming everyone. She showered Skander with rapturous kisses. Kate thought she was going to be ignored but Natalie caught her arm as she passed.

'You are a lucky girl. If I had wanted to break my vows for anyone it would 'ave been for him. *Bonne chance.*'

Almost immediately they ran into Carey and Pigeon, still very much a couple. A glowing Cassy Peck back from a three-month honeymoon, was clutching Jean-François's hand, who looked beside himself with pride. With them was

Neil Hunter, just returned from a trip to Morocco and looking glorious and golden in a Gaultier waistcoat.

Kate very nearly hadn't come. Paris didn't evoke good memories but somehow being with Skander changed all that. He'd been working really hard with the new production and, apart from the dinner at Bea's, this was their first proper night out. He had booked them into the intimate Lancaster Hotel in the rue de Berri, which had small but charming rooms. Although he'd had to spend most of the day caught up in meetings, he had taken time off to have a leisurely lunch with her. Now, lulled by her first glass of champagne and Skander's hand encircling her waist, she was starting to enjoy herself.

The place was crawling with beautiful people. On a raised platform a girl modelled an Yves Saint Laurent gown – it was being raffled to raise money for cancer research. Jean-François bought a block of ten tickets, each costing 1,000 francs, and gave them to Cassy. A brunette, looking somewhat ravaged in an obscenely-tight yellow sequin dress and a black satin bow tied round her neck, rushed over to Neil.

'Neil, darling!' she shrieked, waving her glass of champagne. 'You didn't call me last night, you wicked creature.'

'Filming went on tortuously long. I didn't get to bed until four.'

'I haven't been to bed at all,' said the girl dramatically.

'Could have fooled me,' muttered Skander, spotting an angry love bite the ribbon was obviously supposed to hide. He got nabbed by a stills photographer hoping to break into commercials and was persuaded to join the man at his table.

'Kate, darling. A quick word in your ear.' Neil drew her to one side. 'I wouldn't normally ask. But Grant and I have just declared World War Three and I was wondering if you could put me up when I get to London? Just for the few nights until I get myself sorted.'

'Yes, of course. You two aren't splitting up?'

'Your guess is as good as mine. We adore each other but we just can't live together. By the way,' he said, nodding towards Skander, 'smart move there. Changed your tune a bit since Tuscany, haven't you?'

'Yes,' her voice unconsciously softening, 'I suppose I have.' Somebody turned up the music. Hot House Flowers sang *I can see clearly now,* and suddenly everyone got up to dance.

'Come on, Neil.'

'Okay, but don't go getting any ideas.'

Giggling, she grabbed his arm. What Neil lacked in skill he made up for in enthusiasm. Cutting a sinister look near by was a couple dancing in dark glasses. Neil mimicked the woman's rigid, jerky movements so accurately he soon had Kate sobbing with laughter. Others near by joined in. Always happiest in the limelight, Neil needed no further encouragement.

'You're awful!' said Kate wiping away tears of mirth. 'Look, they've gone to sit down. You should be locked up.'

'Why is it that women are always trying to get me into closets, while men keep taking me out of them? Oh, good. I requested this song.'

Kate stiffened. She stared out through the people, the smoke, her eyes glued to a figure standing by the bar. It couldn't be! Somehow she had expected his looks to have deteriorated over the months, as his image had gradually faded from her mind. But he looked so fit and radiant, as if he'd just come back from a month in Saint Tropez.

Instinctively, it seemed, Roe glanced in her direction and their eyes locked. Music, people, noise dissolved. All she could hear was a roar in her pulse. He bent to whisper something in his blonde companion's ear and then, horror of horrors, started walking towards her. Kate's heart stopped. Don't, please, her eyes implored. She simply wasn't prepared for this. Glancing around anxiously for Skander she saw him trapped on a nearby sofa between two young women deep in conversation.

'Can I butt in?'

'You may.' Neil good-naturedly let her go and suddenly she was back at Castelle's, dancing in Roe's arms for the first time.

'Like old times,' he said, matching her thoughts.

'But I'm older and wiser now.' She was determined to be

light and witty. 'I got the earrings by the way.'

'I wondered if you had. I've missed seeing you.'

Kate tried not to appear fazed. 'I haven't been that hard to track down.'

'Look, I'm going to be in London next week. Can we have dinner?'

'No.'

'Why not?'

'Because I'm busy.'

'I'm talking about dinner, nothing more sinister. Or don't you trust me?'

Tell me who I see when I look in your eyes. Is that you-hoo baby, or just a brilliant disguise, sang Bruce.

'You have an appalling track record.'

'I know. It's destroying my life. How about lunch then? That's nice and safe.'

'You've stayed away this long, why spoil things?'

'I need to see you, Kat. What about Tuesday?'

He was too close. She couldn't think straight.

'No, not Tuesday. I'm working that day.'

Skander was getting up from his table. Oh, God, they mustn't meet.

In a panic she said, 'All right. Wednesday. Make it Wednesday.'

'I'm staying at the Hyde Park. I'll meet you in the lobby at one.'

'I must go.'

'Wear the emeralds,' were his parting words.

'Why is it everyone I meet wants to get into television!' Skander smiled ruefully. 'Hold on, mate, I'll have one of those,' he said, grabbing a drink from a passing tray. 'Have I told you how lovely you look tonight?'

'Twice. But you still haven't danced with me.'

'I couldn't get near enough to ask.'

Right on cue, Bruce slipped into a ballad.

'Well, now's your chance.' Smiling, Kate pulled Skander on to the dance floor keeping a watchful eye on Roe back at the bar.

He hadn't changed. Still the same dynamic, irresistible

Roe! Everything about him so familiar yet strange. The way he held her, the confident touch of his hand against her arm as if he still owned her. It was madness, but she was consumed by desire to be alone with him again. After all this time. Every nerve in her body screamed with anticipation. How would she survive until Wednesday? She caught Skander looking at her and wondered if he'd read anything in her face, but he just smiled one of those Skander smiles which made her feel guilty.

Back in London the following week, Skander gave Kate a lift on his way to a meeting in the city. Although grumpy because he'd been up all night working on his proposal, he touched her often, on the cheek, the neck, brushing the russet strands of hair from her face. As he dropped her off at Knightsbridge tube, Kate wondered if what she had with him was worth putting in jeopardy? But then she hadn't done anything.

'I'll pick you up at your place about six,' he said, ignoring the furious hooting from a woman in the car behind.

'Bye then.'

Kate stepped out into the freezing cold and, hugging her shoulders with crossed arms, moved quickly towards the station. Her heart was thumping. She had an hour. Just enough time to race back to her flat, shower and change.

She arrived at the Hyde Park Hotel a few minutes late. At reception she was told he was still in his room and that she was to go on up. That threw her. She would have preferred to go straight to the restaurant. Stick to neutral ground. Stomach churning, Kate took the lift to the top floor. Was she mad coming here? Wouldn't it just stir up feelings she'd spent so long burying? But the thought of not seeing him was even worse. She had to talk to him, make him realise what she had been through. Last night and then this morning lying in bed as Skander dressed, she had rehearsed what she would say when they were finally alone.

The door to his room had been left slightly ajar. Composing her face into what she hoped was a cool expression, Kate gave it a hesitant tap.

'Roe . . .?'

As the door swung open a pale-blue Louis XV room came into view. The television was on, the windows were steamed up and lying on the huge king-size bed in a hotel robe was Roe. He was on the phone and waved her in. This wasn't something she had bargained for. She entered, closing the door behind her.

How had it happened? They had been standing by the window talking. It seemed as if they'd been talking for hours.

'Funny, I've often thought about us, about what went wrong, but I'd forgotten how beautiful you are.'

'Roe, why stir up the past? It's over. You didn't want me.'

'I always wanted you. You were one of the few good things in my life.'

Kate averted her head and for almost a minute she gazed out at the black sky. Finally she said, 'I'm happy, Roe.'

'Then you have nothing to fear from me.'

The air instantly crackled with sexual chemistry. She had to look at him then. Compelled. Like a starved animal Kate retraced every line and curve on his face with her eyes. She could turn right now, walk through the door and downstairs and never see him again. No regrets, no stirring up the past, no hurting anyone – least of all herself. She could do it, now!

Roe moved behind her. She couldn't see him but she could feel the heat from his body, close, irresistibly close. He caressed her cheek and let his hand run down the side of her neck, across the curving breast, and down further until he heard the soft agonised moan he'd been waiting for. Taking her hand, he led her to the bed.

She had resisted, sort of, but like a drug addict she was lost the moment Roe touched her. She couldn't remember feeling so abandoned, so uninhibited as they explored one another's bodies with a new kind of hunger. Perhaps guilt heightened one's sexual energy, she thought, as at last she fell into an exhausted, dreamless sleep. She had only meant to doze. Then someone was touching her breast. A faint rumble of traffic, TV sounds in the background. She murmured Skander's name and opened her eyes. Roe!

'Hi.' He was fully dressed.

'How long have I been sleeping?'

'Couple of hours. I didn't want to wake you. You looked so peaceful lying there. Besides, I like having you back in my bed.'

That alerted her. 'I must go.' Kate reached for her clothes but was pulled back.

'What's the rush? We've got a lot of catching up to do.'

'Don't . . .' She had to make some effort to keep him off. 'I shouldn't have come here today. It was a mistake.'

'Why? For finally letting go. That's not a mistake, that's a breakthrough!'

'Then why do I feel so ashamed! It took a long time getting over you. I . . .' again she faltered, 'I'm not going through that again.'

'No one's asking you to. Things have changed. You've changed. You never used to be this . . . exciting!'

That stung. 'It's amazing what a bit of practice can do.'

'You always were too sensitive. I want you to come back. To me and to Vaubelle. New terms and better money, of course.'

'I thought you'd signed up Leonora Vaubelle?'

'I did. But she can't compete with you.'

'It's not that simple, Roe. You can't expect to pick up where you left off.'

'Why not? Why does everything have to be so complicated? I can't undo the past but I can work on our future.' He studied her face for a moment. 'This guy you're seeing. Are you committed to him?'

'He's been very good to me.'

'That's no answer, Kat.'

'No, it's not, and he deserves much more than that. I shouldn't have come. If he knew I was here with you now . . .' She looked helplessly out at the wet sky. 'I can't do this!'

He took her head between his hands.

'OK. I'm not going to put any pressure on you. I can see you need time to get used to the idea. Just think about what I've said. I want you back. Rachel wants you back. A great many changes are taking place at Vaubelle. I could own most of the company by the end of the month.'

Business. Why did it always come down to the same thing with Roe?

'I'm here for another week. That should give you enough time to decide. Now, where were we?'

He kissed her very soundly and all thoughts of money dissolved. They went back to bed.

Going home was hell. Skander had said he'd pick her up at six. It was now almost seven thirty. When she got in she'd call and make some excuse. She simply wasn't up to seeing him – to lying. She got the taxi to drop her off by South Kensington tube and walked the rest of the way. She needed time to prepare lines like an actress about to go on stage, hating herself for the deceit almost as much as the infidelity. 'I'm not married to Skander,' she told herself, she owed him nothing. But in her heart she knew it wasn't true. She felt absolutely sick with guilt.

Two blocks before she reached her Cranley Gardens flat she stopped and checked her appearance in a shop mirror for tell-tale signs, half expecting to see red horns sprouting from her head. There were none. When she got to the front door she fumbled for her keys in her bag, but couldn't find them. Funny. She distinctly remembered having them with her when she'd gone out. In a flash, she pictured them lying on Roe's dressing-table. Incriminating evidence! She just hoped Neil was back from work. She rang the bell, jumping at the shrill noise.

Skander opened the door clutching a glass of wine.

'We had a bet it would be you,' he pulled her in, kissing her gently on the forehead in the same place Roe had kissed her less than an hour ago. Traitor! The word vibrated in her head.

'What did you do, forget your keys?'

She followed him into the drawing-room where Neil was sprawled out on the sofa. The fire had been lit and there was an open bottle of red wine on the table.

'This all looks very cosy.'

'So her ladyship's deigned to honour us with her presence after all! Darling, how are you?'

'I'm really sorry I'm late. I should have called.'

'Don't worry about it. Everything's been taken care of. You should see the miracles your boyfriend's been performing in the kitchen. He's given a whole new meaning to the word chef.'

Kate glanced at Skander pouring her a drink.

'By the way, I passed Harrods today and picked up your brochure. It's on the hall table. Not bad for an old scrubber like you.'

Oh God, she wasn't up to this.

'How did it go?' Skander asked, handing her the wine.

Kate looked blank. 'How was what?' She had a gnawing headache.

'The show, dar-ling! Obviously not that memorable. Who did your hair?'

'John Frieda. The make-up was really thick so I took it off.'

'I thought John had gone to New York? Oh, well. That's Grant for you. Always getting his facts wrong.'

It was definitely time to change the subject. Kate turned to Skander. 'How was your afternoon?'

'It started off badly when the Electricity Board cut off all the power in my street without any warning – I was on the word processor at the time and lost half my material. Gave the poor engineer I collared such a bollocking, he'll probably put in for early retirement. Things improved when I signed on a casting director and a scriptwriter who's cheap at the price and a bloody good find.'

'So when do you start casting?'

'As soon as we have a director.'

'Isn't that your department?' asked Neil.

'Not any more. I want to try my hand at producing.'

'Can't fail if it's anything like your cooking.'

'On which note,' said Skander, 'let's eat.'

After they'd cleared the plates and done the washing up, Neil went out. Grant, back from Paris, had rung to apologise and had whisked Neil off to a new gay club. Kate put some music on – anything for a distraction.

'You were very quiet tonight,' said Skander.

She smiled. 'I gave up trying to compete with Neil a long

503

time ago. Would you mind if I ran a bath? I need to unwind.'

She was still fiddling with the stereo.

'First things first.'

This was what she'd been dreading all evening. She kept her back to him, waiting. He reached an arm out and folded her to him, very deliberately removing her hand from the dial. He wrapped his large, comfortable body around her making her feel secure and loved. She experienced a terrible sense of remorse and buried her head against his great barrel-like chest. The familiar smell of skin and Old Holborn was comforting.

'I don't deserve you,' she muttered, as his hands stroked her hair.

'Oh, but I think you do. We make a good match, you and I.' He tilted her head back towards him, but Kate couldn't quite meet his eye.

'Hey. Everything all right?' His voice was gentle, concerned.

For a crazy moment she felt the urge to confess. Would he understand, forgive her?

'Just tired.'

'Come and sit down.' Like a child she obeyed him. 'Now, do you want to tell me where you really were this afternoon?'

'You know very well where I was. I was at Jaeger.'

'This isn't an inquisition, Kate. Only when I popped in to give you a lift home you weren't there.' A hot flush crawled up her neck. 'The manageress told me the show had been cancelled last week.'

'I . . .'

She was saved by the phone. Skander, being nearest, picked it up.

'No, hang on, I'll get her. It's for you.' He handed her the receiver. She knew who it would be.

'Hello,' she said in a voice she didn't recognise.

'Hi, baby. Hope this isn't a bad time to call but you left your keys at my place. Can you talk?'

'Not really.'

'So that *was* my competition who answered the phone. Have you thought about what I said?'

504

'I haven't had a chance.' Kate spoke very slowly as if she were a drunk trying not to slur her words. Why, oh why had she given him her number?

'I want us to spend some time together. Alone. Can you get away next weekend?'

God, he could really turn the charm on. Kate glanced at Skander who had switched on the television. She could tell he was listening.

'Kat, I need to see you, explain the way I feel, everything.'

'I'll have to check with the agency,' she mumbled while a voice in her head screamed, why now, why now! 'Will you be around in the morning?'

'Sure.' His milky voice sounded so warm, 'I'll be making calls from the hotel. Why don't you swing by at about ten. You know my room number.' Kate flinched.

When she put down the phone her hands were shaking. How did women do it, leading double lives? After one evening she was going to pieces.

'Here, drink this.'

Skander handed her the abandoned glass of wine. She sipped it not wanting it, just for something to do. Her head was splitting. Confused. She felt so terribly confused! Shutting her eyes, she massaged her temples.

'Headache?'

'I thought it would go on its own.'

'Don't you think we should talk about it?' he said gently.

'About what?' Kate kept her eyes closed, stalling for time.

'Come on, Kate. It's me you're talking to. I know you. You've been acting like a caged animal all evening. Every time I touch you, you spring away.' Running a hand through his hair he looked suddenly tired. 'You forget I've worked for him too.'

She wanted to deny it all, suddenly afraid. The silence roared in her ears.

'They want me back at Vaubelle and I'm not sure how I feel about it. That's all.'

He didn't look very convinced. 'That isn't what this is about, is it? Kate, I can't do all the guess work. If there are problems then let's talk about it, but don't shut me out.'

505

'I'm not shutting anyone out. I just don't like being spied on!'

'You're avoiding the issue.'

But Kate was crippled with fear. It was as if, by admitting nothing, doing nothing, the problem would go away. She shrank inside herself, feeling cowardly and very sad.

'Are you sleeping with Roe Lewis?'

'I don't want to talk about it.'

'Then maybe I've been right about you all along. I thought you were a fighter.'

They stared at each other, stunned by how quickly their relationship had deteriorated. But it was too late to undo the damage.

Skander got up. 'I'd better go.'

It was awful. Neither of them spoke. Kate kept trying to explain but the words stuck in her throat like ice cubes. Skander collected his jacket in the hall and Kate followed him out, her arms folded defensively across her chest. She thought for one ghastly moment when his hand reached for the door latch that he was going to leave without saying anything. Then he turned and faced her. Here goes, she thought holding her breath.

'I want you to know that I'm trying to understand what's happened. I love you, Kate. You know that. But I'm not going to spend the rest of my life proving it. It's not really your fault that you are the way you are. You live and work in a world of illusion – God knows I understand how hard it is to pull away from that. Deep down you really do want to settle down with a man, but relationships don't work like commercials with neatly-wrapped happy endings. Real people have cracks and flaws and need work, often when you don't feel up to it, but most of us think the investment's worth it. You've got to stop trying to punish the world for your grievances, because in the end you only hurt yourself.'

He took a piece of paper from his jacket pocket and scribbled something on it.

'This is where I'll be from tomorrow. It you want to talk you can get me at Naomi's farm until next Sunday. After that I'll be in New York. I'm not sure when I'll be coming back.'

506

He paused, expecting her to respond, but Kate made no attempt to close the distance, afraid that if she so much as touched him she'd break down.

'He'll never make you happy, Kate, but I suppose you've got to find that out for yourself.'

Quite suddenly he was gone, leaving an awful, empty silence. Her heart was so tight she thought it would split from the strain. She wanted to call out to him, beg him to come back. Apologise. But she could think of nothing to say in her own defence. It was her fault entirely. She deserved nothing. She was guilty. Worthless.

Kate headed straight for the fridge. Her first victim, parked on the top shelf next to the eggs, was a peanut butter jar – she didn't bother using a knife, just scooped out large grooves with her index finger, filling in her mouth, her mistakes, her internal mess. An opened tin of asparagus soup, frozen vegetable pie, pint of milk, olive pâté, two raw chicken fillets, apricot jam and the tail-end of Skander's pasta followed. Stuffing it down, she kept in mind the box of almond brittle Neil had brought her back from Paris. That would be next. As she devoured, reality lost its meaning, her problems pushed to one side by this driven need. She was in a world of must and compulsion.

For half an hour she stood there cramming in food, forcing the turbulent emotion back to its dark, secret place; eat, eat, eat! Fill, fill, fill! When Kate had finished she couldn't believe her eyes. She was swamped with guilt, the terrible shame of what she'd done. Back to reality, she weighed up the consequences; twenty pounds' worth of food and three kilos of fat building on her already fat thighs.

She spent fifteen minutes throwing up. Exhausted (but thin!) she hauled herself upstairs and lay on her bed corpse-like, listening to the click of the digital clock. When finally she let go, she wept for her baby, then for Roe. Why had she slept with him today? Why? It was as if she had deliberately set out to sabotage something good in her life. And to what end? Did she really want Roe back? For so long she had believed that by becoming what she thought he wanted she could win his love. It was finally dawning on her that that was

507

an impossible dream. Roe only wanted what he couldn't have. She turned on her side, wondering if that were really true, then decided that with all the things they'd been through, he must have cared about her. It just hadn't been enough. Any more than it had been with Sophie. For as long as she could remember her mother had left her feeling emotionally short-changed.

Things were now starting to make more sense. Her love for Roe was real but it had been based on childhood events which, though repressed and forgotten (until that night in the rain forest with Skander), she had felt compelled to recreate. She was searching for the familiar, the known, perhaps also attempting to recreate and put right the wrongs of the past. That made sense. Stupid really, but somehow suffering and sinning seemed to bring her peace of mind, because if things were bad, life was reassuringly familiar. Oh God. Was that really how messed up she'd become? She'd always been attracted to Roe because he represented something sexual, dangerous, unpredictable. Perhaps he really did love her but he was as much beyond her grasp as Sophie was. Neither of them truly understood her. She might just as well bang her head against a brick wall.

Later, she heard Neil let himself in. He must have made himself something to eat because she could hear rattling coming from the kitchen. Guiltily she realised he wouldn't find much left. After a few minutes there was a tap at her door. She feigned sleep, too shattered to explain her tears. She'd have to face his penetrating questions soon enough. Curling into a foetal position she gazed unseeingly out at the night. How ironic it was that she took so little joy from her rising career. Nigel raved about her to everyone but instead of feeling good about her success, she had begun to feel like a sham. Sooner or later someone would expose her for the fraud she knew she was. Wasn't that what Skander had thought when they'd worked together in Tuscany: 'You're afraid of anything intimate, Kate. You play games with men then run a mile. Deep down you're just plain scared?' True. He'd been right about her all along. She thought of the peaceful corners of Coochin Coochin and how happy she had been for a few brief weeks; somewhere among her things was a poem she'd written about the place. Once, feeling drunk and rather reckless, she'd fished it out and read it to Skander while he was in the bath. Having expected him to laugh, he surprised her by liking it. Really liking it. They'd talked about it and Skander had encouraged her to continue writing. That moment, sitting on the bathroom floor, hair scraped back, face free of worry and make-up, a dozen written lines had made her feel proud for the first time. Someone had acknowledged her true self and that feeling had lasted for days.

She rolled over on to her other side, smothered with images of Skander. She was running towards him, crying openly, wrapping her arms around his strong wide chest and pulling him close, tightly.

She kept calling his name but the body she held was stiff and distant, arms hanging limply at his side.

'Oh, God!' she sobbed. 'What have I gone and done?'

28

On a wintry Friday morning four days before the launch of the spring/summer *haute couture* Roe called a last-minute meeting of the Vaubelle staff. Miraculously most of them turned up. Rachel (for once ahead of schedule) was very relieved to have most of the *couture* designs ready for Wednesday's show and was discussing the running order with Richard. Brigette, having exhausted her crush on Roe, was back to her old punk ways, four sets of earrings and her old boyfriend Art. She had decided to return to Germany at the end of the season and was being replaced by a young talent hijacked from another *couturier*. A radiant Joni d'Akouri, who had finally given up smoking, had just announced her engagement to an English aristocrat.

'What made you give up?' asked a friend who had been trying to quit for years.

'Happiness!' Joni had replied smugly. 'Pure, unadulterated happiness!'

All the same it had been a job convincing Roe the marriage wouldn't affect her job – her other half was tied up with the Bundesbank and they planned to make their base in Neuilly. Marie-Claire was in less good spirits having just split up with her Serbian boyfriend, but a salary raise and a move up to a new office had helped to soften the blow. Jean-Marc, despite the odds, had finally knuckled down to his job and without Claude Vaubelle to hold him back had more than lived up to the impeccable standards set by Rachel; his latest line of pewter jewellery and belts displaying united flags had become almost a status symbol.

Nicole, still single but happier than she had been for years (which she accredited to Roe – no employer had treated her with such kindness), came back twice to check there were enough bottles of Evian and that everyone had a pencil and pad. Still to come were Sebastian and Roe. There was an air of expectancy in the room. By now they all knew about Carl Elliot's financial collapse. It just remained for Roe to explain where that left the company. And them!

At exactly eleven Roe made his entrance. Watching him stride into the room followed by Pierre, Joni was reminded of the first time she'd set eyes on him. One year ago almost to the day, she marvelled, this complex American had irrevocably turned their lives upside down. In her five years with Vaubelle Roe Lewis had been the first man to really unnerve her. They'd certainly had their share of disputes, God knows. But she had learned to respect him. Always pushing for new ideas, his commitment had enabled the company to forge ahead. What a lot of water under the bridge. Back then it had seemed inconceivable that she might one day be married. Her job had meant everything to her.

In just under an hour Roe had scheduled a press conference to announce his taking control of the company and he was anxious to go over his carefully prepared speech, tucked safely in his breast pocket. The meeting was a little premature, after all Sebastian hadn't actually signed the final contract, but Roe's attorney had been happy to proceed. Roe got to the point right away.

'It's been a difficult few months for us all and by now you'll have heard the rumours circulating about whether we can survive Cortes's collapse. I'm here today to alleviate any fears on that score. Next week I officially take over as Vaubelle's main shareholder, which will give me full control of the company.'

There were several surprised murmurs. 'How will that affect us?' Joni asked anxiously.

'It won't. Things will go on exactly as they have. It just means I no longer have to take issues to a higher authority.'

You never did, thought Richard with a trace of bitterness.

'As a team, you've all worked well together. I see no reason for that to change.' Roe picked up the file in front of

512

him. 'I have here copies of the company report. Brigette, would you pass these round?'

Three men erupted through the door. They were quickly followed by Nicole.

'Sebastian. You're late!' Roe glanced irritably at the strange men. 'This meeting's for staff members only.'

'I know,' Sebastian said pompously.

'Then would you gentlemen mind waiting outside until we're finished?'

'*Non!* I want them to stay.'

'Sebastian,' Roe's voice carried a warning, 'this had better be good.'

'Oh, it will be. I believe you have been outlining your proposed company strategies as chief shareholder?'

'You know damn well what I was outlining,' snapped Roe, running out of patience.

Sebastian smirked. 'Well, you may have been a little hasty.'

'Are you telling me you want to renegotiate?'

'This is not about money,' Sebastian said flatly. 'You, of all people, should know it.'

Roe was suddenly filled with an icy foreboding. Lowering his voice, he said, 'Can we discuss this later?'

'No. I want everyone to hear what I have to say.' Sebastian was going to enjoy this. 'I'm not selling you my shares.'

'What the hell is this!'

Joni and Rachel exchanged anxious looks.

'I never intended selling them to you. You destroyed my father and today I'm repaying the debt.'

For a moment the sinister expression on Sebastian's face reminded Joni of Claude.

'Hey, come on! We've been through all that. Your father was a very sick man, Sebastian. Don't hang his death on me.'

Roe was frantically calculating where he'd gone wrong. Their last discussion had gone so well. He'd thought . . . Oh Christ! What an idiot he'd been.

'I've sold my shares elsewhere.'

'You can't! It was all agreed!'

'Not in writing.'

Roe's eyes glinted dangerously. 'You little shit! Who'd you sell to?'

Rachel gasped as the tall, grey-haired man in the sweeping wool overcoat suddenly stepped forward. 'Mr Vaubelle sold them to me.'

'And who the fuck are you!'

'Toby Wilmot-Smith,' he said smoothly. 'I now own fifty-five per cent of the company.'

'That is correct.' The second man delved into a neat briefcase. 'I have the signed documents here.'

Roe looked at them in disgust. He couldn't quite take in what was happening. All his work, all his dreams for the company. Gone!

'I'm sorry there was no other way of telling you,' said Toby, looking Roe straight in the eye. 'I've been studying last year's reports and you've made some really excellent company changes. I want you to know that you'll be treated with the respect you deserve. But we will have to go over several details, including your future with Vaubelle.'

'I take it that's not all?'

'Not by any means. I'd like to bring my men in first thing tomorrow to go through the restructuring of the company. And,' he continued, glancing at Rachel for the first time, 'we have to talk!'

Then everyone began talking at once. The meeting, if you could call it that, came to an abrupt, rather messy end and Brigette raced off to find a telephone. She couldn't wait to tell Art the scandalous news.

'I don't understand,' stammered Rachel, standing in the corridor with Toby. 'Why have you done this? It's been over six months. You never once phoned me!'

'What could I say? That I was in love with you but another woman was having my child? I did what I thought was right. I've loused things up enough in my life, I wasn't about to mess up yours. That doesn't mean I haven't suffered or not thought about you every moment of every day we've been apart.'

Rachel drank in his presence as he talked. She hadn't

remembered him being so tall! And he'd done something to his hair.

'Why do you think I went back to work? This meeting, my buying the company, even coming here today.'

He could see the bewilderment in her eyes. Putting a hand on the side of each arm, he pulled her closer.

'Don't you understand anything, you brilliant, beautiful fool? I love you. I absolutely adore you!'

All this time not knowing why, thought Rachel in a daze. Now, when she had the chance, her presence of mind suddenly deserted her.

'I don't know what to say?'

'That's a tough one. Say you'll marry me.'

'What!'

'Well, you want to keep your job, don't you? You know the old rule about keeping the boss happy.'

Toby's mouth twitched.

'Oh, get on with it, you two,' said Joni, as she rushed by in a pair of flashing high heels. 'You're obviously crazy about one another.'

'Do you hear that good woman? Someone likes me.'

Rachel giggled. She couldn't help it. There was just something about Toby that made it impossible to stay cross with him.

Once again, Toby was stunned by the way her face lit up when she smiled.

'The suspense is killing me. Will you please say something?'

'I must be completely mad letting you talk me round, I can't take half of this in.'

'Is that a roundabout way of saying yes? Does that mean you'll marry me?'

'It means,' Rachel stressed carefully, 'that we'll discuss it over dinner.'

'Oh, I like the sound of that. The last time I took you to dinner we ended up in bed!'

Sometimes Kate would wake out of a black cloud of sleep with pain waiting for her like a lingering illness. She was miserable. Five days had crawled by and she'd spent most of the time in bed. Her dreams were full of flying. Last night she'd dreamt she was breaking into strange houses, moving from one to another in the dead of night. Whatever it was she was looking for, she never found it.

Propped up against the bedroom phone next to Casper's card was his number. It was looking decidedly grubby from her constant folding and unfolding but she was afraid that if she let it out of her sight she might lose it, her lifeline. Bea, her regular Agony Aunt, was out of the country, and Neil, having patched things up with Grant, had moved back to their flat. By Saturday Kate was so desperate to talk to someone she dropped in at Grantly's Hairdressing Salon. Manning the reception desk was an attractive teenager with slicked-back hair. She wore an 'If it ain't on, it ain't on!' black T-shirt.

'I'm not sure. My husband said not to cut too much off,' said an expensively dressed woman with a short blonde bob. She examined the back of her head in a mirror Grant held up.

'Hi, gorgeous,' he cried, waving Kate over.

'What do you think?' the blonde asked as Kate approached them. 'Don't you think it's a bit short?' She swung her head from side to side as if it helped demonstrate her point.

'I like it but then I'm biased. I've been a fan of Grant's for years.'

Kate kissed his cheek affectionately. 'Is your other half lurking somewhere?'

'Upstairs. Samie! Buzz Neil, will you? Tell him Kate's here and can you ple-case get Mrs Williams's coat.'

He brushed the back of Mrs Williams's tanned neck for stray hairs as she rummaged through her bag for a tip.

Another junior sidled up, his voice almost a whisper, 'Mrs Bottomly's arrived. What do you want me to do with her?'

Grant groaned. 'Someone up there's testing me. I don't know. Use your imagination, just keep her out of sight. She's hardly a good advertisement.'

They all watched a very large woman with purple hair and several Marks and Spencer bags wade in for her monthly perm. Having worked at the Cadogan Club for years before setting up shop on his own, Grant was used to dealing with the very rich. If you didn't have a triple-barrelled name, dress yourself from top to toe in Chanel, and carry a Gold American Express, you didn't make it through the front door, let alone have your hair cut. With one exception. Mrs Bottomly (and Grant kept this very quiet) was his sister's mother-in-law.

'Wash Mrs Bottomly will you, Samie.'

'What! all of her?'

Mrs Williams and Kate exchanged looks in the mirror.

'Cup of tea, then, Mrs Bottomly?'

'There's a luv. It's like trying to shop at the bleedin' FA cup final. Can I put some of me bags out of the way? They're ever so 'eavy.'

'Dar-ling! How long have you been waiting?' It was Neil.

'Not long. Are you busy?'

Neil glanced at his watch. 'My next client isn't in for half an hour. Come on up.'

'Bring me two coffees when you come down?' said Grant, replacing his scissors in the sterilising box. 'Cyanide in you know who's and Valium in mine!'

'Seen this?' said Neil ten minutes later as they sat cupping steaming coffee, milky and sweet the way Kate liked it. He handed her a copy of the *Express* and she read:

One of the sporting world's most celebrated couples are facing an agonising divorce [writes Cameron Ford]. Jack Winger, Scotland's most successful golf player this side of the century, and his pretty wife, Lorna, confirmed yesterday that they were splitting. Despite rumours that Winger, forty-four, was involved with blonde beauty Belinda Parker, most often seen on the international catwalk, friends say they had no idea things had reached this stage. But close friend Yarnton Miller of Wilmot-Palmer Jones Inc. said, 'This relationship is no flash in the pan. They have been together for months and it is no secret how much in love they are. I just feel deeply sorry for Lorna. They've been married a long time.'

A tearful Mrs Winger admitted she had hoped fifteen years of marriage would keep them together. When asked about her Jack's alleged affair, Mrs Winger, looking pale, said, 'You'll have to ask my husband. This was his decision not mine. I just want the whole ghastly ordeal done with so that I can get on with living my life.' The couple have two children, nine-year-old Olivia and Fergus, four.

The Hon. Belinda Parker was not available for comment but was spotted two days ago with Jack at Heathrow heading for a break in the Seychelles.

She threw the paper down. 'Actually they're in Fiji. They just didn't want half of Fleet Street coming with them. I don't think Bea's feet have touched the ground in a month. She's so deliriously happy!'

'Yes, but we can't say the same about you, can we?' Kate tried to muster a smile but failed. 'I thought the Somalian look had gone out of fashion,' Neil said bluntly.

'Thanks! I came here for sympathy not criticism.'

'And much good that will do. You need a kick up the backside, someone to drum some sense into that daft head of yours. Men like Skander only walk through your life once.'

'It's over between us,' she said dully. 'I messed everything up.'

'Why? Because you slept with Roe?'

'News travels fast. How did you know?'

Neil gave her a 'You've got to be joking' look. 'Get real, darling. You can no more resist that man's bed than I can resist silk underwear!'

'It wasn't like that.'

'Then why are you looking so miserable?'

Kate gazed mournfully at the tiled floor. 'Because I don't know what I want any more. I'm so bloody confused!'

'Listen. If you hadn't slept with Roe you might have spent the rest of your life regretting it. Always wondered what if.'

Chewing a nail, eyes anxiously fixed on Neil, Kate felt the first tiny bud of hope.

'So, come on. What did he say when you talked it through?'

'We didn't.' Her voice was small.

'Kate!'

She studied her hands. Neil was right. She should be

ashamed of her lack of courage.

'Far be it from me to preach but when are you going to start showing men how you really feel? Until then nothing's going to change. Darling, do you really want to spend the rest of your life on your own?'

She ran all the way home, oblivious of the frozen air, the hordes of shoppers, the startled looks, carried along by a new and bursting urgency. This morning there had been nothing to live for, now there was hope. She would do it, she would, she would! What a blind, stupid idiot she'd been!

In her nervousness it took her four attempts to fully dial the number. The sudden sharp ringing caused a flood of panic through her veins. She sat down attacking the side of her thumb with her teeth. Of course he wouldn't be there. He'd be at work, or worse! What if he'd already left? It was an appalling prospect. Five, six, the line continued to ring. He had to be there, she had to explain, no matter how clumsily, must make him realise how much she loved him. Dring, dring, eight, nine. On the twelfth ring she would hang up.

The phone suddenly clicked in her ear.

'Yes?' His voice sounded terse.

She almost balked. Admitting she needed him was one of the hardest things she would ever have to do. It was highly likely he was no longer interested. But all her life she'd been running away, putting up ridiculous obstacles to avoid getting hurt. Hadn't she now learned that through pain people found courage and wisdom. Taking risks gave life meaning and gave people hope. Wasn't it time she started taking a few herself?

Kate took a deep breath and jumped.